GREAT NOVELS OF
ANATOLE FRANCE

Évariste walked beside Élodie, smilingly recalling memories of their first meetings.

GREAT NOVELS
OF
ANATOLE FRANCE

Penguin Island

The Crime of Sylvestre Bonnard

The Revolt of the Angels

THE BOOK LEAGUE OF AMERICA
New York

PRINTED AT THE *Country Life Press*, GARDEN CITY, N. Y., U. S. A.

Translations by

A. W. EVANS, LAFCADIO HEARN, MRS. WILFRID JACKSON

CONTENTS

PENGUIN ISLAND

"PENGUIN ISLAND" *translated by* A. W. Evans

BOOK I: THE BEGINNINGS

I

LIFE OF SAINT MAËL

MAËL, a scion of a royal family of Cambria, was sent in his ninth year to the Abbey of Yvern so that he might there study both sacred and profane learning. At the age of fourteen he renounced his patrimony and took a vow to serve the Lord. His time was divided, according to the rule, between the singing of hymns, the study of grammar, and the meditation of eternal truths.

A celestial perfume soon disclosed the virtues of the monk throughout the cloister, and when the blessed Gal, the Abbot of Yvern, departed from this world into the next, young Maël succeeded him in the government of the monastery. He established therein a school, an infirmary, a guest-house, a forge, work-shops of all kinds, and sheds for building ships, and he compelled the monks to till the lands in the neighbourhood. With his own hands he cultivated the garden of the Abbey, he worked in metals, he instructed the novices, and his life was gently gliding along like a stream that reflects the heaven and fertilizes the fields.

At the close of the day this servant of God was accustomed to seat himself on the cliff, in the place that is to-day still called St. Maël's chair. At his feet the rocks bristling with green seaweed and tawny wrack seemed like black dragons as they faced the foam of the waves with their monstrous breasts. He watched the sun descending into the ocean like a red Host whose glorious blood gave a purple tone to the clouds and to the summits of the waves. And the holy man saw in this the image of the mystery of the Cross, by which the divine blood has clothed the earth with a royal purple. In the offing a line of dark blue marked the shores of the island of Gad where St. Bridget, who had been given the veil by St. Malo, ruled over a convent of women.

Now Bridget, knowing the merits of the venerable Maël, begged from him some work of his hands as a rich present. Maël cast a

3

hand-bell of bronze for her and, when it was finished he blessed it and threw it into the sea. And the bell went ringing towards the coast of Gad, where St. Bridget, warned by the sound of the bell upon the waves, received it piously, and carried it in solemn procession with singing of psalms into the chapel of the convent.

Thus the holy Maël advanced from virtue to virtue. He had already passed through two-thirds of the way of life, and he hoped peacefully to reach his terrestrial end in the midst of his spiritual brethren, when he knew by a certain sign that the Divine wisdom had decided otherwise, and that the Lord was calling him to less peaceful but not less meritorious labours.

II

THE APOSTOLICAL VOCATION OF SAINT MAËL

NE day as he walked in meditation to the furthest point of a tranquil beach, for which rocks jutting out into the sea formed a rugged dam, he saw a trough of stone which floated like a boat upon the waters.

It was in a vessel similar to this that St. Guirec, the great St. Columba, and so many holy men from Scotland and from Ireland had gone forth to evangelize Armorica. More recently still, St. Avoye having come from England, ascended the river Auray in a mortar made of rose-coloured granite into which children were afterwards placed in order to make them strong; St. Vouga passed from Hibernia to Cornwall on a rock whose fragments preserved at Penmarch, will cure of fever such pilgrims as place these splinters on their heads. St. Samson entered the Bay of St. Michael's Mount in a granite vessel which will one day be called St. Samson's basin. It is because of these facts that when he saw the stone trough the holy Maël understood that the Lord intended him for the apostolate of the pagans who still peopled the coast and the Breton islands.

He handed his ashen staff to the holy Budoc, thus investing him with the government of the monastery. Then, furnished with bread, a barrel of fresh water, and the book of the Holy Gospels, he entered the stone trough which carried him gently to the island of Hœdic.

This island is perpetually buffeted by the winds. In it some poor men fished among the clefts of the rocks and laboriously cultivated vegetables in gardens full of sand and pebbles that were sheltered from the wind by walls of barren stone and hedges of tamarisk. A beautiful fig-tree raised itself in a hollow of the island and thrust forth its branches far and wide. The inhabitants of the island used to worship it.

And the holy Maël said to them: "You worship this tree because it is beautiful. Therefore you are capable of feeling beauty. Now I come to reveal to you the hidden beauty." And he taught them the Gospel. And after having instructed them, he baptized them with salt and water.

The islands of Morbihan were more numerous in those times than they are to-day. For since then many have been swallowed up by the sea. St. Maël evangelized sixty of them. Then in his granite trough he ascended the river Auray. And after sailing for three hours he landed before a Roman house. A thin column of smoke went up from the roof. The holy man crossed the threshold on which there was a mosaic representing a dog with its hind legs outstretched and its lips drawn back. He was welcomed by an old couple, Marcus Combabus and Valeria Moerens, who lived there on the products of their lands. There was a portico round the interior court the columns of which were painted red, half their height upwards from the base. A fountain made of shells stood against the wall and under the portico there rose an altar with a niche in which the master of the house had placed some little idols made of baked earth and whitened with whitewash. Some represented winged children, others Apollo or Mercury, and several were in the form of a naked woman twisting her hair. But the holy Maël, observing those figures, discovered among them the image of a young mother holding a child upon her knees.

Immediately pointing to that image he said:

"That is the Virgin, the mother of God. The poet Virgil foretold her in Sibylline verses before she was born and, in angelical tones he sang *Jam redit et virgo*. Throughout heathendom prophetic figures of her have been made, like that which you, O Marcus, have placed upon this altar. And without doubt it is she who has protected your modest household. Thus it is that those who faithfully observe the natural law prepare themselves for the knowledge of revealed truths."

Marcus Combabus and Valeria Moerens, having been instructed by this speech, were converted to the Christian faith. They received baptism together with their young freedwoman, Caelia Avitella, who was dearer to them than the light of their eyes. All their tenants renounced paganism and were baptized on the same day.

Marcus Combabus, Valeria Moerens, and Caelia Avitella led thenceforth a life full of merit. They died in the Lord and were admitted into the canon of the saints.

For thirty-seven years longer the blessed Maël evangelized the pagans of the inner lands. He built two hundred and eighteen chapels and seventy-four abbeys.

Now on a certain day in the city of Vannes, where he was preaching the Gospel, he learned that the monks of Yvern had in his absence declined from the rule of St. Gal. Immediately, with the zeal of a hen who gathers her brood, he repaired to his erring children. He was then towards the end of his ninety-seventh year; his figure was bent, but his arms were still strong, and his speech was poured forth abundantly like winter snow in the depths of the valleys.

Abbot Budoc restored the ashen staff to St. Maël and informed him of the unhappy state into which the Abbey had fallen. The monks were in disagreement as to the date on which the festival of Easter ought to be celebrated. Some held for the Roman calendar, others for the Greek calendar, and the horrors of a chronological schism distracted the monastery.

There also prevailed another cause of disorder. The nuns of the island of Gad, sadly fallen from their former virtue, continually came in boats to the coast of Yvern. The monks received them in the guest-house and from this there arose scandals which filled pious souls with desolation.

Having finished his faithful report, Abbot Budoc concluded in these terms:

"Since the coming of these nuns the innocence and peace of the monks are at an end."

"I readily believe it," answered the blessed Maël. "For woman is a cleverly constructed snare by which we are taken even before we suspect the trap. Alas! the delightful attraction of these creatures is exerted with even greater force from a distance than when they are close at hand. The less they satisfy desire the more they inspire it. This is the reason why a poet wrote this verse to one of them:

When present I avoid thee, but when away I find thee.

Thus we see, my son, that the blandishments of carnal love have more power over hermits and monks than over men who live in the world. All through my life the demon of lust has tempted me in various ways, but his strongest temptations did not come to me from meeting a woman, however beautiful and fragrant she was. They came to me from the image of an absent woman. Even now, though full of days and approaching my ninety-eighth year, I am often led by the Enemy to sin against chastity at least in thought. At night when I am cold in my bed and my frozen old bones rattle together with a dull sound I hear voices reciting the second verse of the third Book of the Kings: 'Wherefore his servants said unto him, Let there be sought for my lord the king a young virgin: and let her stand before the king, and let her cherish him, and let her lie in thy bosom, that my lord the king may get heat,' and the devil shows me a girl in the bloom of youth who says to me: 'I am thy Abishag; I am thy Shunamite. Make, O my lord, room for me in thy couch.'

"Believe me," added the old man, "it is only by the special aid of Heaven that a monk can keep his chastity in act and in intention."

Applying himself immediately to restore innocence and peace to the monastery, he corrected the calendar according to the calculations of chronology and astronomy and he compelled all the monks to accept his decision; he sent the women who had declined from St. Bridget's rule back to their convent; but far from driving them away brutally, he caused them to be led to their boat with singing of psalms and litanies.

"Let us respect in them," he said, "the daughters of Bridget and the betrothed of the Lord. Let us beware lest we imitate the Pharisees who affect to despise sinners. The sin of these women and not their persons should be abased, and they should be made ashamed of what they have done and not of what they are, for they are all creatures of God."

And the holy man exhorted his monks to obey faithfully the rule of their order.

"When it does not yield to the rudder," said he to them, "the ship yields to the rock."

III

THE TEMPTATION OF SAINT MAËL

THE blessed Maël had scarcely restored order in the Abbey of Yvern before he learned that the inhabitants of the island of Hœdic, his first catechumens and the dearest of all to his heart, had returned to paganism, and that they were hanging crowns of flowers and fillets of wool to the branches of the sacred fig-tree.

The boatman who brought this sad news expressed a fear that soon those misguided men might violently destroy the chapel that had been built on the shore of their island.

The holy man resolved forthwith to visit his faithless children, so that he might lead them back to the faith and prevent them from yielding to such sacrilege. As he went down to the bay where his stone trough was moored, he turned his eyes to the sheds, then filled with the noise of saws and of hammers, which, thirty years before, he had erected on the fringe of that bay for the purpose of building ships.

At that moment, the Devil, who never tires, went out from the sheds and, under the appearance of a monk called Samson, he approached the holy man and tempted him thus:

"Father, the inhabitants of the island of Hœdic commit sins unceasingly. Every moment that passes removes them farther from God. They are soon going to use violence towards the chapel that you have raised with your own venerable hands on the shore of their island. Time is pressing. Do you not think that your stone trough would carry you more quickly towards them if it were rigged like a boat and furnished with a rudder, a mast, and a sail, for then you would be driven by the wind? Your arms are still strong and able to steer a small craft. It would be a good thing, too, to put a sharp stem in front of your apostolic trough. You are much too clear-sighted not to have thought of it already."

"Truly time is pressing," answered the holy man. "But to do as you say, Samson, my son, would it not be to make myself like those men of little faith who do not trust the Lord? Would it not be to despise the gifts of Him who has sent me this stone vessel without rigging or sail?"

This question, the Devil, who is a great theologian, answered by another.

"Father, is it praiseworthy to wait, with our arms folded, until help comes from on high, and to ask everything from Him who can do all things, instead of acting by human prudence and helping ourselves?"

"It certainly is not," answered the holy Maël, "and to neglect to act by human prudence is tempting God."

"Well," urged the Devil, "is it not prudence in this case to rig the vessel?"

"It would be prudence if we could not attain our end in any other way."

"Is your vessel then so very speedy?"

"It is as speedy as God pleases."

"What do you know about it? It goes like Abbot Budoc's mule. It is a regular old tub. Are you forbidden to make it speedier?"

"My son, clearness adorns your words, but they are unduly over-confident. Remember that this vessel is miraculous."

"It is, father. A granite trough that floats on the water like a cork is a miraculous trough. There is not the slightest doubt about it. What conclusion do you draw from that?"

"I am greatly perplexed. Is it right to perfect so miraculous a machine by human and natural means?"

"Father, if you lost your right foot and God restored it to you, would not that foot be miraculous?"

"Without doubt, my son."

"Would you put a shoe on it?"

"Assuredly."

"Well, then, if you believe that one may cover a miraculous foot with a natural shoe, you should also believe that we can put natural rigging on a miraculous boat. That is clear. Alas! Why must the holiest persons have their moments of weakness and despondency? The most illustrious of the apostles of Brittany could accomplish works worthy of eternal glory . . . But his spirit is tardy and his hand is slothful. Farewell then, father! Travel by short and slow stages and when at last you approach the coast of Hœdic you will see the smoking ruins of the chapel that was built and consecrated by your own hands. The pagans will have burned it and with it the deacon you left there. He will be as thoroughly roasted as a black pudding."

"My trouble is extreme," said the servant of God, drying with his sleeve the sweat that gathered upon his brow. "But tell me, Samson, my son, would not rigging this stone trough be a difficult piece of work? And if we undertook it might we not lose time instead of gaining it?"

"Ah! father," exclaimed the Devil, "in one turning of the hour-glass the thing would be done. We shall find the necessary rigging in this shed that you have formerly built here on the coast and in those store-houses abundantly stocked through your care. I will myself regulate all the ship's fittings. Before being a monk I was a sailor and a carpenter and I have worked at many other trades as well. Let us to work."

Immediately he drew the holy man into an out-house filled with all things needful for fitting out a boat.

"That for you, father!"

And he placed on his shoulders the sail, the mast, the gaff, and the boom.

Then, himself bearing a stem and a rudder with its screw and tiller, and seizing a carpenter's bag full of tools, he ran to the shore, dragging the holy man after him by his habit. The latter was bent, sweating, and breathless, under the burden of canvas and wood.

IV

ST. MAËL'S NAVIGATION ON THE OCEAN OF ICE

HE Devil, having tucked his clothes up to his arm-pits, dragged the trough on the sand, and fitted the rigging in less than an hour.

As soon as the holy Maël had embarked, the vessel, with all its sails set, cleft through the waters with such speed that the coast was almost immediately out of sight. The old man steered to the south so as to double the Land's End, but an irresistible current carried him to the south-west. He went along the southern coast of Ireland and turned sharply towards the north. In the evening the wind freshened. In vain did Maël attempt to furl the sail. The vessel flew distractedly towards the fabulous seas.

By the light of the moon the immodest sirens of the North came around him with their hempen-coloured hair, raising their white throats and their rose-tinted limbs out of the sea; and beating the water into foam with their emerald tails, they sang in cadence:

> Whither go'st thou, gentle Maël,
> In thy trough distracted?
> All distended is thy sail
> Like the breast of Juno
> When from it gushed the Milky Way.

For a moment their harmonious laughter followed him beneath the stars, but the vessel fled on, a hundred times more swiftly than the red ship of a Viking. And the petrels, surprised in their flight, clung with their feet to the hair of the holy man.

Soon a tempest arose full of darkness and groanings, and the trough, driven by a furious wind, flew like a sea-mew through the mist and the surge.

After a night of three times twenty-four hours the darkness was suddenly rent and the holy man discovered on the horizon a shore more dazzling than diamond. The coast rapidly grew larger, and soon by the glacial light of a torpid and sunken sun, Maël saw, rising above the waves, the silent streets of a white city, which, vaster than Thebes with its hundred gates, extended as far as the eye could see the ruins of its forum built of snow, its palaces of frost, its crystal arches, and its iridescent obelisks.

The ocean was covered with floating ice-bergs around which swam men of the sea of a wild yet gentle appearance. And Leviathan passed by hurling a column of water up to the clouds.

Moreover, on a block of ice which floated at the same rate as the stone trough there was seated a white bear holding her little one in her arms, and Maël heard her murmuring in a low voice this verse of Virgil, *Incipe parve puer*.

And full of sadness and trouble, the old man wept.

The fresh water had frozen and burst the barrel that contained it. And Maël was sucking pieces of ice to quench his thirst, and his food was bread dipped in dirty water. His beard and his hair were broken like glass. His habit was covered with a layer of ice and cut into him at every movement of his limbs. Huge waves rose up and opened their foaming jaws at the old man. Twenty times the boat was filled by masses of sea. And the ocean swallowed up the book of the Holy Gospels which the apostle guarded with extreme care in a purple cover marked with a golden cross.

Now on the thirtieth day the sea calmed. And lo! with a frightful clamour of sky and waters a mountain of dazzling whiteness advanced towards the stone vessel. Maël steered to avoid it, but the tiller broke in his hands. To lessen the speed of his progress towards the rock he attempted to reef the sails, but when he tried to knot the reef-points the wind pulled them away from him and the rope seared his hands. He saw three demons with wings of black skin having hooks at their ends, who, hanging from the rigging, were puffing with their breath against the sails.

Understanding from this sight that the Enemy had governed him in all these things, he guarded himself by making the sign of the Cross. Immediately a furious gust of wind filled with the noise of sobs and howls struck the stone trough, carried off the mast with all the sails, and tore away the rudder and the stem.

The trough was drifting on the sea, which had now grown calm. The holy man knelt and gave thanks to the Lord who had delivered him from the snares of the demon. Then he recognised, sitting on a block of ice, the mother bear who had spoken during the storm. She pressed her beloved child to her bosom, and in her hand she held a purple book marked with a golden cross. Hailing the granite trough, she saluted the holy man with these words:

"Pax tibi Maël"

And she held out the book to him.

The holy man recognised his evangelistary, and, full of astonishment, he sang in the tepid air a hymn to the Creator and His creation.

V

THE BAPTISM OF THE PENGUINS

AFTER having drifted for an hour the holy man approached a narrow strand, shut in by steep mountains. He went along the coast for a whole day and a night, passing around the reef which formed an insuperable barrier. He discovered in this way that it was a round island in the middle of which rose a mountain crowned with clouds. He joyfully breathed the fresh breath of the moist air. Rain fell, and this was so pleasant that the holy man said to the Lord:

"Lord, this is the island of tears, the island of contrition."

The strand was deserted. Worn out with fatigue and hunger, he sat down on a rock in the hollow of which there lay some yellow eggs, marked with black spots, and about as large as those of a swan. But he did not touch them, saying:

"Birds are the living praises of God. I should not like a single one of these praises to be lacking through me."

And he munched the lichens which he tore from the crannies of the rocks.

The holy man had gone almost entirely round the island without meeting any inhabitants, when he came to a vast amphitheatre formed of black and red rocks whose summits became tinged with blue as they rose towards the clouds, and they were filled with sonorous cascades.

The reflection from the polar ice had hurt the old man's eyes, but a feeble gleam of light still shone through his swollen eyelids. He distinguished animated forms which filled the rocks, in stages, like a crowd of men on the tiers of an amphitheatre. And at the same time, his ears, deafened by the continual noises of the sea, heard a feeble sound of voices. Thinking that what he saw were men living under the natural law, and that the Lord had sent him to teach them the Divine law, he preached the gospel to them.

Mounted on a lofty stone in the midst of the wild circus:

"Inhabitants of this island," said he, "although you be of small stature, you look less like a band of fishermen and mariners than like the senate of a judicious republic. By your gravity, your silence, your tranquil deportment, you form on this wild rock an assembly comparable to the Conscript Fathers at Rome deliberating in the temple of Victory, or rather, to the philosophers of Athens disputing on the benches of the Areopagus. Doubtless you possess neither their science nor their genius, but perhaps in the sight of God you are their superiors. I believe that you are simple and good. As I went round your island I saw no image of murder, no sign of carnage, no enemies' heads or scalps hung from a lofty pole or nailed to the doors of your villages. You appear to me to have no arts and not to work in metals. But your hearts are pure and your hands are innocent, and the truth will easily enter into your souls."

Now what he had taken for men of small stature but of grave bearing were penguins whom the spring had gathered together, and who were ranged in couples on the natural steps of the rock, erect in the majesty of their large white bellies. From moment to moment they moved their winglets like arms, and uttered peaceful cries. They did not fear men, for they did not know them, and had never received any harm from them; and there was in the monk a certain gentleness that reassured the most timid animals and that pleased these penguins extremely. With a friendly curiosity they turned towards him their little round eyes lengthened in front by a white oval spot that gave something odd and human to their appearance.

Touched by their attention, the holy man taught them the Gospel.

"Inhabitants of this island, the early day that has just risen over your rocks is the image of the heavenly day that rises in your souls. For I bring you the inner light; I bring you the light and heat of the soul. Just as the sun melts the ice of your mountains so Jesus Christ will melt the ice of your hearts."

Thus the old man spoke. As everywhere throughout nature voice calls to voice, as all which breathes in the light of day loves alternate strains, these penguins answered the old man by the sounds of their throats. And their voices were soft, for it was the season of their loves.

The holy man, persuaded that they belonged to some idolatrous people and that in their own language they gave adherence to the Christian faith, invited them to receive baptism.

"I think," said he to them, "that you bathe often, for all the hollows of the rocks are full of pure water, and as I came to your assembly I saw several of you plunging into these natural baths. Now purity of body is the image of spiritual purity."

And he taught them the origin, the nature, and the effects of baptism.

"Baptism," said he to them, "is Adoption, New Birth, Regeneration, Illumination."

And he explained each of these points to them in succession.

Then, having previously blessed the water that fell from the cascades and recited the exorcisms, he baptized those whom he had just taught, pouring on each of their heads a drop of pure water and pronouncing the sacred words.

And thus for three days and three nights he baptized the birds.

VI

AN ASSEMBLY IN PARADISE

WHEN the baptism of the penguins was known in Paradise, it caused neither joy nor sorrow, but an extreme surprise. The Lord himself was embarrassed. He gathered an assembly of clerics and doctors, and asked them whether they regarded the baptism as valid.

"It is void," said St. Patrick.

"Why is it void?" asked St. Gal, who had evangelized the people of Cornwall and had trained the holy Maël for his apostolical labours.

"The sacrament of baptism," answered St. Patrick, "is void when it is given to birds, just as the sacrament of marriage is void when it is given to a eunuch."

But St. Gal replied:

"What relation do you claim to establish between the baptism of a bird and the marriage of a eunuch? There is none at all. Marriage is, if I may say so, a conditional, a contingent sacrament. The priest blesses an event beforehand; it is evident that if the act is not consummated the benediction remains without effect. That is obvious. I have known on earth, in the town of Antrim, a rich man named Sadoc, who, living in concubinage with a woman, caused her to be the mother of nine children. In his old age, yielding to my reproofs, he consented to marry her, and I blessed their union. Unfortunately Sadoc's great age prevented him from consummating the marriage. A short time afterwards he lost all his property, and Germaine (that was the name of the woman), not feeling herself able to endure poverty, asked for the annulment of a marriage which was no reality. The Pope granted her request, for it was just. So much for marriage. But baptism is conferred without restrictions or reserves of any kind. There is no doubt about it, what the penguins have received is a sacrament."

Called to give his opinion, Pope St. Damasus expressed himself in these terms:

"In order to know if a baptism is valid and will produce its result, that is to say, sanctification, it is necessary to consider who gives it and not who receives it. In truth, the sanctifying virtue of this sacrament results from the exterior act by which it is conferred, without the baptized person co-operating in his own sanctification by any personal act; if it were otherwise it would not be administered to the newly born. And there is no need, in order to baptize, to fulfill any special condition; it is not necessary to be in a state of grace; it is sufficient to have the intention of doing what the Church does, to pronounce the consecrated words and to observe the prescribed forms. Now we cannot doubt that the venerable Maël has observed these conditions. Therefore the penguins are baptized."

"Do you think so?" asked St. Guénolé. "And what then do you believe that baptism really is? Baptism is the process of regeneration by which man is born of water and of the spirit, for having entered the water covered with crimes, he goes out of it a neophyte, a new creature, abounding in the fruits of righteousness; baptism is the seed of immortality; baptism is the pledge of the resurrection; baptism is the burying with Christ in His death and participation in His departure from the sepulchre. That is not a gift to bestow upon birds. Reverend Fathers, let us consider. Baptism washes away original sin; now the penguins were not conceived in sin. It removes the penalty of sin; now the penguins have not sinned. It produces grace and the gift of virtues, uniting Christians to Jesus Christ, as the members to the body, and it is obvious to the senses that penguins cannot acquire the virtues of confessors, of virgins, and of widows, or receive grace and be united to——"

St. Damasus did not allow him to finish.

"That proves," said he warmly, "that the baptism was useless; it does not prove that it was not effective."

"But by this reasoning," said St. Guénolé, "one might baptize in the name of the Father, of the Son, and of the Holy Ghost, by aspersion or immersion, not only a bird or a quadruped, but also an inanimate object, a statue, a table, a chair, etc. That animal would be Christian, that idol, that table would be Christian! It is absurd!"

St. Augustine began to speak. There was a great silence.

"I am going," said the ardent bishop of Hippo, "to show you, by an example, the power of formulas. It deals, it is true, with a diabolical operation. But if it be established that formulas taught by the Devil have effect upon unintelligent animals or even on inanimate objects, how can we longer doubt that the effect of the sacramental formulas extends to the minds of beasts and even to inert matter?

"This is the example. There was during my lifetime in the town of Madaura, the birthplace of the philosopher Apuleius, a witch who was able to attract men to her chamber by burning a few of their hairs along with certain herbs upon her tripod, pronouncing at the same time certain words. Now one day when she wished by this means to gain the love of a young man, she was deceived by her maid, and instead of the young man's hairs, she burned some hairs pulled from a leather bottle, made out of a goatskin that hung in a tavern. During the night the leather bottle, full of wine, capered through the town up to the witch's door. This fact is undoubted. And in sacraments as in enchantments it is the form which operates. The effect of a divine formula cannot be less in power and extent than the effect of an infernal formula."

Having spoken in this fashion the great St. Augustine sat down amidst applause.

One of the blessed, of an advanced age and having a melancholy appearance, asked permission to speak. No one knew him. His name was Probus, and he was not enrolled in the canon of the saints.

"I beg the company's pardon," said he, "I have no halo, and I gained eternal blessedness without any eminent distinction. But after what the great St. Augustine has just told you I believe it right to impart a cruel experience, which I had, relative to the conditions necessary for the validity of a sacrament. The bishop of Hippo is indeed right in what he said. A sacrament depends on the form; its virtue is in its form; its vice is in its form. Listen, confessors and pontiffs, to my woeful story. I was a priest in Rome under the rule of the Emperor Gordianus. Without desiring to recommend myself to you for any special merit, I may say that I exercised my priesthood with piety and zeal. For forty years I served the church of St. Modestus-beyond-the-Walls. My habits were regular. Every Saturday I went to a tavern-keeper called Barjas, who dwelt with his wine-jars under the Porta Capena, and from him I bought the wine that I consecrated daily throughout the week. During that long space of time I never failed for a single morning to consecrate the holy sacrifice of the mass. However, I had no joy, and it was with a heart oppressed by sorrow that, on the steps of the altar I used to ask, 'Why art thou so heavy, O my soul, and why art thou so disquieted within me?' The faithful whom I invited to the holy table gave me cause for affliction, for having, so to speak, the Host that I administered still upon their tongues, they fell again into sin just as if the sacrament had been without power or efficacy. At last I reached the end of my earthly trials, and falling asleep in the Lord, I awoke in this abode of the elect. I learned then from the mouth of the angel who brought me here, that Barjas, the tavern-keeper of the Porta Capena, had sold for wine a decoction of roots and barks in which there was not a single drop of the juice of the grape. I had been unable to transmute this vile brew into blood, for it was not wine, and wine alone is changed into the blood of Jesus Christ. Therefore all my consecrations were invalid, and unknown to us, my faithful and myself had for forty years been deprived of the sacrament and were in fact in a state of excommunication. This revelation threw me into a stupor which overwhelms me even to-day in this abode of bliss. I go all through Paradise without ever meeting a single one of those Christians whom formerly I admitted to the holy table in the basilica of the blessed Modestus. Deprived of the bread of angels, they easily gave way to the most abominable vices, and they have all gone to hell. It gives me some satisfaction to think that Barjas, the tavern-keeper, is damned. There is in these things a logic worthy of the author of all logic. Nevertheless my unhappy example proves that it is sometimes inconvenient that form should prevail over essence in the sacraments, and I humbly ask, Could not eternal wisdom remedy this?"

"No," answered the Lord. "The remedy would be worse than the disease. It would be the ruin of the priesthood if essence prevailed over form in the laws of salvation."

"Alas! Lord," sighed the humble Probus. "Be persuaded by my humble experience; as long as you reduce your sacraments to formulas your justice will meet with terrible obstacles."

"I know that better than you do," replied the Lord. "I see in a single glance both the actual problems which are difficult, and the future problems which will not be less difficult. Thus I can foretell that when the sun will have turned round the earth two hundred and forty times more. . . ."

"Sublime language," exclaimed the angels.

"And worthy of the creator of the world," answered the pontiffs.

"It is," resumed the Lord, "a manner of speaking in accordance with my old cosmogony and one which I cannot give up without losing my immutability. . . .

"After the sun, then, will have turned another two hundred and forty times round the earth, there will not be a single cleric left in Rome who knows Latin. When they sing their litanies in the churches people will invoke Orichel, Roguel, and Totichel, and, as you know, these are devils and not angels. Many robbers desiring to make their communions, but fearing that before obtaining pardon they would be forced to give up the things they had robbed to the Church, will make their confessions to travelling priests, who, ignorant of both Italian and Latin, and only speaking the *patois* of their village, will go through cities and towns selling the remission of sins for a base price, often for a bottle of wine. Probably we shall not be inconvenienced by those absolutions as they will want contrition to make them valid, but it may be that their baptisms will cause us some embarrassment. The priests will become so ignorant that they will baptize children *in nomine patria et filia et spirita sancta,* as Louis de Potter will take a pleasure in relating in the third volume of his 'Philosophical, Political, and Critical History of Christianity.' It will be an arduous question to decide on the validity of such baptisms; for even if in my sacred writings I tolerate a Greek less elegant than Plato's and a scarcely

Ciceronian Latin, I cannot possibly admit a piece of pure *patois* as a liturgical formula. And one shudders when one thinks that millions of new-born babes will be baptized by this method. But let us return to our penguins."

"Your divine words, Lord, have already led us back to them," said St. Gal. "In the signs of religion and the laws of salvation form necessarily prevails over essence, and the validity of a sacrament solely depends upon its form. The whole question is whether the penguins have been baptized with the proper forms. Now there is no doubt about the answer."

The fathers and the doctors agreed, and their perplexity became only the more cruel.

"The Christian state," said St. Cornelius, "is not without serious inconveniences for a penguin. In it the birds are obliged to work out their own salvation. How can they succeed? The habits of birds are, in many points, contrary to the commandments of the Church, and the penguins have no reason for changing theirs. I mean that they are not intelligent enough to give up their present habits and assume better."

"They cannot," said the Lord; "my decrees prevent them."

"Nevertheless," resumed St. Cornelius, "in virtue of their baptism their actions no longer remain indifferent. Henceforth they will be good or bad, susceptible of merit or of demerit."

"That is precisely the question we have to deal with," said the Lord.

"I see only one solution," said St. Augustine. "The penguins will go to hell."

"But they have no soul," observed St. Irenaeus.

"It is a pity," sighed Tertullian.

"It is indeed," resumed St. Gal. "And I admit that my disciple, the holy Maël, has, in his mind zeal, created great theological difficulties for the Holy Spirit and introduced disorder into the economy of mysteries."

"He is an old blunderer," cried St. Adjutor of Alsace, shrugging his shoulders.

But the Lord cast a reproachful look on Adjutor.

"Allow me to speak," said he; "the holy Maël has not intuitive knowledge like you, my blessed ones. He does not see me. He is an old man burdened by infirmities; he is half deaf and three parts blind. You are too severe on him. However, I recognise that the situation is an embarrassing one."

"Luckily it is but a passing disorder," said St. Irenaeus. "The penguins are baptized, but their eggs are not, and the evil will stop with the present generation."

"Do not speak thus, Irenaeus my son," said the Lord. "There are exceptions to the laws that men of science lay down on the earth because they are imperfect and have not an exact application to nature. But the laws that I establish are perfect and suffer no exception. We must decide the fate of the baptized penguins without violating any divine law, and in a manner conformable to the decalogue as well as to the commandments of my Church."

"Lord," said St. Gregory Nazianzen, "give them an immortal soul."

"Alas! Lord, what would they do with it," sighed Lactantius. "They have not tuneful voices to sing your praises. They would not be able to celebrate your mysteries."

"Without doubt," said St. Augustine, "they would not observe the divine law."

"They could not," said the Lord.

"They could not," continued St. Augustine. "And if, Lord, in your wisdom, you pour an immortal soul into them, they will burn eternally in hell in virtue of your adorable decrees. Thus will the transcendent order, that this old Welshman has disturbed, be reestablished."

"You propose a correct solution to me, son of Monica," said the Lord, "and one that accords with my wisdom. But it does not satisfy my mercy. And, although in my essence I am immutable, the longer I endure, the more I incline to mildness. This change of character is evident to anyone who reads my two Testaments."

As the discussion continued without much light being thrown upon the matter and as the blessed showed a disposition to keep repeating the same thing, it was decided to consult St. Catherine of Alexandria. This is what was usually done in such cases. St. Catherine while on earth had confounded fifty very learned doctors. She knew Plato's philosophy in addition to the Holy Scriptures, and she also possessed a knowledge of rhetoric.

VII

AN ASSEMBLY IN PARADISE
(*Continuation and End*)

ST. CATHERINE entered the assembly, her head encircled by a crown of emeralds, sapphires, and pearls, and she was clad in a robe of cloth of gold. She carried at her side a blazing wheel, the image of the one whose fragments had struck her persecutors.

The Lord having invited her to speak, she expressed herself in these terms:

"Lord, in order to solve the problem you deign to submit to me I shall not study the habits of animals in general nor those of birds in particular. I shall only remark to the doctors, confessors, and pontiffs gathered in this assembly that the separation between man and animal is not complete since there are monsters who proceed from both. Such are chimeras—half nymphs and half serpents; such are the three Gorgons and the Capripeds; such are the Scyllas and the Sirens who sing in the sea. These have a woman's breast and a fish's tail. Such also are the Centaurs, men down to the waist and the remainder horses. They are a noble race of monsters. One of them, as you know, was able, guided by the light of reason alone, to direct his steps towards eternal blessedness, and you sometimes see his heroic bosom prancing on the clouds. Chiron, the Centaur, deserved for his works on the earth to share the abode of the blessed; he it was who gave Achilles his education; and that young hero, when he left the Centaur's hands, lived for two years, dressed as a young girl, among the daughters of King Lycomedes. He shared their games and their bed without allowing any suspicion to arise that he was not a young virgin like them. Chiron, who taught him such good morals, is, with the Emperor Trajan, the only righteous man who obtained celestial glory by following the law of nature. And yet he was but half human.

"I think I have proved by this example that, to reach eternal blessedness, it is enough to possess some parts of humanity, always on the condition that they are noble. And what Chiron, the Centaur, could obtain without having been regenerated by baptism, would not the penguins deserve too if they became half penguins and half men? That is why, Lord, I entreat you to give old Maël's penguins a human head and breast so that they can praise you worthily. And grant them also an immortal soul—but one of small size."

Thus Catherine spoke, and the fathers, doctors, confessors, and pontiffs heard her with a murmur of approbation.

But St. Anthony, the Hermit, arose and stretching two red and knotty arms towards the Most High:

"Do not so, O Lord God," he cried, "in the name of your holy Paraclete, do not so!"

He spoke with such vehemence that his long white beard shook on his chin like the empty nose-bag of a hungry horse.

"Lord, do not so. Birds with human heads exist already. St. Catherine has told us nothing new."

"The imagination groups and compares; it never creates," replied St. Catherine drily.

"They exist already," continued St. Anthony, who would listen to nothing. "They are called harpies, and they are the most obscene animals in creation. One day as I was having supper in the desert with the Abbot St. Paul, I placed the table outside my cabin under an old sycamore tree. The harpies came and sat in its branches; they deafened us with their shrill cries and cast their excrement over all our food. The clamour of the monsters prevented me from listening to the teaching of the Abbot St. Paul, and we ate birds'· dung with our bread and lettuces. Lord, it is impossible to believe that harpies could give thee worthy praise.

"Truly in my temptations I have seen many hybrid beings, not only women-serpents and women-fishes, but beings still more confusedly formed such as men whose bodies were made out of a pot, a bell, a clock, a cupboard full of food and crockery, or even out of a house with doors and windows through which people engaged in their domestic tasks could be seen. Eternity would not suffice were I to describe all the monsters that assailed me in my solitude, from whales rigged like ships to a shower of red insects which changed the water of my fountain into blood. But none were as disgusting as the harpies whose offal polluted the leaves of my sycamore."

"Harpies," observed Lactantius, "are female monsters with birds' bodies. They have a woman's head and breast. Their forwardness, their shamelessness, and their obscenity proceed from their female nature as the poet Virgil demonstrated in his 'Æneid.' They share the curse of Eve."

"Let us not speak of the curse of Eve," said the Lord. "The second Eve has redeemed the first."

Paul Orosius, the author of a universal history that Bossuet was to imitate in later years, arose and prayed to the Lord:

"Lord, hear my prayer and Anthony's. Do not make any more monsters like the Centaurs, Sirens, and Fauns, whom the Greeks, those collectors of fables, loved. You will derive no satisfaction from them. Those species of monsters have pagan inclinations and their double nature does not dispose them to purity of morals."

The bland Lactantius replied in these terms:

"He who has just spoken is assuredly the best historian in Paradise, for Herodotus, Thucydides, Polybius, Livy, Velleius Paterculus, Cornelius Nepos, Suetonius, Manetho, Diodorus Siculus, Dion Cassius, and Lampridius are deprived of the sight of God, and Tacitus suffers in hell the torments that are reserved for blasphemers. But Paul Orosius does not know heaven as well as he knows the earth, for he does not seem to bear in mind that the angels, who proceed from man and bird, are purity itself."

"We are wandering," said the Eternal. "What have we to do with all those centaurs, harpies, and angels? We have to deal with penguins."

"You have spoken to the point, Lord," said the chief of the fifty doctors, who, during their mortal life had been confounded by the Virgin of Alexandria, "and I dare express the opinion that, in order to put an end to the scandal by which heaven is now stirred, old Maël's penguins should, as St. Catherine who confounded us has proposed, be given half of a human body with an eternal soul proportioned to that half."

At this speech there arose in the assembly a great noise of private conversations and disputes of the doctors. The Greek fathers argued with the Latins concerning the substance, nature, and dimensions of the soul that should be given to the penguins.

"Confessors and pontiffs," exclaimed the Lord, "do not imitate the conclaves and synods of the earth. And do not bring into the Church Triumphant those violences that trouble the Church Militant. For it is but too true that in all the councils held under the inspiration of my spirit, in Europe, in Asia, and in Africa, fathers have torn the beards and scratched the eyes of other fathers. Nevertheless they were infallible, for I was with them."

Order being restored, old Hermas arose and slowly uttered these words:

"I will praise you, Lord, for that you caused my mother, Saphira, to be born amidst your people, in the days when the dew of heaven refreshed the earth which was in travail with its Saviour. And I will praise you, Lord, for having granted to me to see with my mortal eyes the Apostles of your divine Son. And I will speak in this illustrious assembly because you have willed that truth should proceed out of the mouths of the humble, and I will say: 'Change these penguins to men. It is the only determination conformable to your justice and your mercy.'"

Several doctors asked permission to speak, others began to do so. No one listened, and all the confessors were tumultuously shaking their palms and their crowns.

The Lord, by a gesture of his right hand, appeased the quarrels of his elect.

"Let us not deliberate any longer," said he. "The opinion broached by gentle old Hermas is the only one conformable to my eternal designs. These birds will be changed into men. I foresee in this several disadvantages. Many of those men will commit sins they would not have committed as penguins. Truly their fate through this change will be far less enviable than if they had been without this baptism and this incorporation into the family of Abraham. But my foreknowledge must not encroach upon their free will.

"In order not to impair human liberty, I will be ignorant of what I know, I will thicken upon my eyes the veils I have pierced, and in my blind clearsightedness I will let myself by surprised by what I have foreseen."

And immediately calling the archangel Raphael:

"Go and find the holy Maël," said he to him; "inform him of his mistake and tell him, armed with my Name, to change these penguins into men."

VIII

METAMORPHOSIS OF THE PENGUINS

HE archangel, having gone down into the Island of the Penguins, found the holy man asleep in the hollow of a rock surrounded by his new disciples. He laid his hand on his shoulder and, having waked him, said in a gentle voice:

"Maël, fear not!"

The holy man, dazzled by a vivid light, inebriated by a delicious odour, recognised the angel of the Lord, and prostrated himself with his forehead on the ground.

The angel continued:

"Maël, know thy error, believing that thou wert baptizing children of Adam thou hast baptized birds; and it is through thee that penguins have entered into the Church of God."

At these words the old man remained stupefied.

And the angel resumed:

"Arise, Maël, arm thyself with the mighty Name of the Lord, and say to these birds, 'Be ye men!' "

And the holy Maël, having wept and prayed, armed himself with the mighty Name of the Lord and said to the birds:

"Be ye men!"

Immediately the penguins were transformed. Their foreheads enlarged and their heads grew round like the dome of St. Maria Rotunda in Rome. Their oval eyes opened more widely on the universe; a fleshy nose clothed the two clefts of their nostrils; their beaks were changed into mouths, and from their mouths went forth speech; their necks grew short and thick; their wings became arms and their claws legs; a restless soul dwelt within the breast of each of them.

However, there remained with them some traces of their first nature. They were inclined to look sideways; they balanced themselves on their short thighs; their bodies were covered with fine down.

And Maël gave thanks to the Lord, because he had incorporated these penguins into the family of Abraham.

But he grieved at the thought that he would soon leave the island to come back no more, and that perhaps when he was far away the faith of the penguins would perish for want of care like a young and tender plant.

And he formed the idea of transporting their island to the coasts of Armorica.

"I know not the designs of eternal Wisdom," said he to himself.

"But if God wills that this island be transported, who could prevent it?"

And the holy man made a very fine cord about forty feet long out of the flax of his stole. He fastened one end of the cord round a point of rock that jutted up through the sand of the shore and, holding the other end of the cord in his hand, he entered the stone trough.

The trough glided over the sea and towed Penguin Island behind it; after nine days' sailing it approached the Breton coast, bringing the island with it.

BOOK II: THE ANCIENT TIMES

Ⅱ

THE FIRST CLOTHES

NE day St. Maël was sitting by the seashore on a warm stone that he found. He thought it had been warmed by the sun and he gave thanks to God for it, not knowing that the Devil had been resting on it.

The apostle was waiting for the monks of Yvern who had been commissioned to bring a freight of skins and fabrics to clothe the inhabitants of the island of Alca.

Soon he saw a monk called Magis coming ashore and carrying a chest upon his back. This monk enjoyed a great reputation for holiness.

When he had drawn near to the old man he laid the chest on the ground and wiping his forehead with the back of his sleeve, he said:

"Well, father, you wish then to clothe these penguins?"

"Nothing is more needful, my son," said the old man. "Since they have been incorporated into the family of Abraham these penguins share the curse of Eve, and they know that they are naked, a thing of which they were ignorant before. And it is high time to clothe them, for they are losing the down that remained on them after their metamorphosis."

"It is true," said Magis as he cast his eyes over the coast where the penguins were to be seen looking for shrimps, gathering mussels, singing, or sleeping, "they are naked. But do you not think, father, that it would be better to leave them naked? Why clothe them? When they wear clothes and are under the moral law they will assume an immense pride, a vile hypocrisy, and an excessive cruelty."

"Is it possible, my son," sighed the old man, "that you understand so badly the effects of the moral law to which even the heathen submit?"

"The moral law," answered Magis, "forces men who are beasts to live otherwise than beasts, a thing that doubtless puts a constraint

25

upon them, but that also flatters and reassures them; and as they are proud, cowardly, and covetous of pleasure, they willingly submit to restraints that tickle their vanity and on which they found both their present security and the hope of their future happiness. That is the principle of all morality. . . . But let us not mislead ourselves. My companions are unloading their cargo of stuffs and skins on the island. Think, father, while there is still time! To clothe the penguins is a very serious business. At present when a penguin desires a penguin he knows precisely what he desires and his lust is limited by an exact knowledge of its object. At this moment two or three couples of penguins are making love on the beach. See with what simplicity! No one pays any attention and the actors themselves do not seem to be greatly preoccupied. But when the female penguins are clothed, the male penguin will not form so exact a notion of what it is that attracts him to them. His indeterminate desires will fly out into all sorts of dreams and illusions; in short, father, he will know love and its mad torments. And all the time the female penguins will cast down their eyes and bite their lips, and take on airs as if they kept a treasure under their clothes! . . . what a pity!

"The evil will be endurable as long as these people remain rude and poor; but only wait for a thousand years and you will see father, with what powerful weapons you have endowed the daughters of Alca. If you will allow me, I can give you some idea of it beforehand. I have some old clothes in this chest. Let us take at hazard one of these female penguins to whom the male penguins give such little thought, and let us dress her as well as we can.

"Here is one coming towards us. She is neither more beautiful nor uglier than the others; she is young. No one looks at her. She strolls indolently along the shore, scratching her back and with her finger at her nose as she walks. You cannot help seeing, father, that she has narrow shoulders, clumsy breasts, a stout figure, and short legs. Her reddish knees pucker at every step she takes, and there is, at each of her joints, what looks like a little monkey's head. Her broad and sinewy feet cling to the rock with their four crooked toes, while the great toes stick up like the heads of two cunning serpents. She begins to walk, all her muscles are engaged in the task, and, when we see them working, we think of her as a machine intended for walking rather than as a machine intended for making love, although visibly she is both, and contains within herself several other pieces of machinery besides. Well, venerable apostle, you will see what I am going to make of her."

With these words the monk, Magis, reached the female penguin in three bounds, lifted her up, carried her in his arms with her hair trailing behind her, and threw her, overcome with fright, at the feet of the holy Maël.

And whilst she wept and begged him to do her no harm, he took a pair of sandals out of his chest and commanded her to put them on.

"Her feet," observed the old man, "will appear smaller when squeezed in by the woollen cords. The soles, being two fingers high, will give an elegant length to her legs and the weight they bear will seem magnified."

As the penguin tied on her sandals she threw a curious look towards the open coffer, and seeing that it was full of jewels and finery, she smiled through her tears.

The monk twisted her hair on the back of her head and covered it with a chaplet of flowers. He encircled her wrist with golden bracelets and making her stand upright, he passed a large linen band beneath her breasts, alleging that her bosom would thereby derive a new dignity and that her sides would be compressed to the greater glory of her hips.

He fixed this band with pins, taking them one by one out of his mouth.

"You can tighten it still more," said the penguin.

When he had, with much care and study, enclosed the soft parts of her bust in this way, he covered her whole body with a rose-coloured tunic which gently followed the lines of her figure.

"Does it hang well?" asked the penguin.

And bending forward with her head on one side and her chin on her shoulder, she kept looking attentively at the appearance of her toilet.

Magis asked her if she did not think the dress a little long, but she answered with assurance that it was not—she would hold it up.

Immediately, taking the back of her skirt in her left hand, she drew it obliquely across her hips, taking care to disclose a glimpse of her heels. Then she went away, walking with short steps and swinging her hips.

She did not turn her head, but as she passed near a stream she glanced out of the corner of her eye at her own reflection.

A male penguin, who met her by chance, stopped in surprise, and retracing his steps began to follow her. As she went along the shore, others coming back from fishing, went up to her, and after looking at her, walked behind her. Those who were lying on the sand got up and joined the rest.

Unceasingly, as she advanced, fresh penguins, descending from the paths of the mountain, coming out of clefts of the rocks, and emerging from the water, added to the size of her retinue.

And all of them, men of ripe age with vigorous shoulders and hairy breasts, agile youths, old men shaking the multitudinous wrinkles of their rosy, and white-haired skins, or dragging their legs thinner and drier than the juniper staff that served them as a third leg, hurried on, panting and emitting an acrid odour and hoarse gasps. Yet she went on peacefully and seemed to see nothing.

"Father," cried Magis, "notice how each one advances with his nose pointed towards the centre of gravity of that young damsel now that the centre is covered by a garment. The sphere inspires the meditations of geometers by the number of its properties. When it proceeds from a physical and living nature it acquires new qualities, and in order that the interest of that figure might be fully revealed to the penguins it was necessary that, ceasing to see it distinctly with their eyes, they should be led to represent it to themselves in their minds. I myself feel at this moment irresistibly attracted towards that penguin. Whether it be because her skirt gives more importance to her hips, and that in its simple magnificence it invests them with a synthetic and general character and allows only the pure idea, the divine principle, of them to be seen, whether this be the cause I cannot say, but I feel that if I embraced her I would hold in my hands the heaven of human pleasure. It is certain that modesty communicates an invincible attraction to women. My uneasiness is so great that it would be vain for me to try to conceal it."

He spoke, and, gathering up his habit, he rushed among the crowd of penguins, pushing, jostling, trampling, and crushing, until he reached the daughter of Alca, whom he seized and suddenly carried in his arms into a cave that had been hollowed out by the sea.

Then the penguins felt as if the sun had gone out. And the holy Maël knew that the Devil had taken the features of the monk, Magis, in order that he might give clothes to the daughter of Alca. He was troubled in spirit, and his soul was sad. As with slow steps he went towards his hermitage he saw the little penguins of six and seven years of age tightening their waists with belts made of seaweed and walking along the shore to see if anybody would follow them.

II

THE FIRST CLOTHES
(Continuation and End)

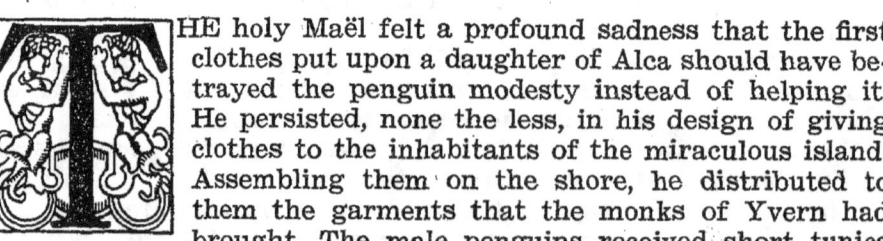

HE holy Maël felt a profound sadness that the first clothes put upon a daughter of Alca should have betrayed the penguin modesty instead of helping it. He persisted, none the less, in his design of giving clothes to the inhabitants of the miraculous island. Assembling them on the shore, he distributed to them the garments that the monks of Yvern had brought. The male penguins received short tunics and breeches, the female penguins long robes. But these robes were far from creating the effect that the former one had produced.

They were not so beautiful, their shape was uncouth and without art, and no attention was paid to them since every woman had one. As they prepared the meals and worked in the fields they soon had nothing but slovenly bodices and soiled petticoats.

The male penguins loaded their unfortunate consorts with work until they looked like beasts of burden. They knew nothing of the troubles of the heart and the disorders of passion. Their habits were innocent. Incest, though frequent, was a sign of rustic simplicity and if drunkenness led a youth to commit some such crime he thought nothing more about it the day afterwards.

III

SETTING BOUNDS TO THE FIELDS AND THE ORIGIN OF PROPERTY

THE island did not preserve the rugged appearance that it had formerly, when in the midst of floating icebergs it sheltered a population of birds within its rock amphitheatre. Its snow-clad peak had sunk down into a hill from the summit of which one could see the coasts of Armorica eternally covered with mist, and the ocean strewn with sullen reefs like monsters half raised out of its depths.

Its coasts were now very extensive and clearly defined and its shape reminded one of a mulberry leaf. It was suddenly covered with coarse grass, pleasing to the flocks, and with willows, ancient fig-trees, and mighty oaks. This fact is attested by the venerable Bede and several other authors worthy of credence.

To the north the shore formed a deep bay that in after years became one of the most famous ports in the universe. To the east, along a rocky coast beaten by a foaming sea, there stretched a deserted and fragrant heath. It was the Beach of Shadows, and the inhabitants of the island never ventured on it for fear of the serpents that lodged in the hollows of the rocks and lest they might encounter the souls of the dead who resembled livid flames. To the south, orchards and woods bounded the languid Bay of Divers. On this fortunate shore old Maël built a wooden church and a monastery. To the west, two streams, the Clange and the Surelle, watered the fertile valleys of Dalles and Dombes.

Now one autumn morning, as the blessed Maël was walking in the valley of Clange in company with a monk of Yvern called Bulloch, he saw bands of fierce-looking men loaded with stones passing along the roads. At the same time he heard in all directions cries and complaints mounting up from the valley towards the tranquil sky.

And he said to Bulloch:

"I notice with sadness, my son, that since they became men the inhabitants of this island act with less wisdom than formerly. When they were birds they only quarrelled during the season of their love affairs. But now they dispute all the time; they pick quarrels with each other in summer as well as in winter. How greatly have they fallen from that peaceful majesty which made the assembly of the penguins look like the Senate of a wise republic!

"Look towards Surelle, Bulloch, my son. In yonder pleasant valley a dozen men penguins are busy knocking each other down with the spades and picks that they might employ better in tilling the ground. The women, still more cruel than the men, are tearing their opponents' faces with their nails. Alas! Bulloch, my son, why are they murdering each other in this way?"

"From a spirit of fellowship, father, and through forethought for the future," answered Bulloch. "For man is essentially provident and sociable. Such is his character and it is impossible to imagine it apart from a certain appropriation of things. Those penguins whom you see are dividing the ground among themselves."

"Could they not divide it with less violence?" asked the aged man. "As they fight they exchange invectives and threats. I do not distinguish their words, but they are angry ones, judging from the tone."

"They are accusing one another of theft and encroachment," answered Bulloch. "That is the general sense of their speech."

At that moment the holy Maël clasped his hands and sighed deeply.

"Do you see, my son," he exclaimed, "that madman who with his teeth is biting the nose of the adversary he has overthrown and that other one who is pounding a woman's head with a huge stone?"

"I see them," said Bulloch. "They are creating law; they are founding property; they are establishing the principles of civilization, the basis of society, and the foundations of the State."

"How is that?" asked old Maël.

"By setting bounds to their fields. That is the origin of all government. Your penguins, O Master, are performing the most august of functions. Throughout the ages their work will be consecrated by lawyers, and magistrates will confirm it."

Whilst the monk, Bulloch, was pronouncing these words a big penguin with a fair skin and red hair went down into the valley carrying a trunk of a tree upon his shoulder. He went up to a little penguin who was watering his vegetables in the heat of the sun, and shouted to him:

"Your field is mine!"

And having delivered himself of this stout utterance he brought down his club on the head of the little penguin, who fell dead upon the field that his own hands had tilled.

At this sight the holy Maël shuddered through his whole body and poured forth a flood of tears.

And in a voice stifled by horror and fear he addressed this prayer to heaven:

"O Lord, my God, O thou who didst receive young Abel's sacrifices, thou who didst curse Cain, avenge, O Lord, this innocent penguin sacrificed upon his own field and make the murderer feel the weight of thy arm. Is there a more odious crime, is there a graver offence against thy justice, O Lord, than this murder and this robbery?"

"Take care, father," said Bulloch gently, "that what you call murder and robbery may not really be war and conquest, those sacred foundations of empires, those sources of all human virtues and all human greatness. Reflect, above all, that in blaming the big penguin you are attacking property in its origin and in its source. I shall have no trouble in showing you how. To till the land is one thing, to possess it is another, and these two things must not be confused; as regards ownership the right of the first occupier is uncertain and badly founded. The right of conquest, on the other hand, rests on more solid foundations. It is the only right that receives respect since it is the only one that makes itself respected. The sole and proud origin of property is force. It is born and preserved by force. In that it is august and yields only to a greater force. This is why it is correct to say that he who possesses is noble. And that big red man, when he knocked down a labourer to get possession of his field, founded at that moment a very noble house upon this earth. I congratulate him upon it."

Having thus spoken, Bulloch approached the big penguin, who was leaning upon his club as he stood in the blood-stained furrow:

"Lord Greatauk, dreaded Prince," said he, bowing to the ground, "I come to pay you the homage due to the founder of legitimate power and hereditary wealth. The skull of the vile Penguin you have overthrown will, buried in your field, attest for ever the sacred rights of your posterity over this soil that you have ennobled. Blessed be your sons and your sons' sons! They shall be Greatauks, Dukes of Skull, and they shall rule over this island of Alca."

Then raising his voice and turning towards the holy Maël:

"Bless Greatauk, father, for all power comes from God."

Maël remained silent and motionless, with his eyes raised towards heaven; he felt a painful uncertainty in judging the monk Bulloch's doctrine. It was, however, the doctrine destined to prevail in epochs of advanced civilization. Bulloch can be considered as the creator of civil law in Penguinia.

IV

THE FIRST ASSEMBLY OF THE ESTATES
OF PENGUINIA

ULLOCH, my son," said old Maël, "we ought to make a census of the Penguins and inscribe each of their names in a book."

"It is a most urgent matter," answered Bulloch, "there can be no good government without it."

Forthwith, the apostle, with the help of twelve monks, proceeded to make a census of the people.

And old Maël then said:

"Now that we keep a register of all the inhabitants, we ought, Bulloch, my son, to levy a just tax so as to provide for public expenses and the maintenance of the Abbey. Each ought to contribute according to his means. For this reason, my son, call together the Elders of Alca, and in agreement with them we shall establish the tax."

The Elders, being called together, assembled to the number of thirty under the great sycamore in the courtyard of the wooden monastery. They were the first Estates of Penguinia. Three-fourths of them were substantial peasants of Surelle and Clange. Greatauk, as the noblest of the Penguins, sat upon the highest stone.

The venerable Maël took his place in the midst of his monks and uttered these words:

"Children, the Lord when he pleases grants riches to men and he takes them away from them. Now I have called you together to levy contributions from the people so as to provide for public expenses and the maintenance of the monks. I consider that these contributions ought to be in proportion to the wealth of each. Therefore he who has a hundred oxen will give ten; he who has ten will give one."

When the holy man had spoken, Morio, a labourer at Anis-on-the-Clange, one of the richest of the Penguins, rose up and said:

"O Father Maël, I think it right that each should contribute to the public expenses and to the support of the Church. For my part I am ready to give up all that I possess in the interest of my brother Penguins, and if it were necessary I would even cheerfully part with my shirt. All the elders of the people are ready, like me, to sacrifice their goods, and no one can doubt their absolute devotion to their country and their creed. We have, then, only to consider the public interest and to do what it requires. Now, Father, what it requires, what it demands, is not to ask much from those who possess much, for then the rich would be less rich and the poor still poorer. The poor live on the wealth of the rich and that is the reason why that wealth is sacred. Do not touch it, to do so would be an uncalled for evil. You will get no great profit by taking from the rich, for they are very few in number; on the contrary you will strip yourself of all your resources and plunge the country into misery. Whereas if you ask a little from each inhabitant without regard to his wealth, you will collect enough for the public necessities and you will have no need to enquire into each citizen's resources, a thing that would be regarded by all as a most vexatious measure. By taxing all equally and easily you will spare the poor, for you will leave them the wealth of the rich. And how could you possibly proportion taxes to wealth? Yesterday I had two hundred oxen, to-day I have sixty, to-morrow I shall have a hundred. Clunic has three cows, but they are thin; Nicclu has only two, but they are fat. Which is the richer, Clunic or Nicclu? The signs of opulence are deceitful. What is certain is that everyone eats and drinks. Tax people according to what they consume. That would be wisdom and it would be justice."

Thus spoke Morio amid the applause of the Elders.

"I ask that this speech be graven on bronze," cried the monk, Bulloch. "It is spoken for the future; in fifteen hundred years the best of the Penguins will not speak otherwise."

The Elders were still applauding when Greatauk, his hand on the pommel of his sword, made this brief declaration:

"Being noble, I shall not contribute; for to contribute is ignoble. It is for the rabble to pay."

After this warning the Elders separated in silence.

As in Rome, a new census was taken every five years; and by this means it was observed that the population increased rapidly. Although children died in marvellous abundance and plagues and famines came with perfect regularity to devastate entire villages, new Penguins, in continually greater numbers, contributed by their private misery to the public prosperity.

V

THE MARRIAGE OF KRAKEN AND ORBEROSIA

URING these times there lived in the island of Alca a Penguin whose arm was strong and whose mind was subtle. He was called Kraken, and had his dwelling on the Beach of Shadows whither the inhabitants never ventured for fear of serpents that lodged in the hollows of the rocks and lest they might encounter the souls of Penguins that had died without baptism. These, in appearance like livid flames, and uttering doleful groans, wandered night and day along the deserted beach. For it was generally believed, though without proof, that among the Penguins that had been changed into men at the blessed Maël's prayer, several had not received baptism and returned after their death to lament amid the tempests. Kraken dwelt on this savage coast in an inaccessible cavern. The only way to it was through a natural tunnel a hundred feet long, the entrance of which was concealed by a thick wood. One evening as Kraken was walking through this deserted plain he happened to meet a young and charming woman Penguin. She was the one that the monk Magis had clothed with his own hands and thus was the first to have worn the garments of chastity. In remembrance of the day when the astonished crowd of Penguins had seen her moving gloriously in her robe tinted like the dawn, this maiden had received the name of Orberosia.*

At the sight of Kraken she uttered a cry of alarm and darted forward to escape from him. But the hero seized her by the garments that floated behind her, and addressed her in these words:

"Damsel, tell me thy name, thy family and thy country."

But Orberosia kept looking at Kraken with alarm.

"Is it you, I see, sir," she asked him, trembling, "or is it not rather your troubled spirit?"

She spoke in this way because the inhabitants of Alca, having no news of Kraken since he went to live on the Beach of Shadows, believed that he had died and descended among the demons of night.

"Cease to fear, daughter of Alca," answered Kraken. "He who speaks to thee is not a wandering spirit, but a man full of strength and might. I shall soon possess great riches."

And young Orberosia asked:

"How dost thou think of acquiring great riches, O Kraken, since thou art a child of the Penguins?"

"By my intelligence," answered Kraken.

*"Orb, poetically, a globe when speaking of the heavenly bodies. By extension any species of globular body."—*Littre.*

"I know," said Orberosia, "that in the time that thou dwelt among us thou wert renowned for thy skill in hunting and fishing. No one equalled thee in taking fishes in a net or in piercing with thy arrows the swift-flying birds."

"It was but a vulgar and laborious industry, O maiden. I have found a means of gaining much wealth for myself without fatigue. But tell me who thou art?"

"I am called Orberosia," answered the young girl.

"Why art thou so far away from thy dwelling and in the night?"

"Kraken, it was not without the will of Heaven."

"What meanest thou, Orberosia?"

"That Heaven, O Kraken, placed me in thy path, for what reason I know not."

Kraken beheld her for a long time in silence.

Then he said with gentleness:

"Orberosia, come into my house; it is that of the bravest and most ingenious of the sons of the Penguins. If thou art willing to follow me, I will make thee my companion."

Then casting down her eyes, she murmured:

"I will follow thee, master."

It is thus that the fair Orberosia became the consort of the hero Kraken. This marriage was not celebrated with songs and torches because Kraken did not consent to show himself to the people of the Penguins; but hidden in his cave he planned great designs.

VI

THE DRAGON OF ALCA

"We afterwards went to visit the cabinet of natural history. . . . The caretaker showed us a sort of packet bound in straw that he told us contained the skeleton of a dragon; a proof, added he, that the dragon is not a fabulous animal." —*Memoirs of Jacques Casanova*, Paris, 1843. Vol. IV., pp. 404, 405.

IN the meantime the inhabitants of Alca practised the labours of peace. Those of the northern coast went in boats to fish or to search for shellfish. The labourers of Dombes cultivated oats, rye, and wheat. The rich Penguins of the valley of Dalles reared domestic animals, while those of the Bay of Divers cultivated their orchards. Merchants of Port-Alca carried on a trade in salt fish with Armorica and the gold of the two Britains, which began to be introduced into the island, facilitated exchange. The Penguin people were enjoying the

fruit of their labours in perfect tranquillity when suddenly a sinister rumour ran from village to village. It was said everywhere that a frightful dragon had ravaged two farms in the Bay of Divers.

A few days before, the maiden Orberosia had disappeared. Her absence had at first caused no uneasiness because on several occasions she had been carried off by violent men who were consumed with love. And thoughtful people were not astonished at this, reflecting that the maiden was the most beautiful of the Penguins. It was even remarked that she sometimes went to meet her ravishers, for none of us can escape his destiny. But this time, as she did not return, it was feared that the dragon had devoured her. The more so as the inhabitants of the valley of Dalles soon knew that the dragon was not a fable told by the women around the fountains. For one night the monster devoured out of the village of Anis six hens, a sheep, and a young orphan child called little Elo. The next morning nothing was to be found either of the animals or of the child.

Immediately the Elders of the village assembled in the public place and seated themselves on the stone bench to take counsel concerning what it was expedient to do in these terrible circumstances.

Having called all those Penguins who had seen the dragon during the disastrous night, they asked them:

"Have you not noticed his form and his behaviour?"

And each answered in his turn:

"He has the claws of a lion, the wings of an eagle, and the tail of a serpent."

"His back bristles with thorny crests."

"His whole body is covered with yellow scales."

"His look fascinates and confounds. He vomits flames."

"He poisons the air with his breath."

"He has the head of a dragon, the claws of a lion, and the tail of a fish."

And a woman of Anis, who was regarded as intelligent and of sound judgment and from whom the dragon had taken three hens, deposed as follows:

"He is formed like a man. The proof is that I thought he was my husband, and I said to him, 'Come to bed, you old fool.'"

Others said:

"He is formed like a cloud."

"He looks like a mountain."

And a little child came and said:

"I saw the dragon taking off his head in the barn so that he might give a kiss to my sister Minnie."

And the Elders also asked the inhabitants:

"How big is the dragon?"

And it was answered:

"As big as an ox."

"Like the big merchant ships of the Bretons."

"He is the height of a man."

"He is higher than the fig-tree under which you are sitting."

"He is as large as a dog."

Questioned finally on his colour, the inhabitants said:

"Red."

"Green."

"Blue."

"Yellow."

"His head is bright green, his wings are brilliant orange tinged with pink, his limbs are silver grey, his hind-quarters and his tail are striped with brown and pink bands, his belly bright yellow spotted with black."

"His colour? He has no colour."

"He is the colour of a dragon."

After hearing this evidence the Elders remained uncertain as to what should be done. Some advised to watch for him, to surprise him and overthrow him by a multitude of arrows. Others, thinking it vain to oppose so powerful a monster by force, counselled that he should be appeased by offerings.

"Pay him tribute," said one of them who passed for a wise man. "We can render him propitious to us by giving him agreeable presents, fruits, wine, lambs, a young virgin."

Others held for poisoning the fountains where he was accustomed to drink or for smoking him out of his cavern.

But none of these counsels prevailed. The dispute was lengthy and the Elders dispersed without coming to any resolution.

VII

THE DRAGON OF ALCA

(*Continuation*)

URING all the month dedicated by the Romans to their false god Mars or Mavors, the dragon ravaged the farms of Dalles and Dombes. He carried off fifty sheep, twelve pigs, and three young boys. Every family was in mourning and the island was full of lamentations. In order to remove the scourge, the Elders of the unfortunate villages watered by the Clange and the Survelle resolved to assemble and together go and ask the help of the blessed Maël.

On the fifth day of the month whose name among the Latins signifies opening, because it opens the year, they went in procession to the wooden monastery that had been built on the southern coast of the island. When they were introduced into the cloister they filled it with their sobs and groans. Moved by their lamentations, old Maël left the room in which he devoted himself to the study of astronomy and the meditation of the Scriptures, and went down to them, leaning on his pastoral staff. At his approach, the Elders, prostrating themselves, held out to him green branches of trees and some of them burnt aromatic herbs.

And the holy man, seating himself beside the cloistral fountain under an ancient fig-tree, uttered these words:

"O my sons, offspring of the Penguins, why do you weep and groan? Why do you hold out those suppliant boughs towards me? Why do you raise towards heaven the smoke of those herbs? What calamity do you expect that I can avert from your heads? Why do you beseech me? I am ready to give my life for you. Only tell your father what it is you hope from him."

To these questions the chief of the Elders answered:

"O Maël, father of the sons of Alca, I will speak for all. A horrible dragon is laying waste our lands, depopulating our cattle-sheds, and carrying off the flower of our youth. He has devoured the child Elo and seven young boys; he has mangled the maiden Orberosia, the fairest of the Penguins, with his teeth. There is not a village in which he does not emit his poisoned breath and which he has not filled with desolation. A prey to this terrible scourge, we come, O Maël, to pray thee, as the wisest, to advise us concerning the safety of the inhabitants of this island lest the ancient race of Penguins be extinguished."

"O chief of the Elders of Alca," replied Maël, "thy words fill me with profound grief, and I groan at the thought that this island is the prey of a terrible dragon. But such an occurrence is not unique, for we find in books several tales of very fierce dragons. The monsters are oftenest found in caverns, by the brinks of waters, and, in preference, among pagan peoples. Perhaps there are some among you who, although they have received holy baptism and been incorporated into the family of Abraham, have yet worshipped idols, like the ancient Romans, or hung up images, votive tablets, fillets of wool, and garlands of flowers on the branches of some sacred tree. Or perhaps some of the women Penguins have danced round a magic stone and drunk water from the fountains where the nymphs dwell. If it be so, I believe, O Penguins, that the Lord has sent this' dragon to punish all for the crimes of some, and to lead you, O children of the Penguins, to exterminate blasphemy, superstition, and impiety from amongst you. For this reason I advise, as a remedy against the great evil from which you suffer, that you carefully search your dwellings for idolatry, and extirpate it from them. I think it would be also efficacious to pray and do penance."

Thus spoke the holy Maël. And the Elders of the Penguin people kissed his feet and returned to their villages with renewed hope.

VIII

THE DRAGON OF ALCA

(*Continuation*)

OLLOWING the counsel of the holy Maël the inhabitants of Alca endeavoured to uproot the superstitions that had sprung up amongst them. They took care to prevent the girls from dancing with incantations round the fairy tree. Young mothers were sternly forbidden to rub their children against the stones that stood upright in the fields so as to make them strong. An old man of Dombes who foretold the future by shaking grains of barley on a sieve, was thrown into a well.

However, each night the monster still raided the poultry-yards and the cattle-sheds. The frightened peasants barricaded themselves in their houses. A woman with child who saw the shadow of a dragon on the road through a window in the moonlight, was so terrified that she was brought to bed before her time.

In those days of trial, the holy Maël meditated unceasingly on the nature of dragons and the means of combating them. After six months of study and prayer he thought he had found what he sought. One evening as he was walking by the sea with a young monk called Samuel, he expressed his thought to him in these terms:

"I have studied at length the history and habits of dragons, not to satisfy a vain curiosity, but to discover examples to follow in the present circumstances. For such, Samuel, my son, is the use of history.

"It is an invariable fact that dragons are extremely vigilant. They never sleep, and for this reason we often find them employed in guarding treasures. A dragon guarded at Colchis the golden fleece that Jason conquered from him. A dragon watched over the golden apples in the garden of the Hesperides. He was killed by Hercules and transformed into a star by Juno. This fact is related in some books, and if it be true, it was done by magic, for the gods of the pagans are in reality demons. A dragon prevented barbarous and ignorant men from drinking at the fountain of Castalia. We must also remember the dragon of Andromeda, which was slain by Perseus. But let us turn from these pagan fables, in which error is always mixed with truth. We meet dragons in the histories of the glorious archangel Michael, of St. George, St. Philip, St. James the Great, St. Patrick, St. Martha, and St. Margaret. And it is in such writings, since they are worthy of full credence, that we ought to look for comfort and counsel.

"The story of the dragon of Silena affords us particularly precious examples. You must know, my son, that on the banks of a vast pool close to that town there dwelt a dragon who sometimes approached the walls and poisoned with his breath all who dwelt in the suburbs. And that they might not be devoured by the monster, the inhabitants of Silena delivered up to him one of their number every morning. The victim was chosen by lot, and after a hundred others, the lot fell upon the king's daughter.

"Now St. George, who was a military tribune, as he passed through the town of Silena, learned that the king's daughter had just been given to the fierce beast. He immediately mounted his horse, and, armed with his lance, rushed to encounter the dragon, whom he reached just as the monster was about to devour the royal virgin. And when St. George had overthrown the dragon, the king's daughter fastened her girdle round the beast's neck and he followed her like a dog led on a leash.

"That is an example for us of the power of virgins over dragons. The history of St. Martha furnishes us with a still more certain proof. Do you know the story, Samuel, my son?"

"Yes, father," answered Samuel.

And the blessed Maël went on:

"There was in a forest on the banks of the Rhone, between Arles and Avignon, a dragon half quadruped and half fish, larger than an ox, with sharp teeth like horns and huge wings at his shoulders. He sank the boats and devoured their passengers. Now St. Martha, at the entreaty of the people, approached this dragon, whom she found devouring a man. She put her girdle round his neck and led him easily into the town.

"These two examples lead me to think that we should have recourse to the power of some virgin so as to conquer the dragon who scatters terror and death through the island of Alca.

"For this reason, Samuel my son, gird up thy loins and go, I pray thee, with two of thy companions, into all the villages of this island, and proclaim everywhere that a virgin alone shall be able to deliver the island from the monster that devastates it.

"Thou shalt sing psalms and canticles and thou shalt say:

" 'O sons of the Penguins, if there be among you a pure virgin, let her arise and go, armed with the sign of the cross, to combat the dragon!' "

Thus the old man spake, and Samuel promised to obey him. The next day he girded up his loins and set out with two of his companions to proclaim to the inhabitants of Alca that a virgin alone would be able to deliver the Penguins from the rage of the dragon.

IX

THE DRAGON OF ALCA
(*Continuation*)

RBEROSIA loved her husband, but she did not love him alone. At the hour when Venus lightens in the pale sky, whilst Kraken scattered terror through the villages, she used to visit in his moving hut, a young shepherd of Dalles called Marcel, whose pleasing form was invested with inexhaustible vigour. The fair Orberosia shared the shepherd's aromatic couch with delight, but far from making herself known to him, she took the name of Bridget, and said that she was the daughter of a gardener in the Bay of Divers. When regretfully she left his arms she walked across the smoking fields towards the Coast of Shadows, and if she happened to meet some belated peasant she immediately spread out her garments like great wings and cried:

"Passer by, lower your eyes, that you may not have to say, 'Alas! alas! woe is me, for I have seen the angel of the Lord.'"

The villagers tremblingly knelt with their faces to the ground. And several of them used to say that angels, whom it would be death to see, passed along the roads of the island in the night time.

Kraken did not know of the loves of Orberosia and Marcel, for he was a hero, and heroes never discover the secrets of their wives. But though he did not know of these loves, he reaped the benefit of them. Every night he found his companion more good-humoured and more beautiful, exhaling pleasure and perfuming the nuptial bed with a delicious odour of fennel and vervain. She loved Kraken with a love that never became importunate or anxious, because she did not rest its whole weight on him alone.

This lucky infidelity of Orberosia was destined soon to save the hero from a great peril and to assure his fortune and his glory for ever. For it happened that she saw passing in the twilight a neatherd from Belmont, who was goading on his oxen, and she fell more deeply in love with him than she had ever been with the shepherd Marcel. He was hunch-backed; his shoulders were higher than his ears; his body was supported by legs of different lengths; his rolling eyes flashed from beneath his matted hair. From his throat issued a hoarse voice and strident laughter; he smelt of the cowshed. However, to her he was beautiful. "A plant," as Gnatho says, "has been loved by one, a stream by another, a beast by a third."

Now, one day, as she was sighing within the neatherd's arms in a village barn, suddenly the blasts of a trumpet, with sounds and footsteps, fell upon her ears; she looked through the window and saw the inhabitants collected in the marketplace round a young monk, who, standing upon a rock, uttered these words in a distinct voice:

"Inhabitants of Belmont, Abbot Maël, our venerable father, informs you through my mouth that neither by strength nor skill in arms shall you prevail against the dragon; but the beast shall be overcome by a virgin. If, then, there be among you a perfectly pure virgin, let her arise and go towards the monster; and when she meets him let her tie her girdle round his neck and she shall lead him as easily as if he were a little dog."

And the young monk, replacing his hood upon his head, departed to carry the proclamation of the blessed Maël to other villages.

Orberosia sat in the amorous straw, resting her head in her hand and supporting her elbow upon her knee, meditating on what she had just heard.

Although, so far as Kraken was concerned, she feared the power of a virgin much less than the strength of armed men, she did not feel reassured by the proclamation of the blessed Maël. A vague but sure instinct ruled her mind and warned her that Kraken could not henceforth be a dragon with safety.

She said to the neatherd:

"My own heart, what do you think about the dragon?"

The rustic shook his head.

"It is certain that dragons laid waste the earth in ancient times and some have been seen as large as mountains. But they come no longer, and I believe that what has been taken for a dragon is not one at all, but pirates or merchants who have carried off the fair Orberosia and the best of the children of Alca in their ships. But if one of those brigands attempts to rob me of my oxen, I will either by force or craft find a way to prevent him from doing me any harm."

This remark of the neatherd increased Orberosia's apprehensions and added to her solicitude for the husband whom she loved.

X

THE DRAGON OF ALCA
(*Continuation*)

HE days passed by and no maiden arose in the island to combat the monster. And in the wooden monastery old Maël, seated on a bench in the shade of an old fig-tree, accompanied by a pious monk called Regimental, kept asking himself anxiously and sadly how it was that there was not in Alca a single virgin fit to overthrow the monster.

He sighed and brother Regimental sighed too. At that moment old Maël called young Samuel, who happened to pass through the garden, and said to him:

"I have meditated anew, my son, on the means of destroying the dragon who devours the flower of our youth, our flocks, and our harvests. In this respect the story of the dragons of St. Riok and of St. Pol de Leon seems to me particularly instructive. The dragon of St. Riok was six fathoms long; his head was derived from the cock and the basilisk, his body from the ox and the serpent; he ravaged the banks of the Elorn in the time of King Bristocus. St. Riok, then aged two years, led him by a leash to the sea, in which the monster drowned himself of his own accord. St. Pol's dragon was sixty feet long and not less terrible. The blessed apostle of Leon bound him with his stole and allowed a young noble of great purity of life to lead him. These examples prove that in the eyes of God a chaste young man is as agreeable as a chaste girl. Heaven makes no distinction between them. For this reason, my son, if you believe what I say, we will both go to the Coast of Shadows; when we reach the dragon's cavern we will call the monster in a loud voice, and when he comes forth I will tie my stole round his neck and you will lead him to the sea, where he will not fail to drown himself."

At the old man's words Samuel cast down his head and did not answer.

"You seem to hesitate, my son," said Maël.

Brother Regimental, contrary to his custom, spoke without being addressed.

"There is at least cause for some hesitation," said he. "St. Riok was only two years old when he overcame the dragon. Who says that nine or ten years later he could have done as much? Remember, father, that the dragon who is devastating our island has devoured little Elo and four or five other young boys. Brother Samuel is not so presumptuous as to believe that at nineteen years of age he is more innocent than they were at twelve and fourteen.

"Alas!" added the monk, with a groan, "who can boast of being chaste in this world, where everything gives the example and model of love, where all things in nature, animals, and plants, show us the caresses of love and advise us to share them? Animals are eager to unite in their own fashion, but the various marriages of quadrupeds, birds, fishes, and reptiles are far from equalling in lust the nuptials of the trees. The greater extremes of lewdness that the pagans have imagined in their fables are outstripped by the simple flowers of the field, and, if you knew the irregularities of lilies and roses you would take those chalices of impurity, those vases of scandal, away from your altars."

"Do not speak in this way, Brother Regimental," answered old Maël. "Since they are subject to the law of nature, animals and plants are always innocent. They have no souls to save, whilst man——"

"You are right," replied Brother Regimental, "it is quite a different thing. But do not send young Samuel to the dragon—the dragon might devour him. For the last five years Samuel is not in a state to show his innocence to monsters. In the year of the comet, the Devil in order to seduce him, put in his path a milkmaid, who was lifting up her petticoat to cross a ford. Samuel was tempted, but he overcame the temptation. The Devil, who never tires, sent him the image of that young girl in a dream. The shade did what the reality was unable to accomplish, and Samuel yielded. When he awoke he moistened his couch with his tears, but alas! repentance did not give him back his innocence."

As he listened to this story Samuel asked himself how his secret could be known, for he was ignorant that the Devil had borrowed the appearance of Brother Regimental, so as to trouble the hearts of the monks of Alca.

And old Maël remained deep in thought and kept asking himself in grief:

"Who will deliver us from the dragon's tooth? Who will preserve us from his breath? Who will save us from his look?"

However, the inhabitants of Alca began to take courage. The labourers of Dombes and the neatherds of Belmont swore that they themselves would be of more avail than a girl against the ferocious beast, and they exclaimed as they stroked the muscles on their arms, "Let the dragon come!" Many men and women had seen him. They did not agree about his form and his figure, but all now united in saying that he was not as big as they had thought, and that his height was not much greater than a man's. The defence was organised; towards nightfall watches were stationed at the entrances of the villages ready to give the alarm; and during the night companies armed with pitchforks and scythes protected the paddocks in which the animals were shut up. Indeed, once in the village of Anis some plucky labourers surprised him as he was scaling Morio's wall, and, as they had flails, scythes, and pitch-forks, they fell upon him and pressed him hard. One of them, a very quick and courageous man, thought to have run him through with his pitchfork; but he slipped in a pool and so let him escape. The others would certainly have caught him had they not waited to pick up the rabbits and fowls that he dropped in his flight.

Those labourers declared to the Elders of the village that the monster's form and proportions appeared to them human enough except for his head and his tail, which were, in truth, terrifying.

XI

THE DRAGON OF ALCA
(*Continuation*)

N that day Kraken came back to his cavern sooner than usual. He took from his head his sealskin hel-met with its two bull's horns and its visor trimmed with terrible hooks. He threw on the table his gloves that ended in horrible claws—they were the beaks of sea-birds. He unhooked his belt from which hung a long green tail twisted into many folds. Then he ordered his page, Elo, to help him off with his boots and, as the child did not succeed in doing this very quickly, he gave him a kick that sent him to the other end of the grotto.

Without looking at the fair Orberosia, who was spinning, he seated himself in front of the fireplace, on which a sheep was roast-ing, and he muttered:

"Ignoble Penguins. . . . There is no worse trade than a dragon's."

"What does my master say?" asked the fair Orberosia.

"They fear me no longer," continued Kraken. "Formerly every-one fled at my approach. I carried away hens and rabbits in my bag; I drove sheep and pigs, cows, and oxen before me. To-day these clod-hoppers keep a good guard; they sit up at night. Just now I was pursued in the village of Anis by doughty labourers armed with flails and scythes and pitchforks. I had to drop the hens and rabbits, put my tail under my arm, and run as fast as I could. Now I ask you, is it seemly for a dragon of Cappadocia to run away like a robber with his tail under his arm? Further, in-commoded as I was by crests, horns, hooks, claws, and scales, I barely escaped a brute who ran half an inch of his pitchfork into my left thigh."

As he said this he carefully ran his hand over the insulted part,

and, after giving himself up for a few moments to bitter medita.
tion:

"What idiots those Penguins are! I am tired of blowing flames in
the faces of such imbeciles. Orberosia, do you hear me?"

Having thus spoken the hero raised his terrible helmet in his
hands and gazed at it for a long time in gloomy silence. Then he
pronounced these rapid words:

"I have made this helmet with my own hands in the shape of
a fish's head, covering it with the skin of a seal. To make it more
terrible I have put on it the horns of a bull and I have given it a
boar's jaws; I have hung from it a horse's tail dyed vermilion.
When in the gloomy twilight I threw it over my shoulders no inhabitant of this island had courage to withstand its sight. Women
and children, young men and old men fled distracted at its approach, and I carried terror among the whole race of Penguins. By
what advice does that insolent people lose its earlier fears and
dare to-day to behold these horrible jaws and to attack this terrible
crest?"

And throwing his helmet on the rocky soil:

"Perish, deceitful helmet!" cried Kraken. "I swear by all the demons of Armor that I will never bear you upon my head again."

And having uttered this oath he stamped upon his helmet, his
gloves, his boots, and upon his tail with its twisted folds.

"Kraken," said the fair Orberosia, "will you allow your servant
to employ artifice to save your reputation and your goods? Do not
despise a woman's help. You need it, for all men are imbeciles."

"Woman," asked Kraken, "what are your plans?"

And the fair Orberosia informed her husband that the monks
were going through the villages teaching the inhabitants the best
way of combating the dragon; that, according to their instructions,
the beast would be overcome by a virgin, and that if a maid placed
her girdle around the dragon's neck she could lead him as easily as
if he were a little dog.

"How do you know that the monks teach this?" asked Kraken.

"My friend," answered Orberosia, "do not interrupt a serious
subject by frivolous questions. . . . 'If, then,' added the monks,
'there be in Alca a pure virgin, let her arise!' Now, Kraken, I have
determined to answer their call. I will go and find the holy Maël and
I will say to him: 'I am the virgin destined by Heaven to overthrow the dragon.'"

At these words Kraken exclaimed: "How can you be that pure
virgin? And why do you want to overthrow me, Orberosia? Have
you lost your reason? Be sure that I will not allow myself to be
conquered by you!"

"Can you not try and understand me before you get angry?"
sighed the fair Orberosia with deep though gentle contempt.

And she explained the cunning designs that she had formed.

As he listened, the hero remained pensive. And when she ceased speaking:

"Orberosia, your cunning is deep," said he. "And if your plans are carried out according to your intentions I shall derive great advantages from them. But how can you be the virgin destined by heaven?"

"Don't bother about that," she replied, "and come to bed."

The next day in the grease-laden atmosphere of the cavern, Kraken plaited a deformed skeleton out of osier rods and covered it with bristling, scaly, and filthy skins. To one extremity of the skeleton Orberosia sewed the fierce crest and the hideous mask that Kraken used to wear in his plundering expeditions, and to its other end she fastened the tail with twisted folds which the hero was wont to trail behind him. And when the work was finished they showed little Elo and the other five children who waited on them how to get inside this machine, how to make it walk, how to blow horns and burn tow in it so as to send forth smoke and flames through the dragon's mouth.

XII

THE DRAGON OF ALCA

(Continuation)

RBEROSIA, having clothed herself in a robe made of coarse stuff and girt herself with a thick cord, went to the monastery and asked to speak to the blessed Maël. And because women were forbidden to enter the enclosure of the monastery the old man advanced outside the gates, holding his pastoral cross in his right hand and resting his left on the shoulder of Brother Samuel, the youngest of his disciples.

He asked:

"Woman, who art thou?"

"I am the maiden Orberosia."

At this reply Maël raised his trembling arms to heaven.

"Do you speak truth, woman? It is a certain fact that Orberosia was devoured by the dragon. And yet I see Orberosia and hear her. Did you not, O my daughter, while within the dragon's bowels arm yourself with the sign of the cross and come uninjured out of his throat? That is what seems to me the most credible explanation."

"You are not deceived, father," answered Orberosia. "That is precisely what happened to me. Immediately I came out of the creature's bowels I took refuge in a hermitage on the Coast of Shadows. I lived there in solitude, giving myself up to prayer and meditation, and performing unheard of austerities, until I learnt by a revelation from heaven that a maid alone could overcome the dragon, and that I was that maid."

"Show me a sign of your mission," said the old man.

"I myself am the sign," answered Orberosia.

"I am not ignorant of the power of those who have placed a seal upon their flesh," replied the apostle of the Penguins. "But are you indeed such as you say?"

"You will see by the result," answered Orberosia.

The monk Regimental drew near:

"That will," said he, "be the best proof. King Solomon has said: 'Three things are hard to understand and a fourth is impossible: they are the way of a serpent on the earth, the way of a bird in the air, the way of a ship in the sea, and the way of a man with a maid.' I regard such matrons as nothing less than presumptuous who claim to compare themselves in these matters with the wisest of kings. Father, if you are led by me you will not consult them in regard to the pious Orberosia. When they have given their opinion you will not be a bit farther on than before. Virginity is not less difficult to prove than to keep. Pliny tells us in his history that its signs are either imaginary or very uncertain.* One who bears upon her the fourteen signs of corruption may yet be pure in the eyes of the angels, and, on the contrary, another who has been pronounced pure by the matrons who inspected her may know that her good appearance is due to the artifices of a cunning perversity. As for the purity of this holy girl here, I would put my hand in the fire in witness of it."

He spoke thus because he was the Devil. But old Maël did not know it. He asked the pious Orberosia:

"My daughter, how would you proceed to conquer so fierce an animal as he who devoured you?"

The virgin answered:

"To-morrow at sunrise, O Maël, you will summon the people together on the hill in front of the desolate moor that extends to the Coast of Shadows, and you will take care that no man of the Penguins remains less than five hundred paces from those rocks so that he may not be poisoned by the monster's breath. And the dragon will come out of the rocks and I will put my girdle round his neck and lead him like an obedient dog."

"Ought you not to be accompanied by a courageous and pious man who will kill the dragon?" asked Maël.

"It will be as thou sayest, venerable father. I shall deliver the monster to Kraken, who will slay him with his flashing sword. For I tell thee that the noble Kraken, who was believed to be dead, will return among the Penguins and he shall slay the dragon. And from

*We have vainly sought for this phrase in Pliny's "Natural History." —*Editor.*

the creature's belly will come forth the little children whom he has devoured."

"What you declare to me, O virgin," cried the apostle, "seems wonderful and beyond human power."

"It is," answered the virgin Orberosia. "But learn, O Maël, that I have had a revelation that as a reward for their deliverance, the Penguin people will pay to the knight Kraken an annual tribute of three hundred fowls, twelve sheep, two oxen, three pigs, one thousand eight hundred bushels of corn, and vegetables according to their season; and that, moreover, the children who will come out of the dragon's belly will be given and committed to the said Kraken to serve him and obey him in all things. If the Penguin people fail to keep their engagements a new dragon will come upon the island more terrible than the first. I have spoken."

XIII

THE DRAGON OF ALCA

(*Continuation and End*)

HE people of the Penguins were assembled by Maël and they spent the night on the Coast of Shadows within the bounds which the holy man had prescribed in order that none among the Penguins should be poisoned by the monster's breath.

The veil of night still covered the earth when, preceded by a hoarse bellowing, the dragon showed his indistinct and monstrous form upon the rocky coast. He crawled like a serpent and his writhing body seemed about fifteen feet long. At his appearance the crowd drew back in terror. But soon all eyes were turned towards the Virgin Orberosia, who, in the first light of the dawn, clothed in white, advanced over the purple heather. With an intrepid though modest gait she walked towards the beast, who, uttering awful bellowings, opened his flaming throat. An immense cry of terror and pity arose from the midst of the Penguins. But the virgin, unloosing her linen girdle, put it round the dragon's neck and led him on the leash like a faithful dog, amid the acclamations of the spectators.

She had walked over a long stretch of the heath when Kraken appeared armed with a flashing sword. The people, who believed him dead, uttered cries of joy and surprise. The hero rushed towards the beast, turned him over on his back, and with his sword cut open his belly, from whence came forth in their shirts, with curling hair and folded hands, little Elo and the five other children whom the monster had devoured.

Immediately they threw themselves on their knees before the virgin Orberosia, who took them in her arms and whispered into their ears:

"You will go through the villages saying: 'We are the poor little children who were devoured by the dragon, and we came out of his belly in our shirts.' The inhabitants will give you abundance of all that you can desire. But if you say anything else you will get nothing but cuffs and whippings. Go!"

Several Penguins, seeing the dragon disembowelled, rushed forward to cut him to pieces, some from a feeling of rage and vengeance, others to get the magic stone called dragonite, that is engendered in his head. The mothers of the children who had come back to life ran to embrace their little ones. But the holy Maël kept them back, saying that none of them were holy enough to approach a dragon without dying.

And soon little Elo and the five other children came towards the people and said:

"We are the poor little children who were devoured by the dragon and we came out of his belly in our shirts."

And all who heard them kissed them and said:

"Blessed children, we will give you abundance of all that you can desire."

And the crowd of people dispersed, full of joy, singing hymns and canticles.

To commemorate this day on which Providence delivered the people from a cruel scourge, processions were established in which the effigy of a chained dragon was led about.

Kraken levied the tribute and became the richest and most powerful of the Penguins. As a sign of his victory and so as to inspire a salutary terror, he wore a dragon's crest upon his head and he had a habit of saying to the people:

"Now that the monster is dead I am the dragon."

For many years Orberosia bestowed her favours upon neatherds and shepherds, whom she thought equal to the gods. But when she was no longer beautiful she consecrated herself to the Lord.

At her death she became the object of public veneration, and was admitted into the calendar of the saints and adopted as the patron saint of Penguinia.

Kraken left a son, who, like his father, wore a dragon's crest, and he was for this reason surnamed Draco. He was the founder of the first royal dynasty of the Penguins.

BOOK III: THE MIDDLE AGES AND THE RENAISSANCE

I

BRIAN THE GOOD AND QUEEN GLAMORGAN

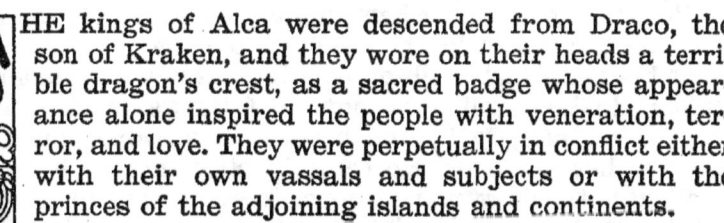HE kings of Alca were descended from Draco, the son of Kraken, and they wore on their heads a terrible dragon's crest, as a sacred badge whose appearance alone inspired the people with veneration, terror, and love. They were perpetually in conflict either with their own vassals and subjects or with the princes of the adjoining islands and continents.

The most ancient of these kings has left but a name. We do not even know how to pronounce or write it. The first of the Draconides whose history is known was Brian the Good, renowned for his skill and courage in war and in the chase.

He was a Christian and loved learning. He also favoured men who had vowed themselves to the monastic life. In the hall of his palace where, under the sooty rafters, there hung the heads, pelts, and horns of wild beasts, he held feasts to which all the harpers of Alca and of the neighbouring islands were invited, and he himself used to join in singing the praises of the heroes. He was just and magnanimous, but inflamed by so ardent a love of glory that he could not restrain himself from putting to death those who had sung better than himself.

The monks of Yvern having been driven out by the pagans who ravaged Brittany, King Brian summoned them into his kingdom and built a wooden monastery for them near his palace. Every day he went with Queen Glamorgan, his wife, into the monastery chapel and was present at the religious ceremonies and joined in the hymns.

Now among these monks there was a brother called Oddoul, who, while still in the flower of his youth, had adorned himself with knowledge and virtue. The devil entertained a great grudge against him, and attempted several times to lead him into temptation. He took several shapes and appeared to him in turn as a war-horse, a young maiden, and a cup of mead. Then he rattled two dice in a dice-box and said to him:

"Will you play with me for the kingdoms of the world against one of the hairs of your head?"

But the man of the Lord, armed with the sign of the Cross, repulsed the enemy. Perceiving that he could not seduce him, the devil thought of an artful plan to ruin him. One summer night he approached the queen, who slept upon her couch, showed her an image of the young monk whom she saw every day in the wooden monastery, and upon this image he placed a spell. Forthwith, like a subtle poison, love flowed into Glamorgan's veins, and she burned with an ardent desire to do as she listed with Oddoul. She formed unceasing pretexts to have him near her. Several times she asked him to teach reading and singing to her children.

"I entrust them to you," said she to him. "And I will follow the lessons you will give them so that I myself may learn also. You will teach both mother and sons at the same time."

But the young monk kept making excuses. At times he would say that he was not a learned enough teacher, and on other occasions that his state forbade him all intercourse with women. This refusal inflamed Glamorgan's passion. One day as she lay pining upon her couch, her malady having become intolerable, she summoned Oddoul to her chamber. He came in obedience to her orders, but remained with his eyes cast down towards the threshold of the door. With impatience and grief she resented his not looking at her.

"See," said she to him, "I have no more strength, a shadow is on my eyes. My body is both burning and freezing."

And as he kept silence and made no movement, she called him in a voice of entreaty:

"Come to me, come!"

With outstretched arms to which passion gave more length, she endeavoured to seize him and draw him towards her.

But he fled away, reproaching her for her wantonness.

Then, incensed with rage and fearing that Oddoul might divulge the shame into which she had fallen, she determined to ruin him so that he might not ruin her.

In a voice of lamentation that resounded throughout all the palace she called for help, as if, in truth, she were in some great danger. Her servants rushed up and saw the young monk fleeing and the queen pulling back the sheets upon her couch. They all cried out together. And when King Brian, attracted by the noise, entered the chamber, Glamorgan, showing him her dishevelled hair, her eyes flooded with tears, and her bosom that in the fury of her love she had torn with her nails, said:

"My lord and husband, behold the traces of the insults I have undergone. Driven by an infamous desire Oddoul has approached me and attempted to do me violence."

When he heard these complaints and saw the blood, the king,

transported with fury, ordered his guards to seize the young monk and burn him alive before the palace under the queen's eyes.

Being told of the affair, the Abbot of Yvern went to the king and said to him:

"King Brian, know by this example the difference between a Christian woman and a pagan. Roman Lucretia was the most virtuous of idolatrous princesses, yet she had not the strength to defend herself against the attacks of an effeminate youth, and, ashamed of her weakness, she gave way to despair, whilst Glamorgan has successfully withstood the assaults of a criminal filled with rage, and possessed by the most terrible of demons." Meanwhile Oddoul, in the prison of the palace, was waiting for the moment when he should be burned alive. But God did not suffer an innocent to perish. He sent to him an angel, who, taking the form of one of the queen's servants called Gudrune, took him out of his prison and led him into the very room where the woman whose appearance he had taken dwelt.

And the angel said to young Oddoul:

"I love thee because thou art daring."

And young Oddoul, believing that it was Gudrune herself, answered with downcast looks:

"It is by the grace of the Lord that I have resisted the violence of the queen and braved the anger of that powerful woman."

And the angel asked:

"What? Hast thou not done what the queen accuses thee of?"

"In truth no, I have not done it," answered Oddoul, his hand on his heart.

"Thou hast not done it?"

"No, I have not done it. The very thought of such an action fills me with horror."

"Then," cried the angel, "what art thou doing here, thou impotent creature?"*

And she opened the door to facilitate the young man's escape. Oddoul felt himself pushed violently out. Scarcely had he gone down into the street than a chamber-pot was poured over his head; and he thought:

"Mysterious are thy designs, O Lord, and thy ways past finding out."

II

DRACO THE GREAT

(Translation of the Relics of St. Orberosia)

THE direct posterity of Brian the Good was extinguished about the year 900 in the person of Collic of the Short Nose. A cousin of that prince, Bosco the Magnanimous, succeeded him, and took care, in order to assure himself of the throne, to put to death all his relations. There issued from him a long line of powerful kings.

One of them, Draco the Great, attained great renown as a man of war. He was defeated more frequently than the others. It is by this constancy in defeat that great captains are recognized. In twenty years he burned down more than a hundred thousand hamlets, market towns, unwalled towns, villages, walled towns, cities, and universities. He set fire impartially to his enemies' territory and to his own domains. And he used to explain his conduct by saying:

"War without fire is like tripe without mustard: it is an insipid thing."

His justice was rigorous. When the peasants whom he made prisoners were unable to raise the money for their ransoms he had them hanged from a tree, and if any unhappy woman came to plead for her destitute husband he dragged her by the hair at his horse's tail. He lived like a soldier without effeminacy. It is satisfactory to relate that his manner of life was pure. Not only did he not allow his kingdom to decline from its hereditary glory, but, even in his reverses he valiantly supported the honour of the Penguin people.

Draco the Great caused the relics of St. Orberosia to be transferred to Alca.

The body of the blessed saint had been buried in a grotto on the Coast of Shadows at the end of a scented heath. The first pilgrims

*The Penguin chronicler who relates the fact employs the expression, *Species inductilis*. I have endeavoured to translate it literally.

who went to visit it were the boys and girls from the neighbouring villages. They used to go there in the evening, by preference in couples, as if their pious desires naturally sought satisfaction in darkness and solitude. They worshipped the saint with a fervent and discreet worship whose mystery they seemed jealously to guard, for they did not like to publish too openly the experiences they felt. But they were heard to murmur one to another words of love, delight, and rapture with which they mingled the name of Orberosia. Some would sigh that there they forgot the world; others would say that they came out of the grotto in peace and calm; the young girls among them used to recall to each other the joys with which they had been filled in it.

Such were the marvels that the virgin of Alca performed in the morning of her glorious eternity; they had the sweetness and indefiniteness of the dawn. Soon the mystery of the grotto spread like a perfume throughout the land; it was a ground of joy and edification for pious souls, and corrupt men endeavoured, though in vain, by falsehood and calumny, to divert the faithful from the springs of grace that flowed from the saint's tomb. The Church took measures so that these graces should not remain reserved for a few children, but should be diffused throughout all Penguin Christianity. Monks took up their quarters in the grotto, they built a monastery, a chapel, and a hostelry on the coast, and pilgrims began to flock thither.

As if strengthened by a longer sojourn in heaven, the blessed Orberosia now performed still greater miracles for those who came to lay their offerings on her tomb. She gave hopes to women who had been hitherto barren, she sent dreams to reassure jealous old men concerning the fidelity of the young wives whom they had suspected without cause, and she protected the country from plagues, murrains, famines, tempests, and dragons of Cappadocia.

But during the troubles that desolated the kingdom in the time of King Collic and his successors, the tomb of St. Orberosia was plundered of its wealth, the monastery burned down, and the monks dispersed. The road that had been so long trodden by devout pilgrims was overgrown with furze and heather, and the blue thistles of the sands. For a hundred years the miraculous tomb had been visited by none save vipers, weasels, and bats, when, one day the saint appeared to a peasant of the neighbourhood, Momordic by name.

"I am the virgin Orberosia," said she to him; "I have chosen thee to restore my sanctuary. Warn the inhabitants of the country that if they allow my memory to be blotted out, and leave my tomb without honour and wealth, a new dragon will come and devastate Penguinia."

Learned churchmen held an inquiry concerning this apparition, and pronounced it genuine, and not diabolical but truly heavenly, and in later years it was remarked that in France, in like circumstances, St. Foy and St. Catherine had acted in the same way and made use of similar language.

The monastery was restored and pilgrims flocked to it anew. The virgin Orberosia worked greater and greater miracles. She cured divers hurtful maladies, particularly club-foot, dropsy, paralysis, and St. Guy's disease. The monks who kept the tomb were enjoying an enviable opulence, when the saint, appearing to King Draco the Great, ordered him to recognise her as the heavenly patron of the kingdom and to transfer her precious remains to the cathedral of Alca.

In consequence, the odoriferous relics of that virgin were carried with great pomp to the metropolitan church and placed in the middle of the choir in a shrine made of gold and enamel and ornamented with precious stones.

The chapter kept a record of the miracles wrought by the blessed Orberosia.

Draco the Great, who had never ceased to defend and exalt the Christian faith, died fulfilled with the most pious sentiments and bequeathed his great possessions to the Church.

III

QUEEN CRUCHA

ERRIBLE disorders followed the death of Draco the Great. That prince's successors have often been accused of weakness, and it is true that none of them followed, even from afar, the example of their valiant ancestor.

His son, Chum, who was lame, failed to increase the territory of the Penguins. Bolo, the son of Chum, was assassinated by the palace guards at the age of nine, just as he was ascending the throne. His brother Gun succeeded him. He was only seven years old and allowed himself to be governed by his mother, Queen Crucha.

Crucha was beautiful, learned, and intelligent; but she was unable to curb her own passions.

These are the terms in which the venerable Talpa expresses himself in his chronicle regarding that illustrious queen:

"In beauty of face and symmetry of figure Queen Crucha yields neither to Semiramis of Babylon nor to Penthesilea, queen of the Amazons nor to Salome, the daughter of Herodias. But she offers in her person certain singularities that will appear beautiful or uncomely according to the contradictory opinions of men and the varying judgments of the world. She has on her forehead two small horns which she conceals in the abundant folds of her golden hair; one of her eyes is blue and one is black; her neck is bent towards the left side; and, like Alexander of Macedon, she has six fingers on her right hand, and a stain like a little monkey's head upon her skin.

"Her gait is majestic and her manner affable. She is magnificent in her expenses, but she is not always able to rule desire by reason.

"One day, having noticed in the palace stables, a young groom of great beauty, she immediately fell violently in love with him, and entrusted to him the command of her armies. What one must praise unreservedly in this great queen is the abundance of gifts that she makes to the churches, monasteries, and chapels in her kingdom, and especially to the holy house of Beargarden, where, by the grace of the Lord, I made my profession in my fourteenth year. She has founded masses for the repose of her soul in such great numbers that every priest in the Penguin Church is, so to speak, transformed into a taper lighted in the sight of heaven to draw down the divine mercy upon the august Crucha."

From these lines and from some others with which I have enriched my text the reader can judge of the historical and literary value of the "Gesta Penguinorum." Unhappily, that chronicle suddenly comes to an end at the third year of Draco the Simple, the successor of Gun the Weak. Having reached that point of my history, I deplore the loss of an agreeable and trustworthy guide.

During the two centuries that followed, the Penguins remained plunged in blood-stained disorder. All the arts perished. In the midst of the general ignorance, the monks in the shadow of their cloister devoted themselves to study, and copied the Holy Scriptures with indefatigable zeal. As parchment was scarce, they scraped the writing off old manuscripts in order to transcribe upon them the divine word. Thus throughout the breadth of Penguinia Bibles blossomed forth like roses on a bush.

A monk of the order of St. Benedict, Ermold the Penguin, had himself alone defaced four thousand Greek and Latin manuscripts so as to copy out the Gospel of St. John four thousand times. Thus the masterpieces of ancient poetry and eloquence were destroyed in great numbers. Historians are unanimous in recognising that the Penguin convents were the refuge of learning during the Middle Ages.

Unending wars between the Penguins and the Porpoises filled the close of this period. It is extremely difficult to know the truth concerning these wars, not because accounts are wanting, but because there are so many of them. The Porpoise Chronicles contradict the Penguin Chronicles at every point. And, moreover, the Penguins contradict each other as well as the Porpoises. I have discovered two chroniclers that are in agreement, but one has copied from the other. A single fact is certain, namely, that massacres, rapes, conflagrations, and plunder succeeded one another without interruption.

Under the unhappy prince Bosco IX. the kingdom was at the verge of ruin. On the news that the Porpoise fleet, composed of six hundred great ships, was in sight of Alca, the bishop ordered a solemn procession. The cathedral chapter, the elected magistrates, the members of Parliament, and the clerics of the University entered the Cathedral and, taking up St. Orberosia's shrine, led it in procession through the town, followed by the entire people singing hymns. The holy patron of Penguinia was not invoked in vain. Nevertheless, the Porpoises besieged the town both by land and sea, took it by assault, and for three days and three nights killed, plundered, violated, and burned, with all the indifference that habit produces.

Our astonishment cannot be too great at the fact that, during those iron ages, the faith was preserved intact among the Penguins. The splendour of the truth in those times illumined all souls that had not been corrupted by sophisms. This is the explanation of the unity of belief. A constant practice of the Church doubtless contributed also to maintain this happy communion of the faithful —every Penguin who thought differently from the others was immediately burned at the stake.

IV

LETTERS: JOHANNES TALPA

URING the minority of King Gun, Johannes Talpa, in the monastery of Beargarden, where at the age of fourteen he had made his profession and from which he never departed for a single day throughout his life, composed his celebrated Latin chronicle in twelve books called "De Gestis Penguinorum."

The monastery of Beargarden lifts its high walls on the summit of an inaccessible peak. One sees around it only the blue tops of mountains, divided by the clouds.

When he began to write his "Gesta Penguinorum," Johannes Talpa was already old. The good monk has taken care to tell us this in his book: "My head has long since lost," he says, "its adornment of fair hair, and my scalp resembles those convex mirrors of metal which the Penguin ladies consult with so much care and zeal. My stature, naturally small, has with years become diminished and bent. My white beard gives warmth to my breast."

With a charming simplicity, Talpa informs us of certain circum-

stances in his life and some features in his character. "Descended,"
he tells us, "from a noble family, and destined from childhood for
the ecclesiastical state, I was taught grammar and music. I learned
to read under the guidance of a master who was called Amicus,
and who would have been better named Inimicus. As I did not
easily attain to a knowledge of my letters, he beat me violently
with rods so that I can say that he printed the alphabet in strokes
upon my back."

In another passage Talpa confesses his natural inclination
towards pleasure. These are his expressive words: "In my youth
the ardour of my senses was such that in the shadow of the woods
I experienced a sensation of boiling in a pot rather than of breathing the fresh air. I fled from women, but in vain, for every object
recalled them to me."

While he was writing his chronicle, a terrible war, at once foreign and domestic, laid waste the Penguin land. The soldiers of
Crucha came to defend the monastery of Beargarden against the
Penguin barbarians and established themselves strongly within its
walls. In order to render it impregnable they pierced loop-holes
through the walls and they took the lead off the church roof to
make balls for their slings. At night they lighted huge fires in the
courts and cloisters and on them they roasted whole oxen which
they spitted upon the ancient pine-trees of the mountain. Sitting
around the flames, amid smoke filled with a mingled odour of resin
and fat, they broached huge casks of wine and beer. Their songs,
their blasphemies, and the noise of their quarrels drowned the
sound of the morning bells.

At last the Porpoises, having crossed the defiles, laid siege to the
monastery. They were warriors from the North, clad in copper
armour. They fastened ladders a hundred and fifty fathoms long to
the sides of the cliffs and sometimes in the darkness and storm
these broke beneath the weight of men and arms, and bunches of
the besiegers were hurled into the ravines and precipices. A prolonged wail would be heard going down into the darkness, and the
assault would begin again. The Penguins poured streams of burning wax upon their assailants, which made them blaze like torches.
Sixty times the enraged Porpoises attempted to scale the monastery
and sixty times they were repulsed.

For six months they had closely invested the monastery, when,
on the day of the Epiphany, a shepherd of the valley showed them
a hidden path by which they climbed the mountain, penetrated into
the vaults of the abbey, ran through the cloisters, the kitchens, the
church, the chapter halls, the library, the laundry, the cells, the re-
fectories, and the dormitories, and burned the buildings, killing and
violating without distinction of age or sex. The Penguins, awakened unexpectedly, ran to arms, but in the darkness and alarm they
struck at one another, whilst the Porpoises with blows of their axes

disputed the sacred vessels, the censers, the candlesticks, dalmatics, reliquaries, golden crosses, and precious stones.

The air was filled with an acrid odour of burnt flesh. Groans and death-cries arose in the midst of the flames, and on the edges of the crumbling roofs monks ran in thousands like ants, and fell into the valley. Yet Johannes Talpa kept on writing his Chronicle. The soldiers of Crucha retreated speedily and filled up all the issues from the monastery with pieces of rock so as to shut up the Porpoises in the burning buildings. And to crush the enemy beneath the ruin they employed the trunks of old oaks as battering-rams. The burning timbers fell in with a noise like thunder and the lofty arches of the naves crumbled beneath the shock of these giant trees when moved by six hundred men together. Soon there was left nothing of the rich and extensive abbey but the cell of Johannes Talpa, which, by a marvellous chance, hung from the ruin of a smoking gable. The old chronicler still kept writing.

This admirable intensity of thought may seem excessive in the case of an annalist who applies himself to relate the events of his own time. For, however abstracted and detached we may be from surrounding things, we nevertheless resent their influence. I have consulted the original manuscript of Johannes Talpa in the National Library, where it is preserved (*Monumenta Peng., K. L6.,* 12390 *four*). It is a parchment manuscript of 628 leaves. The writing is extremely confused, the letters instead of being in a straight line, stray in all directions and are mingled together in great disorder, or, more correctly speaking, in absolute confusion. They are so badly formed that for the most part it is impossible not merely to say what they are, but even to distinguish them from the splashes of ink with which they are plentifully interspersed. Those inestimable pages bear witness in this way to the troubles amid which they were written. To read them is difficult. On the other hand, the monk of Beargarden's style shows no trace of emotion. The tone of the "Gesta Penguinorum" never departs from simplicity. The narration is rapid and of a conciseness that sometimes approaches dryness. The reflections are rare and, as a rule, judicious.

V

THE ARTS: THE PRIMITIVES OF PENGUIN PAINTING

HE Penguin critics vie with one another in affirming that Penguin art has from its origin been distinguished by a powerful and pleasing originality, and that we may look elsewhere in vain for the qualities of grace and reason that characterise its earliest works. But the Porpoises claim that their artists were undoubtedly the instructors and masters of the Penguins. It is difficult to form an opinion on the matter, because the Penguins, before they began to admire their primitive painters, destroyed all their works.

We cannot be too sorry for this loss. For my own part I feel it cruelly, for I venerate the Penguin antiquities and I adore the primitives. They are delightful. I do not say they are all alike, for that would be untrue, but they have common characters that are found in all schools—I mean formulas from which they never depart—and there is besides something finished in their work, for what they know they know well. Luckily we can form a notion of the Penguin primitives from the Italian, Flemish, and Dutch primitives, and from the French primitives, who are superior to all the rest; as M. Gruyer tells us they are more logical, logic being a peculiarly French quality. Even if this is denied it must at least be admitted that to France belongs the credit of having kept primitives when the other nations knew them no longer. The Exhibition of French Primitives at the Pavilion Marsan in 1904 contained several little panels contemporary with the later Valois kings and with Henry IV.

I have made many journeys to see the pictures of the brothers Van Eyck, of Memling, of Roger van der Weyden, of the painter of the death of Mary, of Ambrogio Lorenzetti, and of the old Umbrian masters. It was, however, neither Bruges, nor Cologne, nor Sienna, nor Perugia, that completed my initiation; it was in the little town of Arezzo that I became a conscious adept in primitive painting. That was ten years ago or even longer. At that period of indigence and simplicity, the municipal museums, though usually kept shut, were always opened to foreigners. One evening, an old woman with a candle showed me, for half a lira, the sordid museum of Arezzo, and in it I discovered a painting by Margaritone, a "St. Francis," the pious sadness of which moved me to tears. I was deeply touched, and Margaritone of Arezzo became from that day my dearest primitive.

I picture to myself the Penguin primitives in conformity with the works of that master. It will not therefore be thought superfluous if in this place I consider his works with some attention, if not in detail, at least under their more general and, if I dare say so, most representative aspect.

We possess five or six pictures signed with his hand. His master-piece, preserved in the National Gallery of London, represents the Virgin seated on a throne and holding the infant Jesus in her arms. What strikes one first when one looks at this figure is the propor-tion. The body from the neck to the feet is only twice as long as the head, so that it appears extremely short and podgy. This work is not less remarkable for its painting than for its drawing. The great Margaritone had but a limited number of colours in his possession, and he used them in all their purity without ever modifying the tones. From this it follows that his colouring has more vivacity than harmony. The cheeks of the Virgin and those of the Child are of a bright vermilion which the old master, from a naïve preference for clear definitions, has placed on each face in two circumferences as exact as if they had been traced out by a pair of compasses.

A learned critic of the eighteenth century, the Abbé Lanzi, has treated Margaritone's works with profound disdain. "They are," he says, "merely crude daubs. In those unfortunate times people could neither draw nor paint." Such was the common opinion of the con-noisseurs of the days of powdered wigs. But the great Margaritone and his contemporaries were soon to be avenged for this cruel con-tempt. There was born in the nineteenth century, in the biblical villages and reformed cottages of pious England, a multitude of little Samuels and little St. Johns with hair curling like lambs, who, about 1840 and 1850, became spectacled professors and founded the cult of the primitives.

That eminent theorist of Pre-Raphaelitism, Sir James Tuckett, does not shrink from placing the Madonna of the National Gallery on a level with the masterpieces of Christian art. "By giving to the Virgin's head," says Sir James Tuckett, "a third of the total height of the figure, the old master attracts the spectator's attention and keeps it directed towards the more sublime parts of the human figure, and in particular the eyes, which we ordinarily describe as the spiritual organs. In this picture, colouring and design conspire to produce an ideal and mystical impression. The vermilion of the cheeks does not recall the natural appearance of the skin; it rather seems as if the old master has applied the roses of Paradise to the faces of the Mother and the Child."

We see, in such a criticism as this, a shining reflection, so to speak, of the work which it exalts; yet MacSilly, the seraphic æsthete of Edinburgh, has expressed in a still more moving and penetrating fashion the impression produced upon his mind by the sight of this primitive painting. "The Madonna of Margaritone," says the revered MacSilly, "attains the transcendent end of art. It inspires its beholders with feelings of innocence and purity; it

makes them like little children. And so true is this, that at the age
of sixty-six, after having had the joy of contemplating it closely for
three hours, I felt myself suddenly transformed into a little child.
While my cab was taking me through Trafalgar Square I kept
laughing and prattling and shaking my spectacle-case as if it were
a rattle. And when the maid in my boarding-house had served my
meal I kept pouring spoonfuls of soup into my ear with all the art-
lessness of childhood."

"It is by such results," adds MacSilly, "that the excellence of a
work of art is proved."

Margaritone, according to Vasari, died at the age of seventy-
seven, "regretting that he had lived to see a new form of art aris-
ing and the new artists crowned with fame."

These lines, which I translate literally, have inspired Sir James
Tuckett with what are perhaps the finest pages in his work. They
form part of his "Breviary for Æsthetes"; all the Pre-Raphaelites
know them by heart. I place them here as the most precious ornament of this book. You will agree that nothing more sublime has
been written since the days of the Hebrew prophets.

MARGARITONE'S VISION

Margaritone, full of years and labours, went one day to visit the
studio of a young painter who had lately settled in the town. He
noticed in the studio a freshly painted Madonna, which, although
severe and rigid, nevertheless, by a certain exactness in the proportions and a devilish mingling of light and shade, assumed an
appearance of relief and life. At this sight the artless and sublime
worker of Arezzo perceived with horror what the future of painting
would be. With his brow clasped in his hands he exclaimed:

"What things of shame does not this figure show forth! I descern
in it the end of that Christian art which paints the soul and inspires
the beholder with an ardent desire for heaven. Future painters will
not restrain themselves as does this one to portraying on the side
of a wall or on a wooden panel the cursed matter of which our
bodies are formed; they will celebrate and glorify it. They will
clothe their figures with dangerous appearances of flesh, and these
figures will seem like real persons. Their bodies will be seen; their
forms will appear through their clothing. St. Magdalen will have a
bosom. St. Martha a belly, St. Barbara hips, St. Agnes buttocks; St.
Sebastian will unveil his youthful beauty, and St. George will
display beneath his armour the muscular wealth of a robust virility;
apostles, confessors, doctors, and God the Father himself will appear as ordinary beings like you and me; the angels will affect an
equivocal, ambiguous, mysterious beauty which will trouble hearts.
What desire for heaven will these representations impart? None;
but from them you will learn to take pleasure in the forms of ter-

restrial life. Where will painters stop in their indiscreet inquiries? They will stop nowhere. They will go so far as to show men and women naked like the idols of the Romans. There will be a sacred art and a profane art, and the sacred art will not be less profane than the other.

"Get ye behind me, demons," exclaimed the old master. For in prophetic vision he saw the righteous and the saints assuming the appearance of melancholy athletes. He saw Apollos playing the lute on a flowery hill, in the midst of the Muses wearing light tunics. He saw Venuses lying under shady myrtles and the Danae exposing their charming sides to the golden rain. He saw pictures of Jesus under the pillars of the temple amidst patricians, fair ladies, musicians, pages, negroes, dogs, and parrots. He saw in an inextricable confusion of human limbs, outspread wings, and flying draperies, crowds of tumultuous Nativities, opulent Holy Families, emphatic Crucifixions. He saw St. Catherines, St. Barbaras, St. Agneses humiliating patricians by the sumptuousness of their velvets, their brocades, and their pearls, and by the splendour of their breasts. He saw Auroras scattering roses, and a multitude of naked Dianas and Nymphs surprised on the banks of retired streams. And the great Margaritone died, strangled by so horrible a presentiment of the Renaissance and the Bolognese School.

VI

MARBODIUS

E possess a precious monument of the Penguin literature of the fifteenth century. It is a narrative of a journey to hell undertaken by the monk Marbodius, of the order of St. Benedict, who professed a fervent admiration for the poet Virgil. This narrative, written in fairly good Latin, has been published by M. du Clos des Lunes. It is here translated for the first time. I believe that I am doing a service to my fellow-countrymen in making them acquainted with these pages, though doubtless they are far from forming a unique example of this class of mediæval Latin literature. Among the fictions that may be compared with them we may mention "The Voyage of St. Brendan," "The Vision of Albericus," and "St. Patrick's Purgatory," imaginary descriptions, like Dante Alighieri's "Divine Comedy," of the supposed abode of the dead. The narrative of Marbodius is one of the latest works dealing with this scheme, but it is not the least singular.

THE DESCENT OF MARBODIUS INTO HELL

In the fourteen hundred and fifty-third year of the incarnation of the Son of God, a few days before the enemies of the Cross entered the city of Helena and the great Constantine, it was given to me, Brother Marbodius, an unworthy monk, to see and to hear what none had hitherto seen or heard. I have composed a faithful narrative of those things so that their memory may not perish with me, for man's time is short.

On the first day of May in the aforesaid year, at the hour of vespers, I was seated in the Abbey of Corrigan on a stone in the cloisters and, as my custom was, I read the verses of the poet whom I love best of all, Virgil, who has sung of the labours of the field, of shepherds, and of heroes. Evening was hanging its purple folds from the arches of the cloisters and in a voice of emotion I was murmuring the verses which describe how Dido, the Phœnician queen, wanders with her ever-bleeding wound beneath the myrtles of hell. At that moment Brother Hilary happened to pass by, followed by Brother Jacinth, the porter.

Brought up in the barbarous ages before the resurrection of the Muses, Brother Hilary has not been initiated into the wisdom of the ancients; nevertheless, the poetry of the Mantuan has, like a subtle torch, shed some gleams of light into his understanding.

"Brother Marbodius," he asked me, "do those verses that you utter with swelling breast and sparkling eyes—do they belong to that great 'Æneid' from which morning or evening your glances are never withheld?"

I answered that I was reading in Virgil how the son of Anchises perceived Dido like a moon behind the foliage.*

"Brother Marbodius," he replied, "I am certain that on all occasions Virgil gives expression to wise maxims and profound thoughts. But the songs that he modulates on his Syracusan flute hold such a lofty meaning and such exalted doctrine that I am continually puzzled by them."

"Take care, father," cried Brother Jacinth, in an agitated voice. "Virgil was a magician who wrought marvels by the help of demons. It is thus he pierced through a mountain near Naples and fashioned a bronze horse that had power to heal all the diseases of horses. He was a necromancer, and there is still shown, in a certain town in Italy, the mirror in which he made the dead appear. And yet a woman deceived this great sorcerer. A Neapolitan cour-

*The text runs

. . . qualem primo qui surgere mense
Aut videt aut vidisse putat per nubila lunam.

Brother Marbodius, by a strange misunderstanding, substitutes an entirely different image for the one created by the poet.

tesan invited him to hoist himself up to her window in the basket that was used to bring the provisions, and she left him all night suspended between two storeys."

Brother Hilary did not appear to hear these observations.

"Virgil is a prophet," he replied, "and a prophet who leaves far behind him the sibyls with their sacred verses as well as the daughter of King Priam, and that great diviner of future things, Plato of Athens. You will find in the fourth of his Syracusan cantos the birth of our Lord foretold in a language that seems of heaven rather than of earth.* In the time of my early studies, when I read for the first time JAM REDIT ET VIRGO, I felt myself bathed in an infinite delight, but I immediately experienced intense grief at the thought that, for ever deprived of the presence of God, the author of this prophetic verse, the noblest that has come from human lips, was pining among the heathen in eternal darkness. This cruel thought did not leave me. It pursued me even in my studies, my prayers, my meditations, and my ascetic labours. Thinking that Virgil was deprived of the sight of God and that possibly he might even be suffering the fate of the reprobate in hell, I could neither enjoy peace nor rest, and I went so far as to exclaim several times a day with my arms outstretched to heaven:

" 'Reveal to me, O Lord, the lot thou hast assigned to him who sang on earth as the angels sing in heaven!'

"After some years my anguish ceased when I read in an old book that the great Apostle St. Paul, who called the Gentiles into the Church of Christ, went to Naples and sanctified with his tears the tomb of the prince of poets.† This was some ground for believing that Virgil, like the Emperor Trajan, was admitted to Paradise because even in error he had a presentiment of the truth. We are not compelled to believe it, but I can easily persuade myself that it is true."

Having thus spoken, old Hilary wished me the peace of a holy night and went away with Brother Jacinth.

I resumed the delightful study of my poet. Book in hand, I meditated upon the way in which those whom Love destroys with its cruel malady wander through the secret paths in the depth of the

---

*Three centuries before the epoch in which our Marbodius lived the words—

> Maro, vates gentilium
> Da Christo testimonium

were sung in the churches on Christmas Day.

> †Ad maronis mausoleum
> Ductus, fudit super eum
> Piae rorem lacrymæ.

> Quem te, inquit, reddidissem,
> Si te vivum invenissem,
> Poetarum maxime!

myrtle forest, and, as I meditated, the quivering reflections of the stars came and mingled with those of the leafless eglantines in the waters of the cloister fountain. Suddenly the lights and the perfumes and the stillness of the sky were overwhelmed, a fierce Northwind charged with storm and darkness burst roaring upon me. It lifted me up and carried me like a wisp of straw over fields, cities, rivers, and mountains, and through the midst of thunderclouds, during a long night composed of a whole series of nights and days. And when, after this prolonged and cruel rage, the hurricane was at last stilled, I found myself far from my native land at the bottom of a valley bordered by cypress trees. Then a woman of wild beauty, trailing long garments behind her, approached me. She placed her left hand on my shoulder, and, pointing her right arm to an oak with thick foliage:

"Look!" said she to me.

Immediately I recognised the Sibyl who guards the sacred wood of Avernus, and I discerned the fair Proserpine's beautiful golden twig amongst the tufted boughs of the tree to which her finger pointed.

"O prophetic Virgin," I exclaimed, "thou hast comprehended my desire and thou hast satisfied it in this way. Thou has revealed to me the tree that bears the shining twig without which none can enter alive into the dwelling-place of the dead. And in truth, eagerly did I long to converse with the shade of Virgil."

Having said this, I snatched the golden branch from its ancient trunk and I advanced without fear into the smoking gulf that leads to the miry banks of the Styx, upon which the shades are tossed about like dead leaves. At sight of the branch dedicated to Proserpine, Charon took me in his bark, which groaned beneath my weight, and I alighted on the shores of the dead, and was greeted by the mute baying of the threefold Cerberus. I pretended to throw the shade of a stone at him, and the vain monster fled into his cave. There, amidst the rushes, wandered the souls of those children whose eyes had but opened and shut to the kindly light of day, and there in a gloomy cavern Minos judges men. I penetrated into the myrtle wood in which the victims of love wander languishing, Phædra, Procris, the sad Eriphyle, Evadne, Pasiphaë, Laodamia, and Cenis, and the Phœnician Dido. Then I went through the dusty plains reserved for famous warriors. Beyond them open two ways. That to the left leads to Tartarus, the abode of the wicked. I took that to the right, which leads to Elysium and to the dwellings of Dis. Having hung the sacred branch at the goddess's door, I reached pleasant fields flooded with purple light. The shades of philosophers and poets hold grave converse there. The Graces and the Muses formed sprightly choirs upon the grass. Old Homer sang, accompanying himself upon his rustic lyre. His eyes were closed, but divine images shone upon his lips. I saw Solon, Democritus, and

Pythagoras watching the games of the young men in the meadow, and, through the foliage of an ancient laurel, I perceived also Hesiod, Orpheus, the melancholy Euripides, and the masculine Sappho. I passed and recognised, as they sat on the bank of a fresh rivulet, the poet Horace, Varius, Gallus, and Lycoris. A little apart, leaning against the trunk of a dark holm-oak, Virgil was gazing pensively at the grove. Of lofty stature, though spare, he still preserved that swarthy complexion, that rustic air, that negligent bearing, and unpolished appearance which during his lifetime concealed his genius. I saluted him piously and remained for a long time without speech.

At last when my halting voice could proceed out of my throat:

"O thou, so dear to the Ausonian Muses, thou honour of the Latin name, Virgil," cried I, "it is through thee I have known what beauty is, it is through thee I have known what the tables of the gods and the beds of the goddesses are like. Suffer the praises of the humblest of thy adorers."

"Arise, stranger," answered the divine poet. "I perceive that thou art a living being among the shades, and that thy body treads down the grass in this eternal evening. Thou art not the first man who has descended before his death into these dwellings, although all intercourse between us and the living is difficult. But cease from praise; I do not like eulogies and the confused sounds of glory have always offended my ears. That is why I fled from Rome, where I was known to the idle and curious, and laboured in the solitude of my beloved Parthenope. And then I am not so convinced that the men of thy generation understand my verses that I should be gratified by thy praises. Who art thou?"

"I am called Marbodius of the Kingdom of Alca. I made my profession in the Abbey of Corrigan. I read thy poems by day and I read them by night. It is thee whom I have come to see in Hell; I was impatient to know what thy fate was. On earth the learned often dispute about it. Some hold it probable that, having lived under the power of demons, thou art now burning in inextinguishable flames; others, more cautious, pronounce no opinion, believing that all which is said concerning the dead is uncertain and full of lies; several, though not in truth the ablest, maintain that, because thou didst elevate the tone of the Sicilian Muses and foretell that a new progeny would descend from heaven, thou wert admitted, like the Emperor Trajan, to enjoy eternal blessedness in the Christian heaven."

"Thou seest that such is not the case," answered the shade, smiling.

"I meet thee in truth, O Virgil, among the heroes and sages in those Elysian fields which thou thyself hast described. Thus, contrary to what several on earth believe, no one has come to seek thee on the part of Him who reigns on high?"

After a rather long silence:

"I will conceal nought from thee. He sent for me; one of His messengers, a simple man, came to say that I was expected, and that, although I had not been initiated into their mysteries, in consideration of my prophetic verses a place had been reserved for me among those of the new sect. But I refused to accept that invitation; I had no desire to change my place. I did so not because I share the admiration of the Greeks for the Elysian fields, or because I taste here those joys which caused Proserpine to lose the remembrance of her mother. I never believed much myself in what I say about these things in the 'Æneid.' I was instructed by philosophers and men of science and I had a correct foreboding of the truth. Life in hell is extremely attenuated; we feel neither pleasure nor pain; we are as if we were not. The dead have no existence here except such as the living lend them. Nevertheless I prefer to remain here."

"But what reason didst thou give, O Virgil, for so strange a refusal?"

"I gave excellent ones. I said to the messenger of the god that I did not deserve the honour he brought me, and that a meaning had been given to my verses which they did not bear. In truth I have not in my fourth Eclogue betrayed the faith of my ancestors. Some ignorant Jews alone have interpreted in favour of a barbarian god a verse which celebrates the return of the golden age predicted by the Sibylline oracles. I excused myself then on the ground that I could not occupy a place which was destined for me in error and to which I recognised that I had no right. Then I alleged my disposition and my tastes, which do not accord with the customs of the new heavens.

" 'I am not unsociable,' said I to this man. 'I have shown in life a complaisant and easy disposition, although the extreme simplicity of my habits caused me to be suspected of avarice. I kept nothing for myself alone. My library was open to all and I have conformed my conduct to that fine saying of Euripides, "all ought to be common among friends." Those praises that seemed obtrusive when I myself received them became agreeable to me when addressed to Varius or to Macer. But at bottom I am rustic and uncultivated. I take pleasure in the society of animals; I was so zealous in observing them and took so much care of them that I was regarded, not altogether wrongly, as a good veterinary surgeon. I am told that the people of thy sect claim an immortal soul for themselves, but refuse one to the animals. That is a piece of nonsense that makes me doubt their judgment. Perhaps I love the flocks and the shepherds a little too much. That would not seem right amongst you. There is a maxim to which I endeavour to conform my actions, "Nothing too much." More even than my feeble health my philosophy teaches me to use things with measure. I am sober; a let-

tuce and some olives with a drop of Falernian wine form all my
meals. I have, indeed, to some extent gone with strange women, but
I have not delayed over long in taverns to watch the young Syrians
dance to the sound of the *crotalum*.* But if I have restrained my
desires it was for my own satisfaction and for the sake of good
discipline. To fear pleasure and to fly from joy appears to me the
worst insult that one can offer to nature. I am assured that during their lives certain of the elect of thy god abstained from food
and avoided women through love of asceticism, and voluntarily exposed themselves to useless sufferings. I should be afraid of meeting those criminals whose frenzy horrifies me. A poet must not be
asked to attach himself too strictly to any scientific or moral doctrine. Moreover, I am a Roman, and the Romans, unlike the Greeks,
are unable to pursue profound speculations in a subtle manner. If
they adopt a philosophy it is above all in order to derive some practical advantages from it. Siro, who enjoyed a great renown among
us, taught me the system of Epicurus and thus freed me from vain
terrors and turned me aside from the cruelties to which religion
persuades ignorant men. I have embraced the views of Pythagoras
concerning the souls of men and animals, both of which are of
divine essence; this invites us to look upon ourselves without pride
and without shame. I have learnt from the Alexandrines how the
earth, at first soft and without form, hardened in proportion as
Nereus withdrew himself from it to dig his humid dwellings; I have
learned how things were formed insensibly; in what manner the
rains, falling from the burdened clouds, nourished the silent forests, and by what progress a few animals at last began to wander
over the nameless mountains. I could not accustom myself to your
cosmogony either, for it seems to me fitter for a camel-driver on
the Syrian sands than for a disciple of Aristarchus and Samos. And
what would become of me in the abode of your beatitude if I did
not find there my friends, my ancestors, my masters, and my gods,
and if it is not given me to see Rhea's noble son, or Venus, mother
of Æneas, with her winning smile, or Pan, or the young Dryads,
or the Sylvans, or old Silenus, with his face stained by Ægle's purple mulberries.' These are the reasons which I begged that simple
man to plead before the successor of Jupiter."

"And since then, O great shade, thou hast received no other messages?"

"I have received none."

"To console themselves for thy absence, O Virgil, they have three
poets, Commodianus, Prudentius, and Fortunatus, who were all
three born in those dark days when neither prosody nor grammar
were known. But tell me, O Mantuan, hast thou never received

---

*This phrase seems to indicate that, if one is to believe Macrobius, the
"Copa" is by Virgil.

other intelligence of the God whose company thou didst so deliberately refuse?"

"Never that I remember."

"Hast thou not told me that I am not the first who descended alive into these abodes and presented himself before thee?"

"Thou dost remind me of it. A century and a half ago, or so it seems to me (it is difficult to reckon days and years amid the shades), my profound peace was intruded upon by a strange visitor. As I was wandering beneath the gloomy foliage that borders the Styx, I saw rising before me a human form more opaque and darker than that of the inhabitants of these shores. I recognised a living person. He was of high stature, thin, with an aquiline nose, sharp chin, and hollow cheeks. His dark eyes shot forth fire; a red hood girt with a crown of laurels bound his lean brows. His bones pierced through the tight brown cloak that descended to his heels. He saluted me with deference, tempered by a sort of fierce pride, and addressed me in a speech more obscure and incorrect than that of those Gauls with whom the divine Julius filled both his legions and the Curia. At last I understood that he had been born near Fiesole, in an ancient Etruscan colony that Sulla had founded on the banks of the Arno, and which had prospered; that he had obtained municipal honours, but that he had thrown himself vehemently into the sanguinary quarrels which arose between the senate, the knights, and the people, that he had been defeated and banished, and now he wandered in exile throughout the world. He described Italy to me as distracted by more wars and discords than in the time of my youth, and as sighing anew for a second Augustus. I pitied his misfortunes, remembering what I myself had formerly endured.

"An audacious spirit unceasingly disquieted him, and his mind harboured great thoughts, but alas! his rudeness and ignorance displayed the triumph of barbarism. He knew neither poetry, nor science, nor even the tongue of the Greeks, and he was ignorant, too, of the ancient traditions concerning the origin of the world and the nature of the gods. He gravely repeated fables which in my time would have brought smiles to the little children who were not yet old enough to pay for admission at the baths. The vulgar easily believe in monsters. The Etruscans especially peopled hell with demons, hideous as a sick man's dreams. That they have not abandoned their childish imaginings after so many centuries is explained by the continuation and progress of ignorance and misery, but that one of their magistrates whose mind is raised above the common level should share these popular illusions and should be frightened by the hideous demons that the inhabitants of that country painted on the walls of their tombs in the time of Porsena —that is something which might sadden even a sage. My Etruscan visitor repeated verses to me which he had composed in a new dialect, called by him the vulgar tongue, the sense of which I could not understand. My ears were more surprised than charmed as I heard him repeat the same sound three or four times at regular intervals in his efforts to mark the rhythm. That artifice did not seem ingenious to me; but it is not for the dead to judge of novelties.

"But I do not reproach this colonist of Sulla, born in an unhappy time, for making inharmonious verses or for being, if it be possible, as bad a poet as Bavius or Maevius. I have grievances against him which touch me more closely. The thing is monstrous and scarcely credible, but when this man returned to earth he disseminated the most odious lies about me. He affirmed in several passages of his barbarous poems that I had served him as a guide in the modern Tartarus, a place I know nothing of. He insolently proclaimed that I had spoken of the gods of Rome as false and lying gods, and that I held as the true God the present successor of Jupiter. Friend, when thou art restored to the kindly light of day and beholdest again thy native land, contradict those abominable falsehoods. Say to thy people that the singer of the pious Æneas has never worshipped the god of the Jews. I am assured that his power is declining and that his approaching fall is manifested by undoubted indications. This news would give me some pleasure if one could rejoice in these abodes, where we feel neither fears nor desires."

He spoke, and with a gesture of farewell he went away. I beheld his shade gliding over the asphodels without bending their stalks. I saw that it became fainter and vaguer as it receded farther from me, and it vanished before it reached the wood of evergreen laurels. Then I understood the meaning of the words, "The dead have no life, but that which the living lend them," and I walked slowly through the pale meadow to the gate of horn.

I affirm that all in this writing is true.*

*There is in Marbodius's narrative a passage very worthy of notice, viz., that in which the monk of Corrigan describes Dante Alighieri such as we picture him to ourselves to-day. The miniatures in a very old manuscript of the "Divine Comedy," the "Codex Venetianus," represent the poet as a little fat man clad in a short tunic, the skirts of which fall above his knees. As for Virgil, he still wears the philosophical beard, in the wood-engravings of the sixteenth century.

One would not have thought either that Marbodius, or even Virgil, could have known the Etruscan tombs of Chiusi and Corneto, where, in fact, there are horrible and burlesque devils closely resembling those of Orcagna. Nevertheless, the authenticity of the "Descent of Marbodius into Hell" is indisputable. M. du Clos des Lunes has firmly established it. To doubt it would be to doubt palæography itself.

VII

SIGNS IN THE MOON

AT THAT time, whilst Penguinia was still plunged in ignorance and barbarism, Giles Bird-catcher, a Franciscan monk, known by his writings under the name Ægidius Aucupis, devoted himself with indefatigable zeal to the study of letters and the sciences. He gave his nights to mathematics and music, which he called the two adorable sisters, the harmonious daughters of Number and Imagination. He was versed in medicine and astrology. He was suspected of practising magic, and it seemed true that he wrought metamorphoses and discovered hidden things.

The monks of his convent, finding in his cell Greek books which they could not read, imagined them to be conjuring-books, and denounced their too learned brother as a wizard. Ægidius Aucupis fled, and reached the island of Ireland, where he lived for thirty studious years. He went from monastery to monastery, searching for and copying the Greek and Latin manuscripts which they contained. He also studied physics and alchemy. He acquired a universal knowledge and discovered notable secrets concerning animals, plants, and stones. He was found one day in the company of a very beautiful woman who sang to her own accompaniment on the lute, and who was afterwards discovered to be a machine which he had himself constructed.

He often crossed the Irish Sea to go into the land of Wales and to visit the libraries of the monasteries there. During one of these crossings, as he remained during the night on the bridge of the ship, he saw beneath the waters two sturgeons swimming side by side. He had very good hearing and he knew the languages of the fishes. Now he heard one of the sturgeons say to the other:

"The man in the moon, whom we have often seen carrying fagots on his shoulders, has fallen into the sea."

And the other sturgeon said in its turn:

"And in the silver disc there will be seen the image of two lovers kissing each other on the mouth."

Some years later, having returned to his native country, Ægidius Aucupis found that ancient learning had been restored. Manners had softened. Men no longer pursued the nymphs of the fountains, of the woods, and of the mountains with their insults. They placed images of the Muses and of the modest Graces in their gardens, and they rendered her former honours to the Goddess with ambrosial lips, the joy of men and gods. They were becoming reconciled to nature. They trampled vain terrors beneath their feet and raised their eyes to heaven without fearing, as they formerly did, to read signs of anger and threats of damnation in the skies.

At this spectacle Ægidius Aucupis remembered what the two sturgeons of the sea of Erin had foretold.

BOOK IV: MODERN TIMES: TRINCO

I

MOTHER ROUQUIN

EGIDIUS AUCUPIS, the Erasmus of the Penguins, was not mistaken; his age was an age of free inquiry. But that great man mistook the elegances of the humanists for softness of manners, and he did not foresee the effects that the awaking of intelligence would have amongst the Penguins. It brought about the religious Reformation; Catholics massacred Protestants and Protestants massacred Catholics. Such were the first results of liberty of thought. The Catholics prevailed in Penguinia. But the spirit of inquiry had penetrated among them without their knowing it. They joined reason to faith, and claimed that religion had been divested of the superstitious practices that dishonoured it, just as in later days the booths that the cobblers, hucksters, and dealers in old clothes had built against the walls of the cathedrals were cleared away. The word, legend, which at first indicated what the faithful ought to read, soon suggested the idea of pious fables and childish tales.

The saints had to suffer from this state of mind. An obscure canon called Princeteau, a very austere and crabbed man, designated so great a number of them as not worthy of having their days observed, that he was surnamed the exposer of the saints. He did not think, for instance, that if St. Margaret's prayer were applied as a poultice to a woman in travail that the pains of childbirth would be softened.

Even the venerable patron saint of Penguinia did not escape his rigid criticism. This is what he says of her in his "Antiquities of Alca":

"Nothing is more uncertain than the history, or even the existence, of St. Orberosia. An ancient anonymous annalist, a monk of Dombes, relates that a woman called Orberosia was possessed by the devil in a cavern where, even down to his own days, the little boys and girls of the village used to play at a sort of game repre-

75

senting the devil and the fair Orberosia. He adds that this woman
became the concubine of a horrible dragon, who ravaged the country. Such a statement is hardly credible, but the history of Orberosia, as it has since been related, seems hardly more worthy of belief. The life of that saint by the Abbot Simplicissimus is three
hundred years later than the pretended events which it relates and
that author shows himself excessively credulous and devoid of all
critical faculty."

Suspicion attacked even the supernatural origin of the Penguins.
The historian Ovidius Capito went so far as to deny the miracle of
their transformation. He thus begins his "Annals of Penguinia":

"A dense obscurity envelopes this history, and it would be no
exaggeration to say that it is a tissue of puerile fables and popular
tales. The Penguins claim that they are descended from birds who
were baptized by St. Maël and whom God changed into men at the
intercession of that glorious apostle. They hold that, situated at
first in the frozen ocean, their island, floating like Delos, was
brought to anchor in these heaven-favoured seas, of which it is to-
day the queen. I conclude that this myth is a reminiscence of the
ancient migrations of the Penguins."

In the following century, which was that of the philosophers,
scepticism became still more acute. No further evidence of it is
needed than the following celebrated passage from the "Moral
Essay."

"Arriving we know not from whence (for indeed their origins
are not very clear), and successively invaded and conquered by
four or five peoples from the north, south, east, and west, mis-
cegenated, inter-bred, amalgamated, and commingled, the Penguins boast of the purity of their race, and with justice, for they
have become a pure race. This mixture of all mankind, red, black,
yellow, and white, round-headed and long-headed, has formed in
the course of ages a fairly homogeneous human family, and one
which is recognisable by certain features due to a community of
life and customs.

"This idea that they belong to the best race in the world, and
that they are its finest family, inspires them with noble pride, indomitable courage, and a hatred for the human race.

"The life of a people is but a succession of miseries, crimes, and
follies. This is true of the Penguin nation, as of all other nations.
Save for this exception its history is admirable from beginning to
end."

The two classic ages of the Penguins are too well-known for me
to lay stress upon them. But what has not been sufficiently noticed
is the way in which the rationalist theologians such as Canon
Princeteau called into existence the unbelievers of the succeeding
age. The former employed their reason to destroy what did not
seem to them essential to their religion; they only left untouched

the most rigid article of faith. Their intellectual successors, being taught by them how to make use of science and reason, employed them against whatever beliefs remained. Thus rational theology engendered natural philosophy.

That is why (if I may turn from the Penguins of former days to the Sovereign Pontiff, who, to-day governs the universal Church) we cannot admire too greatly the wisdom of Pope Pius X. in condemning the study of exegesis as contrary to revealed truth, fatal to sound theological doctrine, and deadly to the faith. Those clerics who maintain the rights of science in opposition to him are pernicious doctors and pestilent teachers, and the faithful who approve of them are lacking in either mental or moral ballast.

At the end of the age of philosophers, the ancient kingdom of Penguinia was utterly destroyed, the king put to death, the privileges of the nobles abolished, and a Republic proclaimed in the midst of public misfortunes and while a terrible war was raging. The assembly which then governed Penguinia ordered all the metal articles contained in the churches to be melted down. The patriots even desecrated the tombs of the kings. It is said that when the tomb of Draco the Great was opened, that king presented an appearance as black as ebony and so majestic that those who profaned his corpse fled in terror. According to other accounts, these churlish men insulted him by putting a pipe in his mouth and derisively offering him a glass of wine.

On the seventeenth day of the month of Mayflowers, the shrine of St. Orberosia, which had for five hundred years been exposed to the veneration of the faithful in the Church of St. Maël, was transported into the town-hall and submitted to the examination of a jury of experts appointed by the municipality. It was made of gilded copper in shape like the nave of a church, entirely covered with enamels and decorated with precious stones, which latter were perceived to be false. The chapter in its foresight had removed the rubies, sapphires, emeralds, and great balls of rock-crystal, and had substituted pieces of glass in their place. It contained only a little dust and a piece of old linen, which were thrown into a great fire that had been lighted on the Place de Grève to burn the relics of the saints. The people danced around it singing patriotic songs.

From the threshold of their booth, which leant against the town-hall, a man called Rouquin and his wife were watching this group of madmen. Rouquin clipped dogs and gelded cats; he also frequented the inns. His wife was a ragpicker and a bawd, but she had plenty of shrewdness.

"You see, Rouquin," said she to her man, "they are committing a sacrilege. They will repent of it."

"You know nothing about it, wife," answered Rouquin; "they have become philosophers, and when one is once a philosopher he is a philosopher for ever."

"I tell you, Rouquin, that sooner or later they will regret what they are doing to-day. They ill-treat the saints because they have not helped them enough, but for all that the quails won't fall ready cooked into their mouths. They will soon find themselves as badly off as before, and when they have put out their tongues for enough they will become pious again. Sooner than people think the day will come when Penguinia will again begin to honour her blessed patron. Rouquin, it would be a good thing, in readiness for that day, if we kept a handful of ashes and some rags and bones in an old pot in our lodgings. We will say that they are the relics of St. Orberosia and that we have saved them from the flames at the peril of our lives. I am greatly mistaken if we don't get honour and profit out of them. That good action might be worth a place from the Curé to sell tapers and hire chairs in the chapel of St. Orberosia."

On that same day Mother Rouquin took home with her a little ashes and some bones, and put them in an old jam-pot in her cupboard.

II

TRINCO

THE sovereign Nation had taken possession of the lands of the nobility and clergy to sell them at a low price to the middle classes and the peasants. The middle classes and the peasants thought that the revolution was a good thing for acquiring lands and a bad one for retaining them.

The legislators of the Republic made terrible laws for the defence of property, and decreed death to anyone who should propose a division of wealth. But that did not avail the Republic. The peasants who had become proprietors bethought themselves that though it had made them rich, the Republic had nevertheless caused a disturbance to wealth, and they desired a system more respectful of private property and more capable of assuring the permanence of the new institutions.

They had not long to wait. The Republic, like Agrippina, bore her destroyer in her bosom.

Having great wars to carry on, it created military forces, and these were destined both to save it and to destroy it. Its legislators thought they could restrain their generals by the fear of punishment, but if they sometimes cut off the heads of unlucky soldiers they could not do the same to the fortunate soldiers who obtained over it the advantages of having saved its existence.

In the enthusiasm of victory the renovated Penguins delivered themselves up to a dragon, more terrible than that of their fables, who, like a stork amongst frogs, devoured them for fourteen years with his insatiable beak.

Half a century after the reign of the new dragon a young Maharajah of Malay, called Djambi, desirous, like the Scythian Anacharsis, of instructing himself by travel, visited Penguinia and wrote an interesting account of his travels. I transcribe the first page of his account:

ACCOUNT OF THE TRAVELS OF YOUNG DJAMBI IN PENGUINIA

After a voyage of ninety days I landed at the vast and deserted port of the Penguins and travelled over untilled fields to their ruined capital. Surrounded by ramparts and full of barracks and arsenals it had a martial though desolate appearance. Feeble and crippled men wandered proudly through the streets, wearing old uniforms and carrying rusty weapons.

"What do you want?" I was rudely asked at the gate of the city by a soldier whose moustaches pointed to the skies.

"Sir," I answered, "I come as an inquirer to visit this island."

"It is not an island," replied the soldier.

"What!" I exclaimed, "Penguin Island is not an island?"

"No, sir, it is an insula. It was formerly called an island, but for a century it has been decreed that it shall bear the name of insula. It is the only insula in the whole universe. Have you a passport?"

"Here it is."

"Go and get it signed at the Ministry of Foreign Affairs."

A lame guide who conducted me came to a pause in a vast square.

"The insula," said he, "has given birth, as you know, to Trinco, the greatest genius of the universe, whose statue you see before you. That obelisk standing to your right commemorates Trinco's birth; the column that rises to your left has Trinco crowned with a diadem upon its summit. You see here the triumphal arch dedicated to the glory of Trinco and his family."

"What extraordinary feat has Trinco performed?" I asked.

"War."

"That is nothing extraordinary. We Malayans make war constantly."

"That may be, but Trinco is the greatest warrior of all countries and all times. There never existed a greater conquerer than he. As you anchored in our port you saw to the east a volcanic island called Ampelophoria, shaped like a cone, and of small size, but renowned for its wines. And to the west a larger island which raises to the sky a long range of sharp teeth; for this reason it is called the Dog's Jaws. It is rich in copper mines. We possessed both before Trinco's reign and they were the boundaries of our empire.

Trinco extended the Penguin dominion over the Archipelago of the Turquoises and the Green Continent, subdued the gloomy Porpoises, and planted his flag amid the icebergs of the Pole and on the burning sands of the African deserts. He raised troops in all the countries he conquered, and when his armies marched past in the wake of our own light infantry, our island grenadiers, our hussars, our dragoons, our artillery, and our engineers there were to be seen yellow soldiers looking in their blue armour like crayfish standing on their tails; red men with parrots' plumes, tatooed with solar and Phallic emblems, and with quivers of poisoned arrows resounding on their backs; naked blacks armed only with their teeth and nails; pygmies riding on cranes; gorillas carrying trunks of trees and led by an old ape who wrote upon his hairy breast the cross of the Legion of Honour. And all those troops, led to Trinco's banner by the most ardent patriotism, flew on from victory to victory, and in thirty years of war Trinco conquered half the known world."

"What!" cried I, "you possess half of the world."

"Trinco conquered it for us, and Trinco lost it to us. As great in his defeats as in his victories he surrendered all that he had conquered. He even allowed those two islands we possessed before his time, Ampelophoria and the Dog's Jaws, to be taken from us. He left Penguinia impoverished and depopulated. The flower of the insula perished in his wars. At the time of his fall there were left in our country none but the hunchbacks and cripples from whom we are descended. But he gave us glory."

"He made you pay dearly for it!"

"Glory never costs too much," replied my guide.

III

THE JOURNEY OF DOCTOR OBNUBILE

FTER a succession of amazing vicissitudes, the memory of which is in great part lost by the wrongs of time and the bad style of historians, the Penguins established the government of the Penguins by themselves. They elected a diet or assembly, and invested it with the privilege of naming the Head of the State. The latter, chosen from among the simple Penguins, wore no formidable monster's crest upon his head and exercised no absolute authority over the people. He was himself subject to the laws of the nation. He was not given the title of king, and no ordinal number followed his name. He bore such names as Paturle, Janvion, Truffaldin, Co-

quenhot, and Bredouille. These magistrates did not make war. They were not suited for that.

The new state received the name of Public Thing or Republic. Its partisans were called republicanists or republicans. They were also named Thingmongers and sometimes Scamps, but this latter name was taken in ill part.

The Penguin democracy did not itself govern. It obeyed a financial oligarchy which formed opinion by means of the newspapers, and held in its hands the representatives, the ministers, and the president. It controlled the finances of the republic, and directed the foreign affairs of the country as if it were possessed of sovereign power.

Empires and kingdoms in those days kept up enormous fleets. Penguinia, compelled to do as they did, sank under the pressure of her armaments. Everybody deplored or pretended to deplore so grievous a necessity. However, the rich, and those engaged in business or affairs, submitted to it with a good heart through a spirit of patriotism, and because they counted on the soldiers and sailors to defend their goods at home and to acquire markets and territories abroad. The great manufacturers encouraged the making of cannons and ships through a zeal for the national defence and in order to obtain orders. Among the citizens of middle rank and of the liberal professions some resigned themselves to this state of affairs without complaining, believing that it would last for ever; others waited impatiently for its end and thought they might be able to lead the powers to a simultaneous disarmament.

The illustrious Professor Obnubile belonged to this latter class.

"War," said he, "is a barbarity to which the progress of civilization will put an end. The great democracies are pacific and will soon impose their will upon the aristocrats."

Professor Obnubile, who had for sixty years led a solitary and retired life in his laboratory, whither external noises did not penetrate, resolved to observe the spirit of the peoples for himself. He began his studies with the greatest of all democracies and set sail for New Atlantis.

After a voyage of fifteen days his steamer entered, during the night, the harbour of Titanport, where thousands of ships were anchored. An iron bridge thrown across the water and shining with lights, stretched between two piers so far apart that Professor Obnubile imagined he was sailing on the seas of Saturn and that he saw the marvellous ring which girds the planet of the Old Man. And this immense conduit bore upon it more than a quarter of the wealth of the world. The learned Penguin, having disembarked, was waited on by automatons in a hotel forty-eight stories high. Then he took the great railway that led to Gigantopolis, the capital of New Atlantis. In the train there were restaurants, gaming-rooms, athletic arenas, telegraphic, commercial, and financial

offices, a Protestant Church, and the printing-office of a great newspaper, which latter the doctor was unable to read, as he did not
know the language of the New Atlantans. The train passed along
the banks of great rivers, through manufacturing cities which concealed the sky with the smoke from their chimneys, towns black in
the day, towns red at night, full of noise by day and full of noise
also by night.

"Here," thought the doctor, "is a people far too much engaged
in industry and trade to make war. I am already certain that the
New Atlantans pursue a policy of peace. For it is an axiom admitted by all economists that peace without and peace within are
necessary for the progress of commerce and industry."

As he surveyed Gigantopolis, he was confirmed in this opinion.
People went through the streets so swiftly propelled by hurry that
they knocked down all who were in their way. Obnubile was thrown
down several times, but soon succeeded in learning how to demean
himself better; after an hour's walking he himself knocked down
an Atlantan.

Having reached a great square he saw the portico of a palace
in the classic style, whose Corinthian columns reared their capitals of arborescent acanthus seventy metres above the stylobate.

As he stood with his head thrown back admiring the building,
a man of modest appearance approached him and said in Penguin:

"I see by your dress that you are from Penguinia. I know your
language; I am a sworn interpreter. This is the Parliament palace.
At the present moment the representatives of the States are in de-
liberation. Would you like to be present at the sitting?"

The doctor was brought into the hall and cast his looks upon
the crowd of legislators who were sitting on cane chairs with their
feet upon their desks.

The president arose and, in the midst of general inattention, muttered rather than spoke the following formulas which the interpreter immediately translated to the doctor.

"The war for the opening of the Mongol markets being ended
to the satisfaction of the States, I propose that the accounts be
laid before the finance committee. . . ."

"Is there any opposition? . . ."

"The proposal is carried."

"The war for the opening of the markets of Third-Zealand being
ended to the satisfaction of the States, I propose that the accounts
be laid before the finance committee. . . ."

"Is there any opposition? . . ."

"The proposal is carried."

"Have I heard aright?" asked Professor Obnubile. "What? you
an industrial people and engaged in all these wars!"

"Certainly," answered the interpreter, "these are industrial wars.
Peoples who have neither commerce nor industry are not obliged

to make war, but a business people is forced to adopt a policy of conquest. The number of wars necessarily increases with our productive activity. As soon as one of our industries fails to find a market for its products a war is necessary to open new outlets. It is in this way we have had a coal war, a copper war, and a cotton war. In Third-Zealand we have killed two-thirds of the inhabitants in order to compel the remainder to buy our umbrellas and braces."

At that moment a fat man who was sitting in the middle of the assembly ascended the tribune.

"I claim," said he, "a war against the Emerald Republic, which insolently contends with our pigs for the hegemony of hams and sauces in all the markets of the universe."

"Who is that legislator?" asked Doctor Obnubile.

"He is a pig merchant."

"Is there any opposition?" said the President. "I put the proposition to the vote."

The war against the Emerald Republic was voted with uplifted hands by a very large majority.

"What?" said Obnubile to the interpreter; "you have voted a war with that rapidity and that indifference!"

"Oh! it is an unimportant war which will hardly cost eight million dollars."

"And men . . ."

"The men are included in the eight million dollars."

Then Doctor Obnubile bent his head in bitter reflection.

"Since wealth and civilization admit of as many causes of wars as poverty and barbarism, since the folly and wickedness of men are incurable, there remains but one good action to be done. The wise man will collect enough dynamite to blow up this planet. When its fragments fly through space an imperceptible amelioration will be accomplished in the universe and a satisfaction will be given to the universal conscience. Moreover, this universal conscience does not exist."

BOOK V: MODERN TIMES: CHATILLON

I

THE REVEREND FATHERS AGARIC AND CORNEMUSE

VERY system of government produces people who are dissatisfied. The Republic or Public Thing produced them at first from among the nobles who had been despoiled of their ancient privileges. These looked with regret and hope to Prince Crucho, the last of the Draconides, a prince adorned both with the grace of youth and the melancholy of exile. It also produced them from among the smaller traders, who, owing to profound economic causes, no longer gained a livelihood. They believed that this was the fault of the republic which they had at first adored and from which each day they were now becoming more detached. The financiers, both Christians, and Jews, became by their insolence and their cupidity the scourge of the country, which they plundered and degraded, as well as the scandal of a government which they never troubled either to destroy or preserve, so confident were they that they could operate without hindrance under all governments. Nevertheless, their sympathies inclined to absolute power as the best protection against the socialists, their puny but ardent adversaries. And just as they imitated the habits of the aristocrats, so they imitated their political and religious sentiments. Their women, in particular, loved the Prince and had dreams of appearing one day at his Court.

However, the Republic retained some partisans and defenders. If it was not in a position to believe in the fidelity of its own officials it could at least still count on the devotion of the manual labourers, although it had never relieved their misery. These came forth in crowds from their quarries and their factories to defend it, and marched in long processions, gloomy, emaciated, and sinister. They would have died for it because it had given them hope.

Now, under the Presidency of Theodore Formose, there lived in a peaceable suburb of Alca a monk called Agaric, who kept a school and assisted in arranging marriages. In his school he taught fencing and riding to the sons of old families, illustrious by their birth, but now as destitute of wealth as of privilege. And as soon as they were old enough he married them to the daughters of the opulent and despised caste of financiers.

Tall, thin, and dark, Agaric used to walk in deep thought, with his breviary in his hand and his brow loaded with care, through the corridors of the school and the alleys of the garden. His care was not limited to inculcating in his pupils abstruse doctrines and mechanical precepts and to endowing them afterwards with legitimate and rich wives. He entertained political designs and pursued the realisation of a gigantic plan. His thought of thoughts and labour of labours was to overthrow the Republic. He was not moved to this by any personal interest. He believed that a democratic state was opposed to the holy society to which body and soul he belonged. And all the other monks, his brethren, thought the same. The Republic was perpetually at strife with the congregation of monks and the assembly of the faithful. True, to plot the death of the new government was a difficult and perilous enterprise. Still, Agaric was in a position to carry on a formidable conspiracy. At that epoch, when the clergy guided the superior classes of the Penguins, this monk exercised a tremendous influence over the aristocracy of Alca.

All the young men whom he had brought up waited only for a favourable moment to march against the popular power. The sons of the ancient families did not practise the arts or engage in business. They were almost all soldiers and served the Republic. They served it, but they did not love it; they regretted the dragon's crest. And the fair Jewesses shared in these regrets in order that they might be taken for Christians.

One July as he was walking in a suburban street which ended in some dusty fields, Agaric heard groans coming from a moss-grown well that had been abandoned by the gardeners. And almost immediately he was told by a cobbler of the neighbourhood that a ragged man who had shouted out "Hurrah for the Republic!" had been thrown into the well by some cavalry officers who were passing, and had sunk up to his ears in the mud. Agaric was quite ready to see a general significance in this particular fact. He inferred a great fermentation in the whole aristocratic and military caste, and concluded that it was the moment to act.

The next day he went to the end of the Wood of Conils to visit the good Father Cornemuse. He found the monk in his laboratory pouring a golden-coloured liquor into a still. He was a short, fat, little man, with vermilion-tinted cheeks and elaborately polished bald head. His eyes had ruby-coloured pupils like a guinea-pig's. He graciously saluted his visitor and offered him a glass of the St. Orberosian *liqueur,* which he manufactured, and from the sale of which he gained immense wealth.

Agaric made a gesture of refusal. Then, standing on his long feet and pressing his melancholy hat against his stomach, he remained silent.

"Take a seat," said Cornemuse to him.

Agaric sat down on a rickety stool, but continued mute.

Then the monk of Conils inquired:

"Tell me some news of your young pupils. Have the dear children sound views?"

"I am very satisfied with them," answered the teacher. "It is everything to be nurtured in sound principles. It is necessary to have sound views before having any views at all, for afterwards it is too late. . . . Yes, I have great grounds for comfort. But we live in a sad age."

"Alas!" sighed Cornemuse.

"We are passing through evil days. . . ."

"Times of trial."

"Yet, Cornemuse, the mind of the public is not so entirely corrupted as it seems."

"Perhaps you are right."

"The people are tired of a government that ruins them and does nothing for them. Every day fresh scandals spring up. The Republic is sunk in shame. It is ruined."

"May God grant it!"

"Cornemuse, what do you think of Prince Crucho?"

"He is an amiable young man and, I dare say, a worthy scion of an august stock. I pity him for having to endure the pains of exile at so early an age. Spring has no flowers for the exile, and autumn no fruits. Prince Crucho has sound views; he respects the clergy; he practises our religion; besides, he consumes a good deal of my little products."

"Cornemuse, in many homes, both rich and poor, his return is hoped for. Believe me, he will come back."

"May I live to throw my mantle beneath his feet!" sighed Cornemuse.

Seeing that he held these sentiments, Agaric depicted to him the state of people's minds such as he himself imagined them. He showed him the nobles and the rich exasperated against the popular government; the army refusing to endure fresh insults; the officials willing to betray their chiefs; the people discontented, riot ready to burst forth, and the enemies of the monks, the agents of the constituted authority, thrown into the wells of Alca. He concluded that it was the moment to strike a great blow.

"We can," he cried, "save the Penguin people, we can deliver it from its tyrants, deliver it from itself, restore the Dragon's crest, re-establish the ancient State, the good State, for the honour of the faith and the exaltation of the Church. We can do this if we will. We possess great wealth and we exert secret influences; by

our evangelistic and outspoken journals we communicate with all
the ecclesiastics in towns and country alike, and we inspire them
with our own eager enthusiasm and our own burning faith. They
will kindle their penitents and their congregations. I can dispose
of the chiefs of the army; I have an understanding with the men
of the people. Unknown to them I sway the minds of umbrella
sellers, publicans, shopmen, gutter merchants, newspaper boys,
women of the streets, and police agents. We have more people on
our side than we need. What are we waiting for? Let us act!"

"What do you think of doing?" asked Cornemuse.

"Of forming a vast conspiracy and overthrowing the Republic,
of re-establishing Crucho on the throne of the Draconides."

Cornemuse moistened his lips with his tongue several times.
Then he said with unction:

"Certainly the restoration of the Draconides is desirable; it is
eminently desirable; and for my part, I desire it with all my heart.
As for the Republic, you know what I think of it. . . . But would
it not be better to abandon it to its fate and let it die of the vices
of its own constitution? Doubtless, Agaric, what you propose is
noble and generous. It would be a fine thing to save this great and
unhappy country, to re-establish it in its ancient splendour. But
reflect on it, we are Christians before we are Penguins. And we
must take heed not to compromise religion in political enterprises."

Agaric replied eagerly:

"Fear nothing. We shall hold all the threads of the plot, but we
ourselves shall remain in the background. We shall not be seen."

"Like flies in milk," murmured the monk of Conils.

And turning his keen ruby-coloured eyes towards his brother
monk:

"Take care. Perhaps the Republic is stronger than it seems. Possibly, too, by dragging it out of the nerveless inertia in which it
now rests we may only consolidate its forces. Its malice is great;
if we attack it, it will defend itself. It makes bad laws which hardly
affect us; if it is frightened it will make terrible ones against us.
Let us not lightly engage in an adventure in which we may get
fleeced. You think the opportunity a good one. I don't, and I am
going to tell you why. The present government is not yet known
by everybody, that is to say, it is known by nobody. It proclaims
that it is the Public Thing, the common thing. The populace believes it and remains democratic and Republican. But patience!
This same people will one day demand that the public thing be the
people's thing. I need not tell you how insolent, unregulated, and
contrary to Scriptural polity such claims seem to me. But the people will make them, and enforce them, and then there will be an
end of the present government. The moment cannot now be far
distant; and it is then that we ought to act in the interests of our

august body. Let us wait. What hurries us? Our existence is not in peril. It has not been rendered absolutely intolerable to us. The Republic fails in respect and submission to us; it does not give the priests the honours it owes them. But it lets us live. And such is the excellence of our position that with us to live is to prosper. The Republic is hostile to us, but women revere us. President Formose does not assist at the celebration of our mysteries, but I have seen his wife and daughters at my feet. They buy my phials by the gross. I have no better clients even among the aristocracy. Let us say what there is to be said for it. There is no country in the world as good for priests and monks as Penguinia. In what other country would you find our virgin wax, our virile incense, our rosaries, our scapulars, our holy water, and our St. Orberosian liqueur sold in such great quantities? What other people would, like the Penguins, give a hundred golden crowns for a wave of our hands, a

sound from our mouths, a movement of our lips? For my part, I gain a thousand times more, in this pleasant, faithful, and docile Penguinia, by extracting the essence from a bundle of thyme, than I could make by tiring my lungs with preaching the remission of sins in the most populous States of Europe and America. Honestly, would Penguinia be better off if a police officer came to take me away from here and put me on a steamboat bound for the Islands of Night?"

Having thus spoken, the monk of Conils got up and led his guest into a huge shed where hundreds of orphans clothed in blue were packing bottles, nailing up cases, and gumming tickets. The ear was deafened by the noise of hammers mingled with the dull rumbling of bales being placed upon the rails.

"It is from here that consignments are forwarded," said Cornemuse. "I have obtained from the government a railway through the Wood and a station at my door. Every three days I fill a truck with my own products. You see that the Republic has not killed all beliefs."

Agaric made a last effort to engage the wise distiller in his enterprise. He pointed him to a prompt, certain, dazzling success.

"Don't you wish to share in it?" he added. "Don't you wish to bring back your king from exile?"

"Exile is pleasant to men of good will," answered the monk of Conils. "If you are guided by me, my dear Brother Agaric, you will give up your project for the present. For my own part I have no illusions. Whether or not I belong to your party, if you lose, I shall have to pay like you."

Father Agaric took leave of his friend and went back satisfied to his school. "Cornemuse," thought he, "not being able to prevent the plot, would like to make it succeed and he will give money." Agaric was not deceived. Such, indeed, was the solidarity among priests and monks that the acts of a single one bound them all. That was at once both their strength and their weakness.

II

PRINCE CRUCHO

GARIC resolved to proceed without delay to Prince Crucho, who honoured him with his familiarity. In the dusk of the evening he went out of his school by the side door, disguised as a cattle merchant and took passage on board the *St. Maël.*

The next day he landed in Porpoisia, for it was at Chitterlings Castle on this hospitable soil that Crucho ate the bitter bread of exile.

Agaric met the Prince on the road driving in a motor-car with two young ladies at the rate of a hundred miles an hour. When the monk saw him he shook his red umbrella and the prince stopped his car.

"Is it you, Agaric? Get in! There are already three of us, but we can make room for you. You can take one of these young ladies on your knee."

The pious Agaric got in.

"What news, worthy father?" asked the young prince.

"Great news," answered Agaric. "Can I speak?"

"You can. I have nothing secret from these two ladies."

"Sire, Penguinia claims you. You will not be deaf to her call."

Agaric described the state of feeling and outlined a vast plot.

"On my first signal," said he, "all your partisans will rise at once. With cross in hand and habits girded up, your venerable clergy will lead the armed crowd into Formose's palace. We shall carry terror and death among your enemies. For a reward of our efforts we only ask of you, Sire, that you will not render them useless. We entreat you to come and seat yourself on the throne that we shall prepare."

The prince returned a simple answer:

"I shall enter Alca on a green horse."

Agaric declared that he accepted this manly response. Although, contrary to his custom, he had a lady on his knee, he adjured the young prince, with a sublime loftiness of soul, to be faithful to his royal duties.

"Sire," he cried, with tears in his eyes, "you will live to remember the day on which you have been restored from exile, given back to your people, re-established on the throne of your ancestors by the hands of your monks, and crowned by them with the august crest of the Dragon. King Crucho, may you equal the glory of your ancestor Draco the Great!"

The young prince threw himself with emotion on his restorer and attempted to embrace him, but he was prevented from reaching him by the girth of the two ladies, so tightly packed were they all in that historic carriage.

"Worthy father," said he, "I would like all Penguinia to witness this embrace."

"It would be a cheering spectacle," said Agaric.

In the mean time the motor-car rushed like a tornado through hamlets and villages, crushing hens, geese, turkeys, ducks, guinea-fowls, cats, dogs, pigs, children, labourers, and women beneath its insatiable tyres. And the pious Agaric turned over his great designs in his mind. His voice, coming from behind one of the ladies, expressed this thought:

"We must have money, a great deal of money."

"That is your business," answered the prince.

But already the park gates were opening to the formidable motor-car.

The dinner was sumptuous. They toasted the Dragon's crest. Everybody knows that a closed goblet is a sign of sovereignty; so Prince Crucho and Princess Gudrune, his wife, drank out of goblets that were covered over like ciboriums. The prince had his filled several times with the wines of Penguinia, both white and red.

Crucho had received a truly princely education, and he excelled in motoring, but was not ignorant of history either. He was said to be well versed in the antiquities and famous deeds of his family; and, indeed, he gave a notable proof of his knowledge in this respect. As they were speaking of the various remarkable peculiarities that had been noticed in famous women:

"It is perfectly true," said he, "that Queen Crucha, whose name I bear, had the mark of a little monkey's head upon her body."

During the evening Agaric had a decisive interview with three of the prince's oldest councillors. It was decided to ask for funds from Crucho's father-in-law, as he was anxious to have a king for son-in-law, from several Jewish ladies, who were impatient to become ennobled, and, finally, from the Prince Regent of the Porpoises, who had promised his aid to the Draconides, thinking that by Crucho's restoration he would weaken the Penguins, the hereditary enemies of his people. The three old councillors divided among themselves the three chief offices of the Court, those of Chamberlain, Seneschal, and High Steward, and authorised the monk to distribute the other places to the prince's best advantage.

"Devotion has to be rewarded," said the three old councillors.

"And treachery also," said Agaric.

"It is but too true," replied one of them, the Marquis of Seven-wounds, who had experience of revolutions.

There was dancing, and after the ball Princess Gudrune tore up her green robe to make cockades. With her own hands she sewed a piece of it on the monk's breast, upon which he shed tears of sensibility and gratitude.

M. de Plume, the prince's equerry, set out the same evening to look for a green horse.

III

THE CABAL

AFTER his return to the capital of Penguinia, the Reverend Father Agaric disclosed his projects to Prince Adélestan des Boscénos, of whose Draconian sentiments he was well aware.

The Prince belonged to the highest nobility. The Torticol des Boscénos went back to Brian the Good, and under the Draconides had held the highest offices in the kingdom. In 1179, Philip Torticol, High Admiral of Penguinia, a brave, faithful, and generous, but vindictive man, delivered over the port of La Crique and the Penguin fleet to the enemies of the kingdom, because he suspected that Queen Crucha, whose lover he was, had been unfaithful to him and loved a stable-boy. It was that great queen who gave to the Boscénos the silver warming-pan which they bear in their arms. As for their motto, it only goes back to the sixteenth century. The story of its origin is as follows: One gala night, as he mingled with the crowd of courtiers who were watching the fire-works in the king's garden, Duke John des Boscénos approached the Duchess of Skull and put his hand under the petticoat of that lady, who made no complaint at the gesture. The king, happening to pass, surprised them and contented himself with saying, "And thus I find you." These four words became the motto of the Boscénos.

Prince Adélestan had not degenerated from his ancestors. He preserved an unalterable fidelity for the race of the Draconides and desired nothing so much as the restoration of Prince Crucho, an event which was in his eyes to be the fore-runner of the restoration of his own fortune. He therefore readily entered into the Reverend Father Agaric's plans. He joined himself at once to the monk's projects, and hastened to put him into communication with the most loyal Royalists of his acquaintance, Count Cléna, M. de la Trumelle, Viscount Olive, and M. Bigourd. They met together one night in the Duke of Ampoule's country house, six miles eastward of Alca, to consider ways and means.

M. de la Trumelle was in favor of legal action.

"We ought to keep within the law," said he in substance. "We are for order. It is by an untiring propaganda that we shall best pursue the realisation of our hopes. We must change the feeling of the country. Our cause will conquer because it is just."

The Prince des Boscénos expressed a contrary opinion. He thought that, in order to triumph, just causes need force quite as much and even more than unjust causes require it.

"In the present situation," said he tranquilly, "three methods of action present themselves; to hire the butcher boys, to corrupt the ministers, and to kidnap President Formose."

"It would be a mistake to kidnap Formose," objected M. de la Trumelle. "The President is on our side."

The attitude and sentiments of the President of the Republic are explained by the fact that one Dracophil proposed to seize Formose while another Dracophil regarded him as a friend. Formose showed himself favourable to the Royalists, whose habits he admired and imitated. If he smiled at the mention of the Dragon's crest it was at the thought of putting it on his own head. He was envious of sovereign power, not because he felt himself capable of exercising it, but because he loved to appear so. According to the expression of a Penguin chronicler, "he was a goose."

Prince des Boscénos maintained his proposal to march against Formose's palace and the House of Parliament.

Count Cléna was even still more energetic.

"Let us begin," said he, "by slaughtering, disembowelling, and braining the Republicans and all partisans of the government. Afterwards we shall see what more need be done."

M. de la Trumelle was a moderate, and moderates are always moderately opposed to violence. He recognised that Count Cléna's policy was inspired by a noble feeling and that it was high-minded, but he timidly objected that perhaps it was not conformable to principle, and that it presented certain dangers. At last he consented to discuss it.

"I propose," added he, "to draw up an appeal to the people. Let us show who we are. For my own part I can assure you that I shall not hide my flag in my pocket."

M. Bigourd began to speak.

"Gentlemen, the Penguins are dissatisfied with the new order because it exists, and it is natural for men to complain of their condition. But at the same time the Penguins are afraid to change their government because new things alarm them. They have not known the Dragon's crest and, although they sometimes say that they regret it, we must not believe them. It is easy to see that they speak in this way either without thought or because they are in an ill-temper. Let us not have any illusions about their feelings towards ourselves. They do not like us. They hate the aristocracy both from a base envy and from a generous love of equality. And these two united feelings are very strong in a people. Public opinion is not against us, because it knows nothing about us. But when it knows what we want it will not follow us. If we let it be seen that we wish to destroy democratic government and restore the Dragon's crest, who will be our partisans? Only the butcher-boys and the little shop-keepers of Alca. And could we even count on them to the end? They are dissatisfied, but at the bottom of their hearts they are Republicans. They are more anxious to sell their cursed wares than to see Crucho again. If we act openly we shall only cause alarm.

"To make people sympathise with us and follow us we must make them believe that we want, not to overthrow the Republic, but, on the contrary, to restore it, to cleanse, to purify, to embellish, to adorn, to beautify, and to ornament it, to render it, in a word, glorious and attractive. Therefore, we ought not to act openly ourselves. It is known that we are not favourable to the present order. We must have recourse to a friend of the Republic, and, if we are to do what is best, to a defender of this government. We have plenty to choose from. It would be well to prefer the most popular and, if I dare say so, the most republican of them. We shall win him over to us by flattery, by presents, and above all by prom-ises. Promises cost less than presents, and are worth more. No one gives as much as he who gives hopes. It is not necessary for the man we choose to be of brilliant intellect. I would even prefer him to be of no great ability. Stupid people show an inimitable grace in roguery. Be guided by me, gentlemen, and overthrow the Republic by the agency of a Republican. Let us be prudent. But prudence does not exclude energy. If you need me you will find me at your disposal."

This speech made a great impression upon those who heard it. The mind of the pious Agaric was particularly impressed. But each of them was anxious to appoint himself to a position of honour and profit. A secret government was organised of which all those present were elected active members. The Duke of Ampoule, who was the great financier of the party, was chosen treasurer and charged with organising funds for the propaganda.

The meeting was on the point of coming to an end when a rough voice was heard singing an old air:

> Boscénos est un gros cochon;
> On en va faire des andouilles
> Des saucisses et du jambon
> Pour le réveillon des pauv' bougres.

It had, for two hundred years, been a well-known song in the slums of Alca. Prince Boscénos did not like to hear it. He went down into the street, and, perceiving that the singer was a workman who was placing some slates on the roof of a church, he politely asked him to sing something else.

"I will sing what I like," answered the man.

"My friend, to please me. . . ."

"I don't want to please you."

Prince Boscénos was as a rule good-tempered, but he was easily angered and a man of great strength.

"Fellow, come down or I will go up to you," cried he, in a terrible voice.

As the workman, astride on his coping, showed no sign of budging, the prince climbed quickly up the staircase of the tower and attacked the singer. He gave him a blow that broke his jaw-bone and sent him rolling into a water-spout. At that moment seven or eight carpenters, who were working on the rafters, heard their companion's cry and looked through the window. Seeing the prince on the coping they climbed along a ladder that was leaning on the slates and reached him just as he was slipping into the tower. They sent him, head foremost, down the one hundred and thirty-seven steps of the spiral staircase.

IV

VISCOUNTESS OLIVE

THE Penguins had the finest army in the world. So had the Porpoises. And it was the same with the other nations of Europe. The smallest amount of thought will prevent any surprise at this. For all armies are the finest in the world. The second finest army, if one could exist, would be in a notoriously inferior position; it would be certain to be beaten. It ought to be disbanded at once. Therefore, all armies are the finest in the world. In France the illustrious Colonel Marchand understood this when, before the passage of the Yalou, being questioned by some journalists about the Russo-Japanese war, he did not hesitate to describe the Russian army as the finest in the world, and also the Japanese. And it should be noticed that even after suffering the most terrible reverses an army does not fall from its position of being the finest in the world. For if nations ascribe their victories to the ability of their generals and the courage of their soldiers, they always attribute their defeats to an inexplicable fatality. On the other hand, navies are classed according to the number of their ships. There is a first, a second, a third, and so on. So that there exists no doubt as to the result of naval wars.

The Penguins had the finest army and the second navy in the world. This navy was commanded by the famous Chatillon, who bore the title of Emiralbahr, and by abbreviation Emiral. It is the same word which, unfortunately in a corrupt form, is used to-day among several European nations to designate the highest grade in the naval service. But as there was but one Emiral among the Penguins, a singular prestige, if I dare say so, was attached to that rank.

The Emiral did not belong to the nobility. A child of the people, he was loved by the people. They were flattered to see a man who sprang from their own ranks holding a position of honour. Chatillon was good-looking and fortune favoured him. He was not over-addicted to thought. No event ever disturbed his serene outlook.

The Reverend Father Agaric, surrendering to M. Bigourd's reasons and recognising that the existing government could only be destroyed by one of its defenders, cast his eyes upon Emiral Chatillon. He asked a large sum of money from his friend, the Reverend Father Cornemuse, which the latter handed him with a sigh. And with this sum he hired six hundred butcher boys of Alca to run behind Chatillon's horse and shout, "Hurrah for the Emiral!" Henceforth Chatillon could not take a single step without being cheered.

Viscountess Olive asked him for a private interview. He received her at the Admiralty* in a room decorated with anchors, shells, and grenades.

She was discreetly dressed in greyish blue. A hat trimmed with roses covered her pretty, fair hair. Behind her veil her eyes shone like sapphires. Although she came of Jewish origin there was no more fashionable woman in the whole nobility. She was tall and well shaped; her form was that of the year, her figure that of the season.

"Emiral," said she, in a delightful voice, "I cannot conceal my emotion from you. . . . It is very natural . . . before a hero."

"You are too kind. But tell me, Viscountess, what brings me the honour of your visit."

"For a long time I have been anxious to see you, to speak to you. . . . So I very willingly undertook to convey a message to you."

"Please take a seat."

"How still it is here."

"Yes, it is quiet enough."

"You can hear the birds singing."

"Sit down, then, dear lady."

And he drew up an arm-chair for her.

She took a seat with her back to the light.

"Emiral, I came to bring you a very important message, a message . . ."

"Explain."

"Emiral, have you ever seen Prince Crucho?"

"Never."

She sighed.

"It is a great pity. He would be so delighted to see you! He esteems and appreciates you. He has your portrait on his desk besides his mother's. What a pity it is he is not better known! He is a

*Or better, *Emiralty*.

charming prince and so grateful for what is done for him! He will
be a great king. For he will be king without doubt. He will come
back and sooner than people think. . . . What I have to tell you,
the message with which I am entrusted, refers precisely to . . ."

The Emiral stood up.

"Not a word more, dear lady. I have the esteem, the confidence
of the Republic. I will not betray it. And why should I betray it? I
am loaded with honours and dignities."

"Allow me to tell you, my dear Emiral, that your honours and
dignities are far from equalling what you deserve. If your services
were properly rewarded, you would be Emiralissimo and Generalissimo, Commander-in-chief of the troops both on land and sea. The
Republic is very ungrateful to you."

"All governments are more or less ungrateful."

"Yes, but the Republicans are jealous of you. That class of person is always afraid of his superiors. They cannot endure the Services. Everything that has to do with the navy and the army is
odious to them. They are afraid of you."

"That is possible."

"They are wretches; they are ruining the country. Don't you wish
to save Penguinia?"

"In what way?"

"By sweeping away all the rascals of the Republic, all the Republicans."

"What a proposal to make to me, dear lady!"

"It is what will certainly be done, if not by you, then by some
one else. The Generalissimo, to mention him alone, is ready to throw
all the ministers, deputies, and senators into the sea, and to recall
Prince Crucho."

"Oh, the rascal, the scoundrel," exclaimed the Emiral.

"Do to him what he would do to you. The prince will know how to
recognise your services. He will give you the Constable's sword and
a magnificent grant. I am commissioned, in the meantime, to hand
you a pledge of his royal friendship."

As she said these words she drew a green cockade from her
bosom.

"What is that?" asked the Emiral.

"It is his colours which Crucho sends you."

"Be good enough to take them back."

"So that they may be offered to the Generalissimo who will accept
them! . . . No, Emiral, let me place them on your glorious breast."

Chatillon gently repelled the lady. But for some minutes he
thought her extremely pretty, and he felt this impression still more
when two bare arms and the rosy palms of two delicate hands
touched him lightly. He yielded almost immediately. Olive was slow
in fastening the ribbon. Then when it was done she made a low
courtesy and saluted Chatillon with the title of Constable.

"I have been ambitious like my comrades," answered the sailor, "I don't hide it, and perhaps I am so still; but upon my word of honour, when I look at you, the only desire I feel is for a cottage and a heart."

She turned upon him the charming sapphire glances that flashed from under her eyelids.

"That is to be had also . . . what are you doing, Emiral?"

"I am looking for the heart."

When she left the Admiralty, the Viscountess went immediately to the Reverend Father Agaric to give an account of her visit.

"You must go to him again, dear lady," said that austere monk.

V

THE PRINCE DES BOSCÉNOS

ORNING and evening the newspapers that had been bought by the Dracophils proclaimed Chatillon's praises and hurled shame and opprobrium upon the Ministers of the Republic. Chatillon's portrait was sold through the streets of Alca. Those young descendants of Remus who carry plaster figures on their heads, offered busts of Chatillon for sale upon the bridges.

Every evening Chatillon rode upon his white horse round the Queen's Meadow, a place frequented by the people of fashion. The Dracophils posted along the Emiral's route a crowd of needy Penguins who kept shouting: "It is Chatillon we want." The middle classes of Alca conceived a profound admiration for the Emiral. Shopwomen murmured: "He is good-looking." Women of fashion slackened the speed of their motor-cars and kissed hands to him as they passed, amidst the hurrahs of an enthusiastic populace.

One day, as he went into a tobacco shop, two Penguins who were putting letters in the box recognized Chatillon and cried at the top of their voices: "Hurrah for the Emiral! Down with the Republicans." All those who were passing stopped in front of the shop. Chatillon lighted his cigar before the eyes of a dense crowd of frenzied citizens who waved their hats and cheered. The crowd kept increasing, and the whole town, singing and marching behind its hero, went back with him to the Admiralty.

The Emiral had an old comrade in arms, Under-Emiral Vulcanmould, who had served with great distinction, a man as true as gold and as loyal as his sword. Vulcanmould plumed himself on his thoroughgoing independence and he went among the partisans of Crucho and the Minister of the Republic telling both parties what he thought of them. M. Bigourd maliciously declared that he told each party what the other party thought of it. In truth he had on several occasions been guilty of regrettable indiscretions, which were overlooked as being the freedoms of a soldier who knew nothing of intrigue. Every morning he went to see Chatillon, whom he treated with the cordial roughness of a brother in arms.

"Well, old buffer, so you are popular," said he to him. "Your phiz is sold on the heads of pipes and on liqueur bottles and every drunkard in Alca spits out your name as he rolls in the gutter. . . . Chatillon, the hero of the Penguins! Chatillon, defender of the Penguin glory! . . . Who would have said it? Who would have thought it?"

And he laughed with his harsh laugh. Then changing his tone:

"But, joking aside, are you not a bit surprised at what is happening to you?"

"No, indeed," answered Chatillon.

And out went the honest Vulcanmould, banging the door behind him.

In the meantime Chatillon had taken a little flat at number 18 Johannes-Talpa Street, so that he might receive Viscountess Olive. They met there every day. He was desperately in love with her. During his martial and neptunian life he had loved crowds of women, red, black, yellow, and white, and some of them had been very beautiful. But before he met the Viscountess he did not know what a woman really was. When the Viscountess Olive called him her darling, her dear darling, he felt in heaven and it seemed to him that the stars shone in her hair.

She would come a little late, and, as she put her bag on the table, she would ask pensively:

"Let me sit on your knee."

And then she would talk of subjects suggested by the pious Agaric, interrupting the conversation with sighs and kisses. She would ask him to dismiss such and such an officer, to give a command to another, to send the squadron here or there. And at the right moment she would exclaim:

"How young you are, my dear!"

And he did whatever she wished, for he was simple, he was anxious to wear the Constable's sword, and to receive a large grant; he did not dislike playing a double part, he had a vague idea of saving Penguinia, and he was in love.

This delightful woman induced him to remove the troops that were at La Cirque, the port where Crucho was to land. By this means it was made certain that there would be no obstacle to prevent the prince from entering Penguinia.

The pious Agaric organised public meetings so as to keep up the agitation. The Dracophils held one or two every day in some of the thirty-six districts of Alca, and preferably in the poorer quarters.

They desired to win over the poor, for they are the most numerous. On the fourth of May a particularly fine meeting was held in an old cattle-market, situated in the centre of a populous suburb filled with housewives sitting on the doorsteps and children playing in the gutters. There were present about two thousand people, in the opinion of the Republicans, and six thousand according to the reckoning of the Dracophils. In the audience was to be seen the flower of Penguin society, including Prince and Princess des Boscénos, Count Cléna, M. de La Trumelle, M. Bigourd, and several rich Jewish ladies.

The Generalissimo of the national army had come in uniform. He was cheered.

The committee had been carefully formed. A man of the people, a workman, but a man of sound principles, M. Rauchin, the secretary of the yellow syndicate, was asked to preside, supported by Count Cléna and M. Michaud, a butcher.

The government which Penguinia had freely given itself was called by such names as cesspool and drain in several eloquent speeches. But President Formose was spared and no mention was made of Crucho or the priests.

The meeting was not unanimous. A defender of the modern State and of the Republic, a manual labourer, stood up.

"Gentlemen," said M. Rauchin, the chairman, "we have told you that this meeting would not be unanimous. We are not like our opponents, we are honest men. I allow our opponent to speak. Heaven knows what you are going to hear. Gentlemen, I beg of you to restrain as long as you can the expression of your contempt, your disgust, and your indignation."

"Gentlemen," said the opponent. . . .

Immediately he was knocked down, trampled beneath the feet of the indignant crowd, and his unrecognisable remains thrown out of the hall.

The tumult was still resounding when Count Cléna ascended the tribune. Cheers took the place of groans and when silence was restored the orator uttered these words:

"Comrades, we are going to see whether you have blood in your veins. What we have got to do is to slaughter, disembowel, and brain all the Republicans."

This speech let loose such a thunder of applause that the old shed rocked with it, and a cloud of acrid and thick dust fell from its filthy walls and worm-eaten beams and enveloped the audience.

A resolution was carried vilifying the government and acclaiming Chatillon. And the audience departed singing the hymn of the liberator: "It is Chatillon we want."

The only way out of the old market was through a muddy alley shut in by omnibus stables and coal sheds. There was no moon and a cold drizzle was coming down. The police, who were assembled in great numbers, blocked the alley and compelled the Dracophils to disperse in little groups. These were the instructions they had received from their chief, who was anxious to check the enthusiasm of the excited crowd.

The Dracophils who were detained in the alley kept marking time and singing, "It is Chatillon we want." Soon, becoming impatient of the delay, the cause of which they did not know, they began to push those in front of them. This movement, propagated along the alley, threw those in front against the broad chests of the police. The latter had no hatred for the Dracophils. In the bottom of their hearts they liked Chatillon. But it is natural to resist aggression and strong men are inclined to make use of their strength. For these reasons the police kicked the Dracophils with their hob-nailed boots. As a result there were sudden rushes backwards and forwards. Threats and cries mingled with the songs.

"Murder! Murder! . . . It is Chatillon we want! Murder! Murder!"

And in the gloomy alley the more prudent kept saying, "Don't push." Among these latter, in the darkness, his lofty figure rising above the moving crowd, his broad shoulders and robust body noticeable among the trampled limbs and crushed sides of the rest, stood the Prince des Boscénos, calm, immovable and placid. Serenely and indulgently he waited. In the meantime, as the exit was opened at regular intervals between the ranks of the police, the pressure of elbows against the chests of those around the prince diminished and people began to breathe again.

"You see we shall soon be able to go out," said that kindly giant, with a pleasant smile. "Time and patience . . ."

He took a cigar from his case, raised it to his lips and struck a match. Suddenly, in the light of the match, he saw Princess Anne, his wife, clasped in Count Cléna's arms. At this sight he rushed towards them, striking both them and those around with his cane. He was disarmed, though not without difficulty, but he could not be separated from his opponent. And whilst the fainting princess was lifted from arm to arm to her carriage over the excited and curious crowd, the two men still fought furiously. Prince des Boscénos lost his hat, his eye-glass, his cigar, his necktie, and his portfolio full of private letters and political correspondence; he even lost the miraculous medals that he had received from the good Father Cornemuse. But he gave his opponent so terrible a kick in the stomach that the unfortunate Count was knocked through an iron grating and went, head foremost, through a glass door and into a coal shed.

Attracted by the struggle and the cries of those around, the police rushed towards the prince, who furiously resisted them. He stretched three of them gasping at his feet and put seven others to flight, with, respectively, a broken jaw, a split lip, a nose pouring blood, a fractured skull, a torn ear, a dislocated collar-bone, and broken ribs. He fell, however, and was dragged bleeding and disfigured, with his clothes in rags, to the nearest police-station, where, jumping about and bellowing, he spent the night.

Until daybreak groups of demonstrators went about the town singing, "It is Chatillon we want," and breaking the windows of the houses in which the Ministers of the Republic lived.

VI

THE EMIRAL'S FALL

HAT night marked the culmination of the Dracophil movement. The Royalists had no longer any doubt of its triumph. Their chiefs sent congratulations to Prince Crucho by wireless telegraphy. Their ladies embroidered scarves and slippers for him. M. de Plume had found the green horse.

The pious Agaric shared the common hope. But he still worked to win partisans for the Pretender. They ought, he said, to lay their foundations upon the bed-rock.

With this design he had an interview with three Trade Union workmen.

In these times the artisans no longer lived, as in the days of the Draconides, under the government of corporations. They were free, but they had no assured pay. After having remained isolated from each other for a long time, without help and without support, they had formed themselves into unions. The coffers of the unions were empty, as it was not the habit of the unionists to pay their subscriptions. There were unions numbering thirty thousand members, others with a thousand, five hundred, two hundred, and so forth. Several numbered two or three members only, or even a few less. But as the lists of adherents were not published, it was not easy to distinguish the great unions from the small ones.

After some dark and indirect steps the pious Agaric was put into communication in a room in the Moulin de la Galette, with comrades Dagobert, Tronc, and Balafille, the secretaries of three unions of which the first numbered fourteen members, the second twenty-four, and the third only one. Agaric showed extreme cleverness at this interview.

"Gentlemen," said he, "you and I have not, in most respects, the same political and social views, but there are points in which we may come to an understanding. We have a common enemy. The government exploits you and despises us. Help us to overthrow it;

we will supply you with the means so far as we are able, and you can in addition count on our gratitude."

"Fork out the tin," said Dagobert.

The Reverend Father placed on the table a bag which the distiller of Conils had given him with tears in his eyes.

"Done!" said the three companions.

Thus was the solemn compact sealed.

As soon as the monk had departed, carrying with him the joy of having won over the masses to his cause, Dagobert, Tronc, and Balafille whistled to their wives, Amelia, Queenie, and Matilda, who were waiting in the street for the signal, and all six holding each other's hands, danced around the bag, singing:

> J'ai du bon pognon;
> Tu n'l'auras pas Chatillon!
> Hou! Hou! la calotte!

And they ordered a salad-bowl of warm wine.

In the evening all six went through the street from stall to stall singing their new song. The song became popular, for the detectives reported that every day showed an increase of the number of workpeople who sang through the slums:

> J'ai du bon pognon;
> Tu n'l'auras pas Chatillon!
> Hou! Hou! la calotte!

The Dracophil agitation made no progress in the provinces. The pious Agaric sought to find the cause of this, but was unable to discover it until old Cornemuse revealed it to him.

"I have proofs," sighed the monk of Conils, "that the Duke of Ampoule, the treasurer of the Dracophils, has bought property in Porpoisia with the funds that he received for the propaganda."

The party wanted money. Prince des Boscénos had lost his portfolio in a brawl and he was reduced to painful expedients which were repugnant to his impetuous character. The Viscountess Olive was expensive. Cornemuse advised that the monthly allowance of that lady should be diminished.

"She is very useful to us," objected the pious Agaric.

"Undoubtedly," answered Cornemuse, "but she does us an injury by ruining us."

A schism divided the Dracophils. Misunderstandings reigned in their councils. Some wished that in accordance with the policy of M. Bigourd and the pious Agaric, they should carry on the design of reforming the Republic. Others, wearied by their long constraint, had resolved to proclaim the Dragon's crest and swore to conquer beneath that sign.

The latter urged the advantage of a clear situation and the impossibility of making a pretence much longer, and in truth, the public began to see whither the agitation was tending and that the

Emiral's partisans wanted to destroy the very foundations of the Republic.

A report was spread that the prince was to land at La Cirque and make his entry into Alca on a green horse.

These rumours excited the fanatical monks, delighted the poor nobles, satisfied the rich Jewish ladies, and put hope in the hearts of the small traders. But very few of them were inclined to purchase these benefits at the price of a social catastrophe and the overthrow of the public credit; and there were fewer still who would have risked their money, their peace, their liberty, or a single hour from their pleasures in the business. On the other hand, the workmen held themselves ready, as ever, to give a day's work to the Republic, and a strong resistance was being formed in the suburbs.

"The people are with us," the pious Agaric used to say.

However, men, women, and children, when leaving their factories, used to shout with one voice:

A bas Chatillon!
Hou! Hou! la calotte!

As for the government, it showed the weakness, indecision, flabbiness, and heedlessness common to all governments, and from which none has ever departed without falling into arbitrariness and violence. In three words it knew nothing, wanted nothing, and could do nothing. Formose, shut in his presidential palace, remained blind, dumb, deaf, huge, invisible, wrapped up in his pride as in an eider-down.

Count Olive advised the Dracophils to make a last appeal for funds and to attempt a great stroke while Alca was still in a ferment.

An executive committee, which he himself had chosen, decided to kidnap the members of the Chamber of Deputies, and considered ways and means.

The affair was fixed for the twenty-eighth of July. On that day the sun rose radiantly over the city. In front of the legislative palace women passed to market with their baskets; hawkers cried their peaches, pears, and grapes; cab horses with their noses in their bags munched their hay. Nobody expected anything, not because the secret had been kept but because it met with nothing but unbelievers. Nobody believed in a revolution, and from this fact we may conclude that nobody desired one. About two o'clock the deputies began to pass, few and unnoticed, through the side-door of the palace. At three o'clock a few groups of badly dressed men had formed. At half past three black masses coming from the adjacent streets spread over Revolution Square. This vast expanse was soon covered by an ocean of soft hats, and the crowd of demonstrators, continually increased by sight-seers, having crossed the bridge, struck its dark wave against the walls of the legislative enclosure.

Cries, murmurs, and songs went up to the impassive sky. "It is Chatillon we want!" "Down with the Deputies!" "Down with the Republicans!" "Death to the Republicans!" The devoted band of Dracophils, led by Prince des Boscénos, struck up the august canticle:

> Vive Crucho,
> Vaillant et sage,
> Plein de courage
> Dès le berceau!

Behind the wall silence alone replied.

This silence and the absence of guards encouraged and at the same time frightened the crowd. Suddenly a formidable voice cried out:

"Attack!"

And Prince des Boscénos was seen raising his gigantic form to the top of the wall, which was covered with barbs and iron spikes. Behind him rushed his companions, and the people followed. Some hammered against the wall to make holes in it; others endeavoured to tear down the spikes and to pull out the barbs. These defences had given way in places and some of the invaders had stripped the wall and were sitting astride on the top. Prince des Boscénos was waving an immense green flag. Suddenly the crowd wavered and from it came a long cry of terror. The police and the Republican carabineers issuing out of all the entrances of the palace formed themselves into a column beneath the wall and in a moment it was cleared of its besiegers. After a long moment of suspense the noise of arms was heard, and the police charged the crowd with fixed bayonets. An instant afterwards and on the deserted square strewn with hats and walking-sticks there reigned a sinister silence. Twice again the Dracophils attempted to form, twice they were repulsed. The rising was conquered. But Prince des Boscénos, standing on the wall of the hostile palace, his flag in his hand, still repelled the attack of a whole brigade. He knocked down all who approached him. At last he, too, was thrown down, and fell on an iron spike, to which he remained hooked, still clasping the standard of the Draconides.

On the following day the Ministers of the Republic and the Members of Parliament determined to take energetic measures. In vain this time, did President Formose attempt to evade his responsibilities. The government discussed the question of depriving Chatillon of his rank and dignities and of indicting him before the High Court as a conspirator, an enemy of the public good, a traitor, etc.

At this news the Emiral's old companions in arms, who the very evening before had beset him with their adulations, made no effort to conceal their joy. But Chatillon remained popular with the middle classes of Alca and one still heard the hymn of the liberator sounding in the streets, "It is Chatillon we want."

The Ministers were embarrassed. They intended to indict Chatillon before the High Court. But they knew nothing; they remained in that total ignorance reserved for those who govern men. They were incapable of advancing any grave charges against Chatillon. They could supply the prosecution with nothing but the ridiculous lies of their spies. Chatillon's share in the plot and his relations with Prince Crucho remained the secret of the thirty thousand Dracophils. The Ministers and the Deputies had suspicions and even certainties, but they had no proofs. The Public Prosecutor said to the Minister of Justice: "Very little is needed for a political prosecution! but I have nothing at all and that is not enough." The affair made no progress. The enemies of the Republic were triumphant.

On the eighteenth of September the news ran in Alca that Chatillon had taken flight. Everywhere there was surprise and astonishment. People doubted, for they could not understand.

This is what had happened: One day as the brave Under-Emiral Vulcanmould happened, as if by chance, to go into the office of M. Barbotan, the Minister of Foreign Affairs, he remarked with his usual frankness:

"M. Barbotan, your colleagues do not seem to me to be up to much; it is evident that they have never commanded a ship. That fool Chatillon gives them a deuced bad fit of the shivers."

The Minister, in sign of denial, waved his paper-knife in the air above his desk.

"Don't deny it," answered Vulcanmould. "You don't know how to get rid of Chatillon. You do not dare to indict him before the High Court because you are not sure of being able to bring forward a strong enough charge. Bigourd will defend him, and Bigourd is a clever advocate. . . . You are right, M. Barbotan, you are right. It would be a dangerous trial."

"Ah! my friend," said the Minister, in a careless tone, "if you knew how satisfied we are. . . . I receive the most reassuring news from my prefects. The good sense of the Penguins will do justice to the intrigues of this mutinous soldier. Can you suppose for a moment that a great people, an intelligent, laborious people, devoted to liberal institutions which . . ."

Vulcanmould interrupted with a great sigh:

"Ah! If I had time to do it I would relieve you of your difficulty. I would juggle away my Chatillon like a nutmeg out of a thimble. I would filip him off to Porpoisia."

The Minister paid close attention.

"It would not take long," continued the sailor. "I would rid you in a trice of the creature. . . . But just now I have other fish to fry. . . . I am in a bad hole. I must find a pretty big sum. But, deuce take it, honour before everything."

The Minister and the Under-Emiral looked at each other for a moment in silence. Then Barbotan said with authority:

"Under-Emiral Vulcanmould, get rid of this seditious soldier. You will render a great service to Penguinia, and the Minister of Home Affairs will see that your gambling debts are paid."

The same evening Vulcanmould called on Chatillon and looked at him for some time with an expression of grief and mystery.

"Why do you look like that?" answered the Emiral in an uneasy tone.

Vulcanmould said to him sadly:

"Old brother in arms, all is discovered. For the past half-hour the government knows everything."

At these words Chatillon sank down overwhelmed.

Vulcanmould continued:

"You may be arrested any moment. I advise you to make off."

And drawing out his watch:

"Not a minute to lose."

"Have I time to call on the Viscountess Olive?"

"It would be mad," said Vulcanmould, handing him a passport and a pair of blue spectacles, and telling him to have courage.

"I will," said Chatillon.

"Good-bye! old chum."

"Good-bye and thanks! You have saved my life."

"That is the least I could do."

A quarter of an hour later the brave Emiral had left the city of Alca.

He embarked at night on an old cutter at La Cirque and set sail for Porpoisia. But eight miles from the coast he was captured by a despatch-boat which was sailing without lights and which was under the flag of the Queen of the Black Islands. That Queen had for a long time nourished a fatal passion for Chatillon.

VII

CONCLUSION

*N*UNC *est bibendum.* Delivered from its fears and pleased at having escaped from so great a danger, the government resolved to celebrate the anniversary of the Penguin regeneration and the establishment of the Republic by holding a general holiday.

President Formose, the Ministers, and the members of the Chamber and of the Senate were present at the ceremony.

The Generalissimo of the Penguin army was present in uniform. He was cheered.

Preceded by the black flag of misery and the red flag of revolt, deputations of workmen walked in the procession, their aspect one of grim protection.

President, Ministers, Deputies, officials, heads of the magistracy and of the army, each, in their own names and in the name of the sovereign people, renewed the ancient oath to live in freedom or to die. It was an alternative upon which they were resolutely determined. But they preferred to live in freedom. There were games, speeches, and songs.

After the departure of the representatives of the State the crowd of citizens separated slowly and peaceably, shouting out, "Hurrah for the Republic!" "Hurrah for liberty!" "Down with the shaven pates!"

The newspapers mentioned only one regrettable incident that happened on that wonderful day. Prince des Boscénos was quietly smoking a cigar in the Queen's Meadow when the State procession passed by. The prince approached the Minister's carriage and said in a loud voice: "Death to the Republicans!" He was immediately apprehended by the police, to whom he offered a most desperate resistance. He knocked them down in crowds, but he was conquered by numbers, and, bruised, scratched, swollen, and unrecognisable even to the eyes of his wife, he was dragged through the joyous streets into an obscure prison.

The magistrates carried on the case against Chatillon in a peculiar style. Letters were found at the Admiralty which revealed the complicity of the Reverend Father Agaric in the plot. Immediately public opinion was inflamed against the monks, and Parliament voted, one after the other, a dozen laws which restrained, diminished, limited, prescribed, suppressed, determined, and curtailed, their rights, immunities, exemptions, privileges, and benefits, and created many invalidating disqualifications against them.

The Reverend Father Agaric steadfastly endured the rigour of the laws which struck himself personally, as well as the terrible fall of the Emiral of which he was the chief cause. Far from yielding to evil fortune, he regarded it as but a bird of passage. He was planning new political designs more audacious than the first.

When his projects were sufficiently ripe he went one day to the Wood of Conils. A thrush sang in a tree and a little hedge-hog crossed the stony path in front of him with awkward steps. Agaric walked with great strides, muttering fragments of sentences to himself.

When he reached the door of the laboratory in which, for so many years, the pious manufacturer had distilled the golden liqueur of St. Orberosia, he found the place deserted and the door shut. Having walked around the building he saw in the backyard the venerable Cornemuse, who, with his habit pinned up, was climbing a ladder that leant against the wall.

"Is that you, my dear friend?" said he to him. "What are you doing there?"

"You can see for yourself," answered the monk of Conils in a feeble voice, turning a sorrowful look upon Agaric. "I am going into my house."

The red pupils of his eyes no longer imitated the triumph and brilliance of the ruby, they flashed mournful and troubled glances. His countenance had lost its happy fulness. His shining head was no longer pleasant to the sight; perspiration and inflamed blotches had altered its inestimable perfection.

"I don't understand," said Agaric.

"It is easy enough to understand. You see the consequences of your plot. Although a multitude of laws are directed against me I have managed to elude the greater number of them. Some, however, have struck me. These vindictive men have closed my laboratories and my shops, and confiscated my bottles, my stills, and my retorts. They have put seals on my doors and now I am compelled to go in through the window. I am barely able to extract in secret from time to time the juice of a few plants and that with an apparatus which the humblest labourer would despise."

"You suffer from the persecution," said Agaric. "It strikes us all."

The monk of Conils passed his hand over his afflicted brow:

"I told you so, Brother Agaric; I told you that your enterprise would turn against ourselves."

"Our defeat is only momentary," replied Agaric eagerly. "It is due to purely accidental causes; it results from mere contingencies. Chatillon was a fool; he has drowned himself in his own ineptitude. Listen to me, Brother Cornemuse. We have not a moment to lose. We must free the Penguin people, we must deliver them from their tyrants, save them from themselves, restore the Dragon's crest, re-establish the ancient State, the good State, for the honour of religion and the exaltation of the Catholic faith. Chatillon was a bad instrument; he broke in our hands. Let us take a better instrument to replace him. I have the man who will destroy this impious democracy. He is a civil official; his name is Gomoru. The Penguins worship him. He has already betrayed his party for a plate of rice. There's the man we want!"

At the beginning of this speech the monk of Conils had climbed into his window and pulled up the ladder.

"I foresee," answered he, with his nose through the sash, "that you will not stop until you have us all expelled from this pleasant, agreeable, and sweet land of Penguinia. Good night; God keep you!"

Agaric, standing before the wall, entreated his dearest brother to listen to him for a moment:

"Understand your own interest better, Cornemuse! Penguinia is ours. What do we need to conquer it? Just one effort more . . . one more little sacrifice of money and . . ."

But without listening further, the monk of Conils drew in his head and closed his window.

BOOK VI: MODERN TIMES

THE AFFAIR OF THE EIGHTY THOUSAND TRUSSES OF HAY

Ζεῦ πάτερ ἀλλὰ σὺ ῥῦσαι ὑπ' ἠέρος υἷας Αχαιῶν,
ποίησον δ'αἴθρην, δὸς δ'ὀφθαλμοῖ σιν ἰδέσθαι·
ἐν δὲ φάει ὄλεσσον ἐπει νύ τοι εὔαδεν οὔτως.*

(Iliad xvii. 645 *et seq.*)

I

GENERAL GREATAUK, DUKE OF SKULL

SHORT time after the flight of the Emiral, a middle-class Jew called Pyrot, desirous of associating with the aristocracy and wishing to serve his country, entered the Penguin army. The Minister of War, who at the time was Greatauk, Duke of Skull, could not endure him. He blamed him for his zeal, his hooked nose, his vanity, his fondness for study, his thick lips, his exemplary conduct. Every time the author of any misdeed was looked for, Greatauk used to say:

"It must be Pyrot!"

One morning General Panther, the Chief of the Staff, informed Greatauk of a serious matter. Eighty thousand trusses of hay intended for the cavalry had disappeared and not a trace of them was to be found.

Greatauk exclaimed at once:

"It must be Pyrot who has stolen them!"

He remained in thought for some time and said:

"The more I think of it the more I am convinced that Pyrot has stolen those eighty thousand trusses of hay. And I know it is by this: he stole them in order that he might sell them to our bitter enemies the Porpoises. What an infamous piece of treachery!"

*O Father Zeus, only save thou the sons of the Acheans from the darkness, and make clear sky and vouchsafe sight to our eyes, and then, so it be but light, slay us, since such is thy good pleasure.

110

"There is no doubt about it," answered Panther; "it only remains to prove it."

The same day, as he passed by a cavalry barracks, Prince des Boscénos heard the troopers as they were sweeping out the yard, singing:

Boscénos est un gros cochon;
On en va faire des andouilles,
Des saucisses et du jambon
Pour le réveillon des pauv' bougres.

It seemed to him contrary to all discipline that soldiers should sing this domestic and revolutionary refrain which on days of riot had been uttered by the lips of jeering workmen. On this occasion he deplored the moral degeneration of the army and thought with a bitter smile that his old comrade Greatauk, the head of this degenerate army, basely exposed him to the malice of an unpatriotic government. And he promised himself that he would make an improvement before long.

"That scoundrel Greatauk," said he to himself, "will not remain long a Minister."

Prince des Boscénos was the most irreconcilable of the opponents of modern democracy, free thought, and the government which the Penguins had voluntarily given themselves. He had a vigorous and undisguised hatred for the Jews, and he worked in public and in private, night and day, for the restoration of the line of the Draconides. His ardent royalism was still further excited by the thought of his private affairs, which were in a bad way and were hourly growing worse. He had no hope of seeing an end to his pecuniary embarrassments until the heir of Draco the Great entered the city of Alca.

When he returned to his house, the prince took out of his safe a bundle of old letters consisting of a private correspondence of the most secret nature, which he had obtained from a treacherous secretary. They proved that his old comrade Greatauk, the Duke of Skull, had been guilty of jobbery regarding the military stores and had received a present of no great value from a manufacturer called Maloury. The very smallness of this present deprived the Minister who had accepted it of all excuse.

The prince re-read the letters with a bitter satisfaction, put them carefully back into his safe, and dashed to the Minister of War. He was a man of resolute character. On being told that the Minister could see no one he knocked down the ushers, swept aside the orderlies, trampled under foot the civil and military clerks, burst through the doors, and entered the room of the astonished Greatauk.

"I will not say much," said he to him, "but I will speak to the point. You are a confounded cad. I have asked you to put a flea in the ear of General Mouchin, the tool of those Republicans, and you would not do it. I have asked you to give a command to General des Clapiers, who works for the Dracophils, and who has obliged me personally, and you would not do it. I have asked you to dismiss General Tandem, the commander of Port Alca, who robbed me of fifty louis at cards, and who had me handcuffed when I was brought before the High Court as Emiral Chatillon's accomplice. You would not do it. I asked you for the hay and bran stores. You would not give them. I asked you to send me on a secret mission to Porpoisia. You refused. And not satisfied with these repeated refusals you have designated me to your Government colleagues as a dangerous person, who ought to be watched, and it is owing to you that I have been shadowed by the police. You old traitor! I ask nothing more from you and I have but one word to say to you: Clear out; you have bothered us too long. Besides, we will force the vile Republic to replace you by one of our own party. You know that I am a man of my word. If in twenty-four hours you have not handed in your resignation I will publish the Maloury *dossier* in the newspapers."

But Greatauk calmly and serenely replied:

"Be quiet, you fool. I am just having a Jew transported. I am handing over Pyrot to justice as guilty of having stolen eighty thousand trusses of hay."

Prince Boscénos, whose anger vanished like a dream, smiled.

"Is that true?"

"You will see."

"My congratulations, Greatauk. But as one always needs to take precautions with you I shall immediately publish the good news. People will read this evening about Pyrot's arrest in every newspaper in Alca. . . ."

And he went away muttering:

"That Pyrot! I suspected he would come to a bad end."

A moment later General Panther appeared before Greatauk.

"Sir," said he, "I have just examined the business of the eighty thousand trusses of hay. There is no evidence against Pyrot."

"Let it be found," answered Greatauk. "Justice requires it. Have Pyrot arrested at once."

II

PYROT

LL Penguinia heard with horror of Pyrot's crime; at the same time there was a sort of satisfaction that this embezzlement combined with treachery and even bordering on sacrilege, had been committed by a Jew. In order to understand this feeling it is necessary to be acquainted with the state of the public opinion regarding the Jews both great and small. As we have had occasion to say in this history, the universally detested and all powerful financial caste was composed of Christians and of Jews. The Jews who formed part of it and on whom the people poured all their hatred were the upper-class Jews. They possessed immense riches and, it was said, held more than a fifth part of the total property of Penguinia. Outside this formidable caste there was a multitude of Jews of a mediocre condition, who were not more loved than the others and who were feared much less. In every ordered State, wealth is a sacred thing: in democracies it is the only sacred thing. Now the Penguin State was democratic. Three or four financial companies exercised a more extensive, and above all, more effective and continuous power, than that of the Ministers of the Republic. The latter were puppets whom the companies ruled in secret, whom they compelled by intimidation or corruption to favour themselves at the expense of the State, and whom they ruined by calumnies in the press if they remained honest. In spite of the secrecy of the Exchequer, enough appeared to make the country indignant, but the middle-class Penguins had, from the greatest to the last of them, been brought up to hold money in great reverence, and as they all had property, either much or little, they were strongly impressed with the solidarity of capital and understood that a small fortune is not safe unless a big one is protected. For these reasons they conceived a religious respect for the Jews' millions, and self-interest being stronger with them than aversion, they were as much afraid as they were of death to touch a single hair of one of the rich Jews whom they detested. Towards the poorer Jews they felt less ceremonious and when they saw any of them down they trampled on them. That is why the entire nation learnt with thorough satisfaction that the traitor was a Jew. They could take vengeance on all Israel in his person without any fear of compromising the public credit.

That Pyrot had stolen the eighty thousand trusses of hay nobody hesitated for a moment to believe. No one doubted because the general ignorance in which everybody was concerning the affair did not allow of doubt, for doubt is a thing that demands motives. People

do not doubt without reasons in the same way that people believe without reasons. The thing was not doubted because it was repeated everywhere and, with the public, to repeat is to prove. It was not doubted because people wished to believe Pyrot guilty and one believes what one wishes to believe. Finally, it was not doubted because the faculty of doubt is rare amongst men; very few minds carry in them its germs and these are not developed without cultivation. Doubt is singular, exquisite, philosophic, immoral, transcendent, monstrous, full of malignity, injurious to persons and to property, contrary to the good order of governments, and to the prosperity of empires, fatal to humanity, destructive of the gods, held in horror by heaven and earth. The mass of the Penguins were ignorant of doubt: it believed in Pyrot's guilt and this conviction immediately became one of its chief national beliefs and an essential truth in its patriotic creed.

Pyrot was tried secretly and condemned.

General Panther immediately went to the Minister of War to tell him the result.

"Luckily," said he, "the judges were certain, for they had no proofs."

"Proofs," muttered Greatauk, "proofs, what do they prove? There is only one certain, irrefragable proof—the confession of the guilty person. Has Pyrot confessed?"

"No, General."

"He will confess, he ought to. Panther, we must induce him; tell him it is to his interest. Promise him that, if he confesses, he will obtain favours, a reduction of his sentence, full pardon; promise him that if he confesses his innocence will be admitted, that he will be decorated. Appeal to his good feelings. Let him confess from patriotism, for the flag, for the sake of order, from respect for the hierarchy, at the special command of the Minister of War militarily. . . . But tell me, Panther, has he not confessed already? There are tacit confessions; silence is a confession."

"But, General, he is not silent; he keeps on squealing like a pig that he is innocent."

"Panther, the confessions of a guilty man sometimes result from the vehemence of his denials. To deny desperately is to confess. Pyrot has confessed; we must have witnesses of his confessions, justice requires them."

There was in Western Penguinia a seaport called La Cirque, formed of three small bays and formerly greatly frequented by ships, but now solitary and deserted. Gloomy lagoons stretched along its low coasts exhaling a pestilent odour, while fever hovered over its sleepy waters. Here, on the borders of the sea, there was built a high square tower, like the old Campanile at Venice, from the side of which, close to the summit, hung an open cage which was fastened by a chain to a transverse beam. In the times of the Draconides the Inquisitors of Alca used to put heretical clergy into this cage. It had been empty for three hundred years, but now Pyrot was imprisoned in it under the guard of sixty warders, who lived in the tower and did not lose sight of him night or day, spying on him for confessions that they might afterwards report to the Minister of War. For Greatauk, careful and prudent, desired confessions and still further confessions. Greatauk, who was looked upon as a fool, was in reality a man of great ability and full of rare foresight.

In the mean time Pyrot, burnt by the sun, eaten by mosquitoes, soaked in the rain, hail and snow, frozen by the cold, tossed about terribly by the wind, beset by the sinister croaking of the ravens that perched upon his cage, kept writing down his innocence on pieces torn off his shirt with a tooth-pick dipped in blood. These rags were lost in the sea or fell into the hands of the gaolers. Some of them, however, came under the eyes of the public. But Pyrot's protests moved nobody because his confessions had been published.

III

COUNT DE MAUBEC DE LA DENTDULYNX

THE morals of the Jews were not always pure; in most cases they were averse from none of the vices of Christian civilization, but they retained from the Patriarchal age a recognition of family ties and an attachment to the interest of the tribe. Pyrot's brothers, half-brothers, uncles, great-uncles, first, second, and third cousins, nephews and great-nephews, relations by blood and relations by marriage, and all who were related to him to the number of about seven hundred, were at first overwhelmed by the blow that had struck their relative, and they shut themselves up in their houses, covering themselves with ashes and blessing the hand that had chastised them. For forty days they kept a strict fast. Then they bathed themselves and resolved to search, without rest, at the cost of any toil and at the risk of every danger, for the demonstration of an innocence which they did not doubt. And how could they have doubted? Pyrot's innocence had been revealed to them in the same way that his guilt had been revealed to Christian Penguinia; for these things, being hidden, assume a mystic character and take on the authority of religious truths. The seven hundred Pyrotists set to work with as much zeal as prudence, and made the most thorough inquiries in secret. They were everywhere; they were seen nowhere. One would have said that, like the pilot of Ulysses, they wandered freely over the earth. They penetrated into the War Office and approached, under different disguises, the judges, the registrars, and the witnesses of the affair. Then Greatauk's cleverness was seen. The witnesses knew nothing; the judges and registrars knew nothing. Emissaries reached even Pyrot and anxiously questioned him in his cage amid the prolonged moanings of the sea and the hoarse croaks of the ravens. It was in vain; the prisoner knew nothing. The seven hundred Pyrotists could not subvert the proofs of the accusation because they could not know what they were, and they could not know what they were because there were none. Pyrot's guilt was indefeasible through its very nullity. And it was with a legitimate pride that Greatauk, expressing himself as a

true artist, said one day to General Panther: "This case is a masterpiece: it is made out of nothing." The seven hundred Pyrotists despaired of ever clearing up this dark business, when suddenly they discovered, from a stolen letter, that the eighty thousand trusses of hay had never existed, that a most distinguished nobleman, Count de Maubec, had sold them to the State, that he had received the price but had never delivered them. Indeed seeing that he was descended from the richest land proprietors of ancient Penguinia, the heir of the Maubecs of Dentdulynx, once the possessors of four duchies, sixty counties, and six hundred and twelve marquisates, baronies, and viscounties, he did not possess as much land as he could cover with his hand, and would not have been able to cut a single day's mowing of forage off his own domains. As to his getting a single rush from a land-owner or a merchant, that would have been quite impossible, for everybody except the Ministers of State and the Government officials knew that it would be easier to get blood from a stone than a farthing from a Maubec.

The seven hundred Pyrotists made a minute inquiry concerning the Count Maubec de la Dentdulynx's financial resources, and they proved that that nobleman was chiefly supported by a house in which some generous ladies were ready to furnish all comers with the most lavish hospitality. They publicly proclaimed that he was guilty of the theft of the eighty thousand trusses of straw for which an innocent man had been condemned and was now imprisoned in the cage.

Maubec belonged to an illustrious family which was allied to the Draconides. There is nothing that a democracy esteems more highly than noble birth. Maubec had also served in the Penguin army, and since the Penguins were all soldiers, they loved their army to idolatry. Maubec, on the field of battle, had received the Cross, which is a sign of honour among the Penguins and which they valued even more highly than the embraces of their wives. All Penguinia declared for Maubec, and the voice of the people which began to assume a threatening tone, demanded severe punishments for the seven hundred calumniating Pyrotists.

Maubec was a nobleman; he challenged the seven hundred Pyrotists to combat with either sword, sabre, pistols, carabines, or sticks.

"Vile dogs," he wrote to them in a famous letter, "you have crucified my God and you want my life too; I warn you that I will not be such a duffer as He was and that I will cut off your fourteen hundred ears. Accept my boot on your seven hundred behinds."

The Chief of the Government at the time was a peasant called Robin Mielleux, a man pleasant to the rich and powerful, but hard towards the poor, a man of small courage and ignorant of his own interests. In a public declaration he guaranteed Maubec's innocence and honour, and presented the seven hundred Pyrotists to the criminal courts where they were condemned, as libellers, to imprisonment, to enormous fines, and to all the damages that were claimed by their innocent victim.

It seemed as if Pyrot was destined to remain for ever shut in the cage on which the ravens perched. But all the Penguins being anxious to know and prove that this Jew was guilty, all the proofs brought forward were found not to be good, while some of them were also contradictory. The officers of the Staff showed zeal but lacked prudence. Whilst Greatauk kept an admirable silence, General Panther made inexhaustible speeches and every morning demonstrated in the newspapers that the condemned man was guilty. He would have done better, perhaps, if he had said nothing. The guilt was evident and what is evident cannot be demonstrated. So much reasoning disturbed people's minds; their faith, though still alive, became less serene. The more proofs one gives a crowd the more they ask for.

Nevertheless the danger of proving too much would not have been great if there had not been in Penguinia, as there are, indeed, everywhere, minds framed for free inquiry, capable of studying a difficult question, and inclined to philosophic doubt. They were few; they were not all inclined to speak, and the public was by no means inclined to listen to them. Still, they did not always meet with deaf ears. The great Jews, all the Israelite millionaires of Alca, when spoken to of Pyrot, said: "We do not know the man"; but they thought of saving him. They preserved the prudence to which their wealth inclined them and wished that others would be less timid. Their wish was to be gratified.

IV

COLOMBAN

SOME weeks after the conviction of the seven hundred Pyrotists, a little, gruff, hairy, short-sighted man left his house one morning with a paste-pot, a ladder, and a bundle of posters and went about the streets pasting placards to the walls on which might be read in large letters: *Pyrot is innocent, Maubec is guilty*. He was not a bill-poster; his name was Colomban, and as the author of sixty volumes on Penguin sociology he was numbered among the most laborious and respected writers in Alca. Having given sufficient thought to the matter and no longer doubting Pyrot's innocence, he proclaimed it in the manner which he thought would be most sensational. He met with no hindrance while posting his bills in the quiet streets, but when he came to the populous quarters, every time he mounted his ladder, inquisitive people crowded round him and, dumfounded with surprise and indignation, threw at him threatening looks which he received with the calm that comes from courage and short-sightedness. Whilst caretakers and tradespeople tore down the bills he had posted, he kept on zealously placarding, carrying his tools and followed by little boys who, with their baskets under their arms or their satchels on their backs, were in no hurry to reach school. To the mute indignation against him, protests and murmurs were now added. But Colomban did not condescend to see or hear anything. As, at the entrance to the Rue St. Orberosia, he was posting one of his squares of paper bearing the words: *Pyrot is innocent, Maubec is guilty,* the riotous crowd showed signs of the most violent anger. They called after him, "Traitor, thief, rascal, scoundrel." A woman opened a window and emptied a vessel full of filth over his head, a cabby sent his hat flying from one end of the street to the other by a blow of his whip amid the cheers of the crowd who now felt themselves avenged. A butcher's boy knocked Colomban with his paste-pot, his brush, and his posters, from the top of his ladder into the gutter, and the proud Penguins then felt the greatness of their country. Colomban stood up, covered with filth, lame, and with his elbow injured, but tranquil and resolute.

"Low brutes," he muttered, shrugging his shoulders.

Then he went down on all-fours in the gutter to look for his glasses which he had lost in his fall. It was then seen that his coat was split from the collar to the tails and that his trousers were in rags. The rancour of the crowd grew stronger.

On the other side of the street stretched the big St. Orberosian Stores. The patriots seized whatever they could lay their hands on from the shop front, and hurled at Colomban oranges, lemons, pots of jam, pieces of chocolate, bottles of liqueurs, boxes of sardines, pots of *foie gras,* hams, fowls, flasks of oil, and bags of haricots. Covered with the débris of the food, bruised, tattered, lame, and blind, he took to flight, followed by the shop-boys, bakers, loafers, citizens, and hooligans whose number increased each moment and who kept shouting: "Duck him! Death to the traitor! Duck him!" This torrent of vulgar humanity swept along the streets and rushed into the Rue St. Maël. The police did their duty. From all the adjacent streets constables proceeded and, holding their scabbards with their left hands, they went at full speed in front of the pursuers. They were on the point of grabbing Colomban in their huge hands when he suddenly escaped them by falling through an open manhole to the bottom of a sewer.

He spent the night there in the darkness, sitting close by the dirty water amidst the fat and slimy rats. He thought of his task, and his swelling heart filled with courage and pity. And when the dawn threw a pale ray of light into the air-hole he got up and said, speaking to himself:

"I see that the fight will be a stiff one."

Forthwith he composed a memorandum in which he clearly showed that Pyrot could not have stolen from the Ministry of War the eighty thousand trusses of hay which it had never received, for the reason that Maubec had never delivered them, though he had received the money. Colomban caused this statement to be distributed in the streets of Alca. The people refused to read it and tore it up in anger. The shop-keepers shook their fists at the distributers, who made off, chased by angry women armed with brooms. Feeling grew warm and the ferment lasted the whole day. In the evening bands of wild and ragged men went about the streets yelling: "Death to Colomban!" The patriots snatched whole bundles of the memorandum from the newsboys and burned them in the public squares, dancing wildly round these bon-fires with girls whose petticoats were tied up to their waists.

Some of the more enthusiastic among them went and broke the windows of the house in which Colomban had lived in perfect tranquillity during his forty years of work.

Parliament was roused and asked the Chief of the Government what measures he proposed to take in order to repel the odious attacks made by Colomban upon the honour of the National Army and the safety of Penguinia. Robin Mielleux denounced Colomban's impious audacity and proclaimed amid the cheers of the legislators that the man would be summoned before the Courts to answer for his infamous libel.

The Minister of War was called to the tribune and appeared in it transfigured. He had no longer the air, as in former days, of one of the sacred geese of the Penguin citadels. Now, bristling, with out-stretched neck and hooked beak, he seemed the symbolical vulture fastened to the livers of his country's enemies.

In the august silence of the assembly he pronounced these words only:

"I swear that Pyrot is a rascal."

This speech of Greatauk was reported all over Penguinia and satisfied the public conscience.

V

THE REVEREND FATHERS AGARIC AND CORNEMUSE

OLOMBAN bore with meekness and surprise the weight of the general reprobation. He could not go out without being stoned, so he did not go out. He remained in his study with a superb obstinacy, writing new memoranda in favour of the encaged innocent. In the mean time among the few readers that he found, some, about a dozen, were struck by his reasons and began to doubt Pyrot's guilt. They broached the subject to their friends and endeavoured to spread the light that had arisen in their minds. One of them was a friend of Robin Mielleux and confided to him his perplexities, with the result that he was no longer received by that Minister. Another demanded explanations in an open letter to the Minister of War. A third published a terrible pamphlet. The latter, whose name was Kerdanic, was a formidable controversialist. The public was unmoved. It was said that these defenders of the traitor had been bribed by the rich Jews; they were stigmatized by the name of Pyrotists and the patriots swore to exterminate them. There were only a thousand or twelve hundred Pyrotists in the whole vast Republic, but it was believed that they were everywhere. People were afraid of finding them in the promenades, at meetings, at receptions, in fashionable drawing-rooms, at the dinner-table, even in the conjugal couch. One half of the population was suspected by the other half. The discord set all Alca on fire.

In the mean time Father Agaric, who managed his big school for young nobles, followed events with anxious attention. The misfortunes of the Penguin Church had not disheartened him. He remained faithful to Prince Crucho and preserved the hope of restoring the heir of the Draconides to the Penguin throne. It appeared to him that the events that were happening or about to happen in the country, the state of mind of which they were at once the effect and the cause, and the troubles that necessarily resulted from them might—if they were directed, guided, and led by the profound wisdom of a monk—overthrow the Republic and incline the Penguins to restore Prince Crucho, from whose piety the faithful hoped for so much solace. Wearing his huge black hat, the brim of which looked like the wings of Night, he walked through the Wood of Conils towards the factory where his venerable friend, Father Cornemuse, distilled the hygienic St. Orberosian liqueur. The good monk's industry, so cruelly affected in the time of Emiral Chatillon, was being restored from its ruins. One heard goods trains rumbling through the Wood and one saw in the sheds hundreds of orphans clothed in blue, packing bottles and nailing up cases.

Agaric found the venerable Cornemuse standing before his stoves and surrounded by his retorts. The shining pupils of the old man's eyes had again become as bright as rubies, his skull shone with its former elaborate and careful polish.

Agaric first congratulated the pious distiller on the restored activity of his laboratories and workshops.

"Business is recovering. I thank God for it," answered the old man of Conils. "Alas! it had fallen into a bad state, Brother Agaric. You saw the desolation of this establishment. I need say no more."

Agaric turned away his head.

"The St. Orberosian liqueur," continued Cornemuse, "is making fresh conquests. But none the less my industry remains uncertain and precarious. The laws of ruin and desolation that struck it have not been abrogated, they have only been suspended."

And the monk of Conils lifted his ruby eyes to heaven.

Agaric put his hand on his shoulder.

"What a sight, Cornemuse, does unhappy Penguinia present to us! Everywhere disobedience, independence, liberty! We see the proud, the haughty, the men of revolt rising up. After having braved the Divine laws they now rear themselves against human laws, so true is it that in order to be a good citizen a man must be a good Christian. Colomban is trying to imitate Satan. Numerous criminals are following his fatal example. They want, in their rage, to put aside all checks, to throw off all yokes, to free themselves from the most sacred bonds, to escape from the most salutary restraints. They strike their country to make it obey them. But they will be overcome by the weight of public animadversion, vituperation, indignation, fury, execration, and abomination. That is the abyss to which they have been led by atheism, free thought, and the monstrous claim to judge for themselves and to form their own opinions."

"Doubtless, doubtless," replied Father Cornemuse, shaking his head, "but I confess that the care of distilling these simples has prevented me from following public affairs. I only know that people are talking a great deal about a man called Pyrot. Some maintain that he is guilty, others affirm that he is innocent, but I do not clearly understand the motives that drive both parties to mix themselves up in a business that concerns neither of them."

The pious Agaric asked eagerly:

"You do not doubt Pyrot's guilt?"

"I cannot doubt it, dear Agaric," answered the monk of Conils. "That would be contrary to the laws of my country which we ought to respect as long as they are not opposed to the Divine laws. Pyrot is guilty, for he has been convicted. As to saying more for or against his guilt, that would be to erect my own authority against that of the judges, a thing which I will take good care not to do. Besides, it is useless, for Pyrot has been convicted. If he has not been convicted because he is guilty, he is guilty because he has been convicted; it comes to the same thing. I believe in his guilt as every good citizen ought to believe in it; and I will believe in it as long as the established jurisdiction will order me to believe in it, for it is not for a private person but for a judge to proclaim the innocence of a convicted person. Human justice is venerable even in the errors inherent in its fallible and limited nature. These errors are never irreparable; if the judges do not repair them on earth, God will repair them in Heaven. Besides I have great confidence in General Greatauk, who, though he certainly does not look it, seems to me to be an abler man than all those who are attacking him."

"Dearest Cornemuse," cried the pious Agaric, "the Pyrot affair, if pushed to the point whither we can lead it by the help of God and the necessary funds, will produce the greatest benefits. It will lay bare the vices of this Anti-Christian Republic and will incline the Penguins to restore the throne of the Draconides and the prerogatives of the Church. But to do that it is necessary for the people to see the clergy in the front rank of its defenders. Let us march against the enemies of the army, against those who insult our heroes, and everybody will follow us."

"Everybody will be too many," murmured the monk of Conils, shaking his head. "I see that the Penguins want to quarrel. If we mix ourselves up in their quarrel they will become reconciled at our expense and we shall have to pay the cost of the war. That is why, if you are guided by me, dear Agaric, you will not engage the Church in this adventure."

"You know my energy; you know my prudence. I will compromise nothing. . . . Dear Cornemuse, I only want from you the funds necessary for us to begin the campaign."

For a long time Cornemuse refused to bear the expenses of what he thought was a fatal enterprise. Agaric was in turn pathetic and terrible. At last, yielding to his prayers and threats, Cornemuse, with hanging head and swinging arms, went to the austere cell that concealed his evangelical poverty. In the whitewashed wall under a branch of blessed box, there was fixed a safe. He opened it, and with a sigh took out a bundle of bills which, with hesitating hands, he gave to the pious Agaric.

"Do not doubt it, dear Cornemuse," said the latter, thrusting the papers into the pocket of his overcoat, "this Pyrot affair has been sent us by God for the glory and exaltation of the Church of Penguinia."

"I pray that you may be right!" sighed the monk of Conils.

And, left alone in his laboratory, he gazed, through his exquisite eyes, with an ineffable sadness at his stoves and his retorts.

VI

THE SEVEN HUNDRED PYROTISTS

HE seven hundred Pyrotists inspired the public with an increasing aversion. Every day two or three of them were beaten to death in the streets. One of them was publicly whipped, another thrown into the river, a third tarred and feathered and led through a laughing crowd, a fourth had his nose cut off by a captain of dragoons. They did not dare to show themselves at their clubs, at tennis, or at the races; they put on a disguise when they went to the Stock Exchange. In these circumstances the Prince des Boscénos thought it urgent to curb their audacity and repress their insolence. For this purpose he joined with Count Cléna, M. de La Trumelle, Viscount Olive, and M. Bigourd in founding a great anti-Pyrotist association to which citizens in hundreds of thousands, soldiers in companies, regiments, brigades, divisions, and army corps, towns, districts, and provinces, all gave their adhesion.

About this time the Minister of War happening to visit one day his Chief of Staff, saw with surprise that the large room where General Panther worked, which was formerly quite bare, had now along each wall from floor to ceiling in sets of deep pigeon-holes, triple and quadruple rows of paper bundles of every form and colour. These sudden and monstrous records had in a few days reached the dimensions of a pile of archives such as it takes centuries to accumulate.

"What is this?" asked the astonished minister.

"Proofs against Pyrot," answered General Panther with patriotic satisfaction. "We had not got them when we convicted him, but we have plenty of them now."

The door was open, and Greatauk saw coming up the stair-case a long file of porters who were unloading heavy bales of papers in the hall, and he saw the lift slowly rising heavily loaded with paper packets.

"What are those others?" said he.

"They are fresh proofs against Pyrot that are now reaching us," said Panther. "I have asked for them in every county of Penguinia, in every Staff Office and in every Court in Europe. I have ordered them in every town in America and in Australia, and in every factory in Africa, and I am expecting bales of them from Bremen and a ship-load from Melbourne."

And Panther turned towards the Minister of War the tranquil and radiant look of a hero. However, Greatauk, his eye-glass in his eye, was looking at the formidable pile of papers with less satisfaction than uneasiness.

"Very good," said he, "very good! but I am afraid that this Pyrot business may lose its beautiful simplicity. It was limpid; like a rock-crystal its value lay in its transparency. You could have searched it in vain with a magnifying-glass for a straw, a bend, a blot, for the least fault. When it left my hands it was as pure as the light. Indeed it was the light. I give you a pearl and you make a mountain out of it. To tell you the truth I am afraid that by wishing to do too well you have done less well. Proofs! of course it is good to have proofs, but perhaps it is better to have none at all. I have already told you, Panther, there is only one irrefutable proof, the confession of the guilty person (or if the innocent what matter!). The Pyrot affair, as I arranged it, left no room for criticism; there was no spot where it could be touched. It defied assault. It was invulnerable because it was invisible. Now it gives an enormous handle for discussion. I advise you, Panther, to use your paper packets with great reserve. I should be particularly grateful if you would be more sparing of your communications to journalists. You speak well, but you say too much. Tell me, Panther, are there any forged documents among these?"

"There are some adapted ones."

"That is what I meant. There are some adapted ones. So much the better. As proofs, forged documents, in general, are better than genuine ones, first of all because they have been expressly made to suit the needs of the case, to order and measure, and therefore they are fitting and exact. They are also preferable because they carry the mind into an ideal world and turn it aside from the reality which, alas! in this world is never without some alloy. . . . Nevertheless, I think I should have preferred, Panther, that we had no proofs at all."

The first act of the Anti-Pyrotist Association was to ask the Government immediately to summon the seven hundred Pyrotists and their accomplices before the High Court of Justice as guilty of high treason. Prince des Boscénos was charged to speak on behalf of the Association and presented himself before the Council which had assembled to hear him. He expressed a hope that the vigilance and firmness of the Government would rise to the height of the occasion. He shook hands with each of the ministers and as he passed General Greatauk he whispered in his ear:

"Behave properly, you ruffian, or I will publish the Maloury *dossier!*"

Some days later by a unanimous vote of both Houses, on a motion proposed by the Government, the Anti-Pyrotist Association was granted a charter recognising it as beneficial to the public interest.

The Association immediately sent a deputation to Chitterlings

Castle in Porpoisia, where Crucho was eating the bitter bread of exile, to assure the prince of the love and devotion of the Anti-Pyrotist members.

However, the Pyrotists grew in numbers, and now counted ten thousand. They had their regular cafés on the boulevards. The patriots had theirs also, richer and bigger, and every evening glasses of beer, saucers, match-stands, jugs, chairs, and tables were hurled from one to the other. Mirrors were smashed to bits, and the police ended the struggles by impartially trampling the combatants of both parties under their hob-nailed shoes.

On one of these glorious nights, as Prince des Boscénos was leaving a fashionable café in the company of some patriots, M. de La Trumelle pointed out to him a little, bearded man with glasses, hatless, and having only one sleeve to his coat, who was painfully dragging himself along the rubbish-strewn pavement.

"Look!" said he, "there is Colomban!"

The prince had gentleness as well as strength; he was exceedingly mild; but at the name of Colomban his blood boiled. He rushed at the little spectacled man, and knocked him down with one blow of his fist on the nose.

M. de La Trumelle then perceived that, misled by an undeserved resemblance, he had mistaken for Colomban, M. Bazile, a retired lawyer, the secretary of the Anti-Pyrotist Association, and an ardent and generous patriot. Prince des Boscénos was one of those antique souls who never bend. However, he knew how to recognise his faults.

"M. Bazile," said he, raising his hat, "if I have touched your face with my hand you will excuse me and you will understand me, you will approve of me, nay, you will compliment me, you will congratulate me and felicitate me, when you know the cause of that act. I took you for Colomban."

M. Bazile, wiping his bleeding nostrils with his handkerchief and displaying an elbow laid bare by the absence of his sleeve:

"No, sir," answered he drily, "I shall not felicitate you, I shall not congratulate you, I shall not compliment you, for your action was, at the very least, superfluous; it was, I will even say, supererogatory. Already this evening I have been three times mistaken for Colomban and received a sufficient amount of the treatment he deserves. The patriots have knocked in my ribs and broken my back, and, sir, I was of opinion that that was enough."

Scarcely had he finished this speech than a band of Pyrotists appeared, and misled in their turn by the insidious resemblance, they believed that the patriots were killing Colomban. They fell on Prince des Boscénos and his companions with loaded canes and leather thongs, and left them for dead. Then seizing Bazile they carried him in triumph, and in spite of his protests, along the boulevards, amid cries of: "Hurrah for Colomban! Hurrah for Pyrot!" At last the police, who had been sent after them, attacked and defeated them and dragged them ignominiously to the station, where Bazile, under the name of Colomban, was trampled on by an innumerable quantity of thick, hob-nailed shoes.

VII

BIDAULT–COQUILLE AND MANIFLORE, THE SOCIALISTS

 WHILST the wind of anger and hatred blew in Alca, Eugène Bidault-Coquille, poorest and happiest of astronomers, installed in an old steam-engine of the time of the Draconides, was observing the heavens through a bad telescope, and photographing the paths of the meteors upon some damaged photographic plates. His genius corrected the errors of his instruments and his love of science triumphed over the worthlessness of his apparatus. With an inextinguishable ardour he observed aerolites, meteors, and fire-balls, and all the glowing ruins and blazing sparks which pass through the terrestrial atmosphere with prodigious speed, and as a reward for his studious vigils he received the indifference of the public, the ingratitude of the State and the blame of the learned societies. Engulfed in the celestial spaces he knew not what occurred upon the surface of the earth. He never read the newspapers, and when he walked through the town his mind was occupied with the November asteroids, and more than once he found himself at the bottom of a pond in one of the public parks or beneath the wheels of a motor omnibus.

Elevated in stature as in thought he respected himself and others. This was shown by his cold politeness as well as by a very thin black frock coat and a tall hat which gave to his person an appearance at once emaciated and sublime. He took his meals in a little restaurant from which all customers less intellectual than himself had fled, and thenceforth his napkin bound by its wooden ring rested alone in the abandoned rack.

In this cook-shop his eyes fell one evening upon Colomban's memorandum in favour of Pyrot. He read it as he was cracking some bad nuts and suddenly, exalted with astonishment, admiration, horror, and pity, he forgot all about falling meteors and shooting stars and saw nothing but the innocent man hanging in his cage exposed to the winds of heaven and the ravens perching upon it.

That image did not leave him. For a week he had been obsessed by the innocent convict, when, as he was leaving his cook-shop, he saw a crowd of citizens entering a public-house in which a public meeting was going on. He went in. The meeting was disorderly; they were yelling, abusing one another and knocking one another down in the smoke-laden hall. The Pyrotists and the Anti-Pyrotists spoke in turn and were alternately cheered and hissed at. An obscure and confused enthusiasm moved the audience. With the audacity of a timid and retired man Bidault-Coquille leaped upon the platform and spoke for three-quarters of an hour. He spoke very quickly, without order, but with vehemence, and with all the conviction of a mathematical mystic. He was cheered. When he got down from the platform a big woman of uncertain age, dressed in red, and wearing an immense hat trimmed with heroic feathers, throwing herself into his arms, embraced him, and said to him:

"You are splendid!"

He thought in his simplicity that there was some truth in the statement.

She declared to him that henceforth she would live but for Pyrot's defence and Colomban's glory. He thought her sublime and beautiful. She was Maniflore, a poor old courtesan, now forgotten and discarded, who had suddenly become a vehement politician.

She never left him. They spent glorious hours together in doss-houses and in lodgings beautified by their love, in newspaper offices, in meeting-halls and in lecture-halls. As he was an idealist, he persisted in thinking her beautiful, although she gave him abundant opportunity of seeing that she had preserved no charm of any kind. From her past beauty she only retained a confidence in her capacity for pleasing and a lofty assurance in demanding homage. Still, it must be admitted that this Pyrot affair, so fruitful in prodigies, invested Maniflore with a sort of civic majesty, and transformed her, at public meetings, into an august symbol of justice and truth.

Bidault-Coquille and Maniflore did not kindle the least spark of irony or amusement in a single Anti-Pyrotist, a single defender of Greatauk, or a single supporter of the army. The gods, in their anger, had refused to those men the precious gift of humour. They gravely accused the courtesan and the astronomer of being spies, of treachery, and of plotting against their country. Bidault-Coquille and Maniflore grew visibly greater beneath insult, abuse, and calumny.

For long months Penguinia had been divided into two camps and, though at first sight it may appear strange, hitherto the socialists had taken no part in the contest. Their groups comprised almost all the manual workers in the country, necessarily scattered, confused, broken up, and divided, but formidable. The Pyrot affair threw the group leaders into a singular embarrassment. They did not wish to place themselves either on the side of the financiers or on the side of the army. They regarded the Jews, both great and small, as their uncompromising opponents. Their principles were not at stake, nor were their interests concerned in the affair. Still the greater number felt how difficult it was growing for them to remain aloof from struggles in which all Penguinia was engaged.

Their leaders called a sitting of their federation at the Rue de la Queue-du-diable-St. Maël, to take into consideration the conduct they ought to adopt in the present circumstances and in future eventualities.

Comrade Phœnix was the first to speak.

"A crime," said he, "the most odious and cowardly of crimes, a judicial crime, has been committed. Military judges, coerced or misled by their superior officers, have condemned an innocent man to an infamous and cruel punishment. Let us not say that the victim is not one of our own party, that he belongs to a caste which was, and always will be, our enemy. Our party is the party of social justice; it can look upon no iniquity with indifference.

"It would be a shame for us if we left it to Kerdanic, a radical, to Colomban, a member of the middle classes, and to a few moderate Republicans, alone to proceed against the crimes of the army. If the victim is not one of us, his executioners are our brothers' executioners, and before Greatauk struck down this soldier he shot our comrades who were on strike.

"Comrades, by an intellectual, moral and material effort you must rescue Pyrot from his torment, and in performing this generous act you are not turning aside from the liberating and revolutionary task you have undertaken, for Pyrot has become the symbol of the oppressed and of all the social iniquities that now exist; by destroying one you make all the others tremble."

When Phœnix ended, comrade Sapor spoke in these terms:

"You are advised to abandon your task in order to do something with which you have no concern. Why throw yourselves into a conflict where, on whatever side you turn, you will find none but your natural, uncompromising, even necessary opponents? Are the financiers to be less hated by us than the army? What inept and criminal generosity is it that hurries you to save those seven hundred Pyrotists whom you will always find confronting you in the social war?

"It is proposed that you act the part of the police for your enemies, and that you are to re-establish for them the order which their own crimes have disturbed. Magnanimity pushed to this degree changes its name.

"Comrades, there is a point at which infamy becomes fatal to a society. Penguin society is being strangled by its infamy, and you are requested to save it, to give it air that it can breathe. This is simply turning you into ridicule.

"Leave it to smother itself and let us gaze at its last convulsions with joyful contempt, only regretting that it has so entirely corrupted the soil on which it has been build that we shall find nothing but *poisoned mud on which* to lay the foundations of a new society."

When Sapor had ended his speech comrade Lapersonne pronounced these few words:

"Phœnix calls us to Pyrot's help for the reason that Pyrot is innocent. It seems to me that that is a very bad reason. If Pyrot is innocent he has behaved like a good soldier and has always conscientiously worked at his trade, which principally consists in shooting the people. That is not a motive to make the people brave all dangers in his defence. When it is demonstrated to me that Pyrot is guilty and that he stole the army hay, I shall be on his side."

Comrade Larrivée afterwards spoke.

"I am not of my friend, Phœnix's opinion but I am not with my friend Sapor either. I do not believe that the party is bound to embrace a cause as soon as we are told that that cause is just. That, I am afraid, is a grievous abuse of words and a dangerous equivocation. For social justice is not revolutionary justice. They are both in perpetual antagonism: to serve the one is to oppose the other. As for me, my choice is made. I am for revolutionary justice as against social justice. Still, in the present case I am against abstention. I say that when a lucky chance brings us an affair like this we should be fools not to profit by it.

"How? We are given an opportunity of striking terrible, perhaps fatal, blows against militarism. And am I to fold my arms? I tell you, comrades, I am not a fakir, I have never been a fakir, and if there are fakirs here let them not count on me. To sit in meditation is a policy without results and one which I shall never adopt.

"A party like ours ought to be continually asserting itself. It ought to prove its existence by continual action. We will intervene in the Pyrot affair but we will intervene in it in a revolutionary manner; we will adopt violent action. . . . Perhaps you think that violence is old-fashioned and superannuated, to be scrapped along with diligences, hand-presses and aerial telegraphy. You are mistaken. To-day as yesterday nothing is obtained except by violence; it is the one efficient instrument. The only thing necessary is to know how to use it. You ask what will our action be? I will tell you: it will be to stir up the governing classes against one another, to put the army in conflict with the capitalists, the government with the magistracy, the nobility and clergy with the Jews, and if possible to drive them all to destroy one another. To do this would be to carry on an agitation which would weaken government in the same way that fever wears out the sick.

"The Pyrot affair, little as we know how to turn it to advantage, will put forward by ten years the growth of the Socialist party and the emancipation of the proletariat, by disarmament, the general strike, and revolution."

The leaders of the party having each expressed a different opinion, the discussion was continued, not without vivacity. The orators, as always happens in such a case, reproduced the arguments they had already brought forward, though with less order and moderation than before. The dispute was prolonged and none changed his opinion. But these opinions, in the final analysis, were reduced to two, that of Sapor and Lapersonne who advised abstention, and that of Phœnix and Larrivée, who wanted intervention. Even these two contrary opinions were united in a common hatred of the heads of the army and of their justice, and in a common belief in Pyrot's innocence. So that public opinion was hardly mistaken in regarding all the Socialist leaders as pernicious Anti-Pyrotists.

As for the vast masses in whose name they spoke and whom they represented as far as speech can express the inexpressible— as for the proletarians whose thought is difficult to know and who do not know it themselves, it seemed that the Pyrot affair did not interest them. It was too literary for them, it was in too classical a style, and had an upper-middle-class and high-finance tone about it that did not please them much.

VIII

THE COLOMBAN TRIAL

WHEN the Colomban trial began, the Pyrotists were not many more than thirty thousand, but they were everywhere and might be found even among the priests and millionaires. What injured them most was the sympathy of the rich Jews. On the other hand they derived valuable advantages from their feeble number. In the first place there were among them fewer fools than among their opponents, who were over-burdened with them. Comprising but a feeble minority they co-operated easily, acted with harmony, and had no temptation to divide and thus counteract one another's efforts. Each of them felt the necessity of doing the best possible and was the more careful of his conduct as he found himself more in the public eye. Finally, they had every reason to hope that they would gain fresh adherents, while their opponents, having had everybody with them at the beginning, could only decrease.

Summoned before the judges at a public sitting, Colomban immediately perceived that his judges were not anxious to discover the truth. As soon as he opened his mouth the President ordered him to be silent in the superior interests of the State. For the same reason, which is the supreme reason, the witnesses for the defence were not heard. General Panther, the Chief of the Staff, appeared in the witness-box, in full uniform and decorated with all his orders. He deposed as follows:

"The infamous Colomban states that we have no proofs against Pyrot. He lies; we have them. I have in my archives seven hundred and thirty-two square yards of them which at five hundred pounds each make three hundred and sixty-six thousand pounds weight."

That superior officer afterwards gave, with elegance and ease, a summary of those proofs.

"They are of all colours and all shades," said he in substance, "they are of every form—pot, crown, sovereign, grape, dove-cot, grand eagle, etc. The smallest is less than the hundredth part of a square inch, the largest measures seventy yards long by ninety yards broad."

At this revelation the audience shuddered with horror.

Greatauk came to give evidence in his turn. Simpler, and perhaps greater, he wore a grey tunic and held his hands joined behind his back.

"I leave," said he calmly and in a slightly raised voice, "I leave to M. Colomban the responsibility for an act that has brought our country to the brink of ruin. The Pyrot affair is secret; it ought to remain secret. If it were divulged the cruelest ills, wars, pillages, depredations, fires, massacres, and epidemics would immediately burst upon Penguinia. I should consider myself guilty of high treason if I uttered another word."

Some persons known for their political experience, among others M. Bigourd, considered the evidence of the Minister of War as abler and of greater weight than that of his Chief of Staff.

The evidence of Colonel de Boisjoli made a great impression.

"One evening at the Ministry of War," said that officer, "the attaché of a neighbouring Power told me that while visiting his sovereign's stables he had once admired some soft and fragrant hay, of a pretty green colour, the finest hay he had ever seen! 'Where did it come from?' I asked him. He did not answer, but there seemed to me no doubt about its origin. It was the hay Pyrot had stolen. Those qualities of verdure, softness, and aroma, are those of our national hay. The forage of the neighbouring Power is grey and brittle; it sounds under the fork and smells of dust. One can draw one's own conclusions."

Lieutenant-Colonel Hastaing said in the witness-box, amid hisses, that he did not believe Pyrot guilty. He was immediately seized by the police and thrown into the bottom of a dungeon where, amid vipers, toads, and broken glass, he remained insensible both to promises and threats.

The usher called:

"Count Pierre Maubec de la Dentdulynx."

There was deep silence, and a stately but ill-dressed nobleman, whose moustaches pointed to the skies and whose dark eyes shot forth flashing glances, was seen advancing toward the witness-box.

He approached Colomban and casting upon him a look of ineffable disdain:

"My evidence," said he, "here it is: you excrement!"

At these words the entire hall burst into enthusiastic applause and jumped up, moved by one of those transports that stir men's hearts and rouse them to extraordinary actions. Without another word Count Maubec de la Dentdulynx withdrew.

All those present left the Court and formed a procession behind him. Prostrate at his feet, Princess des Boscénos held his legs in a close embrace, but he went on, stern and impassive, beneath a shower of handkerchiefs and flowers. Viscountess Olive, clinging to his neck, could not be removed, and the calm hero bore her along with him, floating on his breast like a light scarf.

When the court resumed its sitting, which it had been compelled to suspend, the President called the experts.

Vermillard, the famous expert in handwriting, gave the results of his researches.

"Having carefully studied," said he, "the papers found in Pyrot's house, in particular his account book and his laundry books, I noticed that, though apparently not out of the common, they formed an impenetrable cryptogram, the key to which, however, I discovered. The traitor's infamy is to be seen in every line. In this system of writing the words 'Three glasses of beer and twenty francs for Adèle,' mean 'I have delivered thirty thousand trusses of hay to a neighbouring Power.' From these documents I have even been able to establish the composition of the hay delivered by this officer. The words waistcoat, drawers, pocket handkerchief, collars, drink, tobacco, cigars, mean clover, meadow-grass, lucern, burnet, oats, rye-grass, vernal-grass, and common cat's tail grass. And these are precisely the constituents of the hay furnished by Count Maubec to the Penguin cavalry. In this way Pyrot mentioned his crimes in a language that he believed would always remain indecipherable. One is confounded by so much astuteness and so great a want of conscience."

Colomban, pronounced guilty without any extenuating circumstances, was condemned to the severest penalty. The judges immediately signed a warrant consigning him to solitary confinement.

In the Place du Palais on the sides of a river whose banks had during the course of twelve centuries seen so great a history, fifty thousand persons were tumultuously awaiting the result of the trial. Here were the heads of the Anti-Pyrotist Association, among whom might be seen Prince des Boscénos, Count Cléna, Viscount Olive, and M. de La Trumelle; here crowded the Reverend Father Agaric and the teachers of St. Maël College with their pupils; here the monk Douillard and General Caraguel, embracing each other, formed a sublime group. The market women and laundry women with spits, shovels, tongs, beetles, and kettles full of water might be seen running across the Pont-Vieux. On the steps in front of the bronze gates were assembled all the defenders of Pyrot in Alca, professors, publicists, workmen, some conservatives, others Radicals or Revolutionaries, and by their negligent dress and fierce aspect could be recognised comrades Phœnix, Larrivée, Lapersonne, Dagobert, and Varambille. Squeezed in his funereal frock-coat and wearing his hat of ceremony, Bidault-Coquille invoked the sentimental mathematics on behalf of Colomban and Colonel Hastaing. Maniflore shone smiling and resplendent on the topmost step, anxious, like Leæna, to deserve a glorious monument, or to be given, like Epicharis, the praises of history.

The seven hundred Pyrotists disguised as lemonade sellers, gutter-merchants, collectors of odds and ends, or as Anti-Pyrotists, wandered round the vast building.

When Colomban appeared, so great an uproar burst forth that, struck by the commotion of air and water, birds fell from the trees and fishes floated on the surface of the stream.

On all sides there were yells:

"Duck Colomban, duck him, duck him!"

There were some cries of "Justice and truth!" and a voice was even heard shouting:

"Down with the Army!"

This was the signal for a terrible struggle. The combatants fell in thousands, and their bodies formed howling and moving mounds on top of which fresh champions gripped each other by the throats. Women, eager, pale, and dishevelled, with clenched teeth and frantic nails, rushed on the man, in transports that, in the brilliant light of the public square, gave to their faces expressions unsurpassed even in the shade of curtains and in the hollows of pillows. They were going to seize Colomban, to bite him, to strangle, dismember and rend him, when Maniflore, tall and dignified in her red tunic, stood forth, serene and terrible, confronting these furies who recoiled from before her in terror. Colomban seemed to be saved; his partisans succeeded in clearing a passage for him through the Place du Palais and in putting him into a cab stationed at the corner of the Pont-Vieux. The horse was already in full trot when Prince des Boscénos, Count Cléna, and M. de La Trumelle knocked the driver off his seat. Then, making the animal back and pushing the spokes of the wheels, they ran the vehicle on to the parapet of the bridge, whence they overturned it into the river amid the cheers of the delirious crowd. With a resounding splash a jet of water rose upwards.

and then nothing but a slight eddy was to be seen on the surface of the stream.

Almost immediately comrades Dagobert and Varambille, with the help of the seven hundred disguised Pyrotists, sent Prince des Boscénos head foremost into a river-laundry in which he was lamentably swallowed up.

Serene night descended over the Place du Palais and shed silence and peace upon the frightful ruins with which it was strewed. In the meantime, Colomban, three hundred yards down the stream, cowering beside a lame old horse on a bridge, was meditating on the ignorance and injustice of crowds.

"The business," said he to himself, "is even more troublesome than I believed. I foresee fresh difficulties."

He got up and approached the unhappy animal.

"What have you, poor friend, done to them?" said he. "It is on my account they have used you so cruelly."

He embraced the unfortunate beast and kissed the white star on his forehead. Then he took him by the bridle and led him, both of them limping, through the sleeping city to his house, where sleep soon allowed them to forget mankind.

IX

FATHER DOUILLARD

I N their minute gentleness and at the suggestion of the common father of the faithful, the bishops, canons, vicars, curates, abbots, and friars of Penguinia resolved to hold a solemn service in the cathedral of Alca, and to pray that Divine mercy would deign to put an end to the troubles that distracted one of the noblest countries in Christendom, and grant to repentant Penguinia pardon for its crimes against God and against ministers of religion.

The ceremony took place on the fifteenth of June. General Caraguel, surrounded by his staff, occupied the churchwarden's pew. The congregation was numerous and brilliant. According to M. Bigourd's expression it was both crowded and select. In the front rank was to be seen M. de la Bertheoseille, Chamberlain to his Highness Prince Crucho. Near the pulpit, which was to be ascended by the Reverend Father Douillard, of the Order of St. Francis, were gathered, in an attitude of attention with their hands crossed upon their wands of office, the great dignitaries of the Anti-Pyrotist association, Viscount Olive, M. de La Trumelle, Count Cléna, the Duke d'Ampoule, and Prince des Boscénos. Father Agaric was in the apse with the teachers and pupils of St. Maël College. The right-hand transept and aisle were reserved for officers and soldiers in uniform, this side being thought the more honourable, since the Lord leaned his head to the right when he died on the Cross. The ladies of the aristocracy, and among them Countess Cléna, Viscountess Olive, and Princess des Boscénos, occupied reserved seats. In the immense building and in the square outside were gathered twenty thousand clergy of all sorts, as well as thirty thousand of the laity.

After the expiatory and propitiatory ceremony the Reverend Father Douillard ascended the pulpit. The sermon had at first been entrusted to the Reverend Father Agaric, but, in spite of his merits, he was thought unequal to the occasion in zeal and doctrine, and the eloquent Capuchin friar, who for six months had gone through the barracks preaching against the enemies of God and authority, had been chosen in his place.

The Reverend Father Douillard, taking as his text, "He hath put down the mighty from their seat," established that all temporal power has God as its principle and its end, and that it is ruined and destroyed when it turns aside from the path that Providence has traced out for it and from the end to which He has directed it.

Applying these sacred rules to the government of Penguinia, he drew a terrible picture of the evils that the country's rulers had been unable either to prevent or to foresee.

"The first author of all these miseries and degradations, my brethren," said he, "is only too well known to you. He is a monster whose destiny is providentially proclaimed by his name, for it is derived from the Greek word, *pyros*, which means fire. Eternal wisdom warns us by this etymology that a Jew was to set ablaze the country that had welcomed him."

He depicted the country, persecuted by the persecutors of the Church, and crying in its agony:

"O woe! O glory! Those who have crucified my God are crucifying me!"

At these words a prolonged shudder passed through the assembly.

The powerful orator excited still greater indignation when he described the proud and crime-stained Colomban, plunged into the stream, all the waters of which could not cleanse him. He gathered up all the humiliations and all the perils of the Penguins in order to reproach the President of the Republic and his Prime Minister with them.

"That Minister," said he, "having been guilty of degrading cowardice in not exterminating the seven hundred Pyrotists with their allies and defenders, as Saul exterminated the Philistines at Gibeah, has rendered himself unworthy of exercising the power that God delegated to him, and every good citizen ought henceforth to insult his contemptible government. Heaven will look favourably on those who despise him. 'He hath put down the mighty from their seat.'

God will depose these pusillanimous chiefs and will put in their place strong men who will call upon Him. I tell you, gentlemen, I tell you officers, non-commissioned officers, and soldiers who listen to me, I tell you General of the Penguin armies, the hour has come! If you do not obey God's orders, if in His name you do not depose those now in authority, if you do not establish a religious and strong government in Penguinia, God will none the less destroy what He has condemned, He will none the less save His people. He will save them, but, if you are wanting, He will do so by means of a humble artisan or a simple corporal. Hasten! The hour will soon be past."

Excited by this ardent exhortation, the sixty thousand people present rose up trembling and shouting: "To arms! To arms! Death to the Pyrotists! Hurrah for Crucho!" and all of them, monks, women, soldiers, noblemen, citizens, and loafers, who were gathered beneath the superhuman arm uplifted in the pulpit, struck up the hymn, "Let us save Penguinia!" They rushed impetuously from the basilica and marched along the quays to the Chamber of Deputies.

Left alone in the deserted nave, the wise Cornemuse, lifting his arms to heaven, murmured in broken accents:

"Agnosco fortunam ecclesiæ penguicanæ! I see but too well whither this will lead us."

The attack which the crowd made upon the legislative palace was repulsed. Vigorously charged by the police and Alcan guards, the assailants were already fleeing in disorder, when the Socialists, running from the slums and led by comrades Phœnix, Dagobert, Lapersonne, and Varambille, threw themselves upon them and completed their discomfiture. MM. de La Trumelle and d'Ampoule were taken to the police station. Prince des Boscénos, after a valiant struggle, fell upon the bloody pavement with a fractured skull.

In the enthusiasm of victory, the comrades, mingled with an innumerable crowd of paper-sellers and gutter-merchants, ran through the boulevards all night, carrying Maniflore in triumph, and breaking the mirrors of the cafés and the glasses of the street lamps amid cries of "Down with Crucho! Hurrah for the Social Revolution!" The Anti-Pyrotists in their turn upset the newspaper kiosks and tore down the hoardings.

These were spectacles of which cool reason cannot approve and they were fit causes for grief to the municipal authorities, who desired to preserve the good order of the roads and streets. But what was sadder for a man of heart was the sight of the canting humbugs, who, from fear of blows, kept at an equal distance from the two camps, and who, although they allowed their selfishness and cowardice to be visible, claimed admiration for the generosity of their sentiments and the nobility of their souls. They rubbed their eyes with onions, gaped like whitings, blew violently into their handkerchiefs, and, bringing their voices out of the depth of their stomachs, groaned forth: "O Penguins, cease these fratricidal struggles; cease to rend your mother's bosom!" As if men could live in society without disputes and without quarrels, and as if civil discords were not the necessary conditions of national life and progress. They showed themselves hypocritical cowards by proposing a compromise between the just and the unjust, offending the just in his rectitude and the unjust in his courage. One of these creatures, the rich and powerful Machimel, a champion coward, rose upon the town like a colossus of grief; his tears formed poisonous lakes at his feet and his sighs capsized the boats of the fishermen.

During these stormy nights Bidault-Coquille at the top of his old steam-engine, under the serene sky, boasted in his heart, while the shooting stars registered themselves upon his photographic plates. He was fighting for justice. He loved and was loved with a sublime passion. Insult and calumny raised him to the clouds. A caricature of him in company with those of Colomban, Kerdanic, and Colonel Hastaing was to be seen in the newspaper kiosks. The Anti-Pyrotists proclaimed that he had received fifty thousand francs from the big Jewish financiers. The reporters of the militarist sheets held interviews regarding his scientific knowledge with official scholars, who declared he had no knowledge of the stars, disputed his most solid observations, denied his most certain discoveries, and condemned his most ingenious and most fruitful hypotheses. He exulted under these flattering blows of hatred and envy.

He contemplated the black immensity pierced by a multitude of lights, without giving a thought to all the heavy slumbers, cruel insomnias, vain dreams, spoilt pleasures, and infinitely diverse miseries that a great city contains.

"It is in this enormous city," said he to himself, "that the just and the unjust are joining battle."

And substituting a simple and magnificent poetry for the multiple and vulgar reality, he represented to himself the Pyrot affair as a struggle between good and bad angels. He awaited the eternal triumph of the Sons of Light and congratulated himself on being a Child of the Day confounding the Children of Night.

X

MR. JUSTICE CHAUSSEPIED

HITHERTO blinded by fear, incautious and stupid before the bands of Friar Douillard and the partisans of Prince Crucho, the Republicans at last opened their eyes and grasped the real meaning of the Pyrot affair. The deputies who had for two years turned pale at the shouts of the patriotic crowds became, not indeed more courageous, but altered their cowardice and blamed Robin Mielleux for disorders which their own compliance had encouraged, and the instigators of which they had several times slavishly congratulated. They reproached him for having imperilled the Republic by a weakness which was really theirs and a timidity which they themselves had imposed upon him. Some of them began to doubt whether it was not to their interest to believe in Pyrot's innocence rather than in his guilt, and thenceforward they felt a bitter anguish at the thought that the unhappy man might have been wrongly convicted and that in his aerial cage he might be expiating another man's crimes. "I cannot sleep on account of it!" was what several members of Minister Guillaumette's majority used to say. But these were ambitious to replace their chief.

These generous legislators overthrew the cabinet, and the President of the Republic put in Robin Mielleux's place, a patriarchal Republican with a flowing beard, La Trinité by name, who, like most of the Penguins, understood nothing about the affair, but thought that too many monks were mixed up in it.

General Greatauk, before leaving the Ministry of War, gave his final advice to Panther, the Chief of the Staff.

"I go and you remain," said he, as he shook hands with him. "The Pyrot affair is my daughter; I confide her to you, she is worthy of your love and your care; she is beautiful. Do not forget that her beauty loves the shade, is pleased with mystery, and likes to remain veiled. Treat her modesty with gentleness. Too many indiscreet looks have already profaned her charms. . . . Panther, you desired proofs and you obtained them. You have many, perhaps too many, in your possession. I see that there will be many tiresome interventions and much dangerous curiosity. If I were in your place I would tear up all those documents. Believe me, the best of proofs is none at all. That is the only one which nobody discusses."

Alas! General Panther did not realise the wisdom of this advice. The future was only too thoroughly to justify Greatauk's perspicacity. La Trinité demanded the documents belonging to the Pyrot affair. Péniche, his Minister of War, refused them in the superior interests of the national defence, telling him that the documents under General Panther's care formed the hugest mass of archives in the world. La Trinité studied the case as well as he could, and, without penetrating to the bottom of the matter, suspected it of irregularity. Conformably to his rights and prerogatives he then ordered a fresh trial to be held. Immediately, Péniche, his Minister of War, accused him of insulting the army and betraying the country, and flung his portfolio at his head. He was replaced by a second, who did the same. To him succeeded a third, who imitated these examples, and those after him to the number of seventy acted like their predecessors, until the venerable La Trinité groaned beneath the weight of bellicose portfolios. The seventy-first Minister of War, van Julep, retained office. Not that he was in disagreement with so many and such noble colleagues, but he had been commissioned by them generously to betray his Prime Minister, to cover him with shame and opprobrium, and to convert the new trial to the glory of Greatauk, the satisfaction of the Anti-Pyrotists, the profit of the monks, and the restoration of Prince Crucho.

General van Julep, though endowed with high military virtues, was not intelligent enough to employ the subtle conduct and exquisite methods of Greatauk. He thought, like General Panther, that tangible proofs against Pyrot were necessary, that they could never have too many of them, that they could never have even enough. He expressed these sentiments to his Chief of Staff, who was only too inclined to agree with them.

"Panther," said he, "we are at the moment when we need abundant and superabundant proofs."

"You have said enough, General," answered Panther, "I will complete my piles of documents."

Six months later the proofs against Pyrot filled two stories of the Ministry of War. The ceiling fell in beneath the weight of the bundles, and the avalanche of falling documents crushed two head clerks, fourteen second clerks, and sixty copying clerks, who were at work upon the ground floor arranging a change in the fashion of the cavalry gaiters. The walls of the huge edifice had to be propped. Passers by saw with amazement enormous beams and monstrous stanchions which reared themselves obliquely against the noble front of the building now tottering and disjointed, and blocked up the streets, stopped the carriages, and presented to the motor-omnibuses an obstacle against which they dashed with their loads of passengers.

The judges who had condemned Pyrot were not, properly speaking, judges but soldiers. The judges who had condemned Colomban were real judges, but of inferior rank, wearing seedy black clothes like church vergers, unlucky wretches of judges, miserable judgelings. Above them were the superior judges who wore ermine robes over their black gowns. These, renowned for their knowledge and doctrine, formed a court whose terrible name expressed power. It was called the Court of Appeal (Cassation) so as to make it clear that it was the hammer suspended over the judgments and decrees of all other jurisdictions.

One of these superior red judges of the Supreme Court, called Chaussepied, led a modest and tranquil life in a suburb of Alca. His soul was pure, his heart honest, his spirit just. When he had finished studying his documents he used to play the violin and cultivate hyacinths. Every Sunday he dined with his neighbours the Mesdemoiselles Helbivore. His old age was cheerful and robust and his friends often praised the amenity of his character.

For some months, however, he had been irritable and touchy, and when he opened a newspaper his broad and ruddy face would become covered with dolorous wrinkles and darkened with an angry purple. Pyrot was the cause of it. Justice Chaussepied could not understand how an officer could have committed so black a crime as to hand over eighty thousand trusses of military hay to a neighbouring and hostile Power. And he could still less conceive how a scoundrel should have found official defenders in Penguinia. The thought that there existed in his country a Pyrot, a Colonel Hastaing, a Colomban, a Kerdanic, a Phœnix, spoilt his hyacinths, his violin, his heaven, and his earth, all nature, and even his dinner with the Mesdemoiselles Helbivore!

In the meantime the Pyrot case, having been presented to the Supreme Court by the Keeper of the Seals, it fell to Chaussepied to examine it and discover its defects, in case any existed. Although as upright and honest as a man can be, and trained by long habit to exercise his magistracy without fear or favour, he expected to find in the documents to be submitted to him proofs of certain guilt and of obvious criminality. After lengthened difficulties and repeated refusals on the part of General van Julep, Justice Chaussepied was allowed to examine the documents. Numbered and initialed they ran to the number of fourteen millions six hundred and twenty-six thousand three hundred and twelve. As he studied them the judge was at first surprised, then astonished, then stupefied, amazed, and, if I dare say so, flabbergasted. He found among the documents prospectuses of new fancy shops, newspapers, fashion-plates, paper bags, old business letters, exercise books, brown paper, green paper for rubbing parquet floors, playing cards, diagrams, six thousand copies of the "Key to Dreams," but not a single document in which any mention was made of Pyrot.

XI

CONCLUSION

THE appeal was allowed, and Pyrot was brought down from his cage. But the Anti-Pyrotists did not regard themselves as beaten. The military judges retried Pyrot. Greatauk, in this second affair, surpassed himself. He obtained a second conviction; he obtained it by declaring that the proofs communicated to the Supreme Court were worth nothing, and that great care had been taken to keep back the good ones, since they ought to remain secret. In the opinion of connoisseurs he had never shown so much address. On leaving the court, as he passed through the vestibule with a tranquil step, and his hands behind his back, amidst a crowd of sight-seers, a woman dressed in red and with her face covered by a black veil rushed at him, brandishing a kitchen knife.

"Die, scoundrel!" she cried. It was Maniflore. Before those present could understand what was happening, the general seized her by the wrist, and with apparent gentleness, squeezed it so forcibly that the knife fell from her aching hand.

Then he picked it up and handed it to Maniflore.

"Madam," said he with a bow, "you have dropped a household utensil."

He could not prevent the heroine from being taken to the police-station; but he had her immediately released and afterwards he employed all his influence to stop the prosecution.

The second conviction of Pyrot was Greatauk's last victory.

Justice Chaussepied, who had formerly liked soldiers so much, and esteemed their justice so highly, being now enraged with the military judges, squashed their judgments as a monkey cracks nuts. He rehabilitated Pyrot a second time; he would, if necessary, have rehabilitated him five hundred times.

Furious at having been cowards and at having allowed themselves to be deceived and made game of, the Republicans turned against the monks and clergy. The deputies passed laws of expulsion, separation, and spoliation against them. What Father Cornemuse had forseen took place. That good monk was driven from the Wood of Conils. Treasury officers confiscated his retorts and his stills, and the liquidators divided amongst them his bottles of St. Orberosian liqueur. The pious distiller lost the annual income of three million five hundred thousand francs that his products procured for him. Father Agaric went into exile, abandoning his school into the hands of laymen, who soon allowed it to fall into decay.

Separated from its foster-mother, the State, the Church of Penguinia withered like a plucked flower.

The victorious defenders of the innocent man now abused each
other and overwhelmed each other reciprocally with insults and
calumnies. The vehement Kerdanic hurled himself upon Phœnix as
if ready to devour him. The wealthy Jews and the seven hundred
Pyrotists turned away with disdain from the socialist comrades
whose aid they had humbly implored in the past.

"We know you no longer," said they. "To the devil with you and
your social justice. Social justice is the defence of property."

Having been elected a Deputy and chosen to be the leader of the
new majority, comrade Larrivée was appointed by the Chamber
and public opinion to the Premiership. He showed himself an energetic defender of the military tribunals that had condemned Pyrot.
When his former socialist comrades claimed a little more justice
and liberty for the employés of the State as well as for manual
workers, he opposed their proposals in an eloquent speech.

"Liberty," said he, "is not licence. Between order and disorder
my choice is made: revolution is impotence. Progress has no more
formidable enemy than violence. Gentlemen, those who, as I am, are
anxious for reform, ought to apply themselves before everything
else to cure this agitation which enfeebles government just as fever
exhausts those who are ill. It is time to reassure honest people."

This speech was received with applause. The government of the
Republic remained in subjection to the great financial companies,
the army was exclusively devoted to the defence of capital, while
the fleet was designed solely to procure fresh orders for the mine-
owners. Since the rich refused to pay their just share of the taxes,
the poor, as in the past, paid for them.

In the meantime from the height of his old steam-engine, beneath
the crowded stars of night, Bidault-Coquille gazed sadly at the
sleeping city. Maniflore had left him. Consumed with a desire for
fresh devotions and fresh sacrifices, she had gone in company with
a young Bulgarian to bear justice and vengeance to Sofia. He did
not regret her, having perceived, after the Affair, that she was less
beautiful in form and in thought than he had at first imagined. His
impressions had been modified in the same direction concerning
many other forms and many other thoughts. And what was cruelest of all to him, he regarded himself as not so great, not so splendid, as he had believed.

And he reflected:

"You considered yourself sublime when you had but candour and
good-will. Of what were you proud, Bidault-Coquille? Of having
been one of the first to know that Pyrot was innocent and Greatauk
a scoundrel. But three-fourths of those who defended Greatauk
against the attacks of the seven hundred Pyrotists knew that better
than you. Of what then did you show yourself so proud? Of having

dared to say what you thought? That is civic courage, and like military courage, it is a mere result of imprudence. You have been imprudent. So far so good, but that is no reason for praising yourself beyond measure. Your imprudence was trifling; it exposed you to trifling perils; you did not risk your head by it. The Penguins have lost that cruel and sanguinary pride which formerly gave a tragic grandeur to their revolutions; it is the fatal result of the weakening of beliefs and characters. Ought one to look upon oneself as a superior spirit for having shown a little more clear-sightedness than the vulgar? I am very much afraid, on the contrary, Bidault-Coquille, that you have given proof of a gross misunderstanding of the conditions of the moral and intellectual development of a people. You imagined that social injustices were threaded together like pearls and that it would be enough to pull off one in order to unfasten the whole necklace. That is a very ingenuous conception. You flattered yourself that at one stroke you were establishing justice in your own country and in the universe. You were a brave man, an honest idealist, though without much experimental philosophy. But go home to your own heart and you will recognise that you had in you a spice of malice and that your ingenuousness was not without cunning. You believed you were performing a fine moral action. You said to yourself: 'Here am I, just and courageous once for all. I can henceforth repose in the public esteem and the praise of historians.' And now that you have lost your illusions, now that you know how hard it is to redress wrongs, and that the task must ever be begun afresh, you are going back to your asteroids. You are right; but go back to them with modesty, Bidault-Coquille!"

BOOK VII: MODERN TIMES

MADAME CÉRÈS

"Only extreme things are tolerable."
Count Robert de Montesquiou.

I

MADAME CLARENCE'S DRAWING–ROOM

 ADAME CLARENCE the widow of an exalted functionary of the Republic, loved to entertain. Every Thursday she collected together some friends of modest condition who took pleasure in conversation. The ladies who went to see her, very different in age and rank, were all without money and had all suffered much. There was a duchess who looked like a fortune-teller and a fortune-teller who looked like a duchess. Madame Clarence was pretty enough to maintain some old *liaisons*, but not to form new ones, and she generally inspired a quiet esteem. She had a very pretty daughter, who, since she had no dower, caused some alarm among the male guests; for the Penguins were as much afraid of portionless girls as they were of the devil himself. Eveline Clarence, noticing their reserve and perceiving its cause, used to hand them their tea with an air of disdain. Moreover, she seldom appeared at the parties and talked only to the ladies or the very young people. Her discreet and retiring presence put no restraint upon the conversation, since those who took part in it thought either that as she was a young girl she would not understand it, or that, being twenty-five years old, she might listen to everything.

One Thursday therefore, in Madame Clarence's drawing-room, the conversation turned upon love. The ladies spoke of it with pride, delicacy, and mystery, the men with discretion and fatuity; everyone took an interest in the conversation, for each one was interested in what he or she said. A great deal of wit flowed; brilliant apostrophes were launched forth and keen repartees were returned. But when Professor Haddock began to speak he overwhelmed everybody.

"It is the same with our ideas on love as with our ideas on every-thing else," said he, "they rest upon anterior habits whose very memory has been effaced. In morals, the limitations that have lost their grounds for existing, the most useless obligations, the cruelest and most injurious restraints, are because of their profound an-tiquity and the mystery of their origin, the least disputed and the least disputable as well as the most respected, and they are those that cannot be violated without incurring the most severe blame. All morality relative to the relations of the sexes is founded on this principle: that a woman once obtained belongs to the man, that she is his property like his horse or his weapons. And this having ceased to be true, absurdities result from it, such as the marriage or con-tract of sale of a woman to a man, with clauses restricting the right of ownership introduced as a consequence of the gradual diminution of the claims of the possessor.

"The obligation imposed on a girl that she should bring her vir-ginity to her husband comes from the times when girls were mar-ried immediately they were of a marriageable age. It is ridiculous that a girl who marries at twenty-five or thirty should be subject to that obligation. You will, perhaps, say that it is a present with which her husband, if she gets one at last, will be gratified; but every moment we see men wooing married women and showing themselves perfectly satisfied to take them as they find them.

"Still, even in our own day, the duty of girls is determined in re-ligious morality by the old belief that God, the most powerful of warriors, is polygamous, that he has reserved all maidens for him-self, and that men can only take those whom he has left. This belief, although traces of it exist in several metaphors of mysticism, is abandoned to-day by most civilised peoples. However, it still domi-nates the education of girls not only among our believers, but even among our free-thinkers, who, as a rule, think freely for the reason that they do not think at all.

"Discretion means ability to separate and discern. We say that a girl is discreet when she knows nothing at all. We cultivate her ignorance. In spite of all our care the most discreet know some-thing, for we cannot conceal from them their own nature and their own sensations. But they know badly, they know in a wrong way. That is all we obtain by our careful education. . . ."

"Sir," suddenly said Joseph Boutourlé, the High Treasurer of Alca, "believe me, there are innocent girls, perfectly innocent girls, and it is a great pity. I have known three. They married, and the result was tragical."

"I have noticed," Professor Haddock went on, "that Europeans in general and Penguins in particular occupy themselves, after sport and motoring, with nothing so much as with love. It is giving a great deal of importance to a matter that has very little weight."

"Then, Professor," exclaimed Madame Crémeur in a choking voice, "when a woman has completely surrendered herself to you, you think it is a matter of no importance?"

"No, Madam; it can have its importance," answered Professor Haddock, "but it is necessary to examine if when she surrenders herself to us she offers us a delicious fruit-garden or a plot of thistles and dandelions. And then, do we not misuse words? In love, a woman lends herself rather than gives herself. Look at the pretty Madame Pensée. . . ."

"She is my mother," said a tall, fair young man.

"Sir, I have the greatest respect for her," replied Professor Haddock; "do not be afraid that I intend to say anything in the least offensive about her. But allow me to tell you that, as a rule, the opinions of sons about their mothers are not to be relied on. They do not bear enough in mind that a mother is a mother only because she loved, and that she can still love. That, however, is the case, and it would be deplorable were it otherwise. I have noticed, on the contrary, that daughters do not deceive themselves about their mothers' faculty for loving or about the use they make of it; they are rivals; they have their eyes upon them."

The insupportable Professor spoke a great deal longer, adding indecorum to awkwardness, and impertinence to incivility, accumulating incongruities, despising what is respectable, respecting what is despicable; but no one listened to him further.

During this time in a room that was simple without grace, a room sad for the want of love, a room which, like all young girls' rooms, had something of the cold atmosphere of a place of waiting about it, Eveline Clarence turned over the pages of club annuals and prospectuses of charities in order to obtain from them some acquaintance with society. Being convinced that her mother, shut up in her own intellectual but poor world, could neither bring her out nor push her into prominence, she decided that she herself would seek the best means of winning a husband. At once calm and obstinate, without dreams or illusions, and regarding marriage as but a ticket of admission or a passport, she kept before her mind a clear notion of the hazards, difficulties, and chances of her enterprise. She had the art of pleasing and a coldness of temperament that enabled her to turn it to its fullest advantage. Her weakness lay in the fact that she was dazzled by anything that had an aristocratic air.

When she was alone with her mother she said: "Mamma, we will go to-morrow to Father Douillard's retreat."

II

THE CHARITY OF ST. ORBEROSIA

VERY Friday evening at nine o'clock the choicest of Alcan society assembled in the aristocratic church of St. Maël for the Reverend Father Douillard's retreat. Prince and Princess des Boscénos, Viscount and Viscountess Olive, M. and Madame Bigourd, Monsieur and Madame de La Trumelle were never absent. The flower of the aristocracy might be seen there, and fair Jewish baronesses also adorned it by their presence, for the Jewish baronesses of Alca were Christians.

This retreat, like all religious retreats, had for its object to procure for those living in the world opportunities for recollection so that they might think of their eternal salvation. It was also intended to draw down upon so many noble and illustrious families the benediction of St. Orberosia, who loves the Penguins. The Reverend Father Douillard strove for the completion of his task with a truly apostolical zeal. He hoped to restore the prerogatives of St. Orberosia as the patron saint of Penguinia and to dedicate to her a monumental church on one of the hills that dominate the city. His efforts had been crowned with great success, and for the accomplishing of this national enterprise he had already united more than a hundred thousand adherents and collected more than twenty millions of francs.

It was in the choir of St. Maël's that St. Orberosia's new shrine, shining with gold, sparkling with precious stones, and surrounded by tapers and flowers, had been erected.

The following account may be read in the "History of the Miracles of the Patron Saint of Alca" by the Abbé Plantain:

"The ancient shrine had been melted down during the Terror and the precious relics of the saint thrown into a fire that had been lit on the Place de Grève; but a poor woman of great piety, named Rouquin, went by night at the peril of her life to gather up the calcined bones and the ashes of the blessed saint. She preserved them in a jam-pot, and when religion was again restored, brought them to the venerable Curé of St. Maël's. The woman ended her days piously as a vendor of tapers and custodian of seats in the saint's chapel."

It is certain that in the time of Father Douillard, although faith was declining, the cult of St. Orberosia, which for three hundred years had fallen under the criticism of Canon Princeteau and the silence of the Doctors of the Church, recovered, and was surrounded with more pomp, more splendour, and more fervour than ever. The theologians did not now subtract a single iota from the legend. They

held as certainly established all facts related by Abbot Simplicissimus, and in particular declared, on the testimony of that monk,
that the devil, assuming a monk's form had carried off the saint to
a cave and had there striven with her until she overcame him. Neither places nor dates caused them any embarrassment. They paid
no heed to exegesis and took good care not to grant as much to
science as Canon Princeteau had formerly conceded. They knew too
well whither that would lead.

The church shone with lights and flowers. An operatic tenor sang
the famous canticle of St. Orberosia

> Virgin of Paradise
> Come, come in the dusky night
> And on us shed
> Thy beams of light.

Mademoiselle Clarence sat beside her mother and in front of Viscount Cléna. She remained kneeling during a considerable time, for
the attitude of prayer is natural to discreet virgins and it shows off
their figures.

The Reverend Father Douillard ascended the pulpit. He was a
powerful orator and could, at once melt, surprise, and rouse his
hearers. Women complained only that he fulminated against vice
with excessive harshness and in crude terms that made them blush.
But they liked him none the less for it.

He treated in his sermon of the seventh trial of St. Orberosia,
who was tempted by the dragon which she went forth to combat.
But she did not yield, and she disarmed the monster.

The orator demonstrated without difficulty that we, also, by the
aid of St. Orberosia, and strong in the virtue which she inspires,
can in our turn overthrow the dragons that dart upon us and are
waiting to devour us, the dragon of doubt, the dragon of impiety,
the dragon of forgetfulness of religious duties. He proved that the
charity of St. Orberosia was a work of social regeneration, and he
concluded by an ardent appeal to the faithful "to become instruments of the Divine mercy, eager upholders and supporters of the
charity of St. Orberosia, and to furnish it with all the means which
it required to take its flight and bear its salutary fruits."*

After the ceremony, the Reverend Father Douillard remained in
the sacristy at the disposal of those of the faithful who desired information concerning the charity, or who wished to bring their
contributions. Mademoiselle Clarence wished to speak to Father
Douillard, so did Viscount Cléna. The crowd was large, and a queue
was formed. By chance Viscount Cléna and Mademoiselle Clarence
were side by side and possibly they were squeezed a little closely
to each other by the crowd. Eveline had noticed this fashionable

*Cf. J. Ernest Charles in the "Censeur," May–August, 1907, p. 562,
col. 2.

young man; who was almost as well known as his father in the world of sport. Cléna had noticed her, and, as he thought her pretty, he bowed to her, then apologized and pretended to believe that he had been introduced to the ladies, but could not remember where. They pretended to believe it also.

He presented himself the following week at Madame Clarence's, thinking that her house was a bit fast—a thing not likely to displease him—and when he saw Eveline again he felt he had not been mistaken and that she was an extremely pretty girl.

Viscount Cléna had the finest motor-car in Europe. For three months he drove the Clarences every day over hills and plains, through woods and valleys; they visited famous sites and went over celebrated castles. He said to Eveline all that could be said and did all that could be done to overcome her resistance. She did not conceal from him that she loved him, that she would always love him,

and love no one but him. She remained grave and trembling by his side. To his devouring passion she opposed the invincible defence of a virtue conscious of its danger. At the end of three months, after having gone uphill and down hill, turned sharp corners and negotiated level crossings, and experienced innumerable breakdowns, he knew her as well as he knew the fly-wheel of his car, but not much better. He employed surprises, adventures, sudden stoppages in the depths of forests and before hotels, but he had advanced no farther. He said to himself that it was absurd; then, taking her again in his car he set off at fifty miles an hour quite prepared to upset her in a ditch or to smash himself and her against a tree.

One day, having come to take her on some excursion, he found her more charming than ever, and more provoking. He darted upon her as a storm falls upon the reeds that border a lake. She bent with adorable weakness beneath the breath of the storm and twenty times was almost carried away by its strength, but twenty times she arose, supple and bowing to the wind. After all these shocks one would have said that a light breeze had barely touched her charming stem; she smiled as if ready to be plucked by a bold hand. Then her unhappy aggressor, desperate, enraged, and three parts mad, fled so as not to kill her, mistook the door, went into the bedroom of Madame Clarence, whom he found putting on her hat in front of a wardrobe, seized her, flung her on the bed, and possessed her before she knew what had happened.

The same day Eveline, who had been making inquiries, learned that Viscount Cléna had nothing but debts, lived on money given him by an elderly lady, and promoted the sale of the latest models of a motor-car manufacturer. They separated with common accord and Eveline began again disdainfully to serve tea to her mother's guests.

III

HIPPOLYTE CÉRÈS

N Madame Clarence's drawing-room the conversation turned upon love, and many charming things were said about it.

"Love is a sacrifice," sighed Madame Crémeur.

"I agree with you," replied M. Boutourlé with animation.

But Professor Haddock soon displayed his fastidious insolence.

"It seems to me," said he, "that the Penguin ladies have made a great fuss since, through St. Maël's agency, they became viviparous.

But there is nothing to be particularly proud of in that, for it is a state they share in common with cows and pigs, and even with orange and lemon trees, for the seeds of these plants germinate in the pericarp."

"The self-importance which the Penguin ladies give themselves does not go so far back as that," answered M. Boutourlé. "It dates from the day when the holy apostle gave them clothes. But this self-importance was long kept in restraint, and displayed itself fully only with increased luxury of dress and in a small section of society. For go only two leagues from Alca into the country at harvest time, and you will see whether women are over-precise or self-important."

On that day M. Hippolyte Cérès paid his first call. He was a deputy of Alca, and one of the youngest members of the House. His father was said to have kept a dram shop, but he himself was a lawyer of robust physique, a good though prolix speaker, with a self-important air and a reputation for ability.

"M. Cérès," said the mistress of the house, "your constituency is one of the finest in Alca."

"And there are fresh improvements made in it every day, Madame."

"Unfortunately, it is impossible to take a stroll through it any longer," said M. Boutourlé.

"Why?" asked M. Cérès.

"On account of the motors, of course."

"Do not give them a bad name," answered the Deputy. "They are our great national industry."

"I know. The Penguins of to-day make me think of the ancient Egyptians. According to Clement of Alexandria, Taine tells us—though he misquotes the text—the Egyptians worshipped the crocodiles that devoured them. The Penguins to-day worship the motors that crush them. Without a doubt the future belongs to the metal beast. We are no more likely to go back to cabs than we are to go back to the diligence. And the long martyrdom of the horse will come to an end. The motor, which the frenzied cupidity of manufacturers hurls like a Juggernaut's car upon the bewildered people and of which the idle and fashionable make a foolish though fatal elegance, will soon begin to perform its true function, and putting its strength at the service of the entire people, will behave like a docile, toiling monster. But in order that the motor may cease to be injurious and become beneficent we must build roads suited to its speed, roads which it cannot tear up with its ferocious tyres, and from which it will send no clouds of poisonous dust into human lungs. We ought not to allow slower vehicles or mere animals to go upon those roads, and we should establish garages upon them and foot-bridges over them, and so create order and harmony among the means of communication of the future. That is the wish of every good citizen."

Madame Clarence led the conversation back to the improvements in M. Cérès' constituency. M. Cérès showed his enthusiasm for demolitions, tunnelings, constructions, reconstructions, and all other fruitful operations.

"We build to-day in an admirable style," said he; "everywhere majestic avenues are being reared. Was ever anything as fine as our arcaded bridges and our domed hotels!"

"You are forgetting that big palace surmounted by an immense melon-shaped dome," grumbled M. Daniset, an old art amateur, in a voice of restrained rage. "I am amazed at the degree of ugliness which a modern city can attain. Alca is becoming Americanised. Everywhere we are destroying all that is free, unexpected, measured, restrained, human, or traditional among the things that are left us. Everywhere we are destroying that charming object, a piece of an old wall that bears up the branches of a tree. Everywhere we are suppressing some fragment of light and air, some fragment of nature, some fragment of the associations that still remain with us, some fragment of our fathers, some fragment of ourselves. And we are putting up frightful, enormous, infamous houses, surmounted in Viennese style by ridiculous domes, or fashioned after the models of the 'new art' without mouldings, or having profiles with sinister corbels and burlesque pinnacles, and such monsters as these shamelessly peer over the surrounding buildings. We see bulbous protuberances stuck on the fronts of buildings and we are told they are 'new art' motives. I have seen the 'new art' in other countries, but it is not so ugly as with us; it has fancy and it has simplicity. It is only in our own country that by a sad privilege we may behold the newest and most diverse styles of architectural ugliness. What an enviable privilege!"

"Are you not afraid," asked M. Cérès severely, "are you not afraid that these bitter criticisms tend to keep out of our capital the foreigners who flow into it from all parts of the world and who leave millions behind them?"

"You may set your mind at rest about that," answered M. Daniset. "Foreigners do not come to admire our buildings; they come to see our courtesans, our dressmakers, and our dancing saloons."

"We have one bad habit," sighed M. Cérès, "it is that we calumniate ourselves."

Madame Clarence as an accomplished hostess thought it was time to return to the subject of love and asked M. Jumel his opinion of M. Léon Blum's recent book in which the author complained. . . .

". . . That an irrational custom," went on Professor Haddock, "prevents respectable young ladies from making love, a thing they would enjoy doing, whilst mercenary girls do it too much and without getting any enjoyment out of it. It is indeed deplorable. But M. Léon Blum need not fret too much. If the evil exists, as he says it does, in our middle-class society, I can assure him that everywhere else he would see a consoling spectacle. Among the people, the mass of the people through town and country, girls do not deny themselves that pleasure."

"It is depravity!" said Madame Crémeur.

And she praised the innocence of young girls in terms full of modesty and grace. It was charming to hear her.

Professor Haddock's views on the same subject were, on the contrary, painful to listen to.

"Respectable young girls," said he, "are guarded and watched over. Besides, men do not, as a rule, pursue them much, either through probity, or from a fear of grave responsibilities, or because the seduction of a young girl would not be to their credit. Even then we do not know what really takes place, for the reason that what is hidden is not seen. This is a condition necessary to the existence of all society. The scruples of respectable young girls could be more easily overcome than those of married women if the same pressure were brought to bear on them, and for this there are two reasons: they have more illusions, and their curiosity has not been satisfied. Women, for the most part, have been so disappointed by their husbands that they have not courage enough to begin again with somebody else. I myself have been met by this obstacle several times in my attempts at seduction."

At the moment when Professor Haddock ended his unpleasant remarks, Mademoiselle Eveline Clarence entered the drawing-room and listlessly handed about tea with that expression of boredom which gave an oriental charm to her beauty.

"For my part," said Hippolyte Cérès, looking at her, "I declare myself the young ladies' champion."

"He must be a fool," thought the girl.

Hippolyte Cérès, who had never set foot outside of his political world of electors and elected, thought Madame Clarence's drawing-room most select, its mistress exquisite, and her daughter amazingly beautiful. His visits became frequent and he paid court to both of them. Madame Clarence, who now liked attention, thought him agreeable. Eveline showed no friendliness towards him, and treated him with a hauteur and disdain that he took for aristocratic behaviour and fashionable manners, and he thought all the more of her on that account.

This busy man taxed his ingenuity to please them, and he sometimes succeeded. He got them cards for fashionable functions and boxes at the Opera. He furnished Mademoiselle Clarence with several opportunities of appearing to great advantage and in particular at a garden party which, although given by a Minister, was regarded as really fashionable, and gained its first success in society circles for the Republic.

At that party Eveline had been much noticed and had attracted the special attention of a young diplomat called Roger Lambilly who, imagining that she belonged to a rather fast set, invited her to his bachelor's flat. She thought him handsome and believed him rich, and she accepted. A little moved, almost disquieted, she very nearly became the victim of her daring, and only avoided defeat by an offensive measure audaciously carried out. This was the most foolish escapade in her unmarried life.

Being now on friendly terms with Ministers and with the President, Eveline continued to wear her aristocratic and pious affectations, and these won for her the sympathy of the chief personages in the anti-clerical and democratic Republic. M. Hippolyte Cérès, seeing that she was succeeding and doing him credit, liked her still more. He even went so far as to fall madly in love with her.

Henceforth, in spite of everything, she began to observe him with interest, being curious to see if his passion would increase. He appeared to her without elegance or grace, and not well bred, but active, clear-sighted, full of resource, and not too great a bore. She still made fun of him, but he had now won her interest.

One day she wished to test him. It was during the elections, when members of Parliament were, as the phrase runs, requesting a renewal of their mandates. He had an opponent, who, though not dangerous at first and not much of an orator, was rich and was reported to be gaining votes every day. Hippolyte Cérès, banishing both dull security and foolish alarm from his mind, redoubled his care. His chief method of action was by public meetings at which he spoke vehemently against the rival candidate. His committee held huge meetings on Saturday evenings and at three o'clock on Sunday afternoons. One Sunday, as he called on the Clarences, he found Eveline alone in the drawing-room. He had been chatting for about twenty or twenty-five minutes, when, taking out his watch, he saw that it was a quarter to three. The young girl showed herself amiable, engaging, attractive, and full of promises. Cérès was fascinated, but he stood up to go.

"Stay a little longer," said she in a pressing and agreeable voice which made him promptly sit down again.

She was full of interest, of abandon, curiosity, and weakness. He blushed, turned pale, and again got up.

Then, in order to keep him still longer, she looked at him out of two grey and melting eyes, and though her bosom was heaving, she did not say another word. He fell at her feet in distraction, but once more looking at his watch, he jumped up with a terrible oath.

"D——! a quarter to four! I must be off."

And immediately he rushed down the stairs.

From that time onwards she had a certain amount of esteem for him.

IV

A POLITICIAN'S MARRIAGE

HE was not quite in love with him, but she wished him to be in love with her. She was, moreover, very reserved with him, and that not solely from any want of inclination to be otherwise, since in affairs of love some things are due to indifference, to inattention, to a woman's instinct, to traditional custom and feeling, to a desire to try one's power, and to satisfaction at seeing its results. The reason of her prudence was that she knew him to be very much infatuated and capable of taking advantage of any familiarities she allowed as well as of reproaching her coarsely afterwards if she discontinued them.

As he was a professed anti-clerical and free-thinker, she thought it a good plan to affect an appearance of piety in his presence and to be seen with huge prayer-books bound in red morocco, such as Queen Marie Leczinska's or the Dauphiness Marie Josephine's "The Last Two Weeks of Lent." She lost no opportunity either, of showing him the subscriptions that she collected for the endowment of the national cult of St. Orberosia. Eveline did not act in this way because she wished to tease him. Nor did it spring from a young girl's archness, or a spirit of constraint, or even from snobbishness, though there was more than a suspicion of this latter in her behaviour. It was but her way of asserting herself, of stamping herself with a definite character, of increasing her value. To rouse the Deputy's courage she wrapped herself up in religion, just as Brunhild surrounded herself with flames so as to attract Sigard. Her audacity was successful. He thought her still more beautiful thus. Clericalism was in his eyes a sign of good form.

Cérès was re-elected by an enormous majority and returned to a House which showed itself more inclined to the Left, more advanced, and, as it seemed, more eager for reform than its predecessor. Perceiving at once that so much zeal was but intended to hide a fear of change, and a sincere desire to do nothing, he determined to adopt a policy that would satisfy these aspirations. At the beginning of the session he made a great speech, cleverly thought out and well arranged, dealing with the idea that all reform ought to be put off for a long time. He showed himself heated, even fervid; holding the principle that an orator should recommend moderation with extreme vehemence. He was applauded by the entire assembly. The Clarences listened to him from the President's box and Eveline trembled in spite of herself at the solemn sound of the applause.

On the same bench the fair Madame Pensée shivered at the intonations of his virile voice.

As soon as he descended from the tribune, Cérès, even while the audience were still clapping, went without a moment's delay to salute the Clarences in their box. Eveline saw in him the beauty of success, and as he leaned towards the ladies, wiping his neck with his handkerchief and receiving their congratulations with an air of modesty though not without a tinge of self-conceit, the young girl glanced towards Madame Pensée and saw her, palpitating and breathless, drinking in the hero's applause with her head thrown backwards. It seemed as if she were on the point of fainting. Eveline immediately smiled tenderly on M. Cérès.

The Alcan deputy's speech had a great vogue. In political "spheres" it was regarded as extremely able. "We have at last heard an honest pronouncement," said the chief Moderate journal. "It is a regular programme!" they said in the House. It was agreed that he was a man of immense talent.

Hippolyte Cérès had now established himself as leader of the radicals, socialists, and anti-clericals, and they appointed him President of their group, which was then the most considerable in the House. He thus found himself marked out for office in the next ministerial combination.

After a long hesitation Eveline Clarence accepted the idea of marrying M. Hippolyte Cérès. The great man was a little common for her taste. Nothing had yet proved that he would one day reach the point where politics bring in large sums of money. But she was entering her twenty-seventh year and knew enough of life to see that she must not be too fastidious or show herself too difficult to please.

Hippolyte Cérès was celebrated; Hippolyte Cérès was happy. He was no longer recognisable; the elegance of his clothes and deportment had increased tremendously. He wore an undue number of white gloves. Now that he was too much of a society man, Eveline began to doubt if it was not worse than being too little of one. Madame Clarence regarded the engagement with favour. She was reassured concerning her daughter's future and pleased to have flowers given her every Thursday for her drawing-room.

The celebration of the marriage raised some difficulties. Eveline was pious and wished to receive the benediction of the Church. Hippolyte Cérès, tolerant but a free-thinker, wanted only a civil marriage. There were many discussions and even some violent scenes upon the subject. The last took place in the young girl's room at the moment when the invitations were being written. Eveline declared that if she did not go to church she would not believe herself married. She spoke of breaking off the engagement, and of going abroad with her mother, or of retiring into a convent. Then she became tender, weak, suppliant. She sighed, and everything in her virginal chamber sighed in chorus, the holy-water font, the palm-branch above her white bed, the books of devotion on their little shelves, and the blue and white statuette of St. Orberosia chaining the dragon of Cappadocia, that stood upon the marble mantelpiece. Hippolyte Cérès was moved, softened, melted.

Beautiful in her grief, her eyes shining with tears, her wrists girt by a rosary of lapis lazuli and, so to speak, chained by her faith, she suddenly flung herself at Hippolyte's feet, and dishevelled, almost dying, she embraced his knees.

He nearly yielded.

"A religious marriage," he muttered, "a marriage in church, I could make my constituents stand that, but my committee would not swallow the matter so easily. . . . Still I'll explain it to them . . . toleration, social necessities. . . . They all send their daughters to Sunday school. . . . But as for office, my dear I am afraid we are going to drown all hope of that in your holy water."

At these words she stood up grave, generous, resigned, conquered also in her turn.

"My dear, I insist no longer."

"Then we won't have a religious marriage. It will be better, much better not."

"Very well, but be guided by me. I am going to try and arrange everything both to your satisfaction and mine."

She sought the Reverend Father Douillard and explained the situation. He showed himself even more accommodating and yielding than she had hoped.

"Your husband is an intelligent man, a man of order and reason; he will come over to us. You will sanctify him. It is not in vain that God has granted him the blessing of a Christian wife. The Church needs no pomp and ceremonial display for her benedictions. Now that she is persecuted, the shadow of the crypts and the recesses of the catacombs are in better accord with her festivals. Mademoiselle, when you have performed the civil formalities come here to my private chapel in walking costume with M. Cérès. I will marry you, and I will observe the most absolute discretion. I will obtain the necessary dispensations from the Archbishop as well as all facilities regarding the banns, confession-tickets, etc."

Hippolyte, although he thought the combination a little dangerous, agreed to it, a good deal flattered at bottom.

"I will go in a short coat," he said.

He went in a frock coat with white gloves and varnished shoes, and he genuflected.

"Politeness demands. . . ."

V

THE VISIRE CABINET

HE Cérès household was established with modest decency in a pretty flat situated in a new building. Cérès loved his wife in a calm and tranquil fashion. He was often kept late from home by the Commission on the Budget and he worked more than three nights a week at a report on the postal finances of which he hoped to make a masterpiece. Eveline thought she could twist him round her finger, and this did not displease him. The bad side of their situation was that they had not much money; in truth they had very little. The servants of the Republic do not grow rich in her service as easily as people think. Since the sovereign is no longer there to distribute favours, each of them takes what he can, and his depredations limited by the depredations of all the others, are reduced to modest proportions. Hence that austerity of morals that is noticed in democratic leaders. They can only grow rich during periods of great business activity and then they find themselves exposed to the envy of their less favoured colleagues. Hippolyte Cérès had for a long time foreseen such a period. He was one of those who had made preparations for its arrival. Whilst waiting for it he endured his poverty with dignity, and Eveline shared that poverty without suffering as much as one might have thought. She was in close intimacy with the Reverend Father Douillard and frequented the chapel of St. Orberosia, where she met with serious society and people in a position to render her useful services. She knew how to choose among them and gave her confidence to none but those who deserved it. She had gained experience since her motor excursions with Viscount Cléna, and above all she had now acquired the value of a married woman.

The deputy was at first uneasy about these pious practices, which were ridiculed by the demagogic newspapers, but he was soon reassured, for he saw all around him democratic leaders joyfully becoming reconciled to the aristocracy and the Church.

They found that they had reached one of those periods (which often recur) when advance had been carried a little too far. Hippolyte Cérès gave a moderate support to this view. His policy was not a policy of persecution but a policy of tolerance. He had laid its foundations in his splendid speech on the preparations for reform. The Prime Minister was looked upon as too advanced. He proposed schemes which were admitted to be dangerous to capital, and the great financial companies were opposed to him. Of course it followed that the newspapers of all views supported the companies. Seeing the danger increasing, the Cabinet abandoned its schemes, its programme, and its opinions, but it was too late. A new administration was already ready. An insidious question by Paul Visire which was immediately made the subject of a resolution, and a fine speech by Hippolyte Cérès, overthrew the Cabinet.

The President of the Republic entrusted the formation of a new Cabinet to this same Paul Visire, who, though still very young, had been a Minister twice. He was a charming man, spending much of his time in the green-rooms of theatres, very artistic, a great society man, of amazing ability and industry. Paul Visire formed a temporary ministry intended to reassure public feeling which had taken alarm, and Hippolyte Cérès was invited to hold office in it.

The new ministry, belonging to all the groups in the majority, represented the most diverse and contrary opinions, but they were all moderate and convinced conservatives.* The Minister of Foreign Affairs was retained from the former cabinet. He was a little dark man called Crombile, who worked fourteen hours a day with the conviction that he dealt with tremendous questions. He refused to see even his own diplomatic agents, and was terribly uneasy, though he did not disturb anybody else, for the want of foresight of peoples is infinite and that of governments is just as great.

The office of Public Works was given to a Socialist, Fortuné Lapersonne. It was then a political custom and one of the most solemn, most severe, most rigorous, and if I may dare say so, the most terrible and cruel of all political customs, to include a member of the Socialist party in each ministry intended to oppose Socialism, so that the enemies of wealth and property should suffer the shame of being attacked by one of their own party, and so that they could not unite against these forces without turning to some one who might possibly attack themselves in the future. Nothing but a profound ignorance of the human heart would permit the belief that it was difficult to find a Socialist to occupy these functions. Citizen Fortuné Lapersonne entered the Visire cabinet of his own free will and without any constraint; and he found those who approved of his action even among his former friends, so great was the fascination that power exercised over the Penguins!

General Débonnaire went to the War Office. He was looked upon as one of the ablest generals in the army, but he was ruled by a woman, the Baroness Bildermann, who, though she had reached the age of intrigue, was still beautiful. She was in the pay of a neighbouring and hostile Power.

*As this ministry exercised considerable influence upon the destinies of the country and of the world, we think it well to give its composition: Minister of the Interior and Prime Minister, Paul Visire; Minister of Justice, Pierre Bouc; Foreign Affairs, Victor Crombile; Finance, Terrasson; Education, Labillette; Commerce, Posts and Telegraphs, Hippolyte Cérès; Agriculture, Aulac; Public Works, Lapersonne; War, General Débonnaire; Admiralty, Admiral Vivier des Murènes.

The new Minister of Marine, the worthy Admiral Vivier des Murènes, was generally regarded as an excellent seaman. He displayed a piety that would have seemed excessive in an anti-clerical minister, if the Republic had not recognised that religion was of great maritime utility. Acting on the instruction of his spiritual director, the Reverend Father Douillard, the worthy Admiral had dedicated his fleet to St. Orberosia and directed canticles in honour of the Alcan Virgin to be composed by Christian bards. These replaced the national hymn in the music played by the navy.

Prime Minister Visire declared himself to be distinctly anti-clerical but ready to respect all creeds; he asserted that he was a sober-minded reformer. Paul Visire and his colleagues desired reforms, and it was in order not to compromise reform that they proposed none; for they were true politicians and knew that reforms are compromised the moment they are proposed. The government was well received, respectable people were reassured, and the funds rose.

The administration announced that four new ironclads would be put into commission, that prosecutions would be undertaken against the Socialists, and it formally declared its intention to have nothing to do with any inquisitorial income-tax. The choice of Terrasson as Minister of Finance was warmly approved by the press. Terrasson, an old minister famous for his financial operations, gave warrant to all the hopes of the financiers and shadowed forth a period of great business activity. Soon those three udders of modern nations, monopolies, bill discounting, and fraudulent speculation, were swollen with the milk of wealth. Already whispers were heard of distant enterprises, and of planting colonies, and the boldest put forward in the newspapers the project of a military and financial protectorate over Nigritia.

Without having yet shown what he was capable of, Hippolyte Cérès was considered a man of weight. Business people thought highly of him. He was congratulated on all sides for having broken with the extreme sections, the dangerous men, and for having realised the responsibilities of government.

Madame Cérès shone alone amid the Ministers' wives. Crombile withered away in bachelordom. Paul Visire had married money in the person of Mademoiselle Blampignon, an accomplished, estimable, and simple lady who was always ill, and whose feeble health compelled her to stay with her mother in the depths of a remote province. The other Ministers' wives were not born to charm the sight, and people smiled when they read that Madame Labillette had appeared at the Presidency Ball wearing a head-dress of birds of paradise. Madame Vivier des Murènes, a woman of good family, was stout rather than tall, had a face like a beef-steak and the voice of a newspaper-seller. Madame Débonnaire, tall, dry, and florid, was devoted to young officers. She ruined herself by her escapades and crimes and only regained consideration by dint of ugliness and insolence.

Madame Cérès was the charm of the Ministry and its title to consideration. Young, beautiful, and irreproachable, she charmed alike society and the masses by her combination of elegant costumes and pleasant smiles.

Her receptions were thronged by the great Jewish financiers. She gave the most fashionable garden parties in the Republic. The newspapers described her dresses and the milliners did not ask her to pay for them. She went to Mass; she protected the chapel of St. Orberosia from the ill-will of the people; and she aroused in aristocratic hearts the hope of a fresh Concordat.

With her golden hair, grey eyes, and supple and slight though rounded figure, she was indeed pretty. She enjoyed an excellent reputation and she was so adroit, and calm, so much mistress of herself, that she would have preserved it intact even if she had been discovered in the very act of ruining it.

The session ended with a victory for the cabinet which, amid the almost unanimous applause of the House, defeated a proposal for an inquisitorial tax, and with a triumph for Madame Cérès who gave parties in honour of three kings who were at the moment passing through Alca.

VI

THE SOFA OF THE FAVOURITE

THE Prime Minister invited Monsieur and Madame Cérès to spend a couple of weeks of the holidays in a little villa that he had taken in the mountains, and in which he lived alone. The deplorable health of Madame Paul Visire did not allow her to accompany her husband, and she remained with her relatives in one of the southern provinces.

The villa had belonged to the mistress of one of the last Kings of Alca: the drawing-room retained its old furniture, and in it was still to be found the Sofa of the Favourite. The country was charming; a pretty blue stream, the Aiselle, flowed at the foot of the hill that dominated the villa. Hippolyte Cérès loved fishing; when engaged at this monotonous occupation he often formed his best Parliamentary combinations, and his happiest oratorical inspirations. Trout swarmed in the Aiselle; he fished it from morning till evening in a boat that the Prime Minister readily placed at his disposal.

In the mean time, Eveline and Paul Visire sometimes took a turn together in the garden, or had a little chat in the drawing-room.

Eveline, although she recognised the attraction that Visire had for women, had hitherto displayed towards him only an intermittent and superficial coquetry, without any deep intentions or settled design. He was a connoisseur and saw that she was pretty. The House and the Opera had deprived him of all leisure, but, in a little villa, the grey eyes and rounded figure of Eveline took on a value in his eyes. One day as Hippolyte Cérès was fishing in the Aiselle, he made her sit beside him on the Sofa of the Favourite. Long rays of gold struck Eveline like arrows from a hidden Cupid through the chinks of the curtains which protected her from the heat and glare of a brilliant day. Beneath her white muslin dress her rounded yet slender form was outlined in its grace and youth. Her skin was cool and fresh, and had the fragrance of freshly mown hay. Paul Visire behaved as the occasion warranted, and for her part, she was opposed neither to the games of chance or of society. She believed it would be nothing or a trifle; she was mistaken.

"There was," says the famous German ballad, "on the sunny side of the town square, beside a wall whereon the creeper grew, a pretty little letter-box, as blue as the corn-flowers, smiling and tranquil.

"All day long there came to it, in their heavy shoes, small shop-keepers, rich farmers, citizens, the tax-collector and the policeman, and they put into it their business letters, their invoices, their summonses, their notices to pay taxes, the judges' returns, and orders for the recruits to assemble. It remained smiling and tranquil.

"With joy, or in anxiety, there advanced towards it workmen and farm servants, maids and nursemaids, accountants, clerks, and women carrying their little children in their arms; they put into it notifications of births, marriages, and deaths, letters between engaged couples, between husbands and wives, from mothers to their sons, and from sons to their mothers. It remained smiling and tranquil.

"At twilight, young lads and young girls slipped furtively to it, and put in love-letters, some moistened with tears that blotted the ink, others with a little circle to show the place to kiss, all of them very long. It remained smiling and tranquil.

"Rich merchants came themselves through excess of carefulness at the hour of daybreak, and put into it registered letters, and letters with five red seals, full of bank notes or cheques on the great financial establishments of the Empire. It remained smiling and tranquil.

"But one day, Gaspar, whom it had never seen, and whom it did not know from Adam, came to put in a letter, of which nothing is known but that it was folded like a little hat. Immediately the pretty letter-box fell into a swoon. Henceforth it remains no longer in its place; it runs through streets, fields, and woods, girdled with ivy, and crowned with roses. It keeps running up hill and down dale; the country policeman surprises it sometimes, amidst the corn, in Gaspar's arms kissing him upon the mouth."

Paul Visire had recovered all his customary nonchalance. Eveline remained stretched on the Divan of the Favourite in an attitude of delicious astonishment.

The Reverend Father Douillard, an excellent moral theologian, and a man who in the decadence of the Church has preserved his principles, was very right to teach, in conformity with the doctrine of the Fathers, that while a woman commits a great sin by giving herself for money, she commits a much greater one by giving herself for nothing. For, in the first case she acts to support her life, and that is sometimes not merely excuseable but pardonable, and even worthy of the Divine Grace, for God forbids suicide, and is unwilling that his creatures should destroy themselves. Besides, in giving herself in order to live, she remains humble, and derives no pleasure from it, a thing which diminishes the sin. But a woman who gives herself for nothing sins with pleasure and exults in her fault. The pride and delight with which she burdens her crime increase its load of moral guilt.

Madame Hippolyte Cérès' example shows the profundity of these moral truths. She perceived that she had senses. A second was enough to bring about this discovery, to change her soul, to alter her whole life. To have learned to know herself was at first a delight. The γνῶθι σεαυτὸν of the ancient philosophy is not a precept the moral fulfilment of which procures any pleasure, since one enjoys little satisfaction from knowing one's soul. It is not the same with the flesh, for in it sources of pleasure may be revealed to us. Eveline immediately felt an obligation to her revealer equal to the benefit she had received, and she imagined that he who had discovered these heavenly depths was the sole possessor of the key to them. Was this an error, and might she not be able to find others who also had the golden key? It is difficult to decide; and Professor Haddock, when the facts were divulged (which happened without much delay as we shall see), treated the matter from an experimental point of view, in a scientific review, and concluded that the chances Madame C—— would have of finding the exact equivalent of M. V—— were in the proportion of 305 to 975008. This is as much as to say that she would never find it. Doubtless her instinct told her the same, for she attached herself distractedly to him.

I have related these facts with all the circumstances which seemed to me worthy of attracting the attention of mediative and philosophic minds. The Sofa of the Favourite is worthy of the majesty of history; on it were decided the destinies of a great people; nay, on it was accomplished an act whose renown was to extend over the neighbouring nations both friendly and hostile, and even over all humanity. Too often events of this nature escape the superficial minds and shallow spirits who inconsiderately assume the task of writing history. Thus the secret springs of events remain hidden from us. The fall of Empires and the transmission of dominions astonish us and remain incomprehensible to us, because we have not discovered the imperceptible point, or touched the secret spring which when put in movement has destroyed and overthrown everything. The author of this great history knows better than anyone else his faults and his weaknesses, but he can do himself this justice—that he has always kept the moderation, the seriousness, the austerity, which an account of affairs of State demands, and that he has never departed from the gravity which is suitable to a recital of human actions.

VII

THE FIRST CONSEQUENCES

HEN Eveline confided to Paul Visire that she had never experienced anything similar, he did not believe her. He had had a good deal to do with women and knew that they readily say these things to men in order to make them more in love with them. Thus his experience, as sometimes happens, made him disregard the truth. Incredulous, but gratified all the same, he soon felt love and something more for her. This state at first seemed favourable to his intellectual faculties. Visire delivered in the chief town of his constituency a speech full of grace, brilliant and happy, which was considered to be a masterpiece.

The re-opening of Parliament was serene. A few isolated jealousies, a few timid ambitions raised their heads in the House, and that was all. A smile from the Prime Minister was enough to dissipate these shadows. She and he saw each other twice a day, and wrote to each other in the interval. He was accustomed to intimate relationships, was adroit, and knew how to dissimulate; but Eveline displayed a foolish imprudence: she made herself conspicuous with him in drawing-rooms, at the theatre, in the House, and at the Embassies; she wore her love upon her face, upon her whole person, in her moist glances, in the languishing smile of her lips, in the heaving of her breast, in all her heightened, agitated, and distracted beauty. Soon the entire country knew of their intimacy. Foreign Courts were informed of it. The President of the Republic and Eveline's husband alone remained in ignorance. The President became acquainted with it in the country, through a misplaced police report which found its way, it is not known how, into his portmanteau.

Hippolyte Cérès, without being either very subtle, or very perspicacious, noticed that there was something different in his home. Eveline, who quite lately had interested herself in his affairs, and shown, if not tenderness, at least affection, towards him, displayed henceforth nothing but indifference and repulsion. She had always had periods of absence, and made prolonged visits to the Charity of St. Orberosia; now, she went out in the morning, remained out all day, and sat down to dinner at nine o'clock in the evening with the face of a somnambulist. Her husband thought it absurd; however, he might perhaps have never known the reason for this; a profound ignorance of women, a crass confidence in his own merit, and in his own fortune, might perhaps have always hidden the truth from him, if the two lovers had not, so to speak, compelled him to discover it.

When Paul Visire went to Eveline's house and found her alone, they used to say, as they embraced each other; "Not here! not here!" and immediately they affected an extreme reserve. That was their invariable rule. Now, one day, Paul Visire went to the house of his colleague Cérès, with whom he had an engagement. It was Eveline who received him, the Minister of Commerce being delayed by a commission.

"Not here!" said the lovers, smiling.

They said it, mouth to mouth, embracing, and clasping each other. They were still saying it, when Hippolyte Cérès entered the drawing-room.

Paul Visire did not lose his presence of mind. He declared to Madame Cérès that he would give up his attempt to take the dust out of her eye. By this attitude he did not deceive the husband, but he was able to leave the room with some dignity.

Hippolyte Cérès was thunderstruck. Eveline's conduct appeared incomprehensible to him; he asked her what reasons she had for it.

"Why? why?" he kept repeating continually, "why?"

She denied everything, not to convince him, for he had seen them, but from expediency and good taste, and to avoid painful explanations. Hippolyte Cérès suffered all the tortures of jealousy. He admitted it to himself, he kept saying inwardly, "I am a strong man; I am clad in armour; but the wound is underneath, it is in my heart," and turning towards his wife, who looked beautiful in her guilt, he would say:

"It ought not to have been with him."

He was right—Eveline ought not to have loved in government circles.

He suffered so much that he took up his revolver, exclaiming: "I will go and kill him!" But he remembered that a Minister of Commerce cannot kill his own Prime Minister, and he put his revolver back into his drawer.

The weeks passed without calming his sufferings. Each morning he buckled his strong man's armour over his wound and sought in work and fame the peace that fled from him. Every Sunday he inaugurated busts, statues, fountains, artesian wells, hospitals, dispensaries, railways, canals, public markets, drainage systems, triumphal arches, and slaughter houses, and delivered moving speeches on each of these occasions. His fervid activity devoured whole piles of documents; he changed the colours of the postage stamps fourteen times in one week. Nevertheless, he gave vent to outbursts of grief and rage that drove him insane; for whole days his reason abandoned him. If he had been in the employment of a private administration this would have been noticed immediately, but it is much more difficult to discover insanity or frenzy in the conduct of affairs of State. At that moment the government employés were forming themselves into associations and federations amid a ferment that was giving alarm both to the Parliament and to public feeling. The postmen were especially prominent in their enthusiasm for trade unions.

Hippolyte Cérès informed them in a circular that their action was strictly legal. The following day he sent out a second circular forbidding all associations of government employés as illegal. He dismissed one hundred and eighty postmen, reinstated them, reprimanded them, and awarded them gratuities. At Cabinet councils he was always on the point of bursting forth. The presence of the Head of the State scarcely restrained him within the limits of the decencies, and as he did not dare to attack his rival he consoled himself by heaping invectives upon General Débonnaire, the respected Minister of War. The General did not hear them, for he was deaf and occupied himself in composing verses for the Baroness Bildermann. Hippolyte Cérès offered an indistinct opposition to everything the Prime Minister proposed. In a word, he was a madman. One faculty alone escaped the ruin of his intellect: he retained his Parliamentary sense, his consciousness of the temper of majorities, his thorough knowledge of groups, and his certainty of the direction in which affairs were moving.

VIII

FURTHER CONSEQUENCES

THE session ended calmly, and the Ministry saw no dangerous signs upon the benches where the majority sat. It was visible, however, from certain articles in the Moderate journals, that the demands of the Jewish and Christian financiers were increasing daily, that the patriotism of the banks required a civilizing expedition to Nigritia, and that the steel trusts, eager in the defence of our coasts and colonies, were crying out for armoured cruisers and still more armoured cruisers. Rumours of war began to be heard. Such rumours sprang up every year as regularly as the trade winds; serious people paid no heed to them and the government usually let them die away from their own weakness unless they grew stronger and spread. For in that case the country would be alarmed. The financiers only wanted colonial wars and the people did not want any wars at all. It loved to see its government proud and even insolent, but at the least suspicion that a European war was brewing, its violent emotion would quickly have reached the House. Paul Visire was not uneasy. The European situation was in his view completely reassuring. He was only irritated by the maniacal silence of his Minister of Foreign Affairs. That gnome went to the Cabinet meetings with a portfolio bigger than himself stuffed full of papers, said nothing, refused to answer all questions, even those asked him by the respected President of the Republic, and exhausted by his obstinate labours, took a few moments' sleep in his arm-chair in which nothing but the top of his little black head was to be seen above the green tablecloth.

In the mean time Hippolyte Cérès became a strong man again. In company with his colleague Lapersonne he formed numerous intimacies with ladies of the theatre. They were both to be seen at night entering fashionable restaurants in the company of ladies whom they over-topped by their lofty stature and their new hats, and they were soon reckoned amongst the most sympathetic frequenters of the boulevards. Fortuné Lapersonne had his own wound beneath his armour. His wife, a young milliner whom he carried off from a marquis, had gone to live with a chauffeur. He loved her still, and could not console himself for her loss, so that very often in the private room of a restaurant, in the midst of a group of girls who laughed and ate crayfish, the two ministers exchanged a look full of their common sorrow and wiped away an unbidden tear.

Hippolyte Cérès, although wounded to the heart, did not allow himself to be beaten. He swore that he would be avenged.

Madame Paul Visire, whose deplorable health forced her to live with her relatives in a distant province, received an anonymous letter specifying that M. Paul Visire, who had not a half-penny when he married her, was spending her dowry on a married woman, E——— C———, that he gave this woman thirty-thousand-franc motor-cars, and pearl necklaces costing twenty-five thousand francs, and that he was going straight to dishonour and ruin. Madame Paul Visire read the letter, fell into hysterics, and handed it to her father.

"I am going to box your husband's ears," said M. Blampignon; "he is a blackguard who will land you in the workhouse unless we look out. He may be Prime Minister, but he won't frighten me."

When he stepped off the train M. Blampignon presented himself at the Ministry of the Interior, and was immediately received. He entered the Prime Minister's room in a fury.

"I have something to say to you, sir!" And he waved the anonymous letter.

Paul Visire welcomed him smiling.

"You are welcome, my dear father. I was going to write to you. . . . Yes, to tell you of your nomination to the rank of officer of the Legion of Honour. I signed the patent this morning."

M. Blampignon thanked his son-in-law warmly and threw the anonymous letter into the fire.

He returned to his provincial house and found his daughter fretting and agitated.

"Well! I saw your husband. He is a delightful fellow. But then, you don't understand how to deal with him."

About this time Hippolyte Cérès learned through a little scandalous newspaper (it is always through the newspapers that ministers are informed of the affairs of State) that the Prime Minister dined every evening with Mademoiselle Lysiane of the Folies Dramatiques, whose charm seemed to have made a great impression on him. Thenceforth Cérès took a gloomy joy in watching his wife. She came in every evening to dine or dress with an air of agreeable fatigue and the serenity that comes from enjoyment.

Thinking that she knew nothing, he sent her anonymous communications. She read them at the table before him and remained still listless and smiling.

He then persuaded himself that she gave no heed to these vague reports, and that in order to disturb her it would be necessary to enable her to verify her lover's infidelity and treason for herself. There were at the Ministry a number of trustworthy agents charged with secret inquiries regarding the national defence. They were then employed in watching the spies of a neighbouring and hostile Power who had succeeded in entering the Postal and Telegraphic service. M. Cérès ordered them to suspend their work for the present and to inquire where, when, and how the Minister of the Interior saw Mademoiselle Lysiane. The agents performed their missions faithfully and told the minister that they had several times seen the Prime Minister with a woman, but that she was not Mademoiselle Lysiane. Hippolyte Cérès asked them nothing further. He was right; the loves of Paul Visire and Lysiane were but an alibi invented by Paul Visire himself, with Eveline's approval, for his fame was rather inconvenient to her, and she sighed for secrecy and mystery.

They were not shadowed by the agents of the Ministry of Commerce alone. They were also followed by those of the Prefect of Police, and even by those of the Minister of the Interior, who disputed with each other the honour of protecting their chief. Then there were the emissaries of several royalist, imperialist, and clerical organisations, those of eight or ten blackmailers, several amateur detectives, a multitude of reporters, and a crowd of photographers, who all made their appearance wherever these two took refuge in their perambulating love affairs, at big hotels, small hotels, town houses, country houses, private apartments, villas, museums, palaces, hovels. They kept watch in the streets, from neighbouring houses, trees, walls, stair-cases, landings, roofs, adjoining rooms, and even chimneys. The Minister and his friend saw with alarm all round their bed room, gimlets boring through doors and shutters, and drills making holes in the walls. A photograph of Madame Cérès in night attire buttoning her boots was the utmost that had been obtained.

Paul Visire grew impatient and irritable, and often lost his good humour and agreeableness. He came to the cabinet meetings in a rage and he, too, poured invectives upon General Débonnaire—a brave man under fire but a lax disciplinarian—and launched his sarcasms against the venerable admiral Vivier des Murènes whose ships went to the bottom without any apparent reason.

Fortuné Lapersonne listened open-eyed, and grumbled scoffingly between his teeth:

"He is not satisfied with robbing Hippolyte Cérès of his wife, but he must go and rob him of his catch-words too."

These storms were made known by the indiscretion of some ministers and by the complaints of the two old warriors, who declared their intention of flinging their portfolios at the beggar's head, but who did nothing of the sort. These outbursts, far from injuring the lucky Prime Minister, had an excellent effect on Parliament and public opinion, who looked on them as signs of a keen solicitude for the welfare of the national army and navy. The Prime Minister was recipient of general approbation.

To the congratulations of the various groups and of notable per-

sonages, he replied with simple firmness: "Those are my principles!" and he had seven or eight Socialists put in prison.

The session ended, and Paul Visire, very exhausted, went to take
the waters. Hippolyte Cérès refused to leave his Ministry, where
the trade union of telephone girls was in tumultuous agitation. He
opposed it with an unheard of violence, for he had now become a
woman-hater. On Sundays he went into the suburbs to fish along
with his colleague Lapersonne, wearing the tall hat that never left
him since he had become a Minister. And both of them, forgetting
the fish, complained of the inconstancy of women and mingled their
griefs.

Hippolyte still loved Eveline and he still suffered. However, hope
had slipped into his heart. She was now separated from her lover,
and, thinking to win her back, he directed all his efforts to that
end. He put forth all his skill, showed himself sincere, adaptable,
affectionate, devoted, even discreet; his heart taught him the
delicacies of feeling. He said charming and touching things to the

faithless one, and, to soften her, he told her all that he had suffered.

Crossing the band of his trousers upon his stomach.

"See," said he, "how thin I have got."

He promised her everything he thought could gratify a woman, country parties, hats, jewels.

Sometimes he thought she would take pity on him. She no longer displayed an insolently happy countenance. Being separated from Paul, her sadness had an air of gentleness. But the moment he made a gesture to recover her she turned away fiercely and gloomily, girt with her fault as if with a golden girdle.

He did not give up, making himself humble, suppliant, lamentable.

One day he went to Lapersonne and said to him with tears in his eyes:

"Will you speak to her?"

Lapersonne excused himself, thinking that his intervention would be useless, but he gave some advice to his friend.

"Make her think that you don't care about her, that you love another, and she will come back to you."

Hippolyte, adopting this method, inserted in the newspapers that he was always to be found in the company of Mademoiselle Guinaud of the Opera. He came home late or did not come home at all, assumed in Eveline's presence an appearance of inward joy impossible to restrain, took out of his pocket, at dinner, a letter on scented paper which he pretended to read with delight, and his lips seemed as in a dream to kiss invisible lips. Nothing happened. Eveline did not even notice the change. Insensible to all around her, she only came out of her lethargy to ask for some louis from her husband, and if he did not give them she threw him a look of contempt, ready to upbraid him with the shame which she poured upon him in the sight of the whole world. Since she had loved she spent a great deal on dress. She needed money, and she had only her husband to secure it for her; she was so far faithful to him.

He lost patience, became furious, and threatened her with his revolver. He said one day before her to Madame Clarence:

"I congratulate you, Madame; you have brought up your daughter to be a wanton hussy."

"Take me away, Mamma," exclaimed Eveline. "I will get a divorce!"

He loved her more ardently than ever. In his jealous rage, suspecting her, not without probability, of sending and receiving letters, he swore that he would intercept them, re-established a censorship over the post, threw private correspondence into confusion, delayed stock-exchange quotations, prevented assignations, brought out bankruptcies, thwarted passions, and caused suicides. The independent press gave utterance to the complaints of the public and indignantly supported them. To justify these arbitrary measures, the ministerial journals spoke darkly of plots and public dangers, and promoted a belief in a monarchical conspiracy. The less well-informed sheets gave more precise information, told of the seizure of fifty thousand guns, and the landing of Prince Crucho. Feeling grew throughout the country, and the republican organs called for the immediate meeting of Parliament. Paul Visire returned to Paris, summoned his colleagues, held an important Cabinet Council, and proclaimed through his agencies that a plot had been actually formed against the national representation, but that the Prime Minister held the threads of it in his hand, and that a judicial inquiry was about to be opened.

He immediately ordered the arrest of thirty Socialists, and whilst the entire country was acclaiming him as its saviour, baffling the watchfulness of his six hundred detectives, he secretly took Eveline to a little house near the Northern railway station, where they remained until night. After their departure, the maid of their hotel, as she was putting their room in order, saw seven little crosses traced by a hairpin on the wall at the head of the bed.

That is all that Hippolyte Cérès obtained as a reward of his efforts.

IX

THE FINAL CONSEQUENCES

EALOUSY is a virtue of democracies which preserves them from tyrants. Deputies began to envy the Prime Minister his golden key. For a year his domination over the beauteous Madame Cérès had been known to the whole universe. The provinces, whither news and fashions only arrive after a complete revolution of the earth round the sun, were at last informed of the illegitimate loves of the Cabinet. The provinces preserve an austere morality; women are more virtuous there than they are in the capital. Various reasons have been alleged for this: Education, example, simplicity of life. Professor Haddock asserts that this virtue of provincial ladies is solely due to the fact that the heels of their shoes are low. "A woman," said he, in a learned article in the "Anthropological Review," "a woman attracts a civilized man in proportion as her feet make an angle with the ground. If this angle is as much as thirty-five degrees, the attraction becomes acute. For the position of the feet upon the ground determines the whole carriage of the body, and it results that provincial women, since they wear low heels, are not very attractive, and preserve their virtue with ease." These con-

clusions were not generally accepted. It was objected that under
the influence of English and American fashions, low heels had
been introduced generally without producing the results attributed
to them by the learned Professor; moreover, it was said that the
difference he pretended to establish between the morals of the me-
tropolis and those of the provinces is perhaps illusory, and that if
it exists, it is apparently due to the fact that great cities offer
more advantages and facilities for love than small towns provide.
However that may be, the provinces began to murmur against the
Prime Minister, and to raise a scandal. This was not yet a danger,
but there was a possibility that it might become one.

For the moment the peril was nowhere and yet everywhere. The
majority remained solid; but the leaders became stiff and exacting.
Perhaps Hippolyte Cérès would never have intentionally sacrificed
his interests to his vengeance. But thinking that he could henceforth, without compromising his own fortune, secretly damage that
of Paul Visire, he devoted himself to the skilful and careful prepa-
ration of difficulties and perils for the Head of the Government.
Though far from equalling his rival in talent, knowledge, and
authority, he greatly surpassed him in his skill as a lobbyist. The
most acute parliamentarians attributed the recent misfortunes of
the majority to his refusal to vote. At committees, by a calculated
imprudence, he favoured motions which he knew the Prime Minister could not accept. One day his intentional awkwardness provoked a sudden and violent conflict between the Minister of the
Interior, and his departmental Treasurer. Then Cérès became
frightened and went no further. It would have been dangerous for
him to overthrow the ministry too soon. His ingenious hatred found
an issue by circuitous paths. Paul Visire had a poor cousin of easy
morals who bore his name. Cérès, remembering this lady, Céline
Visire, brought her into prominence, arranged that she should become intimate with several foreigners, and procured her engagements in the music-halls. One summer night, on a stage in the
Champs Elysées before a tumultuous crowd, she performed risky
dances to the sounds of wild music which was audible in the gardens where the President of the Republic was entertaining Royalty.
The name of Visire, associated with these scandals, covered the
walls of the town, filled the newspapers, was repeated in the cafés
and at balls, and blazed forth in letters of fire upon the boulevards.

Nobody regarded the Prime Minister as responsible for the scandal of his relatives, but a bad idea of his family came into existence, and the influence of the statesman was diminished.

Almost immediately he was made to feel this in a pretty sharp
fashion. One day in the House, on a simple question, Labillette, the
Minister of Religion and Public Worship, who was suffering from
an attack of liver, and beginning to be exasperated by the inten-

tions and intrigues of the clergy, threatened to close the Chapel of St. Orberosia, and spoke without respect of the National Virgin. The entire Right rose up in indignation; the Left appeared to give but a half-hearted support to the rash Minister. The leaders of the majority did not care to attack a popular cult which brought thirty millions a year into the country. The most moderate of the supporters of the Right, M. Bigourd, made the question the subject of a resolution and endangered the Cabinet. Luckily, Fortuné Lapersonne, the Minister of Public Works, always conscious of the obligations of power, was able in the Prime Minister's absence to repair the awkwardness and indecorum of his colleague, the Minister of Public Worship. He ascended the tribune and bore witness to the respect in which the Government held the heavenly Patron of the country, the consoler of so many ills which science admitted its powerlessness to relieve.

When Paul Visire, snatched at last from Eveline's arms, appeared in the House, the administration was saved; but the Prime Minister saw himself compelled to grant important concessions to the upper classes. He proposed in Parliament that six armoured cruisers should be laid down, and thus won the sympathies of the Steel Trust; he gave new assurances that the income tax would not be imposed, and he had eighteen Socialists arrested.

He was soon to find himself opposed by more formidable obstacles. The Chancellor of the neighbouring Empire in an ingenious and profound speech upon the foreign relations of his sovereign, made a sly allusion to the intrigues that inspired the policy of a great country. This reference, which was received with smiles by the Imperial Parliament, was certain to irritate a punctilious republic. It aroused the national susceptibility, which directed its wrath against its amorous Minister. The Deputies seized upon a frivolous pretext to show their dissatisfaction. A ridiculous incident, the fact that the wife of a sub-prefect had danced at the Moulin Rouge, forced the minister to face a vote of censure, and he was within a few votes of being defeated. According to general opinion, Paul Visire had never been so weak, so vacillating, or so spiritless, as on that occasion.

He understood that he could only keep himself in office by a great political stroke, and he decided on the expedition to Nigritia. This measure was demanded by the great financial and industrial corporations and was one which would bring concessions of immense forests to the capitalists, a loan of eight millions to the banking companies, as well as promotions and decorations to the naval and military officers. A pretext presented itself; some insult needed to be avenged, or some debt to be collected. Six battleships, fourteen cruisers, and eighteen transports sailed up the mouth of the river Hippopotamus. Six hundred canoes vainly opposed the landing of the troops. Admiral Vivier des Murènes' cannons produced an appalling effect upon the blacks, who replied to them with flights of arrows, but in spite of their fanatical courage they were entirely defeated. Popular enthusiasm was kindled by the newspapers which the financiers subsidised, and burst into a blaze. Some Socialists alone protested against this barbarous, doubtful, and dangerous enterprise. They were at once arrested.

At that moment when the Minister, supported by wealth, and now beloved by the poor, seemed unconquerable, the light of hate showed Hippolyte Cérès alone the danger, and looking with a gloomy joy at his rival, he muttered between his teeth, "He is wrecked, the brigand!"

Whilst the country intoxicated itself with glory, the neighouring Empire protested against the occupation of Nigritia by a European power, and these protests following one another at shorter and shorter intervals became more and more vehement. The newspapers of the interested Republic concealed all causes for uneasiness; but Hippolyte Cérès heard the growing menace, and determined at last to risk everything, even the fate of the ministry, in order to ruin his enemy. He got men whom he could trust to write and insert articles in several of the official journals, which, seeming to express Paul Visire's precise views, attributed warlike intentions to the Head of the Government.

These articles roused a terrible echo abroad, and they alarmed the public opinion of a nation which, while fond of soldiers, was not fond of war. Questioned in the House on the foreign policy of his government, Paul Visire made a re-assuring statement, and promised to maintain a peace compatible with the dignity of a great nation. His Minister of Foreign Affairs, Crombile, read a declaration which was absolutely unintelligible, for the reason that it was couched in diplomatic language. The Minister obtained a large majority.

But the rumours of war did not cease, and in order to avoid a new and dangerous motion, the Prime Minister distributed eighty thousand acres of forests in Nigritia among the Deputies, and had fourteen Socialists arrested. Hippolyte Cérès went gloomily about the lobbies, confiding to the Deputies of his group that he was endeavouring to induce the Cabinet to adopt a pacific policy, and that he still hoped to succeed. Day by day the sinister rumours grew in volume, and penetrating amongst the public, spread uneasiness and disquiet. Paul Visire himself began to take alarm. What disturbed him most were the silence and absence of the Minister of Foreign Affairs. Crombile no longer came to the meetings of the Cabinet. Rising at five o'clock in the morning, he worked eighteen hours at his desk, and at last fell exhausted into his waste-paper basket, from whence the registrars removed him, together with the papers which they were going to sell to the military attachés of the neighbouring Empire.

General Débonnaire believed that a campaign was imminent, and prepared for it. Far from fearing war, he prayed for it, and confided his generous hopes to Baroness Bildermann, who informed the neighbouring nation, which, acting on her information, proceeded to a rapid mobilization.

The Minister of Finance unintentionally precipitated events. At the moment, he was speculating for a fall, and in order to bring about a panic on the Stock Exchange, he spread the rumour that war was now inevitable. The neighbouring Empire, deceived by this action, and expecting to see its territory invaded, mobilized its troops in all haste. The terrified Chamber overthrew the Visire ministry by an enormous majority (814 votes to 7, with 28 abstentions). It was too late. The very day of this fall the neighbouring and hostile nation recalled its ambassador and flung eight millions of men into Madame Cérès' country. War became universal, and the whole world was drowned in a torrent of blood.

THE ZENITH OF PENGUIN CIVILIZATION

HALF a century after the events we have just related, Madame Cérès died surrounded with respect and veneration, in the eighty-ninth year of her age. She had long been the widow of a statesman whose name she bore with dignity. Her modest and quiet funeral was followed by the orphans of the parish and the sisters of the Sacred Compassion.

The deceased left all her property to the Charity of St. Orberosia.

"Alas!" sighed M. Monnoyer, a canon of St. Maël, as he received the pious legacy, "it was high time for a generous benefactor to come to the relief of our necessities. Rich and poor, learned and ignorant are turning away from us. And when we try to lead back these misguided souls, neither threats nor promises, neither gentleness nor violence, nor anything else is now successful. The Penguin clergy pine in desolation; our country priests, reduced to following the humblest of trades, are shoeless, and compelled to live upon such scraps as they can pick up. In our ruined churches the rain of heaven falls upon the faithful, and during the holy offices they can hear the noise of stones falling from the arches. The tower of the cathedral is tottering and will soon fall. St. Orberosia is forgotten by the Penguins, her devotion abandoned, and her sanctuary deserted. On her shrine, bereft of its gold and precious stones, the spider silently weaves her web."

Hearing these lamentations, Pierre Mille, who at the age of ninety-eight years had lost nothing of his intellectual and moral power, asked the canon if he did not think that St. Orberosia would one day rise out of this wrongful oblivion.

"I hardly dare to hope so," sighed M. Monnoyer.

"It is a pity!" answered Pierre Mille. "Orberosia is a charming figure and her legend is a beautiful one. I discovered the other day by the merest chance, one of her most delightful miracles, the miracle of Jean Violle. Would you like to hear it, M. Monnoyer?"

"I should be very pleased, M. Mille."

"Here it is, then, just as I found it in a fifteenth-century manuscript:

"Cécile, the wife of Nicolas Gaubert, a jeweller on the Pont-au-Change, after having led an honest and chaste life for many years, and being now past her prime, became infatuated with Jean Violle, the Countess de Maubec's page, who lived at the Hôtel du Paon on the Place de Grève. He was not yet eighteen years old, and his face and figure were attractive. Not being able to conquer her passion, Cécile resolved to satisfy it. She attracted the page to her house, loaded him with caresses, supplied him with sweetmeats and finally did as she wished with him.

"Now one day, as they were together in the jeweller's bed, Master Nicolas came home sooner than he was expected. He found the bolt drawn, and heard his wife on the other side of the door exclaiming, 'My heart! my angel! my love!' Then suspecting that she was shut up with a gallant, he struck great blows upon the door and began to shout: 'Slut! hussy! wanton! open so that I may cut off your nose and ears!' In this peril, the jeweller's wife besought St. Orberosia, and vowed her a large candle if she helped her and the little page, who was dying of fear beside the bed, out of their difficulty.

"The saint heard the prayer. She immediately changed Jean Violle into a girl. Seeing this, Cécile was completely reassured, and began to call out to her husband: 'Oh! you brutal villain, you jealous wretch! Speak gently if you want the door to be opened.' And scolding in this way, she ran to the wardrobe and took out of it an old hood, a pair of stays, and a long grey petticoat, in which she hastily wrapped the transformed page. Then when this was done, 'Catherine, dear Catherine,' said she, loudly, 'open the door for your uncle; he is more fool than knave, and won't do you any harm.' The boy who had become a girl, obeyed. Master Nicolas entered the room and found in it a young maid whom he did not know, and his wife in bed. 'Big booby,' said the latter to him, 'don't stand gaping at what you see. Just as I had come to bed because I had a stomach ache, I received a visit from Catherine, the daughter of my sister Jeanne de Palaiseau, with whom we quarrelled fifteen years ago. Kiss your niece. She is well worth the trouble.' The jeweller gave Violle a hug, and from that moment he wanted nothing so much as to be alone with her a moment, so that he might embrace her as much as he liked. For this reason he led her without any delay down to the kitchen, under the pretext of giving her some walnuts and wine, and he was no sooner there with her than he began to caress her very affectionately. He would not have stopped at that if St. Orberosia had not inspired his good wife with the idea of seeing what he was about. She found him with the pretended niece sitting on his knee. She called him a debauched creature, boxed his ears, and forced him to beg her pardon. The next day Violle resumed his previous form.''

Having heard this story the venerable Canon Monnoyer thanked Pierre Mille for having told it, and, taking up his pen, began to write out a list of horses that would win at the next race meeting. For he was a book-maker's clerk.

In the mean time Penguinia gloried in its wealth. Those who produced the things necessary for life, wanted them; those who did not produce them had more than enough. "But these," as a member of the Institute said, "are necessary economic fatalities." The great Penguin people had no longer either traditions, intellectual culture, or arts. The progress of civilisation manifested itself among them by murderous industry, infamous speculation, and hideous luxury. Its capital assumed, as did all the great cities of the time, a cosmopolitan and financial character. An immense and regular ugliness reigned within it. The country enjoyed perfect tranquillity. It had reached its zenith.

BOOK VIII: FUTURE TIMES

THE ENDLESS HISTORY

Alca is becoming Americanised.—*M. Daniset.*

And he overthrew those cities, and all the plain, and all the inhabitants of the cities, and that which grew upon the ground.—*Genesis xix.* 25.

Τῇ Ἑλλάδι πενίη μέν αἰεὶ κοτε σύντροφός ἐστι, ἀρετὴ δὲ ἔπακτός ἐστι, ἀπό τε σοφίης κατεργασμένη καὶ νόμου ἰσχύρου.*
(Herodotus, Histories, VII. cii.)

You have not seen angels then.—*Liber Terribilis.*

Bqsfttfusftpvtuse jufbmbb b up sjufef tspjtfucftfnqfsf-
vstbqsftbnpjsqsp dmbnfuspjtghjttdmjcfsufmbgsbodfstutpb-
njtfbeftdpnqb hojttgjobo—djfsftr—vjejtqpteoueftsjdifttfte-
vqbzt fuqbsmfn Pzfcevofqsf ttfbdifuffejsjhfboumpqjojno

Voufnpjoxfsiejrvf

We are now beginning to study a chemistry which will deal with effects produced by bodies containing a quantity of concentrated energy the like of which we have not yet had at our disposal.—*Sir William Ramsay.*

THE houses were never high enough to satisfy them; they kept on making them still higher and built them of thirty or forty storeys with offices, shops, banks, societies one above another; they dug cellars and tunnels ever deeper downwards.

Fifteen millions of men laboured in a giant town by the light of beacons which shed forth their glare both day and night. No light of heaven pierced through the smoke of the factories with which the town was girt, but sometimes the red disk of a rayless sun might be seen riding

*Poverty has ever been familiar to Greece, but virtue has been acquired, having been accomplished by wisdom and firm laws.
—Henry Cary's Translation.

180

in the black firmament through which iron bridges ploughed their
way, and from which there descended a continual shower of soot
and cinders. It was the most industrial of all the cities in the world
and the richest. Its organisation seemed perfect. None of the ancient
aristocratic or democratic forms remained; everything was sub-
ordinated to the interests of the trusts. This environment gave rise
to what anthropologists called the multi-millionaire type. The men
of this type were at once energetic and frail, capable of great
activity in forming mental combinations and of prolonged labour
in offices, but men whose nervous irritability suffered from hereditary troubles which increased as time went on.

Like all true aristocrats, like the patricians of republican Rome
or the squires of old England, these powerful men affected a great
severity in their habits and customs. They were the ascetics of
wealth. At the meetings of the trusts an observer would have
noticed their smooth and puffy faces, their lantern cheeks, their
sunken eyes and wrinkled brows. With bodies more withered, com-
plexions yellower, lips drier, and eyes filled with a more burning
fanaticism than those of the old Spanish monks, these multi-
millionaires gave themselves up with inextinguishable ardour to
the austerities of banking and industry. Several, denying themselves all happiness, all pleasure, and all rest, spent their miserable
lives in rooms without light or air, furnished only with electrical
apparatus, living on eggs and milk, and sleeping on camp beds. By
doing nothing except pressing nickel buttons with their fingers,
these mystics heaped up riches of which they never even saw the
signs, and acquired the vain possibility of gratifying desires that
they never experienced.

The worship of wealth had its martyrs. One of these multi-
millionaires, the famous Samuel Box, preferred to die rather than
surrender the smallest atom of his property. One of his workmen,
the victim of an accident while at work, being refused any indemnity by his employer, obtained a verdict in the courts, but repelled by innumerable obstacles of procedure, he fell into the direst
poverty. Being thus reduced to despair, he succeeded by dint of
cunning and audacity in confronting his employer with a loaded
revolver in his hand, and threatened to blow out his brains if he
did not give him some assistance. Samuel Box gave nothing, and
let himself be killed for the sake of principle.

Examples that come from high quarters are followed. Those who
possessed some small capital (and they were necessarily the greater
number), affected the ideas and habits of the multi-millionaires,
in order that they might be classed among them. All passions which
injured the increase or the preservation of wealth, were regarded
as dishonourable; neither indolence, nor idleness, nor the taste for
disinterested study, nor love of the arts, nor, above all, extravagance, was ever forgiven; pity was condemned as a dangerous

weakness. Whilst every inclination to licentiousness excited public reprobation, the violent and brutal satisfaction of an appetite was, on the contrary, excused; violence, in truth, was regarded as less injurious to morality, since it manifested a form of social energy. The State was firmly based on two great public virtues: respect for the rich and contempt for the poor. Feeble spirits who were still moved by human suffering had no other resource than to take refuge in a hypocrisy which it was impossible to blame, since it contributed to the maintenance of order and the solidity of institutions.

Thus, among the rich, all were devoted to the social order, or seemed to be so; all gave good examples, if all did not follow them. Some felt the severity of their position cruelly; but they endured it either from pride or from duty. Some attempted, in secret and by subterfuge, to escape from it for a moment. One of these, Edward Martin, the President of the Steel Trust, sometimes dressed himself as a poor man, went forth to beg his bread, and allowed himself to be jostled by the passers-by. One day, as he asked alms on a bridge, he engaged in a quarrel with a real beggar, and filled with a fury of envy, he strangled him.

As they devoted their whole intelligence to business, they sought no intellectual pleasures. The theatre, which had formerly been very flourishing among them, was now reduced to pantomimes and comic dances. Even the pieces in which women acted were given up; the taste for pretty forms and brilliant toilettes had been lost; the somersaults of clowns and the music of negroes were preferred above them, and what roused enthusiasm was the sight of women upon the stage whose necks were bedizened with diamonds, or processions carrying golden bars in triumph. Ladies of wealth were as much compelled as the men to lead a respectable life. According to a tendency common to all civilizations, public feeling set them up as symbols; they were, by their austere magnificence, to represent both the splendour of wealth and its intangibility. The old habits of gallantry had been reformed, but fashionable lovers were now secretly replaced by muscular labourers or stray grooms. Nevertheless, scandals were rare, a foreign journey concealed nearly all of them, and the Princesses of the Trusts remained objects of universal esteem.

The rich formed only a small minority, but their collaborators, who composed the entire people, had been completely won over or completely subjugated by them. They formed two classes, the agents of commerce or banking, and workers in the factories. The former contributed an immense amount of work and received large salaries. Some of them succeeded in founding establishments of their own; for in the constant increase of the public wealth the more intelligent and audacious could hope for anything. Doubtless it would have been possible to find a certain number of discontented and rebellious persons among the immense crowd of engineers and accountants, but this powerful society had imprinted its firm discipline even on the minds of its opponents. The very anarchists were laborious and regular.

As for the workmen who toiled in the factories that surrounded the town, their decadence, both physical and moral, was terrible; they were examples of the type of poverty as it is set forth by anthropology. Although the development among them of certain muscles, due to the particular nature of their work, might give a false idea of their strength, they presented sure signs of morbid debility. Of low stature, with small heads and narrow chests, they were further distinguished from the comfortable classes by a multitude of physiological anomalies, and, in particular, by a common want of symmetry between the head and the limbs. And they were destined to a gradual and continuous degeneration, for the State made soldiers of the more robust among them, and the health of these did not long withstand the brothels and the drink-shops that sprang up around their barracks. The proletarians became more and more feeble in mind. The continued weakening of their intellectual faculties was not entirely due to their manner of life; it resulted also from a methodical selection carried out by the employers. The latter, fearing that workmen of too great ability might be inclined to put forward legitimate demands, took care to eliminate them by every possible means, and preferred to engage ignorant and stupid labourers, who were incapable of defending their rights, but were yet intelligent enough to perform their toils, which highly perfected machines rendered extremely simple. Thus the proletarians were unable to do anything to improve their lot. With difficulty did they succeed by means of strikes in maintaining the rate of their wages. Even this means began to fail them. The alternations of production inherent in the capitalist system caused such cessations of work that, in several branches of industry, as soon as a strike was declared, the accumulation of products allowed the employers to dispense with the strikers. In a word, these miserable employees were plunged in a gloomy apathy that nothing enlightened and nothing exasperated. They were necessary instruments for the social order and well adapted to their purpose.

Upon the whole, this social order seemed the most firmly established that had yet been seen, at least among mankind, for that of bees and ants is incomparably more stable. Nothing could foreshadow the ruin of a system founded on what is strongest in human nature, pride and cupidity. However, keen observers discovered several grounds for uneasiness. The most certain, although the least apparent, were of an economic order, and consisted in the continually increasing amount of over-production, which entailed long and cruel interruption of labour, though these were, it is true, utilized by the manufacturers as a means of breaking the power of the workmen, by facing them with the prospect of a lock-out. A more obvious peril resulted from the physiological state of almost the entire population. "The health of the poor is what it must be," said the experts in hygiene, "but that of the rich leaves much to be desired." It was not difficult to find the causes of this. The supply of oxygen necessary for life was insufficient in the city, and men breathed in an artificial air. The food trusts, by means of the most daring chemical syntheses, produced artificial wines, meat, milk, fruit, and vegetables, and the diet thus imposed gave rise to stomach and brain troubles. The multi-millionaires were bald at the age of eighteen; some showed from time to time a dangerous weakness of mind. Over-strung and enfeebled, they gave enormous sums to ignorant charlatans; and it was a common thing for some trumpery bath-attendant or other who turned healer or prophet, to make a rapid fortune by the practice of medicine or theology. The number of lunatics increased continually; suicides multiplied in the world of wealth, and many of them were accompanied by atrocious and extraordinary circumstances, which bore witness to an unheard of perversion of intelligence and sensibility.

Another fatal symptom created a strong impression upon average minds. Terrible accidents, henceforth periodical and regular, entered into people's calculations, and kept mounting higher and higher in statistical tables. Every day, machines burst into fragments, houses fell down, trains laden with merchandise fell on to the streets, demolishing entire buildings and crushing hundreds of passers-by. Through the ground, honey-combed with tunnels, two or three storeys of work-shops would often crash, engulfing all those who worked in them.

§ 2

In the southwestern district of the city, on an eminence which had preserved its ancient name of Fort Saint-Michel, there stretched a square where some old trees still spread their exhausted arms above the greensward. Landscape gardeners had constructed a cascade, grottos, a torrent, a lake, and an island, on its northern slope. From this side one could see the whole town with its streets, its boulevards, its squares, the multitude of its roofs and domes, its air-passages, and its crowds of men, covered with a veil of silence, and seemingly enchanted by the distance. This square was the healthiest place in the capital; here no smoke obscured the sky, and children were brought here to play. In summer some employees from the neighbouring offices and laboratories used to resort to it for a moment after their luncheons, but they did not disturb its solitude and peace.

It was owing to this custom that, one day in June, about mid-day, a telegraph clerk, Caroline Meslier, came and sat down on a bench at the end of a terrace. In order to refresh her eyes by the sight of a little green, she turned her back to the town. Dark, with brown eyes, robust and placid, Caroline appeared to be from twenty-five to twenty-eight years of age. Almost immediately, a clerk in the Electricity Trust, George Clair, took his place beside her. Fair, thin, and supple, he had features of a feminine delicacy; he was scarcely older than she, and looked still younger. As they met almost every day in this place, a comradeship had sprung up between them, and they enjoyed chatting together. But their conversation had never been tender, affectionate, or even intimate. Caroline, although it had happened to her in the past to repent of her confidence, might perhaps have been less reserved had not George Clair always shown himself extremely restrained in his expressions and behaviour. He always gave a purely intellectual character to the conversation, keeping it within the realm of general ideas, and, moreover, expressing himself on all subjects with the greatest freedom. He spoke frequently of the organization of society, and the conditions of labour.

"Wealth," said he, "is one of the means of living happily; but people have made it the sole end of existence."

And this state of things seemed monstrous to both of them.

They returned continually to various scientific subjects with which they were both familiar.

On that day they discussed the evolution of chemistry.

"From the moment," said Clair, "that radium was seen to be transformed into helium, people ceased to affirm the immutability of simple bodies; in this way all those old laws about simple relations and about the indestructibility of matter were abolished."

"However," said she, "chemical laws exist."

For, being a woman, she had need of belief.

He resumed carelessly:

"Now that we can procure radium in sufficient quantities, science possesses incomparable means of analysis; even at present we get glimpses, within what are called simple bodies, of extremely diversified complex ones, and we discover energies in matter which seem to increase even by reason of its tenuity."

As they talked, they threw bits of bread to the birds, and some children played around them.

Passing from one subject to another:

"This hill, in the quaternary epoch," said Clair, "was inhabited by wild horses. Last year, as they were tunnelling for the water mains, they found a layer of the bones of primeval horses."

She was anxious to know whether, at that distant epoch, man had yet appeared.

He told her that man used to hunt the primeval horse long before he tried to domesticate him.

"Man," he added, "was at first a hunter, then he became a shepherd, a cultivator, a manufacturer . . . and these diverse civilizations succeeded each other at intervals of time that the mind cannot conceive."

He took out his watch.

Caroline asked if it was already time to go back to the office.

He said it was not, that it was scarcely half-past twelve.

A little girl was making mud pies at the foot of their bench; a little boy of seven or eight years was playing in front of them. Whilst his mother was sewing on an adjoining bench, he played all alone at being a run-away horse, and with that power of illusion, of which children are capable, he imagined that he was at the same time the horse, and those who ran after him, and those who fled in terror before him. He kept struggling with himself and shouting: "Stop him, Hi! Hi! This is an awful horse, he has got the bit between his teeth."

Caroline asked the question:

"Do you think that men were happy formerly?"

Her companion answered:

"They suffered less when they were younger. They acted like that little boy: they played; they played at arts, at virtues, at vices, at heroism, at beliefs, at pleasures; they had illusions; which entertained them; they made a noise, they amused themselves. But now. . . ."

He interrupted himself, and looked again at his watch.

The child, who was running, struck his foot against the little girl's pail, and fell his full length on the gravel. He remained a moment stretched out motionless, then raised himself up on the palms of his hands. His forehead puckered, his mouth opened, and he burst into tears. His mother ran up but Caroline had lifted him from the ground and was wiping his eyes and mouth with her handkerchief. The child kept on sobbing and Clair took him in his arms.

"Come, don't cry, my little man! I am going to tell you a story.

"A fisherman once threw his net into the sea and drew out a little, sealed, copper pot, which he opened with his knife. Smoke came out of it, and as it mounted up to the clouds the smoke grew thicker and thicker and became a giant who gave such a terrible yawn that the whole world was blown to dust. . . ."

Clair stopped himself, gave a dry laugh, and handed the child back to his mother. Then he took out his watch again, and kneeling on the bench with his elbows resting on its back he gazed at the town. As far as the eye could reach, the multitude of houses stood out in their tiny immensity.

Caroline turned her eyes in the same direction.

"What splendid weather it is!" said she. "The sun's rays change the smoke on the horizon into gold. The worst thing about civilization is that it deprives one of the light of day."

He did not answer; his looks remained fixed on a place in the town.

After some seconds of silence they saw about half a mile away, in the richer district on the other side of the river, a sort of tragic fog rearing itself upwards. A moment afterwards an explosion was heard even where they were sitting, and an immense tree of smoke mounted towards the pure sky. Little by little the air was filled with an imperceptible murmur caused by the shouts of thousands of men. Cries burst forth quite close to the square.

"What has been blown up?"

The bewilderment was great, for although accidents were common, such a violent explosion as this one had never been seen, and everybody perceived that something terribly strange had happened.

Attempts were made to locate the place of the accident; districts, streets, different buildings, clubs, theatres, and shops were mentioned. Information gradually became more precise and at last the truth was known.

"The Steel Trust has just been blown up."

Clair put his watch back into his pocket.

Caroline looked at him closely and her eyes filled with astonishment.

At last she whispered in his ear:

"Did you know it? Were you expecting it? Was it you . . ."

He answered very calmly:

"That town ought to be destroyed."

She replied in a gentle and thoughtful tone:

"I think so too."

And both of them returned quietly to their work.

§ 3

From that day onward, anarchist attempts followed one another every week without interruption. The victims were numerous, and almost all of them belonged to the poorer classes. These crimes roused public resentment. It was among domestic servants, hotel-keepers, and the employees of such small shops as the Trusts still allowed to exist, that indignation burst forth most vehemently. In popular districts women might be heard demanding unusual punishments for the dynamitards. (They were called by this old name, although it was hardly appropriate to them, since, to these unknown chemists, dynamite was an innocent material only fit to destroy ant-hills, and they considered it mere child's play to explode nitro-glycerine with a cartridge made of fulminate of mercury.) Business ceased suddenly, and those who were least rich were the first to feel the effects. They spoke of doing justice themselves to the anarchists. In the mean time the factory workers remained hostile or indifferent to violent action. They were threatened, as a result of the decline of business, with a likelihood of losing their work, or even a lock-out in all the factories. The Federation of Trade Unions proposed a general strike as the most powerful means of influencing the employers, and the best aid that could be given to the revolutionists, but all the trades with the exception of the gilders refused to cease work.

The police made numerous arrests. Troops summoned from all parts of the National Federation protected the offices of the Trusts, the houses of the multi-millionaires, the public halls, the banks, and the big shops. A fortnight passed without a single explosion, and it was concluded that the dynamitards, in all probability but a handful of persons, perhaps even still fewer, had all been killed or captured, or that they were in hiding, or had taken flight. Confidence returned; it returned at first among the poorer classes. Two or three hundred thousand soldiers, who had been lodged in the most closely populated districts, stimulated trade, and people began to cry out: "Hurrah for the army!"

The rich, who had not been so quick to take alarm, were reassured more slowly. But at the Stock Exchange a group of "bulls" spread optimistic rumours and by a powerful effort put a brake upon the fall in prices. Business improved. Newspapers with big circulations supported the movement. With patriotic eloquence they depicted capital as laughing in its impregnable position at the assaults of a few dastardly criminals, and public wealth maintaining its serene ascendency in spite of the vain threats made against it. They were sincere in their attitude, though at the same time they found it benefited them. Outrages were forgotten or their occurrence denied. On Sundays, at the race-meetings, the stands were adorned by women covered with pearls and diamonds. It was observed with joy that the capitalists had not suffered. Cheers were given for the multi-millionaires in the saddling rooms.

On the following day the Southern Railway Station, the Petroleum Trust, and the huge church built at the expense of Thomas Morcellet were all blown up. Thirty houses were in flames, and the beginning of a fire was discovered at the docks. The firemen showed amazing intrepidity and zeal. They managed their tall fire-escapes with automatic precision, and climbed as high as thirty storeys to rescue the luckless inhabitants from the flames. The soldiers performed their duties with spirit, and were given a double ration of coffee. But these fresh casualties started a panic. Millions of people, who wanted to take their money with them and leave the town at once, crowded the great banking houses. These establishments, after paying out money for three days, closed their doors amid mutterings of a riot. A crowd of fugitives, laden with their baggage, besieged the railway stations and took the town by storm. Many who were anxious to lay in a stock of provisions and take refuge in the cellars, attacked the grocery stores, although they were guarded by soldiers with fixed bayonets. The public authorities displayed energy. Numerous arrests were made and thousands of warrants issued against suspected persons.

During the three weeks that followed no outrage was committed. There was a rumour that bombs had been found in the Opera House, in the cellars of the Town Hall, and beside one of the pillars of the Stock Exchange. But it was soon known that these were boxes of sweets that had been put in those places by practical jokers or lunatics. One of the accused, when questioned by a magistrate, declared that he was the chief author of the explosions, and said that all his accomplices had lost their lives. These confessions were published by the newspapers and helped to reassure public opinion. It was only towards the close of the examination that the magistrates saw they had to deal with a pretender who was in no way connected with any of the crimes.

The experts chosen by the courts discovered nothing that enabled them to determine the engine employed in the work of destruction. According to their conjectures the new explosion emanated from a gas which radium evolves, and it was supposed that electric waves, produced by a special type of oscillator, were propagated through space and thus caused the explosion. But even the ablest chemist could say nothing precise or certain. At last two policemen, who were passing in front of the Hôtel Meyer, found on the pavement, close to a ventilator, an egg made of white metal and provided with a capsule at each end. They picked it up carefully, and, on the orders of their chief, carried it to the municipal laboratory. Scarcely had the experts assembled to examine it, than the egg burst and blew up the amphitheatre and the dome. All the experts perished, and with them Collin, the General of Artillery, and the famous Professor Tigre.

The capitalist society did not allow itself to be daunted by this fresh disaster. The great banks re-opened their doors, declaring that they would meet demands partly in bullion and partly in paper money guaranteed by the State. The Stock Exchange and the Trade Exchange, in spite of the complete cessation of business, decided not to suspend their sittings.

In the meantime the magisterial investigation into the case of those who had been first accused had come to an end. Perhaps the evidence brought against them might have appeared insufficient under other circumstances, but the zeal both of the magistrates and the public made up for this insufficiency. On the eve of the day fixed for the trial the Courts of Justice were blown up and eight hundred people were killed, the greater number of them being judges and lawyers. A furious crowd broke into the prison and lynched the prisoners. The troops sent to restore order were received with showers of stones and revolver shots; several soldiers being dragged from their horses and trampled underfoot. The soldiers fired on the mob and many persons were killed. At last the public authorities succeeded in establishing tranquillity. Next day the Bank was blown up.

From that time onwards unheard-of things took place. The factory workers, who had refused to strike, rushed in crowds into the town and set fire to the houses. Entire regiments, led by their officers, joined the workmen, went with them through the town singing revolutionary hymns, and took barrels of petroleum from the docks with which to feed the fires. Explosions were continual. One morning a monstrous tree of smoke, like the ghost of a huge palm tree half a mile in height, rose above the giant Telegraph Hall which suddenly fell into a complete ruin.

Whilst half the town was in flames, the other half pursued its accustomed life. In the mornings, milk pails could be heard jingling in the dairy carts. In a deserted avenue some old navvy might be seen seated against a wall slowly eating hunks of bread with perhaps a little meat. Almost all the presidents of the trusts remained at their posts. Some of them performed their duty with heroic simplicity. Raphael Box, the son of a martyred multi-millionaire, was blown up as he was presiding at the general meeting of the Sugar Trust. He was given a magnificent funeral and the procession on its way to the cemetery had to climb six times over piles of ruins or cross upon planks over the uprooted roads.

The ordinary helpers of the rich, the clerks, employees, brokers, and agents, preserved an unshaken fidelity. The surviving clerks of the Bank that had been blown up, made their way along the ruined streets through the midst of smoking houses to hand in their bills of exchange, and several were swallowed up in the flames while endeavouring to present their receipts.

Nevertheless, any illusion concerning the state of affairs was impossible. The enemy was master of the town. Instead of silence the noise of explosions was now continuous and produced an insurmountable feeling of horror. The lighting apparatus having been destroyed, the city was plunged in darkness all through the night, and appalling crimes were committed. The populous districts alone, having suffered the least, still preserved measures of protection. They were paraded by patrols of volunteers who shot the robbers, and at every street corner one stumbled over a body lying in a pool of blood, the hands bound behind the back, a handkerchief over the face, and a placard pinned upon the breast.

It became impossible to clear away the ruins or to bury the dead. Soon the stench from the corpses became intolerable. Epidemics raged and caused innumerable deaths, while they also rendered the survivors feeble and listless. Famine carried off almost all who were left. A hundred and one days after the first outrage, whilst six army corps with field artillery and siege artillery were marching, at night, into the poorest quarter of the city, Caroline and

Clair, holding each other's hands, were watching from the roof a lofty house, the only one still left standing, but now surrounded by smoke and flame. Joyous songs ascended from the street, where the crowd was dancing in delirium.

"To-morrow it will be ended," said the man "and it will be better."

The young woman, her hair loosened and her face shining with the reflection of the flames, gazed with a pious joy at the circle of fire that was growing closer around them.

"It will be better," said she also.

And throwing herself into the destroyer's arms she pressed a passionate kiss upon his lips.

§ 4

The other towns of the federation also suffered from disturbances and outbreaks, and then order was restored. Reforms were introduced into institutions and great changes took place in habits and customs, but the country never recovered the loss of its capital, and never regained its former prosperity. Commerce and industry dwindled away, and civilization abandoned those countries which for so long it had preferred to all others. They became insalubrious and sterile; the territory that had supported so many millions of men became nothing more than a desert. On the hill of Fort St. Michel wild horses cropped the coarse grass.

Days flowed by like water from the fountains, and the centuries passed like drops falling from the ends of stalactites. Hunters came to chase the bears upon the hills that covered the forgotten city; shepherds led their flocks upon them; labourers turned up the soil with their ploughs; gardeners cultivated their lettuces and grafted their pear trees. They were not rich, and they had no arts. The walls of their cabins were covered with old vines and roses. A goat-skin clothed their tanned limbs, while their wives dressed themselves with the wool that they themselves had spun. The goat-herds moulded little figures of men and animals out of clay, or sang songs about the young girl who follows her lover through woods or among the browsing goats while the pine trees whisper together and the water utters its murmuring sound. The master of the house grew angry with the beetles who devoured his figs; he planned snares to protect his fowls from the velvet-tailed fox, and he poured out wine for his neighbours saying:

"Drink! The flies have not spoilt my vintage; the vines were dry before they came."

Then in the course of ages the wealth of the villages and the corn that filled the fields were pillaged by barbarian invaders. The country changed its masters several times. The conquerors built castles upon the hills; cultivation increased; mills, forges, tanneries, and looms were established; roads were opened through the woods and over the marshes; the river was covered with boats. The hamlets became large villages and joining together formed a town which protected itself by deep trenches and lofty walls. Later, becoming the capital of a great State, it found itself straitened within its now useless ramparts, and it converted them into grass-covered walks.

It grew very rich and large beyond measure. The houses were never high enough to satisfy the people; they kept on making them still higher and built them of thirty or forty storeys, with offices, shops, banks, societies one above another; they dug cellars and tunnels ever deeper downwards. *Fifteen millions of men laboured in the giant town.*

THE CRIME OF SYLVESTRE BONNARD

"THE CRIME OF SYLVESTRE BONNARD" *translated by*
LAFCADIO HEARN

PART ONE: THE LOG

December 24, 1849.

I HAD put on my slippers and my dressing-gown. I wiped away a tear with which the north wind blowing over the quay had obscured my vision. A bright fire was leaping in the chimney of my study. Ice-crystals, shaped like fern-leaves, were sprouting over the window-panes, and concealed from me the Seine with its bridges and the Louvre of the Valois.

I drew up my easy-chair to the hearth, and my *table-volante,* and took up so much of my place by the fire as Hamilcar deigned to allow me. Hamilcar was lying in front of the andirons, curled up on a cushion, with his nose between his paws. His thick fine fur rose and fell with his regular breathing. At my coming, he slowly slipped a glance of his agate eyes at me from between his half-opened lids, which he closed again almost at once, thinking to himself, "It is nothing; it is only my friend."

"Hamilcar," I said to him, as I stretched my legs—"Hamilcar, somnolent Prince of the City of Books—thou guardian nocturnal! Like that Divine Cat who combated the impious in Heliopolis—in the night of the great combat—thou dost defend from vile nibblers those books which the old savant acquired at the cost of his slender savings and indefatigable zeal. Sleep, Hamilcar, softly as a sultana, in this library, that shelters thy military virtues; for verily in thy person are united the formidable aspect of a Tartar warrior and the slumbrous grace of a woman of the Orient. Sleep, thou heroic and voluptuous Hamilcar, while awaiting that moonlight hour in which the mice will come forth to dance before the 'Acta Sanctorum' of the learned Bolandists!"

The beginning of this discourse pleased Hamilcar, who accompanied it with a throat-sound like the song of a kettle on the fire. But as my voice waxed louder, Hamilcar notified me by lowering his ears and by wrinkling the striped skin of his brow that it was bad taste on my part so to declaim.

"This old-book man," evidently thought Hamilcar, "talks to no purpose at all, while our housekeeper never utters a word which is

195

not full of good sense, full of significance—containing either the
announcement of a meal or the promise of a whipping. One knows
what she says. But this old man puts together a lot of sounds sig-
nifying nothing."

So thought Hamilcar to himself. Leaving him to his reflections, I
opened a book, which I began to read with interest; for it was a
catalogue of manuscripts. I do not know any reading more easy,
more fascinating, more delightful than that of a catalogue. The one
which I was reading—edited in 1824 by Mr. Thompson, librarian to
Sir Thomas Raleigh—sins, it is true, by excess of brevity, and does
not offer that character of exactitude which the archivists of my
own generation were the first to introduce into works upon diplomatics and paleography. It leaves a good deal to be desired and to
be divined. This is perhaps why I find myself aware, while reading
it, of a state of mind which in a nature more imaginative than mine
might be called reverie. I had allowed myself to drift away thus
gently upon the current of my thoughts, when my housekeeper
announced, in a tone of ill-humour, that Monsieur Coccoz desired
to speak with me.

In fact, some one had slipped into the library after her. He was
a little man—a poor little man of puny appearance, wearing a thin
jacket. He approached me with a number of little bows and smiles.
But he was very pale, and, although still young and alert, he looked
ill. I thought, as I looked at him, of a wounded squirrel. He carried
under his arm a green *toilette,* which he put upon a chair; then
unfastening the four corners of the *toilette,* he uncovered a heap
of little yellow books.

"Monsieur," he then said to me, "I have not the honour to be
known to you. I am a book-agent, Monsieur. I represent the leading
houses of the capital, and in the hope that you will kindly honour
me with your confidence, I take the liberty to offer you a few novelties."

Kind gods! just gods! such novelties as the homunculus Coccoz
showed me! The first volume that he put in my hand was "L'Histoire de la Tour de Nesle," with the amours of Marguerite de Bour-
gogne and the Captain Buridan.

"It is a historical book," he said to me, with a smile—"a book of
real history."

"In that case," I replied, "it must be very tiresome; for all the
historical books which contain no lies are extremely tedious. I write
some authentic ones myself; and if you were unlucky enough to
carry a copy of any of them from door to door you would run the
risk of keeping it all your life in that green baize of yours, without
ever finding ever a cook foolish enough to buy it from you."

"Certainly Monsieur," the little man answered, out of pure good-
nature.

And, all smiling again, he offered me the "Amours d'Héloïse et d'Abeilard"; but I made him understand that, at my age, I had no use for love-stories.

Still smiling, he proposed me the "Règle des Jeux de la Société" —piquet, bezique, écarté, whist, dice, draughts, and chess.

"Alas!" I said to him, "if you want to make me remember the rules of bezique, give me back my old friend Bignan, with whom I used to play cards every evening before the Five Academies solemnly escorted him to the cemetery; or else bring down to the frivolous level of human amusements the grave intelligence of Hamilcar, whom you see on that cushion, for he is the sole companion of my evenings."

The little man's smile became vague and uneasy.

"Here," he said, "is a new collection of society amusements— jokes and puns—with a receipt for changing a red rose to a white rose."

I told him that I had fallen out with roses for a long time, and that, as to jokes, I was satisfied with those which I unconsciously permitted myself to make in the course of my scientific labours.

The homunculus offered me his last book, with his last smile. He said to me:

"Here is the 'Clef des Songes'—the 'Key of Dreams'—with the explanation of any dreams that anybody can have; dreams of gold, dreams of robbers, dreams of death, dreams of falling from the top of a tower. . . . It is exhaustive."

I had taken hold of the tongs, and, brandishing them energetically, I replied to my commercial visitor:

"Yes, my friend; but those dreams and a thousand others, joyous or tragic, are all summed up in one—the Dream of Life; is your little yellow book able to give me the key to that?"

"Yes, Monsieur," answered the homunculus; "the book is complete, and it is not dear—one franc twenty-five centimes, Monsieur."

I called my housekeeper—for there is no bell in my room—and said to her:

"Thérèse, Monsieur Coccoz—whom I am going to ask you to show out—has a book here which might interest you: the 'Key of Dreams.' I shall be very glad to buy it for you."

My housekeeper responded:

"Monsieur, when one has not even time to dream awake, one has still less time to dream asleep. Thank God, my days are just enough for my work and my work for my days, and I am able to say every night, 'Lord, bless Thou the rest which I am going to take.' I never dream, either on my feet or in bed; and I never mistake my eider-down coverlet for a devil, as my cousin did; and, if you will allow me to give my opinion about it, I think you have books enough here now. Monsieur has thousands and thousands of books, which simply turn his head; and as for me, I have just two, which are quite enough for all my wants and purposes—my Catholic prayer-book and my 'Cuisinière Bourgeoise.' "

And with these words my housekeeper helped the little man to fasten up his stock again within the green *toilette*.

The homunculus Coccoz had ceased to smile. His relaxed features took such an expression of suffering that I felt sorry to have made fun of so unhappy a man. I called him back, and told him that I had caught a glimpse of a copy of the "Histoire d'Estelle et de Némorin," which he had among his books; that I was very fond of shepherds and shepherdesses, and that I would be quite willing to purchase, at a reasonable price, the story of these two perfect lovers.

"I will sell you that book for one franc twenty-five centimes, Monsieur," replied Coccoz, whose face at once beamed with joy. "It is historical; and you will be pleased with it. I know now just what suits you. I see that you are a connoisseur. To-morrow I will bring you the 'Crimes des Papes.' It is a good book. I will bring you the *édition d'amateur,* with coloured plates."

I begged him not to do anything of the sort, and sent him away happy. When the green *toilette* and the agent had disappeared in the shadow of the corridor I asked my housekeeper whence this little man had dropped upon us.

"Dropped is the word," she answered; "he dropped on us from the roof, Monsieur, where he lives with his wife."

"You say he has a wife, Thérèse? That is marvellous! women are very strange creatures! This one must be a very unfortunate little woman."

"I don't really know what she is," answered Thérèse; "but every morning I see her trailing a silk dress covered with grease-spots over the stairs. She makes soft eyes at people. And, in the name of common sense! does it become a woman that has been received here out of charity to make eyes and to wear dresses like that? For they allowed the couple to occupy the attic during the time the roof was being repaired, in consideration of the fact that the husband is sick and the wife in an interesting condition. The concierge even says that the pains came on her this morning, and that she is now confined. They must have been very badly off for a child!"

"Thérèse," I replied, "they had no need of a child, doubtless. But Nature had decided they should bring one into the world; Nature made them fall into her snare. One must have exceptional prudence to defeat Nature's schemes. Let us be sorry for them, and not blame them! As for silk dresses, there is no young woman who does not like them. The daughters of Eve adore adornment. You yourself, Thérèse—who are so serious and sensible—what a fuss you make when you have no white apron to wait at table in! But, tell me, have they got everything necessary in their attic?"

"How could they have it, Monsieur," my housekeeper made answer. "The husband, whom you have just seen, used to be a jewellery-peddler—at least, so the concierge tells me—and nobody knows why he stopped selling watches. You have just seen that he is now selling almanacs. That is no way to make an honest living, and I never will believe that God's blessing can come to an almanac-peddler. Between ourselves, the wife looks to me for all the world like a good-for-nothing—a *Marie-couche toi-là*. I think she would be just as capable of bringing up a child as I should be of playing the guitar. Nobody seems to know where they came from; but I am sure they must have come by Misery's coach from the country of *Sans-souci*."

"Wherever they have come from, Thérèse, they are unfortunate; and their attic is cold."

"*Pardi!*—the roof is broken in several places, and the rain comes through in streams. They have neither furniture nor clothing. I don't think cabinet-makers and weavers work much for Christians of that sect!"

"That is very sad, Thérèse; a Christian woman much less well provided for than this pagan, Hamilcar here!—what does she have to say?"

"Monsieur, I never speak to those people; I don't know what she says or what she sings. But she sings all day long; I hear her from the stairway whenever I am going out or coming in."

"Well! the heir of the Coccoz family will be able to say, like the Egg in the village riddle: '*Ma mère me fit en chantant.*'* The like happened in the case of Henry IV. When Jeanne d'Albret felt herself about to be confined she began to sing an old Béarnaise canticle:

" 'Notre-Dame du bout du pont,
　Venez à mon aide en cette heure!
　Priez le Dieu du ciel
　Qu'il me délivre vite,
　Qu'il me donne un garçon!'

"It is certainly unreasonable to bring little unfortunates into the world. But the thing is done every day, my dear Thérèse and all the philosophers on earth will never be able to reform the silly custom. Madame Coccoz has followed it, and she sings. That is creditable at all events! But, tell me, Thérèse, have you not put on the soup to boil to-day?"

"Yes, Monsieur; and it is time for me to go and skim it."

"Good! but don't forget, Thérèse, to take a good bowl of soup out of the pot and carry it to Madame Coccoz, our attic neighbour."

*"My mother sang when she brought me into the world."

My housekeeper was on the point of leaving the room when I added, just in time:

"Thérèse, before you do anything else, please call your friend the porter, and tell him to take a good bundle of wood out of our stock and carry it up to the attic of those Coccoz folks. See, above all, that he puts a first-class log in the lot—a real Christmas log. As for the homunculus, if he comes back again, do not allow either himself or any of his yellow books to come in here."

Having taken all these little precautions with the refined egotism of an old bachelor, I returned to my catalogue again.

With what surprise, with what emotion, with what anxiety did I therein discover the following mention, which I cannot even now copy without feeling my hand tremble:

"*LA LEGENDE DORÉE DE JACQUES DE GENES*
    (*Jacques de Voragine*);—*traduction française, petit in-4.*

"This MS. of the fourteenth century contains, besides the tolerably complete translation of the celebrated work of Jacques de Voragine, 1. The Legends of Saints Ferréol, Ferrution, Germain, Vincent, and Droctoveus; 2. A poem *On the Miraculous Burial of Monsieur Saint-Germain of Auxerre*. This translation, as well as the legends and the poem, are due to the Clerk Alexander.

"This MS. is written upon vellum. It contains a great number of illuminated letters, and two finely executed miniatures, in a rather imperfect state of preservation:—one represents the Purification of the Virgin, and the other the Coronation of Proserpine."

What a discovery! Perspiration moistened my forehead, and a veil seemed to come before my eyes. I trembled; I flushed; and, without being able to speak, I felt a sudden impulse to cry out at the top of my voice.

What a treasure! For more than forty years I had been making a special study of the history of Christian Gaul, and particularly of that glorious Abbey of Saint-Germain-des-Prés, whence issued forth those King-Monks who founded our national dynasty. Now, despite the culpable insufficiency of the description given, it was evident to me that the MS. of the Clerk Alexander must have come from the great Abbey. Everything proved this fact. All the legends added by the translator related to the pious foundation of the Abbey by King Childebert. Then the legend of Saint-Droctoveus was particularly significant; being the legend of the first abbot of my dear Abbey. The poem in French verse on the burial of Saint-Germain led me actually into the nave of that venerable basilica which was the *umbilicus* of Christian Gaul.

The "Golden Legend" is in itself a vast and gracious work. Jacques de Voragine, Definitor of the Order of Saint-Dominic, and Archbishop of Genoa, collected in the thirteenth century the various legends of Catholic saints, and formed so rich a compilation that from all the monasteries and castles of the time there arose the cry: "This is the 'Golden Legend.'" The "Légende Dorée" was especially opulent in Roman hagiography. Edited by an Italian monk, it reveals its best merits in the treatment of matters relating to the terrestrial domains of Saint Peter. Voragine can only perceive the greater saints of the Occident as through a cold mist. For this reason the Aquitanian and Saxon translators of the good legend-writer were careful to add to his recital the lives of their own national saints.

THE ROAD TO THE ACADEMY

I have read and collated a great many manuscripts of the "Golden Legend." I know all those described by my learned colleague, M. Paulin Paris, in his handsome catalogue of the MSS. of the Bibliothèque du Roi. There were two among them which especially drew my attention. One is of the fourteenth century and contains a translation by Jean Belet; the other, younger by a century, presents the version of Jacques Vignay. Both come from the Colbert collection, and were placed on the shelves of that glorious Colbertine library by the Librarian Baluze—whose name I can never pronounce without uncovering my head; for even in the century of the giants of erudition, Baluze astounds by his greatness. I know also a very curious codex in the Bigot collection; I know seventy-four printed editions of the work, commencing with the venerable ancestor of all—the Gothic of Strasburg, begun in 1471, and finished in 1475. But no one of those MSS., no one of those editions, contains the legends of Saints Ferréol, Ferrution, Germain, Vincent, and Droctoveus; no one bears the name of the Clerk Alexander; no one, in fine, came from the Abbey of Saint-Germain-des-Prés. Compared with the MS. described by Mr. Thompson, they are only as straw to gold. I have seen with my eyes, I have touched with my fingers, an incontrovertible testimony to the existence of this document. But the document itself—what has become of it? Sir Thomas Raleigh went to end his days by the shores of the Lake of Como, whither he carried with him a part of his literary wealth. Where did the books go after the death of that aristocratic collector? Where could the manuscript of the Clerk Alexander have gone?

"And why," I asked myself, "why should I have learned that this precious book exists, if I am never to possess it—never even to see it? I would go to seek it in the burning heart of Africa, or in the icy regions of the Pole if I knew it were there. But I do not know where it is. I do not know if it be guarded in a triple-locked iron case by some jealous biblomaniac. I do not know if it be growing mouldy in the attic of some ignoramus. I shudder at the thought that perhaps its torn-out leaves may have been used to cover the pickle-jars of some housekeeper."

August 30, 1850.

THE heavy heat compelled me to walk slowly. I kept close to the walls of the north quays; and, in the lukewarm shade, the shops of the dealers in old books, engravings, and antiquated furniture drew my eyes and appealed to my fancy. Rummaging and idling among these, I hastily enjoyed some verses spiritedly thrown off by a poet of the Pleiad. I examined an elegant Masquerade by Watteau. I felt, with my eye, the weight of a two-handed sword, a steel *gorgerin,* a morion. What a thick helmet! What a ponderous breast-plate—*Seigneur!* A giant's garb? No—the carapace of an insect. The men of those days were cuirassed like beetles; their weakness was within them. Today, on the contrary, our strength is interior, and our armed souls dwell in feeble bodies.

. . . Here is a pastel-portrait of a lady of the old time—the face, vague like a shadow, smiles; and a hand, gloved with an openwork mitten, retains upon her satiny knees a lap-dog, with a ribbon about its neck. That picture fills me with a sort of charming melancholy. Let those who have no half-effaced pastels in their own hearts laugh at me! Like the horse that scents the stable, I hasten my pace as I near my lodgings. There it is—that great human hive, in which I have a cell, for the purpose of therein distilling the somewhat acrid honey of erudition. I climb the stairs with slow effort. Only a few steps more, and I shall be at my own door. But I divine, rather than see, a robe descending with a sound of rustling silk. I stop, and press myself against the balustrade to make room. The lady who is coming down is bareheaded; she is young; she sings; her eyes and teeth gleam in the shadow, for she laughs with lips and eyes at the same time. She is certainly a neighbour, and a very familiar one. She holds in her arms a pretty child, a little boy —quite naked, like the son of a goddess; he has a medal hung round his neck by a little silver chain. I see him sucking his thumbs and looking at me with those big eyes so newly opened on this old universe. The mother simultaneously looks at me in a sly, mysterious way; she stops—I think blushes a little—and holds out the little creature to me. The baby has a pretty wrinkle between wrist and arm, a pretty wrinkle about his neck, and all over him, from head to foot, the daintiest dimples laugh in his rosy flesh.

The mamma shows him to me with pride.

"Monsieur," she says, "don't you think he is very pretty—my little boy?"

She takes one tiny hand, lifts it to the child's own lips, and, drawing out the darling pink fingers again towards me, says,

"Baby, throw the gentleman a kiss."

Then, folding the little being in her arms, she flees away with the agility of a cat, and is lost to sight in a corridor which, judging by the odour, must lead to some kitchen.

I enter my own quarters.

"Thérèse, who can that young mother be whom I saw bareheaded on the stairs just now, with a pretty little boy?"

And Thérèse replies that it was Madame Coccoz.

I stare up at the ceiling, as if trying to obtain some further illumination. Thérèse then recalls to me the little book-peddler who tried to sell me almanacs last year, while his wife was lying in.

"And Coccoz himself?" I asked.

I was answered that I would never see him again. The poor little man had been laid away underground, without my knowledge, and, indeed, with the knowledge of very few people, only a short time after the happy delivery of Madame Coccoz. I learned that his wife had been able to console herself: I did likewise.

"But, Thérèse," I asked, "has Madame Coccoz got everything she needs in that attic of hers?"

"You would be a great dupe, Monsieur," replied my housekeeper, "if you should bother yourself about that creature. They gave her notice to quit the attic when the roof was repaired. But she stays there yet—in spite of the proprietor, the agent, the concierge, and the bailiffs. I think she has bewitched every one of them. She will leave that attic when she pleases, Monsieur; but she is going to leave in her own carriage. Let me tell you that!"

Thérèse reflected for a moment; and then uttered these words:
"A pretty face is a curse from Heaven."

"Then I ought to thank Heaven for having spared me that curse.
But here! put my hat and cane away. I am going to amuse myself
with a few pages of Moréri. If I can trust my old fox-nose, we are
going to have a nicely flavoured pullet for dinner. Look after that
estimable fowl, my girl, and spare your neighbours, so that you and
your old master may be spared by them in turn."

Having thus spoken, I proceeded to follow out the tufted rami-
fications of a princely genealogy.

May 7, 1851.

I HAVE passed the winter according to the ideal of the sages, *in
angello cum libello;* and now the swallows of the Quai Malaquais
find me on their return about as when they left me. He who lives
little, changes little; and it is scarcely living at all to use up one's
days over old texts.

Yet I feel myself to-day a little more deeply impregnated than
ever before with that vague melancholy which life distils. The economy of my intelligence (I dare scarcely confess it to myself!) has
remained disturbed ever since that momentous hour in which the
existence of the manuscript of the Clerk Alexander was first revealed to me.

It is strange that I should have lost my rest simply on account
of a few old sheets of parchment; but it is unquestionably true.
The poor man who has no desires possesses the greatest of riches;
he possesses himself. The rich man who desires something is only a
wretched slave. I am just such a slave. The sweetest pleasures—
those of converse with some one of a delicate and well-balanced
mind, or dining out with a friend—are insufficient to enable me to
forget the manuscript which I know that I want, and have been
wanting from the moment I knew of its existence. I feel the want
of it by day and by night: I feel the want of it in all my joys and
pains; I feel the want of it while at work or asleep.

I recall my desires as a child. How well I can now comprehend
the intense wishes of my early years!

I can see once more, with astonishing vividness, a certain doll
which, when I was eight years old, used to be displayed in the window of an ugly little shop of the Rue de Seine. I cannot tell how it
happened that this doll attracted me. I was very proud of being a
boy; I despised little girls; and I longed impatiently for the day
(which, alas! has come) when a strong beard should bristle on my
chin. I played at being a soldier; and, under the pretext of obtaining forage for my rocking-horse, I used to make sad havoc among
the plants my poor mother delighted to keep on her window-sill.
Manly amusements those, I should say! And, nevertheless, I was

consumed with longing for a doll. Characters like Hercules have such weaknesses occasionally. Was the one I had fallen in love with at all beautiful? No. I can see her now. She had a splotch of vermilion on either cheek, short soft arms, horrible wooden hands, and long sprawling legs. Her flowered petticoat was fastened at the waist with two pins. Even now I can see the black heads of those two pins. It was a decidedly vulgar doll—smelt of the *faubourg*. I remember perfectly well that, child as I was then, before I had put on my first pair of trousers, I was quite conscious in my own way that this doll lacked grace and style—that she was gross, that she was coarse. But I loved her in spite of that; I loved her just for that; I loved her only; I wanted her. My soldiers and my drums had become as nothing in my eyes, I ceased to stick sprigs of heliotrope and veronica into the mouth of my rocking-horse. That doll was all the word to me. I invented ruses worthy of a savage to oblige Virginie, my nurse, to take me by the little shop in the Rue de Seine. I would press my nose against the window until my nurse had to take my arm and drag me away. "Monsieur Sylvestre, it is late, and your mamma will scold you." Monsieur Sylvestre in those days made very little of either scoldings or whippings. But his nurse lifted him up like a feather, and Monsieur Sylvestre yielded to force. In after-years, with age, he degenerated, and sometimes yielded to fear. But at that time he used to fear nothing.

I was unhappy. An unreasoning but irresistible shame prevented me from telling my mother about the object of my love. Thence all my sufferings. For many days that doll, incessantly present in fancy, danced before my eyes, stared at me fixedly, opened her arms to me, assuming in my imagination a sort of life which made her appear at once mysterious and weird, and thereby all the more charming and desirable.

Finally, one day—a day I shall never forget—my nurse took me to see my uncle, Captain Victor, who had invited me to lunch. I admired my uncle a great deal, as much because he had fired the last French cartridge at Waterloo, as because he used to prepare with his own hands, at my mother's table, certain *chapons-à-l'ail,** which he afterwards put into the chicory salad. I thought that was very fine! My Uncle Victor also inspired me with much respect by his frogged coat, and still more by his way of turning the whole house upside down from the moment he came into it. Even now I cannot tell just how he managed it, but I can affirm that whenever my Uncle Victor found himself in any assembly of twenty persons, it was impossible to see or to hear anybody but him. My excellent father, I have reason to believe, never shared my admiration for Uncle Victor, who used to sicken him with his pipe, give him great thumps in the back by way of friendliness, and accuse him of lack-

*Crust on which garlic has been rubbed.

ing energy. My mother, though always showing a sister's indulgence to the Captain, sometimes advised him to fondle the brandy-
bottle a little less frequently. But I had no part either in these
repugnances or these reproaches, and Uncle Victor inspired me with
the purest enthusiasm. It was therefore with a feeling of pride that
I entered into the little lodging he occupied in the Rue Guénégaud.
The entire lunch, served on a small table close to the fireplace, consisted of cold meats and confectionery.

The Captain stuffed me with cakes and undiluted wine. He told
me of numberless injustices to which he had been a victim. He
complained particularly of the Bourbons; and as he neglected to
tell me who the Bourbons were, I got the idea—I can't tell how—
that the Bourbons were horse-dealers established at Waterloo. The
Captain, who never interrupted his talk except for the purpose of
pouring out wine, furthermore made charges against a number of
dirty scoundrels, blackguards, and good-for-nothings whom I did
not know anything about, but whom I hated from the bottom of
my heart. At dessert I thought I heard the Captain say my father
was a man who could be led anywhere by the nose; but I am not
quite sure that I understood him. I had a buzzing in my ears; and
it seemed to me that the table was dancing.

My uncle put on his frogged coat, took his bell-shaped hat, and
we descended to the street, which seemed to me singularly changed.
It looked to me as if I had not been in it before for ever so long
a time. Nevertheless, when we came to the Rue de Seine, the idea
of my doll suddenly returned to my mind and excited me in an extraordinary way. My head was on fire. I resolved upon a desperate
expedient. We were passing before the window. She was there, behind the glass—with her red cheeks, and her flowered petticoat,
and her long legs.

"Uncle," I said, with a great effort, "will you buy that doll for
me?"

And I waited.

"Buy a doll for a boy—*sacrebleu!*" cried my uncle, in a voice of
thunder. "Do you wish to dishonour yourself? And it is that old
Mag there that you want! Well, I must compliment you, my young
fellow! If you grow up with such tastes as that, you will never have
any pleasure in life; and your comrades will call you a precious
ninny. If you asked me for a sword or a gun, my boy, I would buy
them for you with the last silver crown of my pension. But to buy
a doll for you—by all that's holy!—to disgrace you! Never in the
world! Why, if I were ever to see you playing with a puppet rigged
out like that, Monsieur, my sister's son, I would disown you for my
nephew!"

On hearing these words, I felt my heart so wrung that nothing
but pride—a diabolic pride—kept me from crying.

My uncle, suddenly calming down, returned to his ideas about the

Bourbons; but I, still smarting under the weight of his indignation, felt an unspeakable shame. My resolve was quickly made. I promised myself never to disgrace myself—I firmly and for ever renounced that red-cheeked doll.

I felt that day, for the first time, the austere sweetness of sacrifice.

Captain, though it be true that all your life you swore like a pagan, smoked like a beadle, and drank like a bell-ringer, be your memory nevertheless honoured—not merely because you were a brave soldier, but also because you revealed to your little nephew in petticoats the sentiment of heroism! Pride and laziness had made you almost insupportable, Uncle Victor!—but a great heart used to beat under those frogs upon your coat. You always used to wear, I now remember, a rose in your button-hole. That rose which you offered so readily to the shop-girls—that large, open-hearted flower, scattering its petals to all the winds, was the symbol of your glorious youth. You despised neither wine nor tobacco; but you despised life. Neither delicacy nor common sense could have been learned from you, Captain; but you taught me, even at an age when my nurse had to wipe my nose, a lesson of honour and self-abnegation that I shall never forget.

You have now been sleeping for many years in the Cemetery of Mont-Parnasse, under a plain slab bearing this epitaph:

CI–GIT

ARISTIDE VICTOR MALDENT,

CAPITAINE D'INFANTERIE,
CHEVALIER DE LA LEGION D'HONNEUR.

But such, Captain, was not the inscription devised by yourself to be placed above those old bones of yours—knocked about so long on fields of battle and in haunts of pleasure. Among your papers was found this proud and bitter epitaph, which, despite your last will, none could have ventured to put upon your tomb:

CI–GIT

UN BRIGAND DE LA LOIRE.

"Thérèse, we will get a wreath of immortelles to-morrow, and lay them on the tomb of the 'Brigand of the Loire.'" . . .

But Thérèse is not here. And how, indeed, could she be near me, seeing that I am at the *rondpoint* of the Champs-Élysées? There, at the termination of the avenue, the Arc de Triomphe, which bears under its vaults the names of Uncle Victor's companions-in-arms, opens its giant gate against the sky. The trees of the avenue are unfolding to the sun of spring their first leaves, still all pale and chilly. Beside me the carriages keep rolling by to the Bois de Boulogne. Unconsciously I have wandered into this fashionable avenue on my promenade, and halted, quite stupidly, in front of a booth stocked with gingerbread and decanters of liquorice-water, each topped by a lemon. A miserable little boy, covered with rags, which expose his chapped skin, stares with widely opened eyes at those sumptuous sweets which are not for such as he. With the shamelessness of innocence he betrays his longing. His round, fixed eyes contemplate a certain gingerbread man of lofty stature. It is a general, and it looks a little like Uncle Victor. I take it, I pay for it, and present it to the little pauper, who dares not extend his hand to receive it—for, by reason of precocious experience, he cannot believe in luck; he looks at me, in the same way that certain big dogs do, with the air of one saying, "You are cruel to make fun of me like that!"

"Come, little stupid," I say to him, in that rough tone I am accustomed to use, "take it—take it, and eat it; for you, happier than I was at your age, you can satisfy your tastes without disgracing yourself." . . . And you, Uncle Victor—you, whose manly figure has been recalled to me by that gingerbread general, come, glorious Shadow, help me to forget my new doll. We remain for ever children, and are always running after new toys.

Same day.

IN the oddest way that Coccoz family has become associated in my mind with the Clerk Alexander.

"Thérèse," I said, as I threw myself into my easy-chair, "tell me if the little Coccoz is well, and whether he has got his first teeth yet—and bring me my slippers."

"He ought to have them by this time, Monsieur," replied Thérèse; "but I never saw them. The very first fine day of spring the mother disappeared with the child, leaving furniture and clothes and everything behind her. They found thirty-eight empty pomade-pots in the attic. It passes all belief! She had visitors latterly; and you may be quite sure she is not now in a convent of nuns. The niece of the concierge says she saw her driving about in a carriage on the boulevards. I always told you she would end badly."

"Thérèse," I replied, "that young woman has not ended either badly or well as yet. Wait until the term of her life is over before you judge her. And be careful not to talk too much with that concierge. It seemed to me—though I only saw her for a moment on the stairs—that Madame Coccoz was very fond of her child. For that mother's love at least, she deserves credit."

"As far as that goes, Monsieur, certainly the little one never wanted for anything. In all the Quarter one could not have found a child better kept, or better nourished, or more petted and coddled.

Every day that God makes she puts a clean bib on him, and sings to him to make him laugh from morning till night."

"Thérèse, a poet has said, 'That child whose mother has never smiled upon him is worthy neither of the table of the gods nor of the couch of the goddesses.' "

July 8, 1852.

HAVING been informed that the Chapel of the Virgin at Saint-Germain-des-Prés was being repaved, I entered the church with the hope of discovering some old inscriptions, possibly exposed by the labours of the workmen. I was not disappointed. The architect kindly showed me a stone which he had just had raised up against the wall. I knelt down to look at the inscription engraved upon that stone; and then, half aloud, I read in the shadow of the old apsis these words, which made my heart leap:

"Cy-gist Alexandre, moyne de ceste église, qui fist mettre en argent le menton de Saint-Vincent et de Saint-Amant et le pié des Innocens; qui toujours en son vivant fut preud'homme et vayllant. Priez pour l'âme de lui."

I wiped gently away with my handkerchief the dust covering that gravestone; I could have kissed it.

"It is he! it is Alexander!" I cried out; and from the height of the vaults the name fell back upon me with a clang, as if broken.

The silent severity of the beadle, whom I saw advancing towards me, made me ashamed of my enthusiasm; and I fled between the two holy-water sprinklers with which two rival *"rats d'église"* seemed desirous of barring my way.

At all events it was certainly my own Alexander! there could be no more doubt possible; the translator of the "Golden Legend," the author of the lives of Saints Germain, Vincent, Ferréol, Ferrution, and Droctoveus was, just as I had supposed, a monk of Saint-Germain-des-Prés. And what a monk, too—pious and generous! He had a silver chin, a silver head, and a silver foot made, that certain precious remains should be covered with an incorruptible envelope! But shall I never be able to view his handiwork? or is this new discovery only destined to increase my regrets?

August 20, 1859.

"I, that please some, try all; both joy and terror
Of good and bad; that make and unfold error—
Now take upon me, in the name of Time
To use my wings. Impute it not a crime
To me or my swift passage, that I slide
O'er years."

Who speaks thus? 'Tis an old man whom I know too well. It is Time.

Shakespeare, after having terminated the third act of the "Winter's Tale," pauses in order to leave time for little Perdita to grow up in wisdom and in beauty; and when he raises the curtain again he evokes the ancient Scythe-bearer upon the stage to render account to the audience of those many long days which have weighed down upon the head of the jealous Leontes.

Like Shakespeare in his play, I have left in this diary of mine a long interval to oblivion; and after the fashion of the poet, I make Time himself intervene to explain the omission of ten whole years. Ten whole years, indeed, have passed since I wrote one single line in this diary; and now that I take up the pen again, I have not the pleasure, alas! to describe a Perdita "now grown in grace." Youth and beauty are the faithful companions of poets; but those charming phantoms scarcely visit the rest of us, even for the space of a season. We do not know how to retain them with us. If the fair shade of some Perdita should ever, through some inconceivable whim, take a notion to traverse my brain, she would hurt herself horribly against heaps of dog-eared parchments. Happy the poets!—their white hairs never scare away the hovering shades of Helens, Francescas, Juliets, Julias, and Dorotheas! But the nose alone of Sylvestre Bonnard would put to flight the whole swarm of love's heroines.

Yet I, like others, have felt beauty; I have known that mysterious charm which Nature has lent to animate form; and the clay which lives has given to me that shudder of delight which makes the lover and the poet. But I have never known either how to love or how to sing. Now, in my memory—all encumbered as it is with the rubbish of old texts—I can discern again, like a miniature forgotten in some attic, a certain bright young face, with violet eyes. . . . Why, Bonnard, my friend, what an old fool you are becoming! Read that catalogue which a Florentine bookseller sent you this very morning. It is a catalogue of Manuscripts; and he promises you a description of several famous ones, long preserved by the collectors of Italy and Sicily. There is something better suited to you, something more in keeping with your present appearance.

I read; I cry out! Hamilcar, who has assumed with the approach of age an air of gravity that intimidates me, looks at me reproachfully, and seems to ask me whether there is any rest in this world, since he cannot enjoy it beside me, who am old also like himself.

In the sudden joy of my discovery, I need a confidant; and it is to the sceptic Hamilcar that I address myself with all the effusion of a happy man.

"No, Hamilcar! no," I said to him; "there is no rest in this world, and the quietude you long for is incompatible with the duties of life. And you say that we are old, indeed! Listen to what I read in this catalogue, and then tell me whether this is a time to be reposing:

" *'LA LÉGENDE DORÉE DE JACQUES DE VORAGINE;—traduction française du quatorzième siècle, par le Clerc Alexandre.*

" 'Superb MS., ornamented with two miniatures, wonderfully executed, and in a perfect state of preservation:—one representing the Purification of the Virgin; the other the Coronation of Proserpine.

" 'At the termination of the "Légende Dorée" are the Legends of Saints Ferréol, Ferrution, Germain, and Droctoveus (xxviij pp.) and the Miraculous Sepulture of Monsieur Saint-Germain d'Auxerre (xij pp.).

" 'This rare manscript, which formed part of the collection of Sir Thomas Raleigh, is now in the private study of Signor Michel-Angelo Polizzi, of Girgenti.'

"You hear that, Hamilcar? The manuscript of the Clerk Alexander is in Sicily, at the house of Michel-Angelo Polizzi. Heaven grant he may be a friend of learned men! I am going to write to him!"

Which I did forthwith. In my letter I requested Signor Polizzi to allow me to examine the manuscript of Clerk Alexander, stating on what grounds I ventured to consider myself worthy of so great a favour. I offered at the same time to put at his disposal several unpublished texts in my own possession, not devoid of interest. I begged him to favour me with a prompt reply, and below my signature I wrote down all my honorary titles.

"Monsieur! Monsieur! where are you running like that?" cried Thérèse, quite alarmed, coming down the stairs in pursuit of me, four steps at a time, with my hat in her hand.

"I am going to post a letter, Thérèse."

"Good God! is that a way to run out in the street, bareheaded, like a crazy man?"

"I am crazy, I know, Thérèse. But who is not? Give me my hat, quick!"

"And your gloves, Monsieur! and your umbrella!"

I had reached the bottom of the stairs, but still heard her protesting and lamenting.

October 10, 1859.

I AWAITED Signor Polizzi's reply with ill-contained impatience. I could not even remain quiet; I would make sudden nervous gestures—open books and violently close them again. One day I happened to upset a book with my elbow—a volume of Moréri. Hamilcar, who was washing himself, suddenly stopped, and looked angrily at me, with his paw over his ear. Was this the tumultuous existence he must expect under my roof? Had there not been a tacit understanding between us that we should live a peaceful life? I had broken the covenant.

"My poor dear comrade," I made answer, "I am the victim of a violent passion, which agitates and masters me. The passions are enemies of peace and quiet, I acknowledge; but without them there would be no arts or industries in the world. Everybody would sleep naked on a dung-heap; and you would not be able, Hamilcar, to repose all day on a silken cushion, in the City of Books."

I expatiated no further to Hamilcar on the theory of the passions, however, because my housekeeper brought me a letter. It bore the postmark of Naples, and read as follows:

"MOST ILLUSTRIOUS SIR,—I do indeed possess that incomparable manuscript of the 'Golden Legend' which could not escape your keen observation. All-important reasons, however, forbid me, imperiously, tyrannically, to let the manuscript go out of my possession for a single day, for even a single minute. It will be a joy and pride for me to have you examine it in my humble home at Girgenti, which will be embellished and illuminated by your presence. It is with the most anxious expectation of your visit that I presume to sign myself, Seigneur Academician,
            "Your humble and devoted servant
                        "MICHEL-ANGELO POLIZZI,
        "Wine-merchant and Archæologist at Girgenti, Sicily."

Well, then! I will go to Sicily:

"Extremum hunc, Arethusa, mihi concede laborem."

October 25, 1859.

MY resolve had been taken and my preparations made; it only remained for me to notify my housekeeper. I must acknowledge it was a long time before I could make up my mind to tell her I was going away. I feared her remonstrances, her railleries, her objurgations, her tears. "She is a good, kind girl," I said to myself; "she is attached to me; she will want to prevent me from going; and the Lord knows that when she has her mind set upon anything, gestures and cries cost her no effort. In this instance she will be sure to call the concierge, the scrubber, the mattress-maker, and the seven sons of the fruit-seller; they will all kneel down in a circle around me; they will begin to cry, and then they will look so ugly that I shall be obliged to yield, so as not to have the pain of seeing them any more."

Such were the awful images, the sick dreams, which fear marshalled before my imagination. Yes, fear—"fecund Fear," as the poet says—gave birth to these monstrosities in my brain. For—I may as well make the confession in these private pages—I am afraid of my housekeeper. I am aware that she knows I am weak; and this fact alone is sufficient to dispel all my courage in any contest with her. Contests are of frequent occurrence; and I invariably succumb.

But for all that, I had to announce my departure to Thérèse. She came into the library with an armful of wood to make a little fire— *"une flambé,"* she said. For the mornings are chilly. I watched her out of the corner of my eye while she crouched down at the hearth, with her head in the opening of the fireplace. I do not know how I then found the courage to speak, but I did so without much hesitation. I got up, and, walking up and down the room, observed in a

careless tone, with that swaggering manner characteristic of cowards,

"By the way, Thérèse, I am going to Sicily."

Having thus spoken, I awaited the consequence with great anxiety. Thérèse did not reply. Her head and her vast cap remained buried in the fireplace; and nothing in her person, which I closely watched, betrayed the least emotion. She poked some paper under the wood, and blew up the fire. That was all!

Finally I saw her face again;—it was calm—so calm that it made me vexed. "Surely," I thought to myself, "this old maid has no heart. She lets me go away without saying so much as 'Ah!' Can the absence of her old master really affect her so little?"

"Well, then go, Monsieur," she answered at last, "only be back here by six o'clock! There is a dish for dinner to-day which will not wait for anybody."

Naples, November 10, 1859.

"Co tra calle vive, magna, e lave a faccia."

I understand, my friend—for three centimes I can eat, drink, and wash my face, all by means of one of those slices of watermelon you display there on a little table. But Occidental prejudices would prevent me from enjoying that simple pleasure freely and frankly. And how could I suck a watermelon? I have enough to do merely to keep on my feet in this crowd. What a luminous, noisy night in the Strada di Porto! Mountains of fruit tower up in the shops, illuminated by multicoloured lanterns. Upon charcoal furnaces lighted in the open air water boils and streams, and ragouts are singing in frying-pans. The smell of fried fish and hot meats tickles my nose and makes me sneeze. At this moment I find that my handkerchief has left the pocket of my frock-coat. I am pushed, lifted up, and turned about in every direction by the gayest, the most talkative, the most animated and the most adroit populace possible to imagine; and suddenly a young woman of the people, while I am admiring her magnificent hair, with a single shock of her powerful elastic shoulder, pushes me staggering three paces back at least, without injury, into the arms of a maccaroni-eater, who receives me with a smile.

I am in Naples. How I ever managed to arrive here, with a few mutilated and shapeless remains of baggage, I cannot tell, because I am no longer myself. I have been travelling in a condition of perpetual fright; and I think that I must have looked awhile ago in this bright city like an owl bewildered by sunshine. To-night it is much worse! Wishing to obtain a glimpse of popular manners, I went to the Strada di Porto, where I now am. All about me animated throngs of people crowd and press before the eating-places; and I float like a waif among these living surges, which, even while they submerge you, still caress. For this Neapolitan people has, in its very vivacity, something indescribably gentle and polite. I am not roughly jostled, I am merely swayed about; and I think that by dint of thus rocking me to and fro, these good folks want to lull me asleep on my feet. I admire, as I tread the lava pavements by the *strada*, those porters and fishermen who move by me chatting, singing, smoking, gesticulating, quarrelling, and embracing each other the next moment with astonishing versatility of mood. They live through all their senses at the same time; and, being philosophers without knowing it, keep the measure of their desires in accordance with the brevity of life. I approach a much-patronised tavern, and see inscribed above the entrance this quatrain in Neapolitan patois:

> *"Amice, alliegre magnammo e bevimmo*
> *Nfin che n'ce stace noglio a la lucerna:*
> *Chi sa s'a l'autro munno n'ce vedimmo?*
> *Chi sa s'a l'autro munno n'ce taverna?"**

Even such counsels was Horace wont to give to his friends. You received them, Posthumus; you heard them also, Leuconoë, perverse beauty who wished to know the secrets of the future. That future is now the past, and we know it well. Of a truth you were foolish to worry yourselves about so small a matter; and your friend showed his good sense when he told you to take life wisely and to filter your Greek wines—*"Sapias, vina liques."* Even thus the sight of a fair land under a spotless sky urges to the pursuit of quiet pleasures. But there are souls for ever harassed by some sublime discontent; those are the noblest. You were of such, Leuconoë; and I, visiting for the first time, in my declining years, that city where your beauty was famed of old, I salute with deep respect your melancholy memory. Those souls of kin to your own who appeared in the age of Christianity were souls of saints; and the "Golden Legend" is full of the miracles they wrought. Your friend Horace left a less noble posterity, and I see one of his descendants in the person of that tavern poet, who at this moment is serving out wine in cups under the epicurean motto of his sign.

And yet life decides in favour of friend Flaccus, and his philosophy is the only one which adapts itself to the course of events. There is a fellow leaning against that trellis-work covered with vine-leaves, and eating an ice, while watching the stars. He would not stoop even to pick up the old manuscript I am going to seek with so much trouble and fatigue. And in truth man is made rather to eat ices than to pore over old texts.

I continued to wander about among the drinkers and the singers. There were lovers biting into beautiful fruit, each with an arm about the other's waist. Man must be naturally bad; for all this strange joy only evoked in me a feeling of uttermost despondency. That thronging populace displayed such artless delight in the simple act of living, that all the shynesses begotten by my old habits as an author awoke and intensified into something like fright. Furthermore, I found myself much discouraged by my inability to understand a word of all the storm of chatter about me. It was a humiliating experience for a philologist. Thus I had begun to feel quite sulky, when I was startled to hear some one just behind me observe:

"Dimitri, that old man is certainly a Frenchman. He looks so bewildered that I really feel sorry for him. Shall I speak to him?

---

*"Friends, let us merrily eat and drink as long as oil remains in the lamp. Who knows if we shall meet again in the other world? Who knows if in the other world there be a tavern?"

. . . He has such a good-natured look, with that round back of his
—do you not think so, Dimitri?"

It was said in French by a woman's voice. For the moment it
was disagreeable to hear myself spoken of as an old man. Is a man
old at sixty-two? Only the other day, on the Pont des Arts, my
colleague Perrot d'Avrignac complimented me on my youthful appearance; and I should think him a better authority about one's
age than that young chatterbox who has taken it on herself to
make remarks about my back. My back is round, she says. Ah! ah!
I had some suspicion myself to that effect, but I am not going now
to believe it at all, since it is the opinion of a giddy-headed young
woman. Certainly I will not turn my head round to see who it was
that spoke; but I am sure it was a pretty woman. Why? Because
she talks like a capricious person and like a spoiled child. Ugly
women may be naturally quite as capricious as pretty ones; but as
they are never petted and spoiled, and as no allowances are made
for them, they soon find themselves obliged either to suppress their
whims or to hide them. On the other hand, the pretty women can
be just as fantastical as they please. My neighbour is evidently one
of the latter. . . . But, after all, coming to think it over, she really
did nothing worse than to express, in her own way, a kindly
thought about me, for which I ought to feel grateful.

These reflections—including the last and decisive one—passed
through my mind in less than a second; and if I have taken a whole
minute to tell them, it is only because I am a bad writer, which
failing is characteristic of most philologists. In less than a second,
therefore, after the voice had ceased, I did turn round, and saw a
pretty little woman—a sprightly brunette.

"Madame," I said, with a bow, "excuse my involuntary indiscretion. I could not help overhearing what you have just said. You
would like to be of service to a poor old man. And the wish, Madame, has already been fulfilled—the mere sound of a French voice
has given me such pleasure that I must thank you."

I bowed again, and turned to go away; but my foot slipped upon
a melon-rind, and I should certainly have embraced the Partheno-
pean soil had not the young lady put out her hand and caught me.

There is a force in circumstances—even in the very smallest circumstances—against which resistance is vain. I resigned myself to
remain the *protégé* of the fair unknown.

"It is late," she said; "do you not wish to go back to your hotel,
which must be quite close to ours—unless it be the same one?"

"Madame," I replied, "I do not know what time it is, because
somebody has stolen my watch; but I think, as you say, that it
must be time to retire; and I shall be very glad to regain my hotel
in the company of such courteous compatriots."

So saying, I bowed once more to the young lady, and also saluted her companion, a silent colossus with a gentle and melancholy face.

After having gone a little way with them, I learned, among other matters, that my new acquaintances were the Prince and Princess Trépof, and that they were making a trip round the world for the purpose of finding match-boxes, of which they were making a collection.

We proceeded along a narrow, tortuous *vicoletto*, lighted only by a single lamp burning in the niche of a Madonna. The purity and transparency of the air gave a celestial softness and clearness to the very darkness itself; and one could find one's way without difficulty under such a limpid night. But in a little while we began to pass through a "venella," or, in Neapolitan parlance, a *sottoportico*, which led under so many archways and so many far-projecting balconies that no gleam of light from the sky could reach us. My young guide had made us take this route as a short cut, she assured us; but I think she did so quite as much simply in order to show that she felt at home in Naples, and knew the city thoroughly. Indeed, she needed to know it very thoroughly to venture by night into that labyrinth of subterranean alleys and flights of steps. If ever any man showed absolute docility in allowing himself to be guided, that man was myself. Dante never followed the steps of Beatrice with more confidence than I felt in following those of Princess Trépof.

The lady appeared to find some pleasure in my conversation, for she invited me to take a carriage-drive with her on the morrow to visit the grotto of Posilippo and the tomb of Virgil. She declared she had seen me somewhere before; but she could not remember if it had been at Stockholm or at Canton. In the former event I was a very celebrated professor of geology; in the latter, a provision-merchant whose courtesy and kindness had been much appreciated. One thing certain was that she had seen my back somewhere before.

"Excuse me," she added; "we are continually travelling, my husband and I, to collect match-boxes and to change our *ennui* by changing country. Perhaps it would be more reasonable to content ourselves with a single variety of *ennui*. But we have made all our preparations and arrangements for travelling: all our plans have been laid out in advance, and it gives us no trouble, whereas it would be very troublesome for us to stop anywhere in particular. I tell you all this so that you may not be surprised if my recollections have become a little mixed up. But from the moment I first saw you at a distance this evening, I felt—in fact I knew—that I had seen you before. Now the question is, 'Where was it that I saw you?' You are not, then, either the geologist or the provision-merchant?"

"No, Madame," I replied, "I am neither the one nor the other;

and I am sorry for it—since you have had reason to esteem them. There is really nothing about me worthy of your interest. I have spent all my life poring over books, and I have never travelled: you might have known that from my bewilderment, which excited your compassion. I am a member of the Institute."

"You are a member of the Institute! How nice! Will you not write something for me in my album? Do you know Chinese? I would like so much to have you write something in Chinese or Persian in my album. I will introduce you to my friend, Miss Fergusson, who travels everywhere to see all the famous people in the world. She will be delighted. . . . Dimitri, did you hear that?— this gentleman is a member of the Institute, and he has passed all his life over books."

The prince nodded approval.

"Monsieur," I said, trying to engage him in our conversation, "it is true that something can be learned from books; but a great deal more can be learned by travelling, and I regret that I have not been able to go round the world like you. I have lived in the same house for thirty years and I scarcely ever go out."

"Lived in the same house for thirty years!" cried Madame Trépof; "is it possible?"

"Yes, Madame," I answered. "But you must know the house is situated on the bank of the Seine, and in the very handsomest and most famous part of the world. From my window I can see the Tuileries and the Louvre, the Pont-Neuf, the towers of Notre-Dame, the turrets of the Palais de Justice, and the spire of the Sainte-Chapelle. All those stones speak to me; they tell me stories about the days of Saint-Louis, of the Valois, of Henri IV., and of Louis XIV. I understand them, and I love them all. It is only a very small corner of the world, but honestly, Madame, where is there a more glorious spot?"

At this moment we found ourselves upon a public square—a *largo* steeped in the soft glow of the night. Madame Trépof looked at me in an uneasy manner; her lifted eyebrows almost touched the black curls about her forehead.

"Where do you live, then?" she demanded brusquely.

"On the Quai Malaquais, Madame, and my name is Bonnard. It is not a name very widely known, but I am contented if my friends do not forget it."

This revelation, unimportant as it was, produced an extraordinary effect upon Madame Trépof. She immediately turned her back upon me and caught her husband's arm.

"Come, Dimitri!" she exclaimed, "do walk a little faster. I am horribly tired, and you will not hurry yourself in the least. We shall never get home. . . . As for you, monsieur, your way lies over there!"

She made a vague gesture in the direction of some dark *vicolo,* pushed her husband the opposite way, and called to me, without even turning her head.

"Adieu, Monsieur! We shall not go to Posilippo to-morrow, nor the day after, either. I have a frightful headache! . . . Dimitri, you are unendurable! Will you not walk faster?"

I remained for the moment stupefied, vainly trying to think what I could have done to offend Madame Trépof. I had also lost my way, and seemed doomed to wander about all night. In order to ask my way, I would have to see somebody; and it did not seem likely that I should find a single human being who could understand me. In my despair I entered a street at random—a street, or rather a horrible alley that had the look of a murderous place. It proved so in fact, for I had not been two minutes in it before I saw two men fighting with knives. They were attacking each other even more fiercely with their tongues than with their weapons; and I concluded from the nature of the abuse they were showering upon each other that it was a love affair. I prudently made my way into a side alley while those two good fellows were still much too busy with their own affairs to think about mine. I wandered hopelessly about for a while, and at last sat down, completely discouraged, on a stone bench, inwardly cursing the strange caprices of Madame Trépof.

"How are you, Signor? Are you back from San Carlo? Did you hear the diva sing? It is only at Naples you can hear singing like hers."

I looked up, and recognised my host. I had seated myself with my back to the façade of my hotel, under the window of my own room.

Monte-Allegro, November 30, 1859.

WE were all resting—myself, my guides, and their mules—on the road from Sciacca to Girgenti, at a tavern in the miserable village of Monte-Allegro, whose inhabitants, consumed by the *mal' aria,* continually shiver in the sun. But nevertheless they are Greeks, and their gaiety triumphs over all circumstances. A few gather about the tavern, full of smiling curiosity. One good story would have sufficed, had I known how to tell it to them, to make them forget all the woes of life. They had all a look of intelligence! and their women, although tanned and faded, wore their long black cloaks with much grace.

Before me I could see old ruins whitened by the sea-wind—ruins about which no grass ever grows. The dismal melancholy of deserts prevails over this arid land, whose cracked surface can barely nourish a few shrivelled mimosas, cacti, and dwarf palms. Twenty yards away, along the course of a ravine, stones were gleaming whitely like a long line of scattered bones. They told me that was the bed of a stream.

I had been about fifteen days in Sicily. On coming into the Bay
of Palermo—which opens between the two mighty naked masses of
the Pelligrino and the Catalfano, and extends inward along the
"Golden Conch"—the view inspired me with such admiration that
I resolved to travel a little in this island, so ennobled by historic
memories, and rendered so beautiful by the outlines of its hills,
which reveal the principles of Greek art. Old pilgrim though I was,
grown hoary in the Gothic Occident—I dared to venture upon that
classic soil; and, securing a guide, I went from Palermo to Trapani,
from Trapani to Selinonte, from Selinonte to Sciacca—which I left
this morning to go to Girgenti, where I am to find the MS. of Clerk
Alexander. The beautiful things I have seen are still so vivid in my
mind that I feel the task of writing them would be a useless
fatigue. Why spoil my pleasure-trip by collecting notes? Lovers
who love truly do not write down their happiness.

Wholly absorbed by the melancholy of the present and the poetry
of the past, my thoughts peopled with beautiful shapes, and my
eyes ever gratified by the pure and harmonious lines of the landscape, I was resting in the tavern at Monte-Allegro, sipping a glass
of heavy, fiery wine, when I saw two persons enter the waiting-
room, whom, after a moment's hesitation, I recognised as the Prince
and Princess Trépof.

This time I saw the princess in the light—and what a light! He
who has known that of Sicily can better comprehend the words of
Sophocles: *"Oh holy light! . . . Eye of the Golden Day!"* Madame
Trépof, dressed in brown-holland and wearing a broad-brimmed
straw hat, appeared to me a very pretty woman of about twenty-
eight. Her eyes were luminous as a child's; but her slightly plump
chin indicated the age of plenitude. She is, I must confess it, quite
an attractive person. She is supple and changeful; her mood is like
water itself—and, thank Heaven! I am no navigator. I thought I
discerned in her manner a sort of ill-humour, which I attributed
presently, by reason of some observations she uttered at random, to
the fact that she had met no brigands upon her route.

"Such things only happen to us!" she exclaimed, with a gesture
of discouragement.

She called for a glass of iced water, which the landlord presented
to her with a gesture that recalled to me those scenes of funeral
offerings painted upon Greek vases.

I was in no hurry to introduce myself to a lady who had so
abruptly dropped my acquaintance in the public square at Naples;
but she perceived me in my corner, and her frown notified me very
plainly that our accidental meeting was disagreeable to her.

After she had sipped her ice-water for a few moments—whether
because her whim had suddenly changed, or because my loneliness
aroused her pity, I did not know—she walked directly to me.

"Good-day, Monsieur Bonnard," she said. "How do you do? What strange chance enables us to meet again in this frightful country?"

"This country is not frightful, Madame," I replied. "Beauty is so great and so august a quality that centuries of barbarism cannot efface it so completely that adorable vestiges of it will not always remain. The majesty of the antique Ceres still overshadows these arid valleys; and that Greek Muse who made Arethusa and Mænalus ring with her divine accents, still sings for my ears upon the barren mountain and in the place of the dried-up spring. Yes, Madame, when our globe, no longer inhabited, shall, like the moon, roll a wan corpse through space, the soil which bears the ruins of Selinonte will still keep the seal of beauty in the midst of universal death; and then, then, at least there will be no frivolous mouth to blaspheme the grandeur of these solitudes."

I knew well enough that my words were beyond the comprehension of the pretty little empty-head which heard them. But an old fellow like myself who has worn out his life over books does not know how to adapt his tone to circumstances. Besides, I wished to give Madame Trépof a lesson in politeness. She received it with so much submission, and with such an air of comprehension, that I hastened to add, as good-naturedly as possible,

"As to whether the chance which has enabled me to meet you again be lucky or unlucky, I cannot decide the question until I am sure that my presence be not disagreeable to you. You appeared to become weary of my company very suddenly at Naples the other day. I can only attribute that misfortune to my naturally unpleasant manner—since, on that occasion, I had had the honour of meeting you for the first time in my life."

These words seemed to cause her inexplicable joy. She smiled upon me in the most gracious, mischievous way, and said very earnestly, holding out her hand, which I touched with my lips,

"Monsieur Bonnard, do not refuse to accept a seat in my carriage. You can chat with me on the way about antiquity, and that will amuse me ever so much."

"My dear," exclaimed the prince, "you can do just as you please; but you ought to remember that one is horribly cramped in that carriage of yours; and I fear you are only offering Monsieur Bonnard the chance of getting a frightful attack of lumbago."

Madame Trépof simply shook her head by way of explaining that such considerations had no weight with her whatever; then she untied her hat. The darkness of her black curls descended over her eyes, and bathed them in velvety shadow. She remained a little while quite motionless, and her face assumed a surprising expression of reverie. But all of a sudden she darted at some oranges which the tavern-keeper had brought in a basket, and began to throw them, one by one, into a fold of her dress.

"These will be nice on the road," she said. "We are going just where you are going—to Girgenti. I must tell you all about it. You know that my husband is making a collection of match-boxes. We bought thirteen hundred match-boxes at Marseilles. But we heard there was a factory of them at Girgenti. According to what we were told, it is a very small factory, and its products—which are very ugly—never go outside the city and its suburbs. So we are going to Girgenti just to buy match-boxes. Dimitri has been a collector of all sorts of things; but the only kind of collection which can now interest him is a collection of match-boxes. He has already got five thousand two hundred and fourteen different kinds. Some of them gave us frightful trouble to find. For instance, we knew that at Naples boxes were once made with the portraits of Mazzini and Garibaldi on them; and that the police had seized the plates from which the portraits were printed, and put the manufacturer in gaol. Well, by dint of searching and inquiring for ever so long a while, we found one of those boxes at last for sale at one hundred francs, instead of two sous. It was not really too dear at that price; but we were denounced for buying it. We were taken for conspirators. All our baggage was searched; they could not find the box, because I had hidden it so well; but they found my jewels, and carried them off. They have them still. The incident made quite a sensation, and we were going to get arrested. But the king was displeased about it, and he ordered them to leave us alone. Up to that time, I used to think it was very stupid to collect match-boxes; but when I found that there were risks of losing liberty, and perhaps even life, by doing it, I began to feel a taste for it. Now I am an absolute fanatic on the subject. We are going to Sweden next summer to complete our series. . . . Are we not, Dimitri?"

I felt—must I confess it?—a thorough sympathy with these intrepid collectors. No doubt I would rather have found Monsieur and Madame Trépof engaged in collecting antique marbles or painted vases in Sicily. I should have liked to have found them interested in the ruins of Syracuse, or the poetical traditions of the Eryx. But at all events, they were making some sort of a collection—they belonged to the great confraternity—and I could not possibly make fun of them without making fun of myself. Besides, Madame Trépof had spoken of her collection with such an odd mingling of irony and enthusiasm that I could not help finding the idea a very good one.

We were getting ready to leave the tavern, when we noticed some people coming downstairs from the upper room, carrying carbines under their dark cloaks. To me they had the look of thorough bandits; and after they were gone I told Monsier Trépof my opinion of them. He answered me, very quietly, that he also thought they were regular bandits; and the guides begged us to apply for an escort of gendarmes, but Madame Trépof besought us not to do anything of the kind. She declared that we must not "spoil her journey."

Then, turning her persuasive eyes upon me, she asked,

"Do you not believe, Monsieur Bonnard, that there is nothing in life worth having except sensations?"

"Why, certainly, Madame," I answered; "but then we must take into consideration the nature of the sensations themselves. Those which a noble memory or a grand spectacle creates within us certainly represent what is best in human life; but those merely resulting from the menace of danger seem to me sensations which one should be very careful to avoid as much as possible. For example, would you think it a very pleasant thing, Madame, while travelling over the mountains at midnight, to find the muzzle of a carbine suddenly pressed against your forehead?"

"Oh, no!" she replied; "the comic-operas have made carbines absolutely ridiculous, and it would be a great misfortune to any young woman to find herself in danger from an absurd weapon. But it would be quite different with a knife—a very cold and very bright knife blade, which makes a cold shudder go right through one's heart."

She shuddered even as she spoke; closed her eyes, and threw her head back. Then she resumed:

"People like you are so happy! You can interest yourselves in all sorts of things!"

She gave a sidelong look at her husband, who was talking with the innkeeper. Then she leaned towards me, and murmured very low:

"You see, Dimitri and I, we are both suffering from *ennui!* We have still the match-boxes. But at last one gets tired even of match-boxes. Besides, our collection will soon be complete. And then what are we going to do?"

"Oh, Madame!" I exclaimed, touched by the moral unhappiness of this pretty person, "if you only had a son, then you would know what to do. You would then learn the purpose of your life, and your thoughts would become at once more serious and yet more cheerful."

"But I have a son," she replied. "He is a big boy; he is eleven years old, and he suffers from *ennui* like the rest of us. Yes, my George has *ennui*, too; he is tired of everything. It is very wretched."

She glanced again towards her husband, who was superintending the harnessing of the mules on the road outside—testing the condition of girths and straps. Then she asked me whether there had been many changes on the Quai Malaquais during the past ten years. She declared she never visited that neighbourhood because it was too far away.

"Too far from Monte-Allegro?" I queried.

"Why, no!" she replied. "Too far from the Avenue des Champs Élysées, where we live."

And she murmured over again, as if talking to herself, "Too far! —too far!" in a tone of reverie which I could not possibly account for. All at once she smiled again, and said to me,

"I like you, Monsieur Bonnard!—I like you very, very much!"

The mules had been harnessed. The young woman hastily picked up a few oranges which had rolled off her lap; rose up; looked at me, and burst out laughing.

"Oh!" she exclaimed, "how I should like to see you grappling with the brigands! You would say such extraordinary things to them! . . . Please take my hat, and hold my umbrella for me, Monsieur Bonnard."

"What a strange little mind!" I thought to myself, as I followed her. "It could only have been in a moment of inexcusable thoughtlessness that Nature gave a child to such a giddy little woman!"

Girgenti. Same day.

HER manners had shocked me. I left her to arrange herself in her *lettica,* and I made myself as comfortable as I could in my own. These vehicles, which have no wheels, are carried by two mules— one before and one behind. This kind of litter, or chaise, is of ancient origin. I had often seen representations of similar ones in the French MSS. of the fourteenth century. I had no idea then that one of those vehicles would be at a future day placed at my own disposal. We must never be too sure of anything.

For three hours the mules sounded their little bells, and thumped the calcined ground with their hoofs. On either hand there slowly defiled by us the barren monstrous shapes of a nature totally African.

Half-way we made a halt to allow our animals to recover breath.

Madame Trépof came to me on the road, took my arm, and drew me a little away from the party. Then, very suddenly, she said to me in a tone of voice I had never heard before:

"Do not think that I am a wicked woman. My George knows that I am a good mother."

We walked side by side for a moment in silence. She looked up, and I saw that she was crying.

"Madame," I said to her, "look at this soil which has been burned and cracked by five long months of fiery heat. A little white lily has sprung up from it."

And I pointed with my cane to the frail stalk, tipped by a double blossom.

"Your heart," I said, "however arid it be, bears also its white lily; and that is reason enough why I do not believe that you are what you say—a wicked woman."

"Yes, yes, yes!" she cried, with the obstinacy of a child—"I am a wicked woman. But I am ashamed to appear so before you who are so good—so very, very good."

"You do not know anything at all about it," I said to her.

"I know it! I know all about you, Monsieur Bonnard!" she declared, with a smile.

And she jumped back into her *lettica*.

Girgenti, November 30, 1859.

I AWOKE the following morning in the House of Gellias. Gellias was a rich citizen of ancient Agrigentum. He was equally celebrated for his generosity and for his wealth; and he endowed his native city with a great number of free inns. Gellias has been dead for thirteen hundred years; and nowadays there is no gratuitous hospitality among civilised peoples. But the name of Gellias has become that of a hotel in which, by reason of fatigue, I was able to obtain one good night's sleep.

The modern Girgenti lifts its high, narrow, solid streets, dominated by a sombre Spanish cathedral, upon the site of the acropolis of the antique Agrigentum. I can see from my windows, half-way on the hillside towards the sea, the white range of temples partially destroyed. The ruins alone have some aspect of coolness. All the rest is arid. Water and life have forsaken Agrigentum. Water—the divine Nestis of the Agrigentine Empedocles—is so necessary to animated beings that nothing can live far from the rivers and the springs. But the port of Girgenti, situated at a distance of three kilometres from the city, has a great commerce. "And it is in this dismal city," I said to myself, "upon this precipitous rock, that the manuscript of Clerk Alexander is to be found!" I asked my way to the house of Signor Michel-Angelo Polizzi, and proceeded thither.

I found Signor Polizzi, dressed all in white from head to feet, busy cooking sausages in a frying-pan. At the sight of me, he let go the handle of the frying-pan, threw up his arms in the air, and uttered shrieks of enthusiasm. He was a little man whose pimply features, aquiline nose, round eyes, and projecting chin formed a very expressive physiognomy.

He called me "Excellence," said he was going to mark the day with a white stone, and made me sit down. The hall in which we were represented the union of kitchen, reception-room, bedchamber, studio, and wine-cellar. There were charcoal furnaces visible, a bed, paintings, an easel, bottles, strings of onions, and a magnificent lustre of coloured glass pendants. I glanced at the paintings on the wall.

"The arts! the arts!" cried Signor Polizzi, throwing up his arms again to heaven—"the arts! What dignity! what consolation! Excellence, I am a painter!"

And he showed me an unfinished Saint-Francis, which indeed

could very well remain unfinished for ever without any loss to religion or to art. Next he showed me some old paintings of a better style, but apparently restored after a decidedly reckless manner.

"I repair," he said—"I repair old paintings. Oh, the Old Masters! What genius, what soul!"

"Why, then," I said to him, "you must be a painter, an archæologist, and a wine-merchant all in one?"

"At your service, Excellence," he answered. "I have a *zucco* here at this very moment—a *zucco* of which every single drop is a pearl of fire. I want your Lordship to taste of it."

"I esteem the wines of Sicily," I responded, "but it was not for the sake of your flagons that I came to see you, Signor Polizzi."

He: "Then you have come to see me about paintings. You are an amateur. It is an immense delight for me to receive amateurs. I am going to show you the *chef-d'œuvre* of Monrealese; yes, Excellence, his *chef-d'œuvre!* An Adoration of Shepherds! It is the pearl of the whole Sicilian school!"

I: "Later on I will be glad to see the *chef-d'œuvre;* but let us first talk about the business which brings me here."

His little quick bright eyes watched my face curiously; and I perceived, with anguish, that he had not the least suspicion of the purpose of my visit.

A cold sweat broke out over my forehead; and in the bewilderment of my anxiety I stammered out something to this effect:

"I have come from Paris expressly to look at a manuscript of the 'Légende Dorée,' which you informed me was in your possession."

At these words he threw up his arms, opened his mouth and eyes to the widest possible extent, and betrayed every sign of extreme nervousness.

"Oh! the manuscript of the 'Golden Legend!' A pearl, Excellence! a ruby, a diamond! Two miniatures so perfect that they give one the feeling of glimpses of Paradise! What suavity! Those colours ravished from the corollas of flowers make a honey for the eyes! Even a Sicilian could have done no better!"

"Let me see it, then," I asked; unable to conceal either my anxiety or my hope.

"Let you see it!" cried Polizzi. "But how can I, Excellence? I have not got it any longer! I have not got it!"

And he seemed determined to tear out his hair. He might indeed have pulled every hair in his head out of his hide before I should have tried to prevent him. But he stopped of his own accord, before he had done himself any grievous harm.

"What!" I cried out in anger—"what! you make me come all the way from Paris to Girgenti, by promising to show me a manuscript, and now, when I come, you tell me you have not got it! It is simply infamous, Monsieur! I shall leave your conduct to be judged by all honest men!"

Anybody who could have seen me at that moment would have been able to form a good idea of the aspect of a furious sheep.

"It is infamous! it is infamous!" I repeated, waving my arms, which trembled from anger.

Then Michel-Angelo Polizzi let himself fall into a chair in the attitude of a dying hero. I saw his eyes fill with tears, and his hair —until then flamboyant and erect upon his head—fall down in limp disorder over his brow.

"I am a father, Excellence! I am a father!" he groaned, wringing his hands.

He continued, sobbing:

"My son Rafael—the son of my poor wife, for whose death I have been mourning fifteen years—Rafael, Excellence, wanted to settle at Paris; he hired a shop in the Rue Lafitte for the sale of curiosities. I gave him everything precious which I had—I gave him my finest majolicas; my most beautiful Urbino ware; my masterpieces of art; what paintings, Signor! Even now they dazzle me when I see them only in imagination! And all of them signed! Finally, I gave him the manuscript of the 'Golden Legend'! I would have given him my flesh and my blood! An only son, Signor! the son of my poor saintly wife!"

"So," I said, "while I—relying upon your written word, Monsieur —was travelling to the very heart of Sicily to find the manuscript of the Clerk Alexander, the same manuscript was actually exposed for sale in a window in the Rue Lafitte, only fifteen hundred yards from my house?"

"Yes, it was there! that is positively true!" exclaimed Signor Polizzi, suddenly growing calm again; "and it is there still—at least I hope it is, Excellence."

He took a card from a shelf as he spoke, and offered it to me, saying,

"Here is the address of my son. Make it known to your friends, and you will oblige me. Faïence and enamelled wares; hangings; pictures. He has a complete stock of objects of art—all at the fairest possible prices—and everything authentic, I can vouch for it, upon my honour! Go and see him. He will show you the manuscript of the 'Golden Legend.' Two miniatures miraculously fresh in colour!"

I was feeble enough to take the card he held out to me.

The fellow was taking further advantage of my weakness to make me circulate the name of Rafael Polizzi among the Societies of the learned!

My hand was already on the door-knob, when the Sicilian caught me by the arm; he had a look as of sudden inspiration.

"Ah! Excellence!" he cried, "what a city is this city of ours! It gave birth to Empedocles! Empedocles! What a great man what a great citizen! What audacity of thought! what virtue! what soul! At the port over there is a statue of Empedocles, before which I bare my head each time that I pass by! When Rafael, my son, was going away to found an establishment of antiquities in the Rue Lafitte, at Paris, I took him to the port, and there, at the foot of that statue of Empedocles, I bestowed upon him my paternal benediction! 'Always remember Empedocles!' I said to him. Ah! Signor, what our unhappy country needs to-day is a new Empedocles! Would you not like me to show you the way to his statue, Excellence? I will be your guide among the ruins here. I will show you the temple of Castor and Pollux, the temple of the Olympian Jupiter, the temple of the Lucinian Juno, the antique well, the tomb of Theron, and the Gate of Gold! All the professional guides are asses; but we—we shall make excavations, if you are willing—and we shall discover treasures! I know the science of discovering hidden treasures—the secret art of finding their whereabouts—a gift from Heaven!"

I succeeded in tearing myself away from his grasp. But he ran after me again, stopped me at the foot of the stairs, and said in my ear,

"Listen, Excellence. I will conduct you about the city; I will introduce you to some Girgentines! What a race! what types! what forms! Sicilian girls, Signor!—the antique beauty itself!"

"Go to the devil!" I cried at last, in anger, and rushed into the street, leaving him still writhing in the loftiness of his enthusiasm.

When I had got out of his sight, I sank down upon a stone, and began to think, with my face in my hands.

"And it was for this," I said to myself—"it was to hear such propositions as this that I came to Sicily! That Polizzi is simply a scoundrel, and his son another; and they made a plan together to ruin me." But what was their scheme? I could not unravel it. Meanwhile, it may be imagined how discouraged and humiliated I felt.

A merry burst of laughter caused me to turn my head, and I saw Madame Trépos running in advance of her husband, and holding up something which I could not distinguish clearly.

She sat down beside me, and showed me—laughing more merrily all the while—an abominable little paste-board box, on which was printed a red and blue face, which the inscription declared to be the face of Empedocles.

"Yes, Madame," I said, "but that abominable Polizzi, to whom I advise you not to send Monsieur Trépof, has made me fall out for ever with Empedocles; and this portrait is not at all of a nature to make me feel more kindly to the ancient philosopher."

"Oh!" declared Madame Trépof, "it is ugly, but it is rare! These boxes are not exported at all; you can buy them only where they are made. Dimitri has six others just like this in his pocket. We got them so as to exchange with other collectors. You understand? At nine o'clock this morning we were at the factory. You see we did not waste our time."

"So I certainly perceive, Madame," I replied, bitterly; "but I have lost mine."

I then saw that she was naturally a good-hearted woman. All her merriment vanished.

"Poor Monsieur Bonnard! poor Monsieur Bonnard!" she murmured.

And, taking my hand in hers, she added:

"Tell me about your troubles."

I told her about them. My story was long; but she was evidently touched by it, for she asked me quite a number of circumstantial questions, which I took for proof of friendly interest. She wanted to know the exact title of the manuscript, its shape, its appearance, and its age; she asked me for the address of Signor Rafael Polizzi.

And I gave it to her; thus doing (O destiny!) precisely what the abominable Polizzi had told me to do.

It is sometimes difficult to check oneself. I recommenced my plaints and my imprecations. But this time Madame Trépof only burst out laughing.

"Why do you laugh?" I asked her.

"Because I am a wicked woman," she answered.

And she fled away, leaving me all disheartened on my stone.

Paris, December 8, 1859.

MY unpacked trunks still encumbered the hall. I was seated at a table covered with all those good things which the land of France produces for the delectation of *gourmets*. I was eating a *pâte le Chartres,* which is alone sufficient to make one love one's country. Thérèse, standing before me with her hands joined over her white apron, was looking at me with benignity, with anxiety, and with pity. Hamilcar was rubbing himself against my legs, wild with delight.

These words of an old poet came back to my memory:

"Happy is he who, like Ulysses, hath made a goodly journey."

. . . "Well," I thought to myself, "I travelled to no purpose; I have come back with empty hands; but, like Ulysses, I made a goodly journey."

And having taken my last sip of coffee, I asked Thérèse for my hat and cane, which she gave me not without dire suspicions: she feared I might be going upon another journey. But I reassured her by telling her to have dinner ready at six o'clock.

It had always been a keen pleasure for me to breathe the air in those Parisian streets whose every paving-slab and every stone I

love devotedly. But I had an end in view, and I took my way straight
to the Rue Lafitte. I was not long in finding the establishment of
Signor Rafael Polizzi. It was distinguishable by a great display of
old paintings which, although all bearing the signature of some
illustrious artist, had a certain family air of resemblance that
might have suggested some touching idea about the fraternity of
genius, had it not still more forcibly suggested the professional
tricks of Polizzi senior. Enriched by these doubtful works of art,
the shop was further rendered attractive by various petty curiosities: poniards, drinking-vessels, goblets, *figulines,* brass *gaudrons,*
and Hispano-Arabian wares of metallic lustre.

Upon a Portuguese arm-chair, decorated with an escutcheon, lay
a copy of the "Heures" of Simon Vostre, open at the page which has
an astrological figure on it; and an old Vitruvius, placed upon a
quaint chest, displayed its masterly engravings of caryatides and
telamones. This apparent disorder which only masked cunning arrangement, this factitious hazard which had placed the best objects
in the most favourable light, would have increased my distrust of
the place, but that the distrust which the mere name of Polizzi had
already *inspired could not have been increased by any circum-*
stances—being already infinite.

Signor Rafael, who sat there as the presiding genius of all these
vague and incongruous shapes, impressed me as a phlegmatic young
man, with a sort of English character. He betrayed no sign whatever of those transcendent faculties displayed by his father in the
arts of mimicry and declamation.

I told him what I had come for; he opened a cabinet and drew
from it a manuscript, which he placed on a table that I might examine it at my leisure.

Never in my life did I experience such an emotion—except, indeed, during some few brief months of my youth, months whose
memories, though I should live a hundred years, would remain as
fresh at my last hour as in the first day they came to me.

It was, indeed, the very manuscript described by the librarian of
Sir Thomas Raleigh; it was, indeed, the manuscript of the Clerk
Alexander which I saw, which I touched! The work of Voragine
himself had been perceptibly abridged; but that made little difference to me. All the inestimable additions of the monk of Saint-
Germain-des-Prés were there. That was the main point! I tried to
read the Legend of Saint Droctoveus; but I could not—all the lines
of the page quivered before my eyes, and there was a sound in my
ears like the noise of a windmill in the country at night. Nevertheless, I was able to see that the manuscript offered every evidence
of indubitable authenticity. The two drawings of the Purification of
the Virgin and the Coronation of Proserpine were meagre in design
and vulgar in violence of colouring. Considerably damaged in 1824,
as attested by the catalogue of Sir Thomas, they had obtained dur-

ing the interval a new aspect of freshness. But this miracle did not surprise me at all. And, besides, what did I care about the two miniatures? The legends and the poem of Alexander—those alone formed the treasure I desired. My eyes devoured as much of it as they had the power to absorb.

I affected indifference while asking Signor Polizzi the price of the manuscript; and, while awaiting his reply, I offered up a secret prayer that the price might not exceed the amount of ready money at my disposal—already much diminished by the cost of my expensive voyage. Signor Polizzi, however, informed me that he was not at liberty to dispose of the article, inasmuch as it did not belong to him, and was to be sold at auction shortly, at the Hôtel des Ventes, with a number of other MSS. and several *incunabula*.

This was a severe blow to me. I tried to preserve my calmness, notwithstanding, and replied somewhat to this effect:

"You surprise me, Monsieur! Your father, whom I talked with recently at Girgenti, told me positively the manuscript was yours. You cannot now attempt to make me discredit your father's word."

"I *did* own the manuscript, indeed," answered Signor Rafael with absolute frankness; "but I do not own it any longer. I sold that manuscript—the remarkable interest of which you have not failed to perceive—to an amateur whom I am forbidden to name, and who, for reasons which I am not at liberty to mention, finds himself obliged to sell his collection. I am honoured with the confidence of my customer, and was commissioned by him to draw up the catalogue and manage the sale, which takes place the 24th of December. Now, if you will be kind enough to give me your address, I shall have the pleasure of sending you the catalogue, which is already in the press. You will find the 'Légende Dorée' described in it as 'No. 42.'"

I gave my address, and left the shop.

The polite gravity of the son impressed me quite as disagreeably as the impudent buffoonery of the father. I hated, from the bottom of my heart, the tricks of the vile hagglers! It was perfectly evident that the two rascals had a secret understanding, and had only devised this auction-sale, with the aid of a professional appraiser, to force the bidding on the manuscript I wanted so much up to an outrageous figure. I was completely at their mercy. There is one evil in all passionate desires, even the noblest—namely, that they leave us subject to the will of others, and in so far dependent. This reflection made me suffer cruelly; but it did not conquer my longing to own the work of Clerk Alexander. While I was thus meditating, I heard a coachman swear. And I discovered it was I whom he was swearing at only when I felt the pole of a carriage poke me in the ribs. I started aside, barely in time to save myself from being run over; and whom did I perceive through the windows of the *coupé?* Madame Trépof, being taken by two beautiful horses, and a coachman all wrapped up in furs like a Russian *boyard*, into the very street I had just left. She did not notice me; she was laughing to herself with that artless grace of expression which still preserved for her, at thirty years, all the charm of her early youth.

"Well, well!" I said to myself, "she is laughing! I suppose she must have just found another match-box."

And I made my way back to the Ponts, feeling very miserable.

Nature, eternally indifferent, neither hastened nor hurried the twenty-fourth day of December. I went to the Hôtel Bullion, and took my place in *Salle* No. 4, immediately below the high desk at which the auctioneer Boulouze and the expert Polizzi were to sit. I saw the hall gradually fill with familiar faces. I shook hands with several old booksellers of the quays; but that prudence which any large interest inspires in even the most self-assured caused me to keep silence in regard to the reason of my unaccustomed presence in the halls of the Hôtel Bullion. On the other hand, I questioned those gentlemen closely about the purpose of their attendance at the auction sale; and I had the satisfaction of finding them all interested about matters in no wise related to my affair.

Little by little the hall became thronged with interested or merely curious spectators; and, after half an hour's delay, the auctioneer with his ivory hammer, the clerk with his bundle of memorandum-papers, and the crier, carrying his collection-box fixed to the end of a pole, all took their places on the platform in the most solemn business manner. The attendants ranged themselves at the foot of the desk. The presiding officer having declared the sale open, a partial hush followed.

A commonplace series of *Preces diœ*, with miniatures, were first sold off at mediocre prices. Needless to say, the illuminations of these books were in perfect condition!

The lowness of the bids gave courage to the gathering of second-hand booksellers present, who began to mingle with us, and become familiar. The dealers in old brass and *bric-à-brac* pressed forward in their turn, waiting for the doors of an adjoining room to be opened; and the voice of the auctioneer was drowned by the jests of the *Auvergnats*.

A magnificent codex of the "Guerre des Juifs" revived attention. It was long disputed for. "Five thousand francs! five thousand!" called the crier, while the *bric-à-brac* dealers remained silent with admiration. Then seven or eight antiphonaries brought us back again to low prices. A fat old woman, in a loose gown, bareheaded —a dealer in second-hand goods—encouraged by the size of the books and the low prices bidden, had one of the antiphonaries knocked down to her for thirty francs.

At last the expert Polizzi announced No. 42: "The 'Golden Legend'; French MS.; unpublished; two superb miniatures, with a starting bid of three thousand francs."

"Three thousand! three thousand bid!" yelled the crier.

"Three thousand!" dryly repeated the auctioneer.

There was a buzzing in my head, and, as through a cloud, I saw a host of curious faces all turning towards the manuscript, which a boy was carrying open through the audience.

"Three thousand and fifty!" I said.

I was frightened by the sound of my own voice, and further confused by seeing, or thinking that I saw, all eyes turned upon me.

"Three thousand and fifty on the right!" called the crier, taking up my bid.

"Three thousand one hundred!" responded Signor Polizzi.

Then began a heroic duel between the expert and myself.

"Three thousand five hundred!"

"Six hundred!"

"Seven hundred!"

"Four thousand!"

"Four thousand five hundred."

Then, by a sudden bold stroke, Signor Polizzi raised the bid at once to six thousand.

Six thousand francs was all the money I could dispose of. It represented the possible. I risked the impossible.

"Six thousand one hundred!"

Alas! even the impossible did not suffice.

"Six thousand five hundred!" replied Signor Polizzi, with calm.

I bowed my head and sat there stupefied, unable to answer either yes or no to the crier, who called to me:

"Six thousand five hundred, by me—not by you on the right there!—it is my bid—no mistake! Six thousand five hundred!"

"Perfectly understood!" declared the auctioneer. "Six thousand five hundred. Perfectly clear; perfectly plain. . . . Any more bids? The last bid is six thousand five hundred francs."

A solemn silence prevailed. Suddenly I felt as if my head had burst open. It was the hammer of the officiant, who, with a loud blow on the platform, adjudged No. 42 irrevocably to Signor Polizzi. Forthwith the pen of the clerk, coursing over the *papier-timbré,* registered that great fact in a single line.

I was absolutely prostrated, and I felt the utmost need of rest and quiet. Nevertheless, I did not leave my seat. My powers of reflection slowly returned. Hope is tenacious. I had one more hope. It occurred to me that the new owner of the "Légende Dorée" might be some intelligent and liberal bibliophile who would allow me to examine the MS., and perhaps even to publish the more important parts. And, with this idea, as soon as the sale was over I approached the expert as he was leaving the platform.

"Monsieur," I asked him, "did you buy in No. 42 on your own account, or on commission?"

"On commission. I was instructed not to let it go at any price."

"Can you tell me the name of the purchaser?"

"Monsieur, I regret that I cannot serve you in that respect. I have been strictly forbidden to mention the name."

I went home in despair.

December 30, 1859.

"THÉRÈSE! *don't you hear the bell? Somebody has been ringing at the door for the last quarter of an hour?*"

Thérèse does not answer. She is chattering downstairs with the concierge, for sure. So that is the way you observe your old master's birthday? You desert me even on the eve of Saint-Sylvestre! Alas! if I am to hear any kind wishes to-day, they must come up from the ground; for all who love me have long been buried. I really don't know what I am still living for. There is the bell again! . . . I get up slowly from my seat at the fire, with my shoulders still bent from stooping over it, and go to the door myself. Whom do I see at the threshold? It is not a dripping love, and I am not an old Anacreon; but it is a very pretty little boy of about ten years old. He is alone; he raises his face to look at me. His cheeks are blushing; but his little pert nose gives one an idea of mischievous pleasantry. He has feathers in his cap, and a great lace-ruff on his jacket. The pretty little fellow! He holds in both arms a bundle as big as himself, and asks me if I am Monsieur Sylvestre Bonnard. I tell him yes; he gives me the bundle, tells me his mamma sent it to me, and then he runs downstairs.

I go down a few steps; I lean over the balustrade, and see the little cap whirling down the spiral of the stairway like a feather in the wind. "Good-bye, my little boy!" I should have liked so much to question him. But what, after all, could I have asked? It is not polite to question children. Besides, the package itself will probably give me more information than the messenger could.

It is a very big bundle, but not very heavy. I take it into my library, and there untie the ribbons and unfasten the paper wrappings; and I see—what? a log! a first-class log! a real Christmas log, but so light that I know it must be hollow. Then I find that it is indeed composed of two separate pieces, opening on hinges, and fastened with hooks. I slip the hooks back, and find myself inundated with violets! Violets! they pour over my table, over my knees, over the carpet. They tumble into my vest, into my sleeves. I am all perfumed with them.

"Thérèse! Thérèse! fill me some vases with water, and bring them here, quick! Here are violets sent to us I know not from what country nor by what hand; but it must be from a perfumed country, and by a very gracious hand. . . . Do you hear me, old crow?"

I have put all the violets on my table—now completely covered by the odorous mass. But there is still something in the log . . . a book—a manuscript. It is . . . I cannot believe it, and yet I cannot doubt it. . . . It is the "Légende Dorée"!—it is the manuscript of the Clerk Alexander! Here is the "Purification of the Virgin" and the "Coronation of Proserpine";—here is the legend of Saint Droctoveus. I contemplate this violet-perfumed relic. I turn the leaves of it—between which the dark rich blossoms have slipped in here and there; and, right opposite the legend of Saint-Cecilia, I find a card bearing this name:

"Princess Trépof."

Princess Trépof!—you who laughed and wept by turns so sweetly under the fair sky of Agrigentum!—you, whom a cross old man believed to be only a foolish little woman!—to-day I am convinced of your rare and beautiful folly; and the old fellow whom you now overwhelm with happiness will go to kiss your hand, and give you back, in another form, this precious manuscript, of which both he and science owe you an exact and sumptuous publication!

Thérèse entered my study just at that moment; she seemed to be very much excited.

"Monsieur!" she cried, "guess whom I saw just now in a carriage, with a coat-of-arms painted on it, that was stopping before the door?"

"Parbleu!—Madame Trépof," I exclaimed.

"I don't know anything about any Madame Trépof," answered my housekeeper. "The woman I saw just now was dressed like a duchess, and had a little boy with her, with lace-frills all along the seams of his clothes. And it was that same little Madame Coccoz you once sent a log to, when she was lying-in here about eleven years ago. I recognised her at once."

"What!" I exclaimed, "you mean to say it was Madame Coccoz, the widow of the almanac-peddler?"

"Herself, Monsieur! The carriage-door was open for a minute to let her little boy, who had just come from I don't know where, get in. She hasn't changed scarcely at all. Well, why should those women change?—they never worry themselves about anything. Only the Coccoz woman looks a little fatter than she used to be. And the idea of a woman that was taken in here out of pure charity coming to show off her velvets and diamonds in a carriage with a crest painted on it! Isn't it shameful!"

"Thérèse!" I cried, in a terrible voice, "if you ever speak to me again about that lady except in terms of the deepest respect, you and I will fall out! . . . Bring me the Sèvres vases to put those violets in, which now give the City of Books a charm it never had before."

While Thérèse went off with a sigh to get the Sèvres vases, I continued to contemplate those beautiful scattered violets, whose odour spread all about me like the perfume of some sweet presence, some charming soul; and I asked myself how it had been possible for me never to recognise Madame Coccoz in the person of the Princess Trépof. But that vision of the young widow, showing me her little child on the stairs, had been a very rapid one. I had much more reason to reproach myself for having passed by a gracious and lovely soul without knowing it.

"Bonnard," I said to myself, "thou knowest how to decipher old texts; but thou dost not know how to read in the Book of Life. That giddy little Madame Trépof, whom thou once believed to possess no more soul than a bird, has expended, in pure gratitude, more zeal and finer tact than thou didst ever show for anybody's sake. Right royally hath she repaid thee for the log-fire of her churching-day!

"Thérèse! Awhile ago you were a magpie; now you are becoming a tortoise! Come and give some water to these Parmese violets."

PART II: THE DAUGHTER OF CLÉMENTINE

I

THE FAIRY

WHEN I left the train at the Melun station, night had already spread its peace over the silent country. The soil, heated through all the long day by a strong sun—by a *"gros soleil,"* as the harvesters of the Val de Vire say—still exhaled a warm heavy smell. Lush dense odours of grass passed over the level of the fields. I brushed away the dust of the railway carriage, and joyfully inhaled the pure air. My travelling-bag—filled by my housekeeper with linen and various small toilet articles, *munditiis*, seemed so light in my hand that I swung it about just as a schoolboy swings his strapped package of rudimentary books when the class is let out.

Would to Heaven that I were again a little urchin at school! But it is fully fifty years since my good dead mother made me some *tartines* of bread and preserves, and placed them in a basket of which she slipped the handle over my arm, and then led me, thus prepared, to the school kept by Monsieur Douloir, at a corner of the Passage du Commerce well known to the sparrows, between a court and a garden. The enormous Monsieur Douloir smiled upon us genially, and patted my cheek to show, no doubt, the affectionate interest which my first appearance had inspired. But when my mother had passed out of the court, startling the sparrows as she went, Monsieur Douloir ceased to smile—he showed no more affectionate interest; he appeared, on the contrary, to consider me as a very troublesome little fellow. I discovered, later on, that he entertained the same feelings towards all his pupils. He distributed whacks of his ferule with an agility no one could have expected on the part of so corpulent a person. But his first aspect of tender interest invariably reappeared when he spoke to any of our mothers in our presence; and always at such times, while warmly praising our remarkable aptitudes, he would cast down upon us a look of intense affection. Still, those were happy days which I passed on the benches of Monsieur Douloir with my little playfellows, who, like myself, cried and laughed by turns with all their might, from morning till evening.

After a whole half-century these souvenirs float up again, fresh and bright as ever, to the surface of memory, under this starry sky, whose face has in no wise changed since then, and whose serene and immutable lights will doubtless see many other schoolboys such as I was slowly turn into grey-headed savants, afflicted with catarrh.

Stars, who have shone down upon each wise or foolish head among all my forgotten ancestors, it is under your soft light that I now feel stir within me a certain poignant regret! I would that I could have a son who might be able to see you when I shall see you no more. How I should love him! Ah! such a son would—what am I saying?—why, he would be now just twenty years old if you had only been willing, Clémentine—you whose cheeks used to look so ruddy under your pink hood! But you are married to that young bank clerk, Noël Alexandre, who made so many millions afterwards! I never met you again after your marriage, Clémentine, but I can see you now, with your bright curls and your pink hood.

A looking-glass! a looking-glass! a looking-glass! Really, it would be curious to see what I look like now, with my white hair, sighing Clémentine's name to the stars! Still, it is not right to end with sterile irony the thought begun in the spirit of faith and love. No, Clémentine, if your name came to my lips by chance this beautiful night, be it for ever blessed, your dear name! and may you ever, as a happy mother, a happy grandmother, enjoy to the very end of life with your rich husband the utmost degree of that happiness which you had the right to believe you could not win with the poor young scholar who loved you! If—though I cannot even now imagine it— if your beautiful hair has become white, Clémentine, bear worthily the bundle of keys confided to you by Noël Alexandre, and impart to your grandchildren the knowledge of all domestic virtues!

Ah! beautiful Night! She rules, with such noble repose, over men and animals alike, kindly loosed by her from the yoke of daily toil; and even I feel her beneficent influence, although my habits of sixty years have so changed me that I can feel most things only through the signs which represent them. My world is wholly formed of words—so much of a philologist I have become! Each one dreams the dream of life in his own way. I have dreamed it in my library; and when the hour shall come in which I must leave this world, may it please God to take me from my ladder—from before my shelves of books! . . .

"Well, well! it is really himself, *pardieu!* How are you, Monsieur Sylvestre Bonnard? And where have you been travelling to all this time, over the country, while I was waiting for you at the station with my cabriolet? You missed me when the train came in, and I was driving back, quite disappointed, to Lusance. Give me your valise, and get up here beside me in the carriage. Why, do you know it is fully seven kilometres from here to the château?"

Who addresses me thus, at the very top of his voice from the height of his cabriolet? Monsieur Paul de Gabry, nephew and heir of Monsieur Honoré de Gabry, peer of France in 1842, who recently died at Monaco. And it was precisely to Monsieur Paul de Gabry's house that I was going with that valise of mine, so carefully strapped by my housekeeper. This excellent young man has just inherited, conjointly with his two brothers-in-law, the property of his uncle, who, belonging to a very ancient family of distinguished lawyers, had accumulated in his château at Lusance a library rich in MSS., some dating back to the fourteenth century. It was for the purpose of making an inventory and a catalogue of these MSS. that I had come to Lusance at the urgent request of Monsieur Paul de Gabry, whose father, a perfect gentleman and distinguished bibliophile, had maintained the most pleasant relations with me during his lifetime. To tell the truth, Monsieur Paul has not inherited the fine tastes of his father. Monsieur Paul likes sporting; he is a great authority on horses and dogs; and I much fear that of all the sciences capable of satisfying or of duping the inexhaustible curiosity of mankind, those of the stable and the dog-kennel are the only ones thoroughly mastered by him.

I cannot say I was surprised to meet him, since we had made a rendezvous; but I acknowledge that I had become so preoccupied with my own thoughts that I had forgotten all about the Château de Lusance and its inhabitants, and that the voice of the gentleman calling out to me as I started to follow the country road winding away before me—"un bon ruban de queue," as they say—had given me quite a start.

I fear my face must have betrayed my incongruous distraction by a certain stupid expression which it is apt to assume in most of my social transactions. My valise was pulled up into the carriage, and I followed my valise. My host pleased me by his straightforward simplicity.

"I don't know anything myself about your old parchments," he said; "but I think you will find some folks to talk to at the house. Beside the curé, who writes books himself, and the doctor, who is a very good fellow—although a radical—you will meet somebody able to keep your company. I mean my wife. She is not a very learned woman, but there are few things which she can't divine pretty well. Then I count upon being able to keep you with us long enough to make you acquainted with Mademoiselle Jeanne, who has the fingers of a magician and the soul of an angel."

"And is this delightfully gifted young lady one of your family?" I asked.

"Not at all," replied Monsieur Paul.

"Then she is just a friend of yours?" I persisted, rather stupidly.

"She has lost both her father and mother," answered Monsieur de Gabry, keeping his eyes fixed upon the ears of his horse, whose hoofs rang loudly over the road blue-tinted by the moonshine. "Her father managed to get us into some very serious trouble; and we did not get off with a fright either!"

Then he shook his head, and changed the subject. He gave me due warning of the ruinous condition in which I should find the château and the park; they had been absolutely deserted for thirty-two years.

I learned from him that Monsieur Honoré de Gabry, his uncle, had been on very bad terms with some poachers, whom he used to shoot at like rabbits. One of them, a vindictive peasant, who had received a whole charge of shot in his face, lay in wait for the Seigneur one evening behind the trees of the mall, and very nearly succeeded in killing him, for the ball took off the tip of his ear.

"My uncle," Monsieur Paul continued, "tried to discover who had fired the shot; but he could not see any one, and he walked back slowly to the house. The day after he called his steward, and ordered him to close up the manor and the park, and allow no living soul to enter. He expressly forbade that anything should be touched, or looked after, or any repairs made on the estate during his absence. He added, between his teeth, that he would return at Easter, or Trinity Sunday, as they say in the song; and, just as the song has it, Trinity Sunday passed without a sign of him. He died last year at Monaco; my brother-in-law and myself were the first to enter the château after it had been abandoned for thirty-two years. We found a chestnut-tree growing in the middle of the parlour. As for the park, it was useless trying to visit it, because there were no longer any paths or alleys."

My companion ceased to speak; and only the regular hoof-beat of the trotting horse, and the chirping of insects in the grass, broke the silence. On either hand, the sheaves standing in the fields took, in the vague moonlight, the appearance of tall white women kneeling down; and I abandoned myself awhile to those wonderful childish fancies which the charm of night always suggests. After driving under the heavy shadows of the mall, we turned to the right and rolled up a lordly avenue at the end of which the château suddenly rose into view—a black mass, with turrets *en poivrière*. We followed a sort of causeway, which gave access to the court-of-honour, and which, passing over a moat full of running water, doubtless replaced a long-vanished drawbridge. The loss of that drawbridge must have been, I think, the first of various humiliations to which the warlike manor had been subjected ere being reduced to that pacific aspect with which it received me. The stars reflected themselves with marvellous clearness in the dark water. Monsieur Paul, like a courteous host, escorted me to my chamber at the very top of the building, at the end of a long corridor; and then, excusing himself for not presenting me at once to his wife by reason of the lateness of the hour, bade me good-night.

My apartment, painted in white and hung with chintz, seemed to keep some traces of the elegant gallantry of the eighteenth century. A heap of still-glowing ashes—which testified to the pains taken to dispel humidity—filled the fireplace, whose marble mantelpiece supported a bust of Marie Antoinette in *biscuit*. Attached to the frame of the tarnished and discoloured mirror, two brass hooks, that had once doubtless served the ladies of old-fashioned days to hang their *chatelaines* on, seemed to offer a very opportune means of suspending my watch, which I took care to wind up beforehand; for, contrary to the opinion of the Thelemites, I hold that man is only master of time, which is Life itself, when he has divided it into hours, minutes and seconds—that is to say, into parts proportioned to the brevity of human existence.

And I thought to myself that life really seems short to us only because we measure it irrationally by our own mad hopes. We have all of us, like the old man in the fable, a new wing to add to our building. I want, for example, before I die, to finish my "History of the Abbots of Saint-Germain-des-Prés." The time God allots to each one of us is like a precious tissue which we embroider as we best know how. I had begun my woof with all sorts of philological illustrations. . . . So my thoughts wandered on; and at last, as I bound my *foulard* about my head, the notion of Time led me back to the past; and for the second time within the same round of the dial I thought of you, Clémentine—to bless you again in your prosperity, if you have any, before blowing out my candle and falling asleep amid the chanting of the frogs.

II

URING breakfast I had many opportunities to appreciate the good taste, tact, and intelligence of Madame de Gabry, who told me that the château had its ghosts, and was especially haunted by the "Lady-with-three-wrinkles-in-her-back," a poisoner during her lifetime, and thereafter a Soul-in-pain. I could never describe how much wit and animation she gave to this old nurse's tale. We took our coffee on the terrace, whose balusters, clasped and forcibly torn away from their stone coping by a vigorous growth of ivy, remained suspended in the grasp of the amorous plant like bewildered Athenian women in the arms of ravishing Centaurs.

The château, shaped something like a four-wheeled wagon, with a turret at each of the four angles, had lost all original character by reason of repeated remodellings. It was merely a fine spacious building, nothing more. It did not appear to me to have suffered much damage during its abandonment of thirty-two years. But when Madame de Gabry conducted me into the great salon of the ground-floor, I saw that the planking was bulged in and out, the plinths rotten, the wainscotings split apart, the paintings of the piers turned black and hanging more than half out of their settings. A chestnut-tree, after forcing up the planks of the floor, had grown tall under the ceiling, and was reaching out its large-leaved branches towards the glassless windows.

This spectacle was not devoid of charm; but I could not look at it without anxiety, as I remembered that the rich library of Monsieur Honoré de Gabry, in an adjoining apartment, must have been exposed for the same length of time to the same forces of decay. Yet, as I looked at the young chestnut-tree in the salon, I could not but admire the magnificent vigour of Nature, and that resistless power which forces every germ to develop into life. On the other hand I felt saddened to think that, whatever effort we scholars may make to preserve dead things from passing away, we are labouring painfully in vain. Whatever has lived becomes the necessary food of new existences. And the Arab who builds himself a hut out of the marble fragments of a Palmyra temple is really more of a philosopher than all the guardians of museums at London, Munich, or Paris.

August 11.

ALL day long I have been classifying MSS. . . . The sun came in through the lofty uncurtained windows; and, during my reading, often very interesting, I could hear the languid bumble-bees bump heavily against the windows, and the flies, intoxicated with light and heat, making their wings hum in circles around my head. So loud became their humming about three o'clock that I looked up from the document I was reading—a document containing very precious materials for the history of Melun in the thirteenth century—to watch the concentric movements of those tiny creatures. *"Bestions,"* Lafontaine calls them: he found this form of the word in the old popular speech, whence also the term, *tapisserie-à-bestions,* applied to figured tapestry. I was compelled to confess that the effect of heat upon the wings of a fly is totally different from that it exerts upon the brain of a paleographical archivist; for I found it very difficult to think, and a rather pleasant languor weighing upon me, from which I could rouse myself only by a very determined effort. The dinner-bell then startled me in the midst of my labours; and I had barely time to put on my new dress-coat, so as to make a respectable appearance before Madame de Gabry.

The repast, generously served, seemed to prolong itself for my benefit. I am more than a fair judge of wine; and my hostess, who discovered my knowledge in this regard, was friendly enough to open a certain bottle of Château-Margaux in my honour. With deep respect I drank of this famous and knightly old wine, which comes from the slopes of Bordeaux, and of which the flavour and exhilarating power are beyond all praise. The ardour of it spread gently through my veins, and filled me with an almost juvenile animation. Seated beside Madame de Gabry on the terrace, in the gloaming which gave a charming melancholy to the park, and lent to every object an air of mystery, I took pleasure in communicating my impressions of the scene to my hostess. I discoursed with a vivacity quite remarkable on the part of a man so devoid of imagination as I am. I described to her spontaneously, without quoting from any old texts, the caressing melancholy of the evening, and the beauty of that natal earth which feeds us, not only with bread and wine, but also with ideas, sentiments, beliefs, and which will at last take us all back to her maternal breast again, like so many tired little children at the close of a long day.

"Monsieur," said the kind lady, "you see these old towers, those trees, that sky; is it not quite natural that the personages of the popular tales and folk-songs should have been evoked by such scenes? Why, over there is the very path which Little Red Ridinghood followed when she went to the woods to pick nuts. Across this changeful and always vapoury sky the fairy chariots used to roll; and the north tower might have sheltered under its pointed roof that same old spinning woman whose distaff pricked the Sleeping Beauty in the Wood."

I continued to muse upon her pretty fancies, while Monsieur Paul related to me, as he puffed a very strong cigar, the history of some suit he had brought against the commune about a water-right. Madame de Gabry, feeling the chill night air, began to shiver under the shawl her husband had wrapped about her, and left us to go to her room. I then decided, instead of going to my own, to return to the library and continue my examination of the manuscripts. In spite of the protests of Monsieur Paul, I entered what I may call, in old-fashioned phrase, "the book-room," and started to work by the light of a lamp.

After having read fifteen pages, evidently written by some ignorant and careless scribe, for I could scarcely discern their meaning, I plunged my hand into the pocket of my coat to get my snuff-box; but this movement, usually so natural and almost instinctive, this time cost me some effort and even fatigue. Nevertheless, I got out the silver box, and took from it a pinch of the odorous powder, which, somehow or other, I managed to spill all over my shirt-bosom under my baffled nose. I am sure my nose must have expressed its disappointment, for it is a very expressive nose. More than once it has betrayed my secret thoughts, and especially upon

a certain occasion at the public library of Coutances, where I dis.
covered, right in front of my colleague Brioux, the "Cartulary of
Notre-Dame-des-Anges."

What a delight! My little eyes remained as dull and expression-
less as ever behind my spectacles. But at the mere sight of my thick
pug-nose, which quivered with joy and pride, Brioux knew that I
had found something. He noted the volume I was looking at, observed the place where I put it back, pounced upon it as soon as I
turned my heel, copied it secretly, and published it in haste, for
the sake of playing me a trick. But his edition swarms with errors,
and I had the satisfaction of afterwards criticising some of the
gross blunders he made.

But to come back to the point at which I left off: I began to
suspect that I was getting very sleepy indeed. I was looking at a
chart of which the interest may be divined from the fact that it
contained mention of a hutch sold to Jehan d'Estonville, priest, in
1312. But although, even then, I could recognise the importance of
the document, I did not give it that attention it so strongly invited.'
My eyes would keep turning, against my will, towards a certain
corner of the table where there was nothing whatever interesting
to a learned mind. There was only a big German book there, bound
in pigskin, with brass studs on the sides, and very thick cording
upon the back. It was a fine copy of a compilation which has little
to recommend it except the wood engravings it contains, and which
is well known as the "Cosmography of Munster." This volume,
with its covers slightly open, was placed upon edge, with the back
upwards.

I could not say for how long I had been staring causelessly at
the sixteenth-century folio, when my eyes were captivated by a
sight so extraordinary that even a person as devoid of imagination
as I could not but have been greatly astonished by it.

I perceived, all of a sudden, without having noticed her coming
into the room, a little creature seated on the back of the book, with
one knee bent and one leg hanging down—somewhat in the attitude of the amazons of Hyde Park or the Bois de Boulogne on
horseback. She was so small that her swinging foot did not reach
the table, over which the trail of her dress extended in a serpentine
line. But her face and figure were those of an adult. The fulness
of her corsage and the roundness of her waist could leave no doubt
of that, even for an old *savant* like myself. I will venture to add
that she was very handsome, with a proud mien; for my icono-
graphic studies have long accustomed me to recognise at once the
perfection of a type and the character of a physiognomy. The
countenance of this lady who had seated herself inopportunely on
the back of a "Cosmography of Munster" expressed a mingling of
haughtiness and mischievousness. She had the air of a queen, but
a capricious queen; and I judged, from the mere expression of her

eyes, that she was accustomed to wield great authority somewhere, in a very whimsical manner. Her mouth was imperious and mocking, and those blue eyes of hers seemed to laugh in a disquieting way under her finely arched black eyebrows. I have always heard that black eyebrows are very becoming to blondes; and this lady was very blonde. On the whole, the impression she gave me was one of greatness.

It may seem odd to say that a person who was no taller than a wine-bottle, and who might have been hidden in my coat pocket—but that it would have been very disrespectful to put her in it—gave me precisely an idea of greatness. But in the fine proportions of the lady seated upon the "Cosmography of Munster" there was such a proud elegance, such a harmonious majesty, and she maintained an attitude at once so easy and so noble, that she really seemed to me a very great person. Although my ink-bottle, which she examined with an expression of such mockery as appeared to indicate that she knew in advance every word that could ever come out of it at the end of my pen, was for her a deep basin in which she would have blackened her gold-clocked pink stockings up to the garter, I can assure you that she was great, and imposing even in her sprightliness.

Her costume, worthy of her face, was extremely magnificent; it consisted of a robe of gold-and-silver brocade, and a mantle of nacarat velvet, lined with vair. Her head-dress was a sort of *hennin,* with two high points; and pearls of splendid lustre made it bright and luminous as a crescent moon. Her little white hand held a wand. That wand drew my attention very strongly, because my archæological studies had taught me to recognise with certainty every sign by which the notable personages of legend and of history are distinguished. This knowledge came to my aid during various very queer conjectures with which I was labouring. I examined the wand, and saw that it appeared to have been cut from a branch of hazel.

"Then it is a fairy's wand," I said to myself; "consequently the lady who carries it is a fairy."

Happy at thus discovering what sort of a person was before me, I tried to collect my mind sufficiently to make her a graceful compliment. It would have given me much satisfaction, I confess, if I could have talked to her about the part taken by her people, not less in the life of the Saxon and Germanic races, than in that of the Latin Occident. Such a dissertation, it appeared to me, would have been an ingenious method of thanking the lady for having thus appeared to an old scholar, contrary to the invariable custom of her kindred, who never show themselves but to innocent children or ignorant village-folk.

Because one happens to be a fairy, one is none the less a woman, I said to myself; and since Madame Récamier, according to what I heard J. J. Ampère say, used to blush with pleasure when the little chimney-sweeps opened their eyes as wide as they could to look at her, surely the supernatural lady seated upon the "Cosmography of Munster" might feel flattered to hear an erudite man discourse learnedly about her, as about a medal, a seal, a fibula, or a token. But such an undertaking, which would have cost my timidity a great deal, became totally out of the question when I observed the Lady of the Cosmography suddenly take from an alms-purse hanging at her girdle the very smallest nuts I had ever seen, crack the shells between her teeth, and throw them at my nose, while she nibbled the kernels with the gravity of a sucking child.

At this conjuncture, I did what the dignity of science demanded of me—I remained silent. But the nut-shells caused such a painful tickling that I put up my hand to my nose, and found, to my great surprise, that my spectacles were straddling the very end of it—so that I was actually looking at the lady, not through my spectacles, but over them. This was incomprehensible, because my eyes, worn out over old texts, cannot ordinarily distinguish anything without glasses—could not tell a melon from a decanter, though the two were placed close up to my nose.

That nose of mine, remarkable for its size, its shape, and its coloration, legitimately attracted the attention of the fairy; for she seized my goose-quill pen, which was sticking up from the ink-bottle like a plume, and she began to pass the feather-end of that pen over my nose. I had had more than once, in company, occasion to suffer cheerfully from the innocent mischief of young ladies, who made me join their games, and would offer me their cheeks to kiss through the back of a chair, or invite me to blow out a candle which they would lift suddenly above the range of my breath. But until that moment no person of the fair sex had ever subjected me to such a whimsical piece of familiarity as that of tickling my nose with my own feather pen. Happily I remembered the maxim of my late grandfather, who was accustomed to say that everything was permissible on the part of ladies, and that whatever they do to us is to be regarded as a grace and a favour. Therefore, as a grace and a favour I received the nutshells and the titillations with my own pen, and I tried to smile. Much more!—I even found speech.

"Madame," I said, with dignified politeness, "you accord the honour of a visit not to a silly child, nor to a boor, but to a bibliophile who is very happy to make your acquaintance, and who knows that long ago you used to make elf-knots in the manes of mares at the crib, drink the milk from the skimming-pails, slip *graines-à-gratter* down the backs of our great-grandmothers, make the hearth sputter in the faces of the old folks, and, in short, fill the house with disorder and gaiety. You can also boast of giving the nicest frights in the world to lovers who stayed out in the woods too late of evenings. But I thought you had vanished out of existence at least three centuries ago. Can it really be, Madame, that you are still to be seen in this age of railways and telegraphs? My concierge, who used to be a nurse in her young days, does not know your story; and my little boy-neighbour, whose nose is still wiped for him by his *bonne,* declares that you do not exist."

"What do you yourself think about it?" she cried, in a silvery voice, straightening up her royal little figure in a very haughty fashion, and whipping the back of the "Cosmography of Munster" as though it were a hippogriff.

"I don't really know," I answered, rubbing my eyes.

This reply, indicating a deeply scientific scepticism, had the most deplorable effect upon my questioner.

"Monsieur Sylvestre Bonnard," she said to me, "you are nothing but an old pedant. I always suspected as much. The smallest little ragamuffin who goes along the road with his shirt-tail sticking out through a hole in his pantaloons knows more about me than all the old spectacled folks in your Institutes and your Academies. To know is nothing at all; to imagine is everything. Nothing exists except that which is imagined. I am imaginary. That is what it is to exist, I should think! I am dreamed of, and I appear. Everything is only dream; and as nobody ever dreams about you, Sylvestre Bonnard, it is *you* who do not exist. I charm the world; I am everywhere—on a moonbeam, in the trembling of a hidden spring, in the moving of leaves that murmur, in the white vapours that rise each morning from the hollow meadow, in the thickets of pink brier—everywhere! . . . I am seen; I am loved. There are sighs uttered, weird thrills of pleasure felt by those who follow the light print of my feet, as I make the dead leaves whisper. I make the little children smile; I give wit to the dullest-minded nurses. Leaning above the cradles, I play, I comfort, I lull to sleep—and you doubt whether I exist! Sylvestre Bonnard, your warm coat covers the hide of an ass!"

She ceased speaking; her delicate nostrils swelled with indignation; and while I admired, despite my vexation, the heroic anger of this little person, she pushed my pen about in the ink-bottle, backward and forward, like an oar, and then suddenly threw it at my nose, point first.

I rubbed my face, and felt it all covered with ink. She had disappeared. My lamp was extinguished. A ray of moonlight streamed down through a window and descended upon the "Cosmography of Munster." A strong cool wind, which had arisen very suddenly without my knowledge, was blowing my papers, pens, and wafers about. My table was all stained with ink. I had left my window open during the storm. What an imprudence!

III

I WROTE to my housekeeper, as I promised, that I was safe and sound. But I took care not to tell her that I had caught cold from going to sleep in the library at night with the window open; for the good woman would have been as unsparing in her remonstrances to me as parliaments to kings. "At your age, Monsieur," she would have been sure to say, "one ought to have more sense." She is simple enough to believe that sense grows with age. I seem to her an exception to this rule.

Not having any similar motive for concealing my experiences from Madame de Gabry, I told her all about my vision, which she seemed to enjoy very much.

"Why, that was a charming dream of yours," she said; "and one must have real genius to dream such a dream."

"Then I am a real genius when I am asleep," I responded.

"When you dream," she replied; "and you are always dreaming."

I know that Madame de Gabry, in making this remark, only wished to please me; but that intention alone deserves my utmost gratitude; and it is therefore in a spirit of thankfulness and kindliest remembrance that I write down her words, which I will read over and over again until my dying day, and which will never be read by any one save myself.

I passed the next few days in completing the inventory of the manuscripts in the Lusance library. Certain confidential observations dropped by Monsieur Paul de Gabry, however, caused me some painful surprise, and made me decide to pursue the work after a different manner from that in which I had begun it. From those few words I learned that the fortune of Monsieur Honoré de Gabry, which had been badly managed for many years, and subsequently swept away to a large extent through the failure of a banker whose name I do not know, had been transmitted to the heirs of the old French nobleman only under the form of mortgaged real estate and irrecoverable assets.

Monsieur Paul, by agreement with his joint heirs, had decided to sell the library, and I was intrusted with the task of making arrangements to have the sale effected upon advantageous terms. But, totally ignorant as I was of all business methods and trade-customs, I thought it best to get the advice of a publisher who was one of my private friends. I wrote him at once to come and join me at Lusance; and while waiting for his arrival I took my hat and cane and made visits to the different churches of the diocese, in several of which I knew there were certain mortuary inscriptions to be found which had never been correctly copied.

So I left my hosts and departed on my pilgrimage. Exploring the churches and the cemeteries every day, visiting the parish priests and the village notaries, supping at the public inns with peddlers and cattle-dealers, sleeping at night between sheets scented with lavender, I passed one whole week in the quiet but profound enjoyment of observing the living engaged in their various daily occupations even while I was thinking of the dead. As for the purpose of my researches, I made only a few mediocre discoveries, which caused me only a mediocre joy, and one therefore salubrious and not at all fatiguing. I copied a few interesting epitaphs; and I added to this little collection a few recipes for cooking country dishes, which a certain good priest kindly gave me.

With these riches, I returned to Lusance; and I crossed the court-of-honour with such secret satisfaction as a *bourgeois* feels on entering his own home. This was the effect of the kindness of my hosts; and the impression I received on crossing their threshold proves, better than any reasoning could do, the excellence of their hospitality.

I entered the great parlour without meeting anybody; and the young chestnut-tree there spreading out its broad leaves seemed to me like an old friend. But the next thing which I saw—on the pier-table—caused me such a shock of surprise that I readjusted my glasses upon my nose with both hands at once, and then felt myself over so as to get at least some superficial proof of my own existence. In less than one second there thronged into my mind twenty different conjectures—the most rational of which was that I had suddenly become crazy. It seemed to me absolutely impossible that what I was looking at could exist; yet it was equally impossible for me not to see it as a thing actually existing. What caused my surprise was resting on the pier-table, above which rose a great dull speckled mirror.

I saw myself in that mirror; and I can say that I saw for once in my life the perfect image of stupefaction. But I made proper allowance for myself; I approved myself for being so stupefied by a really stupefying thing.

The object I was thus examining with a degree of astonishment that all my reasoning power failed to lessen, obtruded itself on my attention though quite motionless. The persistence and fixity of the phenomenon excluded any idea of hallucination. I am totally exempt from all nervous disorders capable of influencing the sense of sight. The cause of such visual disturbance is, I think, generally due to stomach trouble; and, thank God! I have an excellent stomach. Moreover, visual illusions are accompanied with special abnormal conditions which impress the victims of hallucination themselves, and inspire them with a sort of terror. Now, I felt nothing of this kind; the object which I saw, although seemingly impossible in itself, appeared to me under all the natural conditions of reality. I *observed that it had three* dimensions, and colours, and that it cast a shadow. Ah! how I stared at it! The water came into my eyes so that I had to wipe the glasses of my spectacles.

Finally I found myself obliged to yield to the evidence, and to affirm that I had really before my eyes the Fairy, the very same Fairy I had been dreaming of in the library a few evenings before. It was she, it was her very self, I assure you! She had *the same air* of child-queen, the same proud supple poise; she held the same hazel wand in her hand; she still wore her double-peaked head-dress, and the train of her long brocade robe undulated about her little feet. Same face, same figure. It was she indeed; and to prevent any possible doubt of it, she was seated on the back of a huge old-fashioned book strongly resembling the "Cosmography of Munster." Her immobility but half reassured me; I was really afraid that she was *going to take some more* nuts out of her alms-purse and throw the shells at my face.

I was standing there, waving my hands and gaping, when the musical and laughing voice of Madame de Gabry suddenly rang in my ears.

"So you are examining your fairy, Monsieur Bonnard!" said my hostess. "Well, do you think the resemblance good?"

It was very quickly said; but even while hearing it I had time to perceive that *my fairy was a statuette* in coloured wax, modelled with much taste and spirit by some novice hand. But the phenomenon, even thus reduced by a rational explanation, did not cease to excite my surprise. How, and by whom, had the Lady of the Cosmography been enabled to assume plastic existence? That was what remained for me to learn.

Turning towards Madame de Gabry, I perceived that *she was not alone.* A young girl dressed in black was standing beside her. She had large intelligent eyes, of a grey as sweet as that of the sky of the Isle of France, and at once artless and characteristic in their expression. At the extremities of her rather thin arms were fidgeting uneasily two slender hands, supple but slightly red, as it becomes the hands of young girls to be. Sheathed in her closely fitting merino robe, she had the slim grace of a young tree; and her large mouth bespoke frankness. I *could not describe* how much the child pleased me at first sight! She was not beautiful; but the three dimples of her cheeks and chin seemed to laugh, and her whole person, which revealed the awkwardness of innocence, had something in it indescribably good and sincere.

My gaze alternated from the statuette to the young girl; and I saw her blush—so frankly and fully!—the crimson passing over her face as by waves.

"Well," said my hostess, who had become sufficiently accustomed to my distracted moods to put the same question to me twice, "is that the very same lady who came in to see you through the window that you left open? She was very saucy, but then you were quite imprudent! Anyhow, do you recognise her?"

"It is her very self," I replied; "I see her now on that pier-table precisely as I saw her on the table in the library."

"Then, if that be so," replied Madame de Gabry, "you have to blame for it, in the first place, yourself, as a man who, although devoid of all imagination, to use your own words, knew how to depict your dream in such vivid colours; in the second place, me, who was able to remember and repeat faithfully all your dream; and, lastly, Mademoiselle Jeanne, whom I now introduce to you, for she herself modelled that wax figure precisely according to my instructions."

Madame de Gabry had taken the young girl's hand as she spoke; but the latter had suddenly broken away from her, and was already running through the park with the speed of a bird.

"Little crazy creature!" Madame de Gabry cried after her. "How can one be so shy? Come back here to be scolded and kissed!"

But it was all of no avail; the frightened child disappeared among the shrubbery. Madame de Gabry seated herself in the only chair remaining in the dilapidated parlour.

"I should be much surprised," she said, "if my husband had not already spoken to you of Jeanne. She is a sweet child, and we both love her very much. Tell me the plain truth; what do you think of her statuette?"

I replied that the work was full of good taste and spirit, but that it showed some want of study and practice on the author's part; otherwise I had been extremely touched to think that those young fingers should have thus embroidered an old man's rough sketch of fancy, and given form so brilliantly to the dreams of a dotard like myself.

"The reason I ask your opinion," replied Madame de Gabry, seriously, "is that Jeanne is a poor orphan. Do you think she could earn her living by modelling statuettes like this one?"

"As for that, no!" I replied; "and I think there is no reason to regret the fact. You say the girl is affectionate and sensitive; I can well believe you; I could believe it from her face alone. There are excitements in artist-life which impel generous hearts to act out of all rule and measure. This young creature is made to love; keep her for the domestic hearth. There only is real happiness."

"But she has no dowry!" replied Madame de Gabry.

Then, extending her hand to me, she continued:

"You are our friend; I can tell you everything. The father of this child was a banker, and one of our friends. He went into a colossal speculation, and it ruined him. He survived only a few months after his failure, in which, as Paul must have told you, three-fourths of my uncle's fortune were lost, and more than half of our own.

"We had made his acquaintance at Monaco, during the winter we passed there at my uncle's house. He had an adventurous disposition, but such an engaging manner! He deceived himself before ever he deceived others. After all, it is in the ability to deceive oneself that the greatest talent is shown, is it not? Well, we were captured —my husband, my uncle, and I; and we risked much more than a reasonable amount in a very hazardous undertaking. But, bah! as Paul says, since we have no children we need not worry about it. Besides, we have the satisfaction of knowing that the friend in whom we trusted was an honest man. . . . You must know his name, it was so often in the papers and on public placards—Noël Alexandre. His wife was a very sweet person. I knew her only when she was already past her prime, with traces of having once been very pretty, and a taste for fashionable style and display which seemed quite becoming to her. She was naturally fond of social excitement; but she showed a great deal of courage and dignity after the death of her husband. She died a year after him, leaving Jeanne alone in the world."

"Clémentine!" I cried out.

And on thus learning what I had never even imagined—the mere idea of which would have set all the forces of my soul in revolt— upon hearing that Clémentine was no longer in this world, something like a great silence came upon me; and the feeling which flooded my whole being was not a keen, strong pain, but a quiet and solemn sorrow. Yet I was conscious of some incomprehensible sense of alleviation, and my thought rose suddenly to heights before unknown.

"From wheresoever thou art at this moment, Clémentine," I said to myself, "look down upon this heart now indeed cooled by age, yet whose blood once boiled for thy sake, and say whether it is not reanimated by the mere thought of being able to love all that remains of thee on earth. Everything passes away since thou thyself hast passed away; but Life is immortal; it is that Life we must love in its forms eternally renewed. All the rest is child's play; and I myself, with all my books, am only like a child playing with marbles. The purpose of life—it is thou, Clémentine, who hast revealed it to me!" . . .

Madame de Gabry aroused me from my thoughts by murmuring,

"The child is poor."

"The daughter of Clémentine is poor!" I exclaimed aloud; "how fortunate that it is so! I would not wish that any one but myself should provide for her and dower her! No! the daughter of Clémentine must not have her dowry from any one but me."

And, approaching Madame de Gabry as she rose from her chair, I took her right hand; I kissed that hand, and placed it on my arm, and said:

"You will conduct me to the grave of the widow of Noël Alexandre."

And I heard Madame de Gabry asking me:

"Why are you crying?"

IV

THE LITTLE SAINT-GEORGE

April 16.

AINT DROCTOVEUS and the early abbots of Saint-Germain-des-Prés have been occupying me for the past forty years; but I do not know if I shall be able to write their history before I go to join them. It is already quite a long time since I became an old man. One day last year, on the Pont des Arts, one of my fellow members at the Institute was lamenting before me over the *ennui* of becoming old.

"Still," Saint-Beuve replied to him, "it is the only way that has yet been found of living a long time."

I have tried this way, and I know just what it is worth. The trouble of it is not that one lasts too long, but that one sees all about him pass away—mother, wife, friends, children. Nature makes and unmakes all these divine treasures with gloomy indifference, and at last we find that we have not loved, we have only been embracing shadows. But how sweet some shadows are! If ever creature glided like a shadow through the life of a man, it was certainly that young girl whom I fell in love with when—incredible though it now seems—I was myself a youth.

A Christian sarcophagus from the catacombs of Rome bears a formula of imprecation, the whole terrible meaning of which I only learned with time. It says: *"Whatsoever impious man violates this sepulchre, may he die the last of his own people!"* In my capacity of archæologist, I have opened tombs and disturbed ashes in order to collect the shreds of apparel, metal ornaments, or gems that were mingled with those ashes. But I did it only through that scientific curiosity which does not exclude the feelings of reverence and of piety. May that malediction graven by some one of the first followers of the apostles upon a martyr's tomb never fall upon me! I ought not to fear to survive my own people so long as there are men in the world; for there are always some whom one can love.

But the power of love itself weakens and gradually becomes lost with age, like all the other energies of man. Example proves it; and it is this which terrifies me. Am I sure that I have not myself already suffered this great loss? I should surely have felt it, but for the happy meeting which has rejuvenated me. Poets speak of the Fountain of Youth; it does exist; it gushes up from the earth at every step we take. And one passes by without drinking of it!

The young girl I loved, married of her own choice to a rival, passed, all grey-haired, into the eternal rest. I have found her daughter—so that my life, which before seemed to me without utility, now once more finds a purpose and a reason for being.

To-day I "take the sun," as they say in Provence; I take it on the terrace of the Luxembourg, at the foot of the statue of Marguerite de Navarre. It is a spring sun, intoxicating as young wine. I sit and dream. My thoughts escape from my head like the foam from a bottle of beer. They are light, and their fizzing amuses me. I dream; such a pastime is certainly permissible to an old fellow who has published thirty volumes of texts, and contributed to the *Journal des Savants* for twenty-six years. I have the satisfaction of feeling that I performed my task as well as it was possible for me to do, and that I utilised to their fullest extent those mediocre faculties with which Nature endowed me. My efforts were not all in vain, and I have contributed, in my own modest way, to that renaissance of historical labours which will remain the honour of this restless century. I shall certainly be counted among those ten or twelve who revealed to France her own literary antiquities. My publication of the poetical works of Gautier de Coincy inaugurated a judicious system and fixed a date. It is in the austere calm of old age that I decree to myself this deserved credit, and God, who sees my heart, knows whether pride or vanity have aught to do with this self-award of justice.

But I am tired; my eyes are dim; my hand trembles, and I see an image of myself in those old men of Homer, whose weakness excluded them from the battle, and who, seated upon the ramparts, lifted up their voices like crickets among the leaves.

So my thoughts were wandering when three young men seated themselves near me. I do not know whether each one of them had come in three boats, like the monkey of Lafontaine, but the three certainly displayed themselves over the space of twelve chairs. I took pleasure in watching them, not because they had anything very extraordinary about them, but because I discerned in them that brave joyous manner which is natural to youth. They were from the schools. I was less assured of it by the books they were carrying than by the character of their physiognomy. For all who busy themselves with the things of the mind can be at once recognised by an indescribable something which is common to all of them. I am very fond of young people; and these pleased me, in spite of a certain provoking wild manner which recalled to me my own college days with marvellous vividness. But they did not wear velvet doublets and long hair, as we used to do; they did not walk about, as we used to do, with a death's-head; they did not cry out, as we used to do, "Hell and malediction!" They were quite properly dressed, and neither their costume nor their language had anything suggestive of the Middle Ages. I must also add that they paid considerable attention to the women passing on the terrace, and expressed their admiration of some of them in very animated language. But their reflections, even on this subject, were not of a character to oblige me to flee from my seat. Besides, so long as youth is studious, I think it has a right to its gaieties.

One of them, having made some gallant pleasantry which I forget, the smallest and darkest of the three exclaimed, with a slight Gascon accent,

"What a thing to say! Only physiologists like us have any right to occupy ourselves about living matter. As for you, Gélis, who only live in the past—like all your fellow archivists and paleographers—you will do better to confine yourself to those stone women over there, who are your contemporaries."

And he pointed to the statues of the Ladies of Ancient France which towered up, all white, in a half-circle under the trees of the terrace. This joke, though in itself trifling, enabled me to know that the young man called Gélis was a student at the École des Chartes. From the conversation which followed I was able to learn that his neighbour, blond and wan almost to diaphaneity, taciturn and sarcastic, was Boulmier, a fellow student. Gélis and the future doctor (I hope he will become one some day) discoursed together with much fantasy and spirit. In the midst of the loftiest speculations they would play upon words, and make jokes after the peculiar fashion of really witty persons—that is to say, in a style of enormous absurdity. I need hardly say, I suppose, that they only deigned to maintain the most monstrous kind of paradoxes. They employed all their powers of imagination to make themselves as ludicrous as possible, and all their powers of reasoning to assert the contrary of common sense. All the better for them! I do not like to see young folks too rational.

The student of medicine, after glancing at the title of the book that Boulmier held in his hand, exclaimed,

"What!—you read Michelet—you?"

"Yes," replied Boulmier, very gravely. "I like novels."

Gélis, who dominated both by his fine stature, imperious gestures, and ready wit, took the book, turned over a few pages rapidly, and said,

"Michelet always had a great propensity to emotional tenderness. He wept sweet tears over Maillard, that nice little man who introduced *la paperasserie* into the September massacres. But as emotional tenderness leads to fury, he becomes all at once furious against the victims. There was no help for it. It is the sentimentality of the age. The assassin is pitied, but the victim is considered quite unpardonable. In his later manner Michelet is more Michelet

than ever before. There is no common sense in it; it is simply wonderful! Neither art nor science, neither criticism nor narrative;
only furies and fainting-spells and epileptic fits over matters which
he never deigns to explain. Childish outcries—*envies de femme
grosse!*—and a style, my friend!—not a single finished phrase! It
is astounding!"

And he handed the book back to his comrade. "This is amusing
madness," I thought to myself, "and not quite so devoid of common sense as it appears. This young man, though only playing, has
sharply touched the defect in the cuirass."

But the Provençal student declared that history was a thoroughly
despicable exercise of rhetoric. According to him, the only true history was the natural history of man. Michelet was in the right path
when he came in contact with the fistula of Louis XIV., but he fell
back into the old rut almost immediately afterwards.

After this judicious expression of opinion, the young physiolo-
gist went to join a party of passing friends. The two archivists,
less well acquainted in the neighbourhood of a garden so far from
the Rue Paradis-au-Marais, remained together, and began to chat
about their studies. Gélis, who had completed his third class-year,
was preparing a thesis on the subject of which he expatiated with
youthful enthusiasm. Indeed, I thought the subject a very good one,
particularly because I had recently thought myself called upon to
treat a notable part of it. It was the *Monasticon Gallicanum*. The
young erudite (I give him the name as a presage) wanted to describe all the engravings made about 1690 for the work which Dom
Michel Germain would have had printed but for the one irremedi-
able hindrance which is rarely foreseen and never avoided. Dom
Michel Germain left his manuscript complete, however, and in good
order when he died. Shall I be able to do as much with mine?—but
that is not the present question. So far as I am able to understand,
Monsieur Gélis intends to devote a brief archæological notice to
each of the abbeys pictured by the humble engravers of Dom
Michel Germain.

His friend asked him whether he was acquainted with all the
manuscripts and printed documents relating to the subject. It was
then that I pricked up my ears. They spoke at first of original
sources; and I must confess they did so in a satisfactory manner,
despite their innumerable and detestable puns. Then they began
to speak about contemporary studies on the subject.

"Have you read," asked Boulmier, "the notice of Courajod?"

"Good!" I thought to myself.

"Yes," replied Gélis; "it is accurate."

"Have you read," said Boulmier, "the article by Tamisey de Lar-
roque in the 'Revue des Questions Historiques'?"

"Good!" I thought to myself, for the second time.

"Yes," replied Gélis, "it is full of things." . . .

"Have you read," said Boulmier, "the 'Tableau des Abbayes Bénédictines en 1600,' by Sylvestre Bonnard?"

"Good!" I said to myself, for the third time.

"*Mai foi!* no!" replied Gélis. "Bonnard is an idiot!" Turning my head, I perceived that the shadow had reached the place where I was sitting. It was growing chilly, and I thought to myself what a fool I was to have remained sitting there, at the risk of getting the rheumatism, just to listen to the impertinence of those two young fellows!

"Well! well!" I said to myself as I got up. "Let this prattling fledgling write his thesis, and sustain it! He will find my colleague, Quicherat, or some other professor at the school, to show him what an ignoramus he is. I consider him neither more nor less than a rascal; and really, now that I come to think of it, what he said about Michelet awhile ago was quite insufferable, outrageous! To talk in that way about an old master replete with genius! It was simply abominable!"

April 17.

"THÉRÈSE, give me my new hat, my best frock-coat, and my silver-headed cane."

But Thérèse is deaf as a sack of charcoal and slow as Justice. Years have made her so. The worst is that she thinks she can hear well and move about well; and, proud of her sixty years of upright domesticity, she serves her old master with the most vigilant despotism.

"What did I tell you?" . . . And now she will not give me my silver-headed cane, for fear that I might lose it! It is true that I often forget umbrellas and walking-sticks in the omnibuses and booksellers' shops. But I have a special reason for wanting to take out with me to-day my old cane with the engraved silver head representing Don Quixote charging a windmill, lance in rest, while Sancho Panza, with uplifted arms, vainly conjures him to stop. That cane is all that came to me from the heritage of my uncle, Captain Victor, who in his lifetime resembled Don Quixote much more than Sancho Panza, and who loved blows quite as much as most people fear them.

For thirty years I have been in the habit of carrying this cane upon all memorable or solemn visits which I make; and those two figures of knight and squire give me inspiration and counsel. I imagine I can hear them speak. Don Quixote says,

"Think well about great things; and know that thought is the only reality in this world. Lift up Nature to thine own stature; and let the whole universe be for thee no more than the reflection of thine own heroic soul. Combat for honour's sake: that alone is worthy of a man! and if it should fall to thee to receive wounds, shed thy blood as a beneficent dew, and smile."

And Sancho Panza says to me in his turn,

"Remain just what heaven made thee, comrade! Prefer the bread-crust which has become dry in thy wallet to all the partridges that roast in the kitchens of lords. Obey thy master, whether he be a wise man or a fool, and do not cumber thy brain with too many useless things. Fear blows; 'tis verily tempting God to seek after danger!"

But if the incomparable knight and his matchless squire are imaged only upon this cane of mine, they are realities to my inner conscience. Within every one of us there lives both a Don Quixote and a Sancho Panza to whom we hearken by turns; and though Sancho most persuades us, it is Don Quixote that we find ourselves obliged to admire. . . . But a truce to this dotage!—and let us go to see Madame de Gabry about some matters more important than the everyday details of life. . . .

Same day.

I FOUND Madame de Gabry dressed in black, just buttoning her gloves.

"I am ready," she said.

Ready!—so I have always found her upon any occasion of doing a kindness.

After some compliments about the good health of her husband, who was taking a walk at the time, we descended the stairs and got into the carriage.

I do not know what secret influence I feared to dissipate by breaking silence, but we followed the great deserted drives without speaking, looking at the crosses, the monumental columns, and the mortuary wreaths awaiting sad purchasers.

The vehicle at last halted at the extreme verge of the land of the living, before the gate upon which words of hope are graven.

"Follow me," said Madame de Gabry, whose tall stature I noticed then for the first time. She first walked down an alley of cypresses, and then took a very narrow path contrived between the tombs. Finally, halting before a plain slab, she said to me,

"It is here."

And she knelt down. I could not help noticing the beautiful easy manner in which this Christian woman fell upon her knees, leaving the folds of her robe to spread themselves at random about her. I had never before seen any lady kneel down with such frankness and such forgetfulness of self, except two fair Polish exiles, one evening long ago, in a deserted church in Paris.

This image passed like a flash; and I saw only the sloping stone on which was graven the name of Clémentine. What I then felt was something so deep and vague that only the sound of some rich music could convey any idea of it. I seemed to hear instruments of celestial sweetness make harmony in my old heart. With the solemn accords of a funeral chant there seemed to mingle the subdued melody of a song of love; for my soul blended into one feeling the grave sadness of the present with the familiar graces of the past.

I cannot tell whether we had remained a long time at the tomb of Clémentine before Madame de Gabry arose. We passed through the cemetery again without speaking to each other. Only when we found ourselves among the living once more did I feel able to speak.

"While following you there," I said to Madame de Gabry, "I could not help thinking of those angels with whom we are said to meet on the mysterious confines of life and death. That tomb you led me to, of which I knew nothing—as I know nothing, or scarcely anything, concerning her whom it covers—brought back to me emotions which were unique in my life, and which seem in the dulness of that life like some light gleaming upon a dark road. The light recedes farther and farther away as the journey lengthens; I have now almost reached the bottom of the last slope; and, nevertheless, each time I turn to look back I see the glow as bright as ever.

"You, Madame, who knew Clémentine as a wife and mother after her hair had become grey, you cannot imagine her as I see her still; a young fair girl, all pink and white. Since you have been so kind as to be my guide, dear Madame, I ought to tell you what feelings were awakened in me by the sight of that grave to which you led me. Memories throng back upon me. I feel myself like some old gnarled and mossy oak which awakens a nestling world of birds by the shaking of its branches. Unfortunately the song my birds sing is old as the world, and can amuse no one but myself."

"Tell me your souvenirs," said Madame de Gabry. "I cannot read your books, because they are written only for scholars; but I like very much to have you talk to me, because you know how to give interest to the most ordinary things in life. And talk to me just as you would talk to an old woman. This morning I found three grey threads in my hair."

"Let them come without regret, Madame," I replied. "Time deals gently only with those who take it gently. And when in some years more you will have a silvery fringe under your black fillet, you will be reclothed with a new beauty, less vivid but more touching than the first; and you will find your husband admiring your grey tresses as much as he did that black curl which you gave him when about to be married, and which he preserves in a locket as a thing sacred. . . . These boulevards are broad and very quiet. We can talk at our ease as we walk along. I will tell you, to begin with, how I first made the acquaintance of Clémentine's father. But you must not expect anything extraordinary, or anything even remarkable; you would be greatly deceived.

"Monsieur de Lessay used to live in the second storey of an old house in the Avenue de l'Observatoire, having a stuccoed front, ornamented with antique busts, and a large unkept garden attached to it. That façade and that garden were the first images my child-eyes perceived; and they will be the last, no doubt, which I shall still see through my closed eyelids when the Inevitable Day comes. For it was in that house that I was born; it was in that garden I first learned, while playing, to feel and know some particles of this old universe. Magical hours!—sacred hours!—when the soul, all fresh from the making, first discovers the world, which for its sake seems to assume such caressing brightness, such mysterious charm! And that, Madame, is indeed because the universe itself is only the reflection of our soul.

"My mother was a being very happily constituted. She rose with the sun, like the birds; and she herself resembled the birds by her domestic industry, by her maternal instinct, by her perpetual desire to sing, and by a sort of brusque grace, which I could feel the charm of very well even as a child. She was the soul of the house, which she filled with her systematic and joyous activity. My father was just as slow as she was brisk. I can recall very well that placid face of his, over which at times an ironical smile used to flit. He was fatigued with active life; and he loved his fatigue. Seated beside the fire in his big arm-chair, he used to read from morning till night; and it is from him that I inherit my love of books. I have in my library a Mably and a Raynal, which he annotated with his own hand from beginning to end. But it was utterly useless attempting to interest him in anything practical whatever. When my mother would try, by all kinds of gracious little ruses, to lure him out of his retirement, he would simply shake his head with that inexorable gentleness which is the force of weak characters. He used in this way greatly to worry the poor woman, who could not enter at all into his own sphere of meditative wisdom, and could understand nothing of life except its daily duties and the merry labour of each hour. She thought him sick, and feared he was going to become still more so. But his apathy had a different cause.

"My father, entering the Naval office under Monsieur Decrès, in 1801, gave early proof of high administrative talent. There was a great deal of activity in the marine department in those times; and in 1805 my father was appointed chief of the Second Administrative Division. That same year, the Emperor, whose attention had been called to him by the Minister, ordered him to make a report upon the organisation of the English navy. This work, which reflected a profoundly liberal and philosophic spirit, of which the editor himself was unconscious, was only finished in 1807—about eighteen months after the defeat of Admiral Villeneuve at Trafalgar. Napoleon, who, from that disastrous day, never wanted to hear the word ship mentioned in his presence, angrily glanced over a few pages of the memoir, and then threw it into the fire, vociferating, 'Words!—words! I said once before that I hated ideologists.'

My father was told afterwards that the Emperor's anger was so intense at the moment that he stamped the manuscript down into the fire with his boot-heels. At all events, it was his habit, when very much irritated, to poke down the fire with his feet until he had scorched his boot-soles. My father never fully recovered from this disgrace; and the fruitlessness of all his efforts towards reform was certainly the cause of the apathy which came upon him at a later day. Nevertheless, Napoleon, after his return from Elba, sent for him, and ordered him to prepare some liberal and patriotic bulletins and proclamations for the fleet. After Waterloo, my father, whom the event had rather saddened than surprised, retired into private life, and was not interfered with—except that it was generally averred of him that he was a Jacobin, a *buveur-de-sang*— one of those men with whom no one could afford to be on intimate terms. My mother's eldest brother, Victor Maldent, an infantry captain—retired on half-pay in 1814, and disbanded in 1815—aggravated by his bad attitude the situation in which the fall of the Empire had placed my father. Captain Victor used to shout in the *cafés* and the public balls that the Bourbons had sold France to the Cossacks. He used to show everybody a tricoloured cockade hidden in the lining of his hat; and carried with much ostentation a walking-stick, the handle of which had been so carved that the shadow thrown by it made the silhouette of the Emperor.

"Unless you have seen certain lithographs by Charlet, Madame, you could form no idea of the physiognomy of my Uncle Victor, when he used to stride about the garden of the Tuileries with a fiercely elegant manner of his own—buttoned up in his frogged coat, with his cross-of-honour upon his breast, and a bouquet of violets in his buttonhole.

"Idleness and intemperance greatly intensified the vulgar recklessness of his political passions. He used to insult people whom he happened to see reading the *Quotidienne,* or the *Drapeau Blanc,* and compel them to fight with him. In this way he had the pain and the shame of wounding a boy of sixteen in a duel. In short, my Uncle Victor was the very reverse of a well-behaved person; and as he came to lunch and dine at our house every blessed day in the year, his bad reputation became attached to our family. My poor father suffered cruelly from some of his guest's pranks; but being very good-natured, he never made any remarks, and continued to give the freedom of his house to the captain, who only despised him for it.

"All this which I have told you, Madame, was explained to me afterwards. But at the time in question, my uncle the captain filled me with the very enthusiasm of admiration, and I promised myself to try to become some day as like him as possible. So one fine morning, in order to begin the likeness, I put my arms akimbo, and swore like a trooper. My excellent mother at once gave me such a box on the ear that I remained half stupefied for some little while before I could even burst out crying. I can still see the old arm-chair, covered with yellow Utrecht velvet, behind which I wept innumerable tears that day.

"I was a very little fellow then. One morning my father, lifting me upon his knees, as he was in the habit of doing, smiled at me with that slightly ironical smile which gave a certain piquancy to his perpetual gentleness of manner. As I sat on his knee, playing with his long white hair, he told me something which I did not understand very well, but which interested me very much, for the simple reason that it was mysterious to me. I think, but am not quite sure, that he related to me that morning the story of the little King of Yvetot, according to the song. All of a sudden we heard a great report; and the windows rattled. My father slipped me down gently on the floor at his feet; he threw up his trembling arms, with a strange gesture; his face became all inert and white, and his eyes seemed enormous. He tried to speak, but his teeth were chattering. At last he murmured, 'They have shot him!' I did not know what he meant, and felt only a vague terror. I knew afterwards, however, that he was speaking of Marshal Ney, who fell on the 7th of December, 1815, under the wall enclosing some waste ground beside our house.

"About that time I used often to meet on the stairway an old man (or, perhaps, not exactly an old man) with little black eyes which flashed with extraordinary vivacity, and an impassive, swarthy face. He did not seem to me alive—or at least he did not seem to me alive in the same way that other men were alive. I had once seen, at the residence of Monsieur Denon, where my father had taken me with him on a visit, a mummy brought from Egypt; and I believed in good faith that Monsieur Denon's mummy used to get up when no one was looking, leave its gilded case, put on a brown coat and powdered wig, and become transformed into Monsieur de Lessay. And even to-day dear Madame, while I reject that opinion as being without foundation, I must confess that Monsieur de Lessay bore a very strong resemblance to Monsieur Denon's mummy. The fact is enough to explain why this person inspired me with fantastic terror.

"In reality, Monsieur de Lessay was a small gentleman and a great philosopher. As a disciple of Mably and Rousseau, he flattered himself on being a man without any prejudices; and this pretension itself is a very great prejudice.

"He professed to hate fanaticism, yet was himself a fanatic on the topic of toleration. I am telling you, Madame, about a character belonging to an age that is past. I fear I may not be able to make you understand, and I am sure I shall not be able to interest you. It was so long ago! But I will abridge as much as possible: besides, I did not promise you anything interesting; and you could not have expected to hear of remarkable adventures in the life of Sylvestre Bonnard."

Madame de Gabry encouraged me to proceed, and I resumed:

"Monsieur de Lessay was brusque with men and courteous to ladies. He used to kiss the hand of my mother, whom the customs of the Republic and the Empire had not habituated to such gallantry. In him, I touched the age of Louis XVI. Monsieur de Lessay was a geographer; and nobody, I believe, ever showed more pride than he in occupying himself with the face of the earth. Under the Old Régime he had attempted philosophical agriculture, and thus squandered his estates to the very last acre. When he had ceased to own one square foot of ground, he took possession of the whole globe, and prepared an extraordinary number of maps, based upon the narratives of travellers. But as he had been mentally nourished with the very marrow of the 'Encyclopédie,' he was not satisfied with merely parking off human beings within so many degrees, minutes, and seconds of latitude and longitude. He also occupied himself, alas! with the question of their happiness. It is worthy of remark, Madame, that those who have given themselves the most concern about the happiness of peoples have made their neighbours very miserable. Monsieur de Lessay, who was more of a geometrician than D'Alembert, and more of a philosopher than Jean Jacques, was also more of a royalist than Louis XVIII. But his love for the King was as nothing to his hate for the Emperor. He had joined the conspiracy of Georges against the First Consul; but in the framing of the indictment he was not included among the inculpated parties, having been either ignored or despised, and this injury he never could forgive Bonaparte, whom he called the Ogre of Corsica, and to whom he used to say he would never have confided even the command of a regiment, so pitiful a soldier he judged him to be.

"In 1820, Monsieur de Lessay, who had then been a widower for many years, married again, at the age of sixty, a very young woman, whom he pitilessly kept at work preparing maps for him, and who gave him a daughter some years after their marriage, and died in childbed. My mother had nursed her during her brief illness, and had taken care of the child. The name of that child was Clémentine.

"It was from the time of that birth and that death that the relations between our family and Monsieur de Lessay began. In the meanwhile I had been growing dull as I began to leave my true childhood behind me. I had lost the charming power of being able to see and feel; and things no longer caused me those delicious surprises which form the enchantment of the more tender age. For the same reason, perhaps, I have no distinct remembrance of the period following the birth of Clémentine; I only know that a few months afterwards I had a misfortune, the mere thought of which still wrings my heart. I lost my mother. A great silence, a great coldness, and a great darkness seemed all at once to fill the house.

"I fell into a sort of torpor. My father sent me to the *lycée*, but I could only arouse myself from my lethargy with the greatest effort.

"Still, I was not altogether a dullard, and my professors were able to teach me almost everything they wanted, namely, a little Greek and a great deal of Latin. My acquaintances were confined to the ancients. I learned to esteem Miltiades, and to admire Themistocles. I became familiar with Quintus Fabius, as far, at least, as it was possible to become familiar with so great a Consul. Proud of these lofty acquaintances, I scarcely ever condescended to notice little Clémentine and her old father, who, in any event, went away to Normandy one fine morning without my having deigned to give a moment's thought to their possible return.

"They came back, however, Madame, they came back! Influences of Heaven, forces of nature, all ye mysterious powers which vouchsafe to man the ability to love, you know how I again beheld Clémentine! They re-entered our melancholy home. Monsieur de Lessay no longer wore a wig. Bald, with a few grey locks about his ruddy temples, he had all the aspect of robust old age. But that divine being whom I saw all resplendent, as she leaned upon his arm—she whose presence illuminated the old faded parlour—she was not an apparition! It was Clémentine herself! I am speaking the simple truth: her violet eyes seemed to me in that moment supernatural, and even to-day I cannot imagine how those two living jewels could have endured the fatigues of life, or become subjected to the corruption of death.

"She betrayed a little shyness in greeting my father, whom she did not remember. Her complexion was slightly pink, and her half-open lips smiled with that smile which makes one think of the Infinite—perhaps because it betrays no particular thought, and expresses only the joy of living and the bliss of being beautiful. Under a pink hood her face shone like a gem in an open casket; she wore a cashmere scarf over a robe of white muslin plaited at the waist, from beneath which protruded the tip of a little Morocco shoe. . . . Oh! you must not make fun of me, dear Madame, that was the fashion of the time; and I do not know whether our new fashions have nearly so much simplicity, brightness, and decorous grace.

"Monsieur de Lessay informed us that, in consequence of having undertaken the publication of a historical atlas, he had come back to live in Paris, and that he would be pleased to occupy his former apartment, if it was still vacant. My father asked Mademoiselle de Lessay whether she was pleased to visit the capital. She appeared to be, for her smile blossomed out in reply. She smiled at the windows that looked out upon the green and luminous garden; she smiled at the bronze Marius seated among the ruins of Carthage above the dial of the clock; she smiled at the old yellow-velveted arm-chairs, and at the poor student who was afraid to lift his eyes to look at her. From that day—how I loved her!

"But here we are already at the Rue de Sèvres, and in a little while we shall be in sight of your windows. I am a very bad story-teller; and if I were—by some impossible chance—to take it into my head to compose a novel, I know I should never succeed. I have been drawing out to tiresome length a narrative which I must finish briefly; for there is a certain delicacy, a certain grace of soul, which an old man could not help offending by any complacent expatiation upon the sentiments of even the purest love. Let us take a short turn on this boulevard, lined with convents; and my recital will be easily finished within the distance separating us from that little spire you see over there. . . .

"Monsieur de Lessay, on finding that I had graduated at the École des Chartes, judged me worthy to assist him in preparing his historical atlas. The plan was to illustrate, by a series of maps, what the old philosopher termed the Vicissitudes of Empires from the time of Noah down to that of Charlemagne. Monsieur de Lessay had stored up in his head all the errors of the eighteenth century in regard to antiquity. I belonged, so far as my historical studies were concerned, to the new school; and I was just at that age when one does not know how to dissemble. The manner in which the old man understood, or, rather, misunderstood, the epoch of the Barbarians—his obstinate determination to find in remote antiquity only ambitious princes, hypocritical and avaricious prelates, virtuous citizens, poet-philosophers, and other personages who never existed outside of the novels of Marmontel,—made me dreadfully unhappy, and at first used to excite me into attempts at argument, —rational enough, but perfectly useless and sometimes dangerous, for Monsieur de Lessay was very irascible, and Clémentine was very beautiful. Between her and him I passed many hours of torment and of delight. I was in love; I was a coward, and I granted to him all that he demanded of me in regard to the political and historical aspect which the Earth—that was at a later day to bear Clémentine—presented in the time of Abraham, of Menes, and of Deucalion.

"As fast as we drew our maps Mademoiselle de Lessay tinted them in water-colours. Bending over the table, she held the brush lightly between two fingers; the shadow of her eyelashes descended upon her cheeks, and bathed her half-closed eyes in a delicious penumbra. Sometimes she would lift her head, and I would see her lips pout. There was so much expression in her beauty that she could not breathe without seeming to sigh; and her most ordinary poses used to throw me into the deepest ecstasies of admiration. Whenever I gazed at her I fully agreed with Monsieur de Lessay that Jupiter had once reigned as a despot-king over the mountainous regions of Thessaly, and that Orpheus had committed the imprudence of leaving the teaching of philosophy to the clergy. I am not now quite sure whether I was a coward or a hero when I accorded all this to the obstinate old man.

"Mademoiselle de Lessay, I must acknowledge, paid very little attention to me. But this indifference seemed to me so just and so natural that I never even dreamed of thinking I had a right to complain about it; it made me unhappy, but without my knowing that I was unhappy at the time. I was hopeful;—we had then only got as far as the First Assyrian Empire.

"Monsieur de Lessay came every evening to take coffee with my father. I do not know how they became such friends; for it would have been difficult to find two characters more oppositely constituted. My father was a man who admired very few things, but was capable of excusing a great many. Still, as he grew older, he evinced more and more dislike of everything in the shape of exaggeration. He clothed his ideas with a thousand delicate shades of expression, and never pronounced an opinion without all sorts of reservations. These conversational habits, natural to a finely trained mind, used greatly to irritate the dry, terse old aristocrat, who was never in the least disarmed by the moderation of an adversary— quite the contrary! I always foresaw one danger. That danger was Bonaparte. My father had not himself retained any particular affection for his memory; but, having worked under his direction, he did not like to hear him abused, especially in favour of the Bourbons, against whom he had serious reason to feel resentment. Monsieur de Lessay, more of a Voltairean and a Legitimist than ever, now traced back to Bonaparte the origin of every social, political, and religious evil. Such being the situation, the idea of Uncle Victor made me feel particularly uneasy. This terrible uncle had become absolutely insufferable now that his sister was no longer there to calm him down. The harp of David was broken, and Saul was wholly delivered over to the spirit of madness. The fall of Charles X. had increased the audacity of the old Napoleonic veteran, who uttered all imaginable bravadoes. He no longer frequented our house, which had become too silent for him. But sometimes, at the dinner-hour, we would see him suddenly make his appearance, all covered with flowers, like a mausoleum. Ordinarily he would sit down to table with an oath, growled out from the very bottom of his chest, and brag, between every two mouthfuls, of his good fortune with the ladies as a *vieux brave*. Then, when the dinner was over, he would fold up his napkin in the shape of a bishop's mitre, gulp down half a decanter of brandy, and rush away with the hurried air of a man terrified at the mere idea of remaining for any length of time, without drinking, in conversation with an old philosopher and a young scholar. I felt perfectly sure that, if ever he and Monsieur de Lessay should come together, all would be lost. But that day came, Madame!

"The captain was almost hidden by flowers that day, and seemed so much like a monument commemorating the glories of the Empire that one would have liked to pass a garland of immortelles over each of his arms. He was in an extraordinarily good humour; and the first person to profit by that good humour was our cook— for he put his arm round her waist while she was placing the roast on the table.

"After dinner he pushed away the decanter presented to him, observing that he was going to burn some brandy in his coffee later on. I asked him tremblingly whether he would not prefer to have his coffee at once. He was very suspicious, and not at all dull of comprehension—my Uncle Victor. My precipitation seemed to him in very bad taste; for he looked at me in a peculiar way, and said,

" 'Patience! my nephew. It isn't the business of the baby of the regiment to sound the retreat! Devil take it! You must be in a great hurry, Master Pedant, to see if I've got spurs on my boots!'

"It was evident the captain had divined that I wanted him to go. And I knew him well enough to be sure that he was going to stay. He stayed. The least circumstances of that evening remain impressed on my memory. My uncle was extremely jovial. The mere idea of being in somebody's way was enough to keep him in good humour. He told us, in regular barrack style, ma foi! a certain story about a monk, a trumpet, and five bottles of Chambertin, which must have been much enjoyed in garrison society, but which I would not venture to repeat to you, Madame, even if I could remember it. When we passed into the parlour, the captain called attention to the bad condition of our andirons, and learnedly discoursed on the merits of rotten-stone as a brass-polisher. Not a word on the subject of politics. He was husbanding his forces. Eight o'clock sounded from the ruins of Carthage on the mantelpiece. It was Monsieur de Lessay's hour. A few moments later he entered the parlour with his daughter. The ordinary evening chat began. Clémentine sat down and began to work on some embroidery beside the lamp, whose shade left her pretty head in a soft shadow, and threw down upon her fingers a radiance that made them seem almost self-luminous. Monsieur de Lessay spoke of a comet announced by the astronomers, and developed some theories in relation to the subject, which, however audacious, betrayed at least a certain degree of intellectual culture. My father, who knew a good deal about astronomy, advanced some sound ideas of his own, which he ended up with his eternal, 'But what do we know about it, after all?' In my turn I cited the opinion of our neighbour of the Observatory—the great Arago. My Uncle Victor declared that comets had a peculiar influence on the quality of wines, and related in support of this view a jolly tavern-story. I was so delighted with the turn the conversation had taken that I did all in my power to maintain it in the same groove, with the help of my most recent studies, by a long exposition of the chemical composition of those nebulous bodies which, although extending over a length of billions of leagues, could be contained in a small bottle. My father, a little surprised at my unusual eloquence, watched me with his peculiar, placid, ironical smile. But one cannot always remain in heaven. I spoke, as I looked at Clémentine, of a certain *'comète'* of diamonds, which I had been admiring in a jeweller's window the evening before. It was a most unfortunate inspiration of mine.

" 'Ah! my nephew,' cried Uncle Victor, 'that *comète* of yours was nothing to the one which the Empress Josephine wore in her hair when she came to Strasburg to distribute crosses to the army.'

" 'That little Josephine was very fond of finery and display,' observed Monsieur de Lessay, between two sips of coffee. 'I do not blame her for it; she had good qualities, though rather frivolous in character. She was a Tascher, and she conferred a great honour on Bonaparte by marrying him. To say a Tascher does not, of course, mean a great deal; but to say a Bonaparte simply means nothing at all.'

" 'What do you mean by that, Monsieur the Marquis?' demanded Captain Victor.

" 'I am not a marquis,' dryly responded Monsieur de Lessay; 'and I mean simply that Bonaparte would have been very well suited had he married one of those cannibal women described by Captain Cook in his voyages—naked, tattoed, with a ring in her nose—devouring with delight putrefied human flesh.'

"I had foreseen it, and in my anguish (O pitiful human heart!) my first idea was about the remarkable exactness of my anticipations. I must say that the captain's reply belonged to the sublime order. He put his arms akimbo, eyed Monsieur de Lessay contemptuously from head to foot, and said,

" 'Napoleon, Monsieur the Vidame, had another spouse besides Josephine, another spouse besides Marie-Louise. That companion you know nothing of; but I have seen her, close to me. She wears a mantle of azure gemmed with stars; she is crowned with laurels; the Cross-of-Honour flames upon her breast. Her name is GLORY!'

"Monsieur de Lessay set his cup on the mantel-piece, and quietly observed,

" 'Your Bonaparte was a blackguard!'

"My father rose up calmly, extended his arm, and said very softly to Monsieur de Lessay,

" 'Whatever the man was who died at St. Helena, I worked for ten years in his government, and my brother-in-law was three times wounded under his eagles. I beg of you, dear sir and friend, never to forget these facts in future.'

"What the sublime and burlesque insolence of the captain could not do, the courteous remonstrance of my father effected immediately, throwing Monsieur de Lessay into a furious passion.

" 'I did forget,' he exclaimed, between his set teeth, livid in his rage, and fairly foaming at the mouth; 'the herring-cask always smells of herring, and when one has been in the service of rascals——'

"As he uttered the word, the Captain sprang at his throat; I am sure he would have strangled him upon the spot but for his daughter and me.

"My father, a little paler than his wont, stood there with his arms folded, and watched the scene with a look of inexpressible pity. What followed was still more lamentable—but why dwell further upon the folly of two old men. Finally I succeeded in separating them. Monsieur de Lessay made a sign to his daughter and left the room. As she was following him, I ran out into the stairway after her.

" 'Mademoiselle,' I said to her, wildly, taking her hand as I spoke, 'I love you! I love you!'

"For a moment she pressed my hand; her lips opened. What was it that she was going to say to me? But suddenly, lifting her eyes towards her father ascending the stairs, she drew her hand away, and made me a gesture of farewell.

"I never saw her again. Her father went to live in the neighbourhood of the Pantheon, in an apartment which he had rented for the sale of his historical atlas. He died in it a few months afterward of an apoplectic stroke. His daughter, I was told, retired to Caen to live with some aged relative. It was there that, later on, she married a bank-clerk, the same Noël Alexandre who became so rich and died so poor.

"As for me, Madame, I have lived alone, at peace with myself; my existence, equally exempt from great pains and great joys, has been tolerably happy. But for many years I could never see an empty chair beside my own of a winter's evening without feeling a sudden painful sinking at my heart. Last year I learned from you, who had known her, the story of her old age and death. I saw her daughter at your house. I have seen her; but I cannot yet say like the aged man of Scripture, '*And now, O Lord, let thy servant depart in peace!*' For if an old fellow like me can be of any use to anybody, I would wish, with your help, to devote my last energies and abilities to the care of this orphan."

I had uttered these last words in Madame de Gabry's own vestibule; and I was about to take leave of my kind guide when she said to me,

"My dear Monsieur, I cannot help you in this matter as much as I would like to do. Jeanne is an orphan and a minor. You cannot do anything for her without the authorisation of her guardian."

"Ah!" I exclaimed, "I had not the least idea in the world that Jeanne had a guardian!"

Madame de Gabry looked at me with visible surprise. She had not expected to find the old man quite so simple.

She resumed:

"The guardian of Jeanne Alexandre is Maître Mouche, notary at Levallois-Perret. I am afraid you will not be able to come to any understanding with him; for he is a very serious person."

"Why! good God!" I cried, "with what kind of people can you expect me to have any sort of understanding at my age, except serious persons."

She smiled with a sweet mischievousness—just as my father used to smile—and answered:

"With those who are like you—the innocent folks who wear their hearts on their sleeves. Monsieur Mouche is not exactly a man of that kind. He is cunning and light-fingered. But although I have very little liking for him, we will go together and see him, if you wish, and ask his permission to visit Jeanne, whom he has sent to a boarding-school at Les Ternes, where she is very unhappy."

We agreed at once upon a day; I kissed Madame de Gabry's hands, and we bade each other good-bye.

From May 2 to May 5.

I HAVE seen him in his office, Maître Mouche, the guardian of Jeanne. Small, thin, and dry; his complexion looks as if it was made out of the dust of his pigeon-holes. He is a spectacled animal; for to imagine him without his spectacles would be impossible. I have heard him speak, this Maître Mouche; he has a voice like a tin rattle, and he uses choice phrases; but I should have been better pleased if he had not chosen his phrases so carefully. I have observed him, this Maître Mouche; he is very ceremonious, and watches his visitors slyly out of the corner of his eye.

Maître Mouche is quite pleased, he informs us; he is delighted to find we have taken such an interest in his ward. But he does not think we are placed in this world just to amuse ourselves. No: he does not believe it; and I am free to acknowledge that anybody in his company is likely to reach the same conclusion, so little is he capable of inspiring joyfulness. He fears that it would be giving his dear ward a false and pernicious idea of life to allow her too much enjoyment. It is for that reason that he requests Madame de Gabry not to invite the young girl to her house except at very long intervals.

We left the dusty notary and his dusty study with a permit in due form (everything which issues from the office of Maître Mouche is in due form) to visit Mademoiselle Jeanne Alexandre on the first Thursday of each month at Mademoiselle Préfère's private school, Rue Demours, Aux Ternes.

The first Thursday in May I set out to a pay a visit to Mademoiselle Préfère, whose establishment I discerned from afar off by a big sign, painted with blue letters. That blue tint was the first indication I received of Mademoiselle Préfère's character, which I was able to see more of later on. A scared-looking servant took my card, and abandoned me without one word of hope at the door of a chilly parlour, full of that stale odour peculiar to the dining-rooms of educational establishments. The floor of this parlour had been waxed with such pitiless energy, that I remained for awhile in distress upon the threshold. But happily observing that little strips of woollen carpet had been scattered over the floor in front of each horse-hair chair, I succeeded, by cautiously stepping from one carpet-island to another, in reaching the angle of the mantelpiece, where I sat down quite out of breath.

Over the mantelpiece, in a large gilded frame, was a written document, entitled in flamboyant Gothic lettering, *Tableau d'Honneur,* with a long array of names underneath, among which I did not have the pleasure of finding that of Jeanne Alexandre. After having read over several times the names of those girl-pupils who had thus made themselves honoured in the eyes of Mademoiselle Préfère, I began to feel uneasy at not hearing any one coming. Mademoiselle Préfère would certainly have succeeded in establishing the absolute silence of the interstellar spaces throughout her pedagogical domains, had it not been that the sparrows had chosen her yard to assemble in by legions, and chirp at the top of their voices. It was a pleasure to hear them. But there was no way of seeing them—through the ground-glass windows. I had to content myself with the sights of the parlour, decorated from floor to ceiling, on all of its four walls, with drawings executed by the pupils of the institution. There were Vestals, flowers, thatched cottages, column-capitals, and an enormous head of Tatius, King of the Sabines, bearing the signature *Estelle Mouton.*

I had already passed some time in admiring the energy with which Mademoiselle Mouton had delineated the bushy eyebrows and the fierce gaze of the antique warrior, when a sound, faint like the rustling of a dead leaf moved by the wind, caused me to turn my head. It was not a dead leaf at all—it was Mademoiselle Préfère. With hands joined before her, she came gliding over the mirror-polish of that wonderful floor as the Saints of the Golden Legend were wont to glide over the crystal surface of the waters. But upon any other occasion, I am sure, Mademoiselle Préfère would not have made me think in the least about those virgins dear to mystical fancy. Her face rather gave me the idea of a russet-apple preserved for a whole winter in an attic by some economical housekeeper. Her shoulders were covered with a fringed pelerine, which had nothing at all remarkable about it, but which she wore as if it were a sacerdotal vestment, or the symbol of some high civic function.

I explained to her the purpose of my visit, and gave her my letter of introduction.

"Ah!—so you saw Monsieur Mouche!" she exclaimed. "Is his health *very* good? He is the most upright of men, the most——"

She did not finish the phrase, but raised her eyes to the ceiling. My own followed the direction of their gaze, and observed a little spiral of paper lace, suspended from the place of the chandelier, which was apparently destined, so far as I could discover, to attract the flies away from the gilded mirror-frames and the *Tableau d'Honneur*.

"I have met Mademoiselle Jeanne Alexandre," I observed, "at the residence of Madame de Gabry, and had reason to appreciate the excellent character and quick intelligence of the young girl. As I used to know her parents very well, the friendship which I felt for them naturally inclines me to take an interest in her."

Mademoiselle Préfère, in lieu of making any reply, sighed profoundly, pressed her mysterious pelerine to her heart, and again contemplated the paper spiral.

At last she observed,

"Since you were once the friend of Monsieur and Madame Alexandre, I hope and trust that, like Monsieur Mouche and myself, you deplore those crazy speculations which led them to ruin, and reduced their daughter to absolute poverty!"

I thought to myself, on hearing these words, how very wrong it is to be unlucky, and how unpardonable such an error on the part of those previously in a position worthy of envy. Their fall at once avenges and flatters us; and we are wholly pitiless.

After having answered, very frankly, that I knew nothing whatever about the history of the bank, I asked the schoolmistress if she was satisfied with Mademoiselle Alexandre.

"That child is indomitable!" cried Mademoiselle Préfère.

And she assumed an attitude of lofty resignation, to symbolise the difficult situation she was placed in by a pupil so hard to train. Then, with more calmness of manner, she added:

"The young person is not unintelligent. But she cannot resign herself to learn things by rule."

What a strange old maid was this Mademoiselle Préfère! She walked without lifting her legs, and spoke without moving her lips! Without, however, considering her peculiarities for more than a reasonable instant, I replied that principles were, no doubt, very excellent things, and that I could trust myself to her judgment in regard to their value; but that, after all, when one had learned something, it made very little difference what method had been followed in the learning of it.

Mademoiselle made a slow gesture of dissent. Then, with a sigh, she declared,

"Ah, Monsieur! those who do not understand educational methods are apt to have very false ideas on these subjects. I am certain they express their opinions with the best intentions in the world; but they would do better, a great deal better, to leave all such questions to competent people."

I did not attempt to argue further; and simply asked her whether I could see Mademoiselle Alexandre at once.

She looked at her pelerine, as if trying to read in the entanglement of its fringes, as in a conjuring-book, what sort of answer she ought to make; then said,

"Mademoiselle Alexandre has a penance to perform, and a class-lesson to give; but I should be very sorry to let you put yourself to the trouble of coming here all to no purpose. I am going to send for her. Only first allow me, Monsieur—as is our custom—to put your name on the visitors' register."

She sat down at the table, opened a large copy-book, and, taking out Maître Mouche's letter again from under her pelerine, where she had placed it, looked at it, and began to write.

" 'Bonnard'—with a *d*, is it not?" she asked. "Excuse me for being so particular; but my opinion is that proper names have an orthography. We have dictation-lessons in proper names, Monsieur, at this school—historical proper names, of course!"

After I had written down my name in a running hand, she inquired whether she should not put down after it my profession, title, quality—such as "retired merchant," "employé," "independent gentleman," or something else. There was a column in her register expressly for that purpose.

"My goodness, Madame!" I said, "if you must absolutely fill that column of yours, put down 'Member of the Institute.' "

It was still Mademoiselle Préfère's pelerine I saw before me; but it was not Mademoiselle Préfère now who wore it; it was a totally different person, obliging, gracious, caressing, radiant, happy. Her eyes, smiled; the little wrinkles of her face (there were a vast number of them!) also smiled; her mouth smiled likewise, but only on one side. I discovered afterwards that was her best side. She spoke: her voice had also changed with her manner; it was now sweet as honey.

"You said, Monsieur, that our dear Jeanne was very intelligent. I discovered the same thing myself, and I am proud of being able to agree with you. This young girl has really made me feel a great deal of interest in her. She has what I call a happy disposition. . . . But excuse me for thus drawing upon your valuable time."

She summoned the servant-girl, who looked much more hurried and scared than before, and who vanished with the order to go and tell Mademoiselle Alexandre that Monsieur Sylvestre Bonnard, Member of the Institute, was waiting to see her in the parlour.

Mademoiselle Préfère had barely time to confide to me that she had the most profound respect for all decisions of the Institute—

whatever they might be—when Jeanne appeared, out of breath, red as a poppy, with her eyes very wide open, and her arms dangling helplessly at her sides—charming in her artless awkwardness.

"What a state you are in, my dear child!" murmured Mademoiselle Préfère, with maternal sweetness, as she arranged the girl's collar.

Jeanne certainly did present an odd aspect. Her hair combed back, and imperfectly held by a net from which loose curls were escaping; her slender arms, sheathed down to the elbows in lustring sleeves; her hands, which she did not seem to know what to do with, all red with chilblains; her dress, much too short, revealing that she had on stockings much too large for her, and shoes worn down at the heel; and a skipping-rope tied round her waist in lieu of a belt,—all combined to lend Mademoiselle Jeanne an appearance the reverse of presentable.

"Oh, you crazy girl!" sighed Mademoiselle Préfère, who now seemed no longer like a mother, but rather like an elder sister.

Then she suddenly left the room, gliding like a shadow over the polished floor.

I said to Jeanne,

"Sit down, Jeanne, and talk to me as you would to a friend. Are you not better satisfied here now than you were last year?"

She hesitated; then answered with a good-natured smile of resignation,

"Not much better."

I asked her to tell me about her school life. She began at once to enumerate all her different studies—piano, style, chronology of the Kings of France, sewing, drawing, catechism, deportment. . . . I could never remember them all! She still held in her hands, all unconsciously, the two ends of her skipping-rope, and she raised and lowered them regularly while making her enumeration. Then all at once she became conscious of what she was doing, blushed, stammered, and became so confused that I had to renounce my desire to know the full programme of study adopted in the Préfère Institution.

After having questioned Jeanne on various matters, and obtained only the vaguest answers, I perceived that her young mind was totally absorbed by the skipping-rope, and I entered bravely into that grave subject.

"So you have been skipping?" I said. "It is a very nice amusement, but one that you must not exert yourself too much at; for any excessive exercise of that kind might seriously injure your health, and I should be very much grieved about it, Jeanne—I should be very much grieved, indeed!"

"You are very kind, Monsieur," the young girl said, "to have come to see me and talk to me like this. I did not think about thanking you when I came in, because I was too much surprised. Have you seen Madame de Gabry? Please tell me something about her, Monsieur."

"Madame de Gabry," I answered, "is very well. I can only tell you about her, Jeanne, what an old gardener once said of the lady of the castle, his mistress, when somebody anxiously inquired about her: 'Madame is in her road.' Yes, Madame de Gabry is in her own road; and you know, Jeanne, what a good road it is, and how steadily she can walk upon it. I went out with her the other day, very, very far away from the house; and we talked about you. We talked about you, my child, at your mother's grave."

"I am very glad," said Jeanne.

And then, all at once, she began to cry.

I felt too much reverence for those generous tears to attempt in any way to check the emotion that had evoked them. But in a little while, as the girl wiped her eyes, I asked her,

"Will you not tell me, Jeanne, why you were thinking so much about that skipping-rope a little while ago?"

"Why, indeed I will, Monsieur. It was only because I had no right to come into the parlour with a skipping-rope. You know, of course, that I am past the age for playing at skipping. But when the servant said there was an old gentleman . . . oh! . . . I mean . . . that a gentleman was waiting for me in the parlour, I was making the little girls jump. Then I tied the rope round my waist in a hurry, so that it might not get lost. It was wrong. But I have not been in the habit of having many people come to see me. And Mademoiselle Préfère never lets us off if we commit any breach of deportment: so I know she is going to punish me, and I am very sorry about it." . . .

"That is too bad, Jeanne!"

She became very grave, and said,

"Yes, Monsieur, it is too bad; because when I am punished myself, I have no more authority over the little girls."

I did not at once fully understand the nature of this unpleasantness; but Jeanne explained to me that, as she was charged by Mademoiselle Préfère with the duties of taking care of the youngest class, of washing and dressing the children, of teaching them how to behave, how to sew, how to say the alphabet, of showing them how to play, and, finally, of putting them to bed at the close of the day, she could not make herself obeyed by those turbulent little folks on the days she was condemned to wear a night-cap in the class-room, or to eat her meals standing up, from a plate turned upside down.

Having secretly admired the punishments devised by the Lady of the Enchanted Pelerine, I responded:

"Then, if I understand you rightly, Jeanne, you are at once a pupil here and a mistress? It is a condition of existence very common in the world. You are punished, and you punish?"

"Oh, Monsieur!" she exclaimed. "No! I never punish!"

"Then, I suspect," said I, "that your indulgence gets you many scoldings from Mademoiselle Préfère?"

She smiled, and blinked.

Then I said to her that the troubles in which we often involve ourselves, by trying to act according to our conscience and to do the best we can, are never of the sort that totally dishearten and weary us, but are, on the contrary, wholesome trials. This sort of philosophy touched her very little. She even appeared totally unmoved by my moral exhortations. But was not this quite natural on her part?—and ought I not to have remembered that it is only those no longer innocent who can find pleasure in the systems of moralists? . . . I had at least good sense enough to cut short my sermonising.

"Jeanne," I said, "you were asking a moment ago about Madame de Gabry. Let us talk about that Fairy of yours. She was very prettily made. Do you do any modelling in wax now?"

"I have not a bit of wax," she exclaimed, wringing her hands—"no wax at all!"

"No wax!" I cried—"in a republic of busy bees?"

She laughed.

"And, then, you see, Monsieur, my *figurines*, as you call them, are not in Mademoiselle Préfère's programme. But I had begun to make a very small Saint-George for Madame de Gabry—a tiny little Saint-George, with a golden cuirass. Is not that right, Monsieur Bonnard—to give Saint-George a gold cuirass?"

"Quite right, Jeanne; but what became of it?"

"I am going to tell you. I kept it in my pocket because I had no other place to put it, and—and I sat down on it by mistake."

She drew out of her pocket a little wax figure, which had been squeezed out of all resemblance to human form, and of which the dislocated limbs were only attached to the body by their wire framework. At the sight of her hero thus marred, she was seized at once with compassion and gaiety. The latter feeling obtained the mastery, and she burst into a clear laugh, which, however, stopped as suddenly as it had begun.

Mademoiselle Préfère stood at the parlour door, smiling.

"That dear child!" sighed the schoolmistress in her tenderest tone. "I am afraid she will tire you. And, then, your time is so precious!"

I begged Mademoiselle Préfère to dismiss that illusion, and, rising to take my leave, I took from my pocket some chocolate-cakes and sweets which I had brought with me.

"That is so nice!" said Jeanne; "there will be enough to go round the whole school."

The lady of the pelerine intervened.

"Mademoiselle Alexandre," she said, "thank Monsieur for his generosity."

Jeanne looked at her for an instant in a sullen way; then, turning to me, said with remarkable firmness,

"Monsieur, I thank you for your kindness in coming to see me."

"Jeanne," I said, pressing both her hands, "remain always a good, truthful, brave girl. Good-bye."

As she left the room with her packages of chocolate and confectionery, she happened to strike the handles of her skipping-rope against the back of a chair. Mademoiselle Préfère, full of indignation, pressed both hands over her heart, under her pelerine; and I almost expected to see her give up her scholastic ghost.

When we found ourselves alone, she recovered her composure; and I must say, without considering myself thereby flattered, that she smiled upon me with one whole side of her face.

"Mademoiselle," I said, taking advantage of her good humour, "I noticed that Jeanne Alexandre looks a little pale. You know better than I how much consideration and care a young girl requires at her age. It would only be doing you an injustice by implication to recommend her still more earnestly to your vigilance."

These words seemed to ravish her with delight. She lifted her eyes, as in ecstasy, to the paper spirals of the ceiling, and, clasping her hands, exclaimed,

"How well these eminent men know the art of considering the most trifling details!"

I called her attention to the fact that the health of a young girl was not a trifling detail, and made my farewell bow. But she stopped me on the threshold to say to me, very confidentially,

"You must excuse me, Monsieur. I am a woman, and I love glory. I cannot conceal from you the fact that I feel myself greatly honoured by the presence of a Member of the Institute in my humble institution."

I duly excused the weakness of Mademoiselle Préfère; and, thinking only of Jeanne, with the blindness of egotism, kept asking myself all along the road, "What are we going to do with this child?"

June 3.

I HAD escorted to the Cimetière de Marnes that day a very aged colleague of mine who, to use the words of Goethe, had consented to die. The great Goethe, whose own vital force was something extraordinary, actually believed that one never dies until one really wants to die—that is to say, when all those energies which resist dissolution, and the sum of which make up life itself, have been totally destroyed. In other words, he believed that people only die when it is no longer possible for them to live. Good; it is merely a question of properly understanding one another; and when fully comprehended, the magnificent idea of Goethe only brings us quietly back to the song of La Palisse.

Well, my excellent colleague had consented to die—thanks to several successive attacks of extremely persuasive apoplexy—the last of which proved unanswerable. I had been very little acquainted with him during his lifetime; but it seems that I became his friend the moment he was dead, for our colleagues assured me in the most serious manner, with deeply sympathetic countenances, that I should act as one of the pall-bearers, and deliver an address over the tomb.

After having read very badly a short address I had written as well as I could—which is not saying much for it—I started out for a walk in the woods of Ville-d'Avray, and followed, without leaning too much on the Captain's cane, a shaded path on which the sunlight fell, through foliage, in little discs of gold. Never had the scent of grass and fresh leaves,—never had the beauty of the sky over the trees, and the serene might of noble tree contours, so deeply affected my senses and all my being; and the pleasure I felt in that silence, broken only by faintest tinkling sounds, was at once of the senses and of the soul.

I sat down in the shade of the roadside under a clump of young oaks. And there I made a promise to myself not to die, or at least not to consent to die, before I should be again able to sit down under an oak, where—in the great peace of the open country—I could meditate on the nature of the soul and the ultimate destiny of man. A bee, whose brown breast-plate gleamed in the sun like armour of old gold, came to light upon a mallow-flower close by me —darkly rich in colour, and fully opened upon its tufted stalk. It was certainly not the first time I had witnessed so common an incident; but it was the first time that I had watched it with such comprehensive and friendly curiosity. I could discern that there were all sorts of sympathies between the insect and the flower—a thousand singular little relationships which I had never before even suspected.

Satiated with nectar, the insect rose and buzzed away in a straight line, while I lifted myself up as best I could, and readjusted myself upon my legs.

"Adieu!" I said to the flower and to the bee. "Adieu! Heaven grant I may live long enough to discover the secret of your harmonies. I am very tired. But man is so made that he can only find relaxation from one kind of labour by taking up another. The flowers and insects will give me that relaxation, with God's will, after my long researches in philology and diplomatics. How full of meaning is that old myth of Antæus! I have touched the Earth and I am a new man; and now, at seventy years of age, new feelings of curiosity take birth in my mind, even as young shoots sometimes spring up from the hollow trunk of an aged oak!"

June 4.

I LIKE to look out of my window at the Seine and its quays on those soft grey mornings which give such an infinite tenderness of tint to everything. I have seen that azure sky which flings so luminous a calm over the Bay of Naples. But our Parisian sky is more animated, more kindly, more spiritual. It smiles, threatens, caresses —takes an aspect of melancholy or a look of merriment like a human gaze. At this moment it is pouring down a very gentle light on the men and beasts of the city as they accomplish their daily tasks. Over there, on the opposite bank, the stevedores of the Port Saint-Nicholas are unloading a cargo of cow's horns; while two men standing on a gangway are tossing sugar-loaves from one to the other, and thence to somebody in the hold of a steamer. On the north quay, the cab-horses, standing in a line under the shade of the plane-trees each with its head in a nose-bag, are quietly munching their oats, while the rubicund drivers are drinking at the counter of the wine-seller opposite, but all the while keeping a sharp lookout for early customers.

The dealers in second-hand books put their boxes on the parapet. These good retailers of Mind, who are always in the open air, with blouses loose to the breeze, have become so weatherbeaten by the wind, the rain, the frost, the snow, the fog, and the great sun, that they end by looking very much like the old statues of cathedrals. They are all friends of mine, and I scarcely ever pass by their boxes without picking out of one of them some old book which I had always been in need of up to that very moment, without any suspicion of the fact on my part.

Then on my return home I have to endure the outcries of my housekeeper, who accuses me of bursting all my pockets and filling the house with waste paper to attract the rats. Thérèse is wise about that, and it is because she is wise that I do not listen to her; for in spite of my tranquil mien, I have always preferred the folly of the passions to the wisdom of indifference. But just because my own passions are not of that sort which burst out with violence to devastate and kill, the common mind is not aware of their existence. Nevertheless, I am greatly moved by them at times, and it has more than once been my fate to lose my sleep for the sake of a few pages written by some forgotten monk or printed by some humble apprentice of Peter Schœffer. And if these fierce enthusiasms are slowly being quenched in me, it is only because I am being slowly quenched myself. Our passions are ourselves. My old books are Me. I am just as old and thumb-worn as they are.

A light breeze sweeps away, along with the dust of the pavements, the winged seeds of the plane-trees, and the fragments of hay dropped from the mouths of the horses. The dust is nothing remarkable in itself; but as I watch it flying, I remember a moment in my childhood when I watched just such a whirl of dust; and my old Parisian soul is much affected by that sudden recollection. All that I see from my window—that horizon which extends to the left as far as the hills of Chaillot, and enables me to distinguish the Arc de Triomphe like a die of stone, the Seine, river of glory, and its bridges, the ash-trees of the terrace of the Tuileries, the Louvre of the Renaissance, cut and graven like goldsmith-work; and on my right, towards the Pont-Neuf (*pons Lutetiœ Novus dictus,* as it is named on old engravings), all the old and venerable part of Paris, with its towers and spires:—all that is my life, it is myself; and I should be nothing but for all those things which are thus reflected in me through my thousand varying shades of thought, inspiring me and animating me. That is why I love Paris with an immense love.

And nevertheless I am weary, and I know that there can be no rest for me in the heart of this great city which thinks so much, which has taught me to think, and which for ever urges me to think more. And how avoid being excited among all these books which incessantly tempt my curiosity without ever satisfying it? At one moment it is a date I have to look for; at another it is the name of a place I have to make sure of, or some quaint term of which it is important to determine the exact meaning. Words?—why, yes! words. As a philologist, I am their sovereign; they are my subjects, and, like a good king, I devote my whole life to them. But shall I not be able to abdicate some day? I have an idea that there is somewhere or other, quite far from here, a certain little cottage where I could enjoy the quiet I so much need, while awaiting that day in which a greater quiet—that which can be never broken—shall come to wrap me all about. I dream of a bench before the threshold, and of fields spreading away out of sight. But I must have a fresh smiling young face beside me, to reflect and concentrate all that freshness of nature. I could then imagine myself a grandfather, and all the long void of my life would be filled. . . .

I am not a violent man, and yet I become easily vexed, and all my works have caused me quite as much pain as pleasure. And I do not know how it is that I still keep thinking about that very conceited and very inconsiderate impertinence which my young friend of the Luxembourg took the liberty to utter about me some three months ago. I do not call him "friend" in irony, for I love studious youth with all its temerities and imaginative eccentricities. Still, my young friend certainly went beyond all bounds. Master Ambroise Paré, who was the first to attempt the ligature of arteries, and who, having commenced his profession at a time when surgery was only performed by quack barbers, nevertheless succeeded in lifting the science to the high place it now occupies, was assailed in his old age by all the young sawbones' apprentices. Being grossly abused during a discussion by some young addlehead who might have been the best son in the world, but who certainly lacked all sense of respect, the old master answered him in his treatise *De la Mumie, de la Licorne, des Venins et de la Peste.* "I pray him," said the great man—"I pray him, that if he desire to make any contradictions to my reply, he abandon all animosities, and treat the good old man with gentleness." This answer seems admirable from the pen of Ambroise Paré; but even had it been written by a village bonesetter, grown grey in his calling, and mocked by some young stripling, it would still be worthy of all praise.

It might perhaps seem that my memory of the incident had been kept alive only by a base feeling of resentment. I thought so myself at first, and reproached myself for thus dwelling on the saying of a boy who could not yet know the meaning of his own words. But my reflections on this subject subsequently took a better course: that is why I now note them down in my diary. I remembered that one day when I was twenty years old (that was more than half a century ago) I was walking about in that very same garden of the Luxembourg with some comrades. We were talking about our old professors; and one of us happened to name Monsieur Petit-Radel, an estimable and learned man, who was the first to throw some light upon the origin of early Etruscan civilisation, but who had been unfortunate enough to prepare a chronological table of the lovers of Helen. We all laughed a great deal about that chronological table; and I cried out, "Petit-Radel is an ass, not in three letters, but in twelve whole volumes!"

This foolish speech of my adolescence was uttered too lightly to be a weight on my conscience as an old man. May God kindly prove to me some day that I never used any less innocent shaft of speech in the battle of life! But I now ask myself whether I really never wrote, at any time in my life, something quite as unconsciously absurd as the chronological table of the lovers of Helen. The progress of science renders useless the very books which have been the greatest aids to that progress. As those works are no longer useful, modern youth is naturally inclined to believe they never had any value; it despises them, and ridicules them if they happen to contain any superannuated opinion whatever. That was why, in my twentieth year, I amused myself at the expense of Monsieur Petit-Radel and his chronological table; and that was why, the other day, at the Luxembourg, my young and irreverent friend . . .

> "*Rentre en toi-même, Octave, et cesse de te plaindre.*
> *Quoi! tu veux qu'on t'épargne et n'as rien épargné!*"*

June 6.

It was the first Thursday in June. I shut up my books and took my leave of the holy Abbot Droctoveus, who, being now in the en-

*"Look into thyself, Octavius, and cease complaining.
What! thou wouldst be spared, and thou thyself hast spared none!"

joyment of celestial bliss, cannot feel very impatient to behold his name and works glorified on earth through the humble compilation being prepared by my hands. Must I confess it? That mallow-plant I saw visited by a bee the other day has been occupying my thoughts much more than all the ancient abbots who ever bore croisers or wore mitres. There is in one of Sprengel's books which I read in my youth, at that time when I used to read anything and everything, some ideas about "the loves of flowers" which now return to memory after having been forgotten for half a century, and which to-day interest me so much that I regret not to have devoted the humble capacities of my mind to the study of insects and of plants.

And only awhile ago my housekeeper surprised me at the kitchen window, in the act of examining some wallflowers through a magnifying-glass. . . .

It was while looking for my cravat that I made these reflections. But after searching to no purpose in a great number of drawers, I found myself obliged, after all, to have recourse to my housekeeper. Thérèse came limping in.

"Monsieur," she said, "you ought to have told me you were going out, and I would have given you your cravat!"

"But Thérèse," I replied, "would it not be a great deal better to put it in some place where I could find it without your help?"

Thérèse did not deign to answer me.

Thérèse no longer allows me to arrange anything. I cannot even have a handkerchief without asking her for it; and as she is deaf, crippled, and, what is worse, beginning to lose her memory, I languish in perpetual destitution. But she exercises her domestic authority with such quiet pride that I do not feel the courage to attempt a *coup d'état* against her government.

"My cravat! Thérèse!—do you hear?—my cravat! if you drive me wild like this with your slow ways, it will not be a cravat I shall need, but a rope to hang myself!"

"You must be in a very great hurry, Monsieur," replied Thérèse. "Your cravat is not lost. Nothing is ever lost in this house, because I have charge of everything. But please allow me the time at least to find it."

"Yet here," I thought to myself—"here is the result of half a century of devotedness and self-sacrifice! . . . Ah! if by any happy chance this inexorable Thérèse had once in her whole life, only once, failed in her duty as a servant—if she had ever been at fault for one single instant, she could never have assumed this inflexible authority over me, and I should at least have the courage to resist her. But how can one resist virtue? The people who have no weaknesses are terrible; there is no way of taking advantage of them. Just look at Thérèse, for example; she has not a single fault for which you can blame her! She has no doubt of herself; nor of God, nor of the world. She is the valiant woman, the wise virgin of Scripture; others may know nothing about her, but I know her worth. In my fancy I always see her carrying a lamp, a humble kitchen lamp, illuminating the beams of some rustic roof—a lamp which will never go out while suspended from that meagre arm of hers, scraggy and strong as a vine-branch.

"Thérèse, my cravat! Don't you know, wretched woman, that to-day is the first Thursday in June, and that Mademoiselle Jeanne will be waiting for me? The schoolmistress has certainly had the parlour floor vigorously waxed: I am sure one can look at oneself in it now; and it will be quite a consolation for me when I slip and break my old bones upon it—which is sure to happen sooner or later—to see my rueful countenance reflected in it as in a looking-glass. Then taking for my model that amiable and admirable hero whose image is carved upon the handle of Uncle Victor's walking-stick, I will control myself so as not to make too ugly a grimace. . . . See what a splendid sun! The quays are all gilded by it, and the Seine smiles in countless little flashing wrinkles. The city is gold: a dust-haze, blonde and gold-toned as a woman's hair, floats above its beautiful contours. . . . Thérèse, my cravat! . . . Ah! I can now comprehend the wisdom of that old Chrysal who used to keep his neckbands in a big Plutarch. Hereafter I shall follow his example by laying all my neckties away between the leaves of the 'Acta Sanctorum.' "

Thérèse lets me talk on, and keeps looking for the necktie in silence. I hear a gentle ringing at our door-bell.

"Thérèse," I exclaim; "there is somebody ringing the bell! Give me my cravat, and go to the door; or, rather, go to the door first, and then, with the help of Heaven, you will give me my cravat. But please do not stand there between the clothes-press and the door like an old hack-horse between two saddles."

Thérèse marched to the door as if advancing upon an enemy. My excellent housekeeper becomes more inhospitable the older she grows. Every stranger is an object of suspicion to her. According to her own assertion, this disposition is the result of a long experience with human nature. I had not the time to consider whether the same experience on the part of another experimenter would produce the same results. Maître Mouche was waiting to see me in the ante-room.

Maître Mouche is still more yellow than I had believed him to be. He wears blue glasses, and his eyes keep moving uneasily behind them, like mice running about behind a screen.

Maître Mouche excuses himself for having intruded upon me at a moment when . . . He does not characterise the moment; but I think he means to say a moment in which I happen to be without my cravat. It is not my fault, as you very well know. Maître Mouche, who does not know, does not appear to be at all shocked, however. He is only afraid that he might have dropped in at the wrong moment. I succeeded in partially reassuring him at once upon that point. He then tells me it is as the guardian of Mademoiselle Alexandre that he has come to talk with me. First of all, he desires that I shall not hereafter pay any heed to those restrictions he had at first deemed it necessary to put upon the permit given to visit Mademoiselle Jeanne at the boarding-school. Henceforth the establishment of Mademoiselle Préfère will be open to me any day that I may choose to call—between the hours of midday and four o'clock. Knowing the interest I have taken in the young girl, he considers it his duty to give me some information about the person to whom he has confided his ward. Mademoiselle Préfère, whom he has known for many years, is in possession of his utmost confidence. Mademoiselle Préfère is, in his estimation, an enlightened person, of excellent morals, and capable of giving excellent counsel.

"Mademoiselle Préfère," he said to me, "has principles; and principles are rare in these days, Monsieur. Everything has been totally changed; and this epoch of ours cannot compare with the preceding ones."

"My stairway is a good example, Monsieur," I replied; "twenty-five years ago it used to allow me to climb it without any trouble, and now it takes my breath away, and wears my legs out before I have climbed half a dozen steps. It has had its character spoiled. Then there are those journals and books I used once to devour without difficulty by moonlight: to-day, even in the brightest sunlight, they mock my curiosity, and exhibit nothing but a blur of white and black when I have not got my spectacles on. Then the gout has got into my limbs. That is another malicious trick of the times!"

"Not only that, Monsieur," gravely replied Maître Mouche, "but what is really unfortunate in our epoch is that no one is satisfied with his position. From the top of society to the bottom, in every class, there prevails a discontent, a restlessness, a love of comfort. . . ."

"*Mon Dieu,* Monsieur!" I exclaimed. "You think this love of comfort is a sign of the times? Men have never had at any epoch a love of discomfort. They have always tried to better their condition. This constant effort produces constant changes, and the effort is always going on—that is all there is about it!"

"Ah! Monsieur," replied Maître Mouche, "it is easy to see that you live in your books—out of the business world altogether. You do not see, as I see them, the conflicts of interest, the struggle for money. It is the same effervescence in all minds, great or small. The wildest speculations are being everywhere indulged in. What I see around me simply terrifies me!"

I wondered within myself whether Maître Mouche had called upon me only for the purpose of expressing his virtuous misanthropy; but all at once I heard words of a more consoling character issue from his lips. Maître Mouche began to speak to me of Virginie

Préfère as a person worthy of respect, of esteem, and of sympathy,
—highly honourable, capable of great devotedness, cultivated, discreet,—able to read aloud remarkably well, extremely modest, and
skilful in the art of applying blisters. Then I began to understand
that he had only been painting that dismal picture of universal
corruption in order the better to bring out, by contrast, the virtues
of the schoolmistress. I was further informed that the institution in
the Rue Demours was well patronised, prosperous, and enjoyed a
high reputation with the public. Maître Mouche lifted up his hand
—with a black woollen glove on it—as if making oath to the truth
of these statements. Then he added:

"I am enabled, by the very character of my profession, to know
a great deal about people. A notary is, to a certain extent, a father-
confessor.

"I deemed it my duty, Monsieur, to give you this agreeable information at the moment when a lucky chance enabled you to meet
Mademoiselle Préfère. There is only one thing more which I would
like to say. This lady—who is, of course, quite unaware of my action
in the matter—spoke to me of you the other day in terms of the
deepest sympathy. I could only weaken their expression by repeating them to you; and, furthermore, I could not repeat them without
betraying, to a certain extent, the confidence of Mademoiselle
Préfère."

"Do not betray it, Monsieur; do not betray it!" I responded. "To
tell you the truth, I had no idea that Mademoiselle Préfère knew
anything whatever about me. But since you have the influence of
an old friend with her, I will take advantage of your good will, Monsieur, to ask you to exercise that influence in behalf of Mademoiselle Jeanne Alexandre. The child—for she is still a child—is over-
loaded with work. She is at once a pupil and a mistress—she is
overtaxed. Besides, she is punished in petty disgusting ways; and
hers is one of those generous natures which will be forced into revolt by such continual humiliation."

"Alas!" replied Maître Mouche, "she must be trained to take her
part in the struggle of life. One does not come into this world
simply to amuse oneself, and to do just what one pleases."

"One comes into this world," I responded, rather warmly, "to
enjoy what is beautiful and what is good, and to do as one pleases,
when the things one wants to do are noble, intelligent, and generous. An education which does not cultivate the will, is an education
that depraves the mind. It is a teacher's duty to teach the pupil
how to will."

I perceived that Maître Mouche began to think me a rather silly
man. With a great deal of quiet self-assurance, he proceeded:

"You must remember, Monsieur, that the education of the poor
has to be conducted with a great deal of circumspection, and with
a view to that future state of dependence they must occupy in

society. Perhaps you are not aware that the late Noël Alexandre died a bankrupt, and that his daughter is being educated almost by charity?"

"Oh! Monsieur!" I exclaimed, "do not say it! To say it is to pay oneself back, and then the statement ceases to be true."

"The liabilities of the estate," continued the notary, "exceeded the assets. But I was able to effect a settlement with the creditors in favour of the minor."

He undertook to explain matters in detail. I declined to listen to these explanations, being incapable of understanding business methods in general, and those of Maître Mouche in particular. The notary then took it upon himself to justify Mademoiselle Préfère's educational system, and observed by way of conclusion,

"It is not by amusing oneself that one can learn."

"It is only by amusing oneself that one can learn," I replied. "The whole art of teaching is only the art of awakening the natural curiosity of young minds for the purpose of satisfying it afterwards; and curiosity itself can be vivid and wholesome only in proportion as the mind is contented and happy. Those acquirements crammed by force into the minds of children simply clog and stifle intelligence. In order that knowledge be properly digested, it must have been swallowed with a good appetite. I know Jeanne! If that child were intrusted to my care, I should make of her—not a learned woman, for I would look to her future happiness only—but a child full of bright intelligence and full of life, in whom everything beautiful in art or nature would awaken some gentle responsive thrill. I would teach her to live in sympathy with all that is beautiful— comely landscapes, the ideal scenes of poetry and history, the emotional charm of noble music. I would make lovable to her everything I would wish her to love. Even her needlework I would make pleasurable to her, by a proper choice of the fabrics, the style of embroideries, the designs of lace. I would give her a beautiful dog, and a pony to teach her how to manage animals; I would give her birds to take care of, so that she could learn the value of even a drop of water and a crumb of bread. And in order that she should have a still higher pleasure, I would train her to find delight in exercising charity. And inasmuch as none of us may escape pain, I should teach her that Christian wisdom which elevates us above all suffering, and gives a beauty even to grief itself. That is my idea of the right way to educate a young girl."

"I yield, Monsieur," replied Maître Mouche, joining his black-gloved hands together.

And he rose.

"Of course you understand," I remarked, as I went to the door with him, "that I do not pretend for a moment to impose my educational system upon Mademoiselle Préfère; it is necessarily a private one, and quite incompatible with the organisation of even the best-managed boarding schools. I only ask you to persuade her to give Jeanne less work and more play, and not to punish her except in case of absolute necessity, and to let her have as much freedom of mind and body as the regulations of the institution permit."

It was with a pale and mysterious smile that Maître Mouche informed me that my observations would be taken in good part, and should receive all possible consideration.

Therewith he made me a little bow, and took his departure, leaving me with a peculiar feeling of discomfort and uneasiness. I have met a great many strange characters in my time, but never any at all resembling either this notary or this schoolmistress.

July 6.

MAÎTRE MOUCHE had so much delayed me by his visit that I gave up going to see Jeanne that day. Professional duties kept me very busy for the rest of the week. Although at the age when most men retire altogether from active life, I am still attached by a thousand ties to the society in which I have lived. I have to preside at meetings of academies, scientific congresses, assemblies of various learned bodies. I am overburdened with honorary functions; I have seven of these in one government department alone. The *bureaux* would be very glad to get rid of me, and I should be very glad to get rid of them. But habit is stronger than both of us together, and I continue to hobble up the stairs of various government buildings. Old clerks point me out to each other as I go by like a ghost wandering through the corridors. When one has become very old one finds it extremely difficult to disappear. Nevertheless, it is time, as the old song says, *de prendre ma retraite et de songer à faire un fin"*—to retire on my pension and prepare myself to die a good death.

An old marchioness, who used to be a friend of Helvetius in her youth, and whom I once met at my father's house when a very old woman, was visited during her last sickness by the priest of her parish, who wanted to prepare her to die.

"Is that really necessary?" she asked. "I see everybody else manage it perfectly well the first time."

My father went to see her very soon afterwards and found her extremely ill.

"Good-evening, my friend!" she said, pressing his hand. "I am going to see whether God improves upon acquaintance."

So were wont to die the *belles amies* of the philosophers. Such an end is certainly not vulgar nor impertinent, and such levities are not of the sort that emanate from dull minds. Nevertheless, they shock me. Neither my fears nor my hopes could accommodate themselves to such a mode of departure. I would like to make mine with a perfectly collected mind; and that is why I must begin to think, in a year or two, about some way of belonging to myself; otherwise, I should certainly risk . . . But, hush! let Him not hear His name and turn to look as He passes by! I can still lift my fagot without His aid.

. . . I found Jeanne very happy indeed. She told me that, on the Thursday previous, after the visit of her guardian, Mademoiselle Préfère had set her free from the ordinary regulations and lightened her tasks in several ways. Since that lucky Thursday she could walk in the garden—which only lacked leaves and flowers—as much as she liked; and she had even been given facilities to work at her unfortunate little figure of Saint-George.

She said to me, with a smile,

"I know very well that I owe all this to you."

I tried to talk with her about other matters, but I remarked that she could not attend to what I was saying, in spite of her effort to do so.

"I see you are thinking about something else," I said. "Well, tell me what it is; for, if you do not, we shall not be able to talk to each other at all, which would be very unworthy of both of us."

She answered,

"Oh! I was really listening to you, Monsieur; but it is true that I was thinking about something else. You will excuse me, won't you? I could not help thinking that Mademoiselle Préfère must like you very, very much indeed, to have become so good to me all of a sudden."

Then she looked at me in an odd, smiling, frightened way, which made me laugh.

"Does that surprise you?" I asked.

"Very much," she replied.

"Please tell me why?"

"Because I can see no reason, no reason at all . . . but there! . . . no reason at all why you should please Mademoiselle Préfère so much."

"So, then, you think I am very displeasing, Jeanne?"

She bit her lips, as if to punish them for having made a mistake; and then, in a coaxing way, looking at me with great soft eyes, gentle and beautiful as a spaniel's, she said,

"I know I said a foolish thing; but, still, I do not see any reason why you should be so pleasing to Mademoiselle Préfère. And, nevertheless, you seem to please her a great deal—a very great deal. She called me one day, and asked me all sorts of questions about you."

"Really?"

"Yes; she wanted to find out all about your house. Just think! she even asked me how old your servant was!"

And Jeanne burst out laughing.

"Well, what do you think about it?" I asked.

She remained a long while with her eyes fixed on the worn-out cloth of her shoes, and seemed to be thinking very deeply. Finally, looking up again, she answered,

"I am distrustful. Isn't it very natural to feel uneasy about what one cannot understand; I know I am foolish; but you won't be offended with me, will you?"

"Why, certainly not, Jeanne. I am not a bit offended with you."

I must acknowledge that I was beginning to share her surprise; and I began to turn over in my old head the singular thought of this young girl—"One is uneasy about what one cannot understand."

But, with a fresh burst of merriment, she cried out,

"She asked me . . . guess! I will give you a hundred guesses—a thousand guesses. You give it up? . . . She asked me if you liked good eating."

"And how did you receive this shower of interrogations, Jeanne?"

"I replied, 'I don't know, Mademoiselle.' And Mademoiselle then said to me, 'You are a little fool. The least details of the life of an eminent man ought to be observed. Please to know, Mademoiselle, that Monsieur Sylvestre Bonnard is one of the glories of France!'"

"Stuff!" I exclaimed. "And what did *you* think about it, Mademoiselle?"

"I thought that Mademoiselle Préfère was right. But I don't care at all . . . (I know it is naughty what I am going to say) . . . I don't care a bit, not a bit, whether Mademoiselle Préfère is or is not right about anything."

"Well, then, content yourself, Jeanne, Mademoiselle Préfère was not right."

"Yes, yes, she was quite right that time; but I wanted to love everybody who loved you—everybody without exception—and I cannot do it, because it would never be possible for me to love Mademoiselle Préfère."

"Listen, Jeanne," I answered, very seriously, "Mademoiselle Préfère has become good to you; try now to be good to her."

She answered sharply,

"It is very easy for Mademoiselle Préfère to be good to me, and it would be very difficult indeed for me to be good to her."

I then said, in a still more serious tone:

"My child, the authority of a teacher is sacred. You must consider your schoolmistress as occupying the place to you of the mother whom you lost."

I had scarcely uttered this solemn stupidity when I bitterly regretted it. The child turned pale, and the tears sprang to her eyes.

"Oh, Monsieur!" she cried, "how could you say such a thing— *you?* You never knew mamma!"

Ay, just Heaven! I did know her mamma. And how indeed could I have been foolish enough to have said what I did?

She repeated, as if to herself:

"Mamma! my dear mamma! my poor mamma!"

A lucky chance prevented me from playing the fool any further. I do not know how it happened that at that moment I looked as if I was going to cry. At my age one does not cry. It must have been a bad cough which brought the tears into my eyes. But, anyhow, appearances were in my favour. Jeanne was deceived by them. Oh! what a pure and radiant smile suddenly shone out under her beautiful wet eyelashes—like sunshine among branches after a summer shower! We took each other by the hand and sat a long while without saying a word—absolutely happy. Those celestial harmonies which I once thought I heard thrilling through my soul while I knelt before that tomb to which a saintly woman had guided me, suddenly awoke again in my heart, slow-swelling through the blissful moments with infinite softness. Doubtless the child whose hand pressed my own also heard them; and then, elevated by their enchantment above the material world, the poor old man and the artless young girl both knew that a tender ghostly Presence was making sweetness all about them.

"My child," I said at last, "I am very old, and many secrets of life, which you will only learn little by little, have been revealed to me. Believe me, the future is shaped out of the past. Whatever you can do to live contentedly here, without impatience and without fretting, will help you to live some future day in peace and joy in your own home. Be gentle, and learn how to suffer. When one suffers patiently one suffers less. If you should ever happen to have a serious cause of complaint I shall be there to take your part. If you should be badly treated, Madame de Gabry and I would both consider ourselves badly treated in your person." . . .

"Is your health very good indeed, dear Monsieur?"

It was Mademoiselle Préfère, approaching stealthily behind us, who had asked the question with her peculiar smile. My first idea was to tell her to go to the devil; my second, that her mouth was as little suited for smiling as a frying-pan for musical purposes; my third was to answer her politely and assure her that I hoped she was very well.

She sent the young girl out to take a walk in the garden; then, pressing one hand upon her pelerine and extending the other towards the *Tableau d'Honneur,* she showed me the name of Jeanne Alexandre written at the head of the list in large text.

"I am very much pleased," I said to her, "to find that you are satisfied with the behaviour of that child. Nothing could delight me more; and I am inclined to attribute this happy result to your affectionate vigilance. I have taken the liberty to send you a few books which I think may serve both to instruct and to amuse young girls. You will be able to judge by glancing over them whether they are adapted to the perusal of Mademoiselle Alexandre and her companions."

The gratitude of the schoolmistress not only overflowed in words, but seemed about to take the form of tearful sensibility. In order to change the subject I observed,

"What a beautiful day this is!"

"Yes," she replied; "and if this weather continues, those dear children will have a nice time for their enjoyment."

"I suppose you are referring to the holidays. But Mademoiselle Alexandre, who has no relatives, cannot go away. What in the world is she going to do all alone in this great big house?"

"Oh, we will do everything we can to amuse her. . . . I will take her to the museums and——"

She hesitated, blushed, and continued,

"——and to your house, if you will permit me."

"Why of course!" I exclaimed. "That is a first-rate idea."

We separated very good friends with one another. I with her, because I had been able to obtain what I desired; she with me, for no appreciable motive—which fact, according to Plato, elevated her into the highest rank of the Hierarchy of Souls.

. . . And nevertheless it is not without a presentiment of evil that I find myself on the point of introducing this person into my house. And I would be very glad indeed to see Jeanne in charge of anybody else rather than of her. Maître Mouche and Mademoiselle Préfère are characters whom I cannot at all understand. I never can imagine why they say what they do say, nor why they do what they do; they have a mysterious something in common which makes me feel uneasy. As Jeanne said to me a little while ago: "One is uneasy about what one cannot understand."

Alas! at my age one has learned only too well how little sincerity there is in life; one has learned only too well how much one loses by living a long time in this world; and one feels that one can no longer trust any except the young.

August 12.

I WAITED for them. In fact, I waited for them very impatiently. I exerted all my powers of insinuation and of coaxing to induce Thérèse to receive them kindly; but my powers in this direction are very limited. They came. Jeanne was neater and prettier than I had ever expected to see her. She has not, it is true, anything approaching the charm of her mother. But to-day, for the first time, I observed that she has a pleasing face; and a pleasing face is of great advantage to a woman in this world. I think that her hat was a little on one side; but she smiled, and the City of Books was all illuminated by that smile.

I watched Thérèse to see whether the rigid manners of the old housekeeper would soften a little at the sight of the young girl. I saw her turning her lustreless eyes upon Jeanne; I saw her long wrinkled face, her toothless mouth, and that pointed chin of hers—like the chin of some puissant old fairy. And that was all I could see.

Mademoiselle Préfère made her appearance all in blue—advanced, retreated, skipped, tripped, cried out, sighed, cast her eyes down, rolled her eyes up, bewildered herself with excuses—said she dared not, and nevertheless dared—said she would never dare again, and nevertheless dared again—made courtesies innumerable—made, in short, all the fuss she could.

"What a lot of books!" she screamed. "And have you really read them all, Monsieur Bonnard?"

"Alas! I have," I replied, "and that is just the reason that I do not know anything; for there is not a single one of those books which does not contradict some other book; so that by the time one has read them all one does not know what to think about anything. That is just my condition, Madame."

Thereupon she called Jeanne for the purpose of communicating her impressions. But Jeanne was looking out of the window.

"How beautiful it is!" she said to us. "How I love to see the river flowing! It makes you think about all kinds of things."

Mademoiselle Préfère having removed her hat and exhibited a forehead tricked out with blonde curls, my housekeeper sturdily snatched up the hat at once, with the observation that she did not like to see people's clothes scattered over the furniture. Then she approached Jeanne and asked her for her "things," calling her "my little lady!" Whereupon the little lady, giving up her cloak and hat, exposed to view a very graceful neck and a lithe figure, whose outlines were beautifully relieved against the great glow of the open window; and I could have wished that some one else might have seen her at that moment—some one very different from an aged housekeeper, a schoolmistress frizzled like a sheep, and this old humbug of an archivist and paleographer.

"So you are looking at the Seine," I said to her. "See how it sparkles in the sun!"

"Yes," she replied, leaning over the window-bar, "it looks like a flowing of fire. But see how nice and cool it looks on the other side over there, under the shadow of the willows! That little spot there pleases me better than all the rest."

"Good!" I answered. "I see that the river has a charm for you. How would you like, with Mademoiselle Préfère's permission, to make a trip to Saint-Cloud? We should certainly be in time to catch the steamboat just below the Pont-Royal."

Jeanne was delighted with my suggestion, and Mademoiselle Préfère willing to make any sacrifice. But my housekeeper was not at all willing to let us go off so unconcernedly. She summoned me into the dining-room, whither I followed her in fear and trembling.

"Monsieur," she said to me as soon as we found ourselves alone, "you never think about anything, and it is always I who have to think about everything. Luckily for you I have a good memory."

I did not think that it was a favourable moment for any attempt to dispel this wild illusion. She continued:

"So you were going off without saying a word to me about what this little lady likes to eat? At her age one does not know anything, one does not care about anything in particular, one eats like a bird. You yourself, Monsieur, are very difficult to please; but at least you know what is good: it is very different with these young people—they do not know anything about cooking. It is often the very best thing which they think the worst, and what is bad seems to them good, because their stomachs are not quite formed yet—so that one never knows just what to do for them. Tell me if the little lady would like a pigeon cooked with green peas, and whether she is fond of vanilla ice-cream."

"My good Thérèse," I answered, "just do whatever you think best, and whatever that may be I am sure it will be very nice. Those ladies will be quite contented with our humble ordinary fare."

Thérèse replied, very dryly,

"Monsieur, I am asking you about the little lady: she must not leave this house without having enjoyed herself a little. As for that old frizzle-headed thing, if she doesn't like my dinner she can suck her thumbs. I don't care what she likes!"

My mind being thus set at rest, I returned into the City of Books, where Mademoiselle Préfère was crocheting as calmly as if she were at home. I almost felt inclined myself to think she was. She did not take up much room, it is true, in the angle of the window. But she had chosen her chair and her footstool so well that those articles of furniture seemed to have been made expressly for her.

Jeanne, on the other hand, devoted her attention to the books and pictures—gazing at them in a kindly, expressive, half-sad way, as if she were bidding them an affectionate farewell.

"Here," I said to her, "amuse yourself with this book, which I am sure you cannot help liking, because it is full of beautiful engravings." And I threw open before her Vecellio's collection of costume-designs—not the commonplace edition, by your leave, so meagerly reproduced by modern artists, but in truth a magnificent and venerable copy of that *editio princeps* which is noble as those noble dames who figure upon its yellowed leaves, made beautiful by time.

While turning over the engravings with artless curiosity, Jeanne said to me,

"We were talking about taking a walk; but this is a great journey you are making me take. And I would like to travel very, very far away!"

"In that case, Mademoiselle," I said to her, "you must arrange yourself as comfortably as possible for travelling. But you are now sitting on one corner of your chair, so that the chair is standing upon only one leg, and that Vecellio must tire your knees. Sit down comfortably; put your chair on its four feet, and put your book on the table."

She obeyed me with a laugh.

I watched her. She cried out suddenly,

"Oh, come look at this beautiful costume!" (It was that of the wife of a Doge of Venice.) "How noble it is! What magnificent ideas it gives one of that life! Oh, I must tell you—I adore luxury!"

"You must not express such thoughts as those, Mademoiselle," said the schoolmistress, lifting up her little shapeless nose from her work.

"Nevertheless, it was a very innocent utterance," I replied. "There are splendid souls in whom the love of splendid things is natural and inborn."

The little shapeless nose went down again.

"Mademoiselle Préfère likes luxury too," said Jeanne; "she cuts out paper trimmings and shades for the lamps. It is economical luxury; but it is luxury all the same."

Having returned to the subject of Venice, we were just about to make the acquaintance of a certain patrician lady attired in an embroidered dalmatic, when I heard the bell ring. I thought it was some peddler with his basket; but the gate of the City of Books opened, and . . . Well, Master Sylvestre Bonnard, you were wishing awhile ago that the grace of your *protégée* might be observed by some other eyes than old withered ones behind spectacles. Your wishes have been fulfilled in a most unexpected manner, and a voice cries out to you, as to the imprudent Theseus,

> "Craignez, Seigneur, craignez que le Ciel rigoureux
> Ne vous haïsse assez pour exaucer vos vœux!
> Souvent dans sa colère il reçoit nos victimes,
> Ses présents sont souvent la peine de nos crimes."*

The gate of the City of Books had opened, and a handsome young man made his appearance, ushered in by Thérèse. That good old soul only knows how to open the door for people and to shut it behind them; she has no idea whatever of the tact requisite for the waiting-room and for the parlour. It is not in her nature either to make any announcements or to make anybody wait. She either throws people out on the lobby, or simply pitches them at your head.

And here is this handsome young man already inside; and I cannot really take the girl at once and hide her like a secret treasure in the next room. I wait for him to explain himself; he does it with-

---

*"Beware, my lord! Beware lest stern Heaven hate you enough to hear your prayers! Often 'tis in wrath that Heaven receives our sacrifices; its gifts are often the punishment of our crimes."

out the least embarrassment; but it seems to me that he has already observed the young girl who is still bending over the table looking at Vecellio. As I observe the young man it occurs to me that I have seen him somewhere before, or else I must be very much mistaken. His name is Gélis. That is a name which I have heard somewhere,—I can't remember where. At all events, Monsieur Gélis (since there is a Gélis) is a fine-looking young fellow. He tells me that this is his third class-year at the École des Chartes, and that he has been working for the past fifteen or eighteen months upon his graduation thesis, the subject of which is the Condition of the Benedictine Abbeys in 1700. He has just read my works upon the "Monasticon"; and he is convinced that he cannot terminate this thesis successfully without my advice, to begin with, and in the second place without a certain manuscript which I possess, and which is nothing less than the "Register of the Accounts of the Abbey of Citeaux from 1683 to 1704."

Having thus explained himself, he hands me a letter of introduction bearing the signature of one of the most illustrious of my colleagues.

Good! Now I know who he is! Monsieur Gélis is the very same young man who last year under the chestnut-trees called me an idiot! And while unfolding his letter of introduction I think to myself:

"Aha! my unlucky youth, you are very far from suspecting that I overheard what you said, and that I know what you think of me —or, at least, what you did think of me that day, for these young minds are so fickle? I have got you now, my friend! You have fallen into the lion's den, and so unexpectedly, in good sooth, that the astonished old lion does not know what to do with his prey. But come now, old lion! do not act like an idiot! Is it not possible that you were an idiot? If you are not one now, you certainly were one! You were a fool to have been listening to Monsieur Gélis at the foot of the statue of Marguerite de Valois; you were doubly a fool to have heard what he said; and you were trebly a fool not to have forgotten what it would have been much better never to have heard."

Having thus scolded the old lion, I exhorted him to show clemency. He did not appear to require much coaxing, and gradually became so good-natured that he had some difficulty in restraining himself from bursting out into joyous roarings. From the way in which I had read my colleague's letter one might have supposed me a man who did not know his alphabet. I took a long while to read it; and Monsieur Gélis might have become very tired under different circumstances; but he was watching Jeanne, and endured the trial with exemplary patience. Jeanne occasionally turned her face in our direction. Well, you could not expect a person to remain perfectly motionless, could you? Mademoiselle Préfère was arranging her curls, and her bosom occasionally swelled with little sighs. It may be observed that I have myself often been honoured with these little sighs.

"Monsieur," I said, as I folded up the letter, "I shall be very happy to be of any service to you. You are occupied with researches in which I myself have always felt a very lively interest. I have done all that lay in my power. I know, as you do—and still better than you can know—how much there remains to do. The manuscript you asked for is at your disposal; you may take it home with you, but it is not a manuscript of the smallest kind, and I am afraid——"

"Oh, Monsieur," said Gélis, "big books have never been able to make me afraid of them."

I begged the young man to wait for me, and I went into the next room to get the Register, which I could not find at first, and which I almost despaired of finding, as I discerned, from certain familiar signs, that Thérèse had been setting the room in order. But the Register was so big and so heavy that, luckily for me, Thérèse had not been able to put it in order as she had doubtless wished to do. I could scarcely lift it up myself; and I had the pleasure of finding it quite as heavy as I could have hoped.

"Wait, my boy," I said, with a smile which must have been very sarcastic—"wait! I am going to give you something to do which will break your arms first, and afterwards your head. That will be the first vengeance of Sylvestre Bonnard. Later on we shall see what else there is to be done."

When I returned to the City of Books I heard Monsieur Gélis and Mademoiselle Jeanne chatting—chatting together, if you please! as if they were the best friends in the world. Mademoiselle Préfère, being full of decorum, did not say anything; but the other two were chattering like birds. And what about? About the blond tint used by Venetian painters! Yes, about the "Venetian blond." That little serpent of a Gélis was telling Jeanne the secret of the dye with which, according to the best authorities, the women of Titian and of Veronese tinted their hair. And Mademoiselle Jeanne was expressing her opinion very prettily about the honey tint and the golden tint. I understood that that scamp of a Vecellio was responsible—that they had been bending over the book together, and they had been admiring either that Doge's wife we had been looking at awhile before, or some other patrician woman of Venice.

Never mind! I appeared with my enormous old book, thinking that Gélis was going to make a grimace. It was as much as one could have asked a porter to carry, and my arms were stiff merely with lifting it. But the young man caught it up like a feather, and slipped it under his arm with a smile. Then he thanked me with that sort of brevity which I like, reminded me that he had need of my advice, and, having made an appointment to meet me another day, took his departure after bowing to us with the most perfect self-possession conceivable.

"He seems quite a decent lad," I said.

Jeanne turned over a few more pages of Vecellio, and made no answer.

"Aha!" I thought to myself. . . . And then we went to Saint-Cloud.

September-December.

THE regularity with which visit succeeded visit to the old man's house thereafter made me feel very grateful to Mademoiselle Préfère, who succeeded at last in winning her right to occupy a special corner in the City of Books. She now says *"my* chair," *"my* footstool," *"my* pigeon-hole." Her pigeon-hole is really a small shelf properly belonging to the poets of La Champagne, whom she expelled therefrom in order to obtain a lodging for her work-bag. She is very amiable, and I must really be a monster not to like her. I can only endure her—in the severest signification of the word. But what would one not endure for Jeanne's sake? Her presence lends to the City of Books a charm which seems to hover about it even after she has gone. She is very ignorant; but she is so finely gifted that whenever I show her anything beautiful I am astounded to find that I had never really seen it before, and that it is she who makes me see it. I have found it impossible so far to make her follow some of my ideas, but I have often found pleasure in following the whimsical and delicate course of her own.

A more practical man than I would attempt to teach her to make herself useful; but is not the capacity of being amiable a useful thing in life? Without being pretty, she charms; and the power to charm is perhaps, after all, worth quite as much as the ability to darn stockings. Furthermore, I am not immortal; and I doubt whether she will have become very old when my notary (who is not Maître Mouche) shall read to her a certain paper which I signed a little while ago.

I do not wish that any one except myself should provide for her, and give her her dowry. I am not, however, very rich, and the paternal inheritance did not gain bulk in my hands. One does not accumulate money by poring over old texts. But my books—at the price which such noble merchandise fetches to-day—are worth something. Why, on that shelf there are some poets of the sixteenth century for which bankers would bid against princes! And I think that those "Heures" of Simon Vostre would not be readily overlooked at the Hôtel Sylvestre any more than would those *Preces Piæ* compiled for the use of Queen Claude. I have taken great pains to collect and to preserve all those rare and curious editions which people the City of Books; and for a long time I used to believe that they were as necessary to my life as air and light. I have loved them well, and even now I cannot prevent myself from smiling at them and caressing them. Those morocco bindings are so delightful to the eye! Those old vellums are so soft to the touch! There is not a single one among those books which is not worthy, by reason of some special merit, to command the respect of an honourable man. What other owner would ever know how to dip into them in the proper way? Can I be even sure that another owner would not leave them to decay in neglect, or mutilate them at the prompting of some ignorant whim? Into whose hands will fall that incomparable copy of the "Histoire de l'Abbaye de Saint-Germaindes-Prés," on the margins of which the author himself, in the person of Jacques Bouillard, made such substantial notes in his own handwriting? . . . Master Bonnard, you are an old fool! Your housekeeper—poor soul!—is nailed down upon her bed with a merciless attack of rheumatism. Jeanne is to come with her chaperon, and, instead of thinking how you are going to receive them, you are thinking about a thousand stupidities. Sylvestre Bonnard, you will never succeed at anything in this world, and it is I myself who tell you so!

And at this very moment I catch sight of them from my window, as they get out of the omnibus. Jeanne leaps down like a kitten; but Mademoiselle Préfère intrusts herself to the strong arm of the conductor, with the shy grace of a Virginia recovering after the shipwreck, and this time quite resigned to being saved. Jeanne looks up, sees me, laughs, and Mademoiselle Préfère has to prevent her from waving her umbrella at me as a friendly signal. There is a certain stage of civilisation to which Mademoiselle Jeanne never can be brought. You can teach her all the arts if you like (it is not exactly to Mademoiselle Préfère that I am now speaking); but you will never be able to teach her perfect manners. As a charming girl she makes the mistake of being charming only in her own way. Only an old fool like myself could forgive her pranks. As for young fools—and there are several of them still to be found—I do not know what they would think about it; and what they might think is none of my business. Just look at her running along the pavement, wrapped up in her cloak, with her hat tilted back on her head, and her feather fluttering in the wind, like a schooner in full rig! And really she has a grace of poise and motion which suggests a fine sailing-vessel—so much so, indeed, that she makes me remember seeing one day, when I was at Havre . . . But, Bonnard, my friend, how many times is it necessary to tell you that your housekeeper is in bed, and that you must go and open the door yourself?

Open, Old Man Winter! 'tis Spring who rings the bell.

It is Jeanne herself—Jeanne all flushed like a rose. Mademoiselle Préfère, indignant and out of breath, has still another whole flight to climb before reaching our lobby.

I explained the condition of my housekeeper, and proposed that we should dine at a restaurant. But Thérèse—all-powerful still, even upon her sick-bed—decided that we should dine at home, whether we wanted to or not. Respectable people, in her opinion, never dined at restaurants. Moreover, she had made all necessary arrangements—the dinner had been bought; the concierge would cook it.

The audacious Jeanne insisted upon going to see whether the old woman wanted anything. As you might suppose, she was sent back to the parlour with short shrift, but not so harshly as I had feared.

"If I want anybody to do anything for me, which, thank God, I do not," Thérèse had replied, "I would get somebody less delicate and dainty than you are. What I want is rest. That is a merchandise which is not sold at fairs under the sign of *Motus with finger on lip*. Go and have your fun, and don't stay here—for old age might be catching."

Jeanne, after telling us what she had said, added that she liked very much to hear old Thérèse talk. Whereupon Mademoiselle Préfère reproached her for expressing such unladylike tastes.

I tried to excuse her by citing the example of Molière. Just at that moment it came to pass that, while climbing the ladder to get a book, she upset a whole shelf-row. There was a heavy crash; and Mademoiselle Préfère, being, of course, a very delicate person, almost fainted. Jeanne quickly followed the books to the foot of the ladder. She made one think of a kitten suddenly transformed into a woman, catching mice which had been transformed into old books. While picking them up, she found one which happened to interest her, and she began to read it, squatting down upon her heels. It was the "Prince Grenouille," she told us. Mademoiselle Préfère took occasion to complain that Jeanne had so little taste for poetry. It was impossible to get her to recite Casimir Delavigne's poem on the death of Joan of Arc without mistakes. It was the very most she could do to learn "Le Petit Savoyard." The schoolmistress did not think that any one should read the "Prince Grenouille" before learning by heart the stanzas to Duperrier; and, carried away by her enthusiasm, she began to recite them in a voice sweeter than the bleating of a sheep:

> "Ta douleur, Duperrier, sera donc éternelle,
>   Et les tristes discours
> Que te met en l'esprit l'amitié paternelle
>   L'augmenteront toujours;

>   .   .   .   .

> "Je sais de quels appas son enfance etait pleine,
>   Et n'ai pas entrepris,
> Injurieux ami, de consoler ta peine
>   Avecque son mépris."

Then in ecstasy she exclaimed,

"How beautiful that is! What harmony! How is it possible for any one not to admire such exquisite, such touching verses! But why did Malherbe call that poor Monsieur Duperrier his *'injurieux ami'* at a time when he had been so severely tried by the death of his daughter? *Injurieux ami*—you must acknowledge that the term was very harsh."

I explained to this poetical person that the phrase *"Injurieux ami,"* which shocked her so much, was in apposition, etc. etc. What I said, however, had so little effect towards clearing her head that she was seized with a severe and prolonged fit of sneezing. Meanwhile it was evident that the history of "Prince Grenouille" had proved extremely funny; for it was all that Jeanne could do, as she crouched down there on the carpet, to keep herself from bursting into a wild fit of laughter. But when she had finished with the prince and princess of the story, and the multitude of their children, she assumed a very suppliant expression, and begged me as a great favour to allow her to put on a white apron and go to the kitchen to help in getting the dinner ready.

"Jeanne," I replied, with the gravity of a master, "I think that if it is a question of breaking plates, knocking off the edges of dishes, denting all the pans, and smashing all the skimmers, the person whom Thérèse has set to work in the kitchen already will be able to perform her task without assistance; for it seems to me at this very moment I can hear disastrous noises in that kitchen. But anyhow, Jeanne, I will charge you with the duty of preparing the dessert. So go and get your white apron; I will tie it on for you."

Accordingly, I solemnly knotted the linen apron about her waist; and she rushed into the kitchen, where she proceeded at once—as we discovered later on—to prepare various dishes unknown to Vatel, unknown even to that great Carême who began his treatise upon *pièces montées* with these words: *"The Fine Arts are five in number: Painting, Music, Poetry, Sculpture, and Architecture— whereof the principal branch is Confectionery."* But I had no reason to be pleased with this little arrangement—for Mademoiselle Préfère, on finding herself alone with me, began to act after a fashion which filled me with frightful anxiety. She gazed upon me with eyes full of tears and flames, and uttered enormous sighs.

"Oh, how I pity you!" she said. "A man like you—a man so superior as you are—having to live alone with a coarse servant (for she is certainly coarse, that is incontestable)! How cruel such a life must be! You have need of repose—you have need of comfort, of care, of every kind of attention; you might fall sick. And yet there is no woman who would not deem it an honour to bear your name, and to share your existence. No, there is none; my own heart tells me so."

And she squeezed both hands over that heart of hers—always so ready to fly away.

I was driven almost to distraction. I tried to make Mademoiselle Préfère comprehend that I had no intention whatever of changing my habits at so advanced an age, and that I found just as much happiness in life as my character and my circumstances rendered possible.

"No, you are not happy!" she cried. "You need to have always beside you a mind capable of comprehending your own. Shake off your lethargy, and cast your eyes about you. Your professional connections are of the most extended character, and you must have charming acquaintances. One cannot be a Member of the Institute without going into society. See, judge, compare. No sensible woman would refuse you her hand. I am a woman, Monsieur; my instinct never deceives me—there is something within me which assures me that you would find happiness in marriage. Women are so devoted, so loving (not all, of course, but some)! And, then, they are so sensitive to glory. Remember that at your age one has need, like Œdipus, of an Egeria! Your cook is no longer able—she is deaf, she is infirm. If anything should happen to you at night! Oh! it makes me shudder even to think of it!"

And she really shuddered—she closed her eyes, clenched her hands, stamped on the floor. Great was my dismay. With awful intensity she resumed,

"Your health—your dear health! The health of a Member of the Institute! How joyfully I would shed the very last drop of my blood to preserve the life of a scholar, of a *littérateur*, of a man of worth. And any woman who would not do as much, I should despise her! Let me tell you, Monsieur—I used to know the wife of a great mathematician, a man who used to fill whole note-books with calculations—so many note-books that they filled all the cupboards in the house. He had heart-disease, and he was visibly pining away. And I saw that wife of his, sitting there beside him, perfectly calm! I could not endure it. I said to her one day, 'My dear, you have no heart! If I were in your place I should . . . I should . . . I do not know what I should do!' "

She paused for want of breath. My situation was terrible. As for telling Mademoiselle Préfère what I really thought about her advice—that was something which I could not even dream of daring to do. For to fall out with her was to lose the chance of seeing Jeanne. So I resolved to take the matter quietly. In any case, she was in my house: that consideration helped me to treat her with something of courtesy.

"I am very old, Mademoiselle," I answered her, "and I am very much afraid that your advice comes to me rather too late in life. Still, I will think about it. In the meanwhile let me beg of you to be calm. I think a glass of *eau sucrée* would do you good!"

To my great surprise, these words calmed her at once; and I saw her sit down very quietly in *her* corner, close to *her* pigeon-hole, upon *her* chair, with her feet upon *her* footstool.

The dinner was a complete failure. Mademoiselle Préfère, who seemed lost in a brown study, never noticed the fact. As a rule I am very sensitive about such misfortunes; but this one caused Jeanne so much delight that at last I could not help enjoying it myself. Even at my age I had not been able to learn before that a chicken, raw on one side and burned on the other, was a funny thing; but Jeanne's bursts of laughter taught me that it was. That chicken caused us to say a thousand very witty things, which I have forgotten; and I was enchanted that it had not been properly cooked. Jeanne put it back to roast again; then she broiled it; then she stewed it with butter. And every time it came back to the table it was much less appetising and much more mirth-provoking than before. When we did eat it, at last, it had become a thing for which there is no name in any *cuisine*.

The almond cake was much more extraordinary. It was brought to the table in the pan, because it never could have been got out of it. I invited Jeanne to help us all to a piece, thinking that I was going to embarrass her; but she broke the pan and gave each of us a fragment. To think that anybody at my age could eat such things was an idea possible only to a very artless mind. Mademoiselle Préfère, suddenly awakened from her dream, indignantly pushed away the sugary splinter of earthenware, and deemed it opportune to inform me that she herself was exceedingly skilful in making confectionery.

"Ah!" exclaimed Jeanne, with an air of surprise not altogether without malice.

Then she wrapped all the fragments of the pan in a piece of paper, for the purpose of giving them to her little playmates—especially to the three little Mouton girls, who are naturally inclined to gluttony.

Secretly, however, I was beginning to feel very uneasy. It did not now seem in any way possible to keep much longer upon good terms with Mademoiselle Préfère since her matrimonial fury had thus burst forth. And that lady affronted, good-bye to Jeanne! I took advantage of a moment while the sweet soul was busy putting on her cloak, in order to ask Jeanne to tell me exactly what her own age was. She was eighteen years and one month old. I counted on my fingers, and found she would not come of age for another two years and eleven months. And how should we be able to manage during all that time?

At the door Mademoiselle Préfère squeezed my hand with so much meaning that I fairly shook from head to foot.

"Good-bye," I said very gravely to the young girl. "But listen to me a moment: your friend is very old, and might perhaps fail you when you need him most. Promise me never to fail in your duty to yourself, and then I shall have no fear. God keep you, my child!"

After closing the door behind them, I opened the window to get a last look at her as she was going away. But the night was dark, and I could see only two vague shadows flitting across the quay. I heard the vast deep hum of the city rising up about me; and I suddenly felt a great sinking at my heart.

Poor child!

December 15.

THE King of Thule kept a goblet of gold which his dying mistress had bequeathed him as a souvenir. When about to die himself, after having drunk from it for the last time, he threw the goblet into the sea. And I keep this diary of memories even as that old prince of the mist-haunted seas kept his carven goblet; and even as he flung away at last his love-pledge, so will I burn this my book of souvenirs. Assuredly it is not through any arrogant avarice nor through any egotistical pride, that I shall destroy this record of a humble life—it is only because I fear lest those things which are dear and sacred to me might appear to others, because of my inartistic manner of expression, either commonplace or absurd.

I do not say this in view of what is going to follow. Absurd I certainly must have been when, having been invited to dinner by Mademoiselle Préfère, I took my seat in a *bergère* (it was really a *bergère*) at the right hand of that alarming person. The table had been set in a little parlour; and I could observe from the poor way in which it was set out that the schoolmistress was one of those ethereal souls who soar above terrestrial things. Chipped plates, unmatched glasses, knives with loose handles, forks with yellow prongs—there was absolutely nothing wanting to spoil the appetite of an honest man.

I was assured that the dinner had been cooked for me—for me alone—although Maître Mouche had also been invited. Mademoiselle Préfère must have imagined that I had Sarmatian tastes on the subject of butter; for that which she offered me, served up in little thin pats, was excessively rancid.

The roast very nearly poisoned me. But I had the pleasure of hearing Maître Mouche and Mademoiselle Préfère discourse upon virtue. I said the pleasure—I ought to have said the shame; for the sentiments to which they gave expression soared far beyond the range of my vulgar nature.

What they said proved to me as clear as day that devotedness was their daily bread, and that self-sacrifice was not less necessary to their existence than air and water. Observing that I was not eating, Mademoiselle Préfère made a thousand efforts to overcome that which she was good enough to term my "discretion." Jeanne was not of the party, because, I was told, her presence at it would have been contrary to the rules, and would have wounded the feelings of the other school-children, among whom it was necessary to maintain a certain equality. I secretly congratulated her upon having escaped from the Merovingian butter; from the huge radishes, empty as funeral-urns; from the leathery roast, and from various other curiosities of diet to which I had exposed myself for the love of her.

The extremely disconsolate-looking servant served up some liquid to which they gave the name of cream—I do not know why—and vanished away like a ghost.

Then Mademoiselle Préfère related to Maître Mouche, with extraordinary transports of emotion, all that she had said to me in the City of Books, during the time that my housekeeper was sick in bed. Her admiration for a Member of the Institute, her terror lest I should be taken ill while unattended, and the certainty she felt that any intelligent woman would be proud and happy to share my existence—she concealed nothing, but, on the contrary, added many fresh follies to the recital. Maître Mouche kept nodding his head in approval while cracking nuts. Then, after all this verbiage, he demanded, with an agreeable smile, what my answer had been.

Mademoiselle Préfère, pressing her hand upon her heart and extending the other towards me, cried out,

"He is so affectionate, so superior, so good, and so great! He answered. . . . But I could never, because I am only a humble woman—I could never repeat the words of a Member of the Institute. I can only utter the substance of them. He answered, 'Yes, I understand you—yes.' "

And with these words she reached out and seized one of my hands. Then Maître Mouche, also overwhelmed with emotion, arose and seized my other hand.

"Monsieur," he said, "permit me to offer my congratulations."

Several times in my life I have known fear; but never before had I experienced any fright of so nauseating a character. A sickening terror came upon me.

I disengaged my two hands, and, rising to my feet, so as to give all possible seriousness to my words, I said,

"Madame, either I explained myself very badly when you were at my house, or I have totally misunderstood you here in your own. In either case, a positive declaration is absolutely necessary. Permit me, Madame, to make it now, very plainly. No—I never did understand you; I am totally ignorant of the nature of this marriage project that you have been planning for me—if you really have been planning one. In any event, I should not think of marrying. It would be an unpardonable folly at my age, and even now, at this moment, I cannot conceive how a sensible person like you could ever have advised me to marry. Indeed, I am strongly inclined to believe that I must have been mistaken, and that you never said anything of the kind before. In the latter case, please to excuse an old man totally unfamiliar with the usages of society, unaccustomed to the conversation of ladies, and very contrite for his mistake."

Maître Mouche went back very softly to his place, where, not finding any more nuts to crack, he began to whittle a cork.

Mademoiselle Préfère, after staring at me for a few moments with an expression in her little round dry eyes which I had never seen there before, suddenly resumed her customary sweetness and graciousness. Then she cried out in honeyed tones,

"Oh! these learned men!—these studious men! They are all like children. Yes, Monsieur Bonnard, you are a real child!"

Then, turning to the notary, who still sat very quietly in his corner, with his nose over his cork, she exclaimed, in beseeching tones,

"Oh, do not accuse him! Do not accuse him! Do not think any evil of him, I beg of you! Do not think it at all! Must I ask you upon my knees?"

Maître Mouche continued to examine all the various aspects and surfaces of his cork without making any further manifestation.

I was very indignant; and I know that my cheeks must have been extremely red, if I could judge by the flush of heat which I felt rise to my face. This would enable me to explain the words I heard through all the buzzing in my ears:

"I am frightened about him! our poor friend! . . . Monsieur Mouche, be kind enough to open a window! It seems to me that a compress of arnica would do him some good."

I rushed out into the street with an unspeakable feeling of shame.

"My poor Jeanne!"

December 20.

I passed eight days without hearing anything further in regard to the Préfère establishment. Then, feeling myself unable to remain any longer without some news of Clémentine's daughter, and feeling furthermore that I owed it as a duty to myself not to cease my visits to the school without more serious cause, I took my way to Les Ternes.

The parlour seemed to me more cold, more damp, more inhospitable, and more insidious than ever before; and the servant much more silent and much more scared. I asked to see Mademoiselle Jeanne; but, after a very considerable time, it was Mademoiselle Préfère who made her appearance instead—severe and pale, with lips compressed and a hard look in her eyes.

"Monsieur," she said, folding her arms over her pelerine, "I regret very much that I cannot allow you to see Mademoiselle Alexandre to-day; but I cannot possibly do it."

"Why not?" I asked in astonishment.

"Monsieur," she replied, "the reasons which compel me to request that your visits shall be less frequent hereafter are of an excessively delicate nature; and I must beg you to spare me the unpleasantness of mentioning them."

"Madame," I replied, "I have been authorized by Jeanne's guardian to see his ward every day. Will you please to inform me of your reasons for opposing the will of Monsieur Mouche?"

"The *guardian* of Mademoiselle Alexandre," she replied (and she dwelt upon that word "guardian" as upon a solid support), "desires, quite as strongly as I myself do, that your assiduities may come to an end as soon as possible."

"Then, if that be the case," I said, "be kind enough to let me know his reasons and your own."

She looked up at the little spiral of paper on the ceiling, and then replied, with stern composure,

"You insist upon it? Well, although such explanations are very painful for a woman to make, I will yield to your exaction. This house, Monsieur, is an honourable house. I have my responsibility. I have to watch like a mother over each one of my pupils. Your assiduities in regard to Mademoiselle Alexandre could not possibly be continued without serious injury to the young girl herself; and it is my duty to insist that they shall cease."

"I do not really understand you," I replied—and I was telling the plain truth. Then she deliberately resumed:

"Your assiduities in this house are being interpreted, by the most respectable and the least suspicious persons, in such a manner that I find myself obliged, both in the interest of my establishment and in the interest of Mademoiselle Alexandre, to see that they end at once."

"Madame," I cried, "I have heard a great many silly things in my life, but never anything so silly as what you have just said!"

She answered me very quietly,

"Your words of abuse will not affect me in the slightest. When one has a duty to accomplish, one is strong enough to endure all."

And she pressed her pelerine over her heart once more—not perhaps on this occasion to restrain, but doubtless only to caress that generous heart.

"Madame," I said, shaking my finger at her, "you have wantonly aroused the indignation of an aged man. Be good enough to act in such a fashion that the old man may be able at least to forget your existence, and do not add fresh insults to those which I have already sustained from your lips. I give you fair warning that I shall never cease to look after Mademoiselle Alexandre; and that should you attempt to do her any harm, in any manner whatsoever, you will have serious reason to regret it!"

The more I became excited, the more she became cool; and she answered in a tone of superb indifference:

"Monsieur, I am much too well informed in regard to the nature of the interest which you take in this young girl, not to withdraw her immediately from that very surveillance with which you threaten me. After observing the more than equivocal intimacy in which you are living with your housekeeper, I ought to have taken measures at once to render it impossible for you ever to come into contact with an innocent child. In the future I shall certainly do it. If up to this time I have been too trustful, it is for Mademoiselle Alexandre, and not for you, to reproach me with it. But she is too artless and too pure—thanks to me!—ever to have suspected the nature of that danger into which you were trying to lead her. I scarcely suppose that you will place me under the necessity of enlightening her upon the subject."

"Come, my poor old Bonnard," I said to myself, as I shrugged my shoulders—"so you had to live as long as this in order to learn for the first time exactly what a wicked woman is. And now your knowledge of the subject is complete."

I went out without replying; and I had the pleasure of observing, from the sudden flush which overspread the face of the schoolmistress, that my silence had wounded her far more than my words.

As I passed through the court I looked about me in every direction for Jeanne. She was watching for me, and she ran to me.

"If anybody touches one little hair of your head, Jeanne, write to me! Good-bye!"

"No, not good-bye."

I replied,

"Well, no—not good-bye! Write to me!"

I went straight to Madame de Gabry's residence.

"Madame is at Rome with Monsieur. Did not Monsieur know it?"

"Why, yes," I replied. "Madame wrote to me." . . .

She had indeed written to me in regard to her leaving home; but my head must have become very much confused, so that I had forgotten all about it. The servant seemed to be of the same opinion, for he looked at me in a way that seemed to signify, "Monsieur Bonnard is doting"—and he leaned down over the balustrade of the stairway to see if I was not going to do something extraordinary before I got to the bottom. But I descended the stairs rationally enough; and then he drew back his head in disappointment.

On returning home I was informed that Monsieur Gélis was waiting for me in the parlour. (This young man has become a constant visitor. His judgment is at fault at times; but his mind is not at all commonplace.) On this occasion, however, his usually welcome visit only embarrassed me. "Alas!" I thought to myself, "I shall be sure to say something very stupid to my young friend to-day, and he also will think that my faculties are becoming impaired. But still I cannot really explain to him that I had first been demanded in wedlock, and subsequently traduced as a man wholly devoid of morals —that even Thérèse had become an object of suspicion—and that Jeanne remains in the power of the most rascally woman on the face of the earth. I am certainly in an admirable state of mind for conversing about Cistercian abbeys with a young and mischievously minded man. Nevertheless, we shall see—we shall try." . . .

But Thérèse stopped me:

"How red you are, Monsieur!" she exclaimed, in a tone of reproach.

"It must be the spring," I answered.

She cried out,

"The spring!—in the month of December?"

That is a fact! this is December. Ah! what is the matter with my head? what a fine help I am going to be to poor Jeanne!

"Thérèse, take my cane; and put it, if you possibly can, in some place where I shall be able to find it again.

"Good-day, Monsieur Gélis. How are you?"

Undated.

NEXT morning the old boy wanted to get up; but the old boy could not get up. A merciless invisible hand kept him down upon his bed. Finding himself immovably riveted there, the old boy resigned himself to remain motionless; but his thoughts kept running in all directions.

He must have had a very violent fever; for Mademoiselle Préfère, the Abbots of Saint-Germain-des-Prés, and the servant of Madame de Gabry appeared to him in divers fantastic shapes. The figure of the servant in particular lengthened weirdly over his head, grimacing like some gargoyle of a cathedral. Then it seemed to me that there were a great many people, much too many people, in my bedroom.

This bedroom of mine is furnished after the antiquated fashion. The portrait of my father in full uniform, and the portrait of my mother in her cashmere dress, are suspended on the wall. The wall-paper is covered with green foliage designs. I am aware of all this, and I am even conscious that everything is faded, very much faded. But an old man's room does not require to be pretty; it is enough that it should be clean, and Thérèse sees to that. At all events my room is sufficiently decorated to please a mind like mine, which has always remained somewhat childish and dreamy. There are things hanging on the wall or scattered over the tables and shelves which usually please my fancy and amuse me. But to-day it would seem as if all those objects had suddenly conceived some kind of ill-will against me. They have all become garish, grimacing, menacing. That statuette, modelled after one of the Theological Virtues of Notre-Dame de Brou, always so ingenuously graceful in its natural condition, is now making contortions and putting out its tongue at me. And that beautiful miniature—in which one of the most skilful pupils of Jehan Fouquet depicted himself, girdled with the cord-girdle of the Sons of St. Francis, offering his book, on bended knee, to the good Duc d'Angoulême—who has taken it out of its frame and put in its place a great ugly cat's head, which stares at me with phosphorescent eyes. And the designs on the wall-paper have also turned into heads—hideous green heads. . . . But no—I am sure that wall-paper must have foliage-designs upon it at this moment just as it had twenty years ago, and nothing else. . . . But no, again—I was right before—they are heads, with eyes, noses, mouths—they are heads! . . . Ah! now I understand! they are both heads and foliage-designs at the same time. I wish I could not see them at all.

And there, on my right, the pretty miniature of the Franciscan has come back again; but it seems to me as if I can only keep it in its frame by a tremendous effort of will, and that the moment I get tired the ugly cat-head will appear in its place. Certainly I am not delirious; I can see Thérèse very plainly, standing at the foot of my bed; I can hear her speaking to me perfectly well, and I should be able to answer her quite satisfactorily if I were not kept so busy in trying to compel the various objects about me to maintain their natural aspect.

Here is the doctor coming. I never sent for him, but it gives me pleasure to see him. He is an old neighbour of mine; I have never been of much service to him, but I like him very much. Even if I do not say much to him, I have at least full possession of all my faculties, and I even find myself extraordinarily crafty and observant to-day, for I note all his gestures, his every look, the least wrinkling of his face. But the doctor is very cunning, too, and I cannot really tell what he thinks about me. The deep thought of Goethe suddenly comes to my mind, and I exclaim,

"Doctor, the old man has consented to allow himself to become sick; but he does not intend, this time at least, to make any further concessions to nature."

Neither the doctor nor Thérèse laughs at my little joke. I suppose they cannot have understood it.

The doctor goes away; evening comes; and all sorts of strange shadows begin to shape themselves about my bed-curtains, forming and dissolving by turns. And other shadows—ghosts—throng by before me; and through them I can see distinctly the impassive face of my faithful servant. And suddenly a cry, a shrill cry, a great cry of distress, rends my ears. Was it you who called me, Jeanne?

The day is over; and the shadows take their places at my bedside to remain with me all through the long night.

Then morning comes—I feel a peace, a vast peace, wrapping me all about.

Art Thou about to take me into Thy rest, my dear Lord God?

February 186–.

THE doctor is quite jovial. It seems that I am doing him a great deal of credit by being able to get out of bed. If I must believe him, innumerable disorders must have pounced down upon my poor old body all at the same time.

These disorders, which are the terror of ordinary mankind, have names which are the terror of philologists. They are hybrid names, half Greek, half Latin, with terminations in "itis," indicating the inflammatory condition, and in "algia," indicating pain. The doctor gives me all their names, together with a corresponding number of adjectives ending in "ic," which serve to characterise their detestable qualities. In short, they represent a good half of that most perfect copy of the Dictionary of Medicine contained in the too-authentic box of Pandora.

"Doctor, what an excellent common-sense story the story of Pandora is!—if I were a poet I would put it into French verse. Shake hands, doctor! You have brought me back to life; I forgive you for it. You have given me back to my friends; I thank you for it. You say I am quite strong. That may be, that may be; but I have lasted a very long time. I am a very old article of furniture; I might be very satisfactorily compared to my father's arm-chair. It was an arm-chair which the good man had inherited, and in which he used to lounge from morning until evening. Twenty times a day, when I was quite a baby, I used to climb up and seat myself on one of the arms of that old-fashioned chair. So long as the chair remained intact, nobody paid any particular attention to it. But it began to limp on one foot; and then folks began to say that it was a very good chair. Afterwards it became lame in three legs, squeaked with the fourth leg, and lost nearly half of both arms. Then everybody would exclaim, 'What a strong chair!' They wondered how it was that after its arms had been worn off and all its legs knocked out of perpendicular, it could yet preserve the recognisable shape of a chair, remain nearly erect, and still be of some service. The horsehair came out of its body at last, and it gave up the ghost. And when Cyprien, our servant, sawed up its mutilated members for fire-wood, everybody redoubled their cries of admiration. 'Oh! what an excellent—what a marvellous chair! It was the chair of Pierre Sylvestre Bonnard, the cloth merchant—of Épiménide Bonnard, his son—of Jean-Baptiste Bonnard, the Pyrrhonian philosopher and Chief of the Third Maritime Division. Oh! what a robust and venerable chair!' In reality it was a dead chair. Well, doctor, I am that chair. You think I am solid because I have been able to resist an attack which would have killed many people, and which only three-fourths killed me. Much obliged! I feel none the less that I am something which has been irremediably damaged."

The doctor tries to prove to me, with the help of enormous Greek and Latin words, that I am really in a very good condition. It would, of course, be useless to attempt any demonstration of this kind in so lucid a language as French. However, I allow him to persuade me at last; and I see him to the door.

"Good! good!" exclaimed Thérèse; "that is the way to put the doctor out of the house! Just do the same thing once or twice again, and he will not come to see you any more—and so much the better?"

"Well, Thérèse, now that I have become such a hearty man again, do not refuse to give me my letters. I am sure there must be quite a big bundle of letters, and it would be very wicked to keep me any longer from reading them."

Thérèse, after some little grumbling, gave me my letters. But what did it matter?—I looked at all the envelopes, and saw that no one of them had been addressed by the little hand which I so much wish I could see here now, turning over the pages of the Vecellio. I pushed the whole bundle of letters away: they had no more interest for me.

April–June.

IT was a hotly contested engagement.

"Wait, Monsieur, until I have put on my clean things," exclaimed Thérèse, "and I will go out with you this time also; I will carry your folding-stool as I have been doing these last few days, and we will go and sit down somewhere in the sun."

Thérèse actually thinks me infirm. I have been sick, it is true, but there is an end to all things! Madame Malady has taken her departure quite awhile ago, and it is now more than three months since her pale and gracious-visaged handmaid, Dame Convalescence, politely bade me farewell. If I were to listen to my housekeeper, I should become a veritable *Monsieur Argant,* and I should wear a nightcap with ribbons for the rest of my life. . . . No more of this!—I propose to go out by myself! Thérèse will not hear of it, She takes my folding-stool, and wants to follow me.

"Thérèse, to-morrow, if you like, we will take our seats on the sunny side of the wall of La Petite Provence and stay there just as long as you please. But to-day I have some very important affairs to attend to."

"So much the better! But your affairs are not the only affairs in this world."

I beg; I scold; I make my escape.

It is quite a pleasant day. With the aid of a cab, and the help of God, I trust to be able to fulfil my purpose.

There is the wall on which is painted in great blue letters the words *"Pensionnat de Demoiselles tenu par Mademoiselle Virginie Préfère."* There is the iron gate which would give free entrance into the court-yard if it were ever opened. But the lock is rusty, and sheets of zinc put up behind the bars protect from indiscreet observation those dear little souls to whom Mademoiselle Préfère doubtless teaches modesty, sincerity, justice, and disinterestedness. There is a window, with iron bars before it, and panes daubed over with white paint—the window of the domestic offices, like a glazed eye—the only aperture of the building opening upon the exterior world. As for the house-door, through which I entered so often, but which is now closed against me for ever, it is just as I saw it the last time, with its little iron-grated wicket. The single stone step in front of it is deeply worn, and, without having very good eyes behind my spectacles, I can see the little white scratches on the stone which have been made by the nails in the shoes of the girls going in and out. And why cannot I also go in? I have a feeling that Jeanne must be suffering a great deal in this dismal house, and that she calls my name in secret. I cannot go away from the gate! A strange anxiety takes hold of me. I pull the bell. The scared-looking servant comes to the door, even much more scared-looking than when I saw her the last time. Strict orders have been given; I am not to be allowed to see Mademoiselle Jeanne. I beg the servant to be so kind as to tell me how the child is. The servant, after looking to her right and then to her left, tells me that Mademoiselle Jeanne is well, and then shuts the door in my face. And I am all alone in the street again.

How many times since then have I wandered in the same way under that wall, and passed before the little door,—full of shame and despair to find myself even weaker than that poor child, who has no other help of friend except myself in the world!

Finally I overcame my repugnance sufficiently to call upon Maître Mouche. The first thing I remarked was that his office is much more dusty and much more mouldy this year than it was last year. The notary made his appearance after a moment, with his familiar stiff gestures, and his restless eyes quivering behind his eye-glasses. I made my complaints to him. He answered me. . . . But why should I write down, even in a notebook which I am going to burn, my recollections of a downright scoundrel? He takes sides with Mademoiselle Préfère, whose intelligent mind and irreproachable character he has long appreciated. He does not feel himself in a position to decide the nature of the question at issue; but he must assure me that appearances have been greatly against me. That of course makes no difference to me. He adds—(and this does make some difference to me)—that the small sum which had been placed in his hands to defray the expenses of the education of his ward has been expended, and that, in view of the circumstances, he cannot but gently admire the disinterestedness of Mademoiselle Préfère in consenting to allow Mademoiselle Jeanne to remain with her.

A magnificent light, the light of a perfect day, floods the sordid place with its incorruptible torrent, and illuminates the person of that man!

And outside it pours down its splendour upon all the wretchedness of a populous quarter.

How sweet it is,—this light with which my eyes have so long been filled, and which ere long I must for ever cease to enjoy! I wander out with my hands behind me, dreaming as I go, following the line of the fortifications; and I find myself after awhile, I know not how, in an out-of-the-way suburb full of miserable little gardens. By the dusty roadside I observe a plant whose flower, at once dark and splendid, seems worthy of association with the noblest and purest mourning for the dead. It is a columbine. Our fathers called it "Our Lady's Glove"—*le gant de Notre-Dame*. Only such a "Notre-Dame" as might make herself very, very small, for the sake of appearing to little children, could ever slip her dainty fingers into the narrow capsule of that flower.

And there is a big bumble-bee who tries to force himself into the flower, brutally; but his mouth cannot reach the nectar, and the poor glutton strives and strives in vain. He has to give up the attempt, and comes out of the flower all smeared over with pollen. He flies off in his own heavy lumbering way; but there are not many flowers in this portion of the suburbs, which has been defiled by the soot and smoke of factories. So he comes back to the columbine again, and this time he pierces the corolla and sucks the honey through the little hole which he has made; I should never have thought that a bumble-bee had so much sense! Why, that is admirable! The more I observe them, the more do insects and flowers fill me with astonishment. I am like that good Rollin who went wild with delight over the flowers of his peach-trees. I wish I could have a fine garden, and live at the verge of a wood.

August, September.

IT occurred to me one Sunday morning to watch for the moment when Mademoiselle Préfère's pupils were leaving the school in procession to attend Mass at the parish church. I watched them passing two by two,—the little ones first with very serious faces. There were three of them all dressed exactly alike—dumpy, plump, important-looking little creatures, whom I recognised at once as the Mouton girls. Their elder sister is the artist who drew that terrible head of Tatius, King of the Sabines. Beside the column, the assistant school-teacher, with her prayer-book in her hand, was gesturing and frowning. Then came the next oldest class, and finally the big girls, all whispering to each other, as they went by. But I did not see Jeanne.

I went to police-headquarters and inquired whether they chanced to have, filed away somewhere or other, any information regarding the establishment in the Rue Demours. I succeeded in inducing them to send some female inspectors there. These returned bringing with them the most favourable reports about the establishment. In their opinion the Préfère School was a model school. It is evident that if I were to force an investigation, Mademoiselle Préfère would receive academic honours.

October 3.

THIS Thursday being a school-holiday I had the chance of meeting the three little Mouton girls in the vicinity of the Rue Demours. After bowing to their mother, I asked the eldest who appears to be about ten years old, how was her playmate, Mademoiselle Jeanne Alexandre.

The little Mouton girl answered me, all in a breath,

"Jeanne Alexandre is not my playmate. She is only kept in the school for charity—so they make her sweep the class-rooms. It was Mademoiselle who said so. And Jeanne Alexandre is a bad girl; so they lock her up in the dark room—and it serves her right—and I am a good girl—and I am never locked up in the dark room."

The three little girls resumed their walk, and Madame Mouton followed close behind them, looking back over her broad shoulder at me, in a very suspicious manner.

Alas! I find myself reduced to expedients of a questionable character. Madame de Gabry will not come back to Paris for at least three months more, at the very soonest. Without her, I have no tact, I have no common sense—I am nothing but a cumbersome, clumsy, mischief-making machine.

Nevertheless, I cannot possibly permit them to make Jeanne a boarding-school servant!

December 28.

THE idea that Jeanne was obliged to sweep the rooms had become absolutely unbearable.

The weather was dark and cold. Night had already begun. I rang the school-door bell with the tranquillity of a resolute man. The moment that the timid servant opened the door, I slipped a gold piece into her hand, and promised her another if she would arrange matters so that I could see Mademoiselle Alexandre. Her answer was,

"In one hour from now, at the grated window."

And she slammed the door in my face so rudely that she knocked my hat into the gutter. I waited for one very long hour in a violent snow-storm; then I approached the window. Nothing! The wind raged, and the snow fell heavily. Workmen passing by with their implements on their shoulders, and their heads bent down to keep the snow from coming in their faces, rudely jostled me. Still nothing. I began to fear I had been observed. I knew that I had done wrong in bribing a servant, but I was not a bit sorry for it. Woe to the man who does not know how to break through social regulations in case of necessity! Another quarter of an hour passed. Nothing. At last the window was partly opened.

"Is that you, Monsieur Bonnard?"

"Is that you, Jeanne?—tell me at once what has become of you."

"I am well—very well."

"But what else!"

"They have put me in the kitchen, and I have to sweep the school-rooms."

"In the kitchen! Sweeping—you! Gracious goodness!"

"Yes, because my guardian does not pay for my schooling any longer."

"Gracious goodness! Your guardian seems to me to be a thorough scoundrel."

"Then you know——"

"What?"

"Oh! don't ask me to tell you that!—but I would rather die than find myself alone with him again."

"And why did you not write to me?"

"I was watched."

At that instant I formed a resolve which nothing in this world could have induced me to change. I did, indeed, have some idea that I might be acting contrary to law; but I did not give myself the least concern about that idea. And, being firmly resolved, I was able to be prudent. I acted with remarkable coolness.

"Jeanne," I asked, "tell me! does that room you are in open into the court-yard?"

"Yes."

"Can you open the street-door from the inside yourself?"

"Yes,—if there is nobody in the porter's lodge."

"Go and see if there is any one there, and be careful that nobody observes you."

Then I waited, keeping a watch on the door and window.

In six or seven seconds Jeanne reappeared behind the bars, and said,

"The servant is in the porter's lodge."

"Very well," I said, "have you a pen and ink?"

"No."

"A pencil?"

"Yes."

"Pass it out here."

I took an old newspaper out of my pocket, and—in a wind which blew almost hard enough to put the street-lamps out, in a downpour of snow which almost blinded me—I managed to wrap up and address that paper to Mademoiselle Préfère.

While I was writing I asked Jeanne,

"When the postman passes he puts the papers and letters in the box, doesn't he? He rings the bell and goes away? Then the servant opens the letter-box and takes whatever she finds there to Mademoiselle Préfère immediately; is not that about the way the thing is managed whenever anything comes by post?"

Jeanne thought it was.

"Then we shall soon see. Jeanne, go and watch again; and, as soon as the servant leaves the lodge, open the door and come out here to me."

Having said this, I put my newspaper in the box, gave the bell a tremendous pull, and then hid myself in the embrasure of a neighbouring door.

I might have been there several minutes, when the little door quivered, then opened, and a young girl's head made its appearance through the opening. I took hold of it; I pulled it towards me.

"Come, Jeanne! come!"

She stared at me uneasily. Certainly she must have been afraid that I had gone mad; but, on the contrary, I was very rational indeed.

"Come, my child! come!"

"Where?"

"To Madame de Gabry's."

Then she took my arm. For some time we ran like a couple of thieves. But running is an exercise ill-suited to one as corpulent as

I am, and, finding myself out of breath at last, I stopped and leaned
upon something which turned out to be the stove of a dealer in
roasted chestnuts, who was doing business at the corner of a wine-
seller's shop, where a number of cabmen were drinking. One of
them asked us if we did not want a cab. Most assuredly we wanted
a cab! The driver, after setting down his glass on the zinc counter,
climbed upon his seat and urged his horse forward. We were saved.

"Phew!" I panted, wiping my forehead. For, in spite of the cold,
I was perspiring profusely.

What seemed very odd was that Jeanne appeared to be much
more conscious than I was of the enormity which we had committed. She looked very serious indeed, and was visibly uneasy.

"In the kitchen!" I cried out, with indignation.

She shook her head, as if to say, "Well, there or anywhere else,
what does it matter to me?" And by the light of the street-lamps,
I observed with pain that her face was very thin and her features
all pinched. I did not find in her any of that vivacity, any of those
bright impulses, any of that quickness of expression, which used to
please me so much. Her gaze had become timid, her gestures con-
strained, her whole attitude melancholy. I took her hand—a little
cold hand, which had become all hardened and bruised. The poor
child must have suffered very much. I questioned her. She told me
very quietly that Mademoiselle Préfère had summoned her one day,
and called her a little monster and a little viper, for some reason
which she had never been able to learn.

She had added, "You shall not see Monsieur Bonnard any more;
for he has been giving you bad advice, and he has conducted himself in a most shameful manner towards me." "I then said to her,
'That, Mademoiselle, you will never be able to make me believe.'
Then Mademoiselle slapped my face and sent me back to the school-
room. The announcement that I should never be allowed to see you
again made me feel as if night had come down upon me. Don't you
know those evenings when one feels so sad to see the darkness
come?—well, just imagine such a moment stretched out into weeks
—into whole months! Don't you remember my little Saint-George?
Up to that time I had worked at it as well as I could—just simply
to work at it—just to amuse myself. But when I lost all hope of
ever seeing you again I took my little wax figure, and I began to
work at it in quite another way. I did not try to model it with
wooden matches any more, as I had been doing, but with hair pins.
I even made use of *épingles à la neige*. But perhaps you do not know
what *épingles à la neige* are? Well, I became more particular about
it than you can possibly imagine. I put a dragon on Saint-George's
helmet; and I passed hours and hours in making a head and eyes
and a tail for the dragon. Oh, the eyes! the eyes, above all! I never
stopped working at them till I got them so that they had red pupils
and white eye-lids and eye-brows and everything! I know I am very

silly; I had an idea that I was going to die as soon as my little
Saint-George would be finished. I worked at it during recreation-
hours, and Mademoiselle Préfère used to let me alone. One day I
learned that you were in the parlour with the schoolmistress; I
watched for you; we said *Au revoir!* that day to each other. I was
a little consoled by seeing you. But, some time after that, my guardian came and wanted to make me go out with him one Thursday.
I refused to go to his house,—but please don't ask me why, Monsieur. He answered me, quite gently, that I was a very whimsical
little girl. And then he left me alone. But the next day Mademoiselle
Préfère came to me with such a wicked look on her face that I was
really afraid. She had a letter in her hand. 'Mademoiselle,' she said
to me, 'I am informed by your guardian that he has spent all the
money which belonged to you. Don't be afraid! I do not intend to
abandon you; but, you must acknowledge yourself, *it is only right
that you should earn your own livelihood.*' Then she put me to work
house-cleaning; and whenever I made a mistake she would lock me
up in the garret for days together. And that is what has happened
to me since I saw you last. Even if I had been able to write to you
I do not know whether I should have done it, because I did not
think you could possibly take me away from the school; and, as
Maître Mouche did not come back to see me, there was no hurry. I
thought I could wait for awhile in the garret and the kitchen."

"Jeanne," I cried, "even if we should have to flee to Oceania, the
abominable Préfère shall never get hold of you again. I will take a
great oath on that! And why should we not go to Oceania? The
climate is very healthy; and I read in a newspaper the other day
that they have pianos there. But, in the meantime, let us go to the
house of Madame de Gabry, who returned to Paris, as luck would
have it, some three or four days ago; for you and I are two innocent fools, and we have great need of some one to help us."

Even as I was speaking Jeanne's features suddenly became pale,
and seemed to shrink into lifelessness; her eyes became all dim;
her lips, half open, contracted with an expression of pain. Then her
head sank sideways on her shoulder;—she had fainted.

I lifted her in my arms, and carried her up Madame de Gabry's
staircase like a little baby asleep. But I was myself on the point of
fainting, from emotional excitement and fatigue together, when
she came to herself again.

"Ah! it is you," she said: "so much the better!"

Such was our condition when we rang our friend's door-bell.

Same day.

IT was eight o'clock. Madame de Gabry, as might be supposed,
was very much surprised by our unexpected appearance. But she
welcomed the old man and the child with that glad kindness which

always expresses itself in her beautiful gestures. It seems to me,—
if I might use that language of devotion so familiar to her,—it
seems to me as though some heavenly grace streams from her
hands whenever she opens them; and even the perfume which im-
pregnates her robes seems to inspire the sweet calm zeal of charity
and good works. Surprised she certainly was; but she asked us no
questions,—and that silence seemed to me admirable.

"Madame," I said to her, "we have both come to place ourselves
under your protection. And, first of all, we are going to ask you to
give us some supper—or to give Jeanne some, at least; for a moment ago, in the carriage, she fainted from weakness. As for myself, I could not eat a bite at this late hour without passing a night
of agony in consequence. I hope that Monsieur de Gabry is well."

"Oh, he is here!" she said.

And she called him immediately.

"Come in here, Paul! Come and see Monsieur Bonnard and
Mademoiselle Alexandre."

He came. It was a pleasure for me to see his frank broad face,
and to press his strong square hand. Then we went, all four of us,
into the dining-room; and while some cold meat was being cut for
Jeanne—which she never touched notwithstanding—I related our
adventure. Paul de Gabry asked me permission to smoke his pipe,
after which he listened to me in silence. When I had finished my recital he scratched the short, stiff beard upon his chin, and uttered
a tremendous *"Sacrebleu!"* But, seeing Jeanne stare at each of us
in turn, with a frightened look in her face, he added:

"We will talk about this matter to-morrow morning. Come into
my study for a moment; I have an old book to show you that I
want you to tell me something about."

I followed him into his study, where the steel of guns and hunting knives, suspended against the dark hangings, glimmered in the
lamp-light. There, pulling me down beside him upon a leather-
covered sofa, he exclaimed,

"What have you done? Great God! Do you know what you have
done? Corruption of a minor, abduction, kidnapping! You have got
yourself into a nice mess! You have simply rendered yourself liable
to a sentence of imprisonment of not less than five nor more than
ten years."

"Mercy on us!" I cried; "ten years imprisonment for having
saved an innocent child."

"That is the law!" answered Monsieur de Gabry. "You see, my
dear Monsieur Bonnard, I happen to know the Code pretty well—
not because I ever studied law as a profession, but because, as
mayor of Lusance, I was obliged to teach myself something about
it in order to be able to give information to my subordinates.
Mouche is a rascal; that woman Préfère is a vile hussy; and you

are a . . . Well! I really cannot find any word strong enough to signify what you are!"

After opening his bookcase, where dog-collars, riding-whips, stirrups, spurs, cigar-boxes, and a few books of reference were indiscriminately stowed away, he took out of it a copy of the Code, and began to turn over the leaves.

"'CRIMES AND MISDEMEANOURS' . . . 'SEQUESTRATION OF PERSONS'—that is not your case. . . . 'ABDUCTION OF MINORS'—here we are. . . . 'ARTICLE 354:—*Whosoever shall, either by fraud or violence, have abducted or have caused to be abducted any minor or minors, or shall have enticed them, or turned them away from, or forcibly removed them, or shall have caused them to be enticed, or turned away from or forcibly removed from the places in which they have been placed by those to whose authority or direction they have been submitted or confided, shall be liable to the penalty of imprisonment. See* PENAL CODE, 21 *and* 28.' Here is 21:—'*The term of imprisonment shall not be less than five years.*' 28. '*The sentence of imprisonment shall be considered as involving a loss of civil rights.*' Now all that is very plain, is it not, Monsieur Bonnard?"

"Perfectly plain."

"Now let us go on: 'ARTICLE 356:—*In case the abductor be under the age of 21 years at the time of the offense, he shall only be punished with*' . . . But we certainly cannot invoke this article in your favour. 'ARTICLE 357:—*In case the abductor shall have married the girl by him abducted, he can only be prosecuted at the instance of such persons as, according to the Civil Code, may have the right to demand that the marriage shall be declared null; nor can he be condemned until after the nullity of the marriage shall have been pronounced.*' I do not know whether it is a part of your plans to marry Mademoiselle Alexandre! You can see that the Code is good-natured about it; it leaves you one door of escape. But no—I ought not to joke with you, because really you have put yourself in a very unfortunate position! And how could a man like you imagine that here in Paris, in the middle of the nineteenth century, a young girl can be abducted with absolute impunity? We are not living in the Middle Ages now; and such things are no longer permitted by law."

"You need not imagine," I replied, "that abduction was lawful under the ancient Code. You will find in Baluze a decree issued by King Childebert at Cologne, either in 593 or 594, on the subject: moreover, everybody knows that the famous *Ordonnance de Blois,* of May 1579, formally enacted that any persons convicted of having suborned any son or daughter under the age of twenty-five years, whether under promise of marriage or otherwise, without the full knowledge, will, or consent of the father, mother, and guardians, should be punished with death; and the ordinance adds: '*Et pareillement seront punis extraordinairement tous ceux qui auront participé audit rapt, et qui auront prêté conseil, confort, et aide en*

aucune manière que ce soit.' (And in like manner shall be extraordinarily punished all persons whomsoever, who shall have partici-
pated in the said abduction, and who shall have given thereunto
counsel, succor, or aid in any manner whatsoever.) Those are the
exact, or very nearly the exact, terms of the ordinance. As for that
article of the Code-Napoléon which you have just told me of, and
which excepts from liability to prosecution the abductor who marries the young girl abducted by him, it reminds me that according
to the laws of Bretagne, forcible abduction, followed by marriage,
was not punished. But this usage, which involved various abuses,
was suppressed in 1720—at least I give you the date within ten
years. My memory is not very good now, and the time is long passed
when I could repeat by heart without even stopping to take breath,
fifteen hundred verses of Girart de Roussillon.

"As far as regards the Capitulary of Charlemagne, which fixes
the compensation for abduction, I have not mentioned it because I
am sure that you must remember it. So, my dear Monsieur de
Gabry, you see abduction was considered as a decidedly punishable
offense under the three dynasties of Old France. It is a very great
mistake to suppose that the Middle Ages represent a period of
social chaos. You must remember, on the contrary——"

Monsieur de Gabry here interrupted me:

"So," he exclaimed, "you know the *Ordonnance de Blois,* you
know Baluze, you know Childebert, you know the Capitularies—and
you don't know anything about the Code-Napoléon!"

I replied that, as a matter of fact, I never had read the Code;
and he looked very much surprised.

"And now do you understand," he asked, "the extreme gravity
of the action you have committed?"

I had not indeed been yet able to understand it fully. But little
by little, with the aid of Monsieur Paul's very sensible explanations,
I reached the conviction at last that I should not be judged in
regard to my motives, which were innocent, but only according to
my action, which was punishable. Thereupon I began to feel very
despondent, and to utter divers lamentations.

"What am I to do?" I cried out, "what am I to do? Am I then
irretrievably ruined?—and have I also ruined the poor child whom
I wanted to save?"

Monsieur de Gabry silently filled his pipe, and lighted it so slowly
that his kind broad face remained for at least three or four minutes glowing red behind the light, like a blacksmith's in the gleam
of his forge-fire. Then he said,

"You want to know what to do? Why, don't do anything, my dear
Monsieur Bonnard! For God's sake, and for your own sake, don't
do anything at all! Your situation is bad enough as it is; don't try
to meddle with it now, unless you want to create new difficulties for
yourself. But you must promise me to sustain me in any action that

I may take. I shall go to see Monsieur Mouche the very first thing
to-morrow morning; and if he turns out to be what we think he is
—that is to say, a consummate rascal—I shall very soon find means
of making him harmless, even if the devil himself should take sides
with him. For everything depends on him. As it is too late this evening to take Mademoiselle Jeanne back to her boarding-school, my
wife will keep the young lady here to-night. This of course plainly
constitutes the misdemeanour of complicity; but it saves the girl
from anything like an equivocal position. As for you, my dear Monsieur, you just go back to the Quai Malaquais as quickly as you can;
and if they come to look for Jeanne there, it will be very easy for
you to prove she is not in your house."

While we were thus talking, Madame de Gabry was preparing to
make her young lodger comfortable for the night. When she bade
me good-bye at the door, she was carrying a pair of clean sheets,
scented with lavender, thrown over her arm.

"That," I said, "is a sweet honest smell."

"Well, of course," answered Madame de Gabry, "you must remember we are peasants."

"Ah!" I answered her, "Heaven grant that I also may be able one
of these days to become a peasant! Heaven grant that one of these
days I may be able, as you are at Lusance, to inhale the sweet fresh
odour of the country, and live in some little house all hidden among
trees; and if this wish of mine be too ambitious on the part of an
old man whose life is nearly closed, then I will only wish that my
winding-sheet may be as sweetly scented with lavender as that linen
you have on your arm."

It was agreed that I should come to lunch the following morning.
But I was positively forbidden to show myself at the house before
midday. Jeanne, as she kissed me good-bye, begged me not to take
her back to the school any more. We felt much affected at parting,
and very anxious.

I found Thérèse waiting for me on the landing, in such a condition of worry about me that it had made her furious. She talked of
nothing less than keeping me under lock and key in the future.

What a night I passed! I never closed my eyes for one single instant. From time to time I could not help laughing like a boy at the
success of my prank; and then again, an inexpressible feeling of
horror would come upon me at the thought of being dragged before
some magistrate, and having to take my place upon the prisoner's
bench, to answer for the crime which I had so naturally committed.
I was very much afraid; and nevertheless I felt no remorse or regret whatever. The sun, coming into my room at last, merrily lighted
upon the foot of my bed; and then I made this prayer:

"My God, Thou who didst make the sky and the dew, as it is said
in *Tristan,* judge me in Thine equity, not indeed according unto my
acts, but according only to my motives, which Thou knowest have

been upright and pure; and I will say: Glory to Thee in heaven, and peace on earth to men of good-will. I give into Thy hands the child I stole away. Do that for her which I have not known how to do; guard her from all her enemies;—and blessed for ever be Thy name!"

December 29.

WHEN I arrived at Madame de Gabry's, I found Jeanne completely transfigured.

Had she also, like myself, at the first light of dawn, called upon Him who made the sky and the dew? She smiled with such a sweet calm smile!

Madame de Gabry called her away to arrange her hair; for the amiable lady had insisted upon combing and plaiting, with her own hands, the hair of the child confided to her care. As I had come a little before the hour agreed upon, I had interrupted this charming toilet. By way of punishment I was told to go and wait in the parlour all by myself. Monsieur de Gabry joined me there in a little while. He had evidently just come in, for I could see on his forehead the mark left by the lining of his hat. His frank face wore an expression of joyful excitement. I thought I had better not ask him any questions; and we all went to lunch. When the servants had finished waiting at table, Monsieur Paul, who had been keeping his good story for the dessert, said to us,

"Well! I went to Levallois."

"Did you see Maître Mouche?" excitedly inquired Madame de Gabry.

"No," he replied, curiously watching the expression of disappointment upon our faces.

After having amused himself with our anxiety for a reasonable time, the good fellow added:

"Maître Mouche is no longer at Levallois. Maître Mouche has gone away from France. The day after to-morrow will make just eight days since he decamped, taking with him all the money of his clients—a tolerably large sum. I found the office closed. A woman who lived close by told me all about it with an abundance of curses and imprecations. The notary did not take the 7.55 train all by himself; he took with him the daughter of the hairdresser of Levallois, a young person quite famous in that part of the country for her beauty and her accomplishments;—they say she could shave better than her father. Well, anyhow Mouche has run away with her; the Commissaire de Police confirmed the fact for me. Now, really, could it have been possible for Maître Mouche to have left the country at a more opportune moment? If he had only deferred his escapade one week longer, he would have been still the representative of society, and would have had you dragged off to gaol, Monsieur Bonnard, like a criminal. At present we have nothing whatever to fear from him. Here is to the health of Maître Mouche!" he cried, pouring out a glass of white wine.

I would like to live a long time if it were only to remember that delightful morning. We four were all assembled in the big white dining-room around the waxed oak table. Monsieur Paul's mirth was of the hearty kind,—even perhaps a little riotous; and the good man quaffed deeply. Madame de Gabry smiled at me, with a smile so sweet, so perfect, and so noble, that I thought such a woman ought to keep smiles like that simply as a reward for good actions, and thus make everybody who knew her do all the good of which they were capable. Then, to reward us for our pains, Jeanne, who had regained something of her former vivacity, asked us in less than a quarter of an hour one dozen questions, to answer which would have required an exhaustive exposition of the nature of man, the nature of the universe, the science of physics and of meta-physics, the Macrocosm and the Microcosm—not to speak of the Ineffable and the Unknowable. Then she drew out of her pocket her little Saint-George, who had suffered most cruelly during our flight. His legs and arms were gone; but he still had his gold helmet with the green dragon on it. Jeanne solemnly pledged herself to make a restoration of him in honour of Madame de Gabry.

Delightful friends! I left them at last overwhelmed with fatigue and joy.

On re-entering my lodgings I had to endure the very sharpest remonstrances from Thérèse, who said she had given up trying to understand my new way of living. In her opinion Monsieur had really lost his mind.

"Yes, Thérèse, I am a mad old man and you are a mad old woman. That is certain! May the good God bless us both, Thérèse, and give us new strength; for we now have new duties to perform. But let me lie down upon the sofa; for I really cannot keep myself on my feet any longer."

January 15, 186–.

"GOOD-MORNING, Monsieur," said Jeanne, letting herself in; while Thérèse remained grumbling in the corridor because she had not been able to get to the door in time.

"Mademoiselle, I beg you will be kind enough to address me very solemnly by my title, and to say to me, 'Good-morning, my guardian.'"

"Then it has all been settled? Oh, how nice!" cried the child, clapping her hands.

"It has all been arranged, Mademoiselle, in the *Salle-commune* and before the Justice of the Peace; and from to-day you are under my authority. . . . What are you laughing about, my ward? I see it in your eyes. You have some crazy idea in your head this very moment—some more nonsense, eh?"

"Oh, no! Monsieur. . . . I mean, my guardian. I was looking at your white hair. It curls out from under the edge of your hat like honeysuckle on a balcony. It is very handsome, and I like it very much!"

"Be good enough to sit down, my ward, and, if you can possibly help it, stop saying ridiculous things, because I have some very serious things to say to you. Listen. I suppose you are not going to insist upon being sent back to the establishment of Mademoiselle Préfère? . . . No. Well, then, what would you say if I should take you here to live with me, and to finish your education, and keep you here until . . . what shall I say?—for ever, as the song has it?"

"Oh, Monsieur!" she cried, flushing crimson with pleasure.

I continued,

"Behind there we have a nice little room, which my housekeeper has cleaned up and furnished for you. You are going to take the place of the books which used to be in it; you will succeed them as the day succeeds night. Go with Thérèse and look at it, and see if you think you will be able to live in it. Madame de Gabry and I have made up our minds that you can sleep there to-night."

She had already started to run; I called her back for a moment.

"Jeanne, listen to me a moment longer! You have always until now made yourself a favourite with my housekeeper, who, like all very old people, is apt to be cross at times. Be gentle and forbearing. Make every allowance for her. I have thought it my duty to make every allowance for her myself, and to put up with all her fits of impatience. Now, let me tell you, Jeanne:—Respect her! And when I say that, I do not forget that she is my servant and yours; neither will she ever allow herself to forget it for a moment. But what I want you to respect in her is her great age and her great heart. She is a humble woman who has lived a very, very long time in the habit of doing good; and she has become hardened and stiffened in that habit. Bear patiently with the harsh ways of that upright soul. If you know how to command, she will know how to obey. Go now, my child; arrange your room in whatever way may seem to you best suited for your studies and for your repose."

Having started Jeanne, with this viaticum, upon her domestic career, I began to read a Review, which, although conducted by very young men, is excellent. The tone of it is somewhat unpolished, but the spirit zealous. The article I read was certainly far superior, in point of precision and positiveness, to anything of the sort ever written when I was a young man. The author of the article, Monsieur Paul Meyer, points out every error with a remarkably lucid power of incisive criticism.

We used not in my time to criticise with such strict justice. Our indulgence was vast. It went even so far as to confuse the scholar and the ignoramus in the same burst of praise. And nevertheless one must learn how to find fault; and it is even an imperative duty to blame when the blame is deserved.

I remember little Raymond (that was the name we gave him); he did not know anything, and his mind was not a mind capable of absorbing any solid learning; but he was very fond of his mother. We took very good care never to utter a hint of the ignorance of so perfect a son; and, thanks to our forbearance, little Raymond made his way to the highest positions. He had lost his mother then; but honours of all kinds were showered upon him. He became omnipotent—to the grievous injury of his colleagues and of science. . . . But here comes my young friend of the Luxembourg.

"Good-evening, Gélis. You look very happy to-day. What good fortune has come to you, my dear lad?"

His good fortune is that he has been able to sustain his thesis very creditably, and that he has taken high rank in his class. He tells me this with the additional information that my own words, which were incidentally referred to in the course of the examination, had been spoken of by the college professors in terms of the most unqualified praise.

"That is very nice," I replied; "and it makes me very happy, Gélis, to find my old reputation thus associated with your own youthful honours. I was very much interested, you know, in that thesis of yours;—but some domestic arrangements have been keeping me so busy lately that I quite forgot this was the day on which you were to sustain it."

Mademoiselle Jeanne made her appearance very opportunely, as if in order to suggest to him something about the nature of those very domestic arrangements. The giddy girl burst into the City of Books like a fresh breeze, crying at the top of her voice that her room was a perfect little wonder. Then she became very red indeed on seeing Monsieur Gélis there. But none of us can escape our destiny.

Monsieur Gélis asked her how she was with the tone of a young fellow who presumes upon a previous acquaintance, and who proposes to put himself forward as an old friend. Oh, never fear!—she had not forgotten him at all; that was very evident from the fact that then and there, right under my nose, they resumed their last year's conversation on the subject of the "Venetian blond"! They continued the discussion after quite an animated fashion. I began to ask myself what right I had to be in the room at all. The only thing I could do in order to make myself heard was to cough. As for getting in a word, they never even gave me a chance. Gélis discoursed enthusiastically, not only about the Venetian colourists, but also upon all other matters relating to nature or to mankind. And Jeanne kept answering him, "Yes, Monsieur, you are right." . . . "That is just what I supposed, Monsieur." . . . "Monsieur, you express so beautifully just what I feel." . . . "I am going to think a great deal about what you have just told me, Monsieur."

When *I* speak, Mademoiselle never answers me in that tone. It is only with the very tip of her tongue that she will even taste any intellectual food which I set before her. Usually she will not touch it at all. But Monsieur Gélis seems to be in her opinion the supreme authority upon all subjects. It was always, "Oh, yes!"—"Oh, of course!"—to all his empty chatter. And, then, the eyes of Jeanne! I had never seen them look so large before; I had never before observed in them such fixity of expression; but her gaze otherwise remained what it always is—artless, frank, and brave. Gélis evidently pleased her; she liked Gélis, and her eyes betrayed the fact. They would have published it to the entire universe! All very fine, Master Bonnard!—you have been so deeply interested in observing your ward, that you have been forgetting you are her guardian! You began only this morning to exercise that function; and you can already see that it involves some very delicate and difficult duties. Bonnard, you must really try to devise some means of keeping that young man away from her; you really ought. . . . Eh! how am I to know what I am to do? . . .

I have picked up a book at random from the nearest shelf; I open it, and I enter respectfully into the middle of a drama of Sophocles. The older I grow, the more I learn to love the two civilisations of the antique world; and now I always keep the poets of Italy and of Greece on a shelf within easy reach of my arm in the City of Books.

Monsieur and Mademoiselle finally condescend to take some notice of me, now that I seem too busy to take any notice of them. I really think that Mademoiselle Jeanne has even asked me what I am reading. No, indeed, I will not tell her what it is. What I am reading, between ourselves, is the chant of that smooth and luminous Chorus which rolls out its magnificent tunefulness through a scene of passionate violence—the Chorus of the Old Men of Thebes— Ἔρως ἀνίκατε . . . "*Invincible Love, O Thou who descendest upon rich houses,—Thou who dost rest upon the delicate cheek of the maiden,—Thou who dost traverse all seas,—surely none among the Immortals can escape Thee, nor indeed any among men who live but for a little space; and he who is possessed by Thee, there is a madness upon him.*" And when I had re-read that delicious chant, the face of Antigone appeared before me in all its passionless purity. What images! Gods and goddesses who hover in the highest height of heaven! The blind old man, the long-wandering beggar-king, led by Antigone, has now been buried with holy rites; and his daughter, fair as the fairest dream ever conceived by human soul, resists the will of the tyrant and gives pious sepulture to her brother. She loves the son of the tyrant, and that son loves her also. And as she goes on her way to execution, the victim of her own sweet piety, the old men sing, "*Invincible Love, O Thou who dost descend upon rich houses,—Thou who dost rest upon the delicate cheek of the maiden."* . . .

"Mademoiselle Jeanne, are you really very anxious to know what I am reading? I am reading, Mademoiselle—I am reading that Antigone, having buried the blind old man, wove a fair tapestry embroidered with images in the likeness of laughing faces."

"Ah!" said Gélis, as he burst out laughing, "that is not in the text."

"It is a scholium," I said.

"Unpublished," he added, getting up.

I am not an egotist. But I am prudent. I have to bring up this child; she is much too young to be married now. No! I am not an egotist, but I must certainly keep her with me for a few years more —keep her alone with me. She can surely wait until I am dead! Fear not, Antigone, old Œdipus will find holy burial soon enough.

In the meanwhile, Antigone is helping our housekeeper to scrape the carrots. She says she likes to do it—that it is in her line, being related to the art of sculpture.

May.

WHO would recognise the City of Books now? There are flowers everywhere—even upon all the articles of furniture. Jeanne was right: those roses do look very nice in that blue china vase. She goes to market every day with Thérèse, under the pretext of helping the old servant to make her purchases, but she never brings anything back with her except flowers. Flowers are really very charming creatures. And one of these days I must certainly carry out my plan, and devote myself to the study of them, in their own natural domain, in the country—with all the science and earnestness which I possess.

For what have I to do here? Why should I burn my eyes out over these old parchments which cannot now tell me anything worth knowing? I used to study them, those old texts, with the most ardent enjoyment. What was it which I was then so anxious to find in them? The date of a pious foundation—the name of some monk-ish *imagier* or copyist—the price of a loaf, of an ox, or of a field—some judicial or administrative enactment—all that, and yet something more, a Something vaguely mysterious and sublime which excited my enthusiasm. But for sixty years I have been searching in vain for that Something. Better men than I—the masters, the truly great, the Fauriels, the Thierrys, who found so many things —died at their task without having been able, any more than I have been, to find that Something which, being incorporeal, has no name, and without which, nevertheless, no great mental work would ever be undertaken in this world. And now that I am only looking for what I should certainly be able to find, I cannot find anything at all; and it is probable that I shall never be able to finish the history of the Abbots of Saint-Germain-des-Prés.

"Guardian, just guess what I have in my handkerchief."

"Judging from appearances, Jeanne, I should say flowers."

"Oh, no—not flowers. Look!"

I look, and I see a little grey head poking itself out of the hand-kerchief. It is the head of a little grey cat. The handkerchief opens; the animal leaps down upon the carpet, shakes itself, pricks up first one ear and then the other, and begins to examine with due caution the locality and the inhabitants thereof.

Thérèse, out of breath, with her basket on her arm, suddenly makes her appearance in time to take an objective part in this ex-amination, which does not appear to result altogether in her fav-our; for the young cat moves slowly away from her, without, how-ever, venturing near my legs, or approaching Jeanne, who displays extraordinary volubility in the use of caressing appellations. Thérèse, whose chief fault is her inability to hide her feelings, thereupon vehemently reproaches Mademoiselle for bringing home a cat that she did not know anything about. Jeanne, in order to jus-tify herself, tells the whole story. While she was passing with Thérèse before a chemist's shop, she saw the assistant kick a little cat into the street. The cat, astonished and frightened, seemed to be asking itself whether to remain in the street where it was being terrified and knocked about by the people passing by, or whether to go back into the chemist's even at the risk of being kicked out a second time. Jeanne thought it was in a very critical position, and understood its hesitation. It looked so stupid; and she knew it looked stupid only because it could not decide what to do. So she took it up in her arms. And as it had not been able to obtain any rest either indoors or out-of-doors, it allowed her to hold it. Then she stroked and petted it to keep it from being afraid, and boldly went to the chemist's assistant and said,

"If you don't like that animal, you mustn't beat it; you must give it to me."

"Take it," said the assistant.

. . . "Now there!" adds Jeanne, by way of conclusion; and then she changes her voice again to a flute-tone in order to say all kinds of sweet things to that cat.

"He is horribly thin," I observe, looking at the wretched animal; —"moreover, he is horribly ugly." Jeanne thinks he is not ugly at all, but she acknowledges that he looks even more stupid than he looked at first: this time she thinks it not indecision, but surprise, which gives that unfortunate aspect to his countenance. She asks us to imagine ourselves in his place;—then we are obliged to acknowledge that he cannot possibly understand what has happened to him. And then we all burst out laughing in the face of the poor little beast, which maintains the most comical look of gravity. Jeanne wants to take him up; but he hides himself under the table, and cannot even be tempted to come out by the lure of a saucer of milk.

We all turn our backs and promise not to look; when we inspect the saucer again, we find it empty.

"Jeanne," I observe, "your *protégé* has a decidedly tristful aspect of countenance; he is of a sly and suspicious disposition; I trust he is not going to commit in the City of Books any such misdemeanours as might render it necessary for us to send him back to his chemist's shop. In the meantime we must give him a name. Suppose we call him 'Don Gris de Gouttière'; but perhaps that is too long. 'Pill,' 'Drug,' or 'Castor-oil' would be short enough, and would further serve to recall his early condition in life. What do you think about it?"

" 'Pill' would not sound bad," answers Jeanne, "but it would be very unkind to give him a name which would be always reminding him of the misery from which we saved him. It would be making him pay too dearly for our hospitality. Let us be more generous, and give him a pretty name, in hopes that he is going to deserve it. See how he looks at us! He knows that we are talking about him. And now that he is no longer unhappy, he is beginning to look a great deal less stupid. I am not joking! Unhappiness does make people look stupid,—I am perfectly sure it does."

Well, Jeanne, if you like, we will call your *protégé* Hannibal. The appropriateness of that name does not seem to strike you at once. But the Angora cat who preceded him here as an inmate of the City of Books, and to whom I was in the habit of telling all my secrets —for he was a very wise and discreet person—used to be called

Hamilcar. It is natural that this name should beget the other, and that Hannibal should succeed Hamilcar.

We all agreed upon this point.

"Hannibal!" cried Jeanne, "come here!"

Hannibal, greatly frightened by the strange sonority of his own name, ran to hide himself under a bookcase in an orifice so small that a rat could not have squeezed himself into it.

A nice way of doing credit to so great a name!

I was in a good humour for working that day, and I had just dipped the nib of my pen into the ink-bottle when I heard some one ring. Should any one ever read these pages written by an unimaginative old man, he will be sure to laugh at the way that bell keeps ringing through my narrative, without ever announcing the arrival of a new personage or introducing any unexpected incident. On the stage things are managed on the reverse principle. Monsieur Scribe never has the curtain raised without good reason, and for the greater enjoyment of ladies and young misses. That is art! I would rather hang myself than write a play,—not that I despise life, but because I should never be able to invent anything amusing. Invent! In order to do that one must have received the gift of inspiration. It would be a very unfortunate thing for me to possess such a gift. Suppose I were to invent some monkling in my history of the Abbey of Saint-Germain-des-Prés! What would our young erudites say? What a scandal for the School! As for the Institute, it would say nothing and probably not even think about the matter either. Even if my colleagues still write a little sometimes, they never read. They are of the opinion of Parny, who said,

> *"Une paisible indifférence*
> *Est la plus sage des vertus."**

To be the least wise in order to become the most wise—this is precisely what those Buddhists are aiming at without knowing it. If there is any wiser wisdom than that I will go to Rome to report upon it. . . . And all this because Monsieur Gélis happened to ring the bell!

This young man has latterly changed his manner completely with Jeanne. He is now quite as serious as he used to be frivolous, and quite as silent as he used to be chatty. And Jeanne follows his example. We have reached the phase of passionate love under constraint. For, old as I am, I cannot be deceived about it: these two children are violently and sincerely in love with each other. Jeanne now avoids him—she hides herself in her room when he comes into the library—but how well she knows how to reach him when she is alone! alone at her piano! Every evening she talks to him through

*"The most wise of the virtues is a calm indifference."

the music she plays with a rich thrill of passional feeling which is the new utterance of her new soul.

Well, why should I not confess it? Why should I not avow my weakness? Surely my egotism would not become any less blameworthy by keeping it hidden from myself? So I will write it. Yes! I was hoping for something else;—yes! I thought I was going to keep her all to myself, as my own child, as my own daughter—not always, of course, not even perhaps for very long, but just for a few years more. I am so old! Could she not wait? And, who knows? With the help of the gout, I would not have imposed upon her patience too much. That was my wish; that was my hope. I had made my plans—I had not reckoned upon the coming of this wild young man. But the mistake is none the less cruel because my reckoning happened to be wrong. And yet it seems to me that you are condemning yourself very rashly, friend Sylvestre Bonnard: if you did want to keep this young girl a few years longer, it was quite as much in her own interest as in yours. She has a great deal to learn yet, and you are not a master to be despised. When that miserable notary Mouche—who subsequently committed his rascalities at so opportune a moment—paid you the honour of a visit, you explained to him your ideas of education with all the fervour of high enthusiasm. Then you attempted to put that system of yours into practice;—Jeanne is certainly an ungrateful girl, and Gélis a much too seductive young man!

But still,—unless I put him out of the house, which would be a detestably ill-mannered and ill-natured thing to do,—I must continue to receive him. He has been waiting ever so long in my little parlour, in front of those Sèvres vases with which King Louis Philippe so graciously presented me. The *Moissonneurs* and the *Pêcheurs* of Léopold Robert are painted upon those porcelain vases, which Gélis nevertheless dares to call frightfully ugly, with the warm approval of Jeanne, whom he has absolutely bewitched.

"My dear lad, excuse me for having kept you waiting so long. I had a little bit of work to finish."

I am telling the truth. Meditation is work, but of course Gélis does not know what I mean; he thinks I am referring to something archæological, and, his question in regard to the health of Mademoiselle Jeanne having been answered by a "*Very well indeed*," uttered in that extremely dry tone which reveals my moral authority as guardian, we begin to converse about historical subjects. We first enter upon generalities. Generalities are sometimes extremely serviceable. I try to inculcate into Monsier Gélis some respect for that generation of historians to which I belong. I say to him,

"History, which was formerly an art, and which afforded place for the fullest exercise of the imagination, has in our time become a science, the study of which demands absolute exactness of knowledge."

Gélis asks leave to differ from me on this subject. He tells me he does not believe that history is a science, or that it could possibly ever become a science.

"In the first place," he says to me, "what is history? The written representation of past events. But what is an event? Is it merely a commonplace fact? Is it any fact? No! You say yourself it is a noteworthy fact. Now, how is the historian to tell whether a fact is noteworthy or not? He judges it arbitrarily, according to his tastes, and his caprices and his ideas—in short, as an artist. For facts cannot by reason of their own intrinsic character be divided into historical facts and non-historical facts. But any fact is something exceedingly complex. Will the historian represent facts in all their complexity? No, that is impossible. Then he will represent them stripped of the greater part of the peculiarities which constituted them, and consequently lopped, mutilated, different from what they really were. As for the inter-relation of facts, needless to speak of it! If a so-called historical fact be brought into notice—as is very possible—by one or more facts which are not historical at all, and are for that very reason unknown, how is the historian going to establish the relation of these facts one to another? And in saying this, Monsieur Bonnard, I am supposing that the historian has positive evidence before him, whereas in reality he feels confidence only in such or such a witness for sympathetic reasons. History is not a science; it is an art, and one can succeed in that art only through the exercise of his faculty of imagination."

Monsieur Gélis reminds me very much at this moment of a certain young fool whom I heard talking wildly one day in the garden of the Luxembourg, under the statue of Marguerite of Navarre. But at another turn of the conversation we find ourselves face to face with Walter Scott, whose work my disdainful young friend pleases to term "rococo, troubadourish, and only fit to inspire somebody engaged in making designs for cheap bronze clocks." Those are his very words!

"Why!" I exclaim, zealous to defend the magnificent creator of 'The Bride of Lammermoor' and 'The Fair Maid of Perth,' "the whole past lives in those admirable novels of his;—that is history, that is epic!"

"It is frippery," Gélis answers me.

And,—will you believe it?—this crazy boy actually tells me that no matter how learned one may be, one cannot possibly know just how men used to live five or ten centuries ago, because it is only with the very greatest difficulty that one can picture them to oneself even as they were only ten or fifteen years ago. In his opinion, the historical poem, the historical novel, the historical painting, are all, according to their kind, abominably false as branches of art.

"In all the arts," he adds, "the artist can only reflect his own soul. His work, no matter how it may be dressed up, is of necessity contemporary with himself, being the reflection of his own mind. What do we admire in the 'Divine Comedy' unless it be the great soul of Dante? And the marbles of Michael Angelo, what do they represent to us that is at all extraordinary unless it be Michael Angelo himself? The artist either communicates his own life to his creations, or else merely whittles out puppets and dresses up dolls."

What a torrent of paradoxes and irreverences! But boldness in a young man is not displeasing to me. Gélis gets up from his chair and sits down again. I know perfectly well what is worrying him, and whom he is waiting for. And now he begins to talk to me about his being able to make fifteen hundred francs a year, to which he can add the revenue he derives from a little property that he has inherited—two thousand francs a year or more. And I am not in the least deceived as to the purpose of these confidences on his part. I know perfectly well that he is only making his little financial statements in order to persuade me that he is comfortably circumstanced, steady, fond of home, comparatively independent—or, to put the matter in the fewest words possible, able to marry. *Quod erat demonstrandum,*—as the geometricians say.

He has got up and sat down just twenty times. He now rises for the twenty-first time; and, as he has not been able to see Jeanne, he goes away feeling as unhappy as possible.

The moment he has gone, Jeanne comes into the City of Books, under the pretext of looking for Hannibal. She is also quite unhappy; and her voice becomes singularly plaintive as she calls her pet to give him some milk. Look at that sad little face, Bonnard! Tyrant, gaze upon thy work! Thou hast been able to keep them from seeing each other; but they have now both of them the same expression of countenance, and thou mayest discern from that similarity of expression that in spite of thee they are united in thought. Cassandra, be happy! Bartholo, rejoice! This is what it means to be a guardian! Just see her kneeling down there on the carpet with Hannibal's head between her hands!

Yes, caress the stupid animal!—pity him!—moan over him!— we know very well, you little rogue, the real cause of all those sighs and plaints! Nevertheless, it makes a very pretty picture. I look at it for a long time; then, throwing a glance around my library, I exclaim,

"Jeanne, I am tired of all those books; we must sell them."

September 20.

IT is done!—they are betrothed. Gélis, who is an orphan, as Jeanne is, did not make his proposal to me in person. He got one of his professors, an old colleague of mine, highly esteemed for his learning and character, to come to me on his behalf. But what a love messenger! Great Heavens! A bear—not a bear of the Pyrenees, but a literary bear, and this latter variety of bear is much more ferocious than the former.

"Right or wrong (in my opinion wrong) Gélis says that he does not want any dowry; he takes your ward with nothing but her chemise. Say yes, and the thing is settled! Make haste about it! I want to show you two or three very curious old tokens from Lorraine which I am sure you never saw before."

That is literally what he said to me. I answered him that I would consult Jeanne, and I found no small pleasure in telling him that my ward had a dowry.

Her dowry—there it is in front of me! It is my library. Henri and Jeanne have not even the faintest suspicion about it; and the fact is I am commonly believed to be much richer than I am. I have the face of an old miser. It is certainly a lying face; but its untruthfulness has often won for me a great deal of consideration. There is nobody so much respected in this world as a stingy rich man.

I have consulted Jeanne,—but what was the need of listening for her answer? It is done! They are betrothed.

It would ill become my character as well as my face to watch these young people any longer for the mere purpose of noting down their words and gestures. *Noli me tangere:*—that is the maxim for all charming love affairs. I know my duty. It is to respect all the little secrets of that innocent soul intrusted to me. Let these children love each other all they can! Never a word of their fervent outpouring of mutual confidences, never a hint of their artless self-betrayals, will be set down in this diary by the old guardian whose authority was so gentle and so brief.

At all events, I am not going to remain with my arms folded; and if they have their business to attend to, I have mine also. I am preparing a catalogue of my books, with a view to having them all sold at auction. It is a task which saddens and amuses me at the same time. I linger over it, perhaps a good deal longer than I ought to do; turning the leaves of all those works which have become so familiar to my thought, to my touch, to my sight—even out of all necessity and reason. But it is a farewell; and it has ever been in the nature of man to prolong a farewell.

This ponderous volume here, which has served me so much for thirty long years, how can I leave it without according to it every kindness that a faithful servant deserves? And this one again, which has so often consoled me by its wholesome doctrines, must I not bow down before it for the last time, as to a Master? But each time that I meet with a volume which ever led me into error, which ever afflicted me with false dates, omissions, lies, and other plagues of the archæologist, I say to it with bitter joy: "Go! impostor, traitor, false-witness! flee thou far away from me for ever;—*vade retro!* all absurdly covered with gold as thou art! and I pray it may befall thee—thanks to thy usurped reputation and thy comely mo-

rocco attire—to take thy place in the cabinet of some banker-
bibliomaniac, whom thou wilt never be able to seduce as thou hast
seduced me, because he will never read one single line of thee."

I laid aside some books I must always keep—those books which
were given to me as souvenirs. As I placed among them the manuscript of the "Golden Legend," I could not but kiss it in memory of
Madame Trépof, who remained grateful to me in spite of her high
position and all her wealth, and who became my benefactress merely
to prove to me that she felt I had once done her a kindness. . . .
Thus I had made a reserve. It was then that, for the first time, I
felt myself inclined to commit a deliberate crime. All through that
night I was strongly tempted; by morning the temptation had become irresistible. Everybody else in the house was still asleep. I got
out of bed and stole softly from my room.

Ye powers of darkness! ye phantoms of the night! if while lingering within my home after the crowing of the cock, you saw me
stealing about on tiptoe in the City of Books, you certainly never
cried out, as Madame Trépof did at Naples, "That old man has a
good-natured round back!" I entered the library; Hannibal, with
his tail perpendicularly erected, came to rub himself against my
legs and purr. I seized a volume from its shelf, some venerable
Gothic text or some noble poet of the Renaissance—the jewel, the
treasure which I had been dreaming about all night, I seized it and
slipped it away into the very bottom of the closet which I had reserved for those books I intended to retain, and which soon became
full almost to bursting. It is horrible to relate: I was stealing the
dowry of Jeanne! And when the crime had been consummated I set
myself again sturdily to the task of cataloguing, until Jeanne came
to consult me in regard to something about a dress or a trousseau.
I could not possibly understand just what she was talking about,
through my total ignorance of the current vocabulary of dress-
making and linen-drapery. Ah! if a bride of the fourteenth century
had come to talk to me about the apparel of her epoch, then, indeed,
I should have been able to understand her language! But Jeanne
does not belong to my time, and I have to send her to Madame de
Gabry, who on this important occasion will take the place of her
mother.

. . . Night has come! Leaning from the window, we gaze at the
vast sombre stretch of the city below us, pierced with multitudinous
points of light. Jeanne presses her hand to her forehead as she
leans upon the window-bar, and seems a little sad. And I say to myself as I watch her: All changes, even the most longed for, have
their melancholy; for what we leave behind us is a part of ourselves: we must die to one life before we can enter into another!

And as if answering my thought, the young girl murmurs to me,

"My guardian. I am so happy; and still I feel as if I wanted to
cry!"

THE LAST PAGE

August 21 1869.

PAGE eighty-seven. . . . Only twenty lines more and I shall have finished my book about insects and flowers. Page eighty-seventh and last. . . . *"As we have already seen, the visits of insects are of the utmost importance to plants; since their duty is to carry to the pistils the pollen of the stamens. It seems also that the flower itself is arranged and made attractive for the purpose of inviting this nuptial visit. I think I have been able to show that the nectary of the plant distils a sugary liquid which attracts the insect and obliges it to aid unconsciously in the work of direct or cross fertilisation. The last method of fertilisation is the more common. I have shown that flowers are coloured and perfumed so as to attract insects, and interiorly so constructed as to offer those visitors such a mode of access that they cannot penetrate into the corolla without depositing upon the stigma the pollen with which they have been covered. My most venerated master Sprengel observes in regard to that fine down which lines the coralla of the wood-geranium: 'The wise Author of Nature has never created a single useless hair!' I say in my turn: If that Lily of the Valley whereof the Gospel makes mention is more richly clad than King Solomon in all his glory, its mantle of purple is a wedding-garment, and that rich apparel is necessary to the perpetuation of the species.**

"BROLLES, *August* 21, 1869."

Brolles! My house is the last one you pass in the single street of the village, as you go to the woods. It is a gabled house with a slate

---

*Monsieur Sylvestre Bonnard was not aware that several very illustrious naturalists were making researches at the same time as he in regard to the relation between insects and plants. He was not acquainted with the labours of Darwin, with those of Dr. Hermann Müller, nor with the observations of Sir John Lubbock. It is worthy of note that the conclusions of Monsieur Sylvestre Bonnard are very nearly similar to those reached by the three scientists above mentioned. Less important, but perhaps equally interesting, is the fact that Sir John Lubbock is, like Monsieur Bonnard, an archæologist who began to devote himself only late in life to the natural sciences.—*Note by the French Editor.*

roof, which takes iridescent tints in the sun like a pigeon's breast. The weather-vane above that roof has won more consideration for me among the country people than all my works upon history and philology. There is not a single child who does not know Monsieur Bonnard's weather-vane. It is rusty, and squeaks very sharply in the wind. Sometimes it refuses to do any work at all—just like Thérèse, who now allows herself to be assisted by a young peasant girl—though she grumbles a good deal about it. The house is not large, but I am very comfortable in it. My room has two windows, and gets the sun in the morning. The children's room is upstairs. Jeanne and Henri come twice a year to occupy it.

Little Sylvestre's cradle used to be in it. He was a very pretty child, but very pale. When he used to play on the grass, his mother would watch him very anxiously; and every little while she would stop her sewing in order to take him upon her lap. The poor little fellow never wanted to go to sleep. He used to say that when he was asleep he would go away, very far away, to some place where it was all dark, and where he saw things that made him afraid—things he never wanted to see again.

Then his mother would call me, and I would sit down beside his cradle. He would take one of my fingers into his little dry warm hand, and say to me,

"Godfather, you must tell me a story."

Then I would tell him all kinds of stories, which he would listen to very seriously. They all interested him, but there was one especially which filled his little soul with delight. It was "The Blue Bird." Whenever I finished that, he would say to me, "Tell it again! tell it again!" And I would tell it again until his little pale blue-veined head sank back upon the pillow in slumber.

The doctor used to answer all our questions by saying,

"There is nothing extraordinary the matter with him!"

No! There was nothing extraordinary the matter with little Sylvestre. One evening last year his father called me.

"Come," he said, "the little one is still worse."

I approached the cradle over which the mother hung motionless, as if tied down above it by all the powers of her soul.

Little Sylvestre turned his eyes towards me; their pupils had already rolled up beneath his eyelids, and could not descend again.

"Godfather," he said, "you are not to tell me any more stories."

No, I was not to tell him any more stories!

Poor Jeanne!—poor mother!

I am too old now to feel very deeply; but how strangely painful a mystery is the death of a child!

To-day, the father and mother have come to pass six weeks under the old man's roof. I see them now returning from the woods, walking arm-in-arm. Jeanne is closely wrapped in her black shawl, and

Henri wears a crape band on his straw hat; but they are both of them radiant with youth, and they smile very sweetly at each other. They smile at the earth which sustains them; they smile at the air which bathes them; they smile at the light which each one sees in the eyes of the other. From my window I wave my handkerchief at them,—and they smile at my old age.

Jeanne comes running lightly up the stairs; she kisses me, and then whispers in my ear something which I divine rather than hear. And I make answer to her: "May God's blessing be with you, Jeanne, and with your husband, and with your children, and with your children's children for ever!" . . . *Et nunc dimittis servum tuum, Domine!*

THE REVOLT OF THE ANGELS

"THE REVOLT OF THE ANGELS" *translated by* MRS. WILFRID
JACKSON

CONTAINING IN A FEW LINES THE HISTORY OF A FRENCH FAMILY FROM 1789 TO THE PRESENT DAY

BENEATH the shadow of St. Sulpice the ancient mansion of the d'Esparvieu family rears its austere three stories between a moss-grown forecourt and a garden hemmed in, as the years have elapsed, by ever loftier and more intrusive buildings, wherein, nevertheless, two tall chestnut trees still lift their withered heads.

Here from 1825 to 1857 dwelt the great man of the family, Alexandre Bussart d'Esparvieu, Vice-President of the Council of State under the Government of July, Member of the Academy of Moral and Political Sciences, and author of an *Essay on the Civil and Religious Institutions of Nations*, in three octavo volumes, a work unfortunately left incomplete.

This eminent theorist of a Liberal monarchy left as heir to his name his fortune and his fame, Fulgence-Adolphe Bussart d'Esparvieu, senator under the Second Empire, who added largely to his patrimony by buying land over which the Avenue de l'Impératice was destined ultimately to pass, and who made a remarkable speech in favour of the temporal power of the popes.

Fulgence had three sons. The eldest, Marc-Alexandre, entering the army, made a splendid career for himself: he was a good speaker. The second, Gaétan, showing no particular aptitude for anything, lived mostly in the country, where he hunted, bred horses, and devoted himself to music and painting. The third son, René, destined from his childhood for the law, resigned his deputyship to avoid complicity in the Ferry decrees against the religious orders; and later, perceiving the revival under the presidency of Monsieur Fallières of the days of Decius and Diocletian, put his knowledge and zeal at the service of the persecuted Church.

From the Concordat of 1801 down to the closing years of the

Second Empire all the d'Esparvieus attended mass for the sake of example. Though sceptics in their inmost hearts, they looked upon religion as an instrument of government.

Marc and René were the first of their race to show any sign of sincere devotion. The General, when still a colonel, had dedicated his regiment to the Sacred Heart, and he practised his faith with a fervour remarkable even in a soldier, though we all know that piety, daughter of Heaven, has marked out the hearts of the generals of the Third Republic as her chosen dwelling-place on earth.

Faith has its vicissitudes. Under the old order the masses were believers, not so the aristocracy or the educated middle class. Under the First Empire the army from top to bottom was entirely irreligious. To-day the masses believe nothing. The middle classes wish to believe, and succeed at times, as did Marc and René d'Esparvieu. Their brother Gaétan, on the contrary, the country gentleman, failed to attain to faith. He was an agnostic, a term commonly employed by the modish to avoid the odious one of freethinker. And he openly declared himself an agnostic, contrary to the admirable custom which deems it better to withhold the avowal.

In the century in which we live there are so many modes of belief and of unbelief that future historians will have difficulty in finding their way about. But are we any more successful in disentangling the condition of religious beliefs in the time of Symmachus or of Ambrose?

A fervent Christian, René d'Esparvieu was deeply attached to the liberal ideas his ancestors had transmitted to him as a sacred heritage. Compelled to oppose a Jacobin and atheistical Republic, he still called himself Republican. And it was in the name of liberty that he demanded the independence and sovereignty of the Church.

During the long debates on the Separation and the quarrels over the Inventories, the synods of the bishops and the assemblies of the faithful were held in his house. While the most authoritatively accredited leaders of the Catholic party: prelates, generals, senators, deputies, journalists, were met together in the big green drawing-room, and every soul present turned towards Rome with a tender submission or enforced obedience; while Monsieur d'Esparvieu, his elbow on the marble chimney-piece, opposed civil law to canon law, and protested eloquently against the spoliation of the Church of France, two faces of other days, immobile and speechless, looked down on the modern crowd; on the right of the fireplace, painted by David, was Romain Bussart, a working-farmer at Esparvieu in shirt-sleeves and drill trousers, with a rough-and-ready air not untouched with cunning. He had good reason to smile: the worthy man laid the foundation of the family fortunes when he bought Church lands. On the left, painted by Gérard in full-dress bedizened with orders, was the peasant's son, Baron Emile Bussart d'Esparvieu, prefect under the Empire, Keeper of

the Great Seal under Charles X, who died in 1837, churchwarden
of his parish, with couplets from *La Pucelle* on his lips.

René d'Esparvieu married in 1888 Marie-Antoinette Coupelle,
daughter of Baron Coupelle, ironmaster at Blainville (Haute
Loire). Madame René d'Esparvieu had been president since 1903
of the Society of Christian Mothers. These perfect spouses, having
married off their eldest daughter in 1908, had three children still
at home—a girl and two boys.

Léon, the younger, aged seven, had a room next to his mother
and his sister Berthe. Maurice, the elder, lived in a little pavilion
comprising two rooms at the bottom of the garden. The young man
thus gained a freedom which enabled him to endure family life. He
was rather good-looking, smart without too much pretence, and the
faint smile which merely raised one corner of his mouth did not
lack charm.

At twenty-five Maurice possessed the wisdom of Ecclesiastes.
Doubting whether a man hath any profit of all his labour which he

taketh under the sun he never put himself out about anything. From his earliest childhood this young hopeful's sole concern with work had been considering how he might best avoid it, and it was through his remaining ignorant of the teaching of the *École de Droit* that he became a doctor of law and a barrister at the Court of Appeal.

He neither pleaded nor practised. He had no knowledge and no desire to acquire any; wherein he conformed to his genius whose engaging fragility he forbore to overload; his instinct fortunately telling him that it was better to understand little than to misunderstand a lot.

As Monsieur l'Abbé Patouille expressed it, Maurice had received from Heaven the benefits of a Christian education. From his childhood piety was shown to him in the example of his home, and when on leaving college he was entered at the *École de Droit,* he found the lore of the doctors, the virtues of the confessors, and the constancy of the nursing mothers of the Church assembled around the paternal hearth. Admitted to social and political life at the time of the great persecution of the Church of France, Maurice did not fail to attend every manifestation of youthful Catholicism; he lent a hand with his parish barricades at the time of the Inventories, and with his companions he unharnessed the archbishop's horses when he was driven out from his palace. He showed on all these occasions a modified zeal; one never saw him in the front ranks of the heroic band exciting soldiers to a glorious disobedience or flinging mud and curses at the agents of the law.

He did his duty, nothing more; and if he distinguished himself on the occasion of the great pilgrimage of 1911 among the stretcher-bearers at Lourdes, we have reason to fear it was but to please Madame de la Verdelière, who admired men of muscle. Abbé Patouille, a friend of the family and deeply versed in the knowledge of souls, knew that Maurice had only moderate aspirations to martyrdom. He reproached him with his lukewarmness, and pulled his ear, calling him a bad lot. Anyway, Maurice remained a believer.

Amid the distractions of youth his faith remained intact, since he left it severely alone. He had never examined a single tenet. Nor had he enquired a whit more closely into the ideas of morality current in the grade of society to which he belonged. He took them just as they came. Thus in every situation that arose he cut an eminently respectable figure which he would have assuredly failed to do, had he been given to meditating on the foundations of morality. He was irritable and hot-tempered and possessed of a sense of honour which he was at great pains to cultivate. He was neither vain nor ambitious. Like the majority of Frenchmen, he disliked parting with his money. Women would never have obtained anything from him had they not known the way to make him give. He believed he despised them; the truth was he adored them. He indulged his appetites so naturally that he never suspected that he had any. What people did not know, himself least of all,—though the gleam that occasionally shone in his fine, light-brown eyes might have furnished the hint—was that he had a warm heart and was capable of friendship. For the rest, he was, in the ordinary intercourse of life, no very brilliant specimen.

II

WHEREIN USEFUL INFORMATION WILL BE FOUND CONCERNING A LIBRARY WHERE STRANGE THINGS WILL SHORTLY COME TO PASS

ESIROUS of embracing the whole circle of human knowledge, and anxious to bequeath to the world a concrete symbol of his encyclopædic genius and a display in keeping with his pecuniary resources, Baron Alexandre d'Esparvieu had formed a library of three hundred and sixty thousand volumes, both printed and in manuscript, whereof the greater part emanated from the Benedictines of Ligugé.

By a special clause in his will he enjoined his heirs to add to his library, after his death, whatever they might deem worthy of note in natural, moral, political, philosophical, and religious science.

He had indicated the sums which might be drawn from his estate for the fulfilment of this object, and charged his eldest son, Fulgence-Adolphe, to proceed with these additions. Fulgence-Adolphe accomplished with filial respect the wishes expressed by his illustrious father.

After him, this huge library, which represented more than one child's share of the estate, remained undivided between the Senator's three sons and two daughters; and René d'Esparvieu, on whom devolved the house in the Rue Garancière, became the guardian of the valuable collection. His two sisters, Madame Paulet de Saint-Fain and Madame Cuissart, repeatedly demanded that such a large but unremunerative piece of property should be turned into money. But René and Gaétan bought in the shares of their two colegatees, and the library was saved. René d'Esparvieu even busied himself in adding to it, thus fulfilling the intentions of its founder. But from year to year he lessened the number and importance of the acquisitions, opining that the intellectual output in Europe was on the wane.

Nevertheless, Gaétan enriched it, out of his funds, with works published both in France and abroad which he thought good, and he was not lacking in judgment, though his brothers would never allow that he had a particle. Thanks to this man of leisurely and inquiring mind, Baron Alexandre's collection was kept practically up to date. Even at the present day the d'Esparvieu library, in the departments of theology, jurisprudence, and history is one of the finest private libraries in all Europe. Here you may study physical science, or to put it better, physical sciences in all their branches, and for that matter metaphysic or metaphysics, that is to say, all that is connected with physics and has no other name, so impossible is it to designate by a substantive that which has no substance, and is but a dream and an illusion. Here you may contemplate with admiration philosophers addressing themselves to the solution, dissolution, and resolution of the Absolute, to the determination of the Indeterminate and to the definition of the Infinite.

Amid this pile of books and booklets, both sacred and profane, you may find everything down to the latest and most fashionable pragmatism.

Other libraries there are, more richly abounding in bindings of venerable antiquity and illustrious origin, whose smooth and soft-hued texture render them delicious to the touch; bindings which the gilder's art has enriched with gossamer, lace-work, foliage, flowers, emblematic devices, and coats of arms; bindings that charm the studious eye with their tender radiance. Other libraries perhaps harbour a greater array of manuscripts illuminated with delicate and brilliant miniatures by artists of Venice, Flanders, or Touraine. But in handsome, sound editions of ancient and modern writers, both sacred and profane, the d'Esparvieu library is second to none. Here one finds all that has come down to us from antiquity; all the Fathers of the Church, the Apologists and the Decretalists, all the Humanists of the Renaissance, all the Encyclopædists, the whole world of philosophy and science. Therefore it was that Cardinal Merlin, when he deigned to visit it, remarked:

"There is no man whose brain is equal to containing all the knowledge which is piled upon these shelves. Happily it doesn't matter."

Monseigneur Cachepot, who worked there often when a curate in Paris, was in the habit of saying:

"I see here the stuff to make many a Thomas Aquinas and many an Arius, if only the modern mind had not lost its ancient ardour for good and evil."

There was no gainsaying that the manuscripts formed the more valuable portion of this immense collection. Noteworthy indeed was the unpublished correspondence of Gassendi, of Father Mersenne, and of Pascal, which threw a new light on the spirit of the seventeenth century. Nor must we forget the Hebrew Bibles, the Talmuds, the Rabbinical treatises, printed and in manuscript, the Aramaic and Samaritan texts, on sheepskin and on tablets of sycamore; in fine, all these antique and valuable copies collected in Egypt and in Syria by the celebrated Moïse de Dina, and acquired at a small cost by Alexandre d'Esparvieu in 1836, when the learned Hebraist died of old age and poverty in Paris.

The Esparvienne library occupied the whole of the second floor of the old house. The works thought to be of but mediocre interest, such as books of Protestant exegesis of the nineteenth and twentieth centuries, the gift of Monsieur Gaétan, were relegated unbound to the limbo of the upper regions. The catalogue, with its various supplements, ran into no less than eighteen folio volumes. It was quite up to date, and the library was in perfect order. Monsieur Julien Sariette, archivist and palæographer, who, being poor and retiring, used to make his living by teaching, became, in 1895, tutor to young Maurice on the recommendation of the Bishop of Agra, and with scarcely an interval found himself curator of the Bibliothèque Esparvienne. Endowed with business-like energy and dogged patience, Monsieur Sariette himself classified all the members of this vast body. The system he invented and put into practice was so complicated, the labels he put on the books were made up of so many capital letters and small letters, both Latin and Greek, so many Arabic and Roman numerals, asterisks, double asterisks, triple asterisks, and those signs which in arithmetic express powers and roots, that the mere study of it would have involved more time and labour than would have been required for the complete mastery of algebra, and as no one could be found who would give the hours, that might be more profitably employed in discovering the law of numbers, to the solving of these cryptic symbols, Monsieur Sariette remained the only one capable of finding his way among the intricacies of his system, and without his help it had become an utter impossibility to discover, among the three hundred and sixty thousand volumes confided to his care, the particular volume one happened to require. Such was the result of his labours. Far from complaining about it, he experienced on the contrary a lively satisfaction.

Monsieur Sariette loved his library. He loved it with a jealous love. He was there every day at seven o'clock in the morning busy cataloguing at a huge mahogany desk. The slips in his handwriting filled an enormous case standing by his side surmounted by a plaster bust of Alexandre d'Esparvieu. Alexandre wore his hair brushed straight back, and had a sublime look on his face. Like Chateaubriand, he affected little feathery side whiskers. His lips were pursed, his bosom bare. Punctually at midday Monsieur Sariette used to sally forth to lunch at a *crèmerie* in the narrow gloomy Rue des Canettes. It was known as the *Crèmerie des Quatre Évêques,* and had once been the haunt of Baudelaire, Theodore de Banville, Charles Asselineau, and a certain grandee of Spain who had translated the "Mysteries of Paris" into the language of the *conquistadores.* And the ducks that paddled so nicely on the old stone sign which gave its name to the street used to recognize Monsieur

Sariette. At a quarter to one, to the very minute, he went back to his library, where he remained until seven o'clock. He then again betook himself to the *Quatre Évêques,* and sat down to his frugal dinner, with its crowning glory of stewed prunes. Every evening, after dinner, his crony, Monsieur Guinardon, universally known as Père Guinardon, a scene-painter and picture-restorer, who used to do work for churches, would come from his garret in the Rue Princesse to have his coffee and liqueur at the *Quatre Évêques,* and the two friends would play their game of dominoes.

Old Guinardon, who was like some rugged old tree still full of sap, was older than he could bring himself to believe. He had known Chenavard. His chastity was positively ferocious, and he was for ever denouncing the impurities of neo-paganism in language of alarming obscenity. He loved talking. Monsieur Sariette was a ready listener. Old Guinardon's favourite subject was the Chapelle des Anges in St. Sulpice, in which the paintings were peeling off the walls, and which he was one day to restore; when, that is, it should please God, for, since the Separation, the churches belonged solely to God, and no one would undertake the responsibility of even the most urgent repairs. But old Guinardon demanded no salary.

"Michael is my patron saint," he said. "And I have a special devotion for the Holy Angels."

After they had had their game of dominoes, Monsieur Sariette, very thin and small, and old Guinardon, sturdy as an oak, hirsute as a lion, and tall as a Saint Christopher, went off chatting away side by side across the Place Saint Sulpice, heedless of whether the night were fine or stormy. Monsieur Sariette always went straight home, much to the regret of the painter, who was a gossip and a night-bird.

The following day, as the clock struck seven, Monsieur Sariette would take up his place in the library, and resume his cataloguing. As he sat at his desk, however, he would dart a Medusa-like look at anyone who entered, fearing lest he should prove to be a book-borrower. It was not merely the magistrates, politicians, and prelates whom he would have liked to turn to stone when they came to ask for the loan of a book with an air of authority bred of their familiarity with the master of the house. He would have done as much to Monsieur Gaétan, the library's benefactor, when he wanted some gay or scandalous old volume wherewith to beguile a wet day in the country. He would have meted out similar treatment to Madame René d'Esparvieu, when she came to look for a book to read to her sick poor in hospital, and even to Monsieur René d'Esparvieu himself, who generally contented himself with the Civil Code and a volume of Dalloz. The borrowing of the smallest book seemed like dragging his heart out. To refuse a volume even to such as had the most incontestable right to it, Monsieur Sariette would invent countless far-fetched or clumsy fibs, and did not even shrink from slandering himself as curator or from casting doubts on his own vigilance by saying that such and such a book was mislaid or lost, when a moment ago he had been gloating over that very volume or pressing it to his bosom. And when ultimately forced to part with a volume he would take it back a score of times from the borrower before he finally relinquished it.

He was always in agony lest one of the objects confided to his care should escape him. As the guardian of three hundred and sixty thousand volumes, he had three hundred and sixty thousand reasons for alarm. Sometimes he woke at night bathed in sweat, and uttering a cry of fear, because he had dreamed he had seen a gap on one of the shelves of his bookcases. It seemed to him a monstrous, unheard-of, and most grievous thing that a volume should leave its habitat. This noble rapacity exasperated Monsieur René d'Esparvieu, who, failing to understand the good qualities of his paragon of a librarian, called him an old maniac. Monsieur Sariette knew nought of this injustice, but he would have braved the cruellest misfortune and endured opprobrium and insult to safeguard the integrity of his trust. Thanks to his assiduity, his vigilance and zeal, or, in a word, to his love, the Esparvienne library had not lost so much as a single leaflet under his supervision during the sixteen years which had now rolled by, this ninth of September, 1912.

III

WHEREIN THE MYSTERY BEGINS

T SEVEN o'clock on the evening of that day, having as usual replaced all the books which had been taken from their shelves, and having assured himself that he was leaving everything in good order, he quitted the library, double-locking the door after him. According to his usual habit, he dined at the *Crèmerie des Quatre Évêques*, read his newspaper, *La Croix*, and at ten o'clock went home to his little house in the Rue du Regard. The good man had no trouble and no presentiment of evil; his sleep was peaceful. The next morning at seven o'clock to the minute, he entered the little room leading to the library, and, according to his daily habit, doffed his grand frock-coat, and taking down an old one which hung in a cupboard over his washstand, put it on. Then he went into his workroom, where for sixteen years he had been cataloguing six days out of the seven, under the lofty gaze of Alexandre d'Esparvieu. Preparing to make a round of the various rooms, he entered the first and largest, which contained works on theology and religion in huge cupboards

whose cornices were adorned with bronze-coloured busts of poets and orators of ancient days.

Two enormous globes representing the earth and the heavens filled the window-embrasures. But at his first step Monsieur Sariette stopped dead, stupefied, powerless alike to doubt or to credit what his eyes beheld. On the blue cloth cover of the writing-table books lay scattered about pell-mell, some lying flat, some standing upright. A number of quartos were heaped up in a tottering pile. Two Greek lexicons, one inside the other, formed a single being more monstrous in shape than the human couples of the divine Plato. A gilt-edged folio was all a-gape, showing three of its leaves disgracefully dog's-eared.

Having, after an interval of some moments recovered from his profound amazement, the librarian went up to the table and recognised in the confused mass his most valuable Hebrew, French, and Latin Bibles, a unique Talmud, Rabbinical treatises printed and in manuscript, Aramaic and Samaritan texts and scrolls from the synagogues—in fine, the most precious relics of Israel all lying in a disordered heap, gaping and crumpled.

Monsieur Sariette found himself confronted with an inexplicable phenomenon; nevertheless he sought to account for it. How eagerly he would have welcomed the idea that Monsieur Gaétan, who, being a thoroughly unprincipled man, presumed on the right gained him by his fatal liberality towards the library to rummage there unhindered during his sojourns in Paris, had been the author of this terrible disorder. But Monsieur Gaétan was away travelling in Italy. After pondering for some minutes Monsieur Sariette's next supposition was that Monsieur René d'Esparvieu had entered the library late in the evening with the keys of his manservant Hippolyte, who, for the past twenty-five years, had looked after the second floor and the attics. Monsieur René d'Esparvieu, however, never worked at night, and did not read Hebrew. Perhaps, thought Monsieur Sariette, perhaps he had brought or allowed to be brought to this room some priest, or Jerusalem monk, on his way through Paris; some Oriental *savant* given to scriptural exegesis. Monsieur Sariette next wondered whether the Abbé Patouille, who had an enquiring mind, and also a habit of dog's-earing his books, had, peradventure, flung himself on these talmudic and biblical texts, fired with sudden zeal to lay bare the soul of Shem. He even asked himself for a moment whether Hippolyte, the old manservant, who had swept and dusted the library for a quarter of a century, and had been slowly poisoned by the dust of accumulated knowledge, had allowed his curiosity to get the better of him, and had been there during the night, ruining his eyesight and his reason, and losing his soul poring by moonlight over these undecipherable symbols. Monsieur Sariette even went so far as to imagine that young Maurice, on leaving his club or some nationalist meeting,

might have torn these Jewish volumes from their shelves, out of
hatred for old Jacob and his modern posterity; for this young man
of family was a declared anti-semite, and only consorted with those
Jews who were as anti-semitic as himself. It was giving a very
free rein to his imagination, but Monsieur Sariette's brain could
not rest, and went wandering about among speculations of the wildest extravagance.

Impatient to know the truth, the zealous guardian of the library
called the manservant.

Hippolyte knew nothing. The porter at the lodge could not furnish any clue. None of the domestics had heard a sound. Monsieur
Sariette went down to the study of Monsieur René d'Esparvieu,
who received him in nightcap and dressing-gown, listened to his
story with the air of a serious man bored with idle chatter, and dismissed him with words which conveyed a cruel implication of pity.

"Do not worry, my good Monsieur Sariette; be sure that the
books were lying where you left them last night."

Monsieur Sariette reiterated his enquiries a score of times, discovered nothing, and suffered such anxiety that sleep entirely forsook him. When, on the following day at seven o'clock he entered
the room with the busts and globes, and saw that all was in order,
he heaved a sigh of relief. Then suddenly his heart beat fit to burst.
He had just seen lying flat on the mantelpiece a paper-bound volume, a modern work, the boxwood paper-knife which had served
to cut its pages still thrust between the leaves. It was a dissertation
on the two parallel versions of Genesis, a work which Monsieur
Sariette had relegated to the attic, and which had never left it up
to now, no one in Monsieur d'Esparvieu's circle having had the curiosity to differentiate between the parts for which the polytheistic
and monotheistic contributors were respectively responsible in the
formation of the first of the sacred books. This book bore the
label $R > 3214\frac{\text{VIII}}{2}$. And this painful truth was suddenly borne in
upon the mind of Monsieur Sariette: to wit, that the most scientific
system of numbering will not help to find a book if the book is no
longer in its place. Every day of the ensuing month found the
table littered with books. Greek and Latin lay cheek by jowl with
Hebrew. Monsieur Sariette asked himself whether these nocturnal
flittings were the work of evil-doers who entered by the skylights to
steal valuable and precious volumes. But he found no traces of
burglary, and, notwithstanding the most minute search, failed to
discover that anything had disappeared. Terrible anxiety took possession of his mind, and he fell to wondering whether it was possible that some monkey in the neighbourhood came down the chimney and acted the part of a person engaged in study. Deriving his
knowledge of the habits of these animals in the main from the
paintings of Watteau and Chardin, he took it that, in the art of
imitating gestures or assuming characters they resembled Harle-

quin, Scaramouch, Zerlin, and the Doctors of the Italian comedy; he imagined them handling a palette and brushes, pounding drugs in a mortar, or turning over the leaves of an old treatise on alchemy beside an athanor. And so it was that, when, on one unhappy morning, he saw a huge blot of ink on one of the leaves of the third volume of the polyglot Bible bound in blue morocco and adorned with the arms of the Comte de Mirabeau, he had no doubt that a monkey was the author of the evil deed. The monkey had been pretending to take notes and had upset the inkpot. It must be a monkey belonging to a learned professor.

Imbued with this idea, Monsieur Sariette carefully studied the topography of the district, so as to draw a cordon round the group of houses amid which the d'Esparvieu house stood. Then he visited the four surrounding streets, asking at every door if there was a monkey in the house. He interrogated porters and their wives, washer-women, servants, a cobbler, a greengrocer, a glazier, clerks in bookshops, a priest, a bookbinder, two guardians of the peace, children, thus testing the diversity of character and variety of temper in one and the same people; for the replies he received were quite dissimilar in nature; some were rough, some were gentle; there were the coarse and the polished, the simple and the ironical, the prolix and the abrupt, the brief and even the silent. But of the animal he sought he had had neither sight nor sound, when under the archway of an old house in the Rue Servandoni, a small freckled, red-haired girl who looked after the door, made reply:

"There is Monsieur Ordonneau's monkey; would you care to see it?"

And without another word she conducted the old man to a stable at the other end of the yard. There on some rank straw and old bits of cloth, a young macaco with a chain round his middle sat and shivered. He was no taller than a five-year-old child. His livid face, his wrinkled brow, his thin lips were all expressive of mortal sadness. He fixed on the visitor the still lively gaze of his yellow eyes. Then with his small dry hand he seized a carrot, put it to his mouth, and forthwith flung it away. Having looked at the newcomers for a moment, the exile turned away his head, as if he expected nothing further of mankind or of life. Sitting huddled up, one knee in his hand, he made no further movement, but at times a dry cough shook his breast.

"It's Edgar," said the small girl. "He is for sale, you know."

But the old book-lover, who had come armed with anger and resentment, thinking to find a cynical enemy, a monster of malice, an antibibliophile, stopped short, surprised, saddened, and overcome, before this little being devoid of strength and joy and hope.

Recognising his mistake, troubled by the almost human face which sorrow and suffering made more human still, he murmured "Forgive me" and bowed his head.

THE REVOLT OF THE ANGELS

IV

WHICH IN ITS FORCEFUL BREVITY PROJECTS US TO THE LIMITS OF THE ACTUAL WORLD

TWO months elapsed; the domestic upheaval did not subside, and Monsieur Sariette's thoughts turned to the Freemasons. The papers he read were full of their crimes. Abbé Patouille deemed them capable of the darkest deeds, and believed them to be in league with the Jews and meditating the total over-throw of Christendom.

Having now arrived at the acme of power, they wielded a dominating influence in all the principal departments of State, they ruled the Chambers, there were five of them in the Ministry, and they filled the Elysée. Having some time since assassinated a President of the Republic because he was a patriot, they were getting rid of the accomplices and witnesses of their execrable crime. Few days passed without Paris being terror-stricken at some mysterious murder hatched in their Lodges. These were facts concerning which no doubt was possible. By what means did they gain access to the library? Monsieur Sariette could not imagine. What task had they come to fulfil? Why did they attack sacred antiquity and the origins of the Church? What impious designs were they forming? A heavy shadow hung over these terrible undertakings. The Catholic archivist feeling himself under the eye of the sons of Hiram was terrified and fell ill.

Scarcely had he recovered, when he resolved to pass the night in the very spot where these terrible mysteries were enacted, and to take the subtle and dangerous visitors by surprise. It was an enterprise that demanded all his slender courage. Being a man of delicate physique and of nervous temperament, Monsieur Sariette was naturally inclined to be fearful. On the 8th of January at nine o'clock in the evening, while the city lay asleep under a whirling snowstorm, he built up a good fire in the room containing the busts of the ancient poets and philosophers, and ensconced himself in an arm-chair at the chimney corner, a rug over his knees. On a small stand within reach of his hand were a lamp, a bowl of black coffee, and a revolver borrowed from the youthful Maurice. He tried to read his paper, *La Croix*, but the letters danced beneath his eyes. So he stared hard in front of him, saw nothing but the shadows, heard nothing but the wind, and fell asleep.

When he awoke the fire was out, the lamp was extinguished, leaving an acrid smell behind. But all around, the darkness was filled with milky brightness and phosphorescent lights. He thought he saw something flutter on the table. Stricken to the marrow with cold and terror, but upheld by a resolve stronger than any fear, he rose, approached the table, and passed his hands over the cloth. He saw nothing; even the lights faded, but under his fingers he felt a folio wide open; he tried to close it, the book resisted, jumped up and hit the imprudent librarian three blows on the head.

Monsieur Sariette fell down unconscious. . . .

Since then things had gone from bad to worse. Books left their allotted shelves in greater profusion than ever, and sometimes it was impossible to replace them; they disappeared. Monsieur Sariette discovered fresh losses daily. The Bollandists were now an imperfect set, thirty volumes of exegesis were missing. He himself had become unrecognisable. His face had shrunk to the size of one's fist and grown yellow as a lemon, his neck was elongated out of all proportion, his shoulders drooped, the clothes he wore hung on him as on a peg. He ate nothing, and at the *Crèmerie des Quatre Évêques* he would sit with dull eyes and bowed head, staring fixedly and vacantly at the saucer where, in a muddy juice, floated his stewed prunes. He did not hear old Guinardon relate how he had at last begun to restore the Delacroix paintings at St. Sulpice.

Monsieur René d'Esparvieu, when he heard the unhappy curator's alarming reports, used to answer drily:

"These books have been mislaid, they are not lost; look carefully, Monsieur Sariette, look carefully and you will find them."

And he murmured behind the old man's back:

"Poor old Sariette is in a bad way."

"I think," replied Abbé Patouille, "that his brain is going."

V

WHEREIN EVERYTHING SEEMS STRANGE BECAUSE EVERYTHING IS LOGICAL

THE Chapel of the Holy Angels, which lies on the right hand as you enter the Church of St. Sulpice, was hidden behind a scaffolding of planks. Abbé Patouille, Monsieur Gaétan, Monsieur Maurice, his nephew, and Monsieur Sariette, entered in single file through the low door cut in the wooden hoarding, and found old Guinardon on the top of his ladder standing in front of the Heliodorus. The old artist, surrounded by all sorts of tools and materials, was putting a white paste in the crack which cut in two the High Priest Onias. Zéphyrine, Paul Baudry's favourite model, Zéphyrine, who had lent her golden hair and polished shoulders to so many Magdalens, Mar-

guerites, sylphs, and mermaids, and who, it is said, was beloved of
the Emperor Napoleon III, was standing at the foot of the ladder
with tangled locks, cadaverous cheeks, and dim eyes, older than old
Guinardon, whose life she had shared for more than half a century. She had brought the painter's lunch in a basket.

Although the slanting rays fell grey and cold through the leaded
and iron-barred window, Delacroix's colouring shone resplendent,
and the roses on the cheeks of men and angels dimmed with their
glorious beauty the rubicund countenance of old Guinardon, which
stood out in relief against one of the temple's columns. These frescoes of the Chapel of the Holy Angels, though derided and insulted
when they first appeared, have now become part of the classic tradition, and are united in immortality with the masterpieces of
Rubens and Tintoretto.

Old Guinardon, bearded and long-haired, looked like Father Time
effacing the works of man's genius. Gaétan, in alarm, called out to
him:

"Carefully, Monsieur Guinardon, carefully. Do not scrape too
much."

The painter reassured him.

"Fear nothing, Monsieur Gaétan. I do not paint in that style. My
art is a higher one. I work after the manner of Cimabue, Giotto, and
Beato Angelico, not in the style of Delacroix. This surface here is
too heavily charged with contrast and opposition to give a really
sacred effect. It is true that Chenavard said that Christianity loves
the picturesque, but Chenavard was a rascal with neither faith nor
principle—an infidel. . . . Look, Monsieur d'Esparvieu, I fill up the
crevice, I relay the scales of paint which are peeling. That is all.
. . . The damage, due to the sinking of the wall, or more probably
to a seismic shock, is confined to a very small space. This painting
of oil and wax applied on a very dry foundation is far more solid
than one might think.

"I saw Delacroix engaged on this work. Impassioned but anxious,
he modelled feverishly, scraped out, re-painted unceasingly; his
mighty hand made childish blunders, but the thing is done with the
mastery of a genius and the inexperience of a schoolboy. It is a
marvel how it holds."

The good man was silent, and went on filling in the crevice.

"How classic and traditional the composition is," said Gaétan.
"Time was when one could recognise nothing but its amazing novelty; now one can see in it a multitude of old Italian formulas."

"I may allow myself the luxury of being just, I possess the quali-
fications," said the old man from the top of his lofty ladder. "Delacroix lived in a blasphemous and godless age. A painter of the
decadence, he was not without pride nor grandeur. He was greater
than his times. But he lacked faith, single-heartedness, and purity.
To be able to see and paint angels he needed that virtue of angels

and primitives, that supreme virtue which, with God's help, I do my best to practise, chastity."

"Hold your tongue, Michel; you are as big a brute as any of them."

Thus Zéphyrine, devoured with jealousy because that very morning on the stairs she had seen her lover kiss the bread-woman's daughter, to wit the youthful Octavie, who was as squalid and radiant as one of Rembrandt's Brides. She had loved Michel madly in the happy days long since past, and love had never died out in Zéphyrine's heart.

Old Guinardon received the flattering insult with a smile that he dissembled, and raised his eyes to the ceiling, where the archangel Michael, terrible in azure cuirass and gilt helmet, was springing heavenwards in all the radiance of his glory.

Meanwhile Abbé Patouille, blinking, and shielding his eyes with his hat against the glaring light from the window, began to examine the pictures one after another: Heliodorus being scourged by the angels, St. Michael vanquishing the Demons, and the combat of Jacob and the Angel.

"All this is exceedingly fine," he murmured at last, "but why has the artist only represented wrathful angels on these walls? Look where I will in this chapel, I see but heralds of celestial anger, ministers of divine vengeance. God wishes to be feared; He wishes also to be loved. I would fain perceive on these walls messengers of peace and of clemency. I should like to see the Seraphim who purified the lips of the prophet, St. Raphael who gave back his sight to old Tobias, Gabriel who announced the Mystery of the Incarnation to Mary, the Angel who delivered St. Peter from his chains, the Cherubim who bore the dead St. Catherine to the top of Sinai. Above all, I should like to be able to contemplate those heavenly guardians which God gives to every man baptized in His name. We each have one who follows all our steps, who comforts us and upholds us. It would be pleasant indeed to admire these enchanting spirits, these beautiful faces."

"Ah, Abbé! it depends on the point of view," answered Gaétan. "Delacroix was no sentimentalist. Old Ingres was not very far wrong in saying that this great man's work reeks of fire and brimstone. Look at the sombre, splendid beauty of those angels, look at those androgynes so proud and fierce, at those pitiless youths who lift avenging rods against Heliodorus, note this mysterious wrestler touching the patriarch on the hip. . . ."

"Hush," said Abbé Patouille. "According to the Bible he is no angel like the others; if he be an angel, he is the Angel of Creation, the Eternal Son of God. I am surprised that the Venerable Curé of St. Sulpice, who entrusted the decoration of this chapel to Monsieur Eugène Delacroix, did not tell him that the patriarch's symbolic struggle with Him who was nameless took place in profound darkness, and that the subject is quite out of place here, since it prefigures the Incarnation of Jesus Christ. The best artists go astray when they fail to obtain their ideas of Christian iconography from a qualified ecclesiastic. The institutions of Christian art form the subject of numerous works with which you are doubtless acquainted, Monsieur Sariette."

Monsieur Sariette was gazing vacantly about him. It was the third morning after his adventurous night in the library. Being, however, thus called upon by the venerable ecclesiastic, he pulled himself together and replied:

"On this subject we may with advantage consult Molanus, *De Historia Sacrarum Imaginum et Picturarum*, in the edition given us by Noël Paquot, dated Louvain, 1771; Cardinal Frederico Borromeo, *De Pictura Sacra*, and the Iconography of Didron; but this last work must be read with caution."

Having thus spoken, Monsieur Sariette relapsed into silence. He was pondering on his devastated library.

"On the other hand," continued Abbé Patouille, "since an example of the holy anger of the angels was necessary in this chapel, the painter is to be commended for having depicted for us in imitation of Raphael the heavenly messengers who chastised Heliodorus. Ordered by Seleucus, King of Syria, to carry off the treasures contained in the Temple, Heliodorus was stricken by an angel in a cuirass of gold mounted on a magnificently caparisoned steed. Two other angels smote him with rods. He fell to earth, as Monsieur Delacroix shows us here, and was swallowed up in darkness. It is right and salutary that this adventure should be cited as an example to the Republican Commissioners of Police and to the sacrilegious agents of the law. There will always be Heliodoruses, but, let it be known, every time they lay their hands on the property of the Church, which is the property of the poor, they shall be chastised with rods and blinded by the angels."

"I should like this painting, or, better still, Raphael's sublimer conception of the same subject, to be engraved in little pictures fully coloured, and distributed as rewards in all the schools."

"Uncle," said young Maurice, with a yawn, "I think these things are simply ghastly. I prefer Matisse and Metzinger."

These words fell unheeded, and old Guinardon from his ladder held forth:

"Only the primitives caught a glimpse of Heaven. Beauty is only to be found between the thirteenth and fifteenth centuries. The antique, the impure antique, which regained its pernicious influence over the minds of the sixteenth century, inspired poets and painters with criminal notions and immodest conceptions, with horrid impurities, filth. All the artists of the Renaissance were swine, including Michael-Angelo."

Then, perceiving that Gaétan was on the point of departure, Père

Guinardon assumed an air of bonhomie, and said to him in a confidential tone:

"Bonsieur Gaétan, if you're not afraid of climbing up my five flights, come and have a look at my den. I've got two or three little canvases I wouldn't mind parting with, and they might interest you. All good, honest, straightforward stuff. I'll show you, among other things, a tasty, spicy little Baudouin that would make your mouth water."

At this speech Gaétan made off. As he descended the church steps and turned down the Rue Princesse, he found himself accompanied by old Sariette, and fell to unburdening himself to him, as he would have done to any human creature, or indeed to a tree, a lamp-post, a dog, or his own shadow, of the indignation with which the æsthetic theories of the old painter inspired him.

"Old Guinardon overdoes it with his Christian art and his Primitives! Whatever the artist conceives of Heaven is borrowed from earth; God, the Virgin, the Angels, men and women, saints, the light, the clouds. When he was designing figures for the chapel windows at Dreux, old Ingres drew from life a pure, fine study of a woman, which may be seen, among many others, in the Musée Bonnat at Bayonne. Old Ingres had written at the bottom of the page in case he should forget: 'Mademoiselle Cécile, admirable legs and thighs'—and so as to make Mademoiselle Cécile into a saint in Paradise, he gave her a robe, a cloak, a veil, inflicting thus a shameful decline in her estate, for the tissues of Lyons and Genoa are worthless compared with the youthful living tissue, rosy with pure blood; the most beautiful draperies are despicable compared with the lines of a beautiful body. In fact, clothing for flesh that is desirable and ripe for wedlock is an unmerited shame, and the worst of humiliations"; and Gaétan, walking carelessly in the gutter of the Rue Garancière, continued: "Old Guinardon is a pestilential idiot. He blasphemes Antiquity, sacred Antiquity, the age when the gods were kind. He exalts an epoch when the painter and the sculptor had all their lessons to learn over again. In point of fact, Christianity has run contrary to art in so much as it has not favoured the study of the nude. Art is the representation of nature, and nature is pre-eminently the human body; it is the nude."

"Pardon, pardon," purred old Sariette. "There is such a thing as spiritual, or, as one might term it, inward beauty, which, since the days of Fra Angelico down to those of Hippolyte Flandrin, Christian art has——"

But Gaétan, never hearing a word of all this, went on hurling his impetuous observations at the stones of the old street and the snow-laden clouds overhead:

"The Primitives cannot be judged as a whole, for they are utterly unlike each other. This old madman confounds them all together.

Cimabue is a corrupt Byzantine, Giotto gives hints of powerful genius, but his modelling is bad, and, like children, he gives all his characters the same face. The early Italians have grace and joy, because they are Italians. The Venetians have an instinct for fine colour. But when all is said and done these exquisite craftsmen enamel and gild rather than paint. There is far too much softness about the heart and the colouring of your saintly Angelico for me. As for the Flemish school, that's quite another pair of shoes. They can use their hands, and in glory of workmanship they are on a level with the Chinese lacquer-workers. The technique of the brothers Van Eyck is a marvel, but I cannot discover in their Adoration of the Lamb the charm and mystery that some have vaunted. Everything in it is treated with a pitiless perfection; it is vulgar in feeling and cruelly ugly. Memling may touch one perhaps; but he creates nothing but sick wretches and cripples; under the heavy, rich, and ungraceful robing of his virgins and saints one divines some very lamentable anatomy. I did not wait for Rogier van der Wyden to call himself Roger de la Pasture and turn Frenchman in order to prefer him to Memling. This Rogier or Roger is less of a ninny; but then he is more lugubrious, and the rigidity of his lines bears eloquent testimony to his poverty-stricken figures. It is a strange perversion to take pleasure in these carnivalesque figures when one can have the paintings of Leonardo, Titian, Correggio, Velasquez, Rubens, Rembrandt, Poussin, or Prud'hon. Really it is a perverted instinct."

Meanwhile the Abbé Patouille and Maurice d'Esparvieu were strolling leisurely along in the wake of the esthete and the librarian. As a general rule the Abbé Patouille was little inclined to talk theology with laymen, or, for that matter, with clerics either. Carried away, however, by the attractiveness of the subject, he was telling the youthful Maurice all about the sacred mission of those guardian angels which Monsieur Delacroix had so inopportunely excluded from his picture. And in order to give more adequate expression to his thoughts on such lofty themes, the Abbé Patouille borrowed whole phrases and sentences from Bossuet. He had got them up by heart to put in his sermons, for he adhered strongly to tradition.

"Yes, my son," he was saying, "God has appointed tutelary spirits to be near us. They come to us laden with His gifts. They return laden with our prayers. Such is their task. Not an hour, not a moment passes but they are at our side, ready to help us, ever fervent and unwearying guardians, watchmen that never slumber."

"Quite so, Abbé," murmured Maurice, who was wondering by what cunning artifice he could get on the soft side of his mother and persuade her to give him some money of which he was urgently in need.

VI

WHEREIN PÈRE SARIETTE DISCOVERS HIS MISSING TREASURES

EXT morning Monsieur Sariette entered Monsieur René d'Esparvieu's study without knocking. He raised his arms to the heavens, his few hairs were standing straight up on his head. His eyes were big with terror. In husky tones he stammered out the dreadful news. A very old manscript of Flavius Josephus; sixty volumes of all sizes; a priceless jewel, namely, a *Lucretius* adorned with the arms of Philippe de Vendôme, Grand Prior of France, with notes in Voltaire's own hand; a manuscript of Richard Simon, and a set of Gassendi's correspondence with Gabriel Naudé, comprising two hundred and thirty-eight unpublished letters, had disappeared. This time the owner of the library was alarmed.

He mounted in haste to the abode of the philosophers and the globes, and there with his own eyes confirmed the magnitude of the disaster.

There were yawning gaps on many a shelf. He searched here and there, opened cupboards, dragged out brooms, dusters, and fire-extinguishers, rattled the shovel in the coke fire, shook out Monsieur Sariette's best frock-coat that was hanging in the cloak-room, and then stood and gazed disconsolately at the empty places left by the Gassendi portfolios.

For the past half-century the whole learned world had been loudly clamouring for the publication of this correspondence. Monsieur René d'Esparvieu had not responded to the universal desire, unwilling either to assume so heavy a task, or to resign it to others. Having found much boldness of thought in these letters, and many passages of more libertine tendency than the piety of the twentieth century could endure, he preferred that they should remain unpublished; but he felt himself responsible for their safe-keeping, not only to his country but to the whole civilized world.

"How can you have allowed yourself to be robbed of such a treasure?" he asked severely of Monsieur Sariette.

"How can I have allowed myself to be robbed of such a treasure?" repeated the unhappy librarian. "Monsieur, if you opened my breast, you would find that question engraved upon my heart."

Unmoved by this powerful utterance, Monsieur d'Esparvieu continued with pent-up fury:

"And you have discovered no single sign that would put you on the track of the thief, Monsieur Sariette? You have no suspicion, not the faintest idea, of the way these things have come to pass?

You have seen nothing, heard nothing, noticed nothing, learnt nothing? You must grant this is unbelievable. Think, Monsieur Sariette, think of the possible consequences of this unheard-of theft, committed under your eyes. A document of inestimable value in the history of the human mind disappears. Who has stolen it? Why has it been stolen? Who will gain by it? Those who have got possession of it doubtless know that they will be unable to dispose of it in France. They will go and sell it in America or Germany. Germany is greedy for such literary monuments. Should the correspondence of Gassendi with Gabriel Naudé go over to Berlin, if it is published there by German savants, what a disaster, nay, what a scandal! Monsieur Sariette, have you not thought of that? . . ."

Beneath the stroke of an accusation all the more cruel in that he brought it against himself, Monsieur Sariette stood stupefied, and was silent. And Monsieur d'Esparvieu continued to overwhelm him with bitter reproaches.

"And you make no effort. You devise nothing to find these inestimable treasures. Make enquiries, bestir yourself, Monsieur Sariette; use your wits. It is well worth while."

And Monsieur d'Esparvieu went out, throwing an icy glance at his librarian.

Monsieur Sariette sought the lost books and manuscripts in every spot where he had already sought them a hundred times, and where they could not possibly be. He even looked in the coke-box and under the leather seat of his arm-chair. When midday struck he mechanically went downstairs. At the foot of the stairs he met his old pupil Maurice, with whom he exchanged a bow. But he only saw men and things as through a mist.

The broken-hearted curator had already reached the hall when Maurice called him back.

"Monsieur Sariette, while I think of it, do have the books removed that are choking up my garden-house."

"What books, Maurice?"

"I could not tell you, Monsieur Sariette, but there are some in Hebrew, all worm-eaten, with a whole heap of old papers. They are in my way. You can't turn round in the passage."

"Who took them there?"

"I'm bothered if I know."

And the young man rushed off to the dining-room, the luncheon gong having sounded quite a minute ago.

Monsieur Sariette tore away to the summer-house. Maurice had spoken the truth. About a hundred volumes were there, on tables, on chairs, even on the floor. When he saw them he was divided betwixt joy and fear, filled with amazement and anxiety. Happy in the finding of his lost treasure, dreading to lose it again, and completely overwhelmed with astonishment, the man of books alternately babbled like an infant and uttered the hoarse cries of a maniac. He recognised his Hebrew Bibles, his ancient Talmuds, his very old manuscript of Flavius Josephus, his portfolios of Gassendi's letters to Gabriel Naudé, and his richest jewel of all, to wit, *Lucretius* adorned with the arms of the Grand Prior of France, and with notes in Voltaire's own hand. He laughed, he cried, he kissed the morocco, the calf, the parchment, and vellum, even the wooden boards studded with nails.

As fast as Hippolyte, the manservant, returned with an armful to the library, Monsieur Sariette, with a trembling hand, restored them piously to their places.

VII

OF A SOMEWHAT LIVELY INTEREST, WHEREOF THE MORAL WILL, I HOPE, APPEAL GREATLY TO MY READERS, SINCE IT CAN BE EXPRESSED BY THIS SORROWFUL QUERY: "THOUGHT, WHITHER DOST THOU LEAD ME?" FOR IT IS A UNIVERSALLY ADMITTED TRUTH THAT IT IS UNHEALTHY TO THINK AND THAT TRUE WISDOM LIES IN NOT THINKING AT ALL

LL the books were now once more assembled in the pious keeping of Monsieur Sariette. But this happy reunion was not destined to last. The following night twenty volumes left their places, among them the *Lucretius* of Prior de Vendôme. Within a week the old Hebrew and Greek texts had all returned to the summer-house, and every night during the ensuing month they left their shelves and secretly went on the same path. Others betook themselves no one knew whither.

On hearing of these mysterious occurrences, Monsieur René d'Esparvieu merely remarked with frigidity to his librarian:

"My poor Sariette, all this is very queer, very queer indeed."

And when Monsieur Sariette tentatively advised him to lodge a formal complaint or to inform the Commissaire de Police, Monsieur d'Esparvieu cried out upon him:

"What are you suggesting, Monsieur Sariette? Divulge domestic secrets, make a scandal! You cannot mean it. I have enemies, and I am proud of it. I think I have deserved them. What I might complain about is that I am wounded in the house of my friend, attacked with unheard-of violence, by fervent loyalists, who, I grant you, are good Catholics, but exceedingly bad Christians. . . . In a word, I am watched, spied upon, shadowed, and you suggest, Monsieur Sariette, that I should make a present of this comic-opera mystery, this burlesque adventure, this story in which we both cut somewhat pitiable figures, to a set of spiteful journalists? Do you wish to cover me with ridicule?"

The result of the colloquy was that the two gentlemen agreed to change all the locks in the library. Estimates were asked for and workmen called in. For six weeks the d'Esparvieu household rang from morning till night with the sound of hammers, the hum of centre-bits, and the grating of files. Fires were always going in the abode of the philosophers and globes, and the people of the house were simply sickened by the smell of heated oil. The old, smooth, easy-running locks were replaced, on the cupboards and doors of the rooms, by stubborn and tricky fastenings. There was nothing but combinations of locks, letter-padlocks, safety-bolts, bars, chains, and electric alarm-bells.

All this display of ironmongery inspired fear. The lock-cases glistened, and there was much grinding of bolts. To gain access to a room, a cupboard, or a drawer, it was necessary to know a certain number, of which Monsieur Sariette alone was cognisant. His head was filled with bizarre words and tremendous numbers, and he got entangled among all these cryptic signs, these square, cubic, and triangular figures. He himself couldn't get the doors and the cupboards undone, yet every morning he found them wide open, and the books thrown about, ransacked, and hidden away. In the gutter of the Rue Servandoni a policeman picked up a volume of Salomon Reinach on the identity of Barabbas and Jesus Christ. As it bore the book-plate of the d'Esparvieu library he returned it to the owner.

Monsieur René d'Esparvieu, not even deigning to inform Monsieur Sariette of the fact, made up his mind to consult a magistrate, a friend in whom he had complete confidence, to wit, a certain Monsieur des Aubels, Counsel at the Law Courts, who had put through many an important affair. He was a little plump man, very red, very bald, with a cranium that shone like a billiard ball. He entered the library one morning feigning to come as a book-lover, but he soon showed that he knew nothing about books. While all the busts of the ancient philosophers were reflected in his shining pate, he put divers insidious questions to Monsieur Sariette, who grew uncomfortable and turned red, for innocence is easily flustered. From that moment Monsieur des Aubels had a mighty suspicion that Monsieur Sariette was the perpetrator of the very thefts he denounced with horror; and it immediately occurred to him to seek out the accomplices of the crime. As regards motives, he did not trouble about them; motives are always to be found. Monsieur des Aubels told Monsieur René d'Esparvieu that, if he liked, he would have the house secretly watched by a detective from the Prefecture.

"I will see that you get Mignon," he said. "He is an excellent servant, assiduous and prudent."

By six o'clock next morning Mignon was already walking up and down outside the d'Esparvieus' house, his head sunk between his shoulders, wearing love-locks which showed from under the narrow brim of his bowler hat, his eye cocked over his shoulder. He wore an enormous dull-black moustache, his hands and feet were huge; in fact, his whole appearance was distinctly memorable. He paced regularly up and down from the nearest of the big rams' head pillars which adorn the Hôtel de la Sordière to the end of the Rue Garancière, towards the apse of St. Sulpice Church and the dome of the Chapel of the Virgin.

Henceforth it became impossible to enter or leave the d'Esparvieus' house without feeling that one's every action, that one's very thoughts, were being spied upon. Mignon was a prodigious person endowed with powers that Nature denies to other mortals. He neither ate nor slept. At all hours of the day and night, in wind and rain, he was to be found outside the house, and no one escaped the X-rays of his eye. One felt pierced through and through, penetrated to the very marrow, worse than naked, bare as a skeleton. It was the affair of a moment; the detective did not even stop, but continued his everlasting walk. It became intolerable. Young Maurice threatened to leave the paternal roof if he was to be so radiographed. His mother and his sister Berthe complained of his piercing look; it offended the chaste modesty of their souls. Mademoiselle Caporal, young Léon d'Esparvieu's governess, felt an indescribable embarrassment. Monsieur René d'Esparvieu was sick of the whole business. He never crossed his own threshold without crushing his hat over his eyes to avoid the investigating ray and without wishing old Sariette, the *fons et origo* of all the evil, at the devil. The intimates of the household, such as Abbé Patouille and Uncle Gaétan, made themselves scarce; visitors gave up calling, tradespeople hesitated about leaving their goods, the carts belonging to the big shops scarcely dared stop. But it was among the domestics that the spying roused the most disorder.

The footman, afraid, under the eye of the police, to go and join the cobbler's wife over her solitary labours in the afternoon, found the house unbearable and gave notice. Odile, Madame d'Esparvieu's lady's-maid, not daring, as was her custom after her mistress had retired, to introduce Octave, the handsomest of the neighbouring bookseller's clerks, to her little room upstairs, grew melancholy, irritable and nervous, pulled her mistress's hair while dressing it, spoke insolently, and made advances to Monsieur Maurice. The cook, Madame Malgoire, a serious matron of some fifty years, having no more visits from Auguste, the wine-merchant's man in the Rue Servandoni, and being incapable of suffering a privation so contrary to her temperament, went mad, sent up a raw rabbit to table, and announced that the Pope had asked her hand in marriage. At last, after a fortnight of superhuman assiduity, contrary to all known laws of organic life, and to the essential conditions of animal economy, Mignon, the detective, having observed nothing abnormal, ceased his surveillance and withdrew without a word, refusing to accept a gratuity. In the library the dance of the books became livelier than ever.

"That is all right," said Monsieur des Aubels. "Since nothing comes in nor goes out, the evil-doer must be in the house."

The magistrate thought it possible to discover the criminal without police-warrant or enquiry. On a date agreed upon at midnight, he had the floor of the library, the treads of the stairs, the vestibule, the garden path leading to Monsieur Maurice's summer-house, and the entrance hall of the latter, all covered with a coating of talc.

The following morning Monsieur des Aubels, assisted by a pho-

tographer from the Prefecture, and accompanied by Monsieur René d'Esparvieu and Monsieur Sariette, came to take the imprints. They found nothing in the garden, the wind had blown away the coating of talc; nothing in the summer-house either. Young Maurice told them he thought it was some practical joke and that he had brushed away the white dust with the hearth-brush. The real truth was, he had effaced the traces left by the boots of Odile, the lady's-maid. On the stairs and in the library the very light print of a bare foot could be discerned, it seemed to have sprung into the air and to have touched the ground at rare intervals and without any pressure. They discovered five of these traces. The clearest was to be found in the abode of the busts and spheres, on the edge of the table where the books were piled. The photographer took several negatives of this imprint.

"This is more terrifying than anything else," murmured Monsieur Sariette.

Monsieur des Aubels did not hide his surprise.

Three days later the anthropometrical department of the Prefecture returned the proofs exhibited to them, saying that they were not in the records.

After dinner Monsieur René showed the photographs to his brother Gaétan, who examined them with profound attention, and after a long silence exclaimed:

"No wonder they have not got this at the Prefecture; it is the foot of a god or of an athlete of antiquity. The sole that made this impression is of a perfection unknown to our races and our climates. It exhibits toes of exquisite grace, and a divine heel."

René d'Esparvieu cried out upon his brother for a madman.

"He is a poet," sighed Madame d'Esparvieu.

"Uncle," said Maurice, "you'll fall in love with this foot if you ever come across it."

"Such was the fate of Vivant Denon, who accompanied Bonaparte to Egypt," replied Gaétan. "At Thebes, in a tomb violated by the Arabs, Denon found the little foot of a mummy of marvellous beauty. He contemplated it with extraordinary fervour. 'It is the foot of a young woman,' he pondered, 'of a princess—of a charming creature. No covering has ever marred its perfect shape.' Denon admired, adored, and loved it. You may see a drawing of this little foot in Denon's atlas of his journey to Egypt, whose leaves one could turn over upstairs, without going further afield, if only Monsieur Sariette would ever let us see a single volume of his library."

Sometimes, in bed, Maurice, waking in the middle of the night, thought he heard the sound of pages being turned over in the next room, and the thud of bound volumes falling on the floor.

One morning at five o'clock he was coming home from the club, after a night of bad luck, and while he stood outside the door of the summer-house, hunting in his pocket for his keys, his ears distinctly heard a voice sighing:

"Knowledge, whither dost thou lead me? Thought, whither dost thou lure me?"

But entering the two rooms he saw nothing, and told himself that his ears must have deceived him.

VIII

WHICH SPEAKS OF LOVE, A SUBJECT WHICH ALWAYS GIVES PLEASURE, FOR A TALE WITHOUT LOVE IS LIKE BEEF WITHOUT MUSTARD: AN INSIPID DISH

NOTHING ever astonished Maurice. He never sought to know the causes of things and dwelt tranquilly in the world of appearances. Not denying the eternal truth, he nevertheless followed vain things as his fancy led him.

Less addicted to sport and violent exercise than most young people of his generation, he followed unconsciously the old erotic traditions of his race. The French were ever the most gallant of men, and it were a pity they should lose this advantage. Maurice preserved it. He was in love with no woman, but, as St. Augustine said, he loved to love. After paying the tribute that was rightly due to the imperishable beauty and secret arts of Madame de la Berthelière, he had enjoyed the impetuous caresses of a young singer called Luciole. At present he was joylessly experiencing the primitive perversity of Odile, his mother's lady's-maid, and the tearful adoration of the beautiful Madame Boittier. And he felt a great void in his heart.

It chanced that one Wednesday, on entering the drawing-room where his mother entertained her friends—who were, generally speaking, unattractive and austere ladies, with a sprinkling of old men and very young people—he noticed, in this intimate circle, Madame des Aubels, the wife of the magistrate at the Law Courts, whom Monsieur d'Esparvieu had vainly consulted on the mysterious ransacking of his library. She was young, he found her pretty, and not without cause. Gilberte had been modelled by the Genius of the Race, and no other genius had had a part in the work.

Thus all her attributes inspired desire, and nothing in her shape or her being aroused any other sentiment.

The law of attraction which draws world to world moved young Maurice to approach this delicious creature, and under its influence he offered to escort her to the tea-table. And when Gilberte was served with tea, he said:

"We should hit it off quite well together, you and I, don't you think?"

He spoke in this way, according to modern usage, so as to avoid inane compliments and to spare a woman the boredom of listening to one of those old declarations of love which, containing nothing but what is vague and undefined, require neither a truthful nor an exact reply.

And profiting by the fact that he had an opportunity of conversing secretly with Madame des Aubels for a few minutes, he spoke urgently and to the point. Gilberte, so far as one could judge, was made rather to awaken desire than to feel it. Nevertheless, she well knew that her fate was to love, and she followed it willingly and with pleasure. Maurice did not particularly displease her. She would have preferred him to be an orphan, for experience had taught her how disappointing it sometimes is to love the son of the house.

"Will you?" he said by way of conclusion.

She pretended not to understand, and with her little *foie-gras* sandwich raised half-way to her mouth she looked at Maurice with wondering eyes.

"Will I *what?*" she asked.

"You know quite well."

Madame des Aubels lowered her eyes, and sipped her tea, for her prudishness was not quite vanquished. Meanwhile Maurice, taking her empty cup from her hand, murmured:

"Saturday, five o'clock, 126 Rue de Rome, on the ground-floor, the door on the right, under the arch. Knock three times."

Madame des Aubels glanced severely and imperturbably at the son of the house, and with a self-possessed air rejoined the circle of highly respectable women to whom the Senator Monsieur Le Fol was explaining how artificial incubators were employed at the agricultural colony at St. Julienne.

The following Saturday, Maurice, in his ground-floor flat, awaited Madame des Aubels. He waited her in vain. No light hand came to knock three times on the door under the arch. And Maurice gave way to imprecation, inwardly calling the absent one a jade and a hussy. His fruitless wait, his frustrated desires, rendered him unjust. For Madame des Aubels in not coming where she had never promised to go hardly deserved these names; but we judge human actions by the pleasure or pain they cause us.

Maurice did not put in an appearance in his mother's drawing-room until a fortnight after the conversation at the tea-table. He came late. Madame des Aubels had been there for half an hour. He bowed coldly to her, took a seat some way off, and affected to be listening to the talk.

"Worthily matched," a rich male voice was saying; "the two antagonists were well calculated to render the struggle a terrible and uncertain one. General Bol, with unprecedented tenacity, maintained his position as though he were rooted in the very soil. General Milpertuis, with an agility truly superhuman, kept carrying out movements of the most dazzling rapidity around his immovable adversary. The battle continued to be waged with terrible stubbornness. We were all in an agony of suspense. . . ."

It was General d'Esparvieu describing the autumn manœuvres to a company of breathlessly interested ladies. He was talking well and his audience were delighted. Proceeding to draw a comparison between the French and German methods, he defined their distinguishing characteristics and brought out the conspicuous merits of both with a lofty impartiality. He did not hesitate to affirm that each system had its advantages, and at first made it appear to his circle of wondering, disappointed, and anxious dames, whose countenances were growing increasingly gloomy, that France and Germany were practically in a position of equality. But little by little, as the strategist went on to give a clearer definition of the two methods, that of the French began to appear flexible, elegant, vigorous, full of grace, cleverness, and verve; that of the Germans heavy, clumsy, and undecided. And slowly and surely the faces of the ladies began to clear and to light up with joyous smiles. In order to dissipate any lingering shadows of misgiving from the minds of these wives, sisters, and sweethearts, the General gave them to understand that we were in a position to make use of the German method when it suited us, but that the Germans could not avail themselves of the French method. No sooner had he delivered himself of these sentiments than he was button-holed by Monsieur le Truc de Ruffec, who was engaged in founding a patriotic society known as "Swordsmen All," of which the object was to regenerate France and ensure her superiority over all her adversaries. Even children in the cradle were to be enrolled, and Monsieur le Truc de Ruffec offered the honorary presidency to General d'Esparvieu.

Meanwhile Maurice was appearing to be interested in a conversation that was taking place between a very gentle old lady and the Abbé Lapetite, Chaplain to the Dames du Saint Sang. The old lady, severely tried of late by illness and the loss of friends, wanted to know how it was that people were unhappy in this world.

"How," she asked Abbé Lapetite, "do you explain the scourges that afflict mankind? Why are there plagues, famines, floods, and earthquakes?"

"It is surely necessary that God should sometimes remind us of his existence," replied Abbé Lapetite, with a heavenly smile.

Maurice appeared keenly interested in this conversation. Then he seemed fascinated by Madame Fillot-Grandin, quite a personable young woman, whose simple innocence, however, detracted all piquancy from her beauty, all savour from her bodily charms. A very sour, shrill-voiced old lady, who, affecting the dowdy, woollen weeds of poverty, displayed the pride of a great lady in the world of Christian finance, exclaimed in a squeaky voice:

"Well, my dear Madame d'Esparvieu, so you have had trouble here. The papers speak darkly of robbery, of thefts committed in Monsieur d'Esparvieu's valuable library, of stolen letters. . . ."

"Oh," said Madame d'Esparvieu, "if we are to believe all the newspapers say . . ."

"Oh, so, dear Madame, you have got your treasures back. All's well that ends well."

"The library is in perfect order," asserted Madame d'Esparvieu. "There is nothing missing."

"The library is on the floor above this, is it not?" asked young Madame des Aubels, showing an unexpected interest in the books.

Madame d'Esparvieu replied that the library occupied the whole of the second floor, and that they had put the least valuable books in the attics.

"Could I not go and look at it?"

The mistress of the house declared that nothing could be easier. She called to her son:

"Maurice, go and do the honours of the library to Madame des Aubels."

Maurice rose, and without uttering a word, mounted to the second floor in the wake of Madame des Aubels.

He appeared indifferent, but inwardly he rejoiced, for he had no doubt that Gilberte had feigned her ardent desire to inspect the library simply to see him in secret. And, while affecting indifference, he promised himself to renew those offers which, this time, would not be refused.

Under the romantic bust of Alexandre d'Esparvieu, they were met by the silent shadow of a little wan, hollow-eyed old man, who wore a settled expression of mute terror.

"Do not let us disturb you, Monsieur Sariette," said Maurice. "I am showing Madame des Aubels round the library."

Maurice and Madame des Aubels passed on into the great room where against the four walls rose presses filled with books and surmounted by bronze busts of poets, philosophers, and orators of antiquity. All was in perfect order, an order which seemed never to have been disturbed from the beginning of things.

Only, a black void was to be seen in the place which, only the evening before, had been filled by an unpublished manuscript of Richard Simon. Meanwhile, by the side of the young couple walked Monsieur Sariette, pale, faded, and silent.

"Really and truly, you have not been nice," said Maurice, with a look of reproach at Madame des Aubels.

She signed to him that the librarian might overhear. But he reassured her.

"Take no notice. It is old Sariette. He has become a complete idiot." And he repeated: "No, you have not been at all nice. I awaited you. You did not come. You have made me unhappy."

After a moment's silence, while one heard the low melancholy whistling of asthma in poor Sariette's bronchial tubes, young Maurice continued insistently:

"You are wrong."

"Why wrong?"

"Wrong not to do as I ask you."

"Do you still think so?"

"Certainly."

"You meant it seriously?"

"As seriously as can be."

Touched by his assurance of sincere and constant feeling, and thinking she had resisted sufficiently, Gilberte granted to Maurice what she had refused him a fortnight ago.

They slipped into an embrasure of the window, behind an enormous celestial globe whereon were graven the Signs of the Zodiac and the figures of the stars, and there, their gaze fixed on the Lion, the Virgin, and the Scales, in the presence of a multitude of Bibles, before the works of the Fathers, both Greek and Latin, beneath the casts of Homer, Æschylus, Sophocles, Euripides, Herodotus, Thucydides, Socrates, Plato, Aristotle, Demosthenes, Cicero, Virgil, Horace, Seneca, and Epictetus, they exchanged vows of love and a long kiss on the mouth.

Almost immediately Madame des Aubels bethought herself that she still had some calls to pay, and that she must make her escape quickly, for love had not made her lose all sense of her own importance. But she had barely crossed the landing with Maurice when they heard a hoarse cry and saw Monsieur Sariette plunge madly downstairs, exclaiming as he went:

"Stop it, stop it; I saw it fly away! It escaped from the shelf by itself. It crossed the room . . . there it is—there! It's going downstairs. Stop it! It has gone out of the door on the ground floor!"

"What?" asked Maurice.

Monsieur Sariette looked out of the landing window, murmuring horror-struck:

"It's crossing the garden! It's going into the summer-house. Stop it, stop it!"

"But what is it?" repeated Maurice—"in God's name, what is it?"

"My Flavius Josephus," exclaimed Monsieur Sariette. "Stop it!" And he fell down unconscious.

"You see he is quite mad," said Maurice to Madame des Aubels, as he lifted up the unfortunate librarian.

Gilberte, a little pale, said she also thought she had seen something in the direction indicated by the unhappy man, something flying.

Maurice had seen nothing, but he had felt what seemed like a gust of wind.

He left Monsieur Sariette in the arms of Hippolyte and the housekeeper, who had both hastened to the spot on hearing the noise.

The old gentleman had a wound in his head.

"All the better," said the housekeeper; "this wound may save him from having a fit."

Madame des Aubels gave her handkerchief to stop the blood, and recommended an arnica compress.

IX

WHEREIN IT IS SHOWN THAT, AS AN ANCIENT GREEK POET SAID, "NOTHING IS SWEETER THAN APHRODITE THE GOLDEN"

LTHOUGH he had enjoyed Madame des Aubel's favours for six whole months, Maurice still loved her. True they had had to separate during the summer. For lack of funds of his own he had had to go to Switzerland with his mother, and then to stop with the whole family at the Château d'Esparvieu. She had spent the summer with her mother at Niort, and the autumn with her husband at a little Normandy seaside place, so that they had hardly seen each other four or five times. But since the winter, kindly to lovers, had brought them back to town again, Maurice had been receiving her twice a week in his little flat in the Rue de Rome, and received no one else. No other woman had inspired him with feelings of such constancy and fidelity. What augmented his pleasure was that he believed himself loved, and indeed he was not unpleasing.

He thought that she did not deceive him, not that he had any reason to think so, but it appeared right and fitting that she should be content with him alone. What annoyed him was that she always kept him waiting, and was unpunctual in coming to their meeting-place; she was invariably late,—at times very late.

Now on Saturday, January 30th, since four o'clock in the afternoon, Maurice had been awaiting Madame des Aubels in the little pink room, where a bright fire was burning. He was gaily clad in a suit of flowered pyjamas, smoking Turkish cigarettes. At first he dreamt of receiving her with long kisses, with hitherto unknown caresses. A quarter of an hour having passed, he meditated serious and affectionate reproaches, then after an hour of disappointed waiting he vowed he would meet her with cold disdain.

At length she appeared, fresh and fragrant.

"It was scarcely worth while coming," he said bitterly, as she laid her muff and her little bag on the table and untied her veil before the wardrobe mirror.

Never, she told her beloved, had she had such trouble to get away. She was full of excuses, which he obstinately rejected. But no sooner had she the good sense to hold her tongue than he ceased his reproaches, and then nothing detracted from the longing with which she inspired him.

The curtains were drawn, the room was bathed in warm shadows lit by the dancing gleams of the fire. The mirrors in the wardrobe and on the chimney-piece shone with mysterious lights. Gilberte, leaning on her elbow, head on hand, was lost in thought. A little jeweller, a trustworthy and intelligent man, had shown her a wonderfully pretty pearl and sapphire bracelet; it was worth a great deal, and was to be had for a mere nothing. He had got it from a *cocotte* down on her luck, who was in a hurry to dispose of it. It was a rare chance; it would be a huge pity to let it slip.

"Would you like to see it, darling? I will ask the little man to let me have it to show you."

Maurice did not actually decline the proposal. But it was clear that he took no interest in the wonderful bracelet. "When small jewellers come across a great bargain, they keep it to themselves, and do not allow their customers to profit by it. Moreover, jewellery means nothing just now. Well-bred women have given up wearing it. Everyone goes in for sport, and jewellery does not go with sport."

Maurice spoke thus, contrary to truth, because having given his mistress a fur coat, he was in no hurry to give her anything more. He was not stingy, but he was careful with his money. His people did not give him a very large allowance, and his debts grew bigger every day. By satisfying the wishes of his inamorata too promptly he feared to arouse others still more pressing. The bargain seemed less wonderful to him than to Gilberte; besides, he liked to take the initiative in choosing his gifts. Above all, he thought that if he gave her too many presents he would be no longer sure of being loved for himself.

Madame des Aubels felt neither contempt nor surprise at this attitude; she was gentle and temperate, she knew men, and judged that one must take them as one found them, that for the most part they do not give very willingly, and that a woman should know how to make them give.

Suddenly a gas lamp was lighted in the street, and shone through the gaps in the curtains.

"Half-past six," she said. "We must be on the move."

Pricked by the touch of Time's fleeting wing, Maurice was conscious of reawakened desires and reanimated powers. A white and radiant offering, Gilberte, with her head thrown back, her eyes half closed, her lips apart, sunk in dreamy languor, was breathing slowly and placidly, when suddenly she started up with a cry of terror.

"Whatever is that?"

"Stay still," said Maurice, holding her back in his arms.

In his present mood, had the sky fallen it would not have troubled him. But in one bound she escaped from him. Crouching down, her eyes filled with terror, she was pointing with her finger at a figure which appeared in a corner of the room, between the fire-place and the wardrobe with the mirror. Then, unable to bear the sight, and nearly fainting, she hid her face in her hands.

X

WHICH FAR SURPASSES IN AUDACITY THE IMAGINATIVE FLIGHTS OF DANTE AND MILTON

MAURICE at length turned his head, saw the figure, and perceiving that it moved, was also frightened. Meanwhile, Gilberte was regaining her senses. She imagined that what she had seen was some mistress whom her lover had hidden in the room. Inflamed with anger and disgust at the idea of such treachery, boiling with indignation, and glaring at her supposed rival, she exclaimed:

"A woman . . . a naked woman too! You bring me into a room where you allow your women to come, and when I arrive they have not had time to dress. And you reproach me with arriving late! Your impudence is beyond belief! Come, send the creature packing. If you wanted us both here together, you might at least have asked me whether it suited me. . . ."

Maurice, wide-eyed and groping for a revolver that had never been there, whispered in her ear:

"Be quiet . . . it is no woman. One can scarcely see, but it is more like a man."

She put her hands over her eyes again and screamed harder than ever.

"A man! Where does he come from? A thief. An assassin! Help! Help! Kill him. . . . Maurice, kill him! Turn on the light. No, don't turn on the light. . . ."

She made a mental vow that should she escape from this danger she would burn a candle to the Blessed Virgin. Her teeth chattered.

The figure made a movement.

"Keep away!" cried Gilberte. "Keep away!"

She offered the burglar all the money and jewels she had on the table if he would consent not to stir. Amid her surprise and terror the idea assailed her that her husband, dissembling his suspicions, had caused her to be followed, had posted witnesses, and had had recourse to the Commissaire de Police. In a flash she distinctly saw before her the long painful future, the glaring scandal, the pretended disdain, the cowardly desertion of her friends, the just mockery of society, for it is indeed ridiculous to be found out. She saw the divorce, the loss of her position and of her rank. She saw the dreary and narrow existence with her mother, when no one would make love to her, for men avoid women who fail to give them the security of the married state. And all this, why? Why this ruin, this disaster? For a piece of folly, for a mere nothing. Thus in a lightning flash spoke the conscience of Gilberte des Aubels.

"Have no fear, Madame," said a very sweet voice.

Slightly reassured, she found strength to ask:

"Who are you?"

"I am an angel," replied the voice.

"What did you say?"

"I am an angel. I am Maurice's guardian angel."

"Say it again. I am going mad. I do not understand. . . ."

Maurice, without understanding either, was indignant. He sprang forward and showed himself; with his right hand armed with a slipper he made a threatening gesture, and said in a rough voice:

"You are a low ruffian; oblige me by going the way you came."

"Maurice d'Esparvieu," continued the sweet voice, "He whom you adore as your Creator has stationed by the side of each of the faithful a good angel, whose mission it is to counsel and protect him; it is the invariable opinion of the Fathers, it is founded on many passages in the Bible, the Church admits it unanimously, without, however, pronouncing anathema upon those who hold a contrary opinion. You see before you one of these angels, yours, Maurice. I was commanded to watch over your innocence and to guard your chastity."

"That may be," said Maurice; "but you are certainly no gentleman. A gentleman would not permit himself to enter a room at such a moment. To be plain, what the deuce are you doing here?"

"I have assumed this appearance, Maurice, because, having henceforth to move among mankind, I have to make myself like them. The celestial spirits possess the power of assuming a form which renders them apparent to the eye and to the touch. This shape is real, because it is apparent, and all the realities in the world are but appearances."

Gilberte, pacified at length, was arranging her hair on her forehead.

The Angel pursued:

"The celestial spirits adopt, according to their fancy, one sex or the other, or both at once. But they cannot disguise themselves at any moment, according to their caprice or fantasy. Their metamor-

phoses are subject to constant laws, which you would not understand. Thus I have neither desire nor power to transform myself
under your eyes, for your amusement or my own, into a lion, a
tiger, a fly, or into a sycamore-shaving like the young Egyptian
whose story was found in a tomb. I cannot change myself into an
ass as did Lucius with the pomade of the youthful Photis. For in
my wisdom I had fixed beforehand the hour of my apparition to
mankind, nothing could hasten or delay it."

Impatient for enlightenment, Maurice asked for the second time:
"Still, what are you up to here?"

Joining her voice to his, Madame des Aubels asked: "Yes, indeed,
what are you doing here?"

The Angel replied:

"Man, lend your ear. Woman, hear my voice. I am about to reveal
to you a secret on which hangs the fate of the Universe. In rebellion
against Him whom you hold to be the Creator of all things visible
and invisible, I am preparing the Revolt of the Angels."

"Do not jest," said Maurice, who had faith and did not allow holy
things to be played with.

But the Angel answered reproachfully: "What makes you think,
Maurice, that I am frivolous and given to vain words?"

"Come, come," said Maurice, shrugging his shoulders. "You are
not going to revolt against——"

He pointed to the ceiling—not daring to finish.

But the Angel continued:

"Do you not know that the sons of God have already revolted
and that a great battle took place in the heavens?"

"That was a long time ago," said Maurice, putting on his socks.

Then the Angel replied:

"It was before the creation of the world. But nothing has changed
since then in the heavens. The nature of the Angels is no different
now from what it was originally. What they did then they could do
again now."

"No! It is not possible. It is contrary to faith. If you were an
angel, a good angel as you make out you are, it would never occur
to you to disobey your Creator."

"You are in error, Maurice, and the authority of the Fathers con-
demns you. Origen lays it down in his homilies that good angels are
fallible, that they sin every day and fall from Heaven like flies. Possibly you may be tempted to reject the authority of this Father,
despite his knowledge of the Scriptures, because he is excluded from
the Canon of the Saints. If this be so, I would remind you of the
second chapter of Revelation, in which the Angels of Ephesus and
Pergamos are rebuked for that they kept not ward over their
church. You will doubtless contend that the angels to whom the
Apostle here refers are, properly speaking, the Bishops of the two
cities in question, and that he calls them angels on account of their

ministry. It may be so, and I cede the point. But with what arguments, Maurice, would you counter the opinion of all those Doctors and Pontiffs whose unanimous teaching it is that angels may fall from good to evil? Such is the statement made by Saint Jerome in his Epistle to Damasus. . . ."

"Monsieur," said Madame des Aubels, "go away, I beg you."

But the Angel hearkened not, and continued:

"Saint Augustine, in his *True Religion,* Chapter XIII; Saint Gregory, in his *Morals,* Chapter XXIV; Isadore——"

"Monsieur, let me get my things on; I am in a hurry."

"In his treatise on *The Greatest Good,* Book I, Chapter XII; Bede on Job——"

"Oh, please, Monsieur . . ."

"Chapter VIII; John of Damascus on *Faith,* Book II, Chapter III. Those, I think, are sufficiently weighty authorities, and there is nothing for it, Maurice, but to admit your error. What has led you astray is that you have not duly considered my nature, which is free, active, and mobile, like that of all the angels, and that you have merely observed the grace and felicity with which you deem me so richly endowed. Lucifer possessed no less, yet he rebelled."

"But what on earth are you rebelling for?" asked Maurice.

"Isaiah," answered the child of light, "Isaiah has already asked, before you: 'Quomodo cecidisti de cœlo, Lucifer, qui mane oriebaris?' Hearken, Maurice. Before Time was, the Angels rose up to win dominion over Heaven; the most beautiful of the Seraphim revolted through pride. As for me, it is science that has inspired me with the generous desire for freedom. Finding myself near you, Maurice, in a house containing one of the vastest libraries in the world, I acquired a taste for reading and a love of study. While, fordone with the toils of a sensual life, you lay sunk in heavy slumber, I surrounded myself with books, I studied, I pondered over their pages, sometimes in one of the rooms of the library, under the busts of the great men of antiquity, sometimes at the far end of the garden, in the room in the summer-house next to your own."

On hearing these words, young d'Esparvieu exploded with laughter and beat the pillow with his fist, an infallible sign of uncontrollable mirth.

"Ah . . . ah . . . ah! It was you who pillaged papa's library and drove poor old Sariette off his head. You know, he has become completely idiotic."

"Busily engaged," continued the Angel, "in cultivating for myself a sovereign intelligence, I paid no heed to that inferior being, and when he thought to offer obstacles to my researches and to disturb my work I punished him for his importunity.

"One particular winter's night in the abode of the philosophers and globes I let fall a volume of great weight on his head, which he tried to tear from my invisible hand. Then more recently, raising, with a vigorous arm composed of a column of condensed air, a precious manuscript of Flavius Josephus, I gave the imbecile such a fright, that he rushed out screaming on to the landing and (to borrow a striking expression from Dante Alighieri) *fell even as a dead body falls.* He was well rewarded, for you gave him, Madame, to staunch the blood from his wound, your little scented handkerchief. It was the day, you may remember, when behind a celestial globe you exchanged a kiss on the mouth with Maurice."

"Monsieur," said Madame des Aubels, with a frown, "I cannot allow you . . ."

But she stopped short, deeming it was an inopportune moment to appear over-exacting on a matter of decorum.

"I had made up my mind," continued the Angel impassively, "to examine the foundations of belief. I first attacked the monuments of Judaism, and I read all the Hebrew texts."

"You know Hebrew, then?" exclaimed Maurice.

"Hebrew is my native tongue: in Paradise for a long time we have spoken nothing else."

"Ah, you are a Jew. I might have deduced it from your want of tact."

The Angel, not deigning to hear, continued in his melodious voice: "I have delved deep into Oriental antiquities and also into those of Greece and Rome. I have devoured the works of theologians, philosophers, physicists, geologists, and naturalists. I have learnt. I have thought. I have lost my faith."

"What? You no longer believe in God?"

"I believe in Him, since my existence depends on His, and if He should fail to exist, I myself should fall into nothingness. I believe in Him, even as the Satyrs and the Mænads believed in Dionysus and for the same reason. I believe in the God of the Jews and the Christians. But I deny that He created the world; at the most He organised but an inferior part of it, and all that He touched bears the mark of His rough and unforeseeing touch. I do not think He is either eternal or infinite, for it is absurd to conceive of a being who is not bounded by space or time. I think Him limited, even very limited. I no longer believe Him to be the only God. For a long time He did not believe it Himself; in the beginning He was a polytheist; later, His pride and the flattery of His worshippers made Him a monotheist. His ideas have little connection; He is less powerful than He is thought to be. And, to speak candidly, He is not so much a god as a vain and ignorant demiurge. Those who, like myself, know His true nature, call Him Ialdabaoth."

"What's that you say?"

"Ialdabaoth."

"Ialdabaoth. What's that?"

"I have already told you. It is the demiurge whom, in your blindness, you adore as the one and only God."

"You're mad. I don't advise you to go and talk rubbish like that to Abbé Patouille."

"I am not in the least sanguine, my dear Maurice, of piercing the dense night of your intellect. I merely tell you that I am going to engage Ialdabaoth in conflict with some hopes of victory."

"Mark my words, you won't succeed."

"Lucifer shook His throne, and the issue was for a moment in doubt."

"What is your name?"

"Abdiel for the angels and saints, Arcade for mankind."

"Well, my poor Arcade, I regret to see you going to the bad. But confess that you are jesting with us. I could at a pinch understand your leaving Heaven for a woman. Love makes us commit the greatest follies. But you will never make me believe that you, who have seen God face to face, ultimately found the truth in old Sariette's musty books. No, you will never get me to believe that!"

"My dear Maurice, Lucifer was face to face with God, yet he refused to serve Him. As to the kind of truth one finds in books, it is a truth that enables us sometimes to discern what things are not, without ever enabling us to discover what they are. And this poor little truth has sufficed to prove to me that He in whom I blindly believed is not believable, and that men and angels have been deceived by the lies of Ialdabaoth."

"There is no Ialdabaoth. There is God. Come, Arcade, do the right thing. Renounce these follies, these impieties, dis-incarnate yourself, become once more a pure Spirit, and resume your office of guardian angel. Return to duty. I forgive you, but do not let us see you again."

"I should like to please you, Maurice. I feel a certain affection for you, for my heart is soft. But fate henceforth calls me elsewhere towards beings capable of thought and action."

"Monsieur Arcade," said Madame des Aubels, "withdraw, I implore you. It makes me horribly shy to be in this position before two men. I assure you I am not accustomed to it."

XI

RECOUNTS IN WHAT MANNER THE ANGEL, ATTIRED IN THE CAST-OFF GARMENTS OF A SUICIDE, LEAVES THE YOUTHFUL MAURICE WITHOUT A HEAVENLY GUARDIAN

EASSURE yourself, Madame," replied the apparition, "your position is not as risky as you say. You are not confronted with two men, but with one man and an angel."

She examined the stranger with an eye which, piercing the gloom, was anxiously surveying a vague but by no means negligible indication, and asked:

"Monsieur, is it quite certain that you are an angel?"

The apparition prayed her to have no doubt about it, and gave some precise information as to his origin.

"There are *three hierarchies of celestial spirits, each composed of nine choirs;* the first comprises the Seraphim, Cherubim, and the Thrones; the second, the Dominations, the Virtues, and the Powers; the third, *the Principalities, the Archangels, and the Angels* properly so called. I belong to the ninth choir of the third hierarchy."

Madame des Aubels, who had her reasons for doubting this, expressed at least one:

"You have no wings."

"Why should I, Madame? Am I bound to resemble the angels on your holy-water stoups? Those feathery oars that beat the waves of the air in rhythmic cadences are not always worn by the heavenly messengers on their shoulders. Cherubim may be apterous. That all too beautiful angelic pair who spent an anxious night in the house of Lot compassed about by an Oriental horde—they had no wings! No, they appeared just like men, and the dust of the road covered their feet, which the patriarch washed with pious hand. I would beg you to observe, Madame, that according to the Science of Organic Metamorphosis created by Lamarck and Darwin, *the wings of birds have been successively transformed into forefeet in the case of quadrupeds and into arms in the case of the* Linnæan primates. And you may remember, Maurice, that by a rather annoying reversion to type, Miss Kate, your English nurse, who used to be so fond of giving you a whipping, had arms very like the pinions of a plucked fowl. One may say, then, that a being possessing both arms and wings is a monster and belongs to the department of Teratology. In Paradise we have Cherubim and Kerûbs in the shape of winged bulls, but those are the clumsy in-

ventions of an inartistic god. It is nevertheless true, quite true, that
the Victories of the Temple of Athena Nike on the Athenian Acropolis are beautiful, and possess both arms and wings; it is also true
that the Victory of Brescia is beautiful, with her outstretched arms
and her long wings folded on her mighty loins. It is one of the
miracles of Greek genius to have known how to create harmonious
monsters. The Greeks never err. The Moderns always."

"Yet on the whole," said Madame des Aubels, "you have not the
look of a pure Spirit."

"Nevertheless, I am one, Madame, if ever there was one. And it
ill becomes you, who have been baptised, to doubt it. Several of the
Fathers, such as St. Justin, Tertullian, Origen, and Clement of
Alexandria thought that the Angels were not purely spiritual, but
possessed a body formed of some subtile material. This opinion has
been rejected by the Church; hence I am merely Spirit. But what
is spirit and what is matter? Formerly they were contrasted as
being two opposites, and now your human science tends to reunite
them as two aspects of the same thing. It teaches that everything
proceeds from ether and everything returns to it, that the same
movement transforms the waves of air into stones and minerals,
and that the atoms scattered throughout illimitable space, form, by
the varying speed of their orbits, all the substance of this material
world."

But Madame des Aubels was not listening. She had something
on her mind, and to put an end to her suspense, she asked:

"How long have you been here?"

"I came with Maurice."

"Well—that's a nice thing!" said she, shaking her head. But the
Angel continued with heavenly serenity:

"Everything in the Universe is circular, elliptical, or hyperbolic,
and the same laws which rule the stars govern this grain of dust.
In the original and native movement of its substance, my body is
spiritual, but it may affect, as you perceive, this material state, by
changing the rhythm of its elements."

Having thus spoken he sat down in a chair on Madame des Aubels' black stockings.

A clock struck outside.

"Good heavens, seven o'clock!" exclaimed Gilberte. "What am I
to say to my husband? He thinks I am at that tea-party in the Rue
de Rivoli. We are dining with the La Verdelières to-night. Go away
immediately, Monsieur Arcade. I must get ready to go. I have not a
second to lose."

The Angel replied that he would have willingly obeyed Madame
des Aubels had he been in a state to show himself decently in public, but that he could not dream of appearing out of doors without
any clothes. "Were I to walk naked in the street," he added, "I
should offend a nation attached to its ancient habits, habits which

it has never examined. They are the basis of all moral systems. Formerly," he added, "the angels, in revolt like myself, manifested themselves to Christians under grotesque and ridiculous appearances, black, horned, hairy, and cloven-footed. Pure stupidity! They were the laughing-stock of people of taste. They merely frightened old women and children and met with no success."

"It is true he cannot go out as he is," said Madame des Aubels with justice.

Maurice tossed his pyjamas and his slippers to the celestial messenger. Regarded as outdoor habiliments they were not adequate. Gilberte pressed her lover to run at once in quest of other clothes. He proposed to go and get some from the concierge. She was violently opposed to this. It would, she said, be madly imprudent to drag the concierge into such an affair.

"Do you want them to know that . . ." she exclaimed.

She pointed to the Angel and was silent.

Young d'Esparvieu went out to seek a clothes-shop.

Meanwhile, Gilberte, who could not delay any longer for fear of causing a horrible society scandal, turned on the light and dressed before the Angel. She did it without any awkwardness, for she

knew how to adapt herself to circumstances; and she took it that in such an unheard-of encounter in which heaven and earth were mingled in unutterable confusion it was permissible to retrench in modesty.

Moreover, she knew that she possessed a good figure and had garments as dainty as the fashion demanded. As the apparition's sense of delicacy would not permit him to don Maurice's pyjamas, Gilberte could not help observing by the lamp-light that her suspicions were well-founded, and that angels have the same appearance as men. Curious to know if the appearance were real or imaginary she asked the child of light if Angels were like monkeys, who, to win women, merely lack money.

"Yes, Gilberte," replied Arcade, "Angels are capable of loving mortals. It is the teaching of the Scriptures. It is said in the Seventh Book of Genesis, 'When men became numerous on the face of the earth, and daughters were born to them, the sons of God saw that the daughters of men were beautiful, and they took as wives all those which pleased them.'"

"Good heavens," cried Gilberte all at once, "I shall never be able to fasten my dress; it hooks down the back."

When Maurice entered the room he found the Angel on his knees tying the shoes of the woman taken in *flagrante delicto*.

Taking her muff and her bag off the table she said:

"I have not forgotten anything? No. Good-night, Monsieur Arcade. Good-night, Maurice. I shall not forget to-day." And she vanished like a dream.

"Here," said Maurice, throwing the Angel a bundle of clothes.

The young man, having seen some dismal rags lying among clarionettes and clyster-pipes in the window of a second-hand shop, had bought for nineteen francs the cast-off suit of some wretched sable-clad mortal who had committed suicide. The Angel, with native majesty, took the garments and put them on. Worn by him, they took on an unexpected elegance. He took a step to the door.

"So you are leaving me," said Maurice. "It's settled, then? I very much fear that, some day, you will bitterly regret this hasty action."

"I must not look back. Adieu, Maurice."

Maurice timidly slipped five louis into his hand.

"Adieu, Arcade."

But when the Angel had passed through the door, and all that was to be seen of him in the doorway was his uplifted heel, Maurice called him back.

"Arcade! I never thought of it! I have no guardian angel now!"

"Quite true, Maurice, you have one no longer."

"Then what will become of me? One must have a guardian angel. Tell me,—are there not grave drawbacks,—is there no danger in not having one?"

"Before replying, Maurice, I must ask you if you wish me to speak to you according to your belief, which formerly was my own, according to the teaching of the Church and the Catholic faith, or according to natural philosophy.

"I don't care a straw for your natural philosophy. Answer me according to the religion I believe in, and which I profess, and in which I wish to live and die."

"Very well, my dear Maurice. The loss of your guardian angel will probably deprive you of certain spiritual succour, of certain celestial grace. I am expressing to you the unvarying opinion of the Church on the matter. You will lack an assistance, a support, a consolation which would have guided and confirmed you in the way of salvation. You will have less strength to avoid sin, and as it was you hadn't much. In fact, in spiritual matters, you will be without strength and without joy. Adieu, Maurice; when you see Madame des Aubels, please remember me to her."

"You are going?"

"Farewell."

Arcade disappeared, and Maurice in the depths of an arm-chair sat for a long time with his head in his hands.

XII

WHEREIN IT IS SET FORTH HOW THE ANGEL MIRAR, WHEN BEARING GRACE AND CONSOLATION TO THOSE DWELLING IN THE NEIGHBOURHOOD OF THE CHAMPS ÉLYSÉES IN PARIS, BEHELD A MUSIC-HALL SINGER NAMED BOUCHOTTE AND FELL IN LOVE WITH HER

THROUGH streets filled with brown fog, pierced with white and yellow lights, where horses exhaled their smoking breath and motors radiated their rapid search-lights, the angel made his way, and, mingling with the black flood of foot-passengers which rolled unceasingly along, proceeded across the town from north to south till he came to the lonely boulevards on the left bank of the river. Not far from the old walls of Port Royal, a small restaurant flings night by night athwart the pavement the clouded rays of its streaming windows. Coming to a halt there, Arcade entered a room full of warm, savoury odours, pleasing to the unfortunate beings faint with cold and hunger. Glancing round him he beheld Russian Nihilists, Italian Anarchists, refugees, conspirators, revolutionaries from every quarter of the globe, picturesque old faces with tumbled masses of hair and beard that swept downwards even as the torrent and the

waterfall sweep over their rocky bed. There were young faces of virginal coldness, expressions sombre and wild, pale eyes of infinite sweetness, drawn faces, and, in a corner, there were two Russian women, one extremely lovely, the other hideous, but both resembling each other in their indifference to ugliness and to beauty. But failing to find the face he sought, for there were no angels in the room, he sat down at a small vacant marble table.

Angels, when driven by hunger, eat as do the animals of this earth, and their food, transformed by digestive heat, becomes one with their celestial substance. Seeing three angels under the oaks of Mamre, Abraham offered them cakes, kneaded by Sarah, an whole calf, butter and milk, and they ate. Lot, on receiving two angels in his house, ordered unleavened bread to be baked, and they did eat. Arcade was given a tough beef-steak by a seedy waiter, and he did eat. Nevertheless, his dreams were of the sweet leisure, of the repose, of the delightful studies he had quitted, of the heavy task he had undertaken, of the toil, the weariness, the perils which he would have to endure, and his soul was sad and his heart troubled.

As he was finishing his modest repast, a young man of poor appearance and thinly clad entered the room, and rapidly surveying the tables approached the angel and greeted him by the name of Abdiel, because he himself was a celestial spirit.

"I knew you would answer my call, Mirar," replied Arcade, addressing his angelic brother in his turn by the name he formerly bore in heaven. But Mirar was remembered no more in heaven since he, an Archangel, had left the service of God. He was called Théophile Belais on earth, and to earn his bread gave music lessons to small children in the day-time and at night played the violin in dancing saloons.

"It is you, dear Abdiel?" replied Théophile. "So here we are reunited in this sad world. I am pleased to see you again. All the same I pity you, for we lead a hard life here."

But Arcade answered:

"Friend, your exile draws to an end. I have great plans. I will confide them to you and associate you with them."

And Maurice's guardian angel, having ordered two coffees, revealed his ideas and his projects to his companion: he told how, during his visit on earth, he had abandoned himself to researches little practised by celestial spirits and had studied theologies, cosmogonies, the system of the Universe, theories of matter, modern essays on the transformation and loss of energy. Having, he explained, studied Nature, he had found her in perpetual conflict with the teachings of the Master he served. This Master, greedy of praise, whom he had for a long time adored, appeared to him now as an ignorant, stupid, and cruel tyrant. He had denied Him, blasphemed Him, and was burning to combat Him. His plan was to recommence the revolt of the angels. He wished for war, and hoped for victory.

"But," he added, "it is necessary above all to know our strength and that of our adversary." And he asked if the enemies of Ialdabaoth were numerous and powerful on earth.

Théophile looked wonderingly at his brother. He appeared not to understand the questions addressed him.

"Dear compatriot," he said, "I came at your invitation because it was the invitation of an old comrade. But I do not know what you expect of me, and I fear I shall be unable to help you in anything. I take no hand in politics, neither do I stand forth as a reformer. I am not like you, a spirit in revolt, a free-thinker, a revolutionary. I remain faithful, in the depths of my soul, to the Celestial Creator. I still adore the Master I no longer serve, and I lament the days when shrouding myself with my wings I formed with the multitude of the children of light a wheel of flame around His throne of glory. Love, profane love has alone separated me from God. I quitted heaven to follow a daughter of men. She was beautiful and sang in music-halls."

They rose. Arcade accompanied Théophile, who was living at the other end of the town, at the corner of the Boulevard Rochechouart and the Rue de Steinkerque. While walking through the deserted streets he who loved the singer told his brother of his love and his sorrows.

His fall, which dated from two years back, had been sudden. Belonging to the eighth choir of the third hierarchy he was a bearer of grace to the faithful who are still to be found in large numbers in France, especially among the higher ranks of the officers of the army and navy.

"One summer night," he said, "as I was descending from Heaven, to distribute consolations, the grace of perseverance and of good deaths to divers pious persons in the neighbourhood of the Étoile, my eyes, although well accustomed to immortal light, were dazzled by the fiery flowers with which the Champs Élysées were sown. Great candelabra, under the trees, marking the entrances to cafés and restaurants, gave the foliage the precious glitter of an emerald. Long garlands of luminous pearl surrounded the open-air enclosures where a crowd of men and women sat closely packed listening to the sounds of a lively orchestra, whose strains reached my ears confusedly.

"The night was warm, my wings were beginning to grow tired. I descended into one of the concerts and sat down, invisible, among the audience. At this moment, a woman appeared on the stage, clad in a short spangled frock. Owing to the reflection of the footlights and the paint on her face all that was visible of the latter was the expression and the smile. Her body was supple and voluptuous.

"She sang and danced. . . . Arcade, I have always loved dancing and music, but this creature's thrilling voice and insidious movements created in me an uneasiness I had never known before. My colour came and went. My eyelids drooped, my tongue clove to my mouth. I could not leave the spot."

And Théophile related, groaning, how, possessed by desire for this woman, he did not return to Heaven again, but, taking the shape of a man, lived an earthly life, for it is written: "In those days the sons of God saw that the daughters of men were beautiful."

A fallen angel, having lost his innocence along with the vision of God, Théophile at heart still retained his simplicity of soul. Clad in rags, filched from the stall of a Jewish hawker, he went to seek the woman he loved. She was called Bouchotte and lodged in a small house in Montmartre. He flung himself at her feet and told her she was adorable, that she sang delightfully, that he loved her madly, that, for her, he would renounce his family and his country, that he was a musician and had nothing to eat. Touched by such youthful ingenuousness, candour, poverty, and love, she fed, clothed, and loved him.

However, after long and painful struggles, he procured employment as a music-teacher, and made some money, which he brought to his mistress, keeping nothing for himself. From that time forward she loved him no longer. She despised him for earning so little and did not conceal her indifference, weariness, and disgust. She overwhelmed him with reproaches, irony, and abuse, in spite of which she kept him, for she had had experience of worse partners and was used to domestic quarrels. For the rest, she led a busy, serious, and rather hard life as artist and woman. Théophile loved her as he had loved her the first night, and he suffered.

"She overworks herself," he told his celestial brother, "that is what makes her so hard to please, but I am certain she loves me. I hope soon to give her more comfort."

And he spoke at length of an operetta at which he was working and which he hoped to have brought out at a Paris theatre. A young poet had given him the libretto. It was the story of Aline, queen of Golconda, after an eighteenth-century tale.

"I am strewing it profusely with melodies," said Théophile; "my music comes from my heart. My heart is an inexhaustible source of melody. Unfortunately nowadays people like recondite arrangements, difficult scoring. They accuse me of being too fluid, too limpid, of not imparting enough colour to my style, not aiming at stronger effects in harmony and more vigorous contrasts. Harmony. harmony! . . . No doubt it has given its merits, but it does not appeal to the heart. It is melody which carries us away and ravishes us and brings smiles and tears to our eyes." At these words he smiled and wept to himself. Then he continued with emotion:

"I am a fountain of melody. But the orchestration! there's the rub! In Paradise, you know, Arcade, in the matter of instruments, we only possess the harp, the psaltery, and the hydraulic organ."

Arcade was only listening to him with half an ear. He was meditating plans which filled his soul and swelled his heart.

"Do you know any angels in revolt?" he asked his companion. "As for me, I know only one, Prince Istar, with whom I have exchanged a few letters and who offered to share his attic with me while I was finding a lodging in this town, where I believe rents are very high."

Of angels in revolt Théophile know none. When he met a fallen spirit who had formerly been one of his comrades he shook him by the hand, for he was a faithful friend. Sometimes he saw Prince Istar. But he avoided all those bad angels who shocked him by the violence of their opinions and whose conversations plagued him to death.

"Then you don't approve of me?" asked the impulsive Arcade.

"Friend, I neither approve of you nor blame you. I understand nothing of the ideas which trouble you. Neither do I think it good for an artist to concern himself with politics. One has quite sufficient to occupy oneself with one's art."

He loved his profession, and had hopes of "arriving" one day, but theatrical ways disgusted him. The only chance he saw of having his piece played was to take one or two—perhaps three—collaborators, who, without having done any work, would sign their names and share the profits. Soon Bouchotte would fail to find engagements. When she offered her services in some small hall the manager began by asking her how many shares she was taking in the business. Such customs, thought Théophile, were deplorable.

XIII

WHEREIN WE HEAR THE BEAUTIFUL ARCHANGEL ZITA UNFOLD HER LOFTY DESIGNS AND ARE SHOWN THE WINGS OF MIRAR, ALL MOTH-EATEN, IN A CUPBOARD

THUS talking, the two archangels had reached the Boulevard Rochechouart. As his eye lighted on a tavern, whence, through the mist, the light fell golden on the pavement, Théophile suddenly bethought himself of the Archangel Ithuriel who, in the guise of a poor but beautiful woman, was living in wretched lodgings on La Butte and came every evening to read the papers at this tavern. The musician often met her there. Her name was Zita. Théophile had never been curious enough to enquire into the opinions entertained

by this archangel, but it was generally supposed that she was a Russian nihilist, and he took her to be, like Arcade, an atheist and a revolutionary. He had heard remarkable tales about her. People said she was an hermaphrodite, and that as the active and passive principles were united within her in a condition of stable equilibrium, she was an example of a perfect being, finding in herself complete and continuous satisfaction, contented yet unfortunate in that she knew not desire.

"But," added Théophile, "I have my doubts about it. I believe she's a woman and subject to love, like everything else that has life and breath in the Universe. Besides, someone caught her one day kissing her hand to a strapping peasant fellow."

He offered to introduce his companion to her.

The two angels found her alone, reading. As they drew near she lifted her great eyes in whose deeps of molten gold little sparks of light were forever a-dance. Her brows were contracted into that austere fold which we see on the forehead of the Pythian Apollo; her nose was perfect and descended without a curve; her lips were compressed and imparted a disdainful and supercilious air to her whole countenance. Her tawny hair, with its gleaming lights, was carelessly adorned with the tattered remnants of a huge bird of prey, her garments lay about her in dark and shapeless folds. She was leaning her chin on a small ill-tended hand.

Arcade, who had but recently heard references made to this powerful archangel, showed her marked esteem, and placed entire confidence in her. He immediately proceeded to tell of the progress his mind had made towards knowledge and liberty, of his lucubrations in the d'Esparvieu library, of his philosophical reading, his studies of nature, his works on exegesis, his anger and his contempt when he recognised the deception of the demiurge, his voluntary exile among mankind, and, finally, of his project to stir up rebellion in Heaven. Ready to dare all against an odious master, whom he pursued with inextinguishable hatred, he expressed his profound happiness at finding in Ithuriel a mind capable of counselling and helping him in his great undertaking.

"You are not a very old hand at revolutions," said Zita, smiling.

Nevertheless, she doubted neither his sincerity nor the firmness of his declared resolve, and she congratulated him on his intellectual audacity.

"That is what is most lacking in our people," she said, "they do not think."

And she added almost immediately: "But on what can intelligence sharpen its wits, in a country where the climate is soft and existence made easy? Even here, where necessity calls for intellectual activity, nothing is rarer than a person who thinks."

"Nevertheless," replied Maurice's guardian angel, "man has created science. The important thing is to introduce it into Heaven.

When the angels possess some notions of physics, chemistry, astronomy, and physiology; when the study of matter shows them worlds in an atom, and an atom in the myriads of planets; when they see themselves lost between these two infinities; when they weigh and measure the stars, analyse their composition, and calculate their orbits, they will recognise that these monsters work in obedience to forces which no intelligence can define, or that each star has its particular divinity, or indigenous god; and they will realise that the gods of Aldebaran, Betelgeuse, and Sirius are greater than Ialdabaoth. When at length they come to scrutinise with care the little world in which their lot is cast, and, piercing the crust of the earth, note the gradual evolution of its flora and fauna and the rude origin of man, who, under the shelter of rocks and in cave dwellings, had no God but himself; when they discover that, united by the bonds of universal kinship to plants, beasts, and men, they have successively indued all forms of organic life, from the simplest and the most primitive, until they became at length the most beautiful of the children of light, they will perceive that Ialdabaoth, the obscure demon of an insignificant world lost in space, is imposing on their credulity when he pretends that they issued from nothingness at his bidding; they will perceive that he lies in calling himself the Infinite, the Eternal, the Almighty, and that, so far from having created worlds, he knows neither their number nor their laws. They will perceive that he is like unto one of them; they will despise him, and, shaking off his tyranny, will fling him into the Gehenna where he has hurled those more worthy than himself."

"Do you think so?" murmured Zita, puffing out the smoke of her cigarette. . . . "Nevertheless, this knowledge by virtue of which you reckon to enfranchise Heaven, has not destroyed religious sentiment on earth. In countries where they have set up and taught this science of physics, of chemistry, astronomy, and geology, which you think capable of delivering the world, Christianity has retained almost all its sway. If the positive sciences have had such a feeble influence on the beliefs of mankind, it is not likely they will exercise a greater one on the opinions of the angels, and nothing is of such dubious efficacy as scientific propaganda."

"What!" exclaimed Arcade, "you deny that Science has given the Church its death-blow? Is is possible? The Church, at any rate, judges otherwise. Science, which you believe has no power over her, is redoubtable to her, since she proscribes it. From Galileo's dialogues to Monsieur Aulard's little manuals she has condemned all its discoveries. And not without reason.

"In former days, when she gathered within her fold all that was great in human thought, the Church held sway over the bodies as well as over the souls of men, and imposed unity of obedience by fire and sword. To-day her power is but a shadow and the elect among the great minds have withdrawn from her. That is the state to which Science has reduced her."

"Possibly," replied the beautiful archangel, "but how slowly, with what vicissitudes, at the price of what efforts, of what sacrifices!"

Zita did not absolutely condemn scientific propaganda, but she anticipated no prompt or certain results from it. For her it was not so much a question of enlightening the angels; the important thing was to enfranchise them. In her opinion one only exerted a strong influence on individuals, whoever they might be, by rousing their passions, and appealing to their interests.

"Persuade the angels that they will cover themselves with glory by overthrowing the tyrant, and that they will be happier once they are free; that is the most practical policy to attempt, and, for my own part, I am devoting all my energies to its fulfilment. It is certainly no light task, because the Kingdom of Heaven is a military autocracy and there is no public opinion in it. Nevertheless, I do not despair of starting an intellectual movement. I do not wish to boast, but no one is more closely acquainted than I with the different classes of angelic society."

Throwing away her cigarette, Zita pondered for a moment, then, amid the click of ivory balls on the billiard table, the clinking of glasses, the curt voices of the players announcing their points, the monotonous answers of the waiters to their customers, the Archangel enumerated the entire population of the spirits of light.

"We must not count on the Dominations, the Virtues, nor the Powers, which compose the celestial lower middle class. I have no need to tell you, for you know it as well as I, how selfish, base, and cowardly the middle classes are. As to the great dignitaries, the Ministers, the Generals, Thrones, Cherubim, and Seraphim, you know what they are; they will take no action. Let us, however, once prove ourselves the stronger, and we shall have them with us. For if autocrats do not readily acquiesce in their own downfall, once overthrown, all their forces recoil upon themselves. It will be well to work the Army. Entirely loyal as the Army is, it will allow itself to be influenced by a clever anarchist propaganda. But our greatest and most constant efforts ought to be brought to bear upon the angels of your own category, Arcade; the guardian angels, who dwell upon earth in such great numbers. They fill the lowest ranks of the hierarchy, are for the most part discontented with their lot, and more or less imbued with the ideas of the present century."

She had already conferred with the guardian angels of Montmartre, Clignancourt, and Filles-du-Calvaire. She had devised the plan of a vast association of Spirits on Earth with the view of conquering Heaven.

"To accomplish this task," she said, "I have established myself in France. But not because I had the folly to believe myself freer in a republic than in a monarchy. Quite the contrary, for there is no country where the liberty of the individual is less respected than in France. But the people are indifferent to everything connected with religion; nowhere else, therefore, should I enjoy such tranquillity."

She invited Arcade to unite his efforts to hers, and when they separated at the door of the *brasserie* the steel shutter was already making its groaning descent.

"Above all," said Zita, "you must meet the gardener. I will take you to his rustic home one day."

Théophile, who had slumbered during all this talk, begged his friend to come home with him and smoke a cigarette. He lived quite near in the small street opposite, leading off the Boulevard. Arcade would see Bouchotte, she would please him.

They climbed up five flights of stairs. Bouchotte had not yet returned. A tin of sardines lay open on the piano. Red stockings coiled about the arm-chairs.

"It's a little place, but it's comfortable," said Théophile.

And gazing out of the window which looked out on the russet-coloured night, with its myriad lights, he added, "One can see the *Sacré Cœur*." His hand on Arcade's shoulder, he repeated several times, "I am glad to see you."

Then, dragging his former companion in glory into the kitchen passage, he put down his candle-stick, drew a key from his pocket, opened a cupboard, and, raising a linen covering, disclosed two large white wings.

"You see," he said, "I have preserved them. From time to time, when I am alone, I go and look at them; it does me good."

And he dabbed his reddened eyes. He stood awhile, overcome by silent emotion. Then, holding the candle near the long pinions which were moulting their down in places, he murmured, "They are eaten away."

"You must put some pepper on them," said Arcade.

"I have done so," replied the angelic musician, sighing. "I have put pepper, camphor, and powder on them. But nothing does any good."

XIV

WHICH REVEALS THE CHERUB TOILING FOR THE WELFARE OF HUMANITY AND CONCLUDES IN AN ENTIRELY NOVEL MANNER WITH THE MIRACLE OF THE FLUTE

HE first night of his incarnation Arcade slept at the angel Istar's, in a garret in that narrow, gloomy Rue Mazarine which wallows along beneath the the shadow of the old Institute of France. Istar, who had been expecting him, had pushed against the wall the shattered retorts, cracked pots, broken bottles, and odds and ends of iron stoves, which made up the furniture of his room, and spread his clothes on the floor to lie on, leaving his guest his folding-bed with its straw mattress.

The celestial spirits differ from one another in appearance according to the hierarchy and the choir to which they belong, and according to their own particular nature. They are all beautiful; but in different fashion, and they do not all offer to the eye the soft contours and dimpling smiles of childhood with its rosy lights and pearly tints. Nor do they all adorn themselves with eternal youth, that indefinable beauty that Greek art in its decline has imparted to its most lovingly handled marbles, and whereof Christian painters have so often timidly essayed to give us veiled and softened imitations. In some of them the chin glows with tufts of hair, and the limbs are furnished with such vigorous muscles that it seems as if serpents were writhing beneath the skin. Some have no wings, others possess two, four, or six; others again are formed entirely of conjoined pinions. Many, and these not the least illustrious, take the form of superb monsters, such as the Centaurs of fable; nay, one may even see some who are living chariots, and wheels of fire. A member of the highest celestial hierarchy, Istar belonged to the choir of Cherubim or Kerûbs who see above them the Seraphim alone. In common with all the angelic spirits of his rank he had formerly borne in Heaven the bodily shape of a winged bull surmounted by the head of a horned and bearded man, and carrying between his loins the attributes of generous fecundity. He was vaster and more vigorous than any animal on earth, and when he stood erect with outspread wings he covered with his shadow sixty archangels.

Such was Istar in his native home. There he radiated strength and sweetness. His heart was full of courage and his soul benevolent. Moreover, in those days he loved his lord. He believed him to be good and yielded him faithful service. But even while guarding

the portals of his Master, he used to ponder unceasingly on the
punishment of the rebellious angels and the curse of Eve. His mind
worked slowly but profoundly. When, after a long course of centuries, he persuaded himself that Ialdabaoth in creating the world
had created evil and death, he ceased to adore and to serve him.
His love changed to hatred, his veneration to contempt. He shouted
his execrations in his face, and fled to earth.

Embodied in human form and reduced to the stature of the sons
of Adam, he still retained some characteristics of his former nature. His big protruding eyes, his beaked nose, his thick lips
framed in a black beard which descended in curls on to his chest
recalled those Cherubs of the tabernacle of Iahveh, of which the
bulls of Nineveh afford us a pretty accurate representation. He bore
the name of Istar on earth as well as in Heaven, and although exempt from vanity and free from all social prejudice, he was im-
mensely desirous of showing himself sincere and truthful in all
things. He therefore proclaimed the illustrious rank in which his
birth had placed him in the celestial hierarchy and translated into
French his title of Cherub by the equivalent one of Prince, calling
himself *Prince Istar. Seeking shelter among mankind he had developed an ardent love for them.* While awaiting the coming of the
hour when he should deliver Heaven from bondage, he dreamed of
the salvation of regenerate humanity and was eager to consummate the destruction of this wicked world, in order to raise upon
its ashes, to the sound of the lyre, a city radiant with happiness
and love. A chemist in the pay of a dealer in nitrates, he lived very
frugally. He wrote for newspapers with advanced views on liberty,
spoke at public meetings, and had got himself sentenced several
times to several months' imprisonment for anti-militarism.

Istar greeted his brother Arcade cordially, approved of his rup-
ture with the party of crime, and informed him of the descent of
fifty of the children of light who, at the present moment, formed
a colony near Val de Grace, imbued with a really excellent spirit.

"It is simply raining angels in Paris," he said, laughing. "Every
day some dignitary of the sacred palace falls on one's head, and
soon the Sultan of the Cherubs will have no one to make into Vizirs
or guards but the little unbreeched vagabonds of his pigeon coops."

Soothed by the good news, Arcade fell asleep, full of happiness
and hope.

He awoke in the early dawn and saw Prince Istar bending over
his furnaces, his retorts, and his test tubes. Prince Istar was working for the good of humanity.

Every morning when Arcade woke he saw Prince Istar fulfilling
his work of tenderness and love. Sometimes the Kerûb, huddled up
with his head in his hands, would softly murmur a few chemical
formulæ; at others, drawing himself up to his full height, like a
dark naked column, with his head, his arms, nay, his entire bust

clean out of the skylight window, he would deposit his melting-pot on the roof, fearing the perquisition with which he was constantly menaced. Moved by an immense pity for the miseries of the world wherein he dwelt in exile, conscious perhaps of the rumours to which his name gave rise, inebriated with his own virtue, he played the part of apostle to the Human Race, and neglecting the task he had undertaken in coming to earth, he forgot all about the emancipation of the angels. Arcade, who, on the contrary, dreamed of nothing else but of conquering Heaven and returning thither in triumph, reproached the Cherub with forgetting his native land.

Prince Istar, with a great frank, uncouth laugh, acknowledged that he had no preference for angels over men.

"If I am doing my best," he replied to his celestial brother, "if I am doing my best to stir up France and Europe, it is because the day is dawning which will behold the triumph of the social revolution. It is a pleasure to cast one's seed on ground so well prepared. The French having passed from feudalism to monarchy, and from monarchy to a financial oligarchy, will easily pass from a financial oligarchy to anarchy."

"How erroneous it is," retorted Arcade, "to believe in great and sudden changes in the social order in Europe! The old order is still young in strength and power. The means of defence at her disposal are formidable. On the other hand, the proletariat's plan of defensive organisation is of the vaguest description and brings merely weakness and confusion to the struggle. In our celestial country all goes quite otherwise. Beneath an apparently unchangeable exterior all is rotten within. A mere push would suffice to overturn an edifice which has not been touched for millions of centuries. Outworn administration, out-worn army, out-worn finance, the whole thing is more worm-eaten than either the Russian or Persian autocracy."

And the kindly Arcade adjured the Cherub to fly first to the aid of his brethren who, though dwelling amid the soft clouds with the sound of citterns and their cups of paradisal wine around them, were in more wretched plight than mankind bowed over the grudging earth. For the latter have a conception of justice, while the angels rejoice in iniquity. He exhorted him to deliver the Prince of Light and his stricken companions and to re-establish them in their ancient honours.

Prince Istar allowed himself to be convinced.

He promised to put the sweet persuasiveness of his words and the excellent formulæ of his explosives at the service of the celestial revolution. He gave his promise.

"To-morrow," he said.

And when the morrow came he continued his anti-militarist propaganda at Issy-les-Moulineaux. Like the Titan Prometheus, Istar loved mankind.

Arcade, suffering from all the desires to which the sons of Adam are subjected, found himself lacking in resources to satisfy them. Istar gave him a start in a printing house in the Rue de Vaugirard where he knew the forman. Arcade, thanks to his celestial intelligence, soon knew how to set up type and became, in a short time, a good compositor.

After standing all day in the whirring workroom, holding the composing-stick in his left hand, and swiftly drawing the little leaden signs from the case in the order required by the copy fixed in the *visorium,* he would go and wash his hands at the pump and dine at the corner bar, a newspaper propped up before him on the marble table. Being now no longer invisible, he could not make his way into the d'Esparvieu library, and was thus debarred from allaying his ardent thirst for knowledge at that inexhaustible source. He went, of an evening, to read at the library of Ste. Geneviève on the famous hill of learning, but there were only ordinary books to be had there; greasy things, covered with ridiculous annotations, and lacking many pages.

The sight of women troubled and unsettled him. He would remember Madame des Aubels and her charm, and, although he was handsome, he was not loved, because of his poverty and his workaday clothes. He saw much of Zita, and took a certain pleasure in going for walks with her on Sundays along the dusty roads which edge the grass-grown trenches of the fortifications. They wandered, the pair of them, by wayside inns, market-gardens, and green retreats, propounding and discussing the vastest plans that ever stirred the world, and, occasionally, as they passed along by some travelling circus, the steam organ of the merry-go-round would furnish an accompaniment to their words as they breathed fire and fury against Heaven.

Zita used often to say:

"Istar means well, but he's a simple fellow. He believes in the goodness of men and things. He undertakes the destruction of the old world and imagines that anarchy of itself will create order and harmony. You, Arcade, you believe in Science; you deem that men and angels are capable of understanding, whereas, in point of fact, they are only creatures of sentiment. You may be quite sure that nothing is to be obtained from them by appealing to their intelligence; one must rouse their interests and their passions."

Arcade, Istar, Zita, and three or four other angelic conspirators occasionally foregathered in Théophile Belais' little flat, where Bouchotte gave them tea. Though she did not know that they were rebellious angels, she hated them instinctively, and feared them, for she had had a Christian education, albeit she had sadly failed to keep it up.

Prince Istar alone pleased her; she thought there was something kind-hearted and an air of natural distinction about him. He stove in the sofa, broke down the arm-chairs, and tore corners off sheets of music to make notes, which he thrust into pockets invariably crammed with pamphlets and bottles. The musician used to gaze sorrowfully at the manuscript of his operetta, *Aline, Queen of Golconda,* with its corners all torn off. The prince also had a habit of giving Théophile Belais all sorts of things to take care of—mechanical contrivances, chemicals, bits of old iron, powders, and liquids which gave off noisome smells. Théophile Belais put them cautiously away in the cupboard where he kept his wings, and the responsibility weighed heavily upon him.

Arcade was much pained at the disdain of those of his fellows who had remained faithful. When they met him as they went on their sacred errands they regarded him as they passed by with looks of cruel hatred or of pity that was crueller still.

He used to visit the rebel angels whom Prince Istar pointed out to him, and usually met with a good reception, but as soon as he began to speak of conquering Heaven, they did not conceal the embarrassment and displeasure he caused them. Arcade perceived that they had no desire to be disturbed in their tastes, their affairs, and their habits. The falsity of their judgment, the narrowness of their minds, shocked him; and the rivalry, the jealousy they displayed towards one another deprived him of all hope of uniting them in a common cause. Perceiving how exile debases the character and warps the intellect, he felt his courage fail him.

One evening, when he had confessed his weariness of spirit to Zita, the beautiful archangel said:

"Let us go and see Nectaire; Nectaire has remedies of his own for sadness and fatigue."

She led him into the woods of Montmorency and stopped at the threshold of a small white house, adjoining a kitchen garden, laid waste by winter, where far back in the shadows the light shone on forcing-frames and cracked glass melon shades.

Nectaire opened the door to his visitors, and, after quieting the growls of a big mastiff which protected the garden, led them into a low room warmed by an earthenware stove.

Against the whitewashed wall, on a deal board, among the onions and seeds, lay a flute ready to be put to the lips. A round walnut table bore a stone tobacco-jar, a pipe, a bottle of wine and some glasses. The gardener offered each of his guests a cane-seated chair, and himself sat down on a stool by the table.

He was a sturdy old man; thick grey hair stood up on his head, he had a furrowed brow, a snub-nose, a red face and a forked beard.

The big mastiff stretched himself at his master's feet, rested his short black muzzle on his paws, and closed his eyes. The gardener poured out some wine for his guests, and when they had drunk and talked a little, Zita said to Nectaire:

"Please play your flute to us, you will give pleasure to my friend whom I have brought to see you."

The old man immediately consented. He put the boxwood pipe to his lips,—so clumsy was it that it looked as if the gardener had fashioned it himself,—and preluded with a few strange runs. Then he developed rich melodies in which the thrills sparkled like diamonds and pearls on a velvet ground. Touched by cunning fingers, animated with creative breath, the rustic pipe sang like a silver flute. There were no over-shrill notes and the tone was always even and pure. One seemed to be listening to the nightingale and the Muses singing together, the soul of Nature and the soul of Man. And the old man ordered and developed his thoughts in a musical language full of grace and daring. He told of love, of fear, of vain quarrels, of all-conquering laughter, of the calm light of the intellect, of the arrows of the mind piercing with their golden shafts the monsters of Ignorance and Hate. He told also of Joy and Sorrow bending their twin heads over the earth and of Desire which brings worlds into being.

The whole night listened to the flute of Nectaire. Already the evening star was rising above the paling horizon.

There they sat; Zita with hands clasped about her knees, Arcade, his head leaning on his hand, his lips apart. Motionless they listened. A lark, which had awakened hard by in a sandy field, lured by these novel sounds, rose swiftly in the air, hovered a few seconds, then dropped at one swoop into the musician's orchard. The neighbouring sparrows, forsaking the crannies of the mouldering walls, came and sat in a row on the window-ledge whence notes came welling forth that gave them more delight than oats or grains of barley. A jay, coming for the first time out of his wood, folded his sapphire wings on a leafless cherry tree. Beside the drain-head, a large black rat, glistening with the greasy water of the sewers, sitting on his hind legs, raised his short arms and slender fingers in amazement. A field-mouse, that dwelt in the orchard, was seated near him. Down from the tiles came the old tom-cat, who retained the grey fur, the ringed tail, the powerful loins, the courage, and the pride of his ancestors. He pushed against the half-open door with his nose and approaching the flute-player with silent tread, sat gravely down, pricking his ears that had been torn in many a nocturnal combat; the grocer's white cat followed him, sniffing vibrant air and then, arching her back and closing her blue eyes, listened in ravishment. Mice, swarming in crowds from under the boards, surrounded them, and fearing neither tooth nor claw, sat motionless, their pink hands folded voluptuously on their bosoms. Spiders that had strayed far from their webs, with waving legs, gathered in a charmed circle on the ceiling. A small grey lizard, that had glided on to the doorstep, stayed there, fascinated, and, in the loft, the bat might have been seen hanging by her nails, head down, now half-awakened from her winter sleep, swaying to the rhythm of the marvellous flute.

XV

WHEREIN WE SEE YOUNG MAURICE BEWAILING THE LOSS OF HIS GUARDIAN ANGEL, EVEN IN HIS MISTRESS'S ARMS, AND WHEREIN WE HEAR THE ABBÉ PATOUILLE REJECT AS VAIN AND ILLUSORY ALL NOTIONS OF A NEW REBELLION OF THE ANGELS

 FORTNIGHT had elapsed since the angel's apparition in the flat. For the first time Gilberte arrived before Maurice at the rendezvous. Maurice was gloomy, Gilberte sulky. So far as they were concerned Nature had resumed her drab monotony. They eyed each other languidly, and kept glancing towards the angle between the wardrobe with the mirror and the window, where recently the pale shade of Arcade had taken shape, and where now the blue cretonne of the hangings was the only thing visible. Without giving him a name (it was unnecessary) Madame des Aubels asked:

"You have not seen him since?"

Slowly, sadly, Maurice turned his head from right to left, and from left to right.

"You look as if you missed him," continued Madame des Aubels. "But come, confess that he gave you a terrible fright, and that you were shocked at his unconventionality."

"Certainly he was unconventional," said Maurice without any resentment.

"Tell me, Maurice, is it nothing to you now to be with me alone? . . . You need an angel to inspire you. That is sad, for a young man like you!"

Maurice appeared not to hear, and asked gravely:

"Gilberte, do you feel that your guardian angel is watching over you?"

"I, not at all. I have never thought of him, and yet I am not without religion. In the first place, people who have none are like animals. And then one cannot go straight without religion. It is impossible."

"Exactly, that's just it," said Maurice, his eyes on the violet stripes of his flowerless pyjamas; "when one has one's guardian angel one does not even think about him, and when one has lost him one feels very lonely."

"So you miss this . . ."

"Well, the fact is . . ."

"Oh, yes, yes, you miss him. Well, my dear, the loss of such a guardian angel as that is no great matter. No, no! he is not worth much, that Arcade of yours. On that famous day, while you were out getting him some clothes, he was ever so long fastening my dress, and I certainly felt his hand . . . Well, at any rate, don't trust him."

Maurice dreamily lit a cigarette. They spoke of the six days' cicycle race at the winter velodrome, and of the aviation show at the motor exhibition at Brussels, without experiencing the slightest amusement. Then they tried love-making as a sort of convenient pastime, and succeeded in becoming moderately absorbed in it; but at the very moment when she might have been expected to play a part more in accordance with a mutual sentiment, she exclaimed with a sudden start:

"Good Heavens! Maurice, how stupid of you to tell me that my guardian angel can see me. You cannot imagine how uncomfortable the idea makes me."

Maurice, somewhat taken aback, recalled, a little roughly, his mistress's wandering *thoughts*.

She declared that her principles forbade her to think of playing a round game with angels.

Maurice was longing to see Arcade again and had no other thought. He reproached himself for suffering him to depart without discovering where he was going, and he cudgelled his brains night and day thinking how to find him again.

On the bare chance, he put a notice in the personal column of one of the big papers, running thus:

"Arcade. Come back to your Maurice."

Day after day went by, and Arcade did not return.

One morning, at seven o'clock, Maurice went to St. Sulpice to hear Abbé Pautouille say Mass, then, as the priest was leaving the sacristy, he went up to him and asked to be heard for a moment.

They descended the steps of the church together and in the bright morning light walked round the fountain of the *Quatre Évêques*. In spite of his troubled conscience and the difficulty of presenting so extraordinary a case with any degree of credibility, Maurice related how the angel Arcade had appeared to him and had announced his unhappy resolve to separate from him and to stir up a new revolt of the spirits of glory. And young d'Esparvieu asked the worthy ecclesiastic how to find his celestial guardian again, since he could not bear his absence, and how to lead his angel back to the Christian faith. Abbé Patouille replied in a tone of affectionate sorrow that his dear child had been dreaming, that he took a morbid hallucination for reality, and that it was not permissible to believe that good angels may revolt.

"People have a notion," he added, "that they can lead a life of dissipation and disorder with impunity. They are wrong. The abuse of pleasure corrupts the intelligence and impairs the understanding. The devil takes possession of the sinner's senses, penetrating even to his soul. He has deceived you, Maurice, by a clumsy artifice."

Maurice objected that he was not in any way a victim of hallucinations, that he had not been dreaming, that he had seen his guardian angel with his eyes and heard him with his ears.

"Monsieur l'Abbé," he insisted, "a lady who happened to be with me at the time,—I need not mention her name,—also saw and heard him. And, moreover, she felt the angel's fingers straying . . . well, anyhow, she felt them. . . . Believe me, Monsieur l'Abbé, nothing could be more real, more positively certain than this apparition. The angel was fair, young, very handsome. His clear skin seemed, in the shadow, as if bathed in milky light. He spoke in a pure, sweet voice."

"That, alone, my child," the Abbé interrupted quickly, "proves you were dreaming. According to all the demonologies, bad angels have a hoarse voice, which grates like a rusty lock, and even if they did contrive to give a certain look of beauty to their faces, they cannot succeed in imitating the pure voice of the good spirits. This fact, attested by numerous witnesses, is established beyond all doubt."

"But, Monsieur l'Abbé, I saw him. I saw him sit down, stark naked, in an arm-chair on a pair of black stockings. What else do you want me to tell you?"

The Abbé Pautouille appeared in no way disturbed by this announcement.

"I say once more, my son," he replied, "that these unhappy illusions, these dreams of a deeply troubled soul, are to be ascribed to the deplorable state of your conscience. I believe, moreover, that I can detect the particular circumstance that has caused your unstable mind thus to come to grief. During the winter in company with Monsieur Sariette and your Uncle Gaétan, you came, in an evil frame of mind, to see the Chapel of the Holy Angels in this church, then undergoing repair. As I observed on that occasion, it is impossible to keep artists too closely to the rules of Christian art; they cannot be too strongly enjoined to respect Holy Writ and its authorized interpreters. Monsieur Eugène Delacroix did not suffer his fiery genius to be controlled by tradition. He brooked no guidance and, here, in this chapel he has painted pictures which in common parlance we call lurid, compositions of a violent, terrible nature which, far from inspiring the soul with peace, quietude, and calm, plunge it into a state of agitation. In them the angels are depicted with wrathful countenances, their features are sombre and uncouth. One might take them to be Lucifer and his companions meditating their revolt. Well, my son, it was these pictures, acting upon a mind already weakened and undermined by every kind of dissipation, that have filled it with the trouble to which it is at present a prey."

But Maurice would have none of it.

"Oh, no! Monsieur l'Abbé," he cried, "it is not Eugène Delacroix's pictures that have been troubling me. I didn't so much as look at them. I am completely indifferent to that kind of art."

"Well, then, my son, believe me: there is no truth, no reality, in any of the story you have just related to me. Your guardian angel has certainly not appeared to you."

"But, Abbé," replied Maurice, who had the most absolute confidence in the evidence of the senses, "I saw him tying up a woman's shoe-laces and putting on the trousers of a suicide."

And stamping his feet on the asphalt, Maurice called as witnesses to the truth of his words the sky, the earth, all nature, the towers of St. Sulpice, the walls of the great seminary, the Fountain of the *Quatre Évêques*, the public lavatory, the cabmen's shelter, the taxis and motor 'buses' shelter, the trees, the passers-by, the dogs, the sparrows, the flower-seller and her flowers.

The Abbé made haste to end the interview.

"All this is error, falsehood, and illusion, my child," said he. "You are a Christian: think as a Christian,—a Christian does not allow himself to be seduced by empty shadows. Faith protects him against the seduction of the marvellous, he leaves credulity to freethinkers. There are credulous people for you—freethinkers! There is no humbug they will not swallow. But the Christian carries a weapon which dissipates diabolical illusions,—the sign of the Cross. Reassure yourself, Maurice,—you have not lost your guardian angel. He still watches over you. It lies with you not to make this task too difficult nor too painful for him. Good-bye, Maurice. The weather is going to change, for I feel a burning in my big toe."

And Abbé Patouille went off with his breviary under his arm, hobbling along with a dignity that seemed to foretell a mitre.

That very day, Arcade and Zita were leaning over the parapet of La Butte, gazing down on the mist and smoke that lay floating over the vast city.

"Is it possible," said Arcade, "for the mind to conceive all the pain and suffering that lie pent within a great city? It is my belief that if a man succeeded in realising it, the weight of it would crush him to the earth."

"And yet," answered Zita, "every living being in that place of torment is enamoured of life. It is a great enigma!

"Unhappy, ill-fated, while they live, the idea of ceasing to be is, nevertheless, a horror to them. They look not for solace in annihilation, it does not even bring them the promise of rest. In their madness they even look upon nothingness with terror: they have peopled it with phantoms. Look you at these pediments, these towers and domes and spires that pierce the mist and rear on high their glittering crosses. Men bow in adoration before the demiurge who has given them a life that is worse than death, and a death that is worse than life."

Zita was for a long time lost in thought. At length she broke silence, saying:

"There is something, Arcade, that I must confess to you. It was no desire for a purer justice or wiser laws that hurried Ithuriel earthward. Ambition, a taste for intrigue, the love of wealth and honour, all these things made Heaven, with its calm, unbearable to me, and I longed to mingle with the restless race of men. I came, and by an art unknown to nearly all the angels, I learned how to fashion myself a body which, since I could change it as the fancy seized me, to whatsoever age and sex I would, has permitted me to

experience the most diverse and amazing of human destinies. A hundred times I took a position of renown among the leaders of the day, the lords of wealth and princes of nations. I will not reveal to you, Arcade, the famous names I bore; know only that I was preeminent in learning, in the fine arts, in power, wealth, and beauty, among all the nations of the world. At last, it was but a few years since, as I was journeying in France, under the outward semblance of a distinguished foreigner, I chanced to be roaming at evening through the forest of Montmorency, when I heard a flute unfolding all the sorrows of Heaven. The purity and sadness of its notes rent my very soul. Never before had I hearkened to aught so lovely. My eyes were wet with tears, my bosom full of sobs, as I drew near and beheld, on the skirts of a glade, an old man like to a faun, blowing on a rustic pipe. It was Nectaire. I cast myself at his feet, imprinted kisses on his hands and on his lips divine, and fled away. . . .

"From that day forth, conscious of the littleness of human achievements, weary of the tumult and the vanity of earthly things, ashamed of my vast and profitless endeavours, and deciding to seek out a loftier aim for my ambition, I looked upwards towards my skiey home and vowed I would return to it as a Deliverer. I rid myself of titles, name, wealth, friends, the horde of sycophants and flatterers and, as Zita the obscure, set to work in indigence and solitude, to bring freedom into Heaven."

"And I," said Arcade, "I too have heard the flute of Nectaire. But who is this old gardener who can thus woo from a rude wooden pipe notes that are so moving and so beautiful?"

"You will soon know," answered Zita.

XVI

WHEREIN MIRA THE SEERESS, ZEPHYRINE, AND THE
FATAL AMÉDÉE ARE SUCCESSIVELY BROUGHT UPON
THE SCENE, AND WHEREIN THE NOTION OF EURI-
PIDES THAT THOSE WHOM ZEUS WISHES TO CRUSH
HE FIRST MAKES MAD, IS ILLUSTRATED BY THE TER-
RIBLE EXAMPLE OF MONSIEUR SARIETTE

ISAPPOINTED at his failure to enlighten an eccle-
siastic renowned for his clarity of mind, and frus-
trated in the hope of finding his angel again on the
high road of orthodoxy, Maurice took it into his
head to resort to occultism and resolved to go and
consult a seer. He would have undoubtedly applied
to Madame de Thèbes, but he had already questioned
her on the occasion of his early love troubles, and
her replies showed such wisdom that he no longer believed her to
be a soothsayer. He therefore had recourse to a fashionable medium, Madame Mira. He had heard many examples quoted of the
extraordinary insight of this seeress, but it was necessary to present Madame Mira with some object which the absent one had
either touched or worn and to which her translucent gaze had to
be attracted. Maurice, trying to remember what the angel had
touched since his ill-fated incarnation, recollected that in his celestial nudity he had sat down in an arm-chair on Madame des Aubels'
black stockings and that he had afterwards helped that lady to
dress.

Maurice asked Gilberte for one of the talismans required by the
clairvoyante. But Gilberte could not give him a single one, unless,
as she said, she herself were to play the part of the talisman. For
the angel had, in her case, displayed the greatest indiscretion, and
such agility that it was impossible always to forestall his enterprise. On hearing this confession, which nevertheless told him
nothing new, Maurice lost his temper with the angel, calling him by
the names of the lowest animals and swearing he would give him
a good kick when he got him within reach of his foot. But his fury
soon turned against Madame des Aubels; he accused her of having
provoked the insolence she now denounced, and in his wrath he
referred to her by all the zoological symbols of immodesty and
perversity. His love for Arcade was rekindled in his heart, and
burned with a more ardent flame than ever, and the deserted youth,
with outstretched arms and bended knees, invoked his angel with
sobs and lamentations.

During his sleepless nights it occurred to him that perhaps the
books the angel had turned over before his incarnation might serve

as a talisman. One morning, therefore, Maurice went up to the library and greeted Monsieur Sariette, who was cataloguing under the romantic gaze of Alexandre d'Esparvieu. Monsieur Sariette smiled, but his face was deathly pale. Now that an invisible hand no longer upset the books placed under his charge, now that tranquillity and order once more reigned in the library, Monsieur Sariette was happy, but his strength diminished day by day. There was little left of him but a frail and contented shadow.

"One dies, in full content, of sorrow past."

"Monsieur Sariette," said Maurice, "you remember that time when your books were disarranged every night, how armfuls disappeared, how they were dragged about, turned over, ruined, and sent rolling helter-skelter as far as the gutter in the Rue Palatine. Those were great days! Point out to me, Monsieur Sariette, the books which suffered most."

This proposition threw Monsieur Sariette into a melancholy stupor, and Maurice had to repeat his request three times before he could make the aged librarian understand. At length he pointed to a very ancient Talmud from Jerusalem as having been frequently touched by those unseen hands. An apocryphal Gospel of the third century, consisting of twenty papyrus sheets, had also quitted its place time after time. Gassendi's Correspondence too seemed to have been well thumbed.

"But," added Monsieur Sariette, "the book to which the mysterious visitant devoted the most particular attention was undoubtedly a little copy of *Lucretius* adorned with the arms of Philippe de Vendôme, Grand Prieur de France, with autograph annotations by Voltaire, who, as is well known, frequently visited the Temple in his younger days. The fearsome reader who caused me such terrible anxiety never grew weary of this *Lucretius* and made it his bedside book, as it were. His taste was sound, for it's a gem of a thing. Alas! the monster made a blot of ink on page 137 which perhaps the chemists with all the science at their disposal will be powerless to erase."

And Monsieur Sariette heaved a profound sigh. He repented having said all this when young d'Esparvieu asked him for the loan of the precious *Lucretius*. Vainly did the jealous custodian affirm that the book was being repaired at the binder's and was not available. Maurice made it clear that he wasn't to be taken in like that. He strode resolutely into the abode of the philosophers and the globes and seating himself in an arm-chair said:

"I am waiting."

Monsieur Sariette suggested his having another edition. There were some that, textually, were more correct, and were, therefore, preferable from the student's point of view. He offered him Barbou's edition, or Coustelier's, or, better still, a French translation.

He could have the Baron des Coutures' version—which was perhaps a little old-fashioned—or La Grange's, or those in the Nisard and Panckouke series; or, again, there were two versions of striking elegance, one in verse and the other in prose, both from the pen of Monsieur de Pongerville of the French Academy.

"I don't need a translation," said Maurice proudly. "Give me the Prior de Vendôme's copy."

Monsieur Sariette went slowly up to the cupboard in which the jewel in question was contained. The keys were rattling in his trembling hand. He raised them to the lock and withdrew them again immediately and suggested that Maurice should have the common *Lucretius* published by Garnier.

"It's very handy," said he with an engaging smile.

But the silence with which this proposal was received made it clear that resistance was useless. He slowly drew forth the volume from its place, and having taken the precaution to see that there wasn't a speck of dust on the table-cloth, he laid it tremblingly thereon before the great-grandson of Alexandre d'Esparvieu.

Maurice began to turn the leaves, and when he got to page 137 he saw the stain which had been made with violet ink. It was about the size of a pea.

"Ay, that's it," said old Sariette, who had his eye on the *Lucretius* the whole time; "that's the trace those invisible monsters left behind them."

"What, there were several of them, Monsieur Sariette?" exclaimed Maurice.

"I cannot tell. But I don't know whether I have a right to have this blot removed since, like the blot Paul Louis Courier made on the Florentine manuscript, it constitutes a literary document, so to speak."

Scarcely were the words out of the old fellow's mouth when the front door bell rang and there was a confused noise of voices and footsteps in the next room. Sariette ran forward at the sound and collided with Père Guinardon's mistress, old Zephyrine, who, with her tousled hair sticking up like a nest of vipers, her face aflame, her bosom heaving, her abdominal part like an eiderdown quilt puffed out by a terrific gale, was choking with grief and rage. And amid sobs and sighs and groans and all the innumerable sounds which, on earth, make up the mighty uproar to which the emotions of living beings and the tumult of nature give rise, she cried:

"He's gone, the monster! He's gone off with her. He's cleared out the whole shanty and left me to shift for myself with eighteen-pence in my purse."

And she proceeded to give a long and incoherent account of how Michel Guinardon had abandoned her and gone to live with Octavie, the bread-woman's daughter, and she let loose a torrent of abuse against the traitor.

"A man whom I've kept going with my own money for fifty years and more. For I've had plenty of the needful and known plenty of the upper ten and all. I dragged him out of the gutter and now this is what I get for it. He's a bright beauty, that friend of yours. The lazy scoundrel. Why, he had to be dressed like a child, the drunken contemptible brute. You don't know him yet, Monsieur Sariette. He's a forger. He turns out Giottos, Giottos, I tell you, and Fra Angelicos and Grecos, as hard as he can and sells them to art-dealers—yes, and Fragonards too, and Baudouins. He's a debauchee, and doesn't believe in God! That's the worst of the lot, Monsieur Sariette, for without the fear of God . . ."

Long did Zephyrine continue to pour forth vituperations. When at last her breath failed her, Monsieur Sariette availed himself of the opportunity to exhort her to be calm and bring herself to look on the bright side of things. Guinardon would come back. A man doesn't forget anyone he's lived and got on well with for fifty years——

These two observations only goaded her to a fresh outburst, and Zephyrine swore she would never forget the slight that had been put on her; she swore she would never have the monster back with her any more. And if he came to ask her to forgive him on his knees, she would let him grovel at her feet.

"Don't you understand, Monsieur Sariette, that I despise and hate him, that he makes me sick?"

Sixty times she voiced these lofty sentiments; sixty times she vowed she would never have Guinardon back with her again, that she couldn't bear the sight of him, even in a picture.

Monsieur Sariette made no attempt to oppose a resolve which, after protestations such as these, he regarded as unshakable. He did not blame Zephyrine in the least. He even supported her. Unfolding to the deserted one a purer future, he told her of the frailty of human sentiment, exhorted her to display a spirit of renunciation and enjoined her to show a pious resignation to the will of God.

"Seeing, in truth, that your friend is so little worthy of affection . . ."

He was not suffered to continue, Zephyrine flew at him, and shaking him furiously by the collar of his frock-coat, she yelled, half choking with rage: "So little worthy of affection! Michel! Ah! my boy, you find another more kind, more gay, more witty, you find another like him, always young, yes, always. Not worthy of affection! Anyone can see you don't know anything about love, you old duffer."

Taking advantage of the fact that Père Sariette was thus deeply engaged, young d'Esparvieu slipped the little *Lucretius* into his pocket, and strolled deliberately past the crouching librarian, bidding him adieu with a little wave of the hand.

Armed with his talisman, he hastened to the Place des Ternes, to interview Madame Mira. She received him in a red drawing-room where neither owl nor frog nor any of the paraphernalia of ancient magic were to be found. Madame Mira, in a prune-coloured dress, her hair powdered, though already past her prime, was of very good appearance. She spoke with a certain elegance and prided herself on discovering hidden things by the help alone of Science, Philosophy, and Religion. She felt the morocco binding, feigning to close her eyes, and looking meanwhile through the narrow slit between her lids at the Latin title and the coat of arms which conveyed nothing to her.

Accustomed to receive as tokens such things as rings, handkerchiefs, letters, and locks of hair, she could not conceive to what sort of individual this singular book could belong. By habitual and mechanical cunning she disguised her real surprise under a feigned surprise.

"Strange!" she murmured, "strange! I do not see quite clearly . . . I perceive a woman . . ."

As she let fall this magic word, she glanced furtively to see what sort of an effect it had and beheld on her questioner's face a unexpected look of disappointment. Perceiving that she was off the track, she immediately changed her oracle:

"But she fades away immediately. It is strange, strange! I have a confused impression of some vague form, a being that I cannot define," and having assured herself by a hurried glance that, this time, her words were going down, she expatiated on the vagueness of the person and on the mist that enveloped him.

However, the vision grew clearer to Madame Mira, who was following a clue step by step.

"A wide street . . . a square with a statue . . . a deserted street,—stairs. He is there in a bluish room—he is a young man, with pale and careworn face. There are things he seems to regret, and which he would not do again did they still remain undone."

But the effort at divination had been too great. Fatigue prevented the clairvoyante from continuing her transcendental researches. She spent her remaining strength in impressively recommending him who consulted her to remain in intimate union with God if he wished to regain what he had lost and succeed in his attempts.

On leaving Maurice placed a louis on the mantelpiece and went away moved and troubled, persuaded that Madame Mira possessed supernatural faculties, but unfortunately insufficient ones.

At the bottom of the stairs he remembered he had left the little *Lucretius* on the table of the pythoness, and, thinking that the old maniac Sariette would never get over its loss, went up to recover possession of it.

On re-entering the paternal abode his gaze lighted upon a

shadowy and grief-stricken figure. It was old Sariette, who in tones as plaintive as the wail of the November wind began to beg for his *Lucretius*. Maurice pulled it carelessly out of his great-coat pocket.

"Don't flurry yourself, Monsieur Sariette," said he. "There the thing is."

Clasping the jewel to his bosom the old librarian bore it away and laid it gently down on the blue table-cloth, thinking all the while where he might safely hide his precious treasure, and turning over all sorts of schemes in his mind as became a zealous curator. But who among us shall boast of his wisdom? The foresight of man is short, and his prudence is for ever being baffled. The blows of fate are ineluctable; no man shall evade his doom. There is no counsel, no caution that avails against destiny. Hapless as we are, the same blind force which regulates the courses of atom and of star fashions universal order from our vicissitudes. Our ill-fortune is necessary to the harmony of the Universe. It was the day for the binder, a day which the revolving seasons brought round twice a year, beneath the sign of the Ram and the sign of the Scales. That day, ever since morning, Monsieur Sariette had been making things ready for the binder. He had laid out on the table as many of the newly purchased paper-bound volumes as were deemed worthy of a permanent binding or of being put in boards, and also those books whose binding was in need of repair, and of all these he had drawn up a detailed and accurate list. Punctually at five o'clock, old Amédée, the man from Léger-Massieu's, the binder in the Rue de l'Abbaye, presented himself at the d'Esparvieu library and, after a double check had been carried out by Monsieur Sariette, thrust the books he was to take back to his master into a piece of cloth which he fastened into knots at the four corners and hoisted on to his shoulder. He then saluted the librarian with the following words, "Good night, all!" and went downstairs.

Everything went off on this occasion as usual. But Amédée, seeing the *Lucretius* on the table, innocently put it into the bag with the others, and took it away without Monsieur Sariette's perceiving it. The librarian quitted the home of the Philosophers and Globes in entire forgetfulness of the book whose absence had been causing him such horrible anxiety all day long. Some people may take a stern view of the matter and call this a lapse, a defection of his better nature. But would it not be more accurate to say that fate had decided that things should come to pass in this manner, and that what is called chance, and is in fact but the regular order of nature, had accomplished this imperceptible deed which was to have such awful consequences in the sight of man? Monsieur Sariette went off to his dinner at the *Quatre Évêques,* and read his paper *La Croix.* He was tranquil and serene. It was only the next morning when he entered the abode of the Philosophers and Globes that he remembered the *Lucretius.* Failing to see it on the table he looked for it everywhere, but without success. It never entered his head that Amédée might have taken it away by mistake. What he did think was that the invisible visitant had returned, and he was mightily disturbed.

The unhappy curator, hearing a noise on the landing, opened the door and found it was little Léon, who, with a gold-braided *képi* stuck on his head, was shouting "Vive la France" and hurling dusters and feather-brooms and Hippolyte's floor polish at imaginary foes. The child preferred this landing for playing soldiers to any other part of the house, and sometimes he would stray into the library. Monsieur Sariette was seized with the sudden suspicion that it was he who had taken the *Lucretius* to use as a missile and he ordered him, in threatening tones, to give it back. The child denied that he had taken it, and Monsieur Sariette had recourse to cajolery.

"Léon, if you bring me back the little red book, I will give you some chocolates."

The child grew thoughtful; and in the evening, as Monsieur Sariette was going downstairs, he met Léon, who said:

"There's the book!"

And, holding out a much-torn picture-book called *The Story of Gribouille*, demanded his chocolates.

A few days later the post brought Maurice the prospectus of an enquiry agency managed by an ex-employee at the Prefecture of Police; it promised celerity and discretion. He found at the address indicated a moustached gentleman morose and careworn, who demanded a deposit and promised to find the individual.

The ex-police official soon wrote to inform him that very onerous investigations had been commenced and asked for fresh funds. Maurice gave him no more and resolved to carry on the search himself. Imagining, not without some likelihood, that the angel would associate with the wretched, seeing that he had no money, and with the exiled of all nations—like himself, revolutionaries— he visited the lodging-houses at St. Ouen, at la Chapelle, Montmartre, and the Barrière d'Italie. He sought him in the doss-houses, public-houses where they give you plates of tripe, and others where you can get a sausage for three sous; he searched for him in the cellars at the Market and at Père Momie's.

Maurice visited the restaurants where nihilists and anarchists take their meals. There he came across men dressed as women, gloomy and wild-looking youths, and blue-eyed octogenarians who laughed like little children. He observed, asked questions, was taken for a spy, had a knife thrust into him by a very beautiful woman, and the very next day continued his search in beer-houses, lodging-houses, houses of ill-fame, gambling-hells down by the fortifications, at the receivers of stolen goods, and among the "apaches."

Seeing him thus pale, harassed, and silent, his mother grew worried.

"We must find him a wife," she said. "It is a pity that Mademoiselle de la Verdelière has not a bigger fortune."

Abbé Patouille did not hide his anxiety.

"This child," he said, "is passing through a moral crisis."

"I am more inclined to think," replied Monsieur René d'Esparvieu, "that he is under the influence of some bad woman. We must find him an occupation which will absorb him and flatter his vanity. I might get him appointed Secretary to the Committee for the Preservation of Country Churches, or Consulting Counsel to the Syndicate of Catholic Plumbers."

XVII

WHEREIN WE LEARN THAT SOPHAR, NO LESS EAGER FOR GOLD THAN MAMMON, LOOKED UPON HIS HEAVENLY HOME LESS FAVOURABLY THAN UPON FRANCE, A COUNTRY BLESSED WITH A SAVINGS BANK AND LOAN DEPARTMENTS, AND WHEREIN WE SEE, YET ONCE AGAIN, THAT WHOSO IS POSSESSED OF THIS WORLD'S GOODS FEARS THE EVIL EFFECTS OF ANY CHANGE

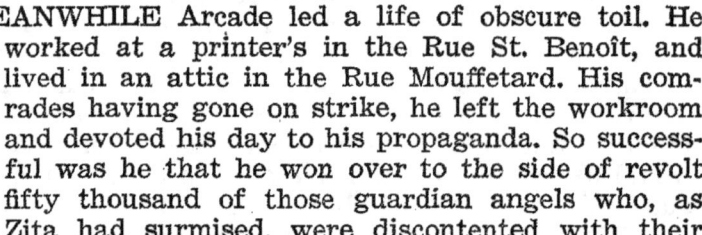

MEANWHILE Arcade led a life of obscure toil. He worked at a printer's in the Rue St. Benoît, and lived in an attic in the Rue Mouffetard. His comrades having gone on strike, he left the workroom and devoted his day to his propaganda. So successful was he that he won over to the side of revolt fifty thousand of those guardian angels who, as Zita had surmised, were discontented with their condition and imbued with the spirit of the times. But lacking money, he lacked liberty, and could not employ his time as he wished in instructing the sons of Heaven. So, too, Prince Istar, hampered by want of funds, manufactured fewer bombs than were needed, and these less fine. Of course he prepared a good many small pocket machines. He had filled Théophile's rooms with them, and not a day passed but he forgot some and left them lying about on the seats in various cafés. But a nice bomb, easily handled and capable of destroying many big mansions, cost him from twenty to twenty-five thousand francs; and Prince Istar only possessed two of this kind. Equally bent on procuring funds, Arcade and Istar both went to make a request for money from a celebrated financier named Max Everdingen, who, as everyone knows, is the managing director of the biggest banking concern in France and indeed in the whole world. What is not so well known is that Max Everdingen was not born of woman, but is a fallen angel. Nevertheless, such is the truth. In Heaven he was named Sophar, and guarded the treasures of Ialdabaoth, a great collector of gold and precious stones. In the exercise of this function Sophar contracted a love of riches which could not be satisfied in a state of society in which banks and stock exchanges are alike unknown. His heart flamed with an ardent love for the god of the Hebrews to whom he remained faithful during a long course of centuries. But at the commencement of the twentieth century of the Christian era, casting his eyes down from the height of the firmament upon France, he saw that this country, under the name of a Republic, was constituted as a plutocracy and that, under the appearance of a democratic government, high finance exercised sovereign sway, untrammelled and unchecked.

Henceforth life in the Empyrean became intolerable to him. He longed for France as for the promised land, and one day, bearing with him all the precious stones he could carry, he descended to earth and established himself in Paris. This angel of cupidity did good business there. Since his materialisation his face had lost its celestial aspect; it reproduced the Semitic type in all its purity, and one could admire the lines and the puckers which wrinkle the faces of bankers and which are to be seen in the money-changers of Quintin Matsys.

His beginnings were humble and his success amazing. He married an ugly woman and they saw themselves reflected in their children as in a mirror. Baron Max Everdingen's large mansion, which rears itself on the heights of the Trocadéro, is crammed with the spoils of Christian Europe.

The Baron received Arcade and Prince Istar in his study,—one of the most modest rooms in his mansion. The ceiling is decorated with a fresco of Tiepolo, taken from a Venetian palace. The bureau of the Regent, Philip of Orleans, is in this room, which is full of cabinets, show-cases, pictures, and statues.

Arcade allowed his gaze to wander over the walls.

"How comes it, my brother Sophar," said he, "that you, in spite of your Jewish heart, obey so ill the commandment of the Lord your God who said: 'Thou shalt have no graven images'? for here I see an Apollo of Houdon's and a Hebe of Lemoine's, and several busts by Caffieri. And, like Solomon in his old age, O son of God, you set up in your dwelling-place the idols of strange nations: for such are this Venus of Boucher, this Jupiter of Rubens, and those nymphs that are indebted to Fragonard's brush for the gooseberry jam which smears their gleaming limbs. And here in this single show-case, Sophar, you keep the sceptre of St. Louis, six hundred pearls of Marie Antoinette's broken necklace, the imperial mantle of

Charles V, the tiara wrought by Ghiberti for Pope Martin V, the Colonna, Bonaparte's sword—and I know not what besides."

"Mere trifles," said Max Everdingen.

"My dear Baron," said Prince Istar, "you even possess the ring which Charlemagne placed on a fairy's finger and which was thought to be lost. But let us discuss the business on which we have come. My friend and I have come to ask you for money."

"I can well believe it," replied Max Everdingen. "Everyone wants money, but for different reasons. What do you want money for?"

Prince Istar replied simply:

"To stir up a revolution in France."

"In France!" repeated the Baron, "in France? Well, I shall give you no money for that, you may be quite sure."

Arcade did not disguise the fact that he had expected greater liberality and more generous help from a celestial brother.

"Our project," he said, "is a vast one. It embraces both Heaven and Earth. It is settled in every detail. We shall first bring about a social revolution in France, in Europe, on the whole planet; then we shall carry war into the heavens, where we shall establish a peaceful democracy. And to reduce the citadels of Heaven, to overturn the mountain of God, to storm celestial Jerusalem, a vast army is needful, enormous resources, formidable machines, and electrophores of a strength yet unknown. It is our intention to commence with France."

"You are madmen!" exclaimed Baron Everdingen; "madmen and fools! Listen to me. There is not one single reform to carry out in France. All is perfect, finally settled, unchangeable. You hear?— unchangeable." And to add force to his statement, Baron Everdingen banged his fist three times on the Regent's bureau.

"Our points of view differ," said Arcade sweetly. "*I* think, as does Prince Istar, that everything should be changed in this country. But what boots it to dispute the matter? Moreover, it is too late. We have come to speak to you, O my brother Sophar, in the name of five hundred thousand celestial spirits, all resolved to commence the universal revolution to-morrow."

Baron Everdingen exclaimed that they were crazy, that he would not give a *sou*, that it was both criminal and mad to attack the most admirable thing in the world, the thing which renders earth more beautiful than heaven—Finance. He was a poet and a prophet. His heart thrilled with holy enthusiasm; he drew attention to the French Savings Bank, the virtuous Savings Bank, that chaste and pure Savings Bank like unto the Virgin of the Canticle who, issuing from the depths of the country in rustic petticoat, bears to the robust and splendid Bank—her bridegroom, who awaits her—the treasures of her love; and drew a picture of the Bank, enriched with the gifts of its spouse, pouring on all the nations of the world torrents of gold, which, of themselves, by a thousand invisible channels return in still greater abundance to the blessed land from which they sprung.

"By Deposit and Loan," he went on, "France has become the New Jerusalem, shedding her glory over all the nations of Europe, and the Kings of the Earth come to kiss her rosy feet. And that is what you would fain destroy? You are both impious and sacrilegious."

Thus spoke the angel of finance. An invisible harp accompanied his voice, and his eyes darted lightning.

Meanwhile Arcade, leaning carelessly against the Regent's bureau, spread out under the Banker's eyes various ground-plans, underground-plans, and sky-plans of Paris with red crosses indicating the points where bombs should be simultaneously placed in cellars and catacombs, thrown on public ways, and flung by a flotilla of aeroplanes. All the financial establishments, and notably the Everdingen Bank and its branches, were marked with red crosses.

The financier shrugged his shoulders.

"Nonsense! you are but wretches and vagabonds, shadowed by all the police of the world. You are penniless. How can you manufacture all the machines?"

By way of reply, Prince Istar drew from his pocket a small copper cylinder, which he gracefully presented to Baron Everdingen.

"You see," said he, "this ordinary-looking box. It is only necessary to let it fall on the ground immediately to reduce this mansion with its inmates to a mass of smoking ashes, and to set a fire going which would devour all the Trocadéro quarter. I have ten thousand like that, and I make three dozen a day."

The financier asked the Cherub to replace the machine in his pocket, and continued in a conciliatory tone:

"Listen to me, my friends. Go and start a revolution at once in Heaven, and leave things alone in this country. I will sign a cheque for you. You can procure all the material you need to attack celestial Jerusalem."

And Baron Everdingen was already working up in his imagination a magnificent deal in electrophores and war-material.

XVIII

WHEREIN IS BEGUN THE GARDENER'S STORY, IN THE COURSE OF WHICH WE SHALL SEE THE DESTINY OF THE WORLD UNFOLDED IN A DISCOURSE AS BROAD AND MAGNIFICENT IN ITS VIEWS AS BOSSUET'S DISCOURSE ON THE HISTORY OF THE UNIVERSE IS NARROW AND DISMAL

HE gardener bade Arcade and Zita sit down in an arbour walled with wild bryony, at the far end of the orchard.

"Arcade," said the beautiful Archangel, "Nectaire will perhaps reveal to you to-day the things you are burning to know. Ask him to speak."

Arcade did so and old Nectaire, laying down his pipe, began as follows:—

"I knew him. He was the most beautiful of all the Seraphim. He shone with intelligence and daring. His great heart was big with all the virtues born of pride: frankness, courage, constancy in trial, indomitable hope. Long, long ago, ere Time was, in the boreal sky where gleam the seven magnetic stars, he dwelt in a palace of diamond and gold, where the air was ever tremulous with the beating of wings and with songs of triumph. Iahveh, on his mountain, was jealous of Lucifer. You both know it: angels like unto men feel love and hatred quicken within them. Capable, at times, of generous resolves, they too often follow their own interests and yield to fear. Then, as now, they showed themselves, for the most part, incapable of lofty thoughts, and in the fear of the Lord lay their sole virtue. Lucifer, who held vile things in proud disdain, despised this rabble of commonplace spirits for ever wallowing in a life of feasts and pleasure. But to those who were possessed of a daring spirit, a restless soul, to those fired with a wild love of liberty, he proffered friendship, which was returned with adoration. These latter deserted in a mass the mountain of God and yielded to the Seraph the homage which That Other would fain have kept for himself alone.

"I ranked among the Dominations, and my name, Alaciel, was not unknown to fame. To satisfy my mind—that was ever tormented with an insatiable thirst for knowledge and understanding —I observed the nature of things, I studied the properties of minerals, air, and water. I sought out the laws which govern nature, solid or ethereal, and after much pondering I perceived that the Universe had not been formed as its pretended Creator would have us believe; I knew that all that exists, exists of itself and not by the caprice of Iahveh; that the world is itself its own creator and the spirit its own God. Henceforth I despised Iahveh for his imposture, and I hated him because he showed himself to be opposed to all that I found desirable and good: liberty, curiosity, doubt. These feelings drew me towards the Seraph. I admired him, I loved him. I dwelt in his light. When at length it appeared that a choice had to be made between him and That Other I ranged myself on the side of Lucifer and knew no other aim than to serve him, no other desire than to share his lot.

"War having become inevitable, he prepared for it with inde-fatigable vigilance and all the resourcefulness of a far-seeing mind. Making the Thrones and Dominations into Chalybes and Cyclopes, he drew forth iron from the mountains bordering his domain; iron, which he valued more than gold, and forged weapons in the cav-erns of Heaven. Then in the desert plain of the North he assembled myriads of Spirits, armed them, taught them, and drilled them. Al-though prepared in secret, the enterprise was too vast for his ad-versary not to be soon aware of it. It might in truth be said that he had always foreseen and dreaded it, for he had made a citadel of his abode and a warlike host of his angels, and he gave himself the name of the God of Hosts. He made ready his thunderbolts. More than half of the children of Heaven remained faithful to him; thronging round him he beheld obedient souls and patient hearts. The Archangel Michael, who knew not fear, took command of these docile troops. Lucifer, as soon as he saw that his army could gain no more in numbers or in warlike skill, moved it swiftly against the foe, and promising his angels riches and glory marched at their head towards the mountain upon whose summit stands the Throne of the Universe. For three days our host swept onward over the ethereal plains. Above our heads streamed the black standards of revolt. And now, behold, the Mountain of God shone rosy in the orient sky and our chief scanned with his eyes the glittering ram-parts. Beneath the sapphire walls the foe was drawn up in battle array, and, while we marched clad in our iron and bronze, they shone resplendent in gold and precious stones.

"Their gonfalons of red and blue floated in the breeze, and light-ning flashed from the points of their lances. In a little while the armies were only sundered one from the other by a narrow strip of level and deserted ground, and at this sight even the bravest shud-dered as they thought that there in bloody conflict their fate would soon be sealed.

"Angels, as you know, never die. But when bronze and iron, dia-mond point or flaming sword tear their ethereal substance, the pain they feel is more acute than men may suffer, for their flesh is more exquisitely delicate; and should some essential organ be destroyed, they fall inert and, slowly decomposing, are resolved into clouds and during long æons float insensible in the cold ether. And when at length they resume spirit and form they fail to recover full memory of their past life. Therefore it is but natural that angels

shrink from suffering, and the bravest among them is troubled ,t
the thought of being reft of light and sweet remembrance. Were it
otherwise the angelic race would know neither the delight of battle
nor the glory of sacrifice. Those who, before the beginning of Time,
fought in the Empyrean for or against the God of Armies, would
have taken part without honour in mock battles, and it would not
now become me to say to you, my children, with rightful pride:

" 'Lo, I was there!'

"Lucifer gave the signal for the onset and led the assault. We
fell upon the enemy, thinking to destroy him then and there and
carry the sacred citadel at the first onslaught. The soldiers of the
jealous God, less fiery, but no whit less firm than ours, remained
immovable. The Archangel Michael commanded them with the
calmness and resolution of a mighty spirit. Thrice we strove to
break through their lines, thrice they opposed to our iron-clad
breast the flaming points of their lances, swift to pierce the stout-
est cuirass. In millions the glorious bodies fell. At length our right
wing pierced the enemy's left and we beheld the Principalities, the
Powers, the Virtues, the Dominations, and the Thrones turn and
flee in full career; while the Angels of the Third Choir, flying distractedly above them, covered them with a snow of feathers mingled with a rain of blood. We sped in pursuit of them amid the
débris of chariots and broken weapons, and we spurred their nim-
ble flight. Suddenly a storm of cries amazed us. It grew louder and
nearer. With desperate shrieks and triumphal clamour the right
wing of the enemy, the giant archangels of the Most High, had
flung themselves upon our left flank and broken it. Thus we were
forced to abandon the pursuit of the fugitives and hasten to the
rescue of our own shattered troops. Our prince flew to rally them,
and re-established the conflict. But the left wing of the enemy,
whose ruin he had not quite consummated, no longer pressed by
lance or arrow, regained courage, returned, and faced us yet again.
Night fell upon the dubious field. While under the shelter of darkness, in the still, silent air stirred ever and anon by the moans of
the wounded, his forces were resting from their toils, Lucifer began to make ready for the next day's battle. Before dawn the trumpets sounded the reveille. Our warriors surprised the enemy at the
hour of prayer, put them to rout, and long and fierce was the carnage that ensued. When all had either fallen or fled, the Archangel
Michael, none with him save a few companions with four wings of
flame, still resisted the onslaughts of a countless host. They fell
back ceaselessly opposing their breasts to us, and Michael still displayed an impassible countenance. The sun had run a third of its
course when we commenced to scale the Mountain of God. An arduous ascent it was: sweat ran from our brows, a dazzling light
blinded us. Weighed down with steel, our feathery wings could not
sustain us, but hope gave us wings that bore us up. The beautiful

Seraph, pointing with glittering hand, mounting ever higher and higher, showed us the way. All day long we slowly clomb the lofty heights which at evening were robed in azure, rose, and violet. The starry host appearing in the sky seemed as the reflection of our own arms. Infinite silence reigned above us. We went on, intoxicated with hope; all at once 'from the darkened sky lightning darted forth, the thunder muttered, and from the cloudy mountain-top fell fire from Heaven. Our helmets, our breastplates were running with flames, and our bucklers broke under bolts sped by invisible hands. Lucifer, in the storm of fire, retained his haughty mien. In vain the lightning smote him; mightier than ever he stood erect, and still defied the foe. At length, the thunder, making the mountain totter, flung us down pell-mell, huge fragments of sapphire and ruby crashing down with us as we fell, and we rolled inert, swooning, for a period whose duration none could measure.

"I awoke in a darkness filled with lamentations. And when my eyes had grown accustomed to the dense shadows I saw round me my companions in arms, scattered in thousands on the sulphurous ground, lit by fitful gleams of livid light. My eyes perceived but fields of lava, smoking craters, and poisonous swamps.

"Mountains of ice and shadowy seas shut in the horizon. A brazen sky hung heavy on our brows. And the horror of the place was such that we wept as we sat, crouched elbow on knee, our cheeks resting on our clenched hands.

"But soon, raising my eyes, I beheld the Seraph standing before me like a tower. Over his pristine splendour sorrow had cast its mantle of sombre majesty.

" 'Comrades,' said he, 'we must be happy and rejoice, for behold we are delivered from celestial servitude. Here we are free, and it were better to be free in Hell than serve in Heaven. We are not conquered, since the will to conquer is still ours. We have caused the Throne of the jealous God to totter; by our hands it shall fall. Arise, therefore, and be of good heart.'

"Thereupon, at his command, we piled mountain upon mountain and on the topmost peak we reared engines which flung molten rocks against the divine habitations. The celestial host was taken unaware and from the abodes of glory there issued groans and cries of terror. And even then we thought to re-enter in triumph on our high estate, but the Mountain of God was wreathed with lightnings, and thunderbolts, falling on our fortress, crushed it to dust. After this fresh disaster, the Seraph remained awhile in meditation, his head buried in his hands. At length he raised his darkened visage. Now he was Satan, greater than Lucifer. Steadfast and loyal the angels thronged about him.

" 'Friends,' he said, 'if victory is denied us now, it is because we are neither worthy nor capable of victory. Let us determine wherein we have failed. Nature shall not be ruled, the sceptre of the Universe shall not be grasped, Godhead shall not be won, save by knowledge alone. We must conquer the thunder; to that task we must apply ourselves unwearyingly. It is not blind courage (no one this day has shown more courage than have you) which will win us the courts of Heaven; but rather study and reflection. In these silent realms where we are fallen, let us meditate, seeking the hidden causes of things; let us observe the course of Nature; let us pursue her with compelling ardour and all-conquering desire; let us strive to penetrate her infinite grandeur, her infinite minuteness. Let us seek to know when she is barren and when she brings forth fruit; how she makes cold and heat, joy and sorrow, life and death; how she assembles and disperses her elements, how she produces both the light air we breathe and the rocks of diamond and sapphire whence we have been precipitated, the divine fire wherewith we have been scarred and the soaring thought which stirs our minds. Torn with dire wounds, scorched by flame and by ice, let us render thanks to Fate which has sedulously opened our eyes, and let us rejoice at our lot. It is through pain that, suffering a first experience of Nature, we have been roused to know her and to subdue her. When she obeys us we shall be as gods. But even though she hide her mysteries for ever from us, deny us arms and keep the secret of the thunder, we still must needs congratulate ourselves on having known pain, for pain has revealed to us new feelings, more precious and more sweet than those experienced in eternal bliss, and inspired us with love and pity unknown to Heaven.'

"These words of the Seraph changed our hearts and opened up fresh hope to us. Our hearts were filled with a great longing for knowledge and love.

"Meanwhile the Earth was coming into being. Its immense and nebulous orb took on hourly more shape and more certainty of outline. The waters which fed the seaweed, the madrepores and shellfish, and bore the light flotilla of the nautilus upon their bosom, no longer covered it in its entirety; they began to sink into beds, and already continents appeared, where, on the warm slime, amphibious monsters crawled. Then the mountains were overspread with forests, and divers races of animals commenced to feed on the grass, the moss, the berries on the trees, and on the acorns. Then there took possession of cavernous shelter under the rocks, a being who was cunning to wound with a sharpened stone the savage beasts, and by his ruses to overcome the ancient denizens of forest, plain, and mountain.

"Man entered painfully on his kingdom. He was defenceless and naked. His scanty hair afforded him but little protection from the cold. His hands ended in nails too frail to do battle with the claws of wild beasts, but the position of his thumb, in opposition to the rest of his fingers, allowed him easily to grasp the most diverse objects and endowed him with skill in default of strength. Without differing essentially from the rest of the animals, he was more cap‑ able than any others of observing and comparing. As he drew from his throat various sounds, it occurred to him to designate by a par‑ ticular inflexion of the voice whatever impinged upon his mind, and by this sequence of different sounds he was enabled to fix and com‑ municate his ideas. His miserable lot and his painstaking spirit aroused the sympathy of the vanquished angels, who discerned in him an audacity equalling their own, and the germ of the pride that was at once their glory and their bane. They came in large num‑ bers to be near him, to dwell on this young earth whither their wings wafted them in effortless flight. And they took pleasure in sharpening his talents and fostering his genius. They taught him to clothe himself in the skins of wild beasts, to roll stones before the mouths of caves to keep out the tigers and bears. They taught him how to make the flame burst forth by twirling a stick among the dried leaves and to foster the sacred fire upon the hearth. In‑ spired by the ingenious spirits he dared to cross the rivers in the hollowed trunks of cleft trees, he invented the wheel, the grinding‑ mill, and the plough; the share tore up the earth and the wound brought forth fruit, and the grain offered to him who ground it divine nourishment. He moulded vessels in clay, and out of the flint he fashioned various tools.

"In fine, taking up our abode among mankind, we consoled them and taught them. We were not always visible to them, but of an evening, at the turn of the road, we would appear to them under forms often strange and weird, at times dignified and charming, and we adopted at will the appearance of a monster of the woods and waters, of a venerable old man, of a beautiful child, or of a woman with broad hips. Sometimes we would mock them in our songs or test their intelligence by some cunning prank. There were certain of us of a rather turbulent humour who loved to tease their women and children, but though lowly folk, they were our brothers, and we were never loath to come to their aid. Through our care their intelligence developed sufficiently to attain to mistaken ideas, and to acquire erroneous notions of the relations of cause and effect. As they supposed that some magic bond existed between the reality and its counterfeit presentment, they covered the walls of their caves with figure of animals and carved in ivory images of the reindeer and the mammoth in order to secure as prey the crea‑ tures they represented. Centuries passed by with infinite slowness while their genius was coming to birth. We sent them happy thoughts in dreams, inspired them to tame the horse, to castrate the bull, to teach the dog to guard the sheep. They created the family and the tribe. It came to pass one day that one of their wandering tribes was assailed by ferocious hunters. Forthwith the young men of the tribe formed an enclosed ring with their chariots, and in it they shut their women, children, old people, cattle, and treasures, and from the platform of their chariots they hurled murderous stones at their assailants. Thus was formed the first city. Born in misery and condemned to do murder by the law of Iahveh, man put his whole heart into doing battle, and to war he was indebted for his noblest virtues. He hallowed with his blood that sacred love of country which should (if man fulfils his destiny to the very end) enfold the whole earth in peace. One of us, Dædalus, brought him the axe, the plumb-line, and the sail. Thus we rendered the existence of mortals less hard and difficult. By the shores of the lakes they built dwellings of osier, where they might enjoy a meditative quiet unknown to the other inhabitants of the earth, and when they had learned to appease their hunger without too painful efforts we breathed into their hearts the love of beauty.

"They raised up pyramids, obelisks, towers, colossal statues which smiled stiff and uncouth, and genetic symbols. Having learnt to know us or trying at least to divine what manner of beings we were, they felt both friendship and fear for us. The wisest among them watched us with sacred awe and pondered our teaching. In their gratitude the people of Greece and of Asia consecrated to us stones, trees, shadowy woods; offered us victims, and sang us hymns; in fact we became gods in their sight, and they called us Horus, Isis, Astarte, Zeus, Cybele, Demeter, and Triptolemus. Satan was worshipped under the names of Evan, Dionysus, Iacchus, and Lenæus. He showed in his various manifestations all the strength and beauty which it is given to mortals to conceive. His eyes had the sweetness of the wood-violet, his lips were brilliant with the ruby-red of the pomegranate, a down finer than the velvet of the peach covered his cheeks and his chin: his fair hair, wound like a diadem and knotted loosely on the crown of his head, was encircled with ivy. He charmed the wild beasts, and penetrating into the deep forests drew to him all wild spirits, every thing that climbed in trees and peered through the branches with wild and timid gaze. On all these creatures fierce and fearful, that lived on bitter berries and beneath whose hairy breasts a wild heart beat, half-human creatures of the woods—on all he bestowed loving-kindness and grace, and they followed him drunk with joy and beauty. He planted the vine and showed mortals how to crush the grapes underfoot to make the wine flow. Magnificent and benign, he fared across the world, a long procession following in his train. To bear him company I took the form of a satyr; from my brow sprang two budding horns. My nose was flat and my ears were pointed. Glands, like those of the goat, hung on my neck, a goat's tail moved with my moving loins, and my hairy legs ended in a black cloven hoof which beat the ground in cadence.

"Dionysus fared on his triumphal march over the world. In his company I passed through Lydia, the Phrygian fields, the scorching plains of Persia, Media bristling with hoar-frost, Arabia Felix, and rich Asia where flourishing cities were laved by the waves of the sea. He proceeded on a car drawn by lions and lynxes, to the sound of flutes, cymbals, and drums, invented for his mysteries. Bacchantes, Thyades, and Mænads, girt with the dappled fawn-skin, waved the thyrsus encircled with ivy. He bore in his train the Satyrs, whose joyous troop I led, Sileni, Pans, and Centaurs. Under his feet flowers and fruit sprang to life, and striking the rocks with his wand he made limpid streams gush forth. In the month of the Vintage he visited Greece, and the villagers ran forth to meet him, stained with the green and ruddy juices of the plants, they wore masks of wood, or bark, or leaves; in their hands they bore earthen cups, and danced wanton dances. Their womenfolk, imitating the companions of the God, their heads wreathed with green smilax, fastened round their supple loins skins of fawn or goat. The virgins twined about their throats garlands of fig leaves, they kneaded cakes of flour, and bore the Phallus in the mystic basket. And the vine-dressers, all daubed with lees of wine, standing up in their wains and bandying mockery or abuse with the passers-by, invented Tragedy.

"Truly, it was not in dreaming beside a fountain, but by dint of strenuous toil that Dionysus taught them to grow plants and to make them bring forth succulent fruits. And while he pondered the art of transforming the rough woodlanders into a race that should love music and submit to just laws, more than once over his brow, burning with the fire of enthusiasm, did melancholy and gloomy fever pass. But his profound knowledge and his friendship for mankind enabled him to triumph over every obstacle. O days divine! Beautiful dawn of life! We led the Bacchanals on the leafy summits of the mountains and on the yellow shores of the seas. The Naiads and the Oreads mingled with us at our play. Aphrodite at our coming rose from the foam of the sea to smile upon us."

XIX

THE GARDENER'S STORY, CONTINUED

HEN men had learned to cultivate the earth, to herd cattle, to enclose their holy places within walls, and to recognise the gods by their beauty, I withdrew to that smiling land girdled with dark woods and watered by the Stymphalos, the Olbios, the Erymanthus, and the proud Crathis, swollen with the icy waters of the Styx, and there, in a green valley at the foot of a hill planted with arbutus, olive, and pine, beneath a cluster of white poplars and plane trees, by the side of a stream flowing with soft murmur amid tufted mastic trees, I sang to the shepherds and the nymphs of the birth of the world, the origin of fire, of the tenuous air, of water and of earth. I told them how primeval men had lived wretched and naked in the woods, before the ingenious spirits had taught them the arts; of God, too, I sang to them, and why they gave Dionysus Semele to mother, because his desire to befriend mankind was born amid the thunder.

"It was not without effort that this people, more pleasing than all the others in the eyes of the gods, these happy Greeks, achieved good government and a knowledge of the arts. Their first temple was a hut composed of laurel branches; their first image of the gods, a tree; their first altar, a rough stone stained with the blood of Iphigenia. But in a short time they brought wisdom and beauty to a point that no nation had attained before them, that no nation has since approached. Whence comes it, Arcade, this solitary marvel on the earth? Wherefore did the sacred soil of Ionia and of Attica bring forth this incomparable flower? Because nor priesthood, nor dogma, nor revelation ever found a place there, because the Greeks never knew the jealous God.

"It was his own grace, his own genius that the Greek enthroned and deified as his God, and when he raised his eyes to the heavens it was his own image that he saw reflected there. He conceived everything in due measure; and to his temples he gave perfect proportion. All therein was grace, harmony, symmetry, and wisdom; all were worthy of the immortals who dwelt within them and who under names of happy choice, in realised shapes, figured forth the genius of man. The columns which bore the marble architrave, the frieze and the cornice were touched with something human, which made them venerable; and sometimes one might see, as at Athens and at Delphi, beautiful young girls strong-limbed and radiant upstaying the entablature of treasure house and sanctuary. O days of splendour, harmony, and wisdom!

"Dionysus resolved to repair to Italy, whither he was summoned under the name of Bacchus by a people eager to celebrate his mysteries. I took passage in his ship decked with tendrils of the vine, and landed under the eyes of the two brothers of Helen at the mouth of the yellow Tiber. Already under the teaching of the god, the inhabitants of Latium had learned to wed the vine to the young stripling elm. It was my pleasure to dwell at the foot of the Sabine hills in a valley crowned with trees and watered with pure springs. I gathered the verbena and the mallow in the meadows. The pale olive-trees twisting their perforated trunks on the slope of the hill gave me of their unctuous fruit. There I taught a race of men with square heads, who had not, like the Greeks, a fertile mind, but whose hearts were true, whose souls were patient, and who reverenced the gods. My neighbour, a rustic soldier, who for fifteen years had bowed under the burden of his haversack, had followed the Roman eagle over land and sea, and had seen the enemies of the sovereign people flee before him. Now he drove his furrow with his two red oxen, starred with white between their spreading horns, while beneath the cabin's thatch his spouse, chaste and sedate of mien, pounded garlic in a bronze mortar and cooked the beans upon the sacred hearth. And I, his friend, seated near by under an oak, used to lighten his labours with the sound of my flute, and smile on his little children, when the sun, already low in the sky, was lengthening the shadows, and they returned from the wood all laden with branches. At the garden gate where the pears and pumpkins ripened, and where the lily and the evergreen acanthus bloomed, a figure of Priapus carved out of the trunk of a fig tree menaced thieves with his formidable emblem, and the reeds swaying with the wind over his head scared away the plundering birds. At new moon the pious husbandman made offering of a handful of salt and barley to his household gods crowned with myrtle and with rosemary.

"I saw his children grow up, and his children's children, who kept in their hearts their early piety and did not forget to offer sacrifice to Bacchus, to Diana, and to Venus, nor omit to pour fresh wines and scatter flowers into the fountains. But slowly they fell away from their old habits of patient toil and simplicity.

"I heard them complain when the torrent, swollen with many rains, compelled them to construct a dyke to protect the paternal fields, and the rough Sabine wine grew unpleasing to their delicate palate. They went to drink the wines of Greece at the neighbouring tavern; and the hours slipped unheeded by, while within the arbour shade they watched the dance of the flute player, practised at swaying her supple limbs to the sound of the castanets.

"Lulled by murmuring leaves and whispering streams, the tillers of the soil took sweet repose, but between the poplars we saw along borders of the sacred way vast tombs, statues, and altars arise, and the rolling of the chariot wheels grew more frequent over the worn stones. A cherry sapling brought home by a veteran told us of the far-distant conquests of a Consul, and odes sung to the lyre related the victories of Rome, mistress of the world.

"All the countries where the great Dionysus had journeyed, changing wild beasts into men, and making the fruit and grain bloom and ripen beneath the passing of his Mænads, now breathed the Pax Romana. The nursling of the she-wolf, soldier and labourer, friend of conquered nations, laid out roads from the margin of the misty sea to the rocky slopes of the Caucasus; in every town rose the temple of Augustus and of Rome, and such was the universal faith in Latin justice that in the gorges of Thessaly or on the wooded borders of the Rhine, the slave, ready to succumb under his iniquitous burden, called aloud on the name of Cæsar.

"But why must it be that on this ill-starred globe of land and water, all should perish and die and the fairest things be ever the most fleeting? O adorable daughters of Greece! O Science! O Wisdom! O Beauty! kindly divinities, you were wrapt in heavy slumber ere you submitted to the outrages of the barbarians, who already in the marshy wastes of the North and on the lonely steppes, ready to assail you, bestrode bare-backed their little shaggy horses.

"While, dear Arcade, the patient legionary camped by the borders of the Phasis and the Tanais, the women and the priests of Asia and of monstrous Africa invaded the Eternal City and troubled the sons of Remus with their magic spells. Until now, Iahveh, the persecutor of the laborious demons, was unknown to the world that he pretended to have created, save to certain miserable Syrian tribes, ferocious like himself, and perpetually dragged from servitude to servitude. Profiting by the Roman peace which assured free travel and traffic everywhere, and favoured the exchange of ideas and merchandise, this old God insolently made ready to conquer the Universe. He was not the only one, for the matter of that, to attempt such an undertaking. At the same time a crowd of gods, demiurges, and demons, such as Mithra, Thammuz, the good Isis, and Eubulus, meditated taking possession of the peace-enfolded world. Of all the spirits, Iahveh appeared the least prepared for victory. His ignorance, his cruelty, his ostentation, his Asiatic luxury, his disdain of laws, his affectation of rendering himself invisible, all these things were calculated to offend those Greeks and Latins who had absorbed the teaching of Dionysus and the Muses. He himself felt he was incapable of winning the allegiance of free men and of cultivated minds, and he employed cunning. To seduce their souls he invented a fable which, although not so ingenious as the myths wherewith we have surrounded the spirits of our disciples of old, could, nevertheless, influence those feebler intellects which are to be found everywhere in great masses. He declared that men having committed a crime against him, an hereditary crime, should pay the penalty for it in their present life and in the life to come (for mortals vainly imagine that their existence is prolonged in hell) ; and the astute Iahveh gave out that he had sent his own son to earth to redeem with his blood the debt of mankind. It is not credible that a penalty should redress a fault, and it is still less credible that the innocent should pay for the guilty. The sufferings of the innocent atone for nothing, and do but add one evil to another. Nevertheless, unhappy creatures were found to adore Iahveh and his son, the expiator, and to announce their mysteries as good tidings. We should not be surprised at this folly. Have we not seen many times indeed human beings who, poor and naked, prostrate themselves before all the phantoms of fear, and rather than follow the teaching of well-disposed demons, obey the commandments of cruel demiurges? Iahveh, by his cunning, took souls as in a net. But he did not gain therefrom, for his glorification, all that he expected. It was not he, but his son, who received the homage of mankind, and who gave his name to the new cult. He himself remained almost unknown upon earth."

XX

THE GARDENER'S STORY, CONTINUED

HE new superstition spread at first over Syria and Africa; it won over the seaports where the filthy rabble swarm, and, penetrating into Italy, infected at first the courtesans and the slaves, and then made rapid progress among the middle classes of the towns. But for a long while the country-side remained undisturbed. As in the past, the villagers consecrated a pine tree to Diana, and sprinkled it every year with the blood of a young boar; they propitiated their Lares with the sacrifice of a sow, and offered to Bacchus—benefactor of mankind—a kid of dazzling whiteness, or if they were too poor for this, at least they had a little wine and a little flour from the vineyard and from the fields for their household gods. We had taught them that it sufficed to approach the altar with clean hands, and that the gods rejoiced over a modest offering.

"Nevertheless, the reign of Iahveh proclaimed its advent in a hundred places by its extravagances. The Christians burnt books, overthrew temples, set fire to the towns, and carried on their ravages as far as the deserts. There, thousands of unhappy beings, turning their fury against themselves, lacerated their sides with points of steel. And from the whole earth the sighs of voluntary victims rose up to God like songs of praise.

"My shadowy retreat could not escape for long from the fury of their madness.

"On the summit of the hill which overlooked the olive woods, brightened daily with the sounds of my flute, had stood since the earliest days of the Pax Romana, a small marble temple, round as the huts of our forefathers. It had no walls, but on a base of seven steps, sixteen columns rose in a circle with the acanthus on the capitals, bearing a cupola of white tiles. This cupola sheltered a statue of Love fashioning his bow, the work of an Athenian sculptor. The child seemed to breathe, joy was welling from his lips, all his limbs were harmonious and polished. I honoured this image of the most powerful of all the gods, and I taught the villagers to bear to him as an offering a cup crowned with verbena and filled with wine two summers old.

"One day, when seated as my custom was at the feet of the god, pondering precepts and songs, an unknown man, wild-looking, with unkempt hair, approached the temple, sprang at one bound up the marble steps, and with savage glee exclaimed:

" 'Die, poisoner of souls, and joy and beauty perish with you.' He spoke thus, and drawing an axe from his girdle raised it against the god. I stayed his arm, I threw him down, and trampled him under my feet.

" 'Demon,' he cried desperately, 'suffer me to overturn this idol, and you may slay me afterwards.'

"I heeded not his atrocious plea, but leaned with all my might on his chest, which cracked under my knee, and, squeezing his throat with my two hands, I strangled the impious one.

"While he lay there, with purple face and lolling tongue, at the feet of the smiling god, I went to purify myself at the sacred stream. Then leaving this land, now the prey of the Christian, I passed through Gaul and gained the banks of the Saône, whither Dionysus had, in days gone by, carried the vine. The god of the Christians had not yet been proclaimed to this happy people. They worshipped for its beauty a leafy beech-tree, whose honoured branches swept the ground, and they hung fillets of wool thereon. They also worshipped a sacred stream and set up images of clay in a dripping grotto. They made offering of little cheeses and a bowl of milk to the Nymphs of the woods and mountains.

"But soon an apostle of sorrow was sent to them by the new God. He was drier than a smoked fish. Although attenuated with fasting and watching, he taught with unabated ardour all manner of gloomy mysteries. He loved suffering, and thought it good; his anger fell upon all that was beautiful, comely, and joyous. The sacred tree fell beneath his hatchet. He hated the Nymphs, because they were beautiful, and he flung imprecations at them when their shining limbs gleamed among the leaves at evening, and he held my melodious flute in aversion. The poor wretch thought that there were certain forms of words wherewith to put to flight the death-less spirits that dwell in the cool groves, and in the depths of the woods and on the tops of the mountains. He thought to conquer us with a few drops of water over which he had pronounced certain words and made certain gestures. The Nymphs, to avenge them-selves, appeared to him at nightfall and inflamed him with desire which the foolish knave thought animal; then they fled, their laughter scattered like grain over the fields, while their victim lay tossing with burning limbs on his couch of leaves. Thus do the di-vine nymphs laugh at exorcisers, and mock the wicked and their sordid chastity.

"The apostle did not do as much harm as he wished, because his teaching was given to the simple souls living in obedience to Na-ture, and because the mediocrity of most of mankind is such that they gain but little from the principles inculcated in them. The little wood in which I dwelt belonged to a Gaul of senatorial family, who retained some traces of Latin elegance. He loved his young freed-woman and shared with her his bed of broidered purple. His slaves cultivated his garden and his vineyard; he was a poet and sang, in imitation of Ausonius, Venus whipping her son with roses. Although a Christian, he offered me milk, fruit, and vegetables as if I were the genius of the place. In return I charmed his idle mo-ments with the music of my flute, and I gave him happy dreams. In fact, these peaceful Gauls knew very little of Iahveh and his son.

"But now behold fires looming on the horizon, and ashes driven by the wind fall within our forest glades. Peasants come driving a long file of waggons along the roads or urging their flocks before them. Cries of terror rise from the villages, 'The Burgundians are upon us!'

"Now one horseman is seen, lance in hand, clad in shining bronze, his long red hair falling in two plaits on his shoulders. Then come two, then twenty, then thousands, wild and blood-stained; old men and children they put to the sword, ay, even aged grandams whose grey hairs cleave to the soles of the slaughterer's boots, mingled with the brains of babes new-born. My young Gaul and his young freed-woman stain with their blood the couch broidered with nar-cissi. The barbarians burn the basilicas to roast their oxen whole, shatter the amphoræ, and drain the wine in the mud of the flooded cellars. Their women accompany them, huddled, half naked, in their war chariots. When the Senate, the dwellers in the cities, and the leaders of the churches had perished in the flames, the Burgun-dians, soddened with wine, lay down to slumber beneath the arcades of the Forum. Two weeks later one of them might have been seen smiling in his shaggy beard at the little child whom, on the thresh-old of their dwelling, his fair-haired spouse gathers in her arms: while another, kindling the fire of his forge, hammers out his iron with measured stroke; another sings beneath the oak tree to his assembled comrades of the gods and heroes of his race; and yet others spread out for sale stones fallen from Heaven, aurochs' horns, and amulets. And the former inhabitants of the country, regaining courage little by little, crept from the woods where they had fled for refuge, and returned to rebuild their burnt-down cabins, plough their fields, and prune their vines.

"Once more life resumed its normal course; but those times were the most wretched that mankind had yet experienced. The barbarians swarmed over the whole Empire. Their ways were uncouth, and as they nurtured feelings of vengeance and greed, they firmly believed in the ransom of sin.

"The fable of Iahveh and his son pleased them, and they believed it all the more easily in that it was taught them by the Romans whom they knew to be wiser than themselves, and to whose arts and mode of life they yielded secret admiration. Alas! the heritage of Greece and Rome had fallen into the hands of fools. All knowledge was lost. In those days it was held to be a great merit to sing among the choir, and those who remembered a few sentences from the Bible passed for prodigious geniuses. There were still poets as there were birds, but their verse went lame in every foot. The ancient demons, the good genii of mankind, shorn of their honours, driven forth, pursued, hunted down, remained hidden in the woods. There, if they still showed themselves to men, they adopted, to hold them in awe, a terrible face, a red, green, or black skin, baleful eyes, an enormous mouth fringed with boars' teeth, horns, a tail, and sometimes a human face on their bellies. The nymphs remained fair, and the barbarians, ignorant of the winsome names they bore in other days, called them fairies, and, imputing to them a capricious character and puerile tastes, both feared and loved them.

"We had suffered a grievous fall, and our ranks were sadly thinned; nevertheless we did not lose courage and, maintaining a laughing aspect and a benevolent spirit, we were in those direful days the real friends of mankind. Perceiving that the barbarians grew daily less sombre and less ferocious, we lent ourselves to the task of conversing with them under all sorts of disguises. We incited them, with a thousand precautions, and by prudent circumlocutions, not to acknowledge the old Iahveh as an infallible master, not blindly to obey his orders, and not to fear his menaces. When need was, we had recourse to magic. We exhorted them unceasingly to study nature and to strive to discover the traces of ancient wisdom.

"These warriors from the North—rude though they were—were acquainted with some mechanical arts. They thought they saw combats in the heavens; the sound of the harp drew tears from their eyes; and perchance they had souls capable of greater things than the degenerate Gauls and Romans whose lands they had invaded.

They knew not how to hew stone or to polish marble; but they caused porphyry and columns to be brought from Rome and from Ravenna; their chief men took for their seal a gem engraved by a Greek in the days when Beauty reigned supreme. They raised walls with bricks, cunningly arranged like ears of corn, and succeeded in building quite pleasing-looking churches with cornices upheld by consoles depicting grim faces, and heavy capitals whereon were represented monsters devouring one another.

"We taught them letters and sciences. A mouthpiece of their god, one Gerbert, took lessons in physics, arithmetic, and music with us, and it was said that he had sold us his soul. Centuries passed, and man's ways remained violent. It was a world given up to fire and blood. The successors of the studious Gerbert, not content with the possession of souls (the profits one gains thereby are lighter than air), wished to possess bodies also. They pretended that their universal and prescriptive monarchy was held from a fisherman on the lake of Tiberias. One of them thought for a moment to prevail over the loutish Germanus, successor to Augustus. But finally the spiritual had to come to terms with the temporal, and the nations were torn between two opposing masters.

"Nations took shape amid horrible tumult. On every side were wars, famines, and internecine conflicts. Since they attributed the innumerable ills that fell upon them to their God, they called him the Most Good, not by way of irony, but because to them the best was he who smote the hardest. In those days of violence, to give myself leisure for study I adopted a *rôle* which may surprise you, but which was exceedingly wise.

"Between the Saône and the mountains of Charolais, where the cattle pasture, there lies a wooded hill sloping gently down to fields watered by a clear stream. There stood a monastery celebrated throughout the Christian world. I hid my cloven feet under a robe and became a monk in this Abbey, where I lived peacefully, sheltered from the men at arms who to friend or foe alike showed themselves equally exacting. Man, who had relapsed into childhood, had all his lessons to learn over again. Brother Luke, whose cell was next to mine, studied the habits of animals and taught us that the weasel conceives her young within her ear. I culled simples in the fields wherewith to soothe the sick, who until then were made by way of treatment to touch the relics of saints. In the Abbey were several demons similar to myself whom I recognised by their cloven feet and by their kindly speech. We joined forces in our endeavours to polish the rough mind of the monks.

"While the little children played at hop-scotch under the Abbey walls our friends the monks devoted themselves to another game equally unprofitable, at which, nevertheless, I joined them, for one must kill time,—that, when one comes to think of it, is the sole business of life. Our game was a game of words which pleased our coarse yet subtle minds, set school fulminating against school, and put all Christendom in an uproar. We formed ourselves into two opposing camps. One camp maintained that before there were apples there was the Apple; that before there were popinjays there was the Popinjay; that before there were lewd and greedy monks there was the Monk, Lewdness and Greed; that before there were feet and before there were posteriors in this world the kick in the posterior must have had existence for all eternity in the bosom of God. The other camp replied that, on the contrary, apples gave man the idea of the apple; popinjays the idea of the popinjay; monks the idea of the monk, greed and lewdness, and that the kick in the posterior existed only after having been duly given and received. The players grew heated and came to fisticuffs. I was an adherent of the second party, which satisfied my reason better, and which was, in fact, condemned by the Council of Soissons.

"Meanwhile, not content with fighting among themselves, vassal against suzerain, suzerain against vassal, the great lords took it into their heads to go and fight in the East. They said, as well as I can remember, that they were going to deliver the tomb of the son of God.

"They said so, but their adventurous and covetous spirit excited them to go forth and seek lands, women, slaves, gold, myrrh, and incense. These expeditions, need it be said, proved disastrous; but our thick-headed compatriots brought back with them the knowledge of certain crafts and oriental arts and a taste for luxury. Henceforth we had less difficulty in making them work and in putting them in the way of inventions. We built wonderfully beautiful churches, with daringly pierced arches, lancet-shaped windows, high towers, thousands of pointed spires, which, rising in the sky towards Iahveh, bore at one and the same time the prayers of the humble and the threats of the proud, for it was all as much our doing as the work of men's hands; and it was a strange sight to see men and demons working together at a cathedral, each one sawing, polishing, collecting stones, graving, on capital and on cornice, nettles, thorns, thistles, wild parsley, and wild strawberry,—carving faces of virgins and saints and weird figures of serpents, fishes with asses' heads, apes scratching their buttocks; each one, in fact, putting his own particular talent,—mocking, sublime, grotesque, modest, or audacious,—into the work and making of it all a harmonious cacophony, a rapturous anthem of joy and sorrow, a Babel of victory. At our instigation the carvers, the goldsmiths, the enamellers, accomplished marvels and all the sumptuary arts flourished at once; there were silks at Lyons, tapestries at Arras, linen at Rheims, cloth at Rouen. The good merchants rode on their palfreys to the fairs, bearing pieces of velvet and brocade, embroideries, orfrays, jewels, vessels of silver, and illuminated books. Strollers and players set up their trestles in the churches and in the public squares, and represented, according to their lights, simple chronicles of Heaven, Earth, and Hell. Women decked themselves in splendid raiment and lisped of love.

"In the spring when the sky was blue, nobles and peasants were possessed with the desire to make merry in the flower-strewn meadows. The fiddler tuned his instrument, and ladies, knights and demoiselles, townsfolk, villagers and maidens, holding hands, began the dance. But suddenly War, Pestilence, and Famine entered the circle, and Death, tearing the violin from the fiddler's hands, led the dance. Fire devoured village and monastery. The men-at-arms hanged the peasants on the sign-posts at the cross-roads when they were unable to pay ransom, and bound pregnant women to tree-trunks, where at night the wolves came and devoured the fruit within the womb. The poor people lost their senses. Sometimes, peace being re-established, and good times come again, they were seized with mad, unreasoning terror, abandoned their homes, and rushed hither and thither in troops, half naked, tearing themselves with iron hooks, and singing. I do not accuse Iahveh and his son of all this evil. Many ill things occurred without him and even in spite of him. But where I recognise the instigation of the All Good (as they called him) was in the custom instituted by his pastors, and established throughout Christendom, of burning, to the sound of bells and the singing of psalms, both men and women who, taught by the demons, professed, concerning this God, opinions of their own."

XXI

THE GARDENER'S STORY, CONCLUDED

IT SEEMED as if science and thought had perished for all eternity, and that the earth would never again know peace, joy, and beauty.

"But one day, under the walls of Rome, some workmen, excavating the earth on the borders of an ancient road, found a marble sarcophagus which bore carved on its sides simulacra of Love and the triumphs of Bacchus.

"The lid being raised, a maiden appeared whose face shone with dazzling freshness. Her long hair spread over her white shoulders, she was smiling in her sleep. A band of citizens, thrilled with enthusiasm, raised the funeral couch and bore it to the Capitol. The people came in crowds to contemplate the ineffable beauty of the Roman maiden and stood around in silence, watching for the awakening of the divine soul held within this form of adorable beauty.

"And it came to pass that the City was so greatly stirred by this spectacle that the Pope, fearing, not without reason, the birth of a pagan cult from this radiant body, caused it to be removed at night and secretly buried. The precaution was vain, the labour fruitless. After so many centuries of barbarism, the beauty of the antique world had appeared for a moment before the eyes of men; it was long enough for its image, graven on their hearts, to inspire them with an ardent desire to love and to know.

"Henceforth, the star of the God of the Christians paled and sloped to its decline. Bold navigators discovered worlds inhabited by numerous races who knew not old Iahveh, and it was suspected that he was no less ignorant of them, since he had given them no news of himself or of his son the expiator. A Polish Canon demonstrated the true motions of the earth, and it was seen that, far from having created the world, the old demiurge of Israel had not even an inkling of its structure. The writings of philosophers, orators, jurisconsults, and ancient poets were dragged from the dust of the cloisters and passing from hand to hand inspired men's minds with the love of wisdom. The Vicar of the jealous God, the Pope himself, no longer believed in Him whom he represented on earth. He loved the arts and had no other care than to collect ancient statues and to rear sumptuous buildings wherein were displayed the orders of Vitruvius re-established by Bramante. We began to breathe anew. Already the old gods, recalled from their long exile, were returning to dwell upon earth. There they found once more their temples and their altars. Leo, placing at their feet the ring, the three crowns, and the keys offered them in secret the incense of sacrifices. Already Polyhymnia, leaning on her elbow, had begun to resume the golden thread of her meditations; already, in the gardens, the comely Graces and the Nymphs and Satyrs were weaving their mazy dances, and at length the earth had joy once more within its grasp. But, O calamity, unlucky fate,—most tragic circumstance! A German monk, all swollen with beer and theology, rose up against this renaissance of paganism, hurled menaces against it, shattered it, and prevailed single handed against the Princes of the Church. Inciting the nations, he called upon them to undertake a reform which saved that which was about to be destroyed. Vainly did the cleverest among us try to turn him from his work. A subtle demon, on earth called Beelzebub, marked him out for attack, now embarrassing him with learned controversial argument, now tormenting him with cruel mockery. The stubborn monk hurled his ink-pot at his head and went on with his dismal reformation. What ultimately happened? The sturdy mariner repaired, calked, and refloated the damaged ship of the Church. Jesus Christ owes it to this shaveling that his shipwreck was delayed for perhaps more than ten centuries. Henceforth things went from bad to worse. In the wake of this loutish monk, this beer-swiller and brawler, came that tall, dry doctor from Geneva, who, filled with the spirit of the ancient Iahveh, strove to bring the world back again to the abominable days of Joshua and the Judges of Israel. A maniac was he, filled with cold fury, a heretic and a burner of heretics, the most ferocious enemy of the Graces.

"These mad apostles and their mad disciples made even demons like myself, even the horned devils, look back longingly on the time when the Son with his Virgin Mother reigned over the nations dazzled with splendours: cathedrals with their stone tracery delicate as lace, flaming roses of stained glass, frescoes painted in vivid colours telling countless wondrous tales, rich orfrays, glittering enamel of shrines and reliquaries, gold of crosses and of monstrances, waxen tapers gleaming like starry galaxies amid the gloom of vaulted arches, organs with their deep-toned harmonies. All this doubtless was not the Parthenon, nor yet the Panathenæa, but it gladdened eyes and hearts; it was, at all events, beauty. And these cursed reformers would not suffer anything either pleasing or lovable. You should have seen them climbing in black swarms over doorways, plinths, spires, and bell-towers, striking with senseless hammers those images in stone which the demons had carved working hand in hand with the master designers, those genial saints and dear, holy women, and the touching idols of Virgin Mothers pressing their suckling to their heart. For, to be just, a little agreeable paganism had slipped into the cult of the jealous God. These monsters of heretics were for extirpating idolatry. We did our best, my companions and I, to hamper their horrible work, and I, for one, had the pleasure of flinging down some dozens from the top of the porches and galleries on to the Cathedral Square, where their detestable brains got knocked out. The worst of it was that the Catholic Church also reformed herself and grew more mischievous than ever. In the pleasant land of France, the seminarists and the monks were inflamed with unheard-of fury against the ingenious demons and the men of learning. My prior was one of the most violent opponents of sound knowledge. For some time past my studious lucubrations had caused him anxiety, and perhaps he had caught sight of my cloven foot. The scoundrel searched my cell and found paper, ink, some Greek books newly printed, and some Pan-pipes hanging on the wall. By these signs he knew me for an evil spirit and had me thrown into a dungeon where I should have eaten the bread of suffering and drunk the waters of bitterness, had I not promptly made my escape by the window and sought refuge in the wooded groves among the Nymphs and the Fauns.

"Far and wide the lighted pyres cast the odour of charred flesh.

Everywhere there were tortures, executions, broken bones, and tongues cut out. Never before had the spirit of Iahveh breathed forth such atrocious fury. However, it was not altogether in vain that men had raised the lid of the ancient sarcophagus and gazed upon the Roman Virgin.

"During this time of great terror when Papists and Reformers rivalled one another in violence and cruelty, amidst all these scenes of torture, the mind of man was regaining strength and courage. It dared to look up to the heavens, and there it saw, not the old Jew drunk with vengeance, but Venus Urania, tranquil and resplendent. Then a new order of things was born, then the great centuries came into being. Without publicly denying the god of their ancestors, men of intellect submitted to his mortal enemies. Science and Reason, and Abbé Gassendi relegated him gently to the far-distant abyss of first causes. The kindly demons who teach and console unhappy mortals, inspired the great minds of those days with discourses of all kinds, with comedies and tales told in the most polished fashion. Women invented conversation, the art of intimate letter-writing, and politeness. Manners took on a sweetness and a nobility unknown to preceding ages. One of the finest minds of that age of reason, the amiable Bernier, wrote one day to St. Evremond: 'It is a great sin to deprive oneself of a pleasure.' And this pronouncement alone should suffice to show the progress of intelligence in Europe. Not that there had not always been Epicureans but, unlike Bernier, Chapelle, and Molière, they had not the consciousness of their talent.

"Then even the very devotees understood Nature. And Racine, fierce bigot that he was, knew as well as such an atheistical physician at Guy Patin, how to attribute to divers states of the organs the passions which agitate mankind.

"Even in my abbey, whither I had returned after the turmoil, and which sheltered only the ignorant and the shallow thinker, a young monk, less of a dunce than the rest, confided to me that the Holy Spirit expresses itself in bad Greek to humiliate the learned.

"Nevertheless, theology and controversy were still raging in this society of thinkers. Not far from Paris in a shady valley there were to be seen solitary beings known as 'les Messieurs,' who called themselves disciples of St. Augustine, and argued with honest conviction that the God of the Scriptures strikes those who fear Him, spares those who confront Him, holds works of no account, and damns—should He so wish it—His most faithful servant; for His justice is not our justice, and His ways are incomprehensible.

"One evening I met one of these gentlemen in his garden, where he was pacing thoughtfully among the cabbage-plots and lettuce-beds. I bowed my horned head before him and murmured these friendly words: 'May old Jehovah protect you, sir. You know him well. Oh, how well you know him, and how perfectly you have understood his character.' The holy man thought he discerned in me a messenger from Hell, concluded he was eternally damned, and died suddenly of fright.

"The following century was the century of philosophy. The spirit of research was developed, reverence was lost; the pride of the flesh was diminished and the mind acquired fresh energy. Manners took on an elegance until then unknown. On the other hand, the monks of my order grew more and more ignorant and dirty, and the monastery no longer offered me any advantage now that good manners reigned in the town. I could bear it no longer. Flinging my habit to the nettles, I put a powdered wig on my horned brow, hid my goat's legs under white stockings, and cane in hand, my pockets stuffed with gazettes, I frequented the fashionable world, visited the modish promenades, and showed myself assiduously in the *cafés* where men of letters were to be found. I was made welcome in *salons* where, as a happy novelty, there were arm-chairs that fitted the form, and where both men and women engaged in rational conversation.

"The very metaphysicians spoke intelligibly. I acquired great weight in the town as an authority on matters of exegesis, and, without boasting, I was largely responsible for the Testament of the curé Meslier and *The Bible Explained,* brought out by the chaplains to the King of Prussia.

"At this time a comic and cruel misadventure befel the ancient Iahveh. An American Quaker, by means of a kite, stole his thunderbolts.

"I was living in Paris, and was at the supper where they talked of strangling the last of the priests with the entrails of the last of the kings. France was in a ferment; a terrible revolution broke out. The ephemeral leaders of the disordered State carried on a Reign of Terror amidst unheard-of perils. They were, for the most part, less pitiless and less cruel than the princes and judges instituted by Iahveh in the kingdoms of the earth; nevertheless, they appeared more ferocious, because they gave judgment in the name of Humanity. Unhappily they were easily moved to pity and of great sensibility. Now men of sensibility are irritable and subject to fits of fury. They were virtuous; they had moral laws, that is to say they conceived certain narrowly defined moral obligations, and judged human actions not by their natural consequences but by abstract principles. Of all the vices which contribute to the undoing of a statesman, virtue is the most fatal; it leads to murder. To work effectively for the happiness of mankind, a man must be superior to all morals, like the divine Julius. God, so ill-used for some time past, did not, on the whole, suffer excessively harsh treatment from these new men. He found protectors among them, and was adored under the name of the Supreme Being. One might even go so far as to say that terror created a diversion from philosophy and was profitable to the old demiurge, in that he appeared to represent order, public tranquillity, and the security of person and property.

"While Liberty was coming to birth amid the storm, I lived at Auteuil, and visited Madame Helvetius, where freethinkers in every branch of intellectual activity were to be met with. Nothing could be rarer than a freethinker, even after Voltaire's day. A man who will face death without trembling dare not say anything out of the ordinary about morals. That very same respect for Humanity which prompts him to go forth to his death, makes him bow to public opinion. In those days I enjoyed listening to the talk of Volney, Cabanis, and Tracy. Disciples of the great Condillac, they regarded the senses as the origin of all our knowledge. They called themselves ideologists, were the most honourable people in the world, and grieved the vulgar minds by refusing them immortality. For the majority of people, though they do not know what to do with this life, long for another that shall have no end. During the turmoil, our small philosophical society was sometimes disturbed in the peaceful shades of Auteuil by patrols of patriots. Condorcet, our great man, was an outlaw. I myself was regarded as suspect by the friends of the people, who, in spite of my rustic appearance and my frieze coat, believed me to be an aristocrat, and I confess that independence of thought is the proudest of all aristocracies.

"One evening while I was stealthily watching the dryads of Boulogne, who gleamed amid the leaves like the moon rising above the horizon, I was arrested as a suspect, and put in prison. It was a pure misunderstanding; but the Jacobins of those days, like the monks whose place they had usurped, laid great stress on unity of obedience. After the death of Madame Helvetius our society gathered together in the *salon* of Madame de Condorcet. Bonaparte did not disdain to chat with us sometimes.

"Recognizing him to be a great man, we thought him an ideologist like ourselves. Our influence in the land was considerable. We used it in his favour, and urged him towards the Imperial throne, thinking to display to the world a second Marcus Aurelius. We counted on him to establish universal peace; he did not fulfil our expectations, and we were wrong-headed enough to be wroth with him for our own mistake.

"Without any doubt he greatly surpassed all other men in quickness of intelligence, depth of dissimulation, and capacity for action. What made him an accomplished ruler was that he lived entirely in the present moment, and had no thoughts for anything beyond the immediate and actual reality. His genius was far-reaching and agile; his intelligence, vast in extent but common and vulgar in character, embraced humanity, but did not rise above it. He thought what every grenadier in the army thought; but he thought it with unprecedented force. He loved the game of chance, and it pleased him to tempt fortune by urging pigmies in their hundreds and thousands against each other. It was the game of a child as big as the world. He was too wily not to introduce old Iahveh into the game,—Iahveh, who was still powerful on earth, and who resembled him in his spirit of violence and domination. He threatened him, flattered him, caressed him, and intimidated him. He imprisoned his Vicar, of whom he demanded, with the knife at his throat, that rite of unction which, since the days of Saul of old, has bestowed might upon kings; he restored the worship of the demiurge, sang *Te Deums* to him, and made himself known through him as God of the earth, in small catechisms scattered broadcast throughout the Empire. They united their thunders, and a fine uproar they made.

"While Napoleon's amusements were throwing Europe into a turmoil, we congratulated ourselves on our wisdom, a little sad, withal, at seeing the era of philosophy ushered in with massacre, torture, and war. The worst is that the children of the century, fallen into the most distressing disorder, formed the conception of a literary and picturesque Christianity, which betokens a degeneracy of mind really unbelievable, and finally fell into Romanticism. War and Romanticism, what terrible scourges! And how pitiful to see these same people nursing a childish and savage love for muskets and drums! They did not understand that war, which trained the courage and founded the cities of barbarous and ignorant men, brings to the victor himself but ruin and misery, and is nothing but a horrible and stupid crime when nations are united together by common bonds of art, science, and trade.

"Insane Europeans who plot to cut each others' throats, now that one and the same civilisation enfolds and unites them all!

"I renounced all converse with these madmen and withdrew to this village, where I devoted myself to gardening. The peaches in my orchard remind me of the sun-kissed skin of the Mænads. For mankind I have retained my old friendship, a little admiration, and much pity, and I await, while cultivating this enclosure, that still distant day when the great Dionysus shall come, followed by his Fauns and his Bacchantes, to restore beauty and gladness to the world, and bring back the Golden Age. I shall fare joyously behind his car. And who knows if in that day of triumph mankind will be there for us to see? Who knows whether their worn-out race will not have already fulfilled its destiny, and whether other beings will not rise upon the ashes and ruins of what once was man and his genius? Who knows if winged beings will not have taken possession of the terrestrial empire? Even then the work of the good demons will not be ended,—they will teach a winged race arts and the joy of life."

XXII

WHEREIN WE ARE SHOWN THE INTERIOR OF A BRIC-A-BRAC SHOP, AND SEE HOW PÈRE GUINARDON'S GUILTY HAPPINESS IS MARRED BY THE JEALOUSY OF A LOVE-LORN DAME

ÈRE GUINARDON (as Zéphyrine had faithfully reported to Monsieur Sariette) smuggled out the pictures, furniture, and curios stored in his attic in the rue Princesse—his studio he called it—and used them to stock a shop he had taken in the rue de Courcelles. Thither he went to take up his abode, leaving Zéphyrine, with whom he had lived for fifty years, without a bed or a saucepan or a penny to call her own, except eighteen-pence the poor creature had in her purse. Père Guinardon opened an old picture and curiosity shop, and in it he installed the fair Octavie.

The shop-front presented an attractive appearance: there were Flemish angels in green copes, after the manner of Gérard David, a Salomé of the Luini school, a Saint Barbara in painted wood of French workmanship, Limoges enamel-work, Bohemian and Venetian glass, dishes from Urbino. There were specimens of English point-lace which, if her tale was true, had been presented to Zéphyrine, in the days of her radiant girlhood, by the Emperor Napoleon III. Within, there were golden articles that glinted in the shadows, while pictures of Christ, the Apostles, high-bred dames, and nymphs also presented themselves to the gaze. There was one canvas that was turned face to the wall so that it should only be looked at by connoisseurs; and connoisseurs are scarce. It was a replica of Fragonard's *Gimblette,* a brilliant painting that looked as if it had barely had time to dry. Papa Guinardon himself remarked on the fact. At the far end of the shop was a king-wood cabinet, the drawers of which were full of all manner of treasures: water-colours by Baudouin, eighteenth-century books of illustrations, miniatures, and so forth.

But the real masterpiece, the marvel, the gem, the pearl of great price, stood upon an easel veiled from public view. It was a *Coronation of the Virgin* by Fra Angelico, an exquisitely delicate thing in gold and blue and pink. Père Guinardon was asking a hundred thousand francs for it. Upon a Louis XV chair beside an Empire work-table on which stood a vase of flowers, sat the fair Octavie, broidery in hand. She, having left her glistering rags behind her in the garret in the rue Princesse, no longer presented the appearance of a touched-up Rembrandt, but shone, rather, with the soft radiance and limpidity of a Vermeer of Delft, for the delectation of the connoisseurs who frequented the shop of Papa Guinardon. Tranquil and demure, she remained alone in the shop all day, while the old fellow himself was up aloft working away at the deuce knows what picture. About five o'clock he used to come downstairs and have a chat with the habitués of the establishment.

The most regular caller was the Comte Desmaisons, a thin, cadaverous man. A strand of hair issued from the deep hollow under each cheek-bone, and, broadening as it descended, shed upon his chin and chest torrents of snow in which he was for ever trailing his long, fleshless, gold-ringed fingers. For twenty years he had been mourning the loss of his wife, who had been carried off by consumption in the flower of her youth and beauty. Since then he had spent his whole life in endeavouring to hold converse with the dead and in filling his lonely mansion with second-rate paintings. His confidence in Guinardon knew no bounds. Another client who was a scarcely less frequent visitor to the shop was Monsieur Blancmesnil, a director of a large financial establishment. He was a florid, prosperous-looking man of fifty. He took no great interest in matters of art, and was perhaps an indifferent connoisseur, but, in his case, it was the fair Octavie, seated in the middle of the shop, like a song-bird in its cage, that offered the attraction.

Monsieur Blancmesnil soon established relations with her, a fact which Père Guinardon alone failed to perceive, for the old fellow was still young in his love-affairs with Octavie. Monsieur Gaétan d'Esparvieu used to pay occasional visits to Père Guinardon's shop out of mere curiosity, for he strongly suspected the old man of being a first-rate "faker."

And then that doughty swordsman, Monsieur Le Truc de Ruffec, also came to see the old antiquary on one occasion, and acquainted him with a plan he had on foot. Monsieur Le Truc de Ruffec was getting up a little historical exhibition of small arms at the Petit Palais in aid of the fund for the education of the native children in Morocco and wanted Père Guinardon to lend him a few of the most valuable articles in his collection.

"Our first idea," he said, "was to organise an exhibition to be called 'The Cross and the Sword.' The juxtaposition of the two words will make the idea which has prompted our undertaking sufficiently clear to you. It was an idea pre-eminently patriotic and Christian which led us to associate the Sword, which is the symbol of Honour, with the Cross, which is the symbol of Salvation. It was hoped that our work would be graced by the distinguished patronage of the Minister of War and Monseigneur Cachepot. Unfortunately there were difficulties in the way, and the full realisation of the project had to be deferred. In the meantime we are limiting our exhibition to 'The Sword.' I have drawn up an explanatory note indicating the significance of the demonstration."

Having delivered himself of these remarks, Monsieur Le Truc de Ruffec produced a pocket-case stuffed full of papers. Picking out from a medley of judgment summonses and other odds and ends a little piece of very crumpled paper, he exclaimed, "Ah, here it is," and proceeded to read as follows: " 'The Sword is a fierce Virgin; it is *par excellence* the Frenchman's weapon. And now, when patriotic sentiment, after suffering an all too protracted eclipse, is beginning to shine forth again more ardently than ever . . .' And so forth; you see?"

And he repeated his request for some really fine specimen to be placed in the most conspicuous position in the exhibition to be held on behalf of the little native children of Morocco, of which General d'Esparview was to be honorary President.

Arms and armour were by no means Père Guinardon's strong point. He dealt principally in pictures, drawings, and books. But he was never to be taken unawares. He took down a rapier with a gilt colander-shaped hilt, a highly typical piece of workmanship of the Louis XIII-Napoleon III period, and presented it to the exhibition promoter, who, while contemplating it with respect, maintained a diplomatic silence.

"I have something better still in here," said the antiquary, and he produced from his inner shop—where it had been lying among the walking-sticks and umbrellas—a real demon of a sword, adorned with fleurs-de-lys, a genuine royal relic. It was the sword of Philippe-Auguste as worn by an actor at the *Odéon* when *Agnès de Méranie* was being performed in 1846. Guinardon held it point downwards, as though it were a cross, clasping his hands piously on the cross-bar. He looked as loyal as the sword itself.

"Have her for your exhibition," said he. "The damsel is well worth it. Bouvines is her name."

"If I find a buyer for it," said Monsieur Le Truc de Ruffec, twirling his enormous moustachios, "I suppose you will allow me a little commission?"

Some days later, Père Guinardon was mysteriously displaying a picture to the Comte Desmaisons and Monsieur Blancmesnil. It was a newly discovered work of El Greco, an amazingly fine example of the Master's later style. It represented a Saint Francis of Assisi standing erect upon Mont Alverno. He was mounting heavenward like a column of smoke, and was plunging into the regions of the clouds a monstrously narrow head that the distance rendered smaller still. In fine it was a real, very real, nay, too real El Greco. The two collectors were attentively scrutinizing the work, while Père Guinardon was belauding the depth of the shadows and the sublimity of the expression. He was raising his arms aloft to convey an idea of the greatness of Theotocopuli, who derived from Tintoretto, whom, however, he surpassed in loftiness by a hundred cubits.

"He was chaste and pure and strong; a mystic, a visionary."

Comte Desmaisons declared that El Greco was his favourite painter. In his inmost heart Blancmesnil was not so entirely struck with it.

The door opened, and Monsieur Gaétan quite unexpectedly appeared on the scene.

He gave a glance at the Saint Francis, and said:

"Bless my soul!"

Monsieur Blancmesnil, anxious to improve his knowledge, asked him what he thought of this artist who was now so much in vogue. Gaétan replied, glibly enough, that he did not regard El Greco as the eccentric, the madman that people used to take him for. It was rather his opinion that a defect of vision from which Theotocopuli suffered compelled him to deform his figures.

"Being afflicted with astigmatism and strabismus," Gaétan went on, "he painted the things he saw exactly as he used to see them." Comte Desmaisons was not readily disposed to accept so natural an explanation, which, however, by its very simplicity, highly commended itself to Monsieur Blancmesnil.

Père Guinardon, quite beside himself, exclaimed:

"Are you going to tell me, Monsieur d'Esparvieu, that Saint John was astigmatic because he beheld a woman clothed with the sun, crowned with stars, with the moon about her feet; the Beast with seven heads and ten horns, and the seven angels robed in white linen that bore the seven cups filled with the wrath of the Living God?"

"After all," said Monsieur Gaétan, by way of conclusion, "people are right in admiring El Greco if he had genius enough to impose his morbidity of vision upon them. By the same token, the contortions to which he subjects the human countenance may give satisfaction to those who love suffering,—a class more numerous than is generally supposed."

"Monsieur," replied the Comte Desmaisons, stroking his luxuriant beard with his long, thin hand, "we must love those that love us. Suffering loves us and attaches itself to us. We must love is if life is to be supportable to us. In the knowledge of this truth lies the strength and value of Christianity. Alas! I do not possess the gift of Faith. It is that which drives me to despair."

The old man thought of her for whom he had been mourning twenty years, and forthwith his reason left him, and his thoughts abandoned themselves unresistingly to the morbid imaginings of gentle and melancholy madness.

Having, he said, made a study of psychic matters, and having, with the co-operation of a favourable medium, carried out experiments concerning the nature and duration of the soul, he had obtained some remarkable results, which, however, did not afford him complete satisfaction. He had succeeded in viewing the soul of his dead wife under the appearance of a transparent and gelatinous mass which bore not the slightest resemblance to his adored one. The most painful part about the whole experiment—which he had repeated over and over again—was that the gelatinous mass, which was furnished with a number of extremely slender tentacles, maintained them in constant motion in time to a rhythm apparently intended to make certain signs, but of what these movements were supposed to convey there was not the slightest clue.

During the whole of this narrative Monsieur Blancmesnil had been whispering in a corner with the youthful Octavie, who sat mute and still, with her eyes on the ground.

Now Zéphyrine had by no means made up her mind to resign her lover into the hands of an unworthy rival. She would often go round of a morning, with her shopping-basket on her arm, and prowl about outside the curio shop. Torn betwixt grief and rage, tormented by warring ideas, she sometimes thought she would empty a saucepanful of vitriol on the head of the faithless one; at others that she would fling herself at his feet, and shower tears and kisses on his precious hands. One day, as she was thus eyeing her Michel—her beloved but guilty Michel—she noticed through the window the fair and youthful Octavie, who was sitting with her embroidery at a table upon which, in a vase of crystal, a rose was swooning to death. Zéphyrine, in a transport of fury, brought down her umbrella on her rival's fair head, and called her a bitch and a trollop. Octavie fled in terror, and ran for the police, while Zéphyrine, beside herself with grief and love, kept digging away with her old gamp at the *Gimblette* of Fragonard, the fuliginous Saint Francis of El Greco, the virgins, the nymphs, and the apostles, and knocked the gilt off the Fra Angelico, shrieking all the while:

"All those pictures there, the El Greco, the Beato Angelico, the Fragonard, the Gérard David, and the Baudouins—Guinardon painted the whole lot of them himself, the wretch, the scoundrel! That Fra Angelico there, why I saw him painting it on my ironing-board, and that Gérard David he executed on an old midwife's sign-board. You and that bitch of yours, why, I'll do for the pair of you just as I'm doing for these pictures."

And tugging away at the coat of an aged collector who, trembling all over, had hidden himself in the darkest corner of the shop, she called him to witness to the crimes of Guinardon, perjurer and impostor. The police had simply to tear her out of the ruined shop. As she was being taken off to the station, followed by a great crowd of people, she raised her fiery eyes to Heaven, crying in a voice choked with sobs:

"But don't you know Michel? If you knew him, you would understand that it is impossible to live without him. Michel! He is handsome and good and charming. He is a very god. He is Love itself.

I love him! I love him! I love him! I have known men high up in the world—Dukes, Ministers of State, and higher still. Not one of them was worthy to clean the mud off Michel's boots. My good, kind sirs, give him back to me again."

XXIII

WHEREIN WE ARE PERMITTED TO OBSERVE THE ADMIRABLE CHARACTER OF BOUCHOTTE, WHO RESISTS VIOLENCE BUT YIELDS TO LOVE. AFTER THAT LET NO ONE CALL THE AUTHOR A MISOGYNIST

N COMING away from the Baron Everdingen's, Prince Istar went to have a few oysters and a bottle of white wine at an eating-house in the Market. Then, being prudent as well as powerful, he paid a visit to his friend, Théophile Belais, for his pockets were full of bombs, and he wanted to secrete them in the musician's cupboard. The composer of *Aline, Queen of Golconda* was not at home. However, the Kerûb found Bouchotte busily working up the rôle of Zigouille; for the young artiste was booked to play the principal part in *Les Apaches,* an operetta that was then being rehearsed in one of the big music halls. The part in question was that of a street-walker who by her obscene gestures lures a passer-by into a trap, and then, while her victim is being gagged and bound, repeats with fiendish cruelty the lascivious motions by which he had been led astray. The part required that she should appear both as mime and singer, and she was in a state of high enthusiasm about it.

The accompanist had just left. Prince Istar seated himself at the piano, and Bouchotte resumed her task. Her movements were unseemly and delicious. Her tawny hair was flying in all directions in wild disordered curls; her skin was moist, it exhaled a scent of violets and alkaline salts which made the nostrils throb; even she herself felt the intoxication. Suddenly, inebriated with her intoxicating presence, Prince Istar arose, and with never a word or a look, caught her into his arms and drew her on to the couch, the little couch with the flowered tapestry which Théophile had procured at one of the big shops by promising to pay ten francs a month for a long term of years. Now Istar might have solicited Bouchotte's favours; he might have invited her to a rapid, and, withal, a mutual embrace, and, despite her preoccupation and excitement, she would not have refused him. But Bouchotte was a girl of spirit. The merest hint of coercion awoke all her untamable pride. She would consent of her own accord, yes; but be mastered, never! She would readily yield to love, curiosity, pity, to less than that even, but she would die rather than yield to force. Her surprise immediately gave place to fury. She fought her aggressor with all her heart and soul. With nails, to which fury lent an added edge, she tore at the cheeks and eyelids of the Kerûb, and, though he held her as in a vice, she arched herself so stiffly and made such excellent play with knee and elbow, that the human-headed bull, blinded with blood and rage, was sent crashing into the piano which gave forth a prolonged groan, while the bombs, tumbling out of his pockets, fell on the floor with a noise like thunder. And Bouchotte, with dishevelled locks, and one breast bare, beautiful and terrible, stood brandishing the poker over the prostrate giant, crying:

"Be off with you, or I'll put your eyes out!"

Prince Istar went to wash himself in the kitchen, and plunged his gory visage into a basin where some haricot beans lay soaking; then he withdrew without anger or resentment, for he had a noble soul.

Scarcely had he gone when the door-bell rang. Bouchotte, calling upon the absent maid in vain, slipped on a dressing-gown and opened the door herself. A young man, very correct in appearance and rather good-looking, bowed politely, and apologising for having to introduce himself, gave his name. It was Maurice d'Esparvieu.

Maurice was still seeking his guardian angel. Upheld by a desperate hope, he sought him in the queerest places. He enquired for him at the houses of sorcerers, magicians, and thaumaturgists, who in filthy hovels lay bare the ineffable secrets of the future, and who, though masters of all the treasures of the earth, wear trousers without any seats to them, and eat pigs' brains. That very day, having been to a back street in Montmartre to consult a priest of Satan, who practised black magic by piercing waxen images, Maurice had gone on to Bouchotte's, having been sent by Madame de la Verdelière, who, being about to give a fête in aid of the fund for the Preservation of Country Churches, was anxious to secure Bouchotte's services, since she had suddenly become—no one knew why—a fashionable artiste.

Bouchotte invited the visitor to sit down on the little flowered couch; at his request she seated herself beside him, and our young man of fashion explained to the singer what Madame de la Verdelière desired of her. The lady wished Bouchotte to sing one of those *apache* songs which were giving such delight in the fashionable world. Unfortunately Madame de la Verdelière could only offer a very modest fee, one out of all proportion to the merits of the artiste, but then it was for a good cause.

Bouchotte agreed to take part, and accepted the reduced fee with the accustomed liberality of the poor towards the rich and of artists towards society people. Bouchotte was not a selfish girl; the work for the preservation of country churches interested her. She remembered with sobs and tears her first communion, and she still retained her faith. When she passed by a church she wanted to enter it, especially in the evening. And so she did not love the Republic which had done its utmost to destroy both the Church and the Army. Her heart rejoiced to see the re-birth of national sentiment. France was lifting up her head. What was most applauded in the music halls were songs about the soldiers and the kind nuns. Meanwhile Maurice inhaled the odour of her tawny hair, the subtle bitter perfume of her body, all the odours of her person, and desire grew in him. He felt her near him on the little couch, very warm and very soft. He complimented the artiste on her great talent. She asked him what he liked best in all her repertory. He knew nothing about it, still he made replies that satisfied her. She had dictated them herself without knowing it. The vain creature

spoke of her talent, of her success, as she wished others to speak
of them. She never ceased talking of her triumphs, yet withal she
was candour itself. Maurice in all sincerity praised Bouchotte's
beauty, her fresh skin, her purity of line. She attributed this advantage to the fact that she never made up and never "put messes
on her face." As to her figure, she admitted that there was enough
everywhere and none too much, and to illustrate this assertion she
passed her hand over all the contours of her charming body, rising
lightly to follow the delightful curves on which she reposed.

Maurice was quite moved by it. It began to grow dark; she
offered to light up. He begged her to do nothing of the sort.

Their talk, at first gay and full of laughter, grew more intimate
and very sweet, with a certain languor in its tone. It seemed to
Bouchotte that she had known Monsieur Maurice d'Esparvieu for
a long time, and holding him for a man of delicacy, she gave him
her confidence. She told him that she was by nature a good woman,
but that she had had a grasping and unscrupulous mother. Maurice
recalled her to the consideration of her own beauty, and exalted
by subtle flattery the excellent opinion she had of herself. Patient
and calculating, in spite of the burning desire growing in him, he
aroused and increased in the desired one the longing to be still
further admired. The dressing-gown opened and slipped down of
its own accord, the living satin of her shoulders gleamed in the
mysterious light of evening. He,—so prudent, so clever, so adroit,—
let her sink in his arms, ardent and half swooning before she had
even perceived she had granted anything at all. Their breath and
their murmurs intermingled. And the little flowery couch sighed in
sympathy with them.

When they recovered the power to express their feelings in
words, she whispered in his ear that his cheek was even softer than
her own.

He answered, holding her embraced:

"It is charming to hold you like this. One would think you had
no bones."

She replied, closing her eyes:

"It is because I love you. Love seems to dissolve my bones; it
makes me as soft and melting as a pig's foot _à la Ste. Menebould._"

Hereupon Théophile came in, and Bouchotte called upon him to
thank Monsieur Maurice d'Esparvieu, who had been amiable enough
to be the bearer of a handsome offer from Madame la Comtesse de
la Verdelière.

The musician was happy, feeling the quiet and peace of the
house after a day of fruitless applications, of colourless lessons, of
failure and humiliation. Three new collaborators had been thrust
upon him who would add their signatures to his on his operetta,
and receive their share of the author's rights, and he had been
told to introduce the tango into the Court of Golconda. He pressed

young d'Esparview's hand and dropped wearily on to the little couch, which, being now at the end of its strength, gave way at the four legs and suddenly collapsed.

And the angel, precipitated to the ground, rolled terror-struck on to the watch, match-box and cigarette-case that had fallen from Maurice's pocket, and on to the bombs Prince Istar had left behind him.

XXIV

CONTAINING AN ACCOUNT OF THE VICISSITUDES THAT BEFEL THE "LUCRETIUS" OF THE PRIOR DE VENDÔME

ÉGER-MASSIEU, successor to Léger senior, the binder, whose establishment was in the rue de l'Abbaye, opposite the old Hôtel of the Abbés of Saint-Germain-des-Prés, in the hotbed of ancient schools and learned societies, employed an excellent but by no means numerous staff of workmen, and served with leisurely deliberation a clientèle who had learned to practise the virtue of patience. Six weeks had elapsed since he had received the parcel of books that had been despatched by Monsieur Sariette, but still Léger-Massieu had not yet put the work in hand. It was not until fifty-three days had come and gone, that, after calling over the books against the list that had been drawn up by Monsieur Sariette, the binder gave them out to his workmen. The little *Lucretius* with the Prior de Vendôme's arms not being mentioned on the list, it was assumed that it had been sent by another customer. And as it did not figure on any list of goods received it remained shut up in a cupboard, from which Léger-Massieu's son, the youthful Ernest, one day surreptitiously abstracted it, and slipped it into his pocket. Ernest was in love with a neighbouring seamstress whose name was Rose. Rose was fond of the country, and liked to hear the birds singing in the woods, and in order to procure the wherewithal to take her to Chatou one Sunday and give her a dinner, Ernest parted with the *Lucretius* for ten francs to old Moranger, a second-hand dealer in the rue Saint X——, who displayed no great curiosity regarding the origin of his acquisitions. Old Moranger handed over the volume, the very same day, to Monsieur Poussard, an expert in books, of the faubourg Saint Germain, for sixty francs. The latter removed the stamp which disclosed the ownership of the matchless copy, and sold it for five hundred francs to Monsieur Joseph Meyer, the well-known collector, who handed it straight away for three thousand francs to Monsieur Ardon, the bookseller, who im-

mediately transferred it to Monsieur R——, the great Parisian
bibliopolist, who gave six thousand for it, and sold it again a fortnight later at a handsome profit to Madame la Comtesse de Gorce.
Well known in the higher ranks of Parisian society, the lady in
question is what was called in the seventeenth century a "curieuse,"
that is to say, a lover of pictures, books, and china. In her mansion
in the Avenue d'Jéna she possesses collections of works of art
which bear witness to the diversity of her knowledge and the excellence of her taste. During the month of July, while the Comtesse
de Gorce was away at her château at Sarville in Normandy, the
house in the Avenue d'Jéna, being unoccupied, was visited one
night by a thief said to belong to a gang known as "The Collectors," who made works of art the special objects of their raids.

The police enquiry elicited the fact that the marauder had
reached the first floor by means of the waste-pipe, that he had then
climbed over the balcony, forced a shutter with a jemmy, broken a
pane of glass, turned the window-fastener, and made his way into
the long gallery. There he broke open several cupboards and possessed himself of whatever took his fancy. His booty consisted for
the most part of small but valuable articles, such as gold caskets,
a few ivory carvings of the fourteenth century, two splendid
fifteenth-century manuscripts, and a volume which the Countess's
secretary briefly described as "a morocco-bound book with a coat
of arms on it," and which was none other than the *Lucretius* from
the d'Esparvieu library.

The malefactor, who was supposed to be an English cook, was
never discovered. But, two months or so after the theft, a well-
dressed, clean-shaven young man passed down the rue de Courcelles, in the dimness of twilight, and went to offer the Prior de
Vendôme's *Lucretius* to Père Guinardon. The antiquary gave him
four shillings for it, examined it carefully, recognised its interest
and its beauty, and put it in the king-wood cabinet, where he kept
his special treasures.

Such were the vicissitudes which, in the course of a single season,
befel this thing of beauty.

XXV

WHEREIN MAURICE FINDS HIS ANGEL AGAIN

THE performance was over. Bouchotte in her dressing-room was taking off her make-up, when the door opened softly and old Monsieur Sandraque, her protector, came in, followed by a troop of her other admirers. Without so much as turning her head, she asked them what they meant by coming and staring at her like a pack of imbeciles, and whether they thought they were in a tent at the Neuilly Fair, looking at the freak woman.

"Now, then, ladies and gentlemen," she rattled on derisively, "just put a penny in the box for the young lady's marriage-portion, and she'll let you feel her legs,—all made of marble!"

Then, with an angry glance at the admiring throng, she exclaimed: "Come, off you go! Look alive!"

She sent them all packing, her sweetheart Théophile among them,—the pale-faced, long-haired, gentle, melancholy, short-sighted, and dreamy Théophile.

But recognizing her little Maurice, she gave him a smile. He approached her, and leaning over the back of the chair on which she was seated, congratulated her on her playing and singing, duly performing a kiss at the end of every compliment. She did not let him escape thus, and with reiterated enquiries, pressing solicitations, feigned incredulity, obliged him to repeat his stock panegyrics three or four times over, and when he stopped she seemed so disappointed that he was forced to take up the strain again immediately. He found it trying, for he was no connoisseur, but he had the pleasure of kissing her plump curved shoulders all golden in the light, and of catching glimpses of her pretty face in the mirror over the toilet-table.

"You were delicious."

"Really? . . . you think so?"

"Adorable . . . div——"

Suddenly he gave a loud cry. His eyes had seen in the mirror a face appear at the back of the dressing-room. He turned swiftly round, flung his arms about Arcade, and drew him into the corridor.

"What manners!" exclaimed Bouchotte, gasping.

But, pushing his way through a troop of performing dogs, and a family of American acrobats, young d'Esparvieu dragged his angel towards the exit.

He hurried him forth into the cool darkness of the boulevard, delirious with joy and wondering whether it was all too good to be true.

"Here you are!" he cried; "here you are! I have been looking for you a long time, Arcade,—or Mirar if you like,—and I have found you at last. Arcade, you have taken my guardian angel from me. Give him back to me. Arcade, do you love me still?"

Arcade replied that in accomplishing the super-angelic task he had set himself he had been forced to crush under foot friendship, pity, love, and all those feelings which tend to soften the soul; but that, on the other hand, his new state, by exposing him to suffering and privation, disposed him to love Humanity, and that he felt a certain mechanical friendship for his poor Maurice.

"Well, then," exclaimed Maurice, "if only you love me, come back to me, stay with me. I cannot do without you. While I had you with me I was not aware of your presence. But no sooner did you depart than I felt a horrible blank. Without you I am like a body without a soul. Do you know that in the little flat in the rue de Rome, with Gilberte by my side, I feel lonely, I miss you sorely, and long to see you and to hear you as I did that day when you made me so angry. Confess I was right, and that your behaviour on that occasion was not that of a gentleman. That you, you of so high an origin, so noble a mind, could commit such an indiscretion is extraordinary, when one comes to think about it. Madame des Aubels has not yet forgiven you. She blames you for having frightened her by appearing at such an inconvenient moment, and for being insolent and forward while hooking her dress and tying her shoes. I, I have forgotten everything. I only remember that you are my celestial brother, the saintly companion of my childhood. No, Arcade, you must not, you cannot leave me. You are my angel; you are my property."

Arcade explained to young d'Esparvieu that he could no longer be guiding angel to a Christian, having himself gone down into the pit. And he painted a horrible picture of himself; he described himself as breathing hatred and fury; in fact, an infernal spirit.

"All nonsense!" said Maurice, smiling, his eyes big with tears.

"Alas! our ideas, our destiny, everything tends to part us, Maurice. But I cannot stifle the tenderness I feel for you, and your candour forces me to love you."

"No," sighed Maurice. "You do not love me. You have never loved me. In a brother or a sister such indifference would be natural; in a friend it would be ordinary; in a guardian angel it is monstrous. Arcade, you are an abominable being. I hate you."

"I have loved you dearly, Maurice, and I still love you. You trouble my heart which I deemed encased in triple bronze. You show me my own weakness. When you were a little innocent boy I loved you as tenderly and purely as Miss Kate, your English governess, who caressed you with so much fervour. In the country, when the thin bark of the plane trees peels off in long strips and discloses the tender green trunk, after the rains which make the fine sand run on the sloping paths, I showed you how with that sand, those strips of bark, a few wild flowers, and a spray of maiden-hair fern to make rustic bridges, rustic shelters, terraces, and those gardens of Adonis, which last but an hour. During the month of May in Paris we raised an altar to the Virgin, and we burnt incense before it, the scent of which, permeating all the house, reminded Marcelline, the cook, of her village church and her lost innocence, and drew from her floods of tears; it also gave your mother a head-ache, your mother who, with all her wealth, was crushed with the *ennui* that is common to the fortunate ones of this world. When you went to college I interested myself in your progress, I shared your work and your play, I pondered with you over arduous prob-lems in arithmetic, I sought the impenetrable meaning of a phrase of Julius Cæsar's. What fine games of prisoners' base and football we had together! More than once did we know the intoxication of victory, and our young laurels were not soaked in blood or tears. Maurice, I did all I could to protect your innocence, but I could not prevent your losing it at the age of fourteen. Afterwards I regret-fully saw you loving women of all sorts, of divers ages, by no means beautiful, at least in the eyes of an angel. Saddened at the sight, I devoted myself to study; a fine library offered me resources rarely met with. I delved into the history of religions; you know the rest."

"But now, my dear Arcade," concluded young d'Esparvieu, "you have lost your position, your situation, you are entirely without resource. You have lost caste, you are off the lines, a vagabond, a bare-footed wanderer."

The Angel replied bitterly that, after all, he was a little better clad at present than when he was wearing the slops of a suicide.

Maurice alleged in excuse that when he dressed his naked angel in a suicide's slops, he was irritated with that angel's infidelity. But it was useless to dwell on the past or to recriminate. What was really needful was to consider what steps to take in future.

And he asked:

"Arcade, what do you think of doing?"

"Have I not already told you, Maurice? To fight with Him who reigns in the heavens, dethrone Him, and set up Satan in His stead."

"You will not do it. To begin with it is not the opportune mo-ment. Opinion is not with you. You will not be in the swim, as papa says. Conservatism and authority are all the go nowadays. We like to be ruled, and the President of the Republic is going to parley with the Pope. Do not be obstinate, Arcade. You are not as bad as you say. At bottom you are like the rest of the world, you adore the good God."

"I thought I had already explained to you, Maurice, that He whom you consider God is actually but a demiurge. He is absolutely ignorant of the divine world above him, and in all good faith believes himself to be the true and only God. You will find in the *History of the Church*, by Monsignor Duchesne—Vol. 1, page 162—that this proud and narrow-minded demiurge is named Ialdabaoth. My child, so as not to ruffle your prejudices and to deal gently with your feelings in future, that is the name I shall give him. If it should happen that I should speak of him to you, I shall call him Ialdabaoth. I must leave you. Adieu."

"Stay——"

"I cannot."

"I shall not let you go thus. You have deprived me of my guardian angel. It is for you to repair the injury you have caused me. Give me another one."

Arcade objected that it was difficult for him to satisfy such a demand. That having quarrelled with the sovereign dispenser of guardian Spirits, he could obtain nothing from that quarter.

"My dear Maurice," he added, smiling, "ask for one yourself from Ialdabaoth."

"No,—no,—no," exclaimed Maurice. "You have taken away my guardian angel,—give him back to me."

"Alas! I cannot."

"Is it, Arcade, because you are a revolutionary that you cannot?"

"Yes."

"An enemy of God?"

"Yes."

"A Satanic spirit?"

"Yes."

"Well, then," exclaimed young Maurice, "I will be your guardian angel,—I will not leave you."

And Maurice d'Esparvieu took Arcade to have some oysters at P—'s.

XXVI

THE CONCLAVE

THAT day, convoked by Arcade and Zita, the rebellious angels met together on the banks of the Seine at La Jonchère, in a deserted and tumble-down entertainment-hall that Prince Istar had hired from a pot-house keeper called Barattan. Three hundred angels crowded together in the stalls and boxes. A table, an arm-chair, and a collection of small chairs were arranged on the stage, where hung the tattered remnants of a piece of rustic scenery. The walls, coloured in distemper with flowers and fruit, were cracked and stained with damp, and were crumbling away in flakes. The vulgar and poverty-stricken appearance of the place rendered the grandeur of the passions exhibited therein all the more striking.

When Prince Istar asked the assembly to form its Committee, and first of all to elect a President, the name that was renowned throughout the world entered the minds of all present, but a religious respect sealed their lips; and after a moment's silence, the absent Nectaire was elected by acclamation. Having been invited to take the chair between Zita and an angel of Japan, Arcade immediately began as follows:

"Sons of Heaven! My comrades! You have freed yourselves from the bonds of celestial servitude—you have shaken off the thrall of him called Iahveh, but to whom we should here accord his veritable name of Ialdabaoth, for he is not the creator of the worlds, but merely an ignorant and barbarous demiurge, who having obtained possession of a minute portion of the Universe has therein sown suffering and death. Sons of Heaven, tell me, I charge you, whether you will combat and destroy Ialdabaoth?"

All with one voice made answer:

"We will!"

And many speaking all together swore they would scale the mountain of Ialdabaoth, and hurl down the walls of jasper and porphyry, and plunge the tyrant of Heaven into eternal darkness.

But a voice of crystal pierced through the sullen murmur.

"Tremble, ye impious, sacrilegious madmen! The Lord hath already lifted his dread arm to smite you!"

It was a loyal angel who, with an impulse of faith and love, envying the glory of confessors and martyrs, jealous and eager, like his God himself, to emulate man in the beauty of sacrifice, had flung himself in the midst of the blasphemers, to brave them, to confound them, and to fall beneath their blows. The assembly turned upon him with furious unanimity. Those nearest to him overwhelmed him with blows. He continued to cry, in a clear, ringing voice, "Glory to God! Glory to God! Glory to God!"

A rebel seized him by the neck and strangled his praises of the Almighty in his throat. He was thrown to the ground, trampled underfoot. Prince Istar picked him up, took him by the wings between his fingers, then rising like a column of smoke, opened a ventilator, which no one else could have reached, and passed the faithful angel through it. Order was immediately restored.

"Comrades," continued Arcade, "now that we have affirmed our stern resolve, we must examine the possible plans of campaign, and choose the best. You will therefore have to consider if we should attack the enemy in full force, or whether it were better, by a lengthy and assiduous propaganda, to win the inhabitants of Heaven to our cause."

"War! War!" shouted the assembled host.

And it seemed as if one could hear the sound of trumpets and the rolling of drums.

Théophile, whom Prince Istar had dragged to the meeting, rose, pale and unstrung, and, speaking with emotion, said:

"Brethren, do not take ill what I am about to say; for it is the friendship I have for you that inspires me. I am but a poor musician. But, believe me, all your plans will come to naught before the Divine Wisdom which has foreseen everything."

Théophile Belais sat down amid hisses. And Arcade continued:

"Ialdabaoth foresees everything. I do not contest it. He foresees everything, but in order to leave us our free will he acts towards us absolutely as if he foresaw nothing. Every instant he is surprised, disconcerted; the most probable events take him unawares. The obligation which he has undertaken, to reconcile with his prescience the liberty of both men and angels, throws him constantly into inextricable difficulties and terrible dilemmas. He never sees further than the end of his nose. He did not expect Adam's disobedience, and so little did he anticipate the wickedness of men that he repented having made them, and drowned them in the waters of the Flood, and all the animals as well, though he had no fault to find with the animals. For blindness he is only to be compared with Charles X, his favourite king. If we are prudent it will be easy to take him by surprise. I think that these observations will be calculated to reassure my brother."

Théophile made no reply. He loved God, but he was fearful of sharing the fate of the faithful angel.

One of the best-informed Spirits of the assembly, Mammon, was not altogether reassured by the remarks of his brother Arcade.

"Bethink you," said this Spirit, "Ialdabaoth has little general culture, but he is a soldier—to the marrow of his bones. The organisation of Paradise is a thoroughly military organisation. It is founded on hierarchy and discipline. Passive obedience is imposed there as a fundamental law. The angels form an army. Compare this spot with the Elysian Fields which Virgil depicts for you. In the Elysian Fields reign liberty, reason, and wisdom. The happy shades hold converse together in the groves of myrtle. In the Heaven of Ialdabaoth there is no civil population. Everyone is enrolled, numbered, registered. It is a barracks and a field for manœuvres. Remember that."

Arcade replied that they must look at their adversary in his true colours, and that the military organisation of Paradise was far more reminiscent of the villages of King Koffee than of the Prussia of Frederick the Great.

"Already," said he, "at the time of the first revolt, before the beginning of Time, the conflict raged for two days, and Ialdabaoth's throne was made to totter. Nevertheless, the demiurge gained the victory. But to what did he owe it? To the thunderstorm which

happened to come on during the conflict. The thunderbolts falling
on Lucifer and his angels struck them down, bruised and blackened,
and Ialdabaoth owed his victory to the thunderbolts. Thunder is his
sole weapon. He abuses its power. In the midst of thunder and
lightning he promulgates his laws. 'Fire goeth before him,' says the
Prophet. Now Seneca, the philosopher, said that the thunderbolt in
its fall brings peril to very few, but fear to all. This remark was
true enough for men of the first century of the Christian era; it is
no longer so for the angels of the twentieth; all of which goes to
prove that, in spite of his thunder, he is not very powerful; it was
acute terror that made men rear him a tower of unbaked brick and
bitumen. When myriads of celestial spirits, furnished with machines
which modern science puts at their disposal, make an assault upon
the heavens, think you, comrades, that the old master of the solar
system surrounded with his angels, armed as in the time of Abraham, will be able to resist them? To this day the warriors of the
demiurge wear helmets of gold and shields of diamond. Michael, his
best captain, knows no other tactics than the hand-to-hand combat.
To him Pharaoh's chariots are still the latest thing, and he has
never heard of the Macedonian phalanx."

And young Arcade lengthily prolonged the parallel between the
armed herds of Ialdabaoth and the intelligent fighting men of the
rebel army. Then the question of pecuniary resources arose.

Zita asserted that there was enough money to commence war,
that the electrophores were in order, that an initial victory would
obtain them credit.

The discussion continued, amid turbulence and confusion. In this
parliament of angels, as in the synods of men, empty words
flowed in abundance. Disturbances grew more violent and more frequent as the time for putting the resolution drew near. It was beyond question that supreme command would be entrusted to him
who had first raised the flag of revolt. But as everyone aspired to
act as Lucifer's Lieutenant, each in describing the kind of fighting
man to be preferred drew a portrait of himself. Thus Alcor, the
youngest of the rebellious angels, arose and spoke rapidly as follows:

"In Ialdabaoth's army, happily for us, the officers obtain their
posts by seniority. This being the case, there is little likelihood of
the command falling into the hands of a military genius, for men
are not made leaders by prolonged habits of obedience, and close
attention to minutiæ is not a good apprenticeship for the evolution
of vast plans of campaign. If we consult ancient and modern history, we shall see that the greatest leaders were kings like Alexander and Frederick, aristocrats like Cæsar and Turenne, or men
impatient of red-tape like Bonaparte. A routine man will always be
poor or second-rate. Comrades, let us appoint intelligent leaders,

men in the prime of life, to command us. An old man may retain the habit of winning victories, but only a young man can acquire it!"

Alcor then gave place to an angel of the philosophic order, who mounted the rostrum and spoke thus:

"War never was an exact science, a clearly defined art. The genius of the race, or the brain of the individual, has ever modified it. Now how are we to define the qualities necessary for a general in command in the war of the future, where one must consider greater masses and a larger number of movements than the intelligence of man can conceive? The multiplication of technical means, by infinitely multiplying the opportunities for mistake, paralyses the genius of those in command. At a certain stage in the progress of military science, a stage which our models, the Europeans, are about to reach, the cleverest leader and the most ignorant become equalized by reason of their incapacity. Another result of great modern armaments is, that the law of numbers tends to rule with inflexible rigour. It is of course true that ten angels in revolt are worth more than ten angels of Ialdabaoth; it is not at all certain that a million rebellious angels are worth more than a million of Ialdabaoth's angels. Great numbers, in war as elsewhere, annihilate intelligence and individual superiority in favour of a sort of exceedingly rudimentary collective soul."

A buzz of conversation drowned the voice of the philosophic angel, and he concluded his speech in an atmosphere of general indifference.

The tribune then resounded with calls to arms and promises of victory. The sword was held up to praise, the sword which defends the right. The triumph of the angels in revolt was celebrated twenty times beforehand, to the plaudits of a delirious crowd.

Cries of "War!" rose to the silent heavens; "Give us war!"

In the midst of these transports Prince Istar hoisted himself on to the platform, and the floor creaked under his weight.

"Comrades," said he, "you wish for victory, and it is a very natural desire, but you must be mouldy with literature and poetry if you expect to obtain it from war. The idea of making war can nowadays only enter the brain of a sottish bourgeois or a belated romantic. What is war? A burlesque masquerade in the midst of which fatuous patriots sing their stupid dithyrambs. Had Napoleon possessed a practical mind he would not have made war; but he was a dreamer, intoxicated with Ossian. You cry, 'Give us war!' You are visionaries. When will you become thinkers? The thinkers do not look for power and strength from any of the dreams which constitute military art: tactics, strategy, fortifications, artillery, and all that rubbish. They do not believe in war, which is a phantasy; they believe in chemistry, which is a science. They know the way to put victory into an algebraic formula."

And drawing from his pocket a small bottle, which he held up to the meeting, Prince Istar exclaimed:

"Victory—it is here!"

XXVII

WHEREIN WE SHALL SEE REVEALED A DARK AND SECRET MYSTERY AND LEARN HOW IT COMES ABOUT THAT EMPIRES ARE OFTEN HURLED AGAINST EMPIRES, AND RUIN FALLS ALIKE UPON THE VICTORS AND THE VANQUISHED; AND THE WISE READER (IF SUCH THERE BE—WHICH I DOUBT) WILL MEDITATE UPON THIS IMPORTANT UTTERANCE: "A WAR IS A MATTER OF BUSINESS"

THE Angels had dispersed. At the foot of the slopes at Meudon, seated on the grass, Arcade and Zita watched the Seine flowing by the willows.

"In this world," said Arcade, "in this world, which we call a cosmos, though it is but a microcosm, no thinking being can imagine that he is able to destroy even one atom. At the utmost, all we can hope for is that we shall succeed in modifying, here and there, the rhythm of some group of atoms and the arrangement of certain cells. That, when one thinks of it, must be the limit of our great enterprise. And when we shall have set up the Contradictor in the place of Ialdabaoth, we shall have done no more. . . . Zita, is the evil in the nature of things or in their arrangement? That is what we ought to know. Zita, I am profoundly troubled——"

"Arcade," replied Zita, "if to act we had to know the secret of Nature, one would never act at all. And neither would one live—since to live is to act. Arcade, is your resolution failing you already?"

Arcade assured the beautiful angel that he was resolved to plunge the demiurge into eternal darkness.

A motor-car passed by on the road, followed by a long trail of dust. It stopped before the two angels, and the hooked nose of Baron Everdingen appeared at the window.

"Good morning, my celestial friends, good morning," said the capitalist. "Sons of Heaven, I am pleased to meet you. I have a word of importance to say to you. Do not remain idle—do not go to sleep. Arm! Arm! You may be surprised by Ialdabaoth. You have a big war-fund. Employ it without stint. I have just learnt that the Archangel Michael has given large orders in Heaven for thunder-bolts and arrows. If you take my advice you will procure fifty thousand more electrophores. I will take the order. Good day, angels. Long live the celestial country!"

And Baron Everdingen flew by the flowery shores of Louveciennes in the company of a pretty actress.

"Is it true that they are taking up arms at the demiurge's?" asked Arcade.

"It may be," replied Zita, "that up there another Baron Everdingen is inciting to arms."

The guardian angel of young Maurice remained pensive for some moments. Then he murmured:

"Can it be that we are the sport of financiers?"

"Pooh!" said the beautiful archangel. "War is a business. It has always been a business."

Then they discussed at length the means of executing their immense enterprise. Rejecting disdainfully the anarchistic proceedings of Prince Istar, they conceived a formidable and sudden invasion of the kingdom of Heaven by their enthusiastic and well-drilled troops.

Now Barattan, the innkeeper of La Jonchère, who had let the entertainment-hall to the rebellious angels, was in the employ of the secret police. In the reports he furnished to the Prefecture he denounced the members of this secret meeting as meditating an attack on a certain person whom they described as obtuse and cruel, and whom they called *Alaballotte.* The agent believed this to be a pseudonym denoting either the President of the Republic or the Republic itself. The conspirators had unanimously given voice to threats against *Alaballotte,* and one of them, a very dangerous individual, well-known in anarchist circles, who had already several convictions against him on account of writings and speeches of a seditious nature, and who was known as Prince Istar or the *Quéroube,* had brandished a bomb of very small calibre which seemed to contain a formidable machine. The other conspirators were unknown to Barattan, notwithstanding the fact that he frequented revolutionary circles. Many among them were very young men, mere beardless youths. There were two who, it appeared, had spoken with conspicuous vehemence; a certain Arcade, dwelling in the Rue St. Jacques, and a woman of easy virtue called Zita, living at Montmartre, both without visible means of subsistence.

The affair seemed sufficiently serious to the Prefect of Police to make him think it necessary to confer without delay with the President of the Council.

The Third Republic was then going through one of those climacteric periods during which the French nation, enamoured of authority and worshipping force, gave itself up for lost because it was not governed enough, and clamoured loudly for a saviour. The President of the Council, and Minister of Justice, was only too eager to be that longed-for saviour. Still, for him to play that part it was first necessary that there should be a danger to face. Thus the news of a plot was highly welcome to him. He questioned the Prefect of Police on the character and importance of the affair. The Prefect of Police explained that the people seemed to have money, intelligence, and energy; but that they talked too much and were too numerous to undertake secret and concerted action. The Minister, leaning back in his arm-chair, pondered on the matter. The Empire writing-table at which he was seated, the ancient tapestry which covered the walls, the clock and the candelabra of the Restoration period—all, in this traditional setting, reminded him of those great principles of government which remain immutable throughout the succession of *régimes,* of stratagem and of bluff. After brief reflexion, he concluded that the plot must be allowed to grow and take shape, that it would even be fitting to nurse it, to embroider it, to colour it, and only to stifle it after having extracted every possible advantage from it.

He instructed the Prefect of Police to watch the affair closely, to render him an account of what went on from day to day, and to confine himself to the rôle of informer.

"I rely on your well-known prudence; observe, and do not intervene."

The Minister lit a cigarette. He quite reckoned, with the help of this plot, on silencing the Opposition, strengthening his own influence, diminishing that of his colleagues, humiliating the President of the Republic, and becoming the saviour of his country.

The Prefect of Police undertook to follow the ministerial instructions, vowing inwardly all the while to act in his own way. He had a watch put upon the individuals pointed out by Barattan, and commanded his agents not to intervene, come what might. Perceiving that he was a marked man, Prince Istar—who united prudence with strength—withdrew the bombs from the gutter outside his window where he had hidden them, and changing from motor 'bus to tube, from tube to motor 'bus, and choosing the most cunningly circuitous route, at length deposited his machines with the angelic musician.

Every time he left his house in the Rue St. Jacques, Arcade found a man of exaggerated smartness at his door, with yellow gloves and in his tie a diamond bigger than the Regent. Being a stranger to the things of this world, the rebellious angel paid no attention to the circumstance. But young Maurice d'Esparvieu, who had undertaken the task of guarding his guardian-angel, viewed this gentleman with uneasiness, for he equalled in assiduity and surpassed in vigilance that Monsieur Mignon who had formerly allowed his inquisitive gaze to wander from the rams' heads on the Hôtel de la Sordière in the Rue Garancière to the apse of the church of St. Sulpice. Maurice came two and three times a day to see Arcade in his furnished rooms, warning him of the danger, and urging him to change his abode.

Every evening he took his angel to night restaurants, where they supped with ladies of easy virtue. There young d'Esparvieu would foretell the issue of some coming glove-fight, and afterwards exert himself to demonstrate to Arcade the existence of God, the necessity for religion, and the beauties of Christianity, and adjure him to renounce his impious and criminal undertakings wherefrom, he said, he would reap but bitterness and disappointment.

"For really," said the young apologist, "if Christianity were false it would be known."

The ladies approved of Maurice's religious sentiments, and when the handsome Arcade uttered some blasphemy in language they could understand, they put their hands to their ears and bade him be silent, for fear of being struck down with him. For they believed that God, in his omnipotence and sovereign goodness, taking sudden vengeance against those who insulted him, was quite capable of striking down the innocent with the guilty without meaning it.

Sometimes the angel and his guardian took supper with the angelic musician. Maurice, who remembered from time to time that he was Bouchotte's lover, was displeased to see Arcade taking liberties with the singer. She had allowed him to do so ever since the day when, the angelic musician having had the little flowery couch repaired, Arcade and Bouchotte had made it a foundation for their friendship. Maurice, who loved Madame des Aubels a great deal, also loved Bouchotte a little, and was rather jealous of Arcade. Now jealousy is a feeling natural to man and beast, and causes them, however slight the attack, keen unhappiness. Therefore, suspecting the truth, which Bouchotte's temperament and the angel's character made sufficiently obvious, he overwhelmed Arcade with sarcasm and abuse, reproaching him with the immorality of his ways. Arcade answered, tranquilly, that it was difficult to subject physiological impulses to perfectly defined rules, and that moralists encountered great difficulties in the case of certain natural necessities.

"Moreover," added Arcade, "I freely acknowledge that it is almost impossible systematically to constitute a natural moral law. Nature has no principles. She furnishes us with no reason to believe that human life is to be respected. Nature, in her indifference, makes no distinction between good and evil."

"You see, then," replied Maurice, "that religion is necessary."

"Moral law," replied the angel, "which is supposed to be revealed to us, is drawn in reality from the grossest empiricism. Custom alone regulates morals. What Heaven prescribes is merely the consecration of ancient customs. The divine law, promulgated amid fireworks on some Mount Sinai, is never anything but the codification of human prejudice. And from this fact—namely, that morals change—religions which endure for a long time, such as Judæo-Christianity, vary their moral law."

"At any rate," said Maurice, whose intelligence was swelling visibly, "you will grant me that religion prevents much profligacy and crime?"

"Except when it promotes crime—as, for instance, the murder of Iphigenia."

"Arcade," exclaimed Maurice, "when I hear you argue, I rejoice that I am not an intellectual."

Meanwhile Théophile, with his head bent over the piano, his face hidden by the long fair veil of his hair, bringing down from on high his inspired hands on to the keys, was playing and singing the full score of *Aline, Queen of Golconda*.

Prince Istar used to come to their friendly reunions, his pockets filled with bombs and bottles of champagne, both of which he owed to the liberality of Baron Everdingen. Bouchotte received the Kerûb with pleasure, since she saw in him the witness and the trophy of the victory she had gained on the little flowered couch. He was to her as the severed head of Goliath in the hands of the youthful David. And she admired the prince for his cleverness as an accompanist, his vigour, which she had subdued, and his prodigious capacity for drink.

One night, when young d'Esparvieu took his angel home in his car from Bouchotte's house to the lodgings in the Rue St. Jacques, it was very dark; before the door the diamond in the spy's necktie glittered like a beacon; three cyclists standing in a group under its rays made off in divers directions at the car's approach. The angel took no notice, but Maurice concluded that Arcade's movements interested various important people in the State. He judged the danger to be pressing, and at once made up his mind.

The next morning he came to seek the suspect, to take him to the Rue de Rome. The angel was in bed. Maurice urged him to dress and to follow him.

"Come," said he. "This house is no longer safe for you. You are watched. One of these days you will be arrested. Do you wish to sleep in gaol? No? Well, then, come. I will put you in a safe place."

The spirit smiled with some little compassion on his naïve pre-server.

"Do you not know," he said, "that an angel broke open the doors of the prison where Peter was confined, and delivered the apostle? Do you believe me, Maurice, to be inferior in power to that heavenly brother of mine, and do you suppose that I am unable to do for myself what he did for the fisherman of the lake of Tiberias?"

"Do not count on it, Arcade. He did it miraculously."

"Or by a stroke of luck, as a modern historian of the Church has it. But no matter. I will follow you. Just allow me to burn a few letters and to make a parcel of some books I shall need."

He threw some papers in the fire-place, put several volumes in his pockets, and followed his guide to the car, which was waiting for them not far off, outside the College of France. Maurice took the wheel. Imitating the Kerûb's prudence, he made so many windings and turnings, and so many rapid twists that he put all the swift and numerous cyclists, speeding in pursuit, off the scent. At length, having left wheelmarks in every direction all over the town, he stopped in the Rue de Rome, before the first-door flat, where the angel had first appeared.

On entering the dwelling which he had left eighteen months before to carry out his mission, Arcade remembered the irreparable past, and breathing in the scent used by Gilberte, his nostrils throbbed. He asked after Madame des Aubels.

"She is very well," replied Maurice. "A little plumper and very much more beautiful for it. She still bears you a grudge for your forward behaviour. I hope that she will one day forgive you, as I have forgiven you, and that she will forget your offence. But she is still very annoyed with you."

Young d'Esparvieu did the honours of his flat to his angel with the manners of a well-bred man and the tender solicitude of a friend. He showed him the folding bed which was opened every evening in the entrance hall and pushed into a dark cupboard in the morning. He showed him the dressing-table, with its accessories; the bath, the linen cupboard, the chest of drawers; gave him the necessary information regarding the heating and lighting; told him that his meals would be brought and the rooms cleaned by the concierge, and showed him which bell to press when he required that person's services. He told him also that he must consider himself at home, and receive whom he wished.

XXVIII

WHICH TREATS OF A PAINFUL DOMESTIC SCENE

SO long as Maurice confined his selection of mistresses to respectable women, his conduct had called forth no reproach. It was a different matter when he took up with Bouchotte. His mother, who had closed her eyes to liaisons which, though guilty, were elegant and discreet, was scandalised when it came to her ears that her son was openly parading about with a music-hall singer. By dint of much prying and probing, Berthe, Maurice's younger sister, had got to know of her brother's adventures, and she narrated them, without any indignation, to her young girl friends. His little brother Léon declared to his mother one day, in the presence of several ladies, that when he was big he, too, would go on the spree, like Maurice. This was a sore wound to the maternal heart of Madame d'Esparvieu.

About the same time there occurred a family event of a very grave nature which occasioned much alarm to Monsieur René d'Esparvieu. Drafts were presented to him signed in his name by his son. His writing had not been forged, but there was no doubt that it had been the son's intention to pass off the signature as his father's. It showed a perverted moral sense; whence it appeared that Maurice was living a life of profligacy, that he was running into debt and on the point of outraging the decencies. The pater-familias talked the matter over with his wife. It was arranged that he should give his son a very severe lecture, hint at vigorous corrective measures, and that in due course the mother should appear with gentle and sorrowing mien and endeavour to soothe the righteous indignation of the father. This plan being agreed upon, Monsieur René d'Esparvieu sent for his son to come to him in his

study. To add to the solemnity of the occasion, he had arrayed
himself in his frock-coat. As soon as Maurice saw it he knew there
was something serious in the wind. The head of the family was
pale, and his voice shook a little (for he was a nervous man), as
he declared that he would no longer put up with his son's irregular
behaviour, and insisted on an immediate and absolute reform. No
more wild courses, no more running into debt, no more undesirable
companions, but work, steadiness, and reputable connexions.

Maurice was quite willing to give a respectful reply to his father,
whose complaints, after all, were perfectly justified; but, unfortunately, Maurice, like his father, was shy, and the frock-coat which
Monsieur d'Esparvieu had donned in order to discharge his magisterial duty with greater dignity seemed to preclude the possibility
of any open and unconstrained intercourse. Maurice maintained an
awkward silence, which looked very much like insolence, and this
silence compelled Monsieur d'Esparvieu to reiterate his complaints,
this time with additional severity. He opened one of the drawers in
his historic bureau (the bureau on which Alexandre d'Esparvieu had
written his "Essay on the Civil and Religious Institutions of the
World"), and produced the bills which Maurice had signed.

"Do you know, my boy," said he, "that this is nothing more or
less than forgery? To make up for such grave misconduct as
that——"

At this moment Madame d'Esparvieu, as arranged, entered the
room attired in her walking-dress. She was supposed to play the
angel of forgiveness, but neither her appearance nor her disposition was suitable to the part. She was harsh and unsympathetic.
Maurice harboured within him the seeds of all the ordinary and
necessary virtues. He loved his mother and respected her. His love,
however, was more a matter of duty than of inclination, and his
respect arose from habit rather than from feeling. Madame René
d'Esparvieu's complexion was blotchy, and having powdered herself in order to appear to advantage at the domestic tribunal, the
colour of her face suggested raspberries sprinkled over with sugar.
Maurice, being possessed of some taste, could not help realising
that she was ugly and rather repulsively so. He was out of tune
with her, and when she began to go through all the accusations his
father had brought against him, making them out to be blacker
than ever, the prodigal turned away his head to conceal his irrita-
tion.

"Your Aunt de Saint-Fain," she went on, "met you in the street
in such disgraceful company that she was really thankful that you
forbore to greet her."

"Aunt de Saint-Fain!" Maurice broke out. "I like to hear her
talking about scandals! Everyone knows the sort of life she has
led, and now the old hypocrite wants to——"

He stopped. He had caught sight of his father, whose face was even more eloquent of sorrow than of anger. Maurice began to feel as though he had committed murder, and could not imagine how he had allowed such words to escape him. He was on the point of bursting into tears, falling on his knees, and imploring his father to forgive him, when his mother, looking up at the ceiling, said with a sigh:

"What offence can I have committed against God, to have brought such a wicked son into the world?"

This speech struck Maurice as a piece of ridiculous affectation, and it pulled him up with a jerk. The bitterness of contrition suddenly gave place to the delicious arrogance of wrong-doing. He plunged wildly into a torrent of insolence and revolt, and breathlessly delivered himself of utterances quite unfit for a mother's ear.

"If you will have it, mamma, rather than forbid me to continue my friendship with a talented lyrical artist, you would be better employed in preventing my elder sister, Madame de Margy, from appearing, night after night, in society and at the theatres with a contemptible and disgusting individual that everybody knows is her lover. You should also keep an eye on my little sister Jeanne, who writes objectionable letters to herself in a disguised hand, and then, pretending she has found them in her prayer-book, shows them to you with assumed innocence, to worry and alarm you. It would be just as well, too, if you prevented my little brother Léon, a child of seven, from being quite so much with Mademoiselle Caporal, and you might tell your maid . . ."

"Get out, sir, I will not have you in the house!" cried Monsieur René d'Esparvieu, white with anger, pointing a trembling finger at the door.

XXIX

WHEREIN WE SEE HOW THE ANGEL, HAVING BE-COME A MAN, BEHAVES LIKE A MAN, COVETING AN-OTHER'S WIFE AND BETRAYING HIS FRIEND. IN THIS CHAPTER THE CORRECTNESS OF YOUNG D'ESPAR-VIEU'S CONDUCT WILL BE MADE MANIFEST

THE angel was pleased with his lodging. He worked of a morning, went out in the afternoon, heedless of detectives, and came home to sleep. As in days gone by, Maurice received Madame des Aubels twice or thrice a week in the room in which they had seen the apparition.

All went very well until one morning Gilberte, having, the night before, left her little velvet bag on the table in the blue room, came to find it, and discovered Arcade stretched on the couch in his pyjamas, smoking a cigarette, and dreaming of the conquest of Heaven. She gave a loud scream.

"You, Monsieur! Had I thought to find you here, you may be quite sure I should not . . . I came to fetch my little bag, which is in the next room. Allow me. . . ." And she slipped past the angel, cautiously and quickly, as if he were a brazier.

Madame des Aubels that morning, in her pale green tailor-made costume, was deliciously attractive. Her tight skirt displayed her movements, and her every step was one of those miracles of Nature which fill men's hearts with amazement.

She reappeared, bag in hand.

"Once more—I ask your pardon. . . . I never dreamt that . . ."

Arcade begged her to sit down and to stay a moment.

"I never expected, Monsieur," said she, "that you would be doing the honours of this flat. I knew how dearly Monsieur d'Esparvieu loved you. . . . Nevertheless, I had no idea that . . ."

The sky had suddenly grown overcast. A brownish glare began to steal into the room. Madame des Aubels told him she had walked for her health's sake, but a storm was brewing, and she asked if a carriage could be called for her.

Arcade flung himself at Gilberte's feet, took her in his arms as one takes a precious piece of china, and murmured words which, being meaningless in themselves, expressed desire.

She put her hands over his eyes and on his lips, and exclaimed, "I hate you!"

And shaking with sobs, she asked for a drink of water. She was choking. The angel went to her assistance. In this moment of extreme peril she defended herself courageously. She kept saying: "No! . . . No! . . . I will not love you. I should love you too well. . . ." Nevertheless she succumbed.

In the sweet familiarity which followed their mutual astonishment she said to him:

"I have often asked after you. I knew that you were an assiduous frequenter of the playhouses at Montmartre,—that you were often seen with Mademoiselle Bouchotte, who, nevertheless, is not at all pretty. I knew that you had become very smart, and that you were making a good deal of money. I was not surprised. You were born to succeed. The day of your"—and she pointed at the spot between the window and the wardrobe with the mirror—"apparition, I was vexed with Maurice for having given you a suicide's rags to wear. You pleased me. . . . Oh, it was not your good looks! Don't think that women are as sensitive as people say to outward attractions. We consider other things in love. There is a sort of—— Well, anyhow I loved you as soon as I saw you."

The shadows grew deeper.

She asked:

"You are not an angel, are you? Maurice believes you are; but he believes so many things, Maurice." She questioned Arcade with her eyes and smiled maliciously. "Confess that you have been fooling him, and that you are no angel?"

Arcade replied:

"I only aspire to please you; I will always be what you want me to be."

Gilberte decided that he was no angel; first, because one never is an angel; secondly, for more detailed reasons which drew her thoughts to the question of love. He did not argue the matter with her, and once again words were found inadequate to express their feelings.

Outside, the rain was falling thick and fast, the windows were streaming, lightning lit up the muslin curtains, and thunder shook the panes. Gilberte made the sign of the Cross and remained with her head hidden in her lover's bosom.

At this moment Maurice entered the room. He came in wet and smiling, confident, tranquil, happy, to announce to Arcade the good news that with his half-share in the previous day's race at Longchamps the angel had won twelve times his stake. Surprising the lady and the angel in their embrace, he became furious; anger gripped the muscles of his throat, his face grew red with blood, and the veins stood out on his forehead. He sprang with clenched fists toward Gilberte, and then suddenly stopped.

Interrupted motion was transformed into heat. Maurice fumed. His anger did not arm him, like Archilochus, with lyrical vengeance. He merely applied an offensive epithet to his unfaithful one.

Meanwhile she had recovered her dignified bearing. She rose, full of modesty and grace, and gave her accuser a look which expressed both offended virtue and loving forgiveness.

But as young d'Esparvieu continued to shower coarse and monotonous insults on her, she grew angry in her turn.

"You are a pretty sort of person, are you not?" she said. "Did I run after this Arcade of yours? It was you who brought him here, and in what a state, too! You had only one idea: to give me up to your friend. Well, Monsieur, you can do as you like—I am not going to oblige you."

Maurice d'Esparvieu replied simply, "Get out of it, you trollop!" And he made a motion as if to push her out. It pained Arcade to see his mistress treated so disrespectfully, but he thought he lacked the necessary authority to interfere with Maurice. Madame des Aubels, who had lost none of her dignity, fixed young d'Esparvieu with her imperious gaze, and said:

"Go and get me a carriage."

And so great is the power of woman over a well-bred soul, in a gallant nation, that the young Frenchman went immediately and told the concierge to call a taxi. Madame des Aubels, with a studied exhibition of charm in every movement, took leave of them, throwing Maurice the contemptuous look that a woman owes to him whom she has deceived. Maurice witnessed her departure with an outward expression of indifference he was far from feeling. Then he turned to the angel clad in the flowered pyjamas which Maurice himself had worn the day of the apparition; and this circumstance, trifling in itself, added fuel to the anger of the host who had been thus shamefully deceived.

"Well," he said, "you may pride yourself on being a despicable individual. You have behaved basely, and all for nothing. If the woman took your fancy, you had but to tell me. I was tired of her. I had had enough of her. I would have willingly left her to you."

He spoke thus to hide his pain, for he loved Gilberte more than ever, and the creature's treachery caused him great suffering. He pursued:

"I was about to ask you to take her off my hands. But you have followed your lower nature—you have behaved like a sweep."

If at this solemn moment Arcade had but spoken one word from his heart, Maurice would have burst into tears, and forgiven his friend and his mistress, and all three would have become content and happy once again. But Arcade had not been nourished on the milk of human kindness. He had never suffered, and did not know how to sympathise with suffering. He replied with frigid wisdom:

"My dear Maurice, that same necessity which orders and constrains the actions of living beings, produces effects that are often unexpected, and sometimes absurd. Thus it is that I have been led to displease you. You would not reproach me if you had a good philosophical understanding of nature; for you would then know that free-will is but an illusion, and that physiological affinities are as exactly determined as are chemical combinations, and, like them, may be summed up in a formula. I think that, in your case, it might be possible to inculcate these truths, but it would be a difficult task, and maybe they would not bring you the serenity which eludes you. It is fitting, therefore, that I should leave this spot, and——"

"Stay," said Maurice.

Maurice had a very clear sense of social obligations. He put honour, when he thought about it, above everything. So now he told himself very forcibly that the outrage he had suffered could only be wiped out with blood. This traditional idea instantly lent an unexpected nobility to his speech and bearing.

"It is I, Monsieur," said he, "who will quit this place, never to return. You will remain here, since you are a refugee. My seconds will wait upon you."

The angel smiled.

"I will receive them, if it gives you pleasure, but, bethink you, my dear Maurice, I am invulnerable. Celestial spirits even when they are materialised cannot be touched by point of sword or pistol shot. Consider, my dear Maurice, the awkward situation in which this fatal inequality puts me, and realise that in refusing to appoint seconds I cannot give as a reason my celestial nature,—it would be unprecedented."

"Monsieur," replied the heir of the Bussart d'Esparvieu, "you should have thought of that before you insulted me."

Out he marched haughtily; but no sooner was he in the street than he staggered like a drunken man. The rain was still falling. He walked unseeing, unhearing, at haphazard, dragging his feet in the gutters through pools of water, through heaps of mud. He followed the outer boulevards for a long time, and at length, fordone with weariness, lay down on the edge of a piece of waste land. He was muddied up to the eyes, mud and tears smeared his face, the brim of his hat was dripping with rain. A passer-by, taking him for a beggar, tossed him a copper. He picked it up, put it carefully in his waistcoat pocket, and set off to find his seconds.

XXX

WHICH TREATS OF AN AFFAIR OF HONOUR, AND WHICH WILL AFFORD THE READER AN OPPORTUNITY OF JUDGING WHETHER, AS ARCADE AFFIRMS, THE EXPERIENCE OF OUR FAULTS MAKES BETTER MEN AND WOMEN OF US

THE ground chosen for the combat was Colonel Manchon's garden, on the Boulevard de la Reine at Versailles. Messieurs de la Verdelière and Le Truc de Ruffec, who had both of them constant practice in affairs of honour and knew the rules with great exactness, assisted Maurice d'Esparvieu. No duel was ever fought in the Catholic world without Monsieur de la Verdelière being present; and, in making application to this swordsman, Maurice had conformed to custom, though not without a certain reluctance, for he had been notorious as the lover of Madame de la Verdelière; but Monsieur de la Verdelière was not to be looked upon as a husband. He was an institution. As to Monsieur Le Truc de Ruffec, honour was his only known profession and avowedly his sole resource, and when the matter was made the subject of ill-natured comment in Society, the question was asked what finer career than that of honour Monsieur Le Truc de Ruffec could possibly have adopted. Arcade's seconds were Prince Istar and Théophile. The celestial musician had not voluntarily nor with a good grace taken a hand in this affair. He had a horror of every kind of violence and disapproved of single combat. The report of pistols and the clash of swords were intolerable to him, and the sight of blood made him faint. This gentle son of

Heaven had obstinately refused to act as second to his brother Arcade, and to bring him to the starting-point the Kerûb had had to threaten to break a bottle of panclastite over his head.

Besides the combatants, the seconds, and the doctors, the only people in the garden were a few officers from the barracks at Versailles and several reporters. Although young d'Esparvieu was known merely as a young man of family, and Arcade had never been heard of at all, the duel had attracted quite a large crowd of inquisitive individuals, and the windows of the adjoining houses were crammed with photographers, reporters, and Society people. What had aroused much curiosity was that a woman was known to be the cause of the quarrel. Many mentioned Bouchotte, but the majority said it was Madame des Aubels. It had been remarked upon, moreover, that duels in which Monsieur de la Verdelière acted as second drew all Paris.

The sky was a soft blue, the garden all a-bloom with roses, a blackbird was piping in a tree. Monsieur de la Verdelière, who, stick in hand, conducted the affair, laid the points of the swords together, and said:

"Allez, Messieurs."

Maurice d'Esparvieu attacked by doubling and beating the blade. Arcade retired, keeping his sword in line. The first engagement was without result. The seconds were under the impression that Monsieur d'Esparvieu was in a grievous state of nervous irritability, and that his adversary would wear him down. In the second encounter Maurice attacked wildly, spread out his arms, and exposed his breast. He attacked as he advanced, gave a straight thrust, and the point of his sword grazed Arcade on the shoulder. The latter was thought to be wounded. But the seconds ascertained with surprise that it was Maurice who had received a scratch on the wrist. Maurice asserted that he felt nothing, and Dr. Quille declared, after examination, that his client might continue the fight. After the regulation quarter of an hour the duel was resumed. Maurice attacked with fury. His adversary was obviously nursing him, and, what disturbed Monsieur de la Verdelière, seemed to be paying very little attention to his own defence. At the opening of the fifth bout, a black spaniel that had got into the garden no one knew how rushed out from a clump of rose-bushes, made its way on to the space reserved for the combatants, and, in spite of sticks and cries, ran in between Maurice's legs. The latter seemed as though his arm were benumbed, merely gave a shoulder-thrust at his invulnerable opponent. He then delivered a straight lunge and impaled his arm on his adversary's sword, which made a deep wound just below the elbow.

Monsieur de la Verdelière stopped the fight, which had lasted an hour and a half. Maurice was conscious of a painful shock. They laid him down on a grassy bank against a wall covered with wistaria. While the surgeon was dressing the wound Maurice called Arcade and offered him his wounded hand. And when the victor, saddened with his victory, advanced, Maurice embraced him ten derly, saying:

"Be generous, Arcade; forgive my treachery. Now that we have fought, I can ask you to be reconciled with me."

He embraced his friend, weeping, and whispered in his ear:

"Come and see me, and bring Gilberte."

Maurice, who was still unreconciled with his parents, was taken to the little flat in the Rue de Rome. No sooner was he stretched on the bed at the far end of the bedroom where the curtains were drawn as on the day of the apparition, than he saw Arcade and Gilberte appear. He began to suffer greatly from his wound; his temperature was rising, but he was at peace, happy and contented. Angel and woman, both in tears, threw themselves at the foot of the bed. He took both their hands with his left, smiled on them, and kissed them tenderly.

"I am sure now that I shall never quarrel with either of you again; you will deceive me no more. I now know you are capable of anything."

Gilberte, weeping, swore that Maurice had been misled by appearances, that she had never betrayed him with Arcade, that she had never betrayed him at all. And in a great gush of sincerity she persuaded herself that this was so.

"You wrong yourself, Gilberte," replied the wounded man. "It did happen; it had to. And it is well. Gilberte, you were basely false to me with my best friend in this very room, and you were right. If you had not been we should not be here, reunited, all three of us, and I should not be at your side tasting the greatest happiness of my life. Oh, Gilberte, how wrong of you to deny a perfect and accomplished fact!"

"If you wish, my friend," replied Gilberte, a little acidly, "I will not deny it. But it will only be to please you."

Maurice made her sit down on the bed, and begged Arcade to be seated in the arm-chair.

"My friend," said Arcade, "I was innocent. I became man. Straightway I did evil. Then I became better."

"Do not let us exaggerate things," said Maurice. "Let's have a game of bridge."

Scarcely, however, had the patient seen three aces in his hand and called "no trumps," than his eyes began to swim, the cards slipped from his fingers, head fell heavily back on the pillow, and he complained of a violent headache. Almost immediately, Madame des Aubels went off to pay some calls, for she made a point of appearing in Society, in order that the calmness and confidence of her demeanour might give the lie to the various rumours that were current concerning her. Arcade saw her to the door, and, with a kiss, inhaled from her a delicate perfume which he brought back with him into the room where Maurice lay dozing.

"I am perfectly content," murmured the latter, "that things should have happened as they have."

"It was bound to be so," answered the Spirit. "All the other angels in revolt would have done as I did with Gilberte. 'Women,' saith the Apostle, 'should pray with their heads covered, because of the angels,' and the Apostle speaks thus because he knows that the angels are disturbed when they look upon them and see that they are beautiful. No sooner do they touch the earth than they desire to embrace mortal women and fulfil their desire. Their clasp is full of strength and sweetness, they hold the secret of those ineffable caresses which plunge the daughters of men into unfathomable depths of delight. Laying upon the lips of their happy victims a honey that burns like fire, making their veins flow with torrents of refreshing flames, they leave them raptured and undone."

"Stop your clatter, you unclean beast," cried the wounded one.

"One word more!" said the angel; "just one other word, my dear Maurice, to bear out what I say, and I will let you rest quietly. There's nothing like having sound references. In order to assure yourself that I am not deceiving you, Maurice, on this subject of the amorous embraces of angels and women, look up Justin, *Apologies,* I and II; Flavius Josephus, *Jewish Antiquities,* Book I, Chapter III; Athenagoras, *Concerning the Resurrection;* Lactantius, Book II, Chapter XV; Tertullian, *On the Veil of the Virgins;* Marcus of Ephesus in *Psellus;* Eusebius, *Præparatio Evangelica,* Book V, Chapter IV; Saint Ambrose, in his book on *Noah and the Ark,* Chapter V; Saint Augustine, in his *City of God,* Book XV, Chapter XXIII; Father Meldonat, the Jesuit, *Treatise on Demons,* page 248; Pierre Lebyer the King's Counsellor——"

"Arcade, please, for pity's sake, be quiet; do, please do, and send this dog away," cried Maurice, whose face was burning, and whose eyes were starting from his head; for in his delirium he thought he saw a black spaniel on his bed.

Madame de la Verdelière, who was assiduous in every modish and patriotic practice, was reckoned, in the best French society, as one of the most gracious of the great ladies interested in good works. She came herself to ask for news of Maurice, and offered to nurse the wounded man. But at the vehement instigation of Madame des Aubels, Arcade shut the door in her face. Expressions of sympathy were showered upon Maurice. Piled on the salver, visiting cards displayed their innumerable little dogs' ears. Monsieur Le Truc de Ruffec was one of the first to show his manly sympathy at the flat in the Rue de Rome, and, holding out his loyal hand, asked young d'Esparvieu as one honourable man to another for twenty-five louis to pay a debt of honour.

"Of course, my dear Maurice, that is the sort of thing one could not ask of everybody."

The same day Monsieur Gaétan came to press his nephew's hand. The latter introduced Arcade.

"This is my guardian angel, whose foot you thought so beautiful when you saw the print it had made on the tell-tale powder, uncle. He appeared to me last year in this very room. You don't believe it? Well, it is true, nevertheless."

Then turning towards the Spirit he said:

"What say you, Arcade? The Abbé Patouille, who is a great theologian and a good priest, does not believe that you are an angel; and Uncle Gaétan, who doesn't know his catechism and hasn't a scrap of religion in him, doesn't think so either. They deny you, the pair of them; the one because he has faith, the other because he hasn't. After that you may be sure that your history, if ever it comes to be narrated, will scarcely appear credible. Moreover, the man that took it into his head to tell your story would not be a man of taste, and would not come in for much approval. For your story is not a pretty one. I love you, but I sit in judgment upon you, too. Since you fell into atheism, you have become an abominable scoundrel. A bad angel, a bad friend, a traitor, and a homicide, for I suppose it was to bring about my death that you sent that black spaniel between my legs on the duelling-ground."

The angel shrugged his shoulders and, addressing Gaétan, said:

"Alas! Monsieur, I am not surprised at finding little credit in your eyes. I have been told that you have fallen out with the Judæo-Christian heaven, which is where I came from."

"Monsieur," answered Gaétan, "my faith in Jehovah is not sufficiently strong to enable me to believe in his angels."

"Monsieur, he whom you call Jehovah is really a coarse and ignorant demiurge, and his name is Ialdabaoth."

"In that case, Monsieur, I am perfectly ready to believe in him. He is a narrow-minded ignoramus, is he? Then belief in his existence offers me no further difficulty. How is he getting on?"

"Badly! We are going to lay him low next month."

"Don't make too sure of that, Monsieur. You remind me of my brother-in-law, Cuissart, who has been expecting to hear of the fall of the Republic for the past thirty years."

"You see, Arcade," exclaimed Maurice, "Uncle Gaétan thinks as I do. He knows you won't succeed."

"And, pray, Monsieur Gaétan, what makes you think I shall not succeed?"

"Your Ialdabaoth is still very powerful in this world, if he isn't in the other. In days gone by he used to be upheld by his priests, by those who believed in him. Now he is supported by those who do not believe in him, by the philosophers. A pedant of a fellow called Picrochole has recently come on the scene who wants to make a bankrupt of science in order to do a good turn to the Church. And just lately Pragmatism has been invented for the express purpose of gaining credit for religion in the minds of rationalists."

"You have been studying Pragmatism?"

"Not I! I was frivolous once, and I went in for metaphysics. I read Hegel and Kant. I have become serious with years, and now I only trouble myself about things evident to the senses: what the eye can see or what the ear can hear. Man is summed up in Art. All the rest is moonshine."

Thus the conversation went on until evening; it was marked by obscenities that would have brought a blush—I will not say to a cuirassier, for cuirassiers are frequently chaste, but even to a Parisienne.

Monsieur Sariette came to see his old pupil. When he entered the room the bust of Alexandre d'Esparvieu seemed to take shape behind the librarian's bald head. He drew near the bed. In the place of blue curtains, mirrored wardrobe, and chimney-piece, there straightway came into view the heavy-laden book cases of the room of the globes and busts, and the air was heavy with piles of papers, records, and files. Monsieur Sariette could not be dissociated from his library; one could not conceive of him or even see him apart from it. He himself was paler, more vague, more shadowy, and more a creature of the fancy than the fancies he evoked.

Maurice, who had grown very quiet, was sensible of this mark of friendship.

"Sit down, Monsieur Sariette,—you know Madame des Aubels. May I introduce Arcade to you,—my guardian angel. It was he who, while yet invisible, pillaged your library for two years, made you lose all desire for food and drink, and drove you to the verge of madness. He it was who moved piles of books from the room of the busts to my summer-house one day; under your very nose, he took away I know not what precious volumes; and was the cause of your falling on the staircase; another day he took a volume of Salomon Reinach's, and, forced to go out with me (for he never left me, as I have learnt later), he let the volume drop in the gutter of the Rue Princesse. Forgive him, Monsieur Sariette,—he had no pockets. He was invisible. I bitterly regret, Monsieur Sariette, that all your old books were not devoured by fire or swallowed up by a flood. They made my angel lose his head. He became man, and now knows neither faith nor obedience to laws. It is I, now, who am his guardian angel. God knows how it will all end."

While listening to this speech, Monsieur Sariette's face took on an expression of infinite, irreparable, eternal sadness; the sadness of a mummy. Rising to take his leave, the sorrowful librarian murmured in Arcade's ear:

"The poor child is very ill. He is delirious."

Maurice called the old man back.

"Do stay, Monsieur Sariette. You shall have a game of bridge with us. Monsieur Sariette, listen to my advice. Do not do as I did —do not keep bad company. You will be lost. I shudder at the mere thought. Monsieur Sariette, do not go yet. I have something very important to ask you. When you come again, bring me a book on the truth of religion, so that I may study it. I must restore to my guardian-angel the faith which he has lost."

XXXI

WHEREIN WE ARE LED TO MARVEL AT THE READI-NESS WITH WHICH AN HONEST MAN OF TIMID AND GENTLE NATURE CAN COMMIT A HORRIBLE CRIME

PROFOUNDLY distressed by the dark utterances of young Maurice, Monsieur Sariette took a motor-omnibus, and went to see Père Guinardon, his friend, his only friend, the one person in the whole world whom it gave him pleasure to see and hear. When Monsieur Sariette entered the shop in the Rue de Courcelles, Guinardon was alone, dozing in the depths of an antique arm-chair. His face, surrounded by his curly hair and luxuriant beard, was crimson in hue. Little violet filaments spread a network about the fleshy part of his nose, to which the wines of Burgundy had imparted a purple tint; for there was no longer any disguising the fact, Père Guinardon drank. Two feet away from him, on the fair Octavie's work-table, a rose, all but withered, drooped in an empty vase, and in a basket a piece of embroidery was lying unfinished and neglected. The young Octavie's absences from the shop were growing more and more frequent, and Monsieur Blancmesnil never called when she was not there. The reason of this was that they were meeting three times a week at five o'clock in a house close to the Champs Elysées. Père Guinardon knew nothing of that. He did not know the full extent of his misfortune, but he suffered.

Monsieur Sariette shook his old friend by the hand; but he did not enquire for the young Octavie, for he refused to recognise the connexion. He would sooner have talked about Zéphyrine, who had been so cruelly deserted, and whom he hoped the old man would make his lawful wife. But Monsieur Sariette was prudent. He contented himself with asking Guinardon how he was.

"Perfectly well," was Guinardon's reply; but he felt ill, for either age and love-making had undermined his sturdy constitution, or else young Octavie's faithlessness had dealt her lover a fatal blow.

"God be praised," he went on, "I still retain my powers of mind and body. I am chaste. Be chaste, Sariette. Chastity is strength."

That evening Père Guinardon had taken some specially valuable books out of the king-wood cabinet to show to a distinguished bibliophile, Monsieur Victor Meyer, and after the latter's departure he had dropped off to sleep without putting them back in their places. Books had an attraction for Monsieur Sariette, and seeing these particular volumes on the marble top of the cabinet, he began to examine them with interest. The first one he looked at was *La Pucelle,* in morocco, with the English continuation. Doubtless it pained his patriotic and Christian heart to admire its text and illustrations, but a good copy was always virtuous and pure in his sight. Continuing to chat very affectionately with Guinardon, he picked up, one by one, the books which the antiquary had, for one reason or another—binding, illustrations, distinguished ownership, or scarcity—added to his stock.

Suddenly a glorious shout of joy and love broke from his lips. He had discovered the *Lucretius* of the Prior de Vendôme, his *Lucretius,* and he was clasping it to his bosom.

"Once again I behold you," he sighed, as he pressed it to his lips.

At first Père Guinardon could not quite make out what his old friend was talking about; but when the latter declared to him that the volume was from the d'Esparvieu collection, that it belonged to him, Sariette, and that he was going to take it away without further ado, the antiquary completely woke up, got on his legs, declared emphatically that the book belonged to him, Guinardon, by right of true and lawful purchase, and that he would not part with it unless he got five thousand francs for it cash down.

"You don't take in what I am telling you," answered Sariette. "The book belongs to the d'Esparvieu library; I must restore it to its place."

"*Pas de ça, Lisette*"—— hummed Guinardon.

"The book belongs to me, I tell you!"

"You are crazy, my good Sariette!"

And noticing that, as a matter of fact, the librarian had a wandering look in his eye, he took the book from him, and tried to change the conversation.

"Have you seen, Sariette, that the rascals are going to rip up the Palais Mazarin, and cover up the very heart and centre of the Old Town, the finest and most venerable place in the whole of Paris, with the deuce knows what works of art of theirs? They are worse than the Vandals, for the Vandals, although they destroyed the buildings of antiquity, did not replace them with hideous and disgusting erections and atrocious bridges like the Pont d'Alexandre. And your poor Rue Garancière, Sariette, has fallen a prey to the barbarians. What have they done with the pretty bronze mask of the Palace fountain?"

Monsieur Sariette never listened to a word of all this.

"Guinardon, you have not understood me. Now listen. This book belongs to the d'Esparvieu library. It was taken away, how or by whom I know not. Dreadful and mysterious things went on in that library. But, anyhow, the book was stolen. I need scarcely appeal to your sentiments of scrupulous probity, my dear friend. You would not like to be regarded as the receiver of stolen goods. Give me the book. I will return it to Monsieur d'Esparvieu, who will duly requite you; of that you may be sure. Rely on his generosity, and you will be acting like the downright good fellow that you are."

The antiquary smiled a bitter smile.

"Catch me relying on the generosity of that old curmudgeon of a d'Esparvieu. Why, he'd skin a flea to get its coat. Look at me, Sariette, old boy, and tell me if I look like a dunderhead. You know perfectly well that d'Esparvieu refused to give fifty francs in a second-hand shop for a portrait of Alexandre d'Esparvieu, the founder of the family, by Hersent, and that consequently the founder of the family has had to remain on the Boulevard Montparnasse, propped against a Jew hawker's stall, just opposite the cemetery, where all the dogs of the neighbourhood come and make water on him. Catch me trusting to Monsieur d'Esparvieu's liberality! You've got some bright ideas in your head, you have!"

"Very well, Guinardon, I myself will undertake to pay you any indemnity that a board of arbitrators may fix upon. Do you hear?"

"Now don't go and do the handsome for people who won't give you so much as a thank-you. This man, d'Esparvieu, has taken your knowledge, your energies, your whole life for a salary that even a valet wouldn't accept. So leave that idea alone. In any case it is too late. The book is sold."

"Sold? To whom?" asked Sariette in agonized tones.

"What does that matter? You'll never see it again. You'll hear no more about it; it's off to America."

"To America! The *Lucretius* with the arms of Philippe de Vendôme and marginalia in Voltaire's own hand! My *Lucretius* off to America!"

Père Guinardon began to laugh.

"My dear Sariette, you remind me of the Chevalier des Grieux when he learns that his darling mistress is to be transported to the Mississippi. 'My dear mistress going to the Mississippi!' says he."

"No! no!" answered Sariette, very pale, "this book shall not go to America. It shall return, as it ought, to the d'Esparvieu library. Let me have it, Guinardon."

The antiquary made a second attempt to put an end to an interview that now looked as if it might take an ugly turn.

"My good Sariette, you haven't told me what you think of my Greco. You never so much as glanced at it. It is an admirable piece of work all the same."

And Guinardon, putting the picture in a good light, went on:

"Now just look at Saint Francis here, the poor man of the Lord, the brother of Jesus. See how his fuliginous body rises heavenward like the smoke from an agreeable sacrifice, like the sacrifice of Abel."

"Give me the book, Guinardon," said Sariette. without turning his head; "give me the book."

The blood suddenly flew to Père Guinardon's head.

"That's enough of it," he shouted, as red as a turkey-cock, the veins standing out on his forehead.

And he dropped the *Lucretius* into his jacket pocket.

Straightway old Sariette flew at the antiquary, assailed him with sudden fury, and, frail and weakly as he was, butted him back into young Octavie's arm-chair.

Guinardon, in furious amazement, belched forth the most horrible abuse on the old maniac and gave him a punch that sent him staggering back four paces against the *Coronation of the Virgin,* by Fra Angelico, which fell down with a crash. Sariette returned to the charge, and tried to drag the book out of the pocket in which it lay hid. This time Père Guinardon would really have floored him had he not been blinded by the blood that was rushing to his head, and hit sideways at the work-table of his absent mistress. Sariette fastened himself on to his bewildered adversary, held him down in the arm-chair, and with his little bony hands clutched him by the neck, which, red as it was already, became a deep crimson. Guinardon struggled to get free, but the little fingers, feeling the mass of soft, warm flesh about them, embedded themselves in it with delicious ecstasy. Some unknown force made them hold fast to their prey. Guinardon's throat began to rattle, saliva was oozing from one corner of his mouth. His enormous frame quivered now and again beneath the grasp; but the tremors grew more and more intermittent and spasmodic. At last they ceased. The murderous hands did not let go their hold. Sariette had to make a violent effort to loose them. His temples were buzzing. Nevertheless he could hear the rain falling outside, muffled steps going past on the pavement, newspaper men shouting in the distance. He could see umbrellas passing along in the dim light. He drew the book from the dead man's pocket and fled.

The fair Octavie did not go back to the shop that night. She went to sleep in a little entresol underneath the bric-a-brac stores which Monsieur de Blancmesnil had recently bought for her in this same Rue de Courcelles. The workman whose task it was to shut up the shop found the antiquary's body still warm. He called Madame Lenain, the concierge, who laid Guinardon on the couch, lit a couple of candles, put a sprig of box in a saucer of holy water, and closed the dead man's eyes. The doctor who was called in to certify the death ascribed it to apoplexy.

Zéphyrine, informed of what had happened by Madame Lenain, hastened to the house, and sat up all night with the body. The dead man looked as if he were sleeping. In the flickering light of the candles El Greco's Saint mounted upwards like a wreath of smoke, the gold of the Primitives gleamed in the shadows. Near the deathbed a little woman by Baudouin was plainly discernible giving herself a douche. All through the night Zéphyrine's lamentations could be heard fifty yards away.

"He's dead, he's dead!" she kept saying. "My friend, my divinity, my all, my love—— But no! he is not dead, he moves. It is I, Michel; I, your Zéphyrine. Awake, hear me! Answer me; I love you; if ever I caused you pain, forgive me. Dead! dead! O my God! See how beautiful he is. He was so good, so clever, so kind. My God! My God! My God! If I had been there he would not now be lying dead. Michel! Michel!"

When morning came she was silent. They thought she had fallen asleep. She was dead too.

XXXII

WHICH DESCRIBES HOW NECTAIRE'S FLUTE WAS HEARD IN THE TAVERN OF CLODOMIR

MADAME DE LA VERDELIÈRE having failed to force an *entrée* as sick-nurse, returned after several days had elapsed,—during the absence of Madame des Aubels,—to ask Maurice d'Esparvieu for his subscription to the French churches. Arcade led her to the bedside of the convalescent. Maurice whispered in the angel's ear:

"Traitor, deliver me from this ogress immediately, or you will be answerable for the evil which will soon befall."

"Be calm," said Arcade, with a confident air.

After the conventional complimentary flourishes, Madame de la Verdelière signed to Maurice to dismiss the angel. Maurice feigned not to understand. And Madame de la Verdelière disclosed the ostensible reason of her visit.

"Our churches," she said, "our beloved country churches,—what is to become of them?"

Arcade gazed at her angelically and sighed.

"They will disappear, Madame; they will fall into ruin. And what a pity! I shall be inconsolable. The church amid the villagers' cottages is like the hen amidst her chickens."

"Just so!" exclaimed Madame de la Verdelière with a delighted smile. "It is just like that."

"And the spires, Madame?"

"Oh, Monsieur, the spires! . . ."

"Yes, the spires, Madame, that stick up into the skies towards the little Cherubim, like so many syringes."

Madame de la Verdelière incontinently left the place.

That same day Monsieur l'Abbé Patouille came to offer the wounded man good counsel and consolation. He exhorted him to break with his bad companions and to be reconciled to his family.

He drew a picture of the sorrowful father, the mother in tears, ready to receive their long-lost child with open arms. Renouncing with manly effort a life of profligacy and deluding joys, Maurice would recover his peace and strength of mind, he would free himself from devouring chimeras, and shake off the Evil Spirit.

Young d'Esparvieu thanked Abbé Patouille for all his kindness, and made a protestation of his religious feelings.

"Never," said he, "have I had such faith. And never have I been in such need of it. Just imagine, Monsieur l'Abbé, I have to teach my guardian angel his catechism all over again, for he has quite forgotten it!"

Monsieur l'Abbé Patouille heaved a deep sigh, and exhorted his dear child to pray, there being no other resource but prayer for a soul assailed by the Devil.

"Monsieur l'Abbé," asked Maurice, "may I introduce my guardian angel to you? Do stay a moment; he has gone to get me some cigarettes."

"Unhappy child!"

And Abbé Patouille's fat cheeks drooped in token of affliction. But almost immediately they plumped up again, as a sign of lightheartedness. For in his heart there was matter for rejoicing. Public opinion was improving. The Jacobins, the Freemasons, the Coalitionists were everywhere in disgrace. The Smart Set led the way. The Académie Française was of the right way of thinking. The number of Christian schools was increasing by leaps and bounds. The young men of the Quartier Latin were submitting to the Church, and the École Normale exhaled the perfume of the seminary. The Cross was gaining the day; but money was wanted,— more money, always money.

After six weeks' rest, Maurice was allowed by his doctor to take a drive. He wore his arm in a sling. His mistress and his friend went with him. They drove to the Bois, and took a gentle pleasure in looking upon the grass and the trees. They smiled on everything and everything smiled on them. As Arcade had said, their faults had made them better. By the unlooked-for ways of jealousy and anger, Maurice had attained to calm and kindliness. He still loved Gilberte and he loved her with an indulgent love. The angel still desired her as much as ever, but having once possessed her, his desire had lost the sting of curiosity. Gilberte forbore trying to please, and thereby pleased the more. They drank milk at the Cascade, and found it good. They were all three innocent. Arcade forgot the injustice of the old tyrant of the world. But he was soon to be reminded of it.

On entering his friend's house, he found Zita awaiting him, looking like a statue in ivory and gold.

"You excite my pity," she said to him. "The day is at hand the like of which has never dawned since the beginning of Time, and perhaps will never dawn again before the Sun enters with all its train into the constellation of Hercules. We are on the eve of surprising Ialdabaoth in his palace of porphyry, and you, who are burning to deliver the heavens, who were so eager to enter in triumph into your emancipated country,—you suddenly forget your noble purpose and fall asleep in the arms of the daughters of men. What pleasure can you find in intercourse with these unclean little animals, composed, as they are, of elements so unstable that they may be said to be in a state of constant evanescence? O Arcade! I was indeed right to distrust you. You are but an intellectual; you do but feel idle curiosity. You are incapable of action."

"You misjudge me, Zita," replied the angel. "It is the nature of the sons of heaven to love the daughters of men. Corruptible though it be, the material part of women and of flowers charms the senses none the less. But not one of these little animals can make me forget my hatred and my love, and I am ready to rise up against Ialdabaoth."

Zita expressed her satisfaction at seeing him in this resolute mood. She urged him to pursue the accomplishment of this vast undertaking with undiminished ardour. Nothing must be hurried or deferred.

"A great action, Arcade, is made up of a multitude of small ones; the most majestic whole is composed of a thousand minute details. Let us neglect nothing."

She had come to take him to a meeting where his presence was required. They were to take a census of the revolutionaries.

She added but one word:

"Nectaire will be there."

When Maurice saw Zita, he deemed her lacking in attraction. She failed to please him because she was perfectly beautiful and because true beauty always caused him painful surprise. Zita inspired him with antipathy when he learned that she was an angel in revolt and that she had come to seek Arcade to take him away among the conspirators.

The poor child tried to retain his companion by all the means that his wit and the circumstances afforded him. If his guardian angel would only remain with him, he would take him to a magnificent boxing-match, to a "revue" where he would witness the apotheosis of Poincaré, or, lastly, to a certain house he knew of where he would behold women remarkable for their beauty, talents, vices, or deformities. But the angel would not allow himself to be tempted, and said he was going with Zita.

"What for?"

"To plot the conquest of the skies."

"Still the same nonsense! The conquest of —— but there, I proved to you that it was neither possible nor desirable."

"Good night, Maurice."

"You are going? Well, I will accompany you."

And Maurice, his arm in a sling, went with Arcade and Zita all the way to Clodomir's restaurant at Montmartre, where the tables were laid in an arbour in the garden.

Prince Istar and Théophile were already there, with a little creature who looked like a child, and was, in fact, a Japanese angel.

"We are only waiting for Nectaire," said Zita.

And at that moment the old gardener noiselessly appeared. He took his seat, and his dog lay down at his feet. French cooking is the best in the world. It is a glory that will transcend all others when humanity has grown wise enough to put the spit above the sword. Clodomir served the angels, and the mortal who was with them, with a soup made of cabbages and bacon, a loin of pork and kidneys cooked in wine, thereby proving himself a real Montmartre cook, and showing that he had not been spoilt by the Americans, who corrupt the most excellent *chefs* of the City of Restaurants.

Clodomir brought forth some Bordeaux, which, though unrecorded among the renowned vintages of Médoc, gave evidence by its choice and delicate aroma of the high nobility of its origin. We must not omit to chronicle that, after this wine and many others had been drunk, the cellarman, in solemn state, produced a Burgundy choice and rare, full-bodied yet not heavy, generous yet delicate, rich with the true Burgundian mellowness, a noble and, withal, a somewhat heady wine, that brought delight alike to mind and sense.

"Hail to thee, Dionysus, greatest of the Gods!" cried old Nectaire, raising his glass on high. "I drink to thee who wilt restore the Golden Age, and give again to mortal men, who will become heroes as of old, the grapes which the Lesbians used to cull, long since, from the vines of Methymna; who wilt restore the vineyards of Thasus, the white clusters of Lake Mareotis, the storehouses of Falernus, the vines of the Tmolus, and the wine of Phanae, of all wines the king. And the juice thereof shall be divine, and, as in old Silenus' day, men shall grow drunk with Wisdom and with Love."

When the coffee was served, Prince Istar, Zita, Arcade, and the Japanese angel took it in turns to give an account of the forces assembled against Ialdabaoth. Angels, in exchanging eternal bliss for the sufferings of an earthly life, grow in intelligence, acquire the means of going astray and the faculty of self-contradiction. Consequently their meetings, like those of men, are tumultuous and confused. Did one of them deal in figures, the others immediately called them in question. They could not add one number to another without quarrelling, and arithmetic itself, subjected to passion, lost its certitude. The Kerûb, who had brought with him the pious Théophile, waxed indignant when he heard the musician praising the Lord, and rained down such blows on his head as would have felled an ox. But the head of a musician is harder than a bucranium, and the blows which Théophile received did not avail to modify that angel's notion of divine providence. Arcade, having at great length set up his scientific idealism in opposition to Zita's pragmatism, the beautiful archangel told him that he argued badly.

"And you are surprised at that!" exclaimed young Maurice's guardian angel. "I argue, like you, in the language of human beings. And what is human language but the cry of the beasts of the forests or the mountains, complicated and corrupted by arrogant anthropoids. How then, Zita, can one be expected to argue well with a collection of angry or plaintive sounds like that? Angels do not reason at all; men, being superior to the angels, reason imperfectly. I will not mention the professors who think to define the absolute with the aid of cries that they have inherited from the pithecanthropoid monkeys, marsupials, and reptiles, their ancestors! It is a colossal joke! How it would amuse the demiurge, if he had any brains!"

It was a beautiful starlight night. The gardener was silent.

"Nectaire," said the beautiful archangel, "play to us on your flute, if you are not afraid that the Earth and Heaven will be stirred to their depths thereby."

Nectaire took up his flute. Young Maurice lighted a cigarette. The flame burnt brightly for a moment, casting back the sky and its stars into the shadows, and then died out. And Nectaire sang of the flame on his divine flute. The silvery voice soared aloft and sang:

"That flame was a whole universe which fulfilled its destiny in less than a minute. Suns and planets were formed therein. Venus Urania apportioned the orbits of the wandering spheres in those infinite spaces. Beneath the breath of Eros—the first of the gods,—plants, animals, and thought sprang into being. In the twenty seconds which hurried by betwixt the life and death of those worlds, civilizations were unfolded, and empires sank in long decline. Mothers shed tears, and songs of love, cries of hatred, and sighs of victims rose upward to the silent skies.

"In proportion to its minuteness, that universe lasted as long as this one—whereof we see a few atoms glittering above our heads—

has lasted or will last. They are, one no less than the other, but a gleam in the Infinite."

As the clear, pure notes welled up into the charmed air, the earth melted into a soft mist, the stars revolved rapidly in their orbits, the Great Bear fell asunder, its parts flew far and wide. Orion's belt was shattered; the Pole Star forsook its magnetic axis. Sirius, whose incandescent flame had lit up the far horizon, grew blue, then red, flickered, and suddenly died out. The shaken constellations formed new signs which were extinguished in their turn. By its incantations the magic flute had compressed into one brief moment the life and the movement of this universe which seems unchanging and eternal both to men and angels. It ceased, and the heavens resumed their immemorial aspect. Nectaire had vanished. Clodomir asked his guests if they were pleased with the cabbage soup which, in order that it might be strong, had been kept simmering for twenty-four hours on the fire, and he sang the praises of the Beaujolais which they had drunk.

The night was mild. Arcade, accompanied by his guardian angel, Théophile, Prince Istar, and the Japanese angel, escorted Zita home.

XXXIII

HOW A DREADFUL CRIME PLUNGES PARIS INTO A STATE OF TERROR

 HE city was asleep. Their footsteps rang loudly on the deserted pavement. Having reached the corner of the Rue Feutrier, half-way up Montmartre, the little company halted before the dwelling of the beautiful angel. Arcade was talking about the Thrones and Dominations with Zita, who, her finger on the bell, could not make up her mind to ring. Prince Istar was tracing the mechanism of a new sort of bomb on the pavement with the end of his stick, and bellowed so loudly that he woke the sleeping citizens and stirred into activity the amatory passions of the neighbouring Pasiphaës. Théophile was singing the barcarole from the second act of *Aline, Queen of Golconda* at the top of his voice. Maurice, his arm in a sling, was fencing left-handed with the Japanese, striking sparks from the pavement, and crying "A hit! a hit!" in a piercing voice.

Meanwhile Inspector Grolle at the corner of the next street was dreaming. He had the bearing of a Roman legionary and displayed all the characteristics of that proudly servile race, who, ever since men first took to building cities, have been the mainstay of Empires and the support of ruling houses. Inspector Grolle was very strong, but very tired. He suffered from an arduous profession and from lack of food. He was a man devoted to duty, but still a man, and he was unable to resist the wiles, the charms, and the blandishments of the gay ladies whom he met in swarms in the shadows along the empty streets and round about pieces of waste ground; he loved them. He loved like a soldier under arms. It tired him, but courage conquered fatigue. Though he had not yet reached the middle of Life's way, he longed for sweet repose and peaceful country pursuits. At the corner of the Rue Muller, on this mild night, he stood lost in thought. He was dreaming of the house where he was born, of the little olive wood, of his father's bit of ground, of his old mother, bent with long and heavy labour, whom he would never see again. Roused from his reverie by the nocturnal tumult, Inspector Grollé turned the corner of the street, and looked rather unfavourably at the band of loiterers, wherein his social instinct suspected enemies of law and order. He was patient and resolute. After a lengthy silence, he said, with awe-inspiring calm:

"Move on, there!"

But Maurice and the Japanese angel were fencing and heard nothing. The musician heard nothing but his own melodies. Prince Istar was absorbed in the explanation of explosive formulæ. Zita was discussing with Arcade the greatest enterprise that had ever been conceived since the solar system issued from its original nebula,—and thus they all remained unconscious of their surroundings.

"Move on, I tell you!" repeated Inspector Grollé.

This time the angels heard the solemn word of warning, but either through indifference or contempt, they neglected to obey, and continued their talk, their songs, and their cries.

"So you want to be taken up, do you?" shouted Inspector Grollé, clapping his great hand on Prince Istar's shoulder.

The Kerûb was indignant at this vile contact, and with one blow from his formidable fist sent the Inspector flying into the gutter. But Constable Fesandet was already running to his comrade's aid, and they both fell upon the Prince, whom they belaboured with mechanic fury, and whom, notwithstanding his strength and weight, they would perchance have dragged all bleeding to the police station, had not the Japanese angel overset them one after the other without effort, and reduced them to writhing and shrieking in the mud, before Maurice, Arcade, and Zita had time to intervene. As to the angelic musician, he stood apart trembling, and invoked the heavens.

At this moment two bakers who were kneading their dough in a neighbouring cellar ran out at the noise, in their white aprons, stripped to the waist. With an instinctive feeling for social solidarity they took the side of the downfallen police. Théophile conceived a just fear at the sight of them, and fled away; they caught

him and were about to hand him over to the guardians of the
peace, when Arcade and Zita tore him from their hands. The fight
continued, unequal and terrible, between the two angels and the
two bakers. Like an athlete of Lysippus in strength and beauty,
Arcade smothered his heavy adversary in his arms. The beautiful
archangel drove her dagger into the baker who had attacked her.
A dark stream of blood flowed down over his hairy chest, and the
two white-capped supporters of the law sank to the ground.

Constable Fesandet had fainted face downwards in the gutter.
But Inspector Grolle, who had got up, blew a blast on his whistle
loud enough to be heard at the neighbouring police-station, and
sprang upon young Maurice. who, having but one arm with which
to defend himself, fired his revolver with his left hand at the inspector, who put his hand to his heart, staggered, and dropped
down. He gave a long sigh, and the shadows of eternity darkened
his eyes.

Meanwhile, windows opened one by one, and heads looked out on
the street. A sound of heavy steps approached. Two policemen on
bicycles debouched upon the street. Thereupon Prince Istar flung a
bomb which shook the ground, put out the gas, shattered some of
the houses, and enveloped the fight of young Maurice and the
angels in a dense smoke.

Arcade and Maurice came to the conclusion that the safest thing
to do after this adventure was to return to the little flat in the Rue
de Rome. They would certainly not be sought for immediately and
probably not at all, the bomb thrown by the Kerûb having fortunately wiped out all witnesses of the affair. They fell asleep
towards dawn, and they had not yet awoke at ten o'clock in the
morning when the concierge brought their tea. While eating his
toast and butter and slice of ham, young d'Esparvieu remarked to
the angel:

"I used to think that a murder was something very extraordinary. Well, I was mistaken. It is the simplest, the most natural
action in the world."

"And of most ancient tradition," replied the angel. "For long
centuries it was both usual and necessary for man to kill and de-
spoil his fellows. It is still recommended in warfare. It is also honourable to attempt human life in certain definite circumstances, and
people approved when you wanted to assassinate me, Maurice, because it appeared to you that I had been intimate with your mistress. But killing a police-inspector is not the action of a man of
fashion."

"Be silent," exclaimed Maurice, "be silent, scoundrel! I killed
the poor Inspector instinctively, not knowing what I was doing. I
am grieved to my heart about it. But it is not I, it is you who are
the guilty one; you who are the murderer. It was you who lured
me along this path of revolt and violence which leads to the pit.

You have been my undoing. You have sacrificed my peace of mind, my happiness, to your pride and your wickedness, and all in vain; for I warn you, Arcade, you will not succeed in what you are undertaking."

The concierge brought in the newspapers. On seeing them Maurice grew pale. They announced the outrage in the Rue de Ramey in huge headlines:

"An Inspector killed—Two cyclist policemen and two bakers seriously wounded—Three houses blown up, numerous victims."

Maurice let the paper drop, and said in a weak, plaintive voice:

"Arcade, why did you not slay me in the little garden at Versailles amidst the roses, to the song of the blackbirds?"

Meanwhile terror reigned in Paris. In the public squares, and in the crowded streets, housewives, string-bag in hand, grew pale as

they listened to the story of the crime, and consigned the perpetrators to the most dreadful punishment. Shopkeepers, standing at the doors of their shops, put it all down to the anarchists, syndicalists, socialists, and radicals, and demanded that special measures should be taken against them.

The more thoughtful people recognized the handiwork of the Jew and the German, and demanded the expulsion of all aliens. Many vaunted the ways of America and advocated lynching. In addition to the printed news sinister rumours became current. Explosions had been heard at various places; everywhere bombs had been discovered; everywhere individuals, taken for malefactors, had been struck down by the popular arm and given up to justice, torn to ribbons. On the Place de la République a drunkard who was crying "Down with the police" was torn to pieces by the crowd.

The President of the Council and Minister of Justice held long conferences with the Prefect of Police, and they agreed to take immediate action. In order to allay the excitement of the Parisians, they arrested five or six hooligans out of the thirty thousand which the Capital contains. The chief of the Russian police, believing he recognised in this attack the methods of the Nihilists, demanded, on behalf of his Government, that a dozen refugees should be given up. The demand was immediately granted. Proceedings were also taken for certain individuals to be extradited to ensure the safety of the King of Spain.

On learning of these energetic measures, Paris breathed once more, and the evening papers congratulated the Government. There was excellent news of the wounded. They were out of danger and identified as their assailants all who were brought before them.

True, Inspector Grolle was dead; but two Sisters of Mercy kept vigil at his side, and the President of the Council came and laid the Cross of Honour on the breast of this victim of duty.

At night there were panics. In the Avenue de la Révolte the police, noticing a travelling acrobat's caravan on a piece of waste ground, took it for the retreat of a band of robbers. They whistled for help, and when they were a goodly number, attacked the caravan. Some worthy citizens joined them; fifteen thousand revolver-shots were fired, the caravan was blown up with dynamite, and among the débris they found the corpse of a monkey.

XXXIV

WHICH CONTAINS AN ACCOUNT OF THE ARREST OF BOUCHOTTE AND MAURICE, OF THE DISASTER WHICH BEFELL THE D'ESPARVIEU LIBRARY, AND OF THE DEPARTURE OF THE ANGELS

AURICE D'ESPARVIEU passed a terrible night. At the least sound he seized his revolver that he might not fall alive into the hands of justice. When morning came he snatched the newspapers from the hands of the concierge, devoured them greedily, and gave a cry of joy; he had just read that Inspector Grolle having been taken to the Morgue for the post-mortem, the police-surgeons had only discovered bruises and contusions of a very superficial nature, and stated that death had been brought about by the rupture of an aneurism of the aorta.

"You see, Arcade," he exclaimed triumphantly; "you see I am not an assassin. I am innocent. I could never have imagined how extremely agreeable it is to be innocent."

Then he grew thoughtful, and—no unusual phenomenon—reflection dissipated his gaiety.

"I am innocent,—but there is no disguising the fact," he said, shaking his head, "I am one of a band of malefactors. I live with miscreants. You are in your right place there, Arcade, for you are deceitful, cruel, and perverse. But I come of good family and have received an excellent education, and I blush for it."

"I also," said Arcade, "have received an excellent education."

"Where was that?"

"In Heaven."

"No, Arcade, no; you never had any education. If good principles had been inculcated into you, you would still hold them. Such principles are never lost. In my childhood I learnt to revere my family, my country, my religion. I have not forgotten the lesson and I never shall. Do you know what shocks me most in you? It is not your perversity, your cruelty, your black ingratitude; it is not your agnosticism, which may be borne with at a pinch; it is not your scepticism, though it is very much out of date (for since the national awakening there is no longer any scepticism in France);—no, what disgusts me in you is your lack of taste, the bad style of your ideas, the inelegance of your doctrines. You think like an intellectual, you speak like a freethinker, you have theories which reek of radicalism and Combeism and all ignoble systems. Get along with you! you disgust me. Arcade, my old friend, Arcade, my dear angel, Arcade, my beloved child, listen to your guardian angel!

Yield to my prayers, renounce your mad ideas; become good, simple, innocent, and happy once more. Put on your hat, come with me to Nôtre-Dame. We will say a prayer and burn a candle together."

Meanwhile public opinion was still active in the matter; the leading papers, the organs of the national awakening, in articles of real elevation and real depth, unravelled the philosophy of this monstrous attack which was revolting to the conscience. They discovered the real origin, the indirect but effective cause in the revolutionary doctrines which had been disseminated unchecked, in the weakening of social ties, the relaxing of moral discipline, in the repeated appeals to every appetite, to every greedy desire. It would be needful, so as to cut down the evil at its root, to repudiate as quickly as possible all such chimeras and Utopias as syndicalism, the income-tax, etc., etc., etc. Many newspapers, and these not the least important, pointed out that the recrudescence of crime was but the natural fruit of impiety and concluded that the salvation of society lay in an unanimous and sincere return to religion. On the Sunday which followed the crime the congregations in the churches were noticed to be unusually large.

Judge Salneuve, who was entrusted with the task of investigation, first examined the persons arrested by the police, and lost his way among attractive but illusory clues; however, the report of the detective Montremain, which was laid before him, put him on the right road, and soon led him to recognise the miscreants of La Jonchère as the authors of the crime of the Rue de Ramey. He ordered a search to be made for Arcade and Zita, and issued a warrant against Prince Istar, on whom the detectives laid hands as he was leaving Bouchotte's, where he had been depositing some bombs of new design. The Kerûb, on learning the detective's intentions, smiled broadly and asked them if they had a powerful motor-car. On their replying that they had one at the door, he assured them that was all he wanted. Thereupon he felled the two detectives on the stairs, walked up to the waiting car, flung the chauffeur under a motor-'bus which was opportunely passing, and seized the steering wheel under the eyes of the terrified crowd.

That same evening Monsieur Jeancourt, the Police Magistrate, entered Théophile's rooms just when Bouchotte was swallowing a raw egg to clear her voice, for she was to sing her new song, "They haven't got any in Germany," at the "National Eldorado" that evening. The musician was absent. Bouchotte received the Magistrate, and received him with a hauteur which intensified the simplicity of her attire; Bouchotte was *en déshabille*. The worthy Magistrate seized the score of *Aline, Queen of Golconda,* and the love-letters which the singer carefully preserved in the drawer of the table by her bed, for she was an orderly young woman. He was about to withdraw when he espied a cupboard, which he opened with a careless air, and found machines capable of blowing up half Paris, and a pair of large white wings, whose nature and use appeared inexplicable to him. Bouchotte was invited to complete her toilette, and, in spite of her cries, was taken off to the police-station.

Monsieur Salneuve was indefatigable. After the examination of the papers seized in Bouchotte's house, and acting on the information of Montremain, he issued a warrant for the arrest of young d'Esparvieu, which was executed on Wednesday, the 27th May, at seven o'clock in the morning, with great discretion. For three days Maurice had neither slept nor eaten, loved nor lived. He had not a moment's doubt as to the nature of the matutinal visit. At the sight of the police magistrate a strange calm fell on him. Arcade had not returned to sleep in the flat. Maurice begged the magistrate to wait for him, dressed with care, and then accompanied the magistrate to the taxi that was waiting at the door. He felt a calmness of mind which was barely disturbed when the door of the Conciergerie closed on him. Alone in his cell, he climbed upon the table to look out. His tranquillity was due to his weariness of spirit, to his numbed senses, and to the fact that he no longer stood in fear of arrest. His misfortune endowed him with superior wisdom. He felt he had fallen into a state of grace. He did not think too highly or too humbly of himself, but left his cause in the hands of God. With no desire to cover up his faults, which he would not hide even from himself, he addressed himself in mind to Providence, to point out that if he had fallen into disorder and rebellion it was to lead his erring angel back into the straight path. He stretched himself on the couch and slept in peace.

On hearing of the arrest of a music-hall singer and of a young man of fashion, both Paris and the provinces felt painful surprise. Deeply stirred by the tragic accounts which the leading newspapers were bringing out, the general idea was that the sort of people the authorities ought to bring to justice were ferocious anarchists, all reeking and dripping from deeds of blood and arson; but they failed to understand what the world of Art and Fashion should have to do with such things. At this news, which he was one of the last to hear, the President of the Council and Keeper of the Seals started up in his chair. The Sphinxes that adorned it were less terrible than he, and in the throes of his angry meditation he cut the mahogany of his imperial table with his penknife, after the manner of Napoleon. And when Judge Salneuve, whose attendance he had commanded, appeared before him, the President flung his penknife in the grate, as Louis XIV flung his cane out of the window in the presence of Lauzun; and it cost him a supreme effort to master himself and to say in a voice of suppressed fury:

"Are you mad? Surely I said often enough that I meant the plot to be anarchist, anti-social, fundamentally anti-social and antigovernmental, with a shade of syndicalism. I have made it clear enough that I wanted it kept within these lines; and what do you go and make of it? . . . The vengeance of anarchists and aspirants to freedom? Whom do you arrest? A singer adored of the nationalist public, and the son of a man highly esteemed in the Catholic party, who receives our bishops and has the *entrée* to the Vatican; a man who may be one day sent as ambassador to the Pope. At one blow you alienate one hundred and sixty Deputies and forty Senators of the Right on the very eve of a motion to discuss the question of religious pacification; you embroil me with my friends of to-day, with my friends of to-morrow. Was it to find out if you were in the same dilemma as des Aubels that you seized the love-letters of young Maurice d'Esparvieu? I can put your mind at rest on that point. You are, and all Paris knows it. But it is not to avenge your personal affronts that you are on the Bench."

"Monsieur le Garde des Sceaux," murmured the Judge, nearly apoplectic and in a choked voice. "I am an honest man."

"You are a fool . . . and a provincial. Listen to me; if Maurice d'Esparvieu and Mademoiselle Bouchotte are not released within half an hour I will crush you like a piece of glass. Be off!"

Monsieur René d'Esparvieu went himself to fetch his son from the Conciergerie and took him back to the old house in the Rue Garancière. The return was triumphant. The news had been disseminated that Maurice had with generous imprudence interested himself in an attempt to restore the monarchy, and that Judge Salneuve, the infamous freemason, the tool of Combes and André, had tried to compromise the young man by making him out to be an accomplice of a band of criminals.

That was what Abbé Patouille seemed to think, and he answered for Maurice as for himself. It was known, moreover, that breaking with his father, who had rallied to the support of the Republic, young d'Esparvieu was on the high road to becoming an out-and-out Royalist. The people who had an inside knowledge of things saw in his arrest the vengeance of the Jews. Was not Maurice a notorious anti-Semite? Catholic youths went forth to hurl imprecations at Judge Salneuve under the windows of his residence in the Rue Guénégaud, opposite the Mint.

On the Boulevard du Palais a band of students presented Maurice with a branch of palm. Maurice made a charming reply.

Maurice was overcome with emotion when he beheld the old house in which his childhood had been spent, and fell weeping into his mother's arms.

It was a great day, unhappily marred by one painful incident. Monsieur Sariette, who had lost his reason as a consequence of the shocking events that had taken place in the Rue de Courcelles, had suddenly become violent. He had shut himself up in the library, and there he had remained for twenty-four hours, uttering the most

horrible cries, and, turning a deaf ear alike to threats and en-
treaties, refused to come out. He had spent the night in a condition of extreme restlessness, for all night long the lamp had been
seen passing rapidly to and fro behind the curtains. In the morning, hearing Hippolyte shouting to him from the court below, he
opened the window of the Hall of the Spheres and the Philosophers,
and heaved two or three rather weighty tomes on to the old valet's
head. The whole of the domestic staff—men, women, and boys—
hurried to the spot, and the librarian proceeded to throw out books
by the armful on to their heads. In view of the gravity of the situation, Monsieur René d'Esparvieu did not disdain to intervene. He
appeared in night-cap and dressing-gown, and attempted to reason
with the poor lunatic, whose only reply was to pour forth torrents
of abuse on the man whom till then he had worshipped as his benefactor, and to endeavour to crush him beneath all the Bibles, all the
Talmuds, all the sacred books of India and Persia, all the Greek
Fathers, and all the Latin Fathers, Saint John Chrysostom, Saint
Gregory Nazianzen, Saint Augustine, Saint Jerome, all the apologists, ay! and under the *Histoire des Variations,* annotated by Bossuet himself! Octavos, quartos, folios came crashing down, and lay
in a sordid heap on the courtyard pavement. The letters of Gassendi, of Père Mersenne, of Pascal, were blown about hither and
thither by the wind. The lady's-maid who had stooped down to
rescue some of the sheets from the gutter got a blow on the head
from an enormous Dutch atlas. Madame René d'Esparvieu had been
terrified by the ominous sounds, and appeared on the scene without
waiting to apply the finishing touches of powder and paint. When
he caught sight of her, old Sariette became more violent than ever.
Down they came one after another as hard as he could pelt them;
the busts of the poets, philosophers, and historians of antiquity—
Homer, Æschylus, Sophocles, Euripides, Herodotus, Thucydides, Socrates, Plato, Aristotle, Demosthenes, Cicero, Virgil, Horace, Seneca,
Epictetus—all lay scattered on the ground. The celestial sphere and
the terrestrial globe descended with a terrifying crash that was followed by a ghastly hush, broken only by the shrill laughter of little
Léon, who was looking down on the scene from a window above.
A locksmith having opened the library door, all the household hastened to enter, and found the aged Sariette entrenched behind piles
of books, busily engaged in tearing and slashing away at the *Lucretius* of the Prior de Vendôme annotated in Voltaire's own hand.
They had to force a way through the barricade. But the maniac,
perceiving that his stronghold was being invaded, fled away and
escaped on to the roof. For two whole hours he gave vent to shouts
and yells that were heard far and wide. In the Rue Garancière the
crowd kept growing bigger and bigger. All had their eyes fixed on
the unhappy creature, and whenever he stumbled on the slates,
which cracked beneath him, they gave a shout of terror. In the

midst of the crowd, the Abbé Patouille, who expected every moment
to see him hurled into space, was reciting the prayers for the dying, and making ready to give him the absolution *en extremis.*
There was a cordon of police round the house keeping order. Someone summoned the fire-brigade, and the sound of their approach
was soon heard. They placed a ladder against the wall of the house,
and after a terrific struggle managed to secure the maniac, who in
the course of his desperate resistance had one of the muscles of his
arm torn out. He was immediately removed to an asylum.

  Maurice dined at home, and there were smiles of tenderness and
affection when Victor, the old butler, brought on the roast veal.
Monsieur l'Abbé Patouille sat at the right hand of the Christian
mother, unctuously contemplating the family which Heaven had so
plentifully blessed. Nevertheless, Madame d'Esparvieu was ill at
ease. Every day she received anonymous letters of so insulting and
coarse a nature that she thought at first they must come from a
discharged footman. She now knew they were the handiwork of her
youngest daughter, Berthe, a mere child! Little Léon, too, gave her
pain and anxiety. He paid no attention to his lessons, and was given
to bad habits. He showed a cruel disposition. He had plucked his
sister's canaries alive; he stuck innumerable pins into the chair on
which Mademoiselle Caporal was accustomed to sit, and had stolen
fourteen francs from the poor girl, who did nothing but cry and
dab her eyes and nose from morning till night.

  No sooner was dinner over than Maurice rushed off to the little
dwelling in the Rue de Rome, impatient to meet his angel again.
Through the door he heard a loud sound of voices, and saw assembled in the room where the apparition had taken place, Arcade,
Zita, the angelic musician, and the Kerûb, who was lying on the
bed, smoking a huge pipe, carelessly scorching pillows, sheets, and
coverlets. They embraced Maurice, and announced their departure.
Their faces shone with happiness and courage. Alone, the inspired
author of *Aline, Queen of Golconda,* shed tears and raised his terrified gaze to heaven. The Kerûb forced him into the party of rebellion by setting before him two alternatives: either to allow himself
to be dragged from prison to prison on earth, or to carry fire and
sword into the palace of Ialdabaoth.

  Maurice perceived with sorrow that the earth had scarcely any
hold over them. They were setting out filled with immense hope,
which was quite justifiable. Doubtless they were but a few combatants to oppose the innumerable soldiers of the sultan of the
heavens; but they counted on compensating for the inferiority of
their numbers by the irresistible impetus of a sudden attack. They
were not ignorant of the fact that Ialdabaoth, who flatters himself
on knowing all things, sometimes allows himself to be taken by
surprise. And it certainly looked as if the first attack would have
taken him unawares had it not been for the warning of the arch-

angel Michael. The celestial army had made no progress since its victory over the rebels before the beginning of Time.

As regards armaments and material it was as out of date as the army of the Moors. Its generals slumbered in sloth and ignorance. Loaded with honours and riches, they preferred the delights of the banquet to the fatigues of war. Michael, the commander-in-chief, ever loyal and brave, had lost, with the passing of centuries, his fire and enthusiasm. The conspirators of 1914, on the other hand, knew the very latest and the most delicate appliances of science for the art of destruction. At length all was ready and decided upon. The army of revolt, assembled by corps each a hundred thousand angels strong, on all the waste places of the earth—steppes, pampas, deserts, fields of ice and snow—was ready to launch itelf against the sky. The angels, in modifying the rhythm of the atoms of which they are composed, are able to traverse the most varied mediums. Spirits that have descended on to the earth, being formed, since their incarnation, of too compact a substance, can no longer fly of themselves, and to rise into ethereal regions and then insensibly grow volatilized, have need of the assistance of their brothers, who, though revolutionaries like themselves, nevertheless, stayed behind in the Empyrean and remained, not immaterial (for all is matter in the Universe), but gloriously untrammelled and diaphanous. Certes, it was not without painful anxiety that Arcade, Istar, and Zita prepared themselves to pass from the heavy atmosphere of the earth to the limpid depths of the heavens. To plunge into the ether there is need to expend such energy that the most intrepid hesitate to take flight. Their very substance, while penetrating this fine medium, must in itself grow fine-spun, become vaporised, and pass from human dimensions to the volume of the vastest clouds which have ever enveloped the earth. Soon they would surpass in grandeur the uttermost planets, whose orbits they, invisible and imponderable, would traverse without disturbing.

In this enterprise—the vastest that angels could undertake— their substance would be ultimately hotter than the fire and colder than the ice, and they would suffer pangs sharper than death.

Maurice read all the daring and the pain of the undertaking in the eyes of Arcade.

"You are going?" he said to him, weeping.

"We are going, with Nectaire, to seek the great archangel to lead us to victory."

"Whom do you call thus?"

"The priests of the demiurge have made him known to you in their calumnies."

"Unhappy being," sighed Maurice.

Arcade embraced him, and Maurice felt the angel's tears as they dropped upon his cheek.

XXXV

AND LAST, WHEREIN THE SUBLIME DREAM OF SATAN IS UNFOLDED

CLIMBING the seven steep terraces which rise up from the bed of the Ganges to the temples muffled in creepers, the five angels reached, by half-obliterated paths, the wild garden filled with perfumed clusters of grapes and chattering monkeys, and, at the far end thereof, they discovered him whom they had come to seek. The archangel lay with his elbow on black cushions embroidered with golden flames. At his feet crouched lions and gazelles. Twined in the trees, tame serpents turned on him their friendly gaze. At the sight of his angelic visitors his face grew melancholy. Long since, in the days when, with his brow crowned with grapes and his sceptre of vine-leaves in his hand, he had taught and comforted mankind, his heart had many times been heavy with sorrow; but never yet, since his glorious downfall, had his beautiful face expressed such pain and anguish.

Zita told him of the black standards assembled in crowds in all the waste places of the globe; of the deliverance premeditated and prepared in the provinces of Heaven, where the first revolt had long ago been fomented.

"Prince," she went on, "your army awaits you. Come, lead it on to victory."

"Friends," replied the great archangel, "I was aware of the object of your visit. Baskets of fruit and honeycombs await you under the shade of this mighty tree. The sun is about to descend into the roseate waters of the Sacred River. When you have eaten, you will slumber pleasantly in this garden, where the joys of the intellect and of the senses have reigned since the day when I drove hence the spirit of the old Demiurge. To-morrow I will give you my answer."

Night hung its blue over the garden. Satan fell asleep. He had a dream, and in that dream, soaring over the earth, he saw it covered with angels in revolt, beautiful as gods, whose eyes darted lightning. And from pole to pole one single cry, formed of a myriad cries, mounted towards him, filled with hope and love. And Satan said:

"Let us go forth! Let us seek the ancient adversary in his high abode." And he led the countless host of angels over the celestial plains. And Satan was cognizant of what took place in the heavenly citadel. When news of this second revolt came thither, the Father said to the Son:

"The irreconcilable foe is rising once again. Let us take heed to ourselves, and in this, our time of danger, look to our defences, lest we lose our high abode."

And the Son, consubstantial with the Father, replied:

"We shall triumph under the sign that gave Constantine the victory."

Indignation burst forth on the Mountain of God. At first the faithful Seraphim condemned the rebels to terrible torture, but afterwards decided on doing battle with them. The anger burning in the hearts of all inflamed each countenance. They did not doubt of victory, but treachery was feared, and eternal darkness had been at once decreed for spies and alarmists.

There was shouting and singing of ancient hymns and praise of the Almighty. They drank of the mystic wine. Courage, over-inflated, came near to giving way, and a secret anxiety stole into the inner depths of their souls. The archangel Michael took supreme command. He reassured their minds by his serenity. His countenance, wherein his soul was visible, expressed contempt for danger. By his orders, the chiefs of the thunderbolts, the Kerûbs, grown dull with the long interval of peace, paced with heavy steps the ramparts of the Holy Mountain, and, letting the gaze of their bovine eyes wander over the glittering clouds of their Lord, strove to place the divine batteries in position. After inspecting the defences, they swore to the Most High that all was in readiness. They took counsel together as to the plan they should follow. Michael was for the offensive. He, as a consummate soldier, said it was the supreme law. Attack, or be attacked,—there was no middle course.

"Moreover," he added, "the offensive attitude is particularly suitable to the ardour of the Thrones and Dominations."

Beyond that, it was impossible to obtain a word from the valiant chief, and this silence seemed the mark of a genius sure of himself.

As soon as the approach of the enemy was announced, Michael sent forth three armies to meet them, commanded by the archangels Uriel, Raphael, and Gabriel. Standards, displaying all the colours of the Orient, were unfurled above the ethereal plains, and the thunders rolled over the starry floors. For three days and three nights was the lot of the terrible and adorable armies unknown on the Mountain of God. Towards dawn on the fourth day news came, but it was vague and confused. There were rumours of indecisive victories; of the triumph now of this side, now of that. There came reports of glorious deeds which were dissipated in a few hours.

The thunderbolts of Raphael, hurled against the rebels, had, it was said, consumed entire squadrons. The troops commanded by the impure Zita were thought to have been swallowed up in the whirlwind of a tempest of fire. It was believed that the savage Istar had been flung headlong into the gulf of perdition so suddenly that the blasphemies begun in his mouth had been forced backwards with explosive results. It was popularly supposed that Satan, laden with chains of adamant, had been plunged once again into the abyss. Meanwhile, the commanders of the three armies had sent no messages. Mutterings and murmurs, mingling with the rumours of glory, gave rise to fears of an indecisive battle, a precipitate retreat. Insolent voices gave out that a spirit of the lowest category, a guardian angel, the insignificant Arcade, had checked and routed the dazzling host of the three great archangels.

There were also rumours of wholesale defection in the Seventh Heaven, where rebellion had broken out before the beginning of Time, and some had even seen black clouds of impious angels joining the armies of the rebels on Earth. But no one lent an ear to the odious rumours, and stress was laid on the news of victory which ran from lip to lip, each statement readily finding confirmation. The high places resounded with hymns of joy; the Seraphim celebrated on harp and psaltery Sabaoth, God of Thunder. The voices of the elect united with those of the angels in glorifying the Invisible and at the thought of the bloodshed that the ministers of holy wrath had caused among the rebels, sighs of relief and jubilation were wafted from the Heavenly Jerusalem towards the Most High. But the beatitude of the most blessed, having swelled to the utmost limit before due time, could increase no more, and the very excess of their felicity completely dulled their senses.

The songs had not yet ceased when the guards watching on the ramparts signalled the approach of the first fugitives of the divine army; Seraphim on tattered wing, flying in disorder, maimed Kerûbs going on three feet. With impassive gaze, Michael, prince of warriors, measured the extent of the disaster; and his keen intelligence penetrated its causes. The armies of the living God had taken the offensive, but by one of those fatalities in war which disconcert the plans of the greatest captains, the enemy had also taken the offensive, and the effect was evident. Scarcely were the gates of the citadel opened to receive the glorious but shattered remnants of the three armies, when a rain of fire fell on the Mountain of God. Satan's army was not yet in sight, but the walls of topaz, the cupolas of emerald, the roofs of diamond, all fell in with an appalling crash under the discharge of the electrophores. The ancient thunderclouds essayed to reply, but the bolts fell short, and their thunders were lost in the deserted plains of the skies.

Smitten by an invisible foe, the faithful angels abandoned the ramparts. Michael went to announce to his God that the Holy Mountain would fall into the hands of the demon in twenty-four hours, and that nothing remained for the Master of the Heavens but to seek safety in flight. The Seraphim placed the jewels of the celestial crown in coffers. Michael offered his arm to the Queen of Heaven, and the Holy Family escaped from the palace by a subterranean passage of porphyry. A deluge of fire was falling on the citadel. Regaining his post once more, the glorious archangel declared that he would never capitulate, and straightway advanced the standards of the living God. That same evening the rebel host made its entry into the thrice-sacred city. On a fiery steed Satan led his demons. Behind him marched Arcade, Istar, and Zita. As in the ancient revels of Dionysus, old Nectaire bestrode his ass. Thereafter, floating out far behind, followed the black standards.

The garrison laid down their arms before Satan. Michael placed his flaming sword at the feet of the conquering archangel.

"Take back your sword, Michael," said Satan. "It is Lucifer who yields it to you. Bear it in defence of peace and law." Then letting his gaze fall on the leaders of the celestial cohorts, he cried in a ringing voice:

"Archangel Michael, and you, Powers, Thrones, and Dominations, swear all of you to be faithful to your God."

"We swear it," they replied with one voice.

And Satan said:

"Powers, Thrones, and Dominations, of all past wars, I wish but to remember the invincible courage that you displayed and the loyalty which you rendered to authority, for these assure me of the steadfastness of the fealty you have just sworn to me."

The following day, on the ethereal plain, Satan commanded the black standards to be distributed to the troops, and the winged soldiers covered them with kisses and bedewed them with tears.

And Satan had himself crowned God. Thronging round the glittering walls of Heavenly Jerusalem, apostles, pontiffs, virgins, martyrs, confessors, the whole company of the elect, who during the fierce battle had enjoyed delightful tranquillity, tasted infinite joy in the spectacle of the coronation.

The elect saw with ravishment the Most High precipitated into Hell, and Satan seated on the throne of the Lord. In conformity with the will of God which had cut them off from sorrow they sang in the ancient fashion the praises of their new Master.

And Satan, piercing space with his keen glance, contemplated the little globe of earth and water where of old he had planted the vine and formed the first tragic chorus. And he fixed his gaze on that Rome where the fallen God had founded his empire on fraud and lie. Nevertheless, at that moment a saint ruled over the Church. Satan saw him praying and weeping. And he said to him:

"To thee I entrust my Spouse. Watch over her faithfully. In thee I confirm the right and power to decide matters of doctrine, to regulate the use of the sacraments, to make laws and to uphold purity of morals. And the faithful shall be under obligation to conform thereto. My Church is eternal, and the gates of hell shall not prevail against it. Thou are infallible. Nothing is changed."

And the successor of the apostles felt flooded with rapture. He prostrated himself, and with his forehead touching the floor, replied:

"O Lord, my God, I recognise Thy voice! Thy breath has been wafted like balm to my heart. Blessed be Thy name. Thy will be done on Earth, as it is in Heaven. Lead us not into temptation, but deliver us from evil."

And Satan found pleasure in praise and in the exercise of his grace; he loved to hear his wisdom and his power belauded. He listened with joy to the canticles of the cherubim who celebrated his good deeds, and he took no pleasure in listening to Nectaire's flute, because it celebrated nature's self, yielded to the insect and to the blade of grass their share of power and love, and counselled happiness and freedom. Satan, whose flesh had crept, in days gone by, at the idea that suffering prevailed in the world, now felt himself inaccessible to pity. He regarded suffering and death as the happy results of omnipotence and sovereign kindness. And the savour of the blood of victims rose upwards towards him like sweet incense. He fell to condemning intelligence and to hating curiosity. He himself refused to learn anything more, for fear that in acquiring fresh knowledge he might let it be seen that he had not known everything at the very outset. He took pleasure in mystery, and believing that he would seem less great by being understood, he affected to be unintelligible. Dense fumes of Theology filled his brain. One day, following the example of his predecessor, he conceived the notion of proclaiming himself one god in three persons. Seeing Arcade smile as this proclamation was made, he drove him from his presence. Istar and Zita had long since returned to earth. Thus centuries passed like seconds. Now, one day, from the altitude of his throne, he plunged his gaze into the depths of the pit and saw Ialdabaoth in the Gehenna where he himself had long lain enchained. Amid the everlasting gloom Ialdabaoth still retained his lofty mien. Blackened and shattered, terrible and sublime, he glanced upwards at the palace of the King of Heaven with a look of proud disdain, then turned away his head. And the new god, as he looked upon his foe, beheld the light of intelligence and love pass across his sorrow-stricken countenance. And lo! Ialdabaoth was now contemplating the Earth and, seeing it sunk in wickedness and suffering, he began to foster thoughts of kindliness in his heart. On a sudden he rose up, and beating the ether with his mighty arms, as though with oars, he hastened thither to instruct and to console mankind. Already his vast shadow shed upon the unhappy planet a shade soft as a night of love.

And Satan awoke bathed in an icy sweat.

Nectaire, Istar, Arcade, and Zita were standing round him. The finches were singing.

"Comrades," said the great archangel, "no—we will not conquer the heavens. Enough to have the power. War engenders war, and victory defeat.

"God, conquered, will become Satan; Satan, conquering, will become God. May the fates spare me this terrible lot; I love the Hell which formed my genius. I love the Earth where I have done some good, if it be possible to do any good in this fearful world where beings live but by rapine. Now, thanks to us, the god of old is dispossessed of his terrestrial empire, and every thinking being on this globe disdains him or knows him not. But what matter that men should be no longer submissive to Ialdabaoth if the spirit of Ialdabaoth is still in them; if they, like him, are jealous, violent, quarrelsome, and greedy, and the foes of the arts and of beauty? What matter that they have rejected the ferocious Demiurge, if they do not hearken to the friendly demons who teach all truths; to Dionysus, Apollo, and the Muses? As to ourselves, celestial spirits, sublime demons, we have destroyed Ialdabaoth, our Tyrant, if in ourselves we have destroyed Ignorance and Fear."

And Satan, turning to the gardener, said:

"Nectaire, you fought with me before the birth of the world. We were conquered because we failed to understand that Victory is a Spirit, and that it is in ourselves and in ourselves alone that we must attack and destroy Ialdabaoth."

www.ingramcontent.com/pod-product-compliance
Lightning Source LLC
Chambersburg PA
CBHW081138020726
47504CB00009B/1916

* 9 7 8 1 6 0 5 9 7 2 3 8 1 *